# 新制多益 New TOEIC

# 閱讀高分金榜演練

## 關鍵10回滿分模擬1000題

 YBM TOEIC R&D  蔡裴驊／賴祖兒／劉嘉珮

# 目錄

# 多益測驗簡介

TOEIC 為 Test of English for International Communication 的縮寫，針對母語非英語的人士所設計，測驗其在日常生活或國際業務上所具備的英語應用能力。該測驗的評量重點在於「與他人溝通的能力」（communication ability），著重「英語的運用與其功能」層面，而非單純針對「英語知識」出題。

1979 年美國 ETS（Educational Testing Service）研發出 TOEIC，而後在全世界 160 個國家中獲得超過 14,000 個機構採用，作為升遷、外派、人才招募的依據，全球每年超過 700 萬人次報考。

## >> 多益測驗題型

| | Part | 測驗題型 | | 題數 | 時間 | 分數 |
|---|---|---|---|---|---|---|
| 聽力 Listening Comprehension | 1 | 照片描述 | | 6 | 45 分鐘 | 495 分 |
| | 2 | 應答問題 | | 25 | | |
| | 3 | 簡短對話 | | 39 | | |
| | 4 | 簡短獨白 | | 30 | | |
| 閱讀 Reading Comprehension | 5 | 句子填空 | | 30 | 75 分鐘 | 495 分 |
| | 6 | 段落填空 | | 16 | | |
| | 7 | 閱測 | 單篇閱讀 | 29 | | |
| | | | 多篇閱讀 | 25 | | |
| 總計 | | | | 200 | 約 150 分鐘 ✷ | 990 分 |

✷ 含基本資料及問卷填寫

### >> 報名方式

請上官網 www.toeic.com.tw 確認測驗日期、報名時間等相關細節。報名時，請先查看定期場次和新增場次的時間，再選擇欲報考的測驗日期。完成報名後，請務必再次確認報考測驗日期與應試地點。

### >> 應試攜帶物品

- **指定身分證件**：國民身分證、有效期限內之護照等，詳細資訊請以多益官網公告為準（如未攜帶者，不得入場考試）。
- **考試用具**：2B 鉛筆和橡皮擦（不可使用原子筆或簽字筆）。
- **手錶**：指針式手錶（不可使用電子手錶）。

### >> 成績查詢

通常於測驗後的二至三週內開放網路查詢。成績單將於測驗結束後 12 個工作日（不含假日）寄發，一般郵局大宗郵件平信寄送作業約需 3–5 個工作天（不含假日）。申請成績單補發／證書的期限為自測驗日起的兩年內。

### >> 多益測驗如何計分？

多益分數分為聽力與閱讀部分的分數，每部分的分數以 5 分為單位，範圍在 5 分至 495 分，總分則會落在 10 分至 990 分。多益測驗成績會針對題本內容，設定不同量尺轉換方法，最後分數是以「答對」的題數，經過量尺轉換而來。

共 30 題

## PART 5 句子填空 Incomplete Sentences

### >> 文法題

**時態**和**代名詞**的文法題各會出現 **2 題**；**限定詞**和**分詞**的文法題則各會出現 **1 題**。與時態有關的文法題中，可能會同時考**主動**語態／**被動**語態，以及**主詞與動詞的單複數一致性**。此外也會出現專門考限定詞、主動語態／被動語態、不定詞和動名詞的考題。

### >> 詞彙題

**動詞**、**名詞**、**形容詞**及**副詞**的詞彙題各會出現 **2** 至 **3 題**；**介系詞**詞彙題通常會有 **3 題**。另外，**連接詞**或**片語**相關詞彙題可能**完全不會出現**，有時則會考 **3 題**。

### >> 詞性題

**名詞**及**副詞**的考題約會出現 **2** 至 **3 題**；相較之下，形容詞考題的出題頻率較低。

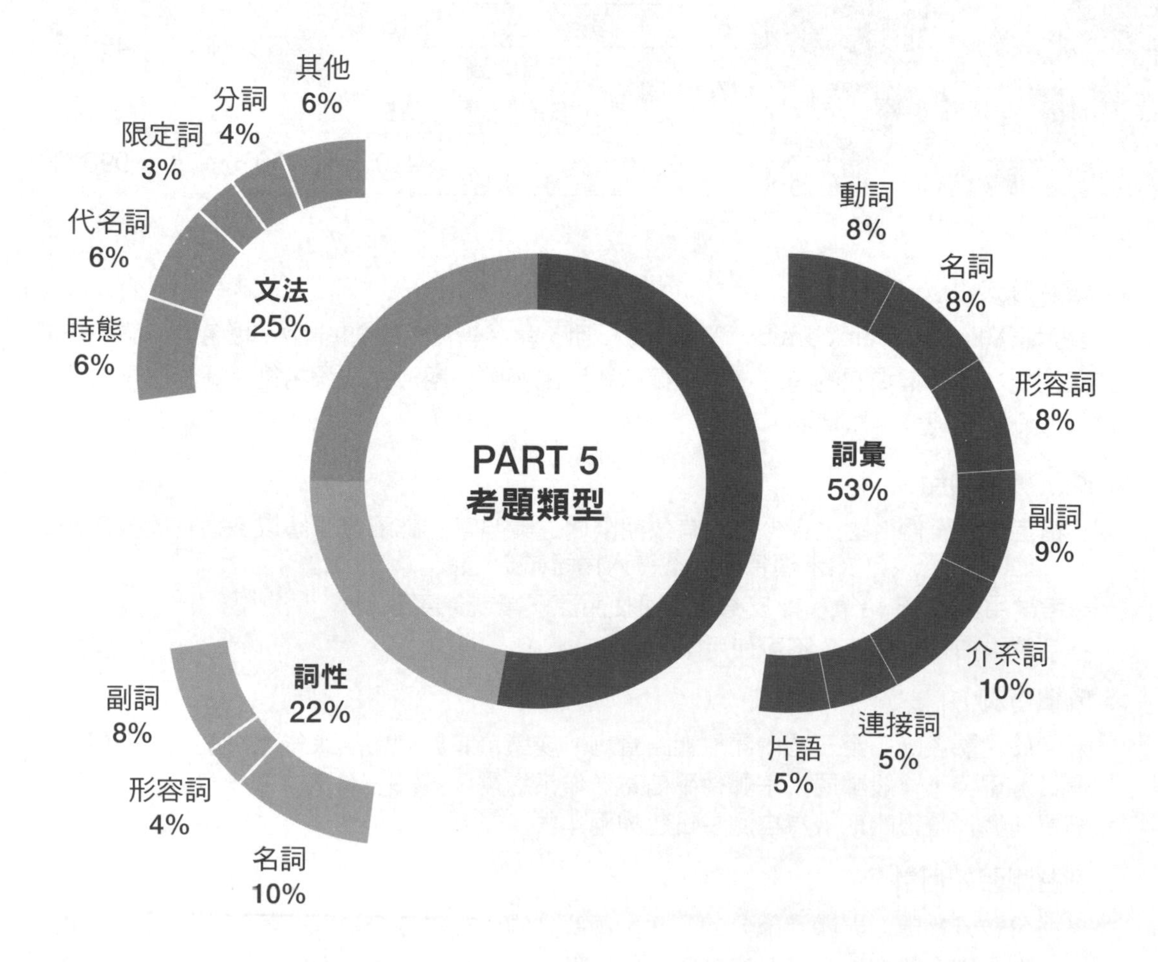

共 4 篇文章，共 16 題（每篇 4 題）

## PART 6 段落填空 Text Completion

一篇文章題組共有 4 題，平均會考詞彙題 2 題、詞性或文法題 1 題、句子插入題 1 題。
除了句子插入題之外，其他考題的類型幾乎與第五大題相同。

### >> 詞彙題

**動詞**、**名詞**、**副詞**和**片語**的詞彙題每次約出現 **1** 至 **2 題**。若為副詞詞彙題，最常出現的是能夠**自然連接上下文**的副詞，像是 therefore（因此）或 however（然而）。

### >> 文法題

與**文意密切相關**的時態題約會出現 **2 題**，可能同時會考**主動**語態／**被動**語態以及**主詞動詞的單複數一致性**。此外也會考代名詞、主動語態／被動語態、不定詞、連接詞、介系詞等。

### >> 句子插入題

每篇文章都會考 **1 題**句子插入題。最常出現在 4 題中的**第 2 題**，其次依序為 4 題中的第 3 題、第 4 題、第 1 題。

### >> 詞性題

**名詞**或**形容詞**的考題，出題頻率較副詞考題高。

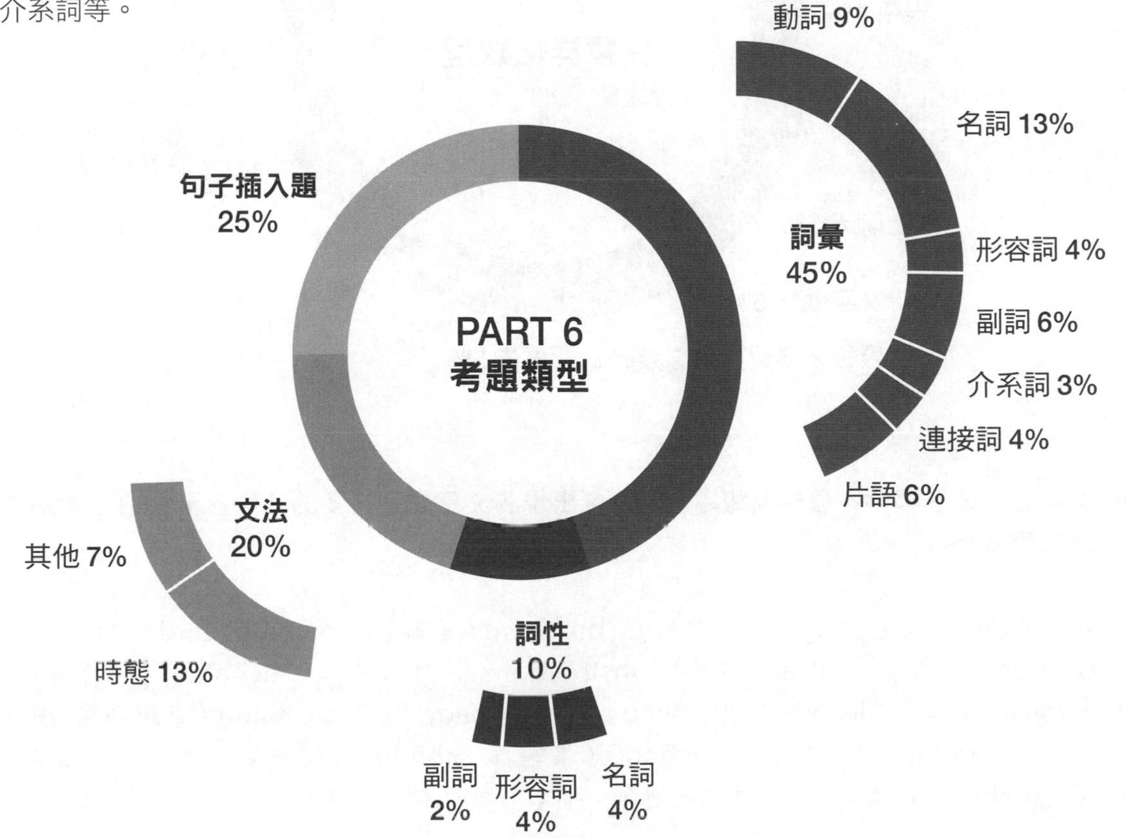

共 15 篇文章，共 54 題（每篇含 2 至 5 題）

## PART 7 閱讀理解 Reading Comprehension

| 文章類型 | 每篇文章的題數 | 文章數量 | 百分比（%） |
|---|---|---|---|
| 單篇閱讀 | 2 題 | 4 篇 | 約 15% |
| | 3 題 | 3 篇 | 約 16% |
| | 4 題 | 3 篇 | 約 22% |
| 雙篇閱讀 | 5 題 | 2 篇 | 約 19% |
| 多篇閱讀 | 5 題 | 3 篇 | 約 28% |

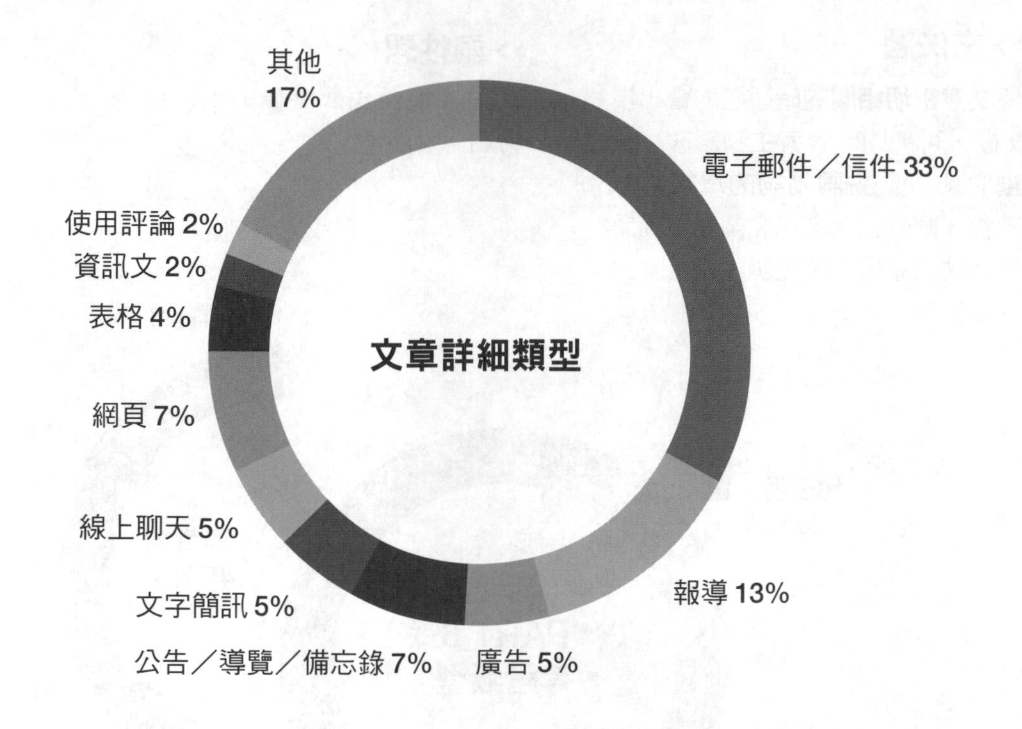


- 基本上，**電子郵件**、**信件**及**報導**是一定會出現的文章類型，多的時候甚至會佔整大題的 **50% 至 60%**。

- 其他類型的文章包含 agenda（議程）、brochure（手冊）、comment card（評論卡）、coupon（優惠券）、flyer（傳單）、instructions（使用說明）、invitation（邀請函）、invoice（收據）、list（清單）、menu（菜單）、page from a catalog（目錄冊頁面）、policy statement（政策通知）、report（報導）、schedule（時程表）、survey（調查）和 voucher（兌換券）等各類型的資訊，平均出現於本大題中。

（若將雙篇閱讀與多篇閱讀的文章各以 2 篇和 3 篇計算，則本大題共有 23 篇文章）

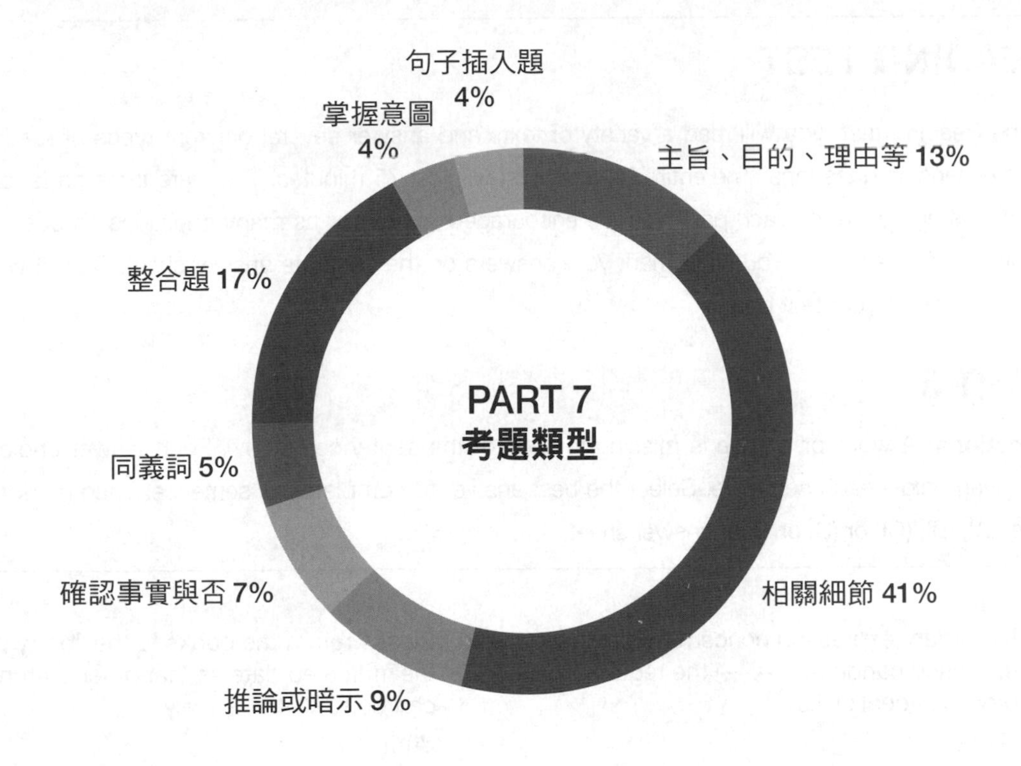


◆ **同義詞**考題主要出現在**雙篇**閱讀或**多篇**閱讀中。

◆ **整合題**一般會在**雙篇**閱讀中考 **1 題**，在**多篇**閱讀中考 **2 題**。

◆ **掌握意圖**的考題會出現在 **text-message chain**（文字訊息串）及 **online chat discussion**（線上聊天室）的文章裡，各考 2 題。

◆ **句子插入題**會考 **2 題**，主要出現在報導、電子郵件、信件和備忘錄的文章裡。

# ACTUAL TEST 

## READING TEST

In the Reading test, you will read a variety of texts and answer several different types of reading comprehension questions. The entire Reading test will last 75 minutes. There are three parts, and directions are given for each part. You are encouraged to answer as many questions as possible within the time allowed. You must mark your answers on the separate answer sheet. Do not write your answers in your test book.

## PART 5

**Directions:** A word or phrase is missing in each of the sentences below. Four answer choices are given below each sentence. Select the best answer to complete the sentence. Then mark the letter (A), (B), (C), or (D) on your answer sheet.

**101.** Mr. Ardary expressed concern that the proposed candidate ------- the required organizational skills.

(A) fails
(B) struggles
(C) lacks
(D) limits

**102.** Rayville's Public Works Department hired local ------- to clean up the lakeside.

(A) contract
(B) contracted
(C) contractor
(D) contractors

**103.** Submissions of translated writings must include the original text ------- your translation.

(A) along
(B) as well as
(C) altogether
(D) also

**104.** ------- a temporary problem with the speaker system, the product launch event went as planned.

(A) Apart from
(B) After all
(C) Instead of
(D) Not only

**105.** Please return the books to the library by the indicated date so that other patrons can borrow ------- freely.

(A) it
(B) its own
(C) them
(D) themselves

**106.** ------- this drug to strong light or heat will reduce its effectiveness.

(A) Consuming
(B) Handling
(C) Allowing
(D) Exposing

**107.** When the machine is out of paper or ------- unable to function, a notification will appear on the display screen.

(A) otherwise
(B) however
(C) in case
(D) anymore

**108.** The ------- of a MimEx smartphone may be extended by filling out an online form.

(A) warranty
(B) lifespan
(C) design
(D) vendor

109. In order to boost participation, ------- who enters the photo contest will receive a small gift.
(A) those
(B) everyone
(C) they
(D) many

110. The bulk of Eltis Automotive's financial resources is being directed ------- developing new vehicles.
(A) by
(B) besides
(C) towards
(D) onto

111. The radio towers will provide park rangers with a ------- means of communication despite the mountainous terrain.
(A) reliable
(B) reliably
(C) reliability
(D) reliant

112. Arrange the plants as ------- as possible on the aquarium's floor to create the ideal environment for your fish.
(A) densest
(B) densely
(C) density
(D) denser

113. Ms. Muir argues that technological advancements in manufacturing have led to ------- prices for consumers.
(A) comparable
(B) full
(C) market
(D) better

114. Grelf, Inc. held a press conference yesterday to announce plans to expand, ------- its rivals in the mining industry.
(A) surprised
(B) surprising
(C) surprises
(D) surprise

115. As Brenford Grill's most popular dish, Corinne's Chili Cheeseburger is ------- featured in advertisements for the restaurant.
(A) prominently
(B) inadvertently
(C) rapidly
(D) respectively

116. Hyall Health, Inc.'s claims about the benefits of its aromatherapy oils do not have scientific -------.
(A) result
(B) verification
(C) experiment
(D) excuse

117. Television advertising is appropriate for products with broad target markets, ------- mobile advertising is more suited to niche products.
(A) in spite of
(B) contrary to
(C) whereas
(D) only if

118. This memo details our proposal ------- the secondary storage closet into a small meeting space.
(A) will convert
(B) conversion
(C) was converted
(D) to convert

119. Assembly line workers may have facial hair as long as it does not ------- with their work.
(A) affect
(B) disrupt
(C) interfere
(D) compromise

120. The survey data show that interns found the written training materials more ------- than the video.
(A) informing
(B) information
(C) informatively
(D) informative



GO ON TO THE NEXT PAGE

121. New employees will be asked to wear temporary badges ------- their official identification cards are issued.

(A) whether
(B) rather than
(C) as though
(D) until

122. Thanks to Ms. Perry's tireless campaigning, education ------- as the central issue of the city council election.

(A) emerging
(B) will be emerged
(C) is emerging
(D) has been emerged

123. The commission system gives sales associates a strong ------- to work hard.

(A) incentive
(B) satisfaction
(C) supervision
(D) approach

124. As its name suggests, "Painting for Beginners" caters ------- to those who have never studied the craft before.

(A) specify
(B) specific
(C) specified
(D) specifically

125. The technical support department's budget is no longer ------- to cover its staffing expenses.

(A) vital
(B) plentiful
(C) accustomed
(D) sufficient

126. Taskko software helps managers ensure that tasks are being distributed ------- among the members of their team.

(A) briefly
(B) loosely
(C) evenly
(D) newly

127. Our services include the ------- of any required import and export documents.

(A) supplies
(B) supplier
(C) supplying
(D) supplied

128. Hogan & Partners' internship program gives law students the chance to learn ------- the guidance of seasoned attorneys.

(A) within
(B) under
(C) behind
(D) among

129. If his flight from Madrid had arrived on time, Mr. Martín ------- the conference's welcome reception.

(A) was attending
(B) could have attended
(C) can attend
(D) had attended

130. The success of its new line of beverages has reduced Genvia's ------- on its flagship snack bars for revenue.

(A) expertise
(B) dependence
(C) perspective
(D) shortage

## PART 6

**Directions:** Read the texts that follow. A word, phrase, or sentence is missing in parts of each text. Four answer choices for each question are given below the text. Select the best answer to complete the text. Then mark the letter (A), (B), (C), or (D) on your answer sheet.

**Questions 131–134** refer to the following Web page.

www.vegashift.com

**VegaShift**

VegaShift is a mobile app that gives restaurants, stores, and other shift-based businesses a fast, simple way to facilitate shift trades. Workers offer unwanted shifts ------- (131.) to their coworkers, who can choose whether or not to take them. This enables employees to increase the flexibility of their working hours without inconveniencing their supervisors. ------- (132.), VegaShift allows management to retain control of the schedule. Supervisors can require all trades to be approved so that no workers are scheduled to work more than their ------- (133.) hours. The app can also alert management to added costs that may arise due to differences in employees' hourly pay.

We are so confident in VegaShift's quality that we give businesses the chance to use it for a whole month at no cost. ------- (134.) .

**131.** (A) directs
(B) directly
(C) directing
(D) direction

**132.** (A) As a result
(B) In other words
(C) On the contrary
(D) At the same time

**133.** (A) permitted
(B) shortened
(C) preferred
(D) extra

**134.** (A) Learn why *Tech Z* named us one of the industry's top employers.
(B) Enter your information below to start your free trial today.
(C) For a full list of products, click on "Offerings."
(D) Additional technical support is available at 1-800-555-0184.

*GO ON TO THE NEXT PAGE*

**Questions 135–138** refer to the following article.

**Reyno to Host National Science Festival**

REYNO (December 11)—The National Department of Science and Technology (NDST) has announced that the city of Reyno will host the second annual National Science Festival in June.

NDST spokesperson Isaac Hodges said that ------- (**135.**) for the honor was fierce, but Reyno was chosen because of its "fast-growing agricultural science and biotechnology industry." He also mentioned the city's recent establishment of the Reyno 300 complex for technology start-ups. ------- (**136.**).

The National Science Festival is a weeklong event showcasing the country's scientific achievements and projects. It features lectures that introduce cutting-edge concepts to the general public, exhibitions for all ages, and ------- (**137.**) demonstrations. The first one ------- (**138.**) in Oglesby.

**135.** (A) selection
(B) opportunity
(C) competition
(D) recommendation

**136.** (A) Visitors hoping to stay there should make their reservations soon.
(B) He has initiated several such projects during his time in city government.
(C) Companies accepted as tenants there receive special funding and advice.
(D) There is concern that its construction will cause traffic problems during the festival.

**137.** (A) fascinating
(B) fascinatingly
(C) fascinated
(D) fascinates

**138.** (A) was being held
(B) was held
(C) is held
(D) will be held

**Questions 139–142** refer to the following e-mail.

From: Patrick Holbrook
To: Library Services Staff
Subject: Peer Evaluations
Date: November 15
Attachment: Evaluation Forms

Hi all,

Your yearly employee performance evaluations will take place over the next month. As before, evaluations will be conducted by me but will include input ------- (139.) your peers in the Library Services Department. To gather this feedback, I need each of you to fill out and send back the evaluation forms in the attached file. Please ------- (140.) one for every member of the department. ------- (141.). Like last time, you will be asked to first rate your coworker's performance in a range of areas and then write a paragraph explaining and expanding on your answers. However, I urge you to take special care with the latter part this year. Remember, thoughtful feedback can benefit your peers ------- (142.).

Patrick Holbrook
Vice Director of Library Services

**139.** (A) from
(B) on
(C) like
(D) over

**140.** (A) grant
(B) compile
(C) complete
(D) attend

**141.** (A) Surveys were distributed to library patrons as well.
(B) The format of the questionnaires has not been altered.
(C) Head Director Htun will be present at each review.
(D) You appear to have left some boxes blank.

**142.** (A) consider
(B) considers
(C) considerable
(D) considerably

*GO ON TO THE NEXT PAGE*

**Questions 143–146** refer to the following notice.

## NOTICE TO CUSTOMERS

Due to increases in the cost of raw materials such as paper and ink, Wheeler Printing Shop has decided to raise the prices of our printing services as of February 1. -------. **143.**

This is our first such ------- **144.** in over five years. We have delayed it out of respect for our customers, but it has now become unavoidable because of the abovementioned economic factors. ------- **145.** our prices is necessary to enable us to continue providing top-notch service well into the future.

Our price list boards will be updated on February 1 to reflect the changes, and employees will be encouraged to state the cost of all printing services upfront to avoid misunderstandings. Questions about this matter ------- **146.** to Lucia Zaiser, our manager. Thank you for your understanding.

**143.** (A) We are not able to accept any other digital file formats.
(B) Our regular business hours will resume on February 8.
(C) To print packaging materials, please visit our Holloway location.
(D) The prices of our graphic design services will remain the same.

**144.** (A) adjustment
(B) expenditure
(C) departure
(D) error

**145.** (A) Having raised
(B) Raised
(C) To be raised
(D) Raising

**146.** (A) have been addressed
(B) can be addressed
(C) are addressing
(D) will be addressing

# PART 7

**Directions:** In this part you will read a selection of texts, such as magazine and newspaper articles, e-mails, and instant messages. Each text or set of texts is followed by several questions. Select the best answer for each question and mark the letter (A), (B), (C), or (D) on your answer sheet.

**Questions 147–148** refer to the following information.

*Howell Airlines*

**Howell Sky Lounge Guest Policy**

Sky Lounge members are allowed to bring holders of tickets for same-day Howell Airlines flights into the lounge as guests. Platinum Membership holders may bring two guests or a spouse and any children under 21 years of age into the Sky Lounge at no cost; Gold Membership holders may do the same for a fee of $25 per person. Guests must be accompanied by the admitted member for the duration of their visit. They are also subject to Sky Lounge rules regarding attire, behavior, and use of lounge amenities.

**147.** According to the information, what is different between membership types?
(A) The amount of time guests can stay
(B) The number of guests allowed
(C) The cost of bringing a guest
(D) The qualifications required of guests

**148.** What must guests do after entering the Sky Lounge?
(A) Remain with an escort
(B) Wear a form of identification
(C) Leave baggage in a designated area
(D) Pay a fee for amenities

GO ON TO THE NEXT PAGE

**Questions 149–150** refer to the following e-mail.

E-Mail message

| | |
|---|---|
| **From:** | Natasha Akers |
| **To:** | Satchelton Running Club |
| **Subject:** | March events |
| **Date:** | February 28 |

Hi runners! Isn't it great that the weather is starting to get warmer? Soon we'll have a lot of greenery to admire during our outings.

Here's what will be going on in the club in March:

- Nearby event alert: the Spratt City Marathon. Details are below. If you're interested in carpooling to the city the night before, contact me by the race registration deadline.
  - Date: March 30
  - Location: Spratt
  - Course length: 26.2 miles
  - Registration deadline: March 16
  - Web site: www.sprattcitymarathon.com
- We'll continue going on group runs every Sunday at 10 A.M. (seven-mile course) and Wednesday at 7 P.M. (five-mile course) at Cosmon Park. Remember to sign up in advance on the club Web site so I know to send you text message notifications about cancellations or other changes.

I hope to see you on the course!

-Natasha

**149.** By what date should Ms. Akers be contacted about sharing transportation to Spratt?

(A) February 28
(B) March 16
(C) March 29
(D) March 30

**150.** What does Ms. Akers remind recipients to do?

(A) Send her a text message on Sundays
(B) Warm up before going on a group run
(C) Register to receive updates about events
(D) Study course routes in advance

**Questions 151–153** refer to the following e-mail.

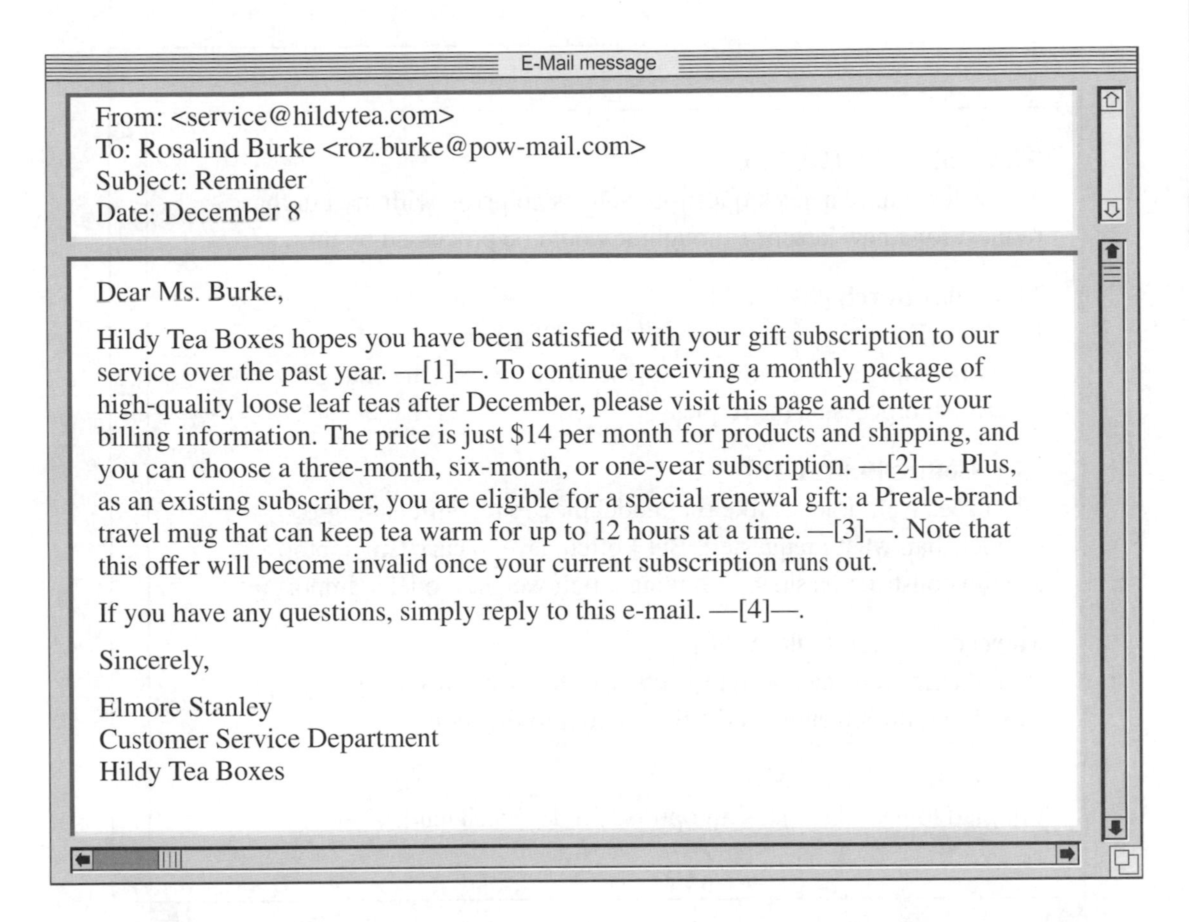

E-Mail message

From: <service@hildytea.com>
To: Rosalind Burke <roz.burke@pow-mail.com>
Subject: Reminder
Date: December 8

Dear Ms. Burke,

Hildy Tea Boxes hopes you have been satisfied with your gift subscription to our service over the past year. —[1]—. To continue receiving a monthly package of high-quality loose leaf teas after December, please visit this page and enter your billing information. The price is just $14 per month for products and shipping, and you can choose a three-month, six-month, or one-year subscription. —[2]—. Plus, as an existing subscriber, you are eligible for a special renewal gift: a Preale-brand travel mug that can keep tea warm for up to 12 hours at a time. —[3]—. Note that this offer will become invalid once your current subscription runs out.

If you have any questions, simply reply to this e-mail. —[4]—.

Sincerely,

Elmore Stanley
Customer Service Department
Hildy Tea Boxes

**151.** Why was the e-mail sent to Ms. Burke?
(A) She complained about Hildy Tea Boxes.
(B) She referred a friend to Hildy Tea Boxes.
(C) A new product has become available.
(D) Her subscription period will end soon.

**152.** What does Mr. Stanley offer to Ms. Burke?
(A) A drinking container
(B) Some cold-weather apparel
(C) Free shipping for one year
(D) Advance notice of a sales promotion

**153.** In which of the positions marked [1], [2], [3], and [4] does the following sentence best belong?
"I or another representative will respond within 24 hours."
(A) [1]
(B) [2]
(C) [3]
(D) [4]

*GO ON TO THE NEXT PAGE*

**Questions 154–155** refer to the following online chat discussion.

**Alex Collins [9:02 A.M.]**
Mercedes, I have a quick question. What's going on with my purchase request for a new laptop? I thought it would be processed by now.

**Mercedes Burch [9:03 A.M.]**
Hi, Alex. Didn't you get my e-mail? The IT department is recommending a different model. Once you approve the change, we can finish processing the request.

**Alex Collins [9:07 A.M.]**
Oh, I see. Well, it looks like the model they're recommending is heavier than what I requested. But I often have to carry my laptop around construction sites, so having a lightweight model is important.

**Mercedes Burch [9:08 A.M.]**
In that case, you can oppose the change. Just write a short paragraph explaining the situation, and I'll append it to the request.

**Alex Collins [9:08 A.M.]**
I'm glad to hear that that's an option. I'll do that. Thanks.

**154.** At 9:03 A.M., what does Ms. Burch imply when she writes, "Didn't you get my e-mail"?

(A) Her e-mail provides an explanation for a delay.
(B) Her e-mail gives notification of the conclusion of a process.
(C) Her e-mail describes a change to a policy.
(D) Her e-mail announces a staff transfer.

**155.** What does Mr. Collins state that his job frequently requires?

(A) Carrying out training
(B) Visiting work sites
(C) Doing persuasive writing
(D) Researching personal electronics

**Questions 156–157** refer to the following notice.

## NOTICE FOR RESIDENTS OF SANDLING APARTMENTS

Over the past few months, the volume of tenants' packages being delivered to the apartment management office has grown beyond our capacity to handle them. The result has been an excessive amount of work for our employees, reduced space in our facility, and several incidents of packages being lost. Therefore, the office will no longer accept delivery of packages for tenants from Monday, October 1. Please take advantage of this ample advance notice to make other arrangements for any packages that will likely arrive on or after that date. These could be taking delivery at the door of your building or a third location like a post office box or your workplace.

- Sandling Apartments Management

**156.** What are apartment residents mainly being notified of?
(A) The holding of a tenant meeting
(B) The elimination of a receiving service
(C) The installation of a convenience facility
(D) The misplacement of some goods

**157.** What is suggested about Sandling Apartments?
(A) Its office is closed on weekends.
(B) It will soon be under new management.
(C) It recently reduced its number of employees.
(D) It occupies multiple buildings.

*GO ON TO THE NEXT PAGE*

**Questions 158–160** refer to the following memo.

From: Shane Maxwell
To: All employees
Re: Announcement
Date: May 8

It's the time of year when Goldwin Publishing gives all of its employees a chance to show their creativity. We are again seeking proposals for innovative additions to our range of Spanish language education solutions. Any type of product that is among those we already offer—books, flash cards, board games, etc.—or reasonably similar to them is welcome.

We believe that valuable contributions can come from unconventional sources, so employees in every area are encouraged to participate. Last year, Lois Edwards in the accounting department suggested a book that not only was published but ended up selling very well. If you have a fresh idea, we urge you to temporarily put aside your regular workload and write a proposal for it.

Each employee can submit up to two proposals. There is no specific format for proposals, but they should include a detailed description of the product and its target market. To keep submissions manageable, however, we do ask that they be no more than one page in length. Please send them to my assistant, Ivan Briggs, at ivan@goldwinpublishing.com by Friday, May 19.

**158.** What does Mr. Maxwell ask recipients of the memo to submit?
(A) Reviews of existing products
(B) Ideas for potential new products
(C) Applications for joining a product development team
(D) Proposals for improving the product development process

**159.** Who most likely was Ms. Edwards's book intended for?
(A) Board game fans
(B) Amateur cooks
(C) Language learners
(D) Accounting students

**160.** What is indicated about submissions?
(A) They should be sent to two people.
(B) They are accepted twice a year.
(C) They can be up to two pages long.
(D) They must include two pieces of information.

**Questions 161–164** refer to the following Web page.

www.shopslam.com/hiring/faq

## Frequently Asked Questions about Hiring at Shopslam

Due to our exciting work environment and excellent employee benefits, thousands of people each year express interest in becoming part of the Shopslam team. Our recruiters cannot respond to all of the inquiries that we receive, so we have collected some common questions and their answers on this page.

**1. Can I apply for more than one job?**

This is permitted. However, we strongly recommend that you focus on the position for which you are best qualified.

**2. Do you provide disability accommodations during the hiring process?**

We are happy to offer accommodations such as sign language interpreters, wheelchair-accessible hotels for interviewees coming from out of town, etc. Simply fill out the optional "Accessibility Request Form" and include it with your other application materials.

**3. Will you notify me if my application is rejected?**

The high volume of applications means that we are only able to send updates about the hiring process to successful candidates.

**4. After being rejected, can I reapply for the same job?**

Yes, but if it is a technical position, we ask that you gain substantial additional experience before doing so.

**161.** What is most likely true about Shopslam?
(A) It hires thousands of people annually.
(B) It sends recruiters to university campuses.
(C) It has lower requirements for some technical jobs.
(D) It has a reputation for being a good employer.

**162.** What is mentioned as an example of a disability accommodation?
(A) Help with in-person communication
(B) Forms with large lettering
(C) An easily accessible interview site
(D) Additional time to fill out paperwork

**163.** According to the Web page, what should job applicants do?
(A) Check a Web page for hiring updates
(B) Concentrate their efforts on a single opening
(C) Include work samples with their application materials
(D) Review a list of commonly asked interview questions

**164.** Which question does NOT receive an affirmative reply?
(A) 1
(B) 2
(C) 3
(D) 4

*GO ON TO THE NEXT PAGE*

**Questions 165-168** refer to the following text-message chain.

**Lynne Fleming** **[1:45 P.M.]**
Johnny, are you still at the supermarket?

**John Rivera** **[1:47 P.M.]**
No, I'm on my way back. I pulled over to the side of the road to answer your text. Why do you ask?

**Lynne Fleming** **[1:48 P.M.]**
I was just cleaning up the Rose Room for the guests who are coming at five, and I ran out of some of our cleaning supplies. Would you mind going back and picking some up? I know it's inconvenient.

**John Rivera** **[1:49 P.M.]**
Well, I am right by Nash Mart.

**Lynne Fleming** **[1:50 P.M.]**
Oh, that would work! We need paper towels and window cleaner.

**John Rivera** **[1:51 P.M.]**
Really? We're out of paper towels? I bought a 12-pack just last week.

**Lynne Fleming** **[1:52 P.M.]**
Yes, the family with young kids that stayed in the Lilac Suite last weekend used a lot of them to clean up spills. Why don't you get a 24-pack this time? That should last us for a while.

**John Rivera** **[1:53 P.M.]**
OK, will do. I should be back in half an hour.

**Lynne Fleming** **[1:53 P.M.]**
Great. Don't forget to get a receipt for this purchase too.

**165.** Where do the writers most likely work?
(A) At a small hotel
(B) At a landscaping firm
(C) At a cleaning company
(D) At an educational institution

**166.** At 1:49 P.M., what does Mr. Rivera mean when he writes, "I am right by Nash Mart"?
(A) His journey is progressing quickly.
(B) He might be able to shop at Nash Mart.
(C) He would like Ms. Fleming to pick him up.
(D) Ms. Fleming should be able to see him from her location.

**167.** What most likely surprises Mr. Rivera?
(A) That he has been chosen to do a task
(B) That Ms. Fleming is aware of a problem
(C) That it has been a full week since an event occurred
(D) That some supplies have been used up

**168.** What does Ms. Fleming remind Mr. Rivera to do?
(A) Put fuel in a vehicle
(B) Avoid spilling a liquid
(C) Receive proof of a payment
(D) Send a notification to a coworker

**Questions 169–171** refer to the following e-mail.

| | |
|---|---|
| **From:** | Wally Barnes <w.barnes@mclerdon.com> |
| **To:** | Araceli Diaz <araceli@hevneymanufacturing.com> |
| **Subject:** | Request |
| **Date:** | April 28 |

Dear Ms. Diaz,

My name is Wally Barnes, and I am a marketing specialist at McLerdon, Inc. My department was established earlier this year thanks to growth fueled by the loyal patronage of clients like Hevney Manufacturing. Your account manager, Mr. Quinn, has told me that McLerdon staff have had the honor of guarding Hevney's factory premises for nearly five years now.

In addition to introducing myself, I am writing to make a request. I am currently adding client logos to McLerdon's Web site and would like to include your company's. This would normally be authorized by the service agreement between your company and ours, but our low level of marketing expertise at the time the contract was written meant that no such provision was included. If you agree to this request, all we need is a clear image of your current logo at a size of 150 pixels by 150 pixels. However, if you prefer that we do not display your logo, please do not hesitate to let me know.

McLerdon thanks you again for your business. We hope to hear from you soon.

Best regards,

Wally Barnes
McLerdon, Inc.

**169.** What is suggested about Mr. Barnes?
(A) Mr. Quinn is his manager.
(B) He helped draft an agreement.
(C) He holds a newly-created position.
(D) He has visited Hevney Manufacturing's Web site.

**170.** What most likely does McLerdon, Inc. do for its clients?
(A) Conduct marketing campaigns
(B) Provide security personnel
(C) Repair factory equipment
(D) Give legal advice

**171.** What does Mr. Barnes ask Ms. Diaz for?
(A) A client testimonial
(B) A signed copy of a contract
(C) Confirmation of a machine's dimensions
(D) Permission to use an image

GO ON TO THE NEXT PAGE

**Questions 172–175** refer to the following article.

## *Doretta* Creates Stir in Podcast Industry

By Filip Knutsen

Fans of *Doretta*, the eight-episode audio podcast chronicling the life of novelist Doretta Worth, will soon have many similar offerings to listen to. *Doretta*'s success has inspired its production company, Elgior Media, and several other podcast giants to develop scripted podcasts depicting interesting events and people in history. —[1]—.

According to podcast industry analytics firm Casteye, the majority of the top ten most popular podcasts are usually current events or interview shows. That is why *Doretta*'s achievement of mainstream popularity has made such an impression. As a historical fiction podcast, the show featured scripted dialogue performed by professional actors, sound effects, and a musical score. —[2]—. And yet, in the second month of its run, it reached number four on Casteye's ranking list. The show still has an active discussion board on Elgior's Web site, and the cast gave five sold-out live performances of an abridged version of its story shortly after it ended.

Some have speculated that *Doretta*'s distinctness was the cause of its popularity instead of a barrier to it. —[3]—. However, Casteye analyst Cynthia Myers disagrees. "After all, *Doretta* was not the first historical fiction podcast," she said. "Our research indicates that it was the excellence of the show's writing and performances that appealed to listeners."

Still, the industry believes that there is now an audience for similar projects. Elgior offered Kent Mulligan, *Doretta*'s creator, a lucrative deal to develop another historical fiction podcast next year. —[4]—. Meanwhile, Lenston Studios will release *1955*, a podcast detailing a championship season for the Marchand Panthers, next month, and Carryover Radio says it is currently in production on a show depicting the Murrell v. Talbert court case.

**172.** What is indicated about *Doretta*?
(A) It was based on a bestselling book.
(B) It was expected to run for more episodes.
(C) It was in a different genre from other popular podcasts.
(D) It was the first show made by its production company.

**173.** What can *Doretta* fans most likely do on Elgior Media's Web site?
(A) Purchase themed merchandise
(B) Post messages to each other
(C) Read some biographical facts
(D) View photographs of a performance

**174.** What does Ms. Myers provide an expert opinion on?
(A) The cause of *Doretta*'s success
(B) The historical accuracy of *Doretta*
(C) The reliability of Casteye's rankings
(D) The future prospects of Elgior Media

**175.** In which of the positions marked [1], [2], [3], and [4] does the following sentence best belong?
"A spokesperson for the company said it would deal with the building of Corbitt Bridge."
(A) [1]
(B) [2]
(C) [3]
(D) [4]



GO ON TO THE NEXT PAGE

**Questions 176–180** refer to the following e-mail and Web page.

| | |
|---|---|
| **From:** | Yeon-Hee Nam |
| **To:** | Research Team |
| **Subject:** | Workshop |
| **Date:** | January 30 |

Hi all,

I'm sure most of you have heard of Slinview, the new data visualization software. Well, Vazent Tech, its maker, is going to hold an educational workshop here next month. At just $40 per person for eight hours of instruction, this would be a great chance for us to become familiar with Slinview before investing a large sum of money to purchase it. I'd like to send two members of the team to attend the workshop and determine if it would benefit Fannon Agricultural Consulting to adopt Slinview.

You can find information about the workshop on this page. Note that we'll pay for your lunch at a nearby restaurant, but you'll need to coordinate your own transportation to the Grenory Hotel and get there by 8 A.M.

If you're interested, respond to this e-mail by the end of the day with a brief outline of the arguments for sending you. I'll notify those chosen tomorrow and have my assistant call to sign them up.

–Yeon-Hee

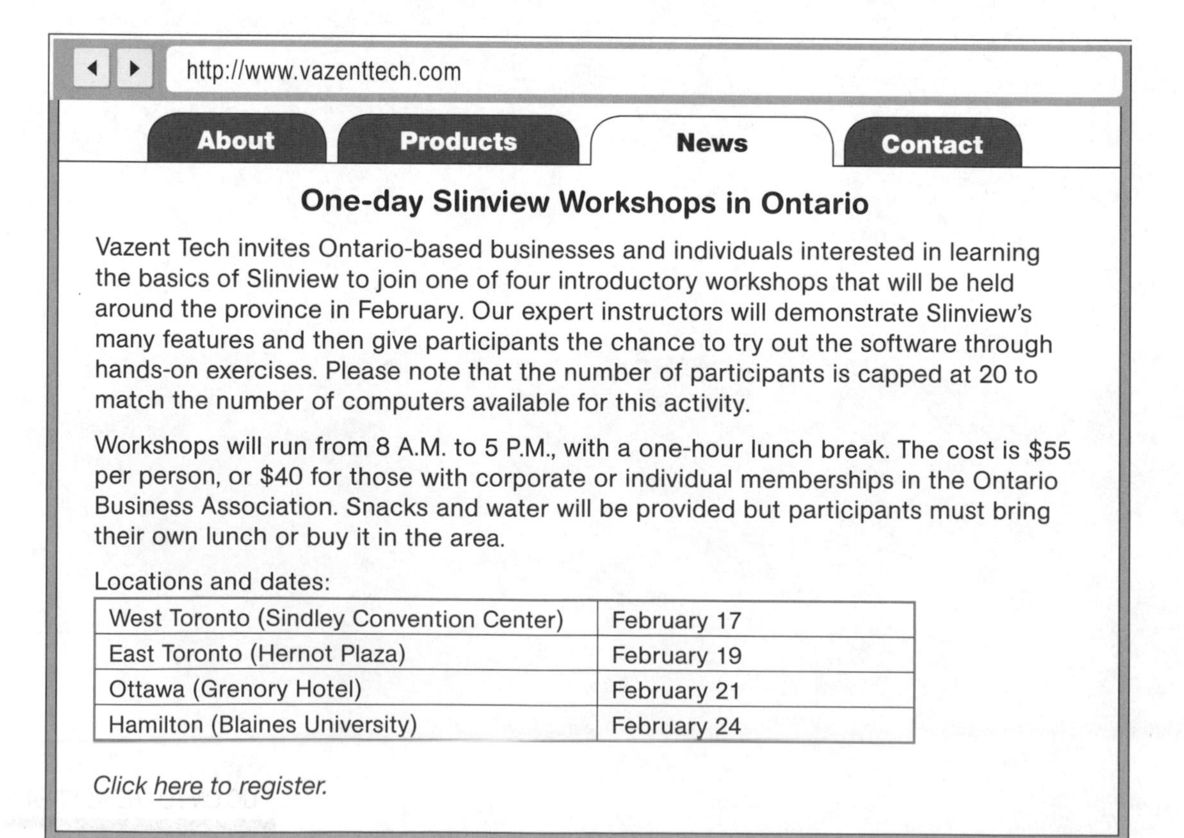

http://www.vazenttech.com

About | Products | News | Contact

**One-day Slinview Workshops in Ontario**

Vazent Tech invites Ontario-based businesses and individuals interested in learning the basics of Slinview to join one of four introductory workshops that will be held around the province in February. Our expert instructors will demonstrate Slinview's many features and then give participants the chance to try out the software through hands-on exercises. Please note that the number of participants is capped at 20 to match the number of computers available for this activity.

Workshops will run from 8 A.M. to 5 P.M., with a one-hour lunch break. The cost is $55 per person, or $40 for those with corporate or individual memberships in the Ontario Business Association. Snacks and water will be provided but participants must bring their own lunch or buy it in the area.

Locations and dates:

| | |
|---|---|
| West Toronto (Sindley Convention Center) | February 17 |
| East Toronto (Hernot Plaza) | February 19 |
| Ottawa (Grenory Hotel) | February 21 |
| Hamilton (Blaines University) | February 24 |

*Click here to register.*

**176.** Who most likely is Ms. Nam?
(A) A team manager
(B) A software developer
(C) An executive assistant
(D) A freelance event coordinator

**177.** In the e-mail, the word "arguments" in paragraph 3, line 2, is closest in meaning to
(A) procedures
(B) attitudes
(C) disputes
(D) reasons

**178.** What is implied about Fannon Agricultural Consulting?
(A) It is located on the west side of Toronto.
(B) It regularly pays for its staff to undergo skills training.
(C) It belongs to the Ontario Business Association.
(D) It recently adopted a new technique for data collection.

**179.** Which detail given by Ms. Nam about the workshops differs from the information in the Web page?
(A) The time she recommends arriving
(B) The method she describes for registering
(C) The place where she expects participants to eat
(D) The duration she attributes to the instructional portion

**180.** According to the Web page, why is the number of workshop participants limited?
(A) To ensure that participants can practice using the software
(B) To prevent venues from becoming difficult to access
(C) To allow participants to speak with the instructor
(D) To generate interest in an exclusive experience

***GO ON TO THE NEXT PAGE***

**Questions 181–185** refer to the following article and e-mail.

## Shrader Extension to Offer Certificate in Remote Work

SHRADER CITY (December 1)—The University of Shrader Extension has announced that it will begin offering a "Remote Work Proficiency Certificate."

Operated by the university, the extension is a Shrader-wide network of offices that is charged with sharing knowledge through continuing education classes and other programs. The extension's dean, Dr. Irwin Hirano, said that the goal of this program is to give opportunities to underemployed people in rural areas: "We want them to be able to make a living while remaining a part of their community, instead of feeling forced to move to a city."

For students' convenience, the program will be administered entirely online.
Dr. Hirano explained, "All that people will need is a computer, moderate computer literacy, and a good Internet connection." He did point out that a background in fields like marketing or graphic design is helpful, but said that "there are remote work jobs, like customer service representative, that require little previous work experience."

The five-week program, which will cost nothing for residents of certain rural areas, centers around a course teaching the technological tools and job skills needed for remote work. Once the course ends, certificate-holders will have access to a career coach as they launch their job search.

Potential students must register by December 26 for the inaugural session, which will begin classes on January 2, and by February 24 for the session beginning March 3. More information about the program can be found at www.extension.shrader.edu/rwpc.

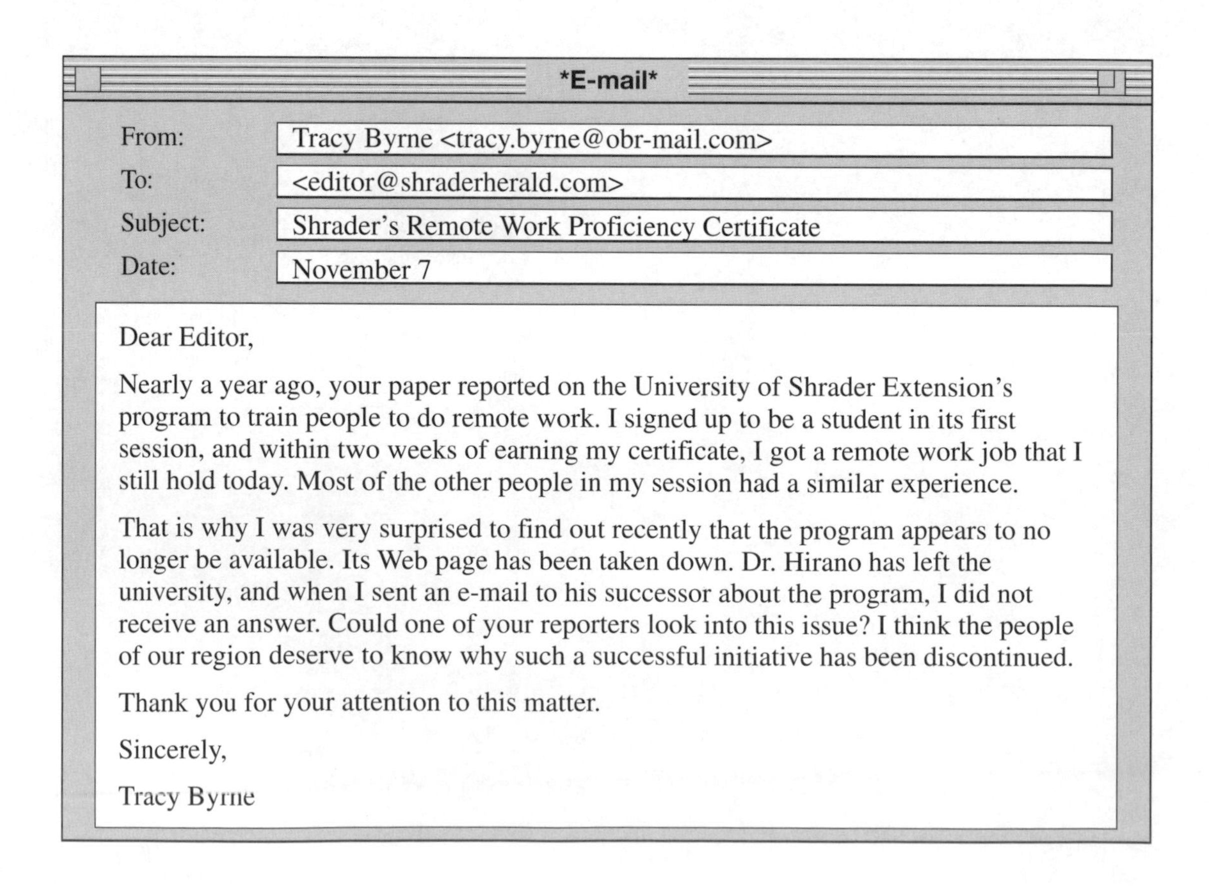

*E-mail*

From: Tracy Byrne <tracy.byrne@obr-mail.com>
To: <editor@shraderherald.com>
Subject: Shrader's Remote Work Proficiency Certificate
Date: November 7

Dear Editor,

Nearly a year ago, your paper reported on the University of Shrader Extension's program to train people to do remote work. I signed up to be a student in its first session, and within two weeks of earning my certificate, I got a remote work job that I still hold today. Most of the other people in my session had a similar experience.

That is why I was very surprised to find out recently that the program appears to no longer be available. Its Web page has been taken down. Dr. Hirano has left the university, and when I sent an e-mail to his successor about the program, I did not receive an answer. Could one of your reporters look into this issue? I think the people of our region deserve to know why such a successful initiative has been discontinued.

Thank you for your attention to this matter.

Sincerely,

Tracy Byrne

181. What kind of people is the program intended for?
(A) People who live in areas with low population density
(B) People who have family care responsibilities
(C) People who do not have university degrees
(D) People who previously worked in certain industries

182. What does the article state about the program's course?
(A) Its contents include a final exam.
(B) Some of its students are charged a reduced fee.
(C) Some of its classes are held at university extension offices.
(D) Its graduates can get job seeking assistance.

183. What is the purpose of the e-mail?
(A) To ask for an investigation into the program's status
(B) To complain about changes to the program's design
(C) To recommend the program to other potential students
(D) To thank a publication for promoting the program

184. What did Ms. Byrne most likely do on January 2?
(A) Notice an article
(B) Complete enrollment
(C) Start her course
(D) Receive her certificate

185. What is suggested about the University of Shrader Extension?
(A) It is Ms. Byrne's current employer.
(B) It did not fulfill a promise it made to Ms. Byrne.
(C) It no longer has an online presence.
(D) It has a new dean.



GO ON TO THE NEXT PAGE

**Questions 186–190** refer to the following Web pages and e-mail.

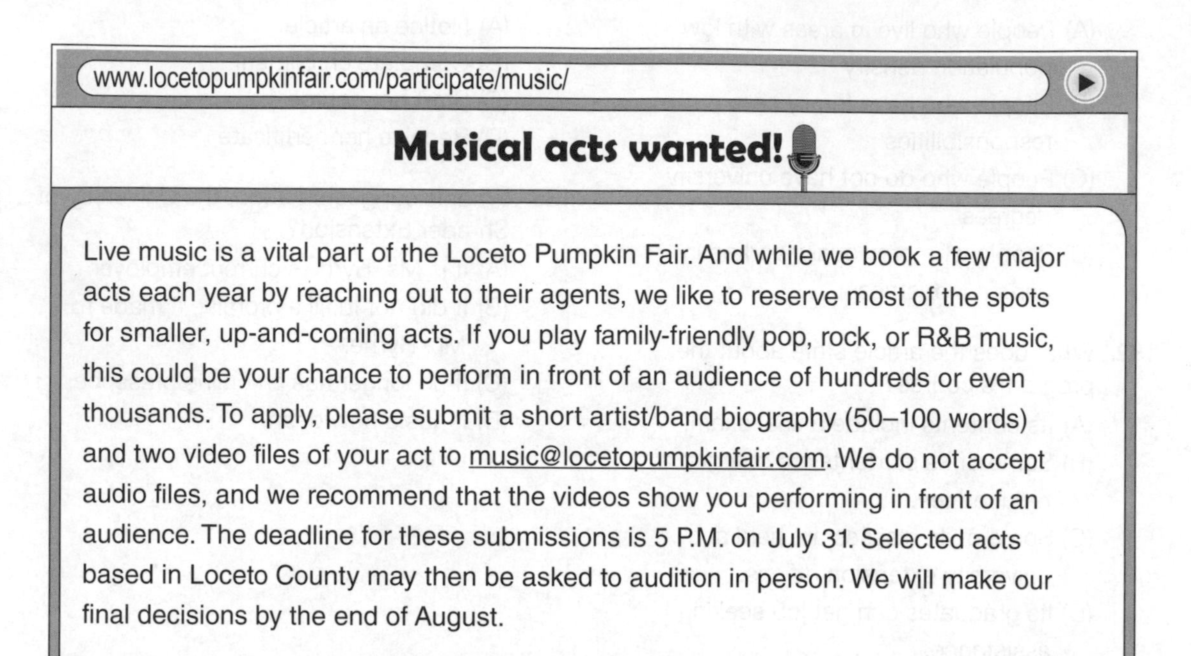

www.locetopumpkinfair.com/participate/music/

## Musical acts wanted!

Live music is a vital part of the Loceto Pumpkin Fair. And while we book a few major acts each year by reaching out to their agents, we like to reserve most of the spots for smaller, up-and-coming acts. If you play family-friendly pop, rock, or R&B music, this could be your chance to perform in front of an audience of hundreds or even thousands. To apply, please submit a short artist/band biography (50–100 words) and two video files of your act to music@locetopumpkinfair.com. We do not accept audio files, and we recommend that the videos show you performing in front of an audience. The deadline for these submissions is 5 P.M. on July 31. Selected acts based in Loceto County may then be asked to audition in person. We will make our final decisions by the end of August.

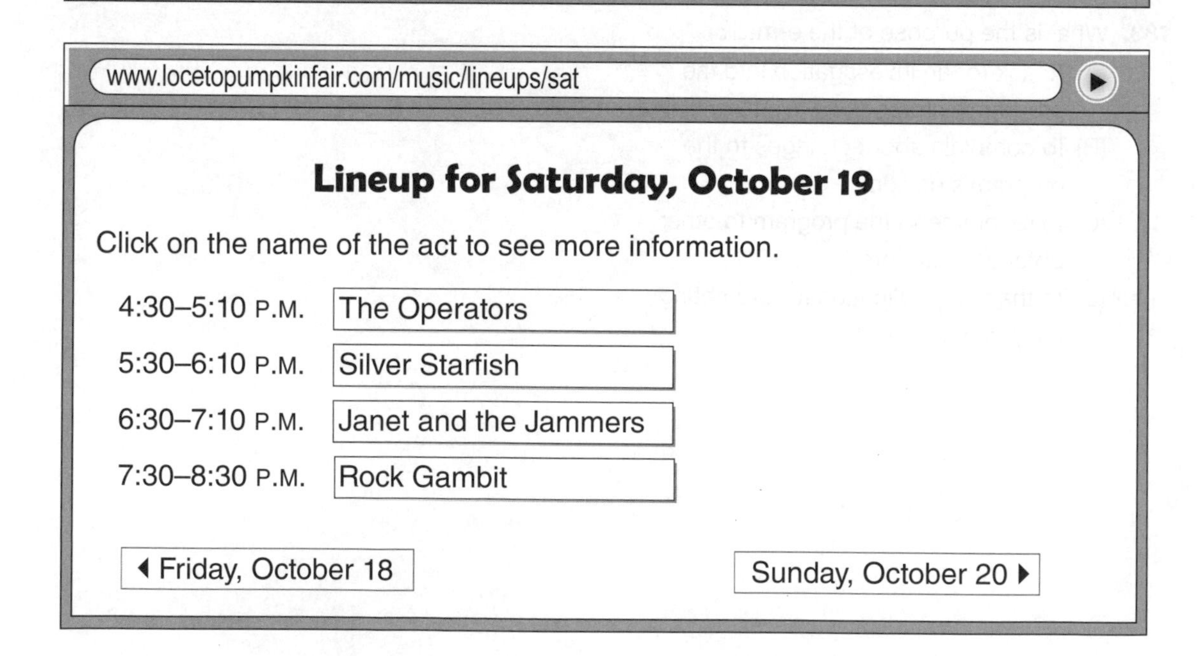

www.locetopumpkinfair.com/music/lineups/sat

## Lineup for Saturday, October 19

Click on the name of the act to see more information.

| | |
|---|---|
| 4:30–5:10 P.M. | The Operators |
| 5:30–6:10 P.M. | Silver Starfish |
| 6:30–7:10 P.M. | Janet and the Jammers |
| 7:30–8:30 P.M. | Rock Gambit |

◀ Friday, October 18 Sunday, October 20 ▶

| From: | <music@locetopumpkinfair.com> |
|---|---|
| To: | Lora Gordon <lora.g@pmt-mail.com> |
| Subject: | Loceto Pumpkin Fair |
| Date: | September 23 |

Dear Ms. Gordon,

One of the bands scheduled to perform at the Loceto Pumpkin Fair on October 19 has dropped out unexpectedly, and we would like to offer your band the chance to take its place. As I mentioned in my earlier e-mail, the other members of the music committee and I were very impressed by the Hairpins' audition and were sorry that we were initially unable to offer you a spot. You're the first act we're contacting about this opening.

You would play a 40-minute set starting at 4:30 P.M., and the pay is $300. We understand that the Hairpins may have found another engagement that day, so please discuss our offer with your bandmates and let us know what you decide. We need to hear from you by the end of the day tomorrow.

Thanks,

Wendell Fox
Loceto Pumpkin Fair Music Committee

**186.** What does the first Web page indicate about the application process?
(A) It is simpler than it was the previous year.
(B) There is a video guide explaining it.
(C) Some bands do not go through it.
(D) It requires applicants to submit a payment.

**187.** In the first Web page, the word "reserve" in paragraph 1, line 2, is closest in meaning to
(A) possess
(B) set aside
(C) take over
(D) exert

**188.** What is the purpose of the e-mail?
(A) To offer Ms. Gordon an opportunity
(B) To revise the terms of an offer
(C) To give some preparation instructions
(D) To warn Ms. Gordon about a problem

**189.** What is most likely true about the Hairpins?
(A) It plays R&B music.
(B) It gave a performance on July 31.
(C) It is represented by a professional agent.
(D) Its members live in Loceto County.

**190.** Which band will NOT perform on October 19 ?
(A) The Operators
(B) Silver Starfish
(C) Janet and the Jammers
(D) Rock Gambit

GO ON TO THE NEXT PAGE

**Questions 191–195** refer to the following advertisement, e-mail, and bill.

## High Efficiency Fume Hoods from Belker Science

Almost every type of laboratory needs fume hoods so that its scientists can safely work with chemicals that give off hazardous gases. Unfortunately, fume hoods are also among the most energy-hungry pieces of lab equipment. That is why Belker Science created its range of high efficiency fume hoods. Each has a sophisticated controller and three-speed blower that together can reduce the hood's airflow usage and thus its energy requirements. In addition, the special motor uses less energy than a traditional motor. Available in 2-foot, 4-foot, 6-foot, and 8-foot models, the hoods also feature a vertical safety glass sash for maximum safety and usability.

Visit www.belkerscience.com today to learn more about these and other innovative products.

| | |
|---|---|
| **From:** | Linda Murphy <l.murphy@simonroylabs.com> |
| **To:** | Jabril Nasser <j.nasser@simonroylabs.com> |
| **Date:** | February 2 |
| **Subject:** | Replacing fume hoods |

Hi Jabril,

As you requested, I spent last week's trade fair looking for ways for the lab to save money, and I was most impressed by what I saw at Belker Science's booth. Their high efficiency fume hoods seem to be just what we're looking for. Our fume hoods are all over 10 years old, so I'm sure that replacing them would result in noticeably lower energy bills. Plus, the salesperson mentioned that Wisenway, our energy provider, is offering an "EE" (energy efficiency) rebate through May, so if we hurry, we can get a rebate of up to $500 for upgrading.

You can see the collection of models at www.belkerscience.com/fumehoods/he. I think we should take advantage of the change to move up a size from our current 4-foot hoods, but I know that depends on our budget.

I hope this recommendation is helpful!

-Linda

**Wisenway Energy**

Simonroy Laboratories
540 Cole Lane
Crawfend, CO 80022

Account #: 4018532
**Amount due: $648.86**
**Due date: July 22**

***Energy Bill***

Billing period: June 1–June 30
**Energy usage: 7,348 kWh**
Meter #: 8231004248
Read date: June 30
Rate type: Commercial

Historical usage:
- Previous billing period: 8,011 kWh
- This billing period last year: 8,104 kWh

| **Charge type** | **Rate** | **Total charge** |
| --- | --- | --- |
| Energy | $0.120 per kWh | $ 881.76 |
| Distribution | $0.032 per kWh | $ 235.14 |
| System Access | $7.00 per month | $ 7.00 |
| EE Rebate | -$500.00 (one-time) | -$ 500.00 |
| | Subtotal | $ 623.90 |
| | Taxes (4.0%) | $ 24.96 |
| | **Total** | **$ 648.86** |

*See reverse for payment options. →*

**191.** Which part of the fume hoods is NOT described as increasing energy efficiency?
(A) The controller
(B) The blower
(C) The sash
(D) The motor

**192.** In the e-mail, the word "spent" in paragraph 1, line 1, is closest in meaning to
(A) contributed
(B) passed
(C) paid
(D) clarified

**193.** What size of fume hood does Ms. Murphy suggest buying?
(A) 2-foot
(B) 4-foot
(C) 6-foot
(D) 8-foot

**194.** What is implied about a rebate program?
(A) It has been extended.
(B) Its maximum amount was raised.
(C) It is now offered by two organizations.
(D) Its name has been changed.

**195.** What does the bill indicate about Simonroy Laboratories?
(A) Its current bill is due at the end of the next billing period.
(B) It has been a Wisenway Energy customer for at least a year.
(C) Its energy expenses are automatically withdrawn from its bank account.
(D) All of its regular energy charges vary based on its energy usage.

GO ON TO THE NEXT PAGE

**Questions 196–200** refer to the following advertisement and e-mails.

## Flickinger Corporate Dining Services

www.delicious-fcds.com

Flickinger Corporate Dining Services (FCDS) has become the number-one operator of corporate cafeterias in the Birmingham area because of our dedication to excellence and range of flexible services. We can plan the creation of a new cafeteria or take over operation of an existing facility from an in-house provider to increase efficiency. If desired, we can serve meals from 6 A.M. to 10 P.M. For businesses with environmental concerns, we offer menu plans with dishes made only with foods from regional suppliers. Above all, we guarantee delicious, nutritious meals and snacks. Visit our Web site for more information and resources, including footage of our chefs at work.

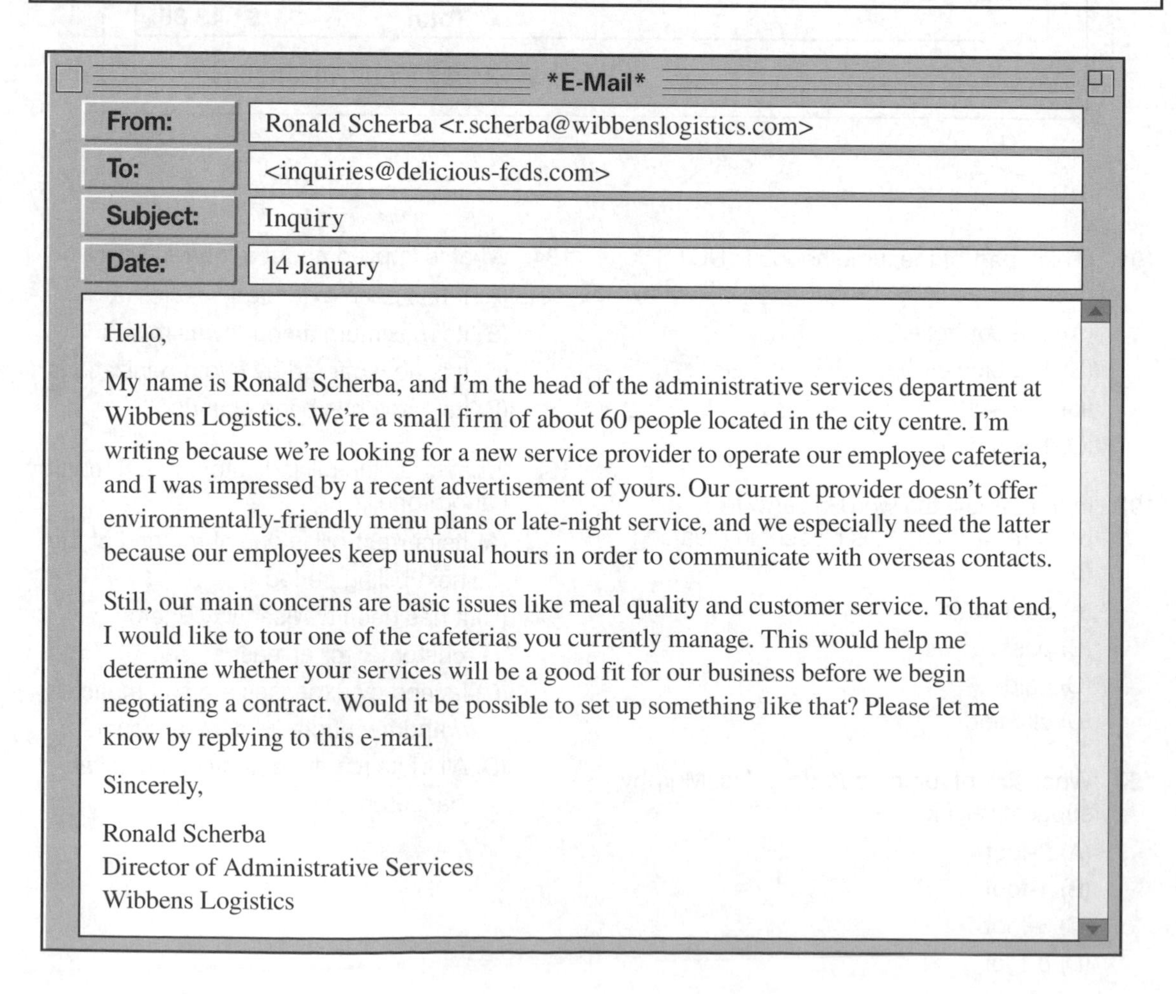

*E-Mail*

| | |
|---|---|
| **From:** | Ronald Scherba <r.scherba@wibbenslogistics.com> |
| **To:** | <inquiries@delicious-fcds.com> |
| **Subject:** | Inquiry |
| **Date:** | 14 January |

Hello,

My name is Ronald Scherba, and I'm the head of the administrative services department at Wibbens Logistics. We're a small firm of about 60 people located in the city centre. I'm writing because we're looking for a new service provider to operate our employee cafeteria, and I was impressed by a recent advertisement of yours. Our current provider doesn't offer environmentally-friendly menu plans or late-night service, and we especially need the latter because our employees keep unusual hours in order to communicate with overseas contacts.

Still, our main concerns are basic issues like meal quality and customer service. To that end, I would like to tour one of the cafeterias you currently manage. This would help me determine whether your services will be a good fit for our business before we begin negotiating a contract. Would it be possible to set up something like that? Please let me know by replying to this e-mail.

Sincerely,

Ronald Scherba
Director of Administrative Services
Wibbens Logistics

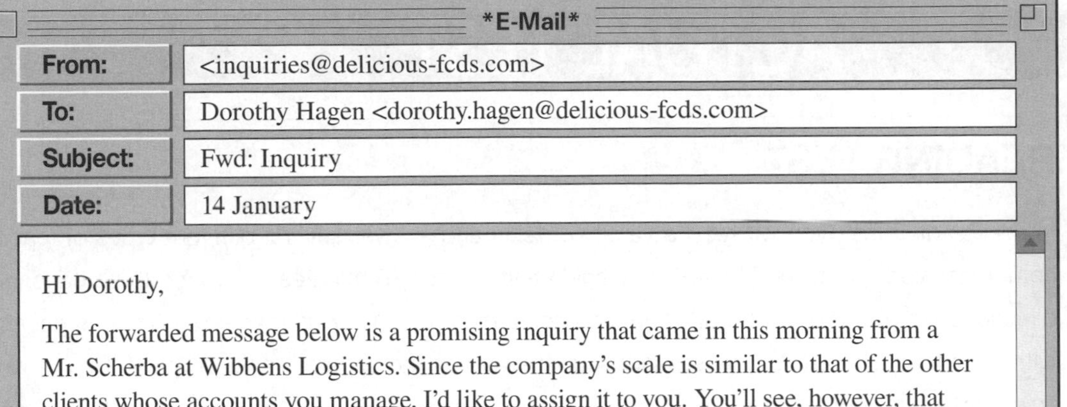
*E-Mail*

From: <inquiries@delicious-fcds.com>

To: Dorothy Hagen <dorothy.hagen@delicious-fcds.com>

Subject: Fwd: Inquiry

Date: 14 January

Hi Dorothy,

The forwarded message below is a promising inquiry that came in this morning from a Mr. Scherba at Wibbens Logistics. Since the company's scale is similar to that of the other clients whose accounts you manage, I'd like to assign it to you. You'll see, however, that Mr. Scherba makes an unusual request in his e-mail. Could you come to my office at 2 P.M. to talk about the best way to handle it? If I don't receive a reply from you by 1:30, I'll contact you through the company messaging service.

Thanks,

Vincent Porter

**196.** According to the advertisement, what can visitors to FCDS's Web site do?

(A) Read comments made by current customers
(B) Access a variety of sample menu plans
(C) See a list of the company's suppliers
(D) Watch videos of meals being prepared

**197.** What is a service mentioned in the advertisement Mr. Scherba does NOT inquire about?

(A) Special occasion catering
(B) Cafeteria construction planning
(C) A locally-sourced food program
(D) Extended serving hours

**198.** What does Mr. Scherba hope to arrange?

(A) A visit to a food service facility
(B) A conference call with FCDS staff
(C) A delivery of informational materials
(D) A collaboration between two food service providers

**199.** What is most likely true about Ms. Hagen?

(A) She manages all clients within a certain city district.
(B) She met Mr. Scherba at a networking event.
(C) She has experience with small firms.
(D) She specializes in overseas accounts.

**200.** Why is Ms. Hagen asked to go to Mr. Porter's office?

(A) To present the results of some research
(B) To assist with assigning tasks to other employees
(C) To discuss strategies for responding to a request
(D) To resolve an issue with some software

**Stop! This is the end of the test. If you finish before time is called, you may go back to Parts 5, 6, and 7 and check your work.**

# ACTUAL TEST

## READING TEST

In the Reading test, you will read a variety of texts and answer several different types of reading comprehension questions. The entire Reading test will last 75 minutes. There are three parts, and directions are given for each part. You are encouraged to answer as many questions as possible within the time allowed. You must mark your answers on the separate answer sheet. Do not write your answers in your test book.

## PART 5

**Directions:** A word or phrase is missing in each of the sentences below. Four answer choices are given below each sentence. Select the best answer to complete the sentence. Then mark the letter (A), (B), (C), or (D) on your answer sheet.

**101.** Authorities ------- a warning to drivers about poor road conditions caused by the recent storm.

(A) is issuing
(B) was issued
(C) will be issued
(D) have issued

**102.** Ben Johnson was ------- one of the most influential photographers of the year.

(A) easy
(B) ease
(C) easily
(D) easiest

**103.** The city is considering turning the vacant land ------- a small playground or some plots for community gardening.

(A) into
(B) apart
(C) across
(D) only

**104.** Since Ms. Huff's lecture dealt with the most controversial topic, the audience directed the majority of its questions to -------.

(A) herself
(B) hers
(C) her
(D) she

**105.** Collis Group regularly appears ------- lists of banks with the highest level of customer satisfaction.

(A) at
(B) on
(C) of
(D) to

**106.** Please confirm that you have closed the paper drawers ------- before attempting to operate the printer.

(A) securely
(B) widely
(C) hardly
(D) strictly

**107.** The release of the SwiftPlay game console was ------- timed to occur at the start of the holiday shopping season.

(A) strategy
(B) strategized
(C) strategic
(D) strategically

**108.** Flexible working arrangements are increasingly favored by full-time and part-time workers -------.

(A) neither
(B) alike
(C) both
(D) same

**109.** After careful consideration, Mr. Marsh's reasons for requesting a deadline ------- were determined to be insufficient.

(A) extension
(B) extended
(C) extendable
(D) extensions

**110.** Candidates may be asked to provide ------- of their qualifications in the form of diplomas, certificates, etc.

(A) access
(B) renewal
(C) evidence
(D) compensation

**111.** Alonta Associates requires its employees to ------- the company of a change in their home address.

(A) note
(B) reveal
(C) educate
(D) inform

**112.** ------- draws readers to the *Willard Daily News* is our commitment to fair and honest reporting.

(A) Something
(B) What
(C) Whom
(D) Whoever

**113.** Bailey Studios' new comedy has performed ------- better at the box office than movie industry analysts predicted it would.

(A) far
(B) so
(C) very
(D) beyond

**114.** ------- the construction permit application took longer than the contractor had anticipated.

(A) Prepare
(B) Preparing
(C) Preparation
(D) Prepared

**115.** At the orientation, trainees should listen attentively while the representative from headquarters ------- our corporate values.

(A) described
(B) has described
(C) describe
(D) is describing

**116.** Bauft Software's booth was crowded with visitors ------- its inconvenient placement in a back corner of the exhibition hall.

(A) despite
(B) between
(C) except
(D) unlike

**117.** ------- upgraded with the latest hardware, our data centers offer safe, reliable data storage.

(A) Frequent
(B) Frequenting
(C) Frequency
(D) Frequently

**118.** The year-end report your department will produce must include summaries of both concluded and ------- projects.

(A) multiple
(B) ambitious
(C) tailored
(D) ongoing

**119.** Due to the mild weather, this seems likely to be Jennings Winter Recreation Area's ------- season of the past fifteen years.

(A) shorten
(B) shortest
(C) shorter
(D) shortly

**120.** The office's energy ------- has been successfully reduced by the campaign to power down idle electronics at night.

(A) transition
(B) efficiency
(C) consumption
(D) awareness



GO ON TO THE NEXT PAGE

**121.** An e-mail notification about an upcoming series of training sessions was sent to -------.

(A) recruiter
(B) recruits
(C) recruit
(D) recruiting

**122.** The recipe calls for one pound of ground beef, but this can be replaced with an ------- amount of a vegetarian substitute such as cooked lentils.

(A) existing
(B) accountable
(C) equivalent
(D) overall

**123.** The business world and the academic community must be encouraged to collaborate with ------- to engage in practical research.

(A) other
(B) which
(C) itself
(D) one another

**124.** Moxis Motors ------- to supply transportation providers with economical, fuel-efficient commercial vehicles.

(A) strives
(B) conforms
(C) discontinues
(D) specializes

**125.** The final step of the licensing process is a practical exam that verifies applicants' ------- in the art of styling hair.

(A) insight
(B) privilege
(C) proficiency
(D) compliance

**126.** ------- joining Keller Fox Ltd., Ms. Jang was the vice president of sales at Cortiss Hotels.

(A) Prior to
(B) Compared to
(C) Ever since
(D) According to

**127.** The IT director has assured us that the technicians ------- the system repairs by this time tomorrow.

(A) will have finished
(B) have finished
(C) are finishing
(D) were finishing

**128.** Mr. Easton released a statement ------- his spokesperson instead of speaking directly to the press.

(A) even
(B) officially
(C) announced
(D) through

**129.** The committee proposed ------- the Sparks and Corgan courts in a new building to be located in western Corgan.

(A) expediting
(B) consolidating
(C) delegating
(D) waiving

**130.** Wunch Consulting's strategic planning services will assist you in determining your business objectives ------- evaluating your progress in achieving them.

(A) yet
(B) beside
(C) and
(D) in regard to

# PART 6

**Directions:** Read the texts that follow. A word, phrase, or sentence is missing in parts of each text. Four answer choices for each question are given below the text. Select the best answer to complete the text. Then mark the letter (A), (B), (C), or (D) on your answer sheet.



**Questions 131–134** refer to the following letter.

February 25

Diana Townsend
407 Robin Rd.
Burkett, ME 04007

Ms. Townsend,

You are hereby invited to a community meeting on the proposal to construct an express train line paralleling part of the Gold Line. The meeting will be held in the auditorium of the Powlar Community Center from 6 to 8 P.M. on Thursday, March 18. -------. **131.**

------- **132.** described in detail in the enclosure, the express line would run from Burkett to Grenham Central Station with just two stops in between. Therefore, it would enable ------- **133.** journeys to and from the city center.

The meeting will be a chance for Burkett residents to provide input on the proposal. The agenda includes a presentation ------- **134.** by transit officials and a question-and-answer session. We hope you will attend.

Sincerely,

Gary Murphy
Director, Grenham Regional Transit Authority

Encl.

**131.** (A) Unfortunately, this date does not suit my schedule.
(B) The center is located at 150 Second Street, Burkett.
(C) We expect construction to be nearly done by then.
(D) Please come prepared with a revised draft of the proposal.

**132.** (A) Upon
(B) For
(C) Until
(D) As

**133.** (A) swifter
(B) cozier
(C) more scenic
(D) cheaper

**134.** (A) will conduct
(B) was conducted
(C) to conduct
(D) conducted

GO ON TO THE NEXT PAGE

**Questions 135–138** refer to the following e-mail.

From: Gwendolyn Ramsey
To: All volunteers
Subject: Policy
Date: 16 December

Dear Lyndie Fashion Museum volunteers,

I recently overheard a volunteer guide giving incorrect information ------- **135.** a tour of our exhibits. Please do not do this. I understand that it may be embarrassing to be asked a question that you can't answer. ------- **136.**, the correct response in that situation is to direct the visitor to our educational staff. ------- **137.**. It's also wise to learn the answer yourself to prevent the problem from recurring.

I wanted to spell this policy out to all of you, as it's not clear ------- **138.** the incident I witnessed was a one-time mistake or part of a widespread problem. Please reply briefly to confirm that you've read and understood this e-mail.

Thanks,

Gwendolyn Ramsey
Volunteer Coordinator
Lyndie Fashion Museum

**135.** (A) like
(B) during
(C) though
(D) while

**136.** (A) Likewise
(B) On the contrary
(C) More importantly
(D) Nevertheless

**137.** (A) They will be able to give an overview of our event calendar.
(B) The museum is open from 10 A.M. to 6 P.M., Tuesday through Sunday.
(C) If they are unavailable, the visitor may e-mail them later at info@lfm.org.nz.
(D) We are always seeking additional volunteers to lead tours.

**138.** (A) whether
(B) based on
(C) after all
(D) when

**Questions 139–142** refer to the following information.

*Thank you for ordering from Sarinta Studio!*

The enclosed candle was handmade with high-quality ingredients. -------(139.) its wick trimmed to a 1/8-inch length for best results. We also advise burning it until the top layer of wax melts completely each time to keep the top from becoming uneven.

If you are displeased with your purchase for any reason, please don't hesitate to contact us. -------(140.). Our decades of fragrance expertise are at your disposal. We are happy to recommend another -------(141.) for you or even create a customized one. We can be reached by e-mail at sarinta@pexo-market.com or by phone during regular business hours at (864) 555-0192.

On the other hand, if you are satisfied with your Sarinta candle, please let -------(142.) know! You can leave a positive review of our studio at www.pexo-market.com/sarinta. We would deeply appreciate the support.

**139.** (A) To keep
(B) Having kept
(C) Keeping
(D) Keep

**140.** (A) At present, Sarinta Studio does not operate any offline stores.
(B) Our social media accounts are often updated with photos of new products.
(C) Take 15% off of your next order with the coupon code "MYSARINTA."
(D) Along with returns and exchanges, we can offer helpful advice.

**141.** (A) scent
(B) shape
(C) texture
(D) pattern

**142.** (A) her
(B) some
(C) others
(D) them



GO ON TO THE NEXT PAGE

**Questions 143–146** refer to the following memo.

To: All Pengler employees
Re: Rouse Commercial Services

I'm writing to share with you all a recent success story for our company.

Rouse Commercial Services, a maintenance and repair provider, used to have a paperwork problem. Its service visit report forms were long and easy to misplace. Customers complained about paying for the time technicians spent ------- them by hand after every visit, while lost forms often made it difficult for the company to bill correctly for the services it had provided.
**143.**

Fortunately, Rouse chose to buy tablet computers and begin using Pengler Business. Its technicians ------- fill out electronic forms that are automatically saved to a shared, well-organized folder.
**144.**

Rouse's service business supervisor told us, "You've made it possible for our technicians to be much more productive. -------." Thanks to these benefits, the company ------- its investment in just one year.
**145.** **146.**

We should all be proud of the assistance that Pengler provided for Rouse Commercial Services. Let's keep up the good work.

Gun-Woo Han
Chief Executive Officer

**143.** (A) on completion
(B) that complete
(C) completing
(D) completed

**144.** (A) now
(B) then
(C) rarely
(D) still

**145.** (A) We employ specialists in plumbing, electricity, and building repair.
(B) And just as importantly, we no longer lose money to underbilling.
(C) We want customers to know that we are keeping their data safe.
(D) As a matter of fact, we are exploring that possibility right now.

**146.** (A) reserved
(B) recovered
(C) maintained
(D) encouraged

# PART 7

**Directions:** In this part you will read a selection of texts, such as magazine and newspaper articles, e-mails, and instant messages. Each text or set of texts is followed by several questions. Select the best answer for each question and mark the letter (A), (B), (C), or (D) on your answer sheet.



**Questions 147–148** refer to the following e-mail.

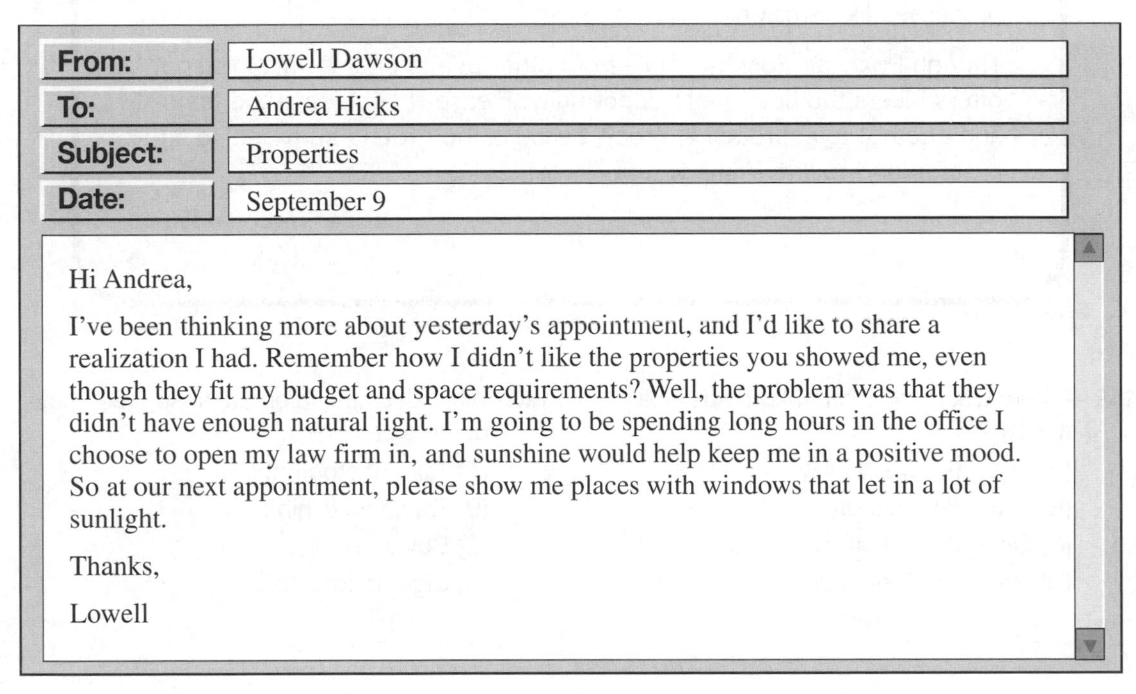

| | |
|---|---|
| **From:** | Lowell Dawson |
| **To:** | Andrea Hicks |
| **Subject:** | Properties |
| **Date:** | September 9 |

Hi Andrea,

I've been thinking more about yesterday's appointment, and I'd like to share a realization I had. Remember how I didn't like the properties you showed me, even though they fit my budget and space requirements? Well, the problem was that they didn't have enough natural light. I'm going to be spending long hours in the office I choose to open my law firm in, and sunshine would help keep me in a positive mood. So at our next appointment, please show me places with windows that let in a lot of sunlight.

Thanks,

Lowell

**147.** Why did Mr. Dawson send the e-mail?
(A) To confirm a choice
(B) To inquire about a budget
(C) To provide a specification
(D) To make an appointment

**148.** What is suggested about Mr. Dawson?
(A) He will be spending a lot of time outdoors soon.
(B) He wants to upgrade some lighting fixtures.
(C) He is concerned about a property law.
(D) He plans to start his own business.

GO ON TO THE NEXT PAGE

**Questions 149–150** refer to the following information.

## Foxhead Rock

Foxhead Rock is the large rock formation visible on the rise opposite this point. Named for its resemblance to the head of a fox, it is one of the most famous geological features in the park. The 27-foot structure is made of sandstone shaped over millions of years by natural processes like erosion.

Though Foxhead Rock is visible from other points on the trail, this spot offers hikers the best photo opportunity. Please do not leave the trail and attempt to approach the rock, because the ground surrounding it is steep and rocky. Thank you.

*Lundes National Park*

**149.** Where would the information most likely appear?

(A) In a museum display
(B) In a park brochure
(C) On a product label
(D) On an outdoor sign

**150.** What does the information suggest that readers can do?

(A) Take photographs
(B) Touch an exhibit
(C) Buy souvenirs
(D) Sign up for a tour

**Questions 151–152** refer to the following text-message chain.

**Herman Ahderom [3:02 P.M.]**
Ms. Ryan, the candidate you brought to us isn't responding to my attempts to video chat with him.

**Eleanor Ryan [3:03 P.M.]**
Matthew Kasper? The applicant for the data-entry position?

**Herman Ahderom [3:03 P.M.]**
That's right.

**Eleanor Ryan [3:04 P.M.]**
I'm sorry about that. Let me check in with him.

**Eleanor Ryan [3:05 P.M.]**
I think there must be a misunderstanding. He says he's online.

**Herman Ahderom [3:06 P.M.]**
Let's confirm our information. I'm calling him using the program "Chatrich," and his user name is "matthew_kasper," right?

**Eleanor Ryan [3:07 P.M.]**
Actually, it's "matthew.kasper," according to my materials. Try that.

**Herman Ahderom [3:09 P.M.]**
OK, now the call is going through. Thank you. I'll call you afterwards to let you know how the interview went.

**151.** Who most likely is Ms. Ryan?
(A) A computer technician
(B) A political reporter
(C) An event planner
(D) A job recruiter

**152.** At 3:07 P.M., what does Ms. Ryan recommend doing when she writes, "Try that"?
(A) Using different contact information
(B) Restarting a software program
(C) Reading some instructional materials
(D) Changing a computer's display setting



GO ON TO THE NEXT PAGE

**Questions 153–154** refer to the following Web page.

http://www.scheelerexpress.com/rail

## Scheeler Express Rail Services

Rail can be an excellent way to move large amounts of freight. When compared with trucking, the other major over-the-land shipping method, rail can be slower and less convenient but offers increased safety and causes less harm to the environment. It is best suited to businesses that need to transport large amounts of freight over a long distance on a regular basis.

Scheeler Express's transportation experts can advise you on whether railway transport is right for your company. If you decide it is, we can assist you with navigating the complex systems of different railway companies on your route. We maintain relationships with all major operators, which enables us to stay up-to-date on their constantly changing technology.

Contact us today to get started.

**153.** Who is the Web page intended for?

(A) Employees commuting to work
(B) Companies shipping cargo
(C) Tourists visiting a certain region
(D) Train operators seeking repair services

**154.** According to the Web page, what is one advantage of Scheeler Express?

(A) It offers long hours of operation.
(B) It employs advanced technology.
(C) It has connections with other companies.
(D) It has exclusive use of a rail route.

**Questions 155–157** refer to the following e-mail.

E-Mail message

From: Zaters Hardware
To: Wallace Glover
Subject: Announcement
Date: November 1

Dear Valued Customer,

Zaters Hardware is sorry to announce the discontinuation of our Zaters Points program. For the last eight years, Zaters Points have been a great way for our customers to earn discounts on our products. Unfortunately, the cost of running the program has grown to the point where it no longer makes sense to continue offering it. Starting today, no new applications for the program will be accepted. However, we will allow existing participants to continue accruing Zaters Points until November 30 and spending them until January 31. Please keep the latter deadline in mind as you determine how to use your remaining points. We will send out periodic reminder e-mails about the situation as well.

As always, thank you for being a loyal Zaters Hardware customer.

Sincerely,

Darryl Harmon, CEO
Zaters Hardware

**155.** What does the e-mail notify recipients of ?
(A) The closing of a retail store
(B) The end of a loyalty program
(C) The replacement of an executive
(D) The recall of a hardware product

**156.** According to the e-mail, what was the reason for the decision?
(A) A security issue
(B) A legal dispute
(C) Financial considerations
(D) Business restructuring

**157.** What are recipients asked to do?
(A) Fill out a form
(B) Wait for a future e-mail
(C) Choose between two options
(D) Remember a date



GO ON TO THE NEXT PAGE

**Questions 158–160** refer to the following Web page.

http://www.olimmer.com/purchase/step2

**Step 2: Choose Your Subscription**

Thank you for creating an Olimmer account, Ms. Garza. Now it is time to decide how long you want to be able to access our vast library of templates, themes, and graphics to make first-rate online content for your clients. Please review the following information and select the subscription you would like in the drop-down menu at the bottom of the page.

Pricing:

- 3-month subscription ($90)
- 6-month subscription ($160)
- 1-year subscription ($270)
- 2-year subscription ($410)

As you can see, we offer great deals for longer-term subscriptions. Our 2-year subscription costs just $0.56 per day—barely half as much as our 3-month subscription, which is still reasonable at $0.98 per day. Our 6-month and 1-year subscriptions are also wonderful options at $0.88 and $0.73 per day, respectively.

Payment:

Payments can be made monthly or yearly. Your first payment is due immediately. We accept credit and debit cards. You will be asked for your payment details on the following screen.

Changing your subscription term:

This can be done at any time at no charge. A new billing cycle will be started, and your first invoice will include a credit for the unused time on your previous subscription.

**Subscription:** 1-year   **Next ▶**

**158.** Who most likely is Olimmer intended for?
(A) Freelance accountants
(B) Web designers
(C) Librarians
(D) Journalists

**159.** How much will Ms. Garza pay per day for her subscription?
(A) $0.56
(B) $0.73
(C) $0.88
(D) $0.98

**160.** What is stated about Olimmer subscriptions?
(A) They can be cancelled at any time.
(B) Their prices reflect the services they allow access to.
(C) There is no fee for switching from one to another.
(D) They must be paid for on a monthly basis.

**Questions 161–163** refer to the following memo.

To: All employees
From: Diane Erickson
Re: Flexible hours

It has recently come to my attention that there is some confusion among employees about Prask's policy with regard to flexible working hours. —[1]—. I have rewritten the employee handbook as follows to clarify the issue:

"Prask requires all full-time employees to work in the office for 40 hours each week. —[2]—. However, employees approved to work flextime may fulfill this requirement by working any combination of hours between 7 A.M. and 8 P.M., Monday through Friday. Flextime is only available to employees whose job duties do not require them to be in the office at specific times. Employees must receive managerial approval in order to work flexible hours. The privilege of working flextime may be revoked at any time due to business needs or employee performance issues. —[3]—."

If you believe that you are eligible to work flextime and would like to do so, you should begin by creating a proposed schedule, and then meet with your manager to discuss it. Please do not bring flextime requests directly to the HR department. However, general inquiries about the policy can be made to our department by contacting John Burrows (ext. 72, john.burrows@prask.com). —[4]—.

Diane Erickson
Director of Human Resources

**161.** What is indicated about Prask's flextime policy?
(A) It allows weekend work.
(B) It was recently implemented.
(C) It excludes some employees.
(D) It is popular with staff.

**162.** According to the memo, what should an employee interested in working flextime do first?
(A) Determine their desired working hours
(B) Ask a manager for permission
(C) Submit a request to Human Resources
(D) Earn a positive performance evaluation

**163.** In which of the positions marked [1], [2], [3], and [4] does the following sentence best belong?
"In either case, the employee's manager should clearly explain the situation and give the employee advance notice of the change."
(A) [1]
(B) [2]
(C) [3]
(D) [4]



GO ON TO THE NEXT PAGE

**Questions 164–167** refer to the following online chat discussion.

**Lana Norton** **[11:54 A.M.]**
Hi, everyone. I'm at a doctor's appointment that's running long, so I'm not going to be able to teach my 1 P.M. aerobics class today. Kyeong-Mo told me to text all of you to see if one of you could do it for me.

**Henry Russell** **[11:54 A.M.]**
I would, but I'll be in the middle of a pilates class at that time.

**Kenya Hunt** **[11:55 A.M.]**
I'm finished with my scheduled classes for the day. Could you give me some more details?

**Lana Norton** **[11:55 A.M.]**
It's a low-intensity, dance-centered class that runs from 1:00 to 1:50 in Studio 3. It doesn't require any equipment, and the students are usually older women.

**Kenya Hunt** **[11:56 A.M.]**
OK, that sounds doable. I'll take it. What kind of music do you usually play?

**Kyeong-Mo Jeon** **[11:57 A.M.]**
Thank you, Kenya. I'll send out a text to let the regular attendees know that the class will go forward with a different instructor.

**Lana Norton** **[11:58 A.M.]**
I actually have a video of the class that I recorded a few weeks ago. It should give you an idea of the music to play and the kind of moves that we usually do. What's your e-mail address?

**Kenya Hunt** **[11:58 A.M.]**
It's kenya.hunt@pnb-mail.com. Thanks! That'll be really helpful.

**Lana Norton** **[11:59 A.M.]**
No, thank you for volunteering to substitute! Let me know if you have any more questions. I should be able to check my phone periodically during the rest of my appointment.

**164.** Why does Ms. Norton message the other participants?
(A) To ask for a favor
(B) To promote an event
(C) To apologize for a situation
(D) To announce a schedule

**165.** At 11:56 A.M., what does Ms. Hunt most likely mean when she writes, "I'll take it"?
(A) She is accepting a teaching opportunity.
(B) She is volunteering to move an item.
(C) She would like to keep some equipment.
(D) She is interested in acquiring a new skill.

**166.** What is NOT indicated about the 1 P.M. class?
(A) It lasts for less than an hour.
(B) It requires registration in advance.
(C) It involves relatively easy exercise.
(D) It is attended routinely by some people.

**167.** What most likely will Ms. Norton e-mail to Ms. Hunt?
(A) A video clip
(B) A list of songs
(C) A sign-up sheet
(D) A neighborhood map

**Questions 168–171** refer to the following letter.

Claire Fields
390 Holt Drive
4C24+8G Bridgetown

18 March

Ruthie's
2090 Philip Road
3CV4+9Q Bridgetown

To Whom It May Concern:

My name is Claire Fields, and I am a frequent customer at your shop. I love your iced mochas, and I think your service is excellent. However, as a wheelchair user, there is an accessibility issue that I would like to bring to your attention. Your service counter is quite high. It seems like it is about 150 centimeters off the floor. I cannot see things that are set on it, I struggle to reach over it, and it even obstructs my view of your menu.

It would probably be quite expensive to replace your counter, so I am not asking you to do that. Instead, I am writing because I heard that you are opening new locations in other areas of Bridgetown. Please consider equipping them with more wheelchair-friendly facilities. Also, I suggest contacting the Barbados Disability Authority (BDA) for more tips on accessible design. Its Web site is www.bda.bb.

Thank you for taking the time to read my letter, and good luck! It is always exciting to see locally-owned businesses thrive.

Sincerely,

*Claire Fields*

**168.** What kind of business is Ruthie's?
(A) A café
(B) A hair salon
(C) A flower shop
(D) A clothing store

**169.** What problem does Ms. Fields describe?
(A) A doorway is too narrow.
(B) The text on a sign is too small.
(C) Some flooring is too uneven.
(D) A piece of furniture is too tall.

**170.** What is indicated about Ruthie's?
(A) It is currently expanding.
(B) It offers an unusual service.
(C) It employs people with disabilities.
(D) It is an international chain.

**171.** Why does Ms. Fields recommend contacting the BDA?
(A) To schedule an inspection
(B) To receive further information
(C) To apply for financial support
(D) To report a difficulty



GO ON TO THE NEXT PAGE

**Questions 172–175** refer to the following article.

# Evarson Farmers' Petition Introduced in State Parliament

SCAVELL (8 September)—Today, member of State Parliament Naomi Black submitted a petition created by farmers in the Evarson area protesting a government plan to reduce their water licences.

Water licences authorize their holders to use specific, large amounts of groundwater. —[1]—. The government's reduction plan would slowly shrink the amount of water that licence-holders in the agricultural industry are entitled to by 10% over the next five years. It was developed by the Evarson Water and Agriculture Taskforce (EWAT) as a way to combat the regions increasing dryness.

"Everyone has to adjust," said Alvin Brooks, EWAT's chair. "The state government has already cut its own water use through actions like replacing grass in public parks with stone gravel. The licence plan will encourage farmers to use water more efficiently."

However, the farmers complain that the reductions will unfairly devalue their land and damage the local economy. —[2]—. Courtney Grant, head of the Evarson Farmers Association (EFA) and one of the creators of the petition, said, "We already use water efficiently. All that the reductions will do is lower our output."

EWAT representatives and EFA members discussed the plan at a public meeting soon after its announcement last month, but were unable to find a mutually acceptable compromise. —[3]—. The association then wrote and circulated the "Petition for Responsible Water Resources Management."

The petition proposes that the state government invest in finding or developing additional water sources instead. —[4]—. Now that it has been officially introduced into State Parliament, it will be referred to the appropriate parliamentary committee for review.

**172.** What does EWAT propose doing?
(A) Subsidizing water-efficient technology
(B) Allocating less water to farming efforts
(C) Raising the qualifications for water licences
(D) Using water-conserving landscaping on public property

**173.** What is suggested about EWAT's plan?
(A) It was developed without input from EFA.
(B) It will be implemented after a delay of several years.
(C) It is similar to proposals made in other states.
(D) It will require a large investment of government funds.

**174.** Who most likely is Ms. Black?
(A) A university professor
(B) A produce grower
(C) A regional politician
(D) An environmental activist

**175.** In which of the positions marked [1], [2], [3], and [4] does the following sentence best belong?
"It garnered more than 1,000 signatures in two weeks."
(A) [1]
(B) [2]
(C) [3]
(D) [4]



GO ON TO THE NEXT PAGE

**Questions 176–180** refer to the following chart and e-mail.

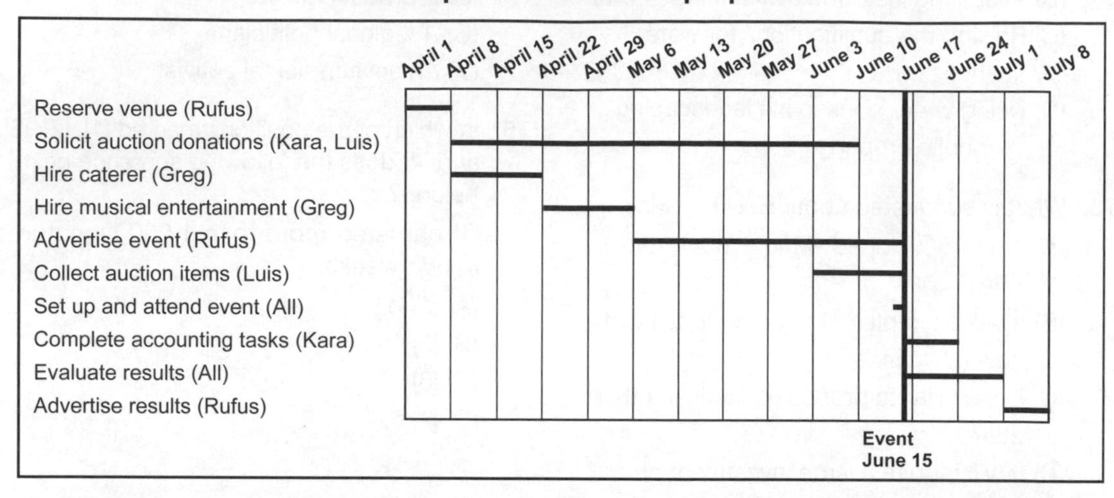


| | |
|---|---|
| **From:** | Kara Griffin |
| **To:** | Luis Rodriguez |
| **Subject:** | Good news |
| **Date:** | April 24 |

Hi Luis,

I have some good news from my meeting with Mr. Bobrova at Falcon Gallery this morning—he agreed to donate a Gabrielle Searcy painting! It's valued at nearly $500, so it could bring in a pretty high bid. It turns out that Mr. Bobrova loves Felix Forest, so he was very happy to help with our conservation efforts.

You should talk to him in advance about how to collect and transport the piece, though, because I suspect that that might be difficult. If you do need to use a packing or transportation service, make sure you keep the receipts and any other paperwork. We'll need them for accounting purposes after the event.

How are your efforts going? Have you heard back from the amusement park yet? Their admission tickets would be such an attractive item for families.

Also, I noticed that Greg hasn't met his first deadline. Do you know why? I thought that you might have heard something since your desk is next to his.

- Kara

**176.** According to the chart, what is Rufus NOT responsible for?

(A) Reserving a site
(B) Hiring a food provider
(C) Publicizing the event
(D) Setting up a venue

**177.** What has Ms. Griffin obtained a donation of?

(A) An artwork
(B) A gallery tour
(C) A set of painting lessons
(D) A meal with an artist

**178.** Who most likely would need the paperwork mentioned in the e-mail?

(A) Rufus
(B) Ms. Griffin
(C) Greg
(D) Ms. Searcy

**179.** What deadline did Greg fail to meet?

(A) April 8
(B) April 15
(C) April 22
(D) May 6

**180.** In the e-mail, what is suggested about the event that is being planned?

(A) It had to be rescheduled.
(B) It will require special transportation for attendees.
(C) It is being sponsored by an entertainment business.
(D) It will benefit an environmental cause.



GO ON TO THE NEXT PAGE

**Questions 181–185** refer to the following invoice and e-mail.

## INVOICE

**Brendan Echevarria Services**
P.O. Box 10392
Toronto ON M4N 3P6
647-555-0129
www.brendanechevarria.com

Invoice #: 62
Work period: January 1–January 31
Date issued: February 1
**Date due: March 2**

Client: Baldora Online
Attn: Amanda Aoki
780 Richmond St.
Toronto ON M6J 1B9
416-555-0105

| Service | Rate | Total |
|---|---|---|
| 300-word news article on Werra, Inc. expansion | $0.30/word | $90.00 |
| 450-word informative article on management skills | $0.50/word | $225.00 |
| 30-minute phone call with client | $5/15 minutes | $10.00 |
| Revision of 450-word article | $0.10/word | $45.00 |
| | **Total:** | **$370.00** |

Payment can be made by check to the above physical address or by WeisPay to payment@brendanechevarria.com.

*Thank you for your business!*

***E-mail***

From: Brendan Echevarria <contact@brendanechevarria.com>
To: Amanda Aoki <amanda.aoki@baldora.com>
Subject: Re: Questions
Date: February 5

Dear Amanda,

I'm happy to address your question about my invoice for this month. First, you are correct that my rewriting rate increased this year. I'm sorry if it took you by surprise, but the new rate was stated in the rate sheet that I sent to your predecessor in December, and he agreed to it. I'll forward you the e-mail exchange separately so that you can confirm this. My guess is that he forgot to update my information in your company files.

As for your request to recommend other potential contributors, I do know someone that you may be interested in. Her name is Melody Thorpe, and she's a former colleague of mine from the *Yorkville Herald* who recently became a freelance science writer. She has a simple, engaging style that you can see in her old articles on the *Herald's* Web site. If you decide you'd like to contact her, her e-mail address is m.thorpe@vct-mail.com.

Let me know if you have any further questions or concerns. Unless you tell me otherwise, I'll continue working on my current 250-word news article.

Sincerely,

Brendan

**181.** What did Mr. Echevarria write about for Baldora Online in January?

(A) Sports
(B) Politics
(C) Business
(D) Entertainment

**182.** What is the purpose of the e-mail?

(A) To answer some client inquiries
(B) To report a problem with a payment
(C) To discuss changes to a project
(D) To apologize for a billing mistake

**183.** Which rate does Mr. Echevarria indicate recently changed?

(A) $0.30 per word
(B) $0.50 per word
(C) $5.00 for 15 minutes
(D) $0.10 per word

**184.** In the e-mail, the word "exchange" in paragraph 1, line 4, is closest in meaning to

(A) trade
(B) market
(C) conversion
(D) correspondence

**185.** What does the e-mail indicate about Ms. Thorpe?

(A) She is one of Mr. Echevarria's clients.
(B) She has a degree in a science field.
(C) She no longer has a full-time employer.
(D) She responded to an advertisement on a Web site.



GO ON TO THE NEXT PAGE

**Questions 186–190** refer to the following e-mail, form, and note.

| | |
|---|---|
| **From:** | Ed Padgett |
| **To:** | Rose Tate |
| **Subject:** | Office decoration |
| **Date:** | September 30 |
| **Attachment:** | Office_decoration_request |

Dear Ms. Tate,

Welcome to Lunsford & Associates! My name is Ed Padgett, and I'm the office administrator for your floor. Since you'll be very busy after you begin work, you might want to start shopping for your new office now. Our office decoration policies are as follows:

- Employees who have private offices (hereafter, "officeholders") should decorate them within one month in order to make a good impression on clients.
- Upon hiring or promotion, new officeholders may spend up to $1000 on office decoration.
- Purchases can be requested by submitting an electronic Office Decoration Request form to an office administrator.
- Requests to spend any additional funds at this or a later time must be approved by the officeholder's manager.
- Decorations must be tasteful and professional.
- Nearby officeholders should be notified of decorating activities in advance in case it may disturb their work.

For reference, your office is roughly 10 feet long by 10 feet wide. Also, you may remember from your visit that it has grey marble floors and already contains a desk, a small sofa, and a bookcase—but of course you can replace any of those items if you'd like.

I've attached the necessary form to this e-mail. Please let me know if you have any questions about this information.

Sincerely,

Ed

## Office Decoration Request

Name: Rose Tate
Job Title: Senior Accountant

Effective Date of Hiring/Promotion: October 4
Office No.: 305

| Item description | Seller | Web page link | Quantity | Approx. Total Price* |
|---|---|---|---|---|
| Desk chair | Mallorin | www.mallorin.com/4024 | 1 | $235.00 |
| Art print | Nicole Phan | Not available | 1 | $175.00 |
| Armchair | Bohn Homes | www.bohnhomes.com/3421 | 2 | $210.00 |
| End table | Bohn Homes | www.bohnhomes.com/0257 | 1 | $65.00 |
| Coat rack | Bohn Homes | www.bohnhomes.com/6369 | 1 | $40.00 |
| | | Estimated Total: | | $725.00 |

Date of Submission: October 6

Submitted to: Ed Padgett

*Price estimates must include potential shipping/delivery/installation charges.

Hi Audrey,

I just wanted to let you know that I need to do some decorating in my office this morning. Please tell me if there are any times that would be especially inconvenient for you, because I have some flexibility on that.

Thanks,

Rose



**186.** What information does Mr. Padgett NOT provide about Ms. Tate's office?
(A) Its dimensions
(B) Its existing contents
(C) Its flooring material
(D) Its location

**187.** In the e-mail, the word "professional" in paragraph 6, line 1, is closest in meaning to
(A) receiving money
(B) durable
(C) appropriate for business
(D) polite

**188.** What is suggested about Ms. Tate's request?
(A) It will not require managerial approval.
(B) It includes replacements for some used furniture.
(C) It was submitted later than recommended.
(D) It has already been revised once.

**189.** What is indicated about the products listed on the form?
(A) One of them will be customized.
(B) Not all of them are sold online.
(C) Some of them are used items.
(D) They are all made by the same manufacturer.

**190.** What is implied about Audrey?
(A) She does not work in the mornings.
(B) Her office is near Ms. Tate's.
(C) She is a maintenance supervisor.
(D) Her job title is the same as Mr. Padgett's.

GO ON TO THE NEXT PAGE

**Questions 191–195** refer to the following article and Web pages.

### Hammell Wins Best Actor Prize at Vellon Springs

VELLON SPRINGS (May 17)—At its awards ceremony on Sunday night, the jury of the Vellon Springs Film Festival awarded Best Actor to veteran actor Christopher Hammell. Other big winners among the 22 independent films and countless performers competing in the festival included *Shouting in the Wind* (Best Picture) and Sylvia Mathis (Best Actress for her role in *The Advance*).

Mr. Hammell won for his superb performance in *Our Fence*. Directed by Vitomir Holmwood and costarring Felicia Carlson, *Our Fence* tells the story of a retired Seattle truck driver (Mr. Hammell) who finds his quiet life interrupted when an artist (Ms. Carlson) and her young daughter move in to the house next door. The moving film was an audience favorite and has been picked up for late summer distribution across the United States by RTY Films.

The award may represent a career comeback for Mr. Hammell, who stopped appearing in major studio-produced films about a decade ago after a string of disappointing box-office results. He has worked steadily in theater productions and smaller films since that time, but *Our Fence* is the first to gain widespread recognition.

During his acceptance speech onstage at the Vellon Theater, Mr. Hammell thanked Mr. Holmwood, Ms. Carlson, and the festival jury, and finished by saying, "It feels like I've been given a second chance. I can't believe it."

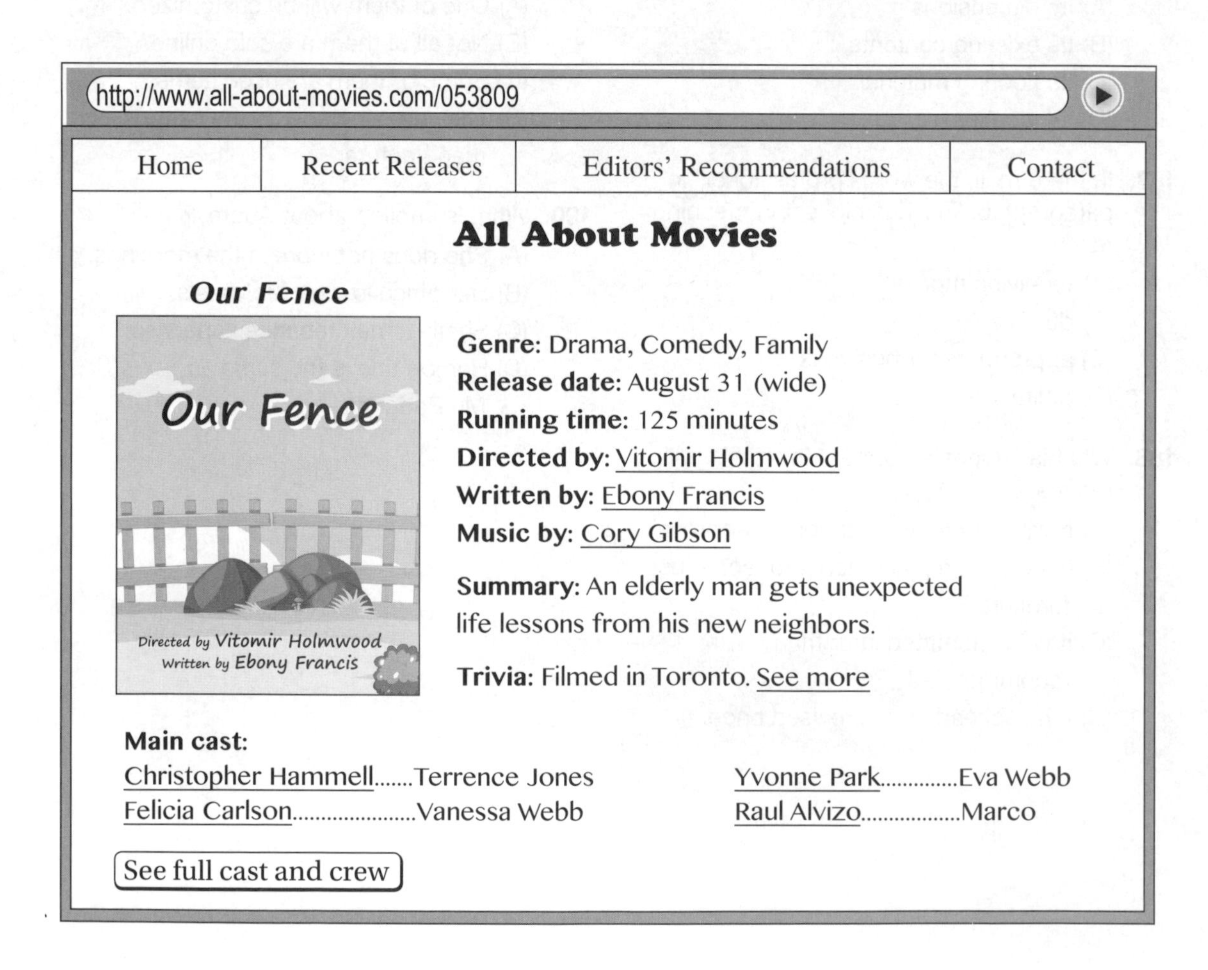
http://www.all-about-movies.com/053809

| Home | Recent Releases | Editors' Recommendations | Contact |
|---|---|---|---|

**All About Movies**

***Our Fence***



**Genre**: Drama, Comedy, Family
**Release date:** August 31 (wide)
**Running time:** 125 minutes
**Directed by:** Vitomir Holmwood
**Written by:** Ebony Francis
**Music by:** Cory Gibson

**Summary:** An elderly man gets unexpected life lessons from his new neighbors.

**Trivia:** Filmed in Toronto. See more

**Main cast:**

Christopher Hammell.......Terrence Jones
Felicia Carlson.....................Vanessa Webb
Yvonne Park.............Eva Webb
Raul Alvizo.................Marco

See full cast and crew

| Home | Recent Releases | Editors' Recommendations | Contact |
|---|---|---|---|

**All About Movies**

Reviews of: ***Our Fence***

**"More drama than comedy"** ★★★☆☆
I went to see this movie because the TV commercials for it made it look really fun, but it turned out to be quite sad in some parts. I'd still give it a positive review, though. The cast was great.
*Silvia Flores, Sept. 3*

**"Great job all around!"** ★★★★☆
Christopher Hammell definitely earns his festival award, but I think Ebony Francis is the real talent involved in this film. I'll certainly be seeking out more of her work.
*Kurt Stewart, Sept. 1*



**191.** What information does the article provide about the film festival?
(A) The president of its jury
(B) The length of time it lasts
(C) The number of times it has been held
(D) The venue of its awards ceremony

**192.** What does the article suggest that Mr. Hammell has done in recent years?
(A) Acted in independent films
(B) Worked as a film producer
(C) Taught students in a theater program
(D) Participated in a fund-raising campaign

**193.** What is most likely true about *Our Fence*?
(A) Its wide release was delayed.
(B) It was shortened after the film festival.
(C) It was not filmed where its story takes place.
(D) Its poster was not approved by RTY Films.

**194.** Why did Ms. Flores decide to see *Our Fence*?
(A) She read positive audience reviews of it.
(B) She is a fan of one of its cast members.
(C) She wanted to know more about its subject matter.
(D) She liked its promotional materials.

**195.** What did Mr. Stewart most appreciate about *Our Fence*?
(A) Its performances
(B) Its direction
(C) Its writing
(D) Its music

GO ON TO THE NEXT PAGE

**Questions 196–200** refer to the following Web page, warranty, and e-mail.

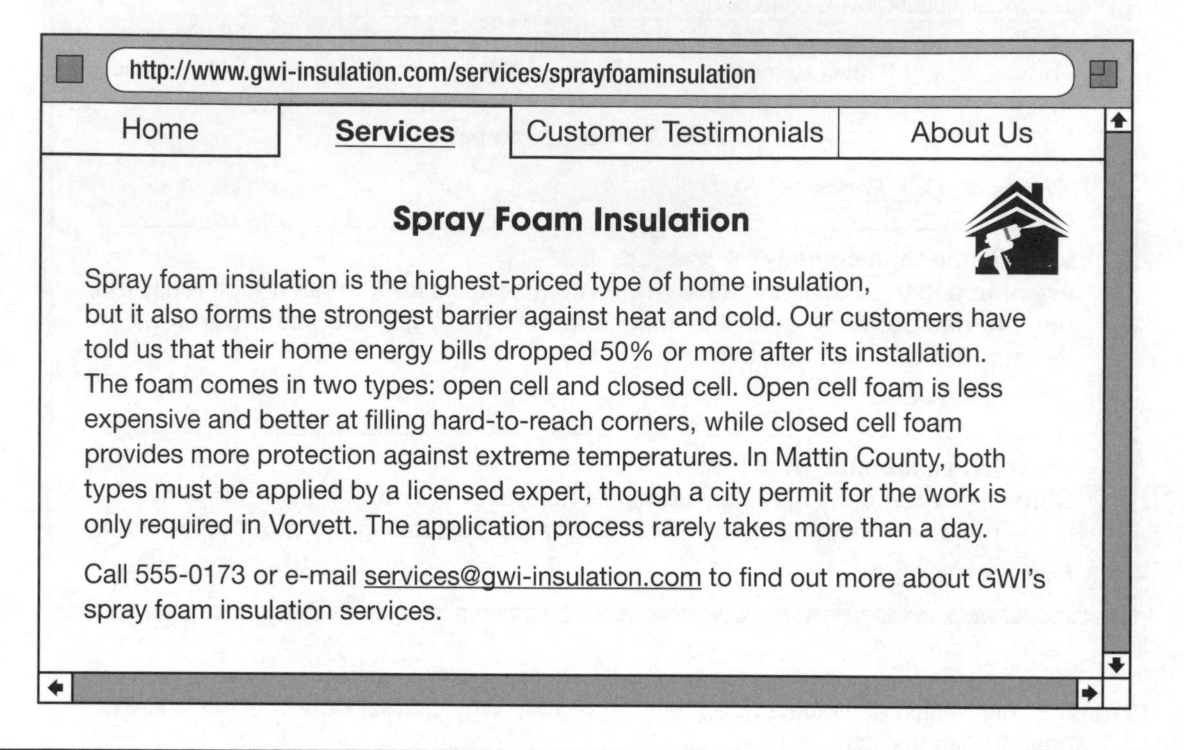
http://www.gwi-insulation.com/services/sprayfoaminsulation

Home | **Services** | Customer Testimonials | About Us

**Spray Foam Insulation**

Spray foam insulation is the highest-priced type of home insulation, but it also forms the strongest barrier against heat and cold. Our customers have told us that their home energy bills dropped 50% or more after its installation. The foam comes in two types: open cell and closed cell. Open cell foam is less expensive and better at filling hard-to-reach corners, while closed cell foam provides more protection against extreme temperatures. In Mattin County, both types must be applied by a licensed expert, though a city permit for the work is only required in Vorvett. The application process rarely takes more than a day.

Call 555-0173 or e-mail services@gwi-insulation.com to find out more about GWI's spray foam insulation services.

*GWI Insulation*

**Warranty**

**Work Information**

GWI Insulation installed open-cell insulation foam in the attic of the house located at 450 Brewer Street, Vorvett, at the request of its owner, Albert Mackie.

**Coverage**

GWI Insulation will provide labor and goods at no charge to repair any problems with the insulation that arise from defective products or work performed incorrectly at the time of installation.

This warranty is valid throughout the life of the structure and can be transferred along with the ownership of the structure.

**Exclusions**

GWI Insulation will not be held responsible for problems with insulation in the following cases:

1. It or the surrounding area has been altered or replaced by the homeowner or another company.
2. It has been damaged by extreme wind, rain, or other natural occurrences.
3. The surface to which it has been attached is damaged by the collapse or shifting of the structure's foundation or walls.
4. The surface to which it has been attached is suffering from mildew, mold, or natural aging.

*Lillian Thiel*

Lillian Thiel

President, GWI Insulation

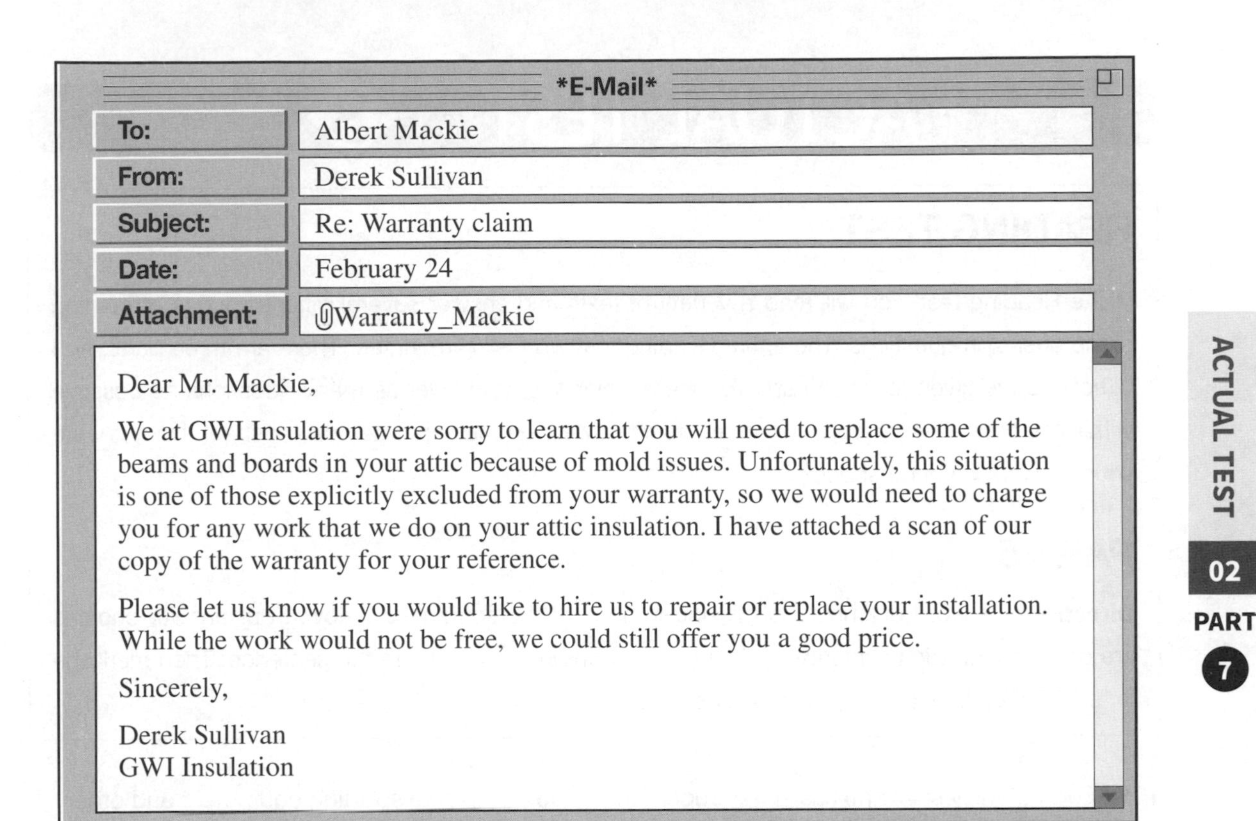
*E-Mail*

To: Albert Mackie
From: Derek Sullivan
Subject: Re: Warranty claim
Date: February 24
Attachment: Warranty_Mackie

Dear Mr. Mackie,

We at GWI Insulation were sorry to learn that you will need to replace some of the beams and boards in your attic because of mold issues. Unfortunately, this situation is one of those explicitly excluded from your warranty, so we would need to charge you for any work that we do on your attic insulation. I have attached a scan of our copy of the warranty for your reference.

Please let us know if you would like to hire us to repair or replace your installation. While the work would not be free, we could still offer you a good price.

Sincerely,

Derek Sullivan
GWI Insulation



**196.** According to the Web page, what have GWI Insulation's customers reported?
(A) Lower energy costs
(B) Better indoor air quality
(C) Reduced noise pollution
(D) Increased structural strength

**197.** What is suggested about the work done on Mr. Mackie's house?
(A) It was carried out in an underground space.
(B) It took place with a city government's permission.
(C) It involved the more expensive type of spray foam.
(D) It required more than one day to complete.

**198.** What is stated about the warranty?
(A) It has an expiration date.
(B) Mr. Mackie paid extra to obtain it.
(C) It will still be valid even if Mr. Mackie sells the house.
(D) It does not cover the cost of products needed for repairs.

**199.** Which exclusion in the warranty does Mr. Sullivan refer to?
(A) Exclusion 1
(B) Exclusion 2
(C) Exclusion 3
(D) Exclusion 4

**200.** In the e-mail, the word "learn" in paragraph 1, line 1, is closest in meaning to
(A) master
(B) discover
(C) memorize
(D) experience

**Stop! This is the end of the test. If you finish before time is called, you may go back to Parts 5, 6, and 7 and check your work.**

# ACTUAL TEST 

## READING TEST

In the Reading test, you will read a variety of texts and answer several different types of reading comprehension questions. The entire Reading test will last 75 minutes. There are three parts, and directions are given for each part. You are encouraged to answer as many questions as possible within the time allowed. You must mark your answers on the separate answer sheet. Do not write your answers in your test book.

## PART 5

**Directions:** A word or phrase is missing in each of the sentences below. Four answer choices are given below each sentence. Select the best answer to complete the sentence. Then mark the letter (A), (B), (C), or (D) on your answer sheet.

**101.** Edith Stanley says she has ------- regretted switching her university major from finance to engineering.
(A) never
(B) enough
(C) very
(D) less

**102.** Users should avoid closing the copy machine's lid more ------- than necessary.
(A) forceful
(B) forcefully
(C) forcing
(D) force

**103.** Mr. Hawkins hoped that hiring the career coach would enable ------- to pursue certain goals.
(A) himself
(B) him
(C) his
(D) he

**104.** Quezada Grill offers free delivery to locations ------- five miles of its store but charges relatively high fees for longer trips.
(A) about
(B) on
(C) within
(D) up to

**105.** Seasonal sporting equipment and other infrequently used items ------- in the apartment complex's basement.
(A) can be stored
(B) should store
(C) are storing
(D) stored

**106.** Just a few weeks after ------- responsibility for factory operations, Ms. Jennings began making changes to increase efficiency.
(A) assumes
(B) assuming
(C) assumed
(D) assume

**107.** With the exception of morning rush hour, the study found that city buses are ------- on time throughout the day.
(A) general
(B) generalized
(C) generally
(D) generalizing

**108.** Though this cannot be proven conclusively, archaeologists believe it is ------- that the object was used in preparing food.
(A) actual
(B) functional
(C) usual
(D) probable

**109.** Modern fans of Mr. Montano's books may be surprised to learn that few of ------- were popular with critics upon release.

(A) theirs
(B) their
(C) them
(D) themselves

**110.** In spite of the recent failure of her juice bar franchise, Ms. Diaz remains ------- among investors for her early success with Diaz Café.

(A) respectful
(B) respecting
(C) respectably
(D) respected

**111.** The Rostan Building has never been ------- popular before, though it has been considered a Hentville landmark for years.

(A) this
(B) high
(C) how
(D) much

**112.** The crew tasked with resurfacing Maple Street will begin at its intersection with Higgs Road and proceed in the ------- of Leskett Avenue.

(A) director
(B) most direct
(C) directing
(D) direction

**113.** ------- the Boyce Eagles have reached the final round of the Wicks Cup several times, they have not yet managed to win it.

(A) While
(B) Even
(C) Whenever
(D) Despite

**114.** Dr. Bak's article in *Organizational Psychology* explains how people ------- to strong leadership have difficulty in horizontally-structured workplaces.

(A) respond
(B) responsive
(C) responsively
(D) responded

**115.** Your signature will indicate your agreement ------- abide by the terms of this contract.

(A) with
(B) through
(C) regarding
(D) to

**116.** As of today, special bins for the disposal of used batteries ------- in front of all of the city's public libraries.

(A) have been placed
(B) placed
(C) will place
(D) is being placed

**117.** ------- the latest market report, the cosmetics industry will continue to expand thanks to growth in income levels.

(A) Except for
(B) Through
(C) In addition to
(D) According to

**118.** Our negotiator ------- Silmond Software to discount its services in exchange for a positive customer testimonial.

(A) argued
(B) persuaded
(C) assured
(D) settled

**119.** Jeralt, Inc., employees appreciate that telecommuting is ------- and very easy to arrange via an online scheduling system.

(A) permit
(B) permitting
(C) permission
(D) permitted

**120.** There is some evidence that regular tea drinkers have a reduced ------- of heart disease.

(A) treatment
(B) progress
(C) risk
(D) diagnosis



GO ON TO THE NEXT PAGE

**121.** When our employee complained about the issue, the hotel manager ------- offered to upgrade her to a better room.

(A) greatly
(B) collectively
(C) randomly
(D) readily

**122.** Air Primera will begin offering increased leg room on flights to ensure passenger -------.

(A) comforting
(B) comfortable
(C) comfort
(D) comfortably

**123.** The law requiring hospital fees to be published online is intended to make the medical industry's pricing more ------- to patients.

(A) transparent
(B) equivalent
(C) adequate
(D) knowledgeable

**124.** During the banquet, the recipient of the Reilter Prize will be introduced and given the opportunity to make remarks in ------- of the honor.

(A) reaction
(B) acceptance
(C) gratitude
(D) analysis

**125.** Our training courses are constantly updated to ensure that they ------- with the requirements of the workforce.

(A) collaborate
(B) implement
(C) equip
(D) align

**126.** Prost Agriculture's booth features a video screen ------- displays pictures taken by the trade show's attendees.

(A) whose
(B) just
(C) that
(D) of

**127.** Human resources staff must demonstrate ------- in handling the private information of their coworkers.

(A) prosperity
(B) discretion
(C) consensus
(D) aspiration

**128.** In preparation for their stay in Japan, the JFLT program provides its participants with 50 hours of Japanese language -------.

(A) instruction
(B) instructed
(C) instructive
(D) instructors

**129.** Goines Corporation will ------- construction of the building when all necessary approvals have been obtained.

(A) redeem
(B) exercise
(C) commence
(D) maneuver

**130.** The decrease in Sparont's revenues is the ------- effect of a drop in demand for digital cameras, its chief product.

(A) scarce
(B) inevitable
(C) competent
(D) cooperative

# PART 6

**Directions:** Read the texts that follow. A word, phrase, or sentence is missing in parts of each text. Four answer choices for each question are given below the text. Select the best answer to complete the text. Then mark the letter (A), (B), (C), or (D) on your answer sheet.

**Questions 131–134** refer to the following article.

**Groundswork to Hold 1,000th Weekly Garden Clean-up**

Nonprofit organization Groundswork will hold its 1,000th Weekly Garden Clean-up this Saturday, September 8, at Schuler Park.

Since its ------- (**131.**) by a group of local conservationists, Groundswork has strived to promote a love of nature among Mellin County residents. The enthusiastic volunteers ------- (**132.**) to Schuler Park nearly every weekend are a major part of these efforts. Overseen by park staff, they have been picking up trash and helping with plant care tasks for over 19 years. The organization also holds regular hikes and classes on nature-related topics for all ages.

Groundswork plans to celebrate the ------- (**133.**) with a party after Saturday's clean-up. ------- (**134.**). Those interested in attending should visit its Web site, www.groundswork.org, for more information.

**131.** (A) granting
(B) achieving
(C) founding
(D) joining

**132.** (A) have been sent
(B) it sends
(C) that send
(D) are sending

**133.** (A) milestone
(B) acquisition
(C) improvement
(D) decision

**134.** (A) Applications for membership are welcomed year-round.
(B) In fact, a clean-up plan must be submitted for all park events.
(C) It will feature music, family-friendly games, and refreshments.
(D) Mayor Chan even posted a congratulatory message on social media.

**Questions 135–138** refer to the following e-mail.

From: Imani Jackson
To: Toby Ortega
Subject: Receptionist job candidates
Date: April 2
Attachments: Candidate spreadsheet

Hi Toby,

As you may remember, the application period for the receptionist position ended last Friday. I'm happy to report that we received résumés from more than 50 people! -------. **135.**

Anyway, I've narrowed down the candidate pool in accordance with the requirements that you specified, and the top ten prospects ------- **136.** in the attached spreadsheet. Please ------- **137.** the file when you have time and choose the people you would like to interview. ------- **138.**, we should follow the timetable stated in the ad and begin calling them this week.

Let me know if there's anything else you need.

Sincerely,

Imani

**135.** (A) Posting the ad on that job seeking Web site certainly made a difference.
(B) However, that is why we were unable to respond promptly to your application.
(C) It may not be so difficult to fill all ten openings by the end of April after all.
(D) It is lucky that Mark will have time next week to help me review each one.

**136.** (A) have described
(B) having described
(C) being described
(D) are described

**137.** (A) pass up
(B) call for
(C) look over
(D) turn around

**138.** (A) If possible
(B) Instead
(C) Therefore
(D) In particular

**Questions 139–142** refer to the following letter.

**Lauryl County Toll Road Authority**

430 Main Street, Carlson, VA 22432

April 10
Melba Graves
108 Franklin Lane
Carlson, VA 22433

Dear Ms. Graves,

You are receiving this letter because a vehicle registered to you used Knapp Toll Road on April 2. As the vehicle is not enrolled in Lauryl County's Electronic Toll Collection System (ETCS), this action was a violation of county law. Please see the enclosed -------. **139.** The amount requested on it must be paid by May 2. Note that if your payment has not been received by -------, **140.** you will be charged an additional fee.

Also, if you are likely to use a toll road again in the future, we strongly suggest that you enroll in the ETCS. -------. **141.** Enrollment is free and will prevent ------- **142.** issues of this sort.

If you believe you have received this notice in error, follow the instructions on the back of this page to dispute it.

Encl.

**139.** (A) invoice
(B) photograph
(C) manual
(D) license

**140.** (A) many
(B) then
(C) yourself
(D) tomorrow

**141.** (A) The money collected from tolls is used for road upkeep projects.
(B) It has eased traffic congestion in other neighborhoods as well.
(C) This can be done by visiting our office at the address above.
(D) A device in your vehicle transmits an electronic signal each time.

**142.** (A) total
(B) identical
(C) valuable
(D) further



*GO ON TO THE NEXT PAGE*

**Questions 143–146** refer to the following information.

## Verification of Information

As an open-source online encyclopedia whose contributors may not be experts, Calhoun Science Encyclopedia takes the verification of information -------. Contributors must specify
**143.**
the source of ------- content they add to the encyclopedia's articles. To do this, append a
**144.**
footnote link to the relevant part of the text and give all necessary information in the connected footnote. (See this page for information on footnote formatting.) Sources must be reliable and professionally published. -------. Content that is not accompanied by a
**145.**
footnote citing such a source should be -------. The reason for the removal should be
**146.**
explained in the article's discussion page so that others can review it. Finally, in the case that trustworthy sources disagree, contributors should provide a neutral account of the positions of all sides.

**143.** (A) serious
(B) seriously
(C) seriousness
(D) more serious

**144.** (A) any
(B) either
(C) which
(D) another

**145.** (A) The latter kind of claim requires additional verification.
(B) Ideal examples are academic journal articles and textbooks.
(C) Otherwise, the quotation might violate publishing copyrights.
(D) This includes the title, author, publisher, and date of the work.

**146.** (A) highlighted
(B) reorganized
(C) condensed
(D) deleted

# PART 7

**Directions:** In this part you will read a selection of texts, such as magazine and newspaper articles, e-mails, and instant messages. Each text or set of texts is followed by several questions. Select the best answer for each question and mark the letter (A), (B), (C), or (D) on your answer sheet.



**Questions 147–148** refer to the following notice.

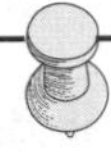

## NOTICE OF STREET TREE TRIMMING

The trees on your street will be trimmed between the hours of 8 A.M. and 5 P.M. on June 28–29. Branches hanging less than thirteen feet above the street or eight feet above the sidewalk will be trimmed or removed.

The Dawston Parks Department regularly performs this work in city parks and adjacent streets in order to improve the trees' structural stability and protect them from damage caused by possible breakages. A certified tree care professional supervises our crew to make certain that the work is done properly.

Please keep the street clear on these days by parking automobiles in driveways or on other streets. Also, we ask for your understanding regarding the loud noise made by the trimming machinery.

**147.** Why are the trees being trimmed?
(A) To protect residents' automobiles
(B) To prevent damage to power lines
(C) To improve their appearance
(D) To maintain their well-being

**148.** According to the notice, how will the city ensure the work is done well?
(A) By having an expert monitor it
(B) By incorporating feedback from citizens
(C) By sending multiple work crews
(D) By using special machinery

GO ON TO THE NEXT PAGE

**Questions 149–150** refer to the following receipt.

**Barry's Books #4**

47 Fir Street
Central City, IL 61087
555-0161

Store number: 4 Register number: 3 Cashier: Kate G.
Card: Barry's Loyalty Club Member Expires: May 11

Book: *Heritage in Mumbai* $26.00
10% member card discount(-2.60) →$23.40

Magazine: *Movie Monthly* $7.00
10% member card discount(-0.70) →$6.30

Sale subtotal $29.70

Customer special order #1127
*In-store pickup
*Notification method: text message

Book: *Bold Architecture* $34.00
Promotion 2848 – 50% off (-17.00) $17.00
10% member card discount (-1.70) $15.30

Special order subtotal $15.30

**TOTAL** **$45.00**
CASH PAID $50.00
CHANGE $ 5.00

*Visit our in-store café - open during regular store hours*
*Date/time of purchase*: March 7 04:09 P.M.

**149.** What is NOT indicated on the receipt about Barry's Books?

(A) It only accepts returns for a limited period.
(B) It has a customer loyalty program.
(C) It has more than one store.
(D) It also operates a café.

**150.** According to the receipt, what is true about *Bold Architecture*?

(A) It can only be purchased online.
(B) It was part of a sales promotion.
(C) It was ordered by telephone.
(D) It was a staff recommendation.

**Questions 151–152** refer to the following text-message chain.

**Jody Rodriguez (1:43 P.M.)**
Grady, are you on the construction site right now?

**Grady Webb (1:44 P.M.)**
Yes, I'm over on the north side talking to the electrical team. What's up?

**Jody Rodriguez (1:44 P.M.)**
I wanted to check with you that it's all right to send up the RBX80.

**Grady Webb (1:45 P.M.)**
The RBX80? I'm sorry, but I don't know what that is.

**Jody Rodriguez (1:46 P.M.)**
Oh, it's a new technology. It's a drone aircraft equipped with cameras. We're going to fly it around the outsides of the building to make sure there are no problems in the walls that have been put up so far.

**Grady Webb (1:47 P.M.)**
Ah, I see. That should be fine, but please give advance notice to the teams that are working on any of the floors you'll be looking at—especially the high ones. It could be dangerous to surprise them.

**Jody Rodriguez (1:48 P.M.)**
I'll send out a group text to the team leaders now.

**151.** At 1:46 P.M., what does Ms. Rodriguez mean when she writes, "it's a new technology"?
(A) She cannot guarantee that the RBX80 will work well.
(B) Mr. Webb's unfamiliarity with the RBX80 is understandable.
(C) A problem that occurred in the past will be avoided today.
(D) Her team will need time to prepare for a procedure.

**152.** What is suggested about the building being constructed?
(A) It has a round shape.
(B) It has brick walls.
(C) It is in an airport.
(D) It will be tall.

*GO ON TO THE NEXT PAGE*

**Questions 153–154** refer to the following advertisement.

## The Forance Company

*Announcing: the Blue Sky Line of Greeting Cards*

When Rufus Forance started The Forance Company more than 70 years ago to publish a lifestyle magazine, he did not imagine what it would become. Rufus only began making greeting cards to earn extra profit via his printing presses. However, the cards, designed by the magazine's staff artists, were an instant success, and Rufus soon decided to focus exclusively on them. Since then, The Forance Company has become one of the nation's most trusted sources of beautiful, thoughtful greeting cards.

Now, The Forance Company is proud to add a new line of cards to our catalog: the Blue Sky line. Blue Sky cards are for sending heartfelt messages of love, support, and friendship in everyday life. Their simple, charming style is designed to put the focus on the sender's words. Instead of waiting for a birthday or holiday, let people know you care about them right now. Visit any major stationery store to browse the Blue Sky line today.

**153.** What is mentioned about The Forance Company?

(A) It is still owned by the Forance family.
(B) It began with 70 employees.
(C) It achieved success through print advertising.
(D) It used to make a different type of product.

**154.** What is the Blue Sky line intended to enable customers to do?

(A) Customize the design of a greeting card
(B) Express goodwill outside of special occasions
(C) Send positive messages electronically
(D) Support local artists through their purchase

**Questions 155–157** refer to the following e-mail.

E-Mail message

**From:** Simon Burgess
**To:** Viola McDonald
**Subject:** Re: Inquiry
**Date:** July 30

Dear Ms. McDonald,

Thank you for your inquiry regarding Rolent smart glass. From what you wrote, I believe that our RC-2 Glass would be an excellent fit for your project. In its transparent setting, it will eliminate the dark, cramped feeling you describe your building as having, and in its opaque "frosted" setting, it will provide your conference rooms, copy rooms, etc. with the same privacy you currently enjoy.

I can also address your concern about cost. Though smart glass does require electric power to switch settings, it does not need electricity to maintain either setting. None of our many satisfied clients have found it to have a significant impact on their utility bills.

I would be happy to visit your site to provide more information on RC-2 Glass and suggestions on its best use in your project. If you are interested, please reply to this e-mail or call me at 555-0196.

Sincerely,

Simon Burgess
Sales Associate, Rolent Ltd.

**155.** What most likely is Ms. McDonald planning to do?
(A) Construct a building
(B) Improve a vehicle's design
(C) Renovate an office
(D) Create an outdoor display

**156.** What does Mr. Burgess write to reassure Ms. McDonald about smart glass?
(A) It does not use much energy.
(B) It is not expensive to install.
(C) It is not difficult to keep clean.
(D) It does not break easily.

**157.** What does Mr. Burgess offer Ms. McDonald?
(A) A reference
(B) A consultation
(C) A demonstration
(D) A discount

**Questions 158–160** refer to the following notice.

*Thornton Burger, Lakeside Branch*

# Notice

Our staff workshop is due to take place next Tuesday from 9 A.M. to 12 P.M. It is mandatory for all staff regardless of seniority level, so the restaurant will be closed during those hours. If you have a prior commitment, please contact your line manager to make appropriate arrangements. —[1]—.

The workshop's leader will be Karen Downing. She will be talking about maintaining hygiene standards at our restaurant. —[2]—. Ms. Downing has already delivered this workshop at branches all over the country and is up to date with the latest regulations and research. —[3]—. I am sure you will find it to be an informative day.

You have all been pre-registered for this event automatically. Uniforms are not required for this day. —[4]—. See the relevant section of the employee handbook.

**158.** What is the notice announcing?
(A) A training event
(B) A job opening
(C) A facility inspection
(D) A new dress code

**159.** What is indicated about Ms. Downing?
(A) She was recently promoted to management.
(B) She will observe the restaurant's operations.
(C) She proposed some company regulations.
(D) She is an expert in food hygiene.

**160.** In which of the positions marked [1], [2], [3], and [4] does the following sentence best belong?
"However, we expect you to wear company-recognized business casual clothing."
(A) [1]
(B) [2]
(C) [3]
(D) [4]

**Questions 161–163** refer to the following agreement.

## Leopard Automotive

I may, during my period of employment, be exposed to information confidential to Leopard Automotive. This includes but is not limited to technical specifications of automobiles and manufacturing equipment, business practices, company plans, data from market research, sales and revenue information, and details about security procedures. I understand that this category also includes information and materials that I myself develop while employed at Leopard Automotive.

I will not disclose such information to third parties, including competitors, journalists and members of the public, during or following my employment at Leopard Automotive.

At the end of my employment period, I will immediately return to the company all physical security credentials and company-issued devices, and supply all passwords to company systems.

I have been provided with a copy of this document for my own records.

Signed: *Jeremy Fulton*

Title: *Manufacturing Manager*

Date: *November 19*

**161.** What is suggested about the agreement?
(A) It must also be signed by a company representative.
(B) It extends past Mr. Fulton's period of employment.
(C) It cannot be removed from the business's premises.
(D) It has been modified at Mr. Fulton's request.

**162.** What is NOT mentioned as confidential information?
(A) Results of consumer studies
(B) Company earnings
(C) Names of suppliers
(D) Vehicle specifications

**163.** What does the agreement specify?
(A) What Mr. Fulton should do upon leaving his job
(B) What penalties Mr. Fulton may face for violating it
(C) Whom Mr. Fulton may share some information with
(D) How Mr. Fulton may use company-issued devices



GO ON TO THE NEXT PAGE

**Questions 164–167** refer to the following e-mail.

| | |
|---|---|
| To: | Louise Anderson |
| From: | Jesse Reed |
| Subject: | Panel discussion invitation |
| Date: | 18 June |

Dear Ms. Anderson,

Hello. My name is Jesse Reed, and I am one of the organizers of IT Healthlink. IT Healthlink has become one of the UK's most exciting conferences on information technology in healthcare, bringing together hundreds of medical care providers, entrepreneurs, investors, government representatives, and others annually. —[1]—. We are currently seeking speakers and panelists for this year's conference, which will be held in London's Fiore Hall on 5–7 October.

The particular session I am contacting you about is an hour-long panel discussion titled "The Next Generation of Health Tech." —[2]—. We have already engaged Clive Minamore, Kwame Obeng, Logan Norwick, and Andrew Earle, four of the industry's most innovative young minds, to participate. However, as you might have realized immediately, there is something missing from that group—a female perspective. So I asked around my network for recommendations, and Harold Kirby said he was very impressed with your speech at Health Liverpool last year. —[3]—. After watching the video of it that is available online, I am too. It would be an honor if you would join our panel to share your inventive ideas with our attendees.

If you are interested, all you need to do at this stage is respond to this e-mail with your affirmative answer and, for our Web site, a professional headshot and your official job title. I would send you the speaking agreement with all of the details of the event by the end of this month. —[4]—. Alternatively, if you have any questions or concerns, you can reply to this e-mail or call me at 020-7043-5214 during business hours.

I hope to hear from you soon.

Sincerely,

Jesse Reed

**164.** What is stated about the panel discussion?

(A) It will take place on October 7.
(B) It will be moderated by Mr. Kirby.
(C) It is not currently scheduled to include any women.
(D) It has been part of previous conferences.

**165.** How did Mr. Reed find out about Ms. Anderson?

(A) By attending a talk
(B) By reading a newspaper
(C) By searching the Internet
(D) By receiving a referral

**166.** What should Ms. Anderson provide first if she wants to participate?

(A) A photograph of herself
(B) A signed contract
(C) A fee quote
(D) A suggested topic

**167.** In which of the positions marked [1], [2], [3], and [4] does the following sentence best belong?

"Over the three-day event, participants form connections, share practical tips, and discuss big ideas."

(A) [1]
(B) [2]
(C) [3]
(D) [4]

**Questions 168–171** refer to the following online article.

## Auckland Business News

(19 February)—Christine Redman recently found herself unable to pay for the iced latte she had ordered at her favorite coffee shop—even though she had plenty of cash. "They'd made the switch to electronic payments a few weeks before," Ms. Redman explained. "But that day, I forgot to bring my debit card. It was embarrassing."

The coffee shop, Seeley's Beans, is one of several New Zealand retailers that have stopped accepting cash at their stores. Supporters of the trend say that electronic payments have benefits like faster transactions, error-free record-keeping, and less handling of potentially-unsanitary bills and coins. Seeley's Beans spokesperson Sharon Wright said, "It was an easy choice, frankly."

Consumers, however, are not convinced. Although there has been a steady move toward using cards and apps instead of paper money, many still prefer to use cash or at least to have the option of doing so. "For me, it's about privacy. I wouldn't go to a cashless store, because I don't like the credit card company knowing everything I buy," said Auckland citizen Chad Williams.

Similar consumer resistance has led some city governments in the United States to prohibit businesses from going cashless. Retail analyst Sang-Wook Jung believes that could happen here as well, but not right away. "At this point, there are only a few cashless places, so it's not a big inconvenience. But if a lot of stores start to switch over, we may see a backlash too."

*Have you visited a cashless store? Tell us about it in the comments! (Note that commenters must create an Auckland Tribune account.)*

**168.** What is the article about?
(A) A trend in retail payment methods
(B) The expansion of a coffee shop chain
(C) A proposal for a city ordinance
(D) A dispute between a customer and a store

**169.** What is implied about Mr. Williams?
(A) He works in the finance field.
(B) He will not patronize cafés like Seeley's Beans.
(C) He spoke with Ms. Redman earlier in February.
(D) He hopes to become a local politician.

**170.** Why does the article mention another country?
(A) To explain a management practice's origin
(B) To highlight a company's structure
(C) To introduce a situation's potential outcome
(D) To express pride about a region's achievements

**171.** What are readers of the article encouraged to do?
(A) Sign up to receive updates on a story
(B) Discuss any relevant experiences
(C) Look at a list of similar writings
(D) Report any factual errors

*GO ON TO THE NEXT PAGE*

**Questions 172–175** refer to the following online chat discussion.

| | |
|---|---|
| **Monica Dietrich [2:11 P.M.]** | Great news! A representative from Ramona Enterprises has finally agreed to do an interview with me! |
| **Tao Hou [2:12 P.M.]** | That's wonderful! Our readers will be thrilled to get some insights into one of the fastest-growing software companies in the industry. When will you go there? |
| **Monica Dietrich [2:14 P.M.]** | Next Monday at 2 P.M. That doesn't give me much time to prepare, and I've only been given a one-hour time slot, but I'll take what I can get. |
| **Roxanne Toro [2:16 P.M.]** | Jacques, are you free to go with Monica and take pictures? |
| **Monica Dietrich [2:17 P.M.]** | Actually, I'm the only one who will be allowed in the offices. The company said it prefers to supply its own pictures. |
| **Jacques Favreau [2:18 P.M.]** | That's a shame. I would love to see their offices. I heard that employees are allowed to personalize their workspaces, so you see everything from standing desks with treadmills to recliner chairs. |
| **Monica Dietrich [2:19 P.M.]** | I'll be sure to let you know if that's true! |
| **Roxanne Toro [2:22 P.M.]** | Will you have the article ready in time for this month's issue? The deadline is March 18, just two days after you visit Ramona Enterprises. |
| **Monica Dietrich [2:23 P.M.]** | I don't think that's a good idea. |
| **Tao Hou [2:24 P.M.]** | I agree. Quality has to be the top priority. |

**172.** What is suggested about Ms. Dietrich?
(A) She used to be employed by Ramona Enterprises.
(B) She made multiple requests to Ramona Enterprises.
(C) She checks Ramona Enterprises' Web site regularly.
(D) She has confirmed a sale to Ramona Enterprises.

**173.** Where most likely do the writers work?
(A) At a technology company
(B) At a news station
(C) At a recruiting agency
(D) At a magazine publisher

**174.** Why is Mr. Favreau unable to accompany Ms. Dietrich?
(A) He is too far away to arrive in time.
(B) He has not been granted access.
(C) He is busy with other work.
(D) He is not qualified for an assignment.

**175.** At 2:23 P.M., what does Ms. Dietrich mean when she writes, "I don't think that's a good idea"?
(A) She plans to supervise a process.
(B) She prefers to meet in-person.
(C) She wants more time for a task.
(D) She thinks a workspace policy is unwise.



GO ON TO THE NEXT PAGE

**Questions 176–180** refer to the following e-mail and article.

E-Mail message

From: Megan Danner
To: Liling Yang
Subject: Request
Date: 3 September
Attachment: 7 files

Dear Professor Yang,

Hello! I hope this e-mail finds you well. I'm writing to take you up on the offer you made when I graduated last summer. In particular, I've decided to enter the Queensland Young Designers Contest, and I'm hoping that you'll review my submission before I turn it in.

I suspect you're already familiar with the contest, but let me give you an overview just in case. It's organised by the Queensland Fashion Council in order to support talented young designers. The first prize winner is featured in the council yearbook, but I'm just hoping for one of the top five spots, as all of them come with an invitation to the council's yearly fashion show. As for the entries, contestants have to submit three collections. Each collection consists of sketches of three clothing designs connected by a creative concept chosen by the applicant.

So, I'm sending you my sketches and the accompanying explanations of the creative concepts I chose. I've also included a document listing the judging criteria, for reference. I know you are busy, but I would be very grateful if you could take a look at these materials sometime before 10 September and share any comments that come to mind. Thank you in advance for any help you can give.

Sincerely,

Megan

## Queensland Young Designers Contest Award Winner Announced

BRISBANE (12 December)—The Queensland Fashion Council (QFC) revealed the winner of its fourth annual contest for young fashion designers yesterday. Jacquelyn Abbot, an assistant buyer at Sandpace Apparel and a recent graduate of Wilburt University, took first place among nearly 500 entrants.

The QFC has over 3,000 members, including designers, other industry employees, and investors, and the judges committee for the Queensland Young Designers Contest consists of some of the top names in eastern Australian fashion.

Ms. Abbot's design entry, which embodied the concepts "Fresh," "Reflections," and "Flight," impressed the judges with its original interpretations of classic styles. Gary Odell, the chair of the committee and a member of the QFC board, said, "Ms. Abbot's clothes and accessories are fascinating, becoming more complex the longer you look at them. We think she has a bright future in this industry."

Ms. Abbot, as well as top runners-up Jedda Ryan, Hayden Noe, Megan Danner, and Kevin Naylor, will receive a range of support services from the council.

**176.** Why was the e-mail sent?
(A) To request clarification about a requirement
(B) To respond to a suggestion to enter a contest
(C) To ask for feedback on some entry materials
(D) To provide a reminder about a deadline

**177.** What is NOT attached to the e-mail?
(A) A sample template for a document
(B) A list of some evaluation standards
(C) Descriptions of design concepts
(D) Drawings of fashion items

**178.** What is suggested about Ms. Danner?
(A) She completed an internship at the QFC.
(B) She will be promoted in an annual publication.
(C) She wrote an e-mail to a Wilburt University professor.
(D) She will receive a pass to a fashion event.

**179.** According to the article, what is true about the QFC?
(A) It has around 500 members.
(B) Its board of directors is headed by Mr. Odell.
(C) It has held the competition three times before.
(D) It is affiliated with Sandpace Apparel.

**180.** In the article, the word "bright" in paragraph 3, line 9, is closest in meaning to
(A) sunny
(B) cheerful
(C) promising
(D) clever



GO ON TO THE NEXT PAGE

**Questions 181–185** refer to the following meeting agenda and e-mail.

## Thornwood Monthly City Council Meeting

Room 105, Thornwood Community Center
Tuesday, February 10, 7 P.M.

**Attendance:** 10 out of 12 council members **Absent:** Patrick Chu, Tamara Walton
Minutes from January's meeting were read and approved.

| **Department Reports:** |
| --- |
| Finance: Request for March's operating expenses approved<br>Parks and Recreation: Explanation of park improvement grant |
| **Public Presentations:** |
| Suggestions for the usage of the grant funds at Randall Park<br>-Richard Dejean, former council member: building a covered picnic shelter with several picnic tables<br>-Lorena Palermo, Thornwood resident: adding an asphalt path that joggers can use to exercise in the park<br>-Veer Kamath, Thornwood resident: installing a fenced-in basketball court near the soccer fields<br>-Heather Bolin, president of the Nature Now charity: planting a flower garden to enhance the park's appearance |
| **Deliberation:** |
| Council members debated the merits of the various proposals. |
| **Next Meeting (March 13):** |
| The council will vote on the park improvement grant. The meeting will be held in the main auditorium because unusually large attendance is predicted. |

| | |
| --- | --- |
| **To:** | Lewis Knutson <lknutson@thornwood.gov> |
| **From:** | Victoria Pickard <vpickard@thornwood.gov> |
| **Date:** | March 15 |
| **Subject:** | Randall Park Project |

Hi Lewis,

Now that we have selected the project for Randall Park, we need to get started on the planning. I would like to sit down with the director and assistant director of the parks and recreation department sometime this week—could you arrange that? We need to get an accurate map of where the jogging path will be installed.

Once a tentative plan is in place, we can begin advertising the project and collecting bids from construction companies. I believe this project will be an excellent use of the grant funds we received. However, I'm worried that the process will be much lengthier than citizens expect. We'll have to hurry if we want it to be ready by the end of the summer.

Please keep me posted on your progress.

Thanks!

Victoria

**181.** What is NOT indicated about the February meeting?

(A) A monthly budget was approved.
(B) A charity representative gave a presentation.
(C) The majority of council members were present.
(D) There was a debate over the venue of the next meeting.

**182.** What does the meeting agenda suggest about the vote on the park improvement grant?

(A) Some council members would not participate in it.
(B) It was supposed to take place in February.
(C) It would be broadcast to local audiences.
(D) It was expected to attract a lot of public interest.

**183.** Whose proposal was successful?

(A) Mr. Dejean's
(B) Ms. Palermo's
(C) Mr. Kamath's
(D) Ms. Bolin's

**184.** What is Mr. Knutson asked to do this week?

(A) Train some volunteers
(B) Set up a meeting
(C) Contact construction companies
(D) Post an advertisement

**185.** What does Ms. Pickard mention about the park improvement project?

(A) A grant organization may not approve plans for it.
(B) It will not use all of the available funds.
(C) She is concerned about its duration.
(D) It may disrupt a seasonal festival.



*GO ON TO THE NEXT PAGE*

**Questions 186–190** refer to the following Web page and e-mails.

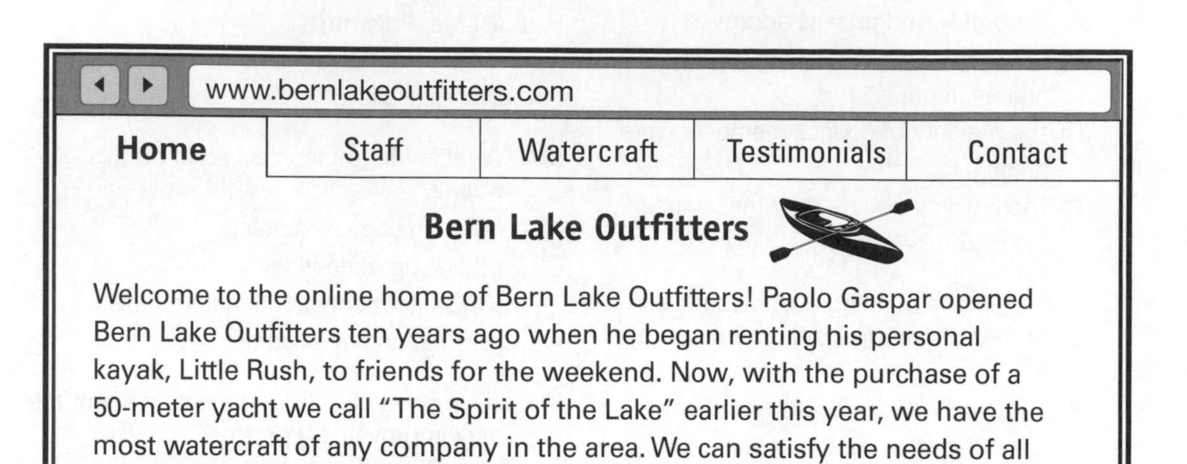

www.bernlakeoutfitters.com

**Home** | Staff | Watercraft | Testimonials | Contact

## Bern Lake Outfitters

Welcome to the online home of Bern Lake Outfitters! Paolo Gaspar opened Bern Lake Outfitters ten years ago when he began renting his personal kayak, Little Rush, to friends for the weekend. Now, with the purchase of a 50-meter yacht we call "The Spirit of the Lake" earlier this year, we have the most watercraft of any company in the area. We can satisfy the needs of all customers, whether they want to participate in fast-paced aquatic sports with one of our Golden Blaze speedboats, or spend an afternoon fishing with a few friends in a Quiet Ripple rowboat.

****If you're staying in the area, let us help you with your lodgings. We can get you a discounted rate at our longtime partner hotel, the Laguna Lodge.*

E-Mail message

**From:** <chloeblosser@sod.ch>
**To:** <paolo@bernlakeoutfitters.com>
**Subject:** Inquiry
**Date:** January 15

Hello,

I'm writing on behalf of the Swiss Organization of Dentists. Our annual conference will be held close to Bern Lake in June, and I'm in charge of organizing the closing dinner. It will be an informal event for us to unwind and have fun together, so I thought it would be nice to have it on the lake. There will be about 40 of us. Do you have a boat big enough to handle that many people?

I would also welcome any tips you have about accommodations.

Thank you,

Chloe Blosser
Swiss Organization of Dentists

E-Mail message

| | |
|---|---|
| **From:** | <paolo@bernlakeoutfitters.com> |
| **To:** | <chloeblosser@sod.ch> |
| **Subject:** | RE: Inquiry |
| **Date:** | January 15 |

Dear Ms. Blosser,

Thanks for getting in touch!

Our operation certainly has a boat that can suit your needs. Could you let me know the exact date in June you'll need it?

As far as your inquiry about accommodations goes—I know that the Laguna Lodge has some openings for that time frame, while the Brand New Sunset Hotel may be a less pricey option, if it's not fully booked already. Let me know what you decide, because depending on which one you choose, we may be able to make bookings for you at a discounted rate.

Sincerely,

Paolo Gaspar



**186.** What is mentioned as a special characteristic of Bern Lake Outfitters?

(A) The length of its history

(B) The rental price of its boats

(C) The convenience of its locations

(D) The number of boats it owns

**187.** Why is Ms. Blosser visiting the Bern Lake area?

(A) To attend a professional gathering

(B) To take an overseas vacation

(C) To watch a series of sporting events

(D) To conduct scientific research

**188.** Which boat will most likely be recommended to Ms. Blosser?

(A) The Little Rush

(B) The Spirit of the Lake

(C) The Golden Blaze

(D) The Quiet Ripple

**189.** In the second e-mail, the word "goes" in paragraph 3, line 1, is closest in meaning to

(A) is available

(B) is concerned

(C) functions

(D) departs

**190.** What does Mr. Gaspar indicate about Bern Lake Outfitters' partner hotel?

(A) It is relatively inexpensive.

(B) It recently reopened.

(C) It currently has vacancies for June.

(D) There is a dining establishment in it.

*GO ON TO THE NEXT PAGE*

**Questions 191–195** refer to the following article, e-mail, and order form.

## Making the World a Better Place

(August 4)—Though corporate social responsibility is becoming more important to consumers around the world, some companies are finding that giving back can be tricky.

Pinflash was embarrassed last year when a Charity Monitor report gave its main charitable partner a "D" rating because of its lack of impact. Similarly, Dunne Galloway recently ended its relationship with an arts nonprofit because of a disagreement over accounting processes.

This is why Peter Gandy started Giveler, a for-profit company that tries to make corporate giving as easy and efficient as possible.

"We do it all," says Mr. Gandy. "We help businesses choose a cause to support, connect them with a reputable charity or nonprofit organization, handle the donation logistics, and supply publicity tools."

In the two years it has been in business, Giveler has served over one hundred corporations and estimates that its clients have donated roughly three million dollars to various causes.

Among these successes, Mr. Gandy says he is most proud of Rickard Paper Co.: "We set up a program in which a tree is planted for almost every stationery product they sell. Not only have 56,000 trees been planted so far, but the publicity from the program has led to a 10% bump in Rickard's sales. That's the kind of mutually beneficial relationship we want for all of our clients and their partner organizations."

**From:** Samuel Akagi <samuel.akagi@giveler.com>
**To:** Janelle Hawn <janelle.hawn@weatherfordpro.com>
**Subject:** Potential partners
**Date:** August 24
**Attachment:** Nonprofit Review

Dear Janelle,

It was a pleasure to meet you yesterday. As I promised then, I'm now sending you an overview of our process for connecting corporations with partner charities and nonprofits. I believe it will relieve the concerns you mentioned about experiencing the same setback as Dunne Galloway.

In addition, here are some organizations that we think might be a good fit for Weatherford Pro:

- Kirchner Foundation - Operates free rural summer camp for kids
- Green Now! - Lobbies government to expand national parks
- Withrow Society - Protects endangered animals in a variety of habitats
- Mission Clean - Removes garbage from beaches and oceans

The Web site of each one is linked in its name so that you can learn a little more about them. If some questions come up or you feel ready to make a selection, just e-mail or give me a call at 555-0186.

Sincerely,

Samuel Akagi
Client Account Manager

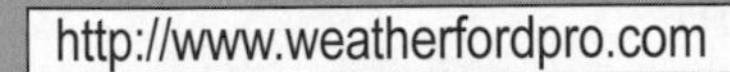


HOME | PRODUCTS | PROMOTIONS | ABOUT

## Weatherford Pro

Shipping Information: Victoria Cole
340 Griffin St.
Pueblo, CO 81008

Billing Address: Same as shipping ☑
Payment Method: PayRight
Account: vicky100@efr-mail.com

| Product No. | Description | Quantity | Price |
|---|---|---|---|
| H2420 | Trail Master Backpack – Navy | 1 | $59.99 |
| R4371 | Onivin Trekking Shoes – Size 10 | 1 | $89.99 |
| | | Subtotal | $149.98 |
| | | Taxes | $10.50 |
| | | Total | $160.48 |

**Did you know?** Weatherford Pro passes on 5% of each pre-tax sale to the Withrow Society! Click "Complete My Order" to help us donate $7.50 right now.

**Complete My Order**

**191.** What is the purpose of the article?
(A) To examine some corporations' mistakes
(B) To profile a local entrepreneur
(C) To promote a company's services
(D) To urge consumers to make certain choices

**192.** In the article, the word "bump" in paragraph 6, line 6, is closest in meaning to
(A) difficulty
(B) collision
(C) opportunity
(D) increase

**193.** What is implied about Ms. Hawn?
(A) She thinks that publicity methods should be simple.
(B) She hopes to avoid becoming engaged in a financial dispute.
(C) She is worried about the effectiveness of potential partner organizations.
(D) She is concerned about accidentally breaking a law.

**194.** What is Ms. Cole ordering from Weatherford Pro?
(A) Bicycling gear
(B) Camping supplies
(C) Fishing equipment
(D) Hiking accessories

**195.** What cause did Weatherford Pro choose to support?
(A) Saving rare animals from extinction
(B) Enabling children to spend time outdoors
(C) Affecting government policy on nature areas
(D) Clearing waste from coastal habitats



GO ON TO THE NEXT PAGE

**Questions 196–200** refer to the following Web page and e-mails.

http://www.kurgess.com/packages

| HOME | ABOUT | PACKAGES | CONTACT |
|---|---|---|---|

Kurgess Property Management offers a range of packages representing different levels of involvement in the management of your house, apartment, or condominium. Whichever you choose, you can be certain that all services will be performed by dedicated specialists committed to taking care of your property.

- Bronze – Services include property showings, rental application processing, credit and background checks, tenancy agreement signing, and deposit collection.
  Cost: 100% of the monthly rental fee (one time).
- Silver – All services in the bronze package plus collection of monthly rent.
  Cost: 4% of the monthly rental fee (monthly).
- Gold – All services in the silver package plus maintenance and repair services.
  Cost: 6% of the monthly rental fee (monthly).
- Gold Plus – All services in the gold package but offered at a discount for those who hire Kurgess to manage three or more properties.
  Cost: For each property, 5% of the monthly rental fee (monthly).

E-Mail message

From: Rex Campbell <rex@kurgess.com>
To: Dora McLaughlin <d.mclaughlin@rui-mail.com>
Subject: Good news
Date: March 21
Attachment: Application, Background Check, Credit Check, Contract

Dear Ms. McLaughlin,

I am pleased to notify you that we have found a suitable tenant for your property located at 682 Perry Road in Hennisberg. We have carried out his credit and background checks with a high degree of thoroughness; the results are attached for your perusal. As you can see, Isaiah Pritchard has a steady job as a high school teacher and a history of financial responsibility. Also, of course, he is willing to agree to all of the property usage terms you specified.

Mr. Pritchard would like to begin his one-year lease on Saturday, April 14. If you are satisfied with the information we have provided, please print out the contract, sign it, and send it to my office by certified mail as soon as possible. Thank you.

Regards,

Rex Campbell
Account Manager
Kurgess Property Management
Hennisberg Branch

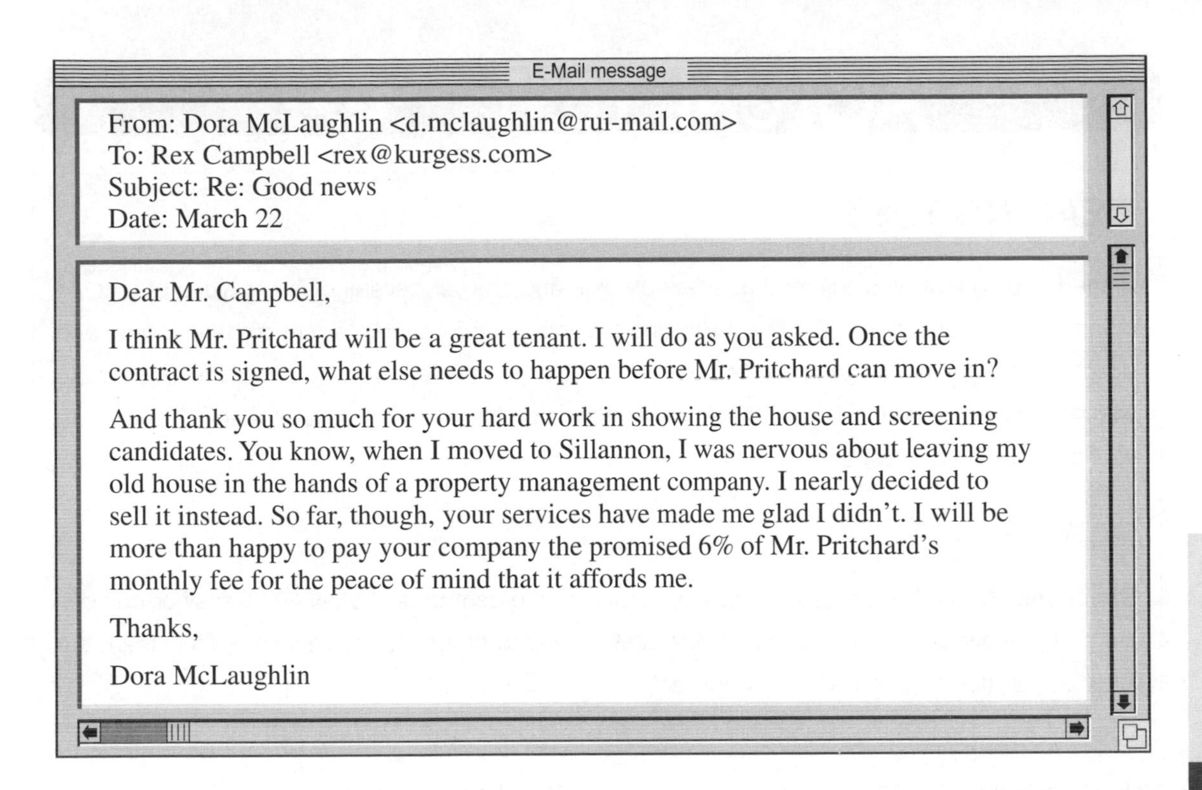

E-Mail message

From: Dora McLaughlin <d.mclaughlin@rui-mail.com>
To: Rex Campbell <rex@kurgess.com>
Subject: Re: Good news
Date: March 22

Dear Mr. Campbell,

I think Mr. Pritchard will be a great tenant. I will do as you asked. Once the contract is signed, what else needs to happen before Mr. Pritchard can move in?

And thank you so much for your hard work in showing the house and screening candidates. You know, when I moved to Sillannon, I was nervous about leaving my old house in the hands of a property management company. I nearly decided to sell it instead. So far, though, your services have made me glad I didn't. I will be more than happy to pay your company the promised 6% of Mr. Pritchard's monthly fee for the peace of mind that it affords me.

Thanks,

Dora McLaughlin

**196.** What is suggested about Kurgess Property Management?
(A) It outsources some of its maintenance services.
(B) It handles only residential properties.
(C) It requires an advance deposit.
(D) It offers a discount to clients after three years.

**197.** What is mentioned as a positive characteristic of Mr. Pritchard?
(A) A history of home ownership
(B) A flexible move-in date
(C) A stable career
(D) A lack of pet animals

**198.** What service package did Ms. McLaughlin most likely choose?
(A) Bronze
(B) Silver
(C) Gold
(D) Gold Plus

**199.** What does Ms. McLaughlin ask about?
(A) Some steps in a process
(B) Some changes to an agreement
(C) The reason for a recommendation
(D) The person responsible for a task

**200.** What is implied about Ms. McLaughlin?
(A) She will visit Kurgess Property Management's offices.
(B) She will move out of her current house by April 14.
(C) She will call Mr. Campbell's work phone.
(D) She will send some paperwork to Hennisberg.

**Stop! This is the end of the test. If you finish before time is called, you may go back to Parts 5, 6, and 7 and check your work.**

# ACTUAL TEST 

## READING TEST

In the Reading test, you will read a variety of texts and answer several different types of reading comprehension questions. The entire Reading test will last 75 minutes. There are three parts, and directions are given for each part. You are encouraged to answer as many questions as possible within the time allowed. You must mark your answers on the separate answer sheet. Do not write your answers in your test book.

## PART 5

**Directions:** A word or phrase is missing in each of the sentences below. Four answer choices are given below each sentence. Select the best answer to complete the sentence. Then mark the letter (A), (B), (C), or (D) on your answer sheet.

**101.** In her e-mail, the CEO assured shareholders that she was ------- in control of the situation.

(A) filling
(B) filled
(C) fuller
(D) fully

**102.** Mr. Moss and I attended the conference and shared what ------- had learned there with the rest of the team upon returning.

(A) we
(B) us
(C) our
(D) ourselves

**103.** Train conductors are ------- to reduce the machines' speed during heavy rainfall.

(A) examined
(B) instructed
(C) referred
(D) fixed

**104.** Mr. Maeda urges readers not to overlook ------- effects of social media use.

(A) benefited
(B) benefit
(C) beneficial
(D) beneficially

**105.** The registration ------- for our classes will last ten business days in total.

(A) requirement
(B) administrator
(C) period
(D) form

**106.** The recent improvements to the Walton Ballroom ------- its popularity as a venue for formal events.

(A) enhances
(B) have enhanced
(C) are enhanced
(D) enhancing

**107.** Customers wishing to use the free parking lot should drive ------- the Botanic Garden Café and take a left on Elm Street.

(A) between
(B) upon
(C) past
(D) through

**108.** Ms. Yates agreed to photograph Emburg's daylong dance ------- for a national newspaper.

(A) competed
(B) competitor
(C) competitors
(D) competition

109. As its manager, Mr. Staley is ------- for the outcome of the building project.

(A) confident
(B) accountable
(C) sensible
(D) obliged

110. Although Warron's spreadsheet software is widely used, ------- are aware of its specialty functions.

(A) few
(B) that
(C) each
(D) many

111. Cobb Buffet is booked solid in December, ------- you will need to find a different site for the year-end banquet.

(A) until
(B) then
(C) but
(D) so

112. Angul Timepieces will make a series of animated advertisements in an attempt to be ------- in its marketing.

(A) creatively
(B) creative
(C) creators
(D) creations

113. It is necessary for receptionists to answer the telephone promptly, ------- busy they may be.

(A) very
(B) even
(C) likewise
(D) however

114. Mr. Woods will require assistance in order to finish the budget report ------- before its deadline.

(A) successfully
(B) succeeded
(C) successful
(D) success

115. The Franklin Warehouse was built to enable faster ------- of our products in the region.

(A) proximity
(B) destination
(C) distribution
(D) fulfillment

116. Jocabia Market will reopen now that its organizers have ------- a dispute with the city over the market's operating license.

(A) settled
(B) resigned
(C) conveyed
(D) elected

117. Luigi Mancini, ------- achievements as a player included winning a "Most Valuable Player" award, has been hired to coach the Ardshire Ravens.

(A) whichever
(B) whose
(C) who
(D) his

118. Some offices prefer Horizon air purifiers due to their ------- size and portability.

(A) brief
(B) compact
(C) demanding
(D) authentic

119. The services Sephat Hotel offers ------- the needs of travelers on the go include digital check-in.

(A) accommodate
(B) accommodated
(C) are accommodating
(D) to accommodate

120. The Zambardi-Z backpack has side pockets to allow easy ------- to essential items such as water bottles and snacks.

(A) accesses
(B) accessing
(C) access
(D) accessed



GO ON TO THE NEXT PAGE

**121.** While the staff handbook prohibits smartphone use on the job, it does not specify the ------- of breaking this rule.

(A) offenders

(B) consequences

(C) alternatives

(D) objectives

**122.** Woolio uses information gathered through its mobile app to improve its own services, but it does not share customer data -------.

(A) externally

(B) inaccurately

(C) meticulously

(D) originally

**123.** The mayor's attendance at the gathering marked his first public appearance ------- nearly a month.

(A) in

(B) over

(C) since

(D) around

**124.** Storgan Education's language programs produce self-motivated learners capable of ------- to new circumstances.

(A) cooperating

(B) converting

(C) addressing

(D) adapting

**125.** One of the duties of the stock clerk is to ensure that all of the merchandise ------- in the store is placed on the right shelves.

(A) are selling

(B) will sell

(C) being sold

(D) have sold

**126.** Our monthly utility bills have been ------- ower since the new temperature control system was installed.

(A) deeply

(B) forcefully

(C) substantially

(D) extremely

**127.** Ms. Ok has been tasked with investigating ------- standard procedures are being properly followed.

(A) into

(B) whether

(C) before

(D) any

**128.** The establishment of the call center complex will make Blundell's economy less ------- on manufacturing.

(A) reliance

(B) relying

(C) reliant

(D) reliable

**129.** Despite their careful preparations, the party's caterers were forced to ------- when the refrigeration unit suddenly broke down.

(A) improvise

(B) designate

(C) condense

(D) attain

**130.** The most popular of Mortel Consulting's leadership seminars teaches managers how to foster teamwork while respecting employee -------.

(A) individual

(B) individually

(C) individualized

(D) individuality

# PART 6

**Directions:** Read the texts that follow. A word, phrase, or sentence is missing in parts of each text. Four answer choices for each question are given below the text. Select the best answer to complete the text. Then mark the letter (A), (B), (C), or (D) on your answer sheet.

**Questions 131–134** refer to the following article.

*City News Times* *Week of March 3*

The highly anticipated grand opening of Fusion Foods, ------- **131.** chef David Huu's new restaurant, is scheduled for Thursday, March 13 at 5 P.M. The event ------- **132.** a ribbon-cutting ceremony and reception with complimentary delicacies.

During his 24-year career, Mr. Huu has become one of the region's most prominent and popular chefs. ------- **133.** His first eatery, Café West 24, opened early last year to strong reviews and continues to be a popular option for city diners. ------- **134.** running his own restaurants, Mr. Huu worked for a decade as head chef at Gianmati's Bistro on Third Street.

Fusion Foods is located at 3402 Jordan Street. From March 14, it will be open for lunch and dinner, Tuesday through Sunday. Its menu is already available online at www.fusion-food.com.

**131.** (A) aspiring
(B) visiting
(C) retired
(D) noted

**132.** (A) featured
(B) would have featured
(C) is to feature
(D) will have featured

**133.** (A) He currently teaches culinary arts classes there.
(B) Fusion Foods is his second restaurant.
(C) Fusion Foods may change ownership soon.
(D) He also plans to extend its business hours.

**134.** (A) As soon as
(B) Prior to
(C) Afterward
(D) In addition

*GO ON TO THE NEXT PAGE*

**Questions 135–138** refer to the following e-mail.

To: <customerservice@romerouniforms.com>
From: <natasha.maxwell@odn-mail.com>
Subject: Uniform logo
Date: November 25
Attachment: lion_image

Hello,

I'm trying to use your Web site to order customized uniforms for the youth basketball team I coach, but it doesn't seem to be working ------- **135.** We are the Lions, and one of our team member's parents designed an image of a lion that we plan to use as our logo. ------- **136.**, when we upload it to your site, it looks distorted in the uniform preview image. We've tried different image sizes and all of the possible file types, but the issue ------- **137.** So, I'm sending you the image as an attachment to this e-mail. ------- **138.** I'm not sure if this matters, but we've chosen the "Winner Diamond Dunk" uniform style with an emerald green background and white diamonds.

Thanks,

Natasha Maxwell

**135.** (A) corrected
(B) correct
(C) correctly
(D) corrections

**136.** (A) Instead
(B) Namely
(C) Similarly
(D) Unfortunately

**137.** (A) persists
(B) resides
(C) determines
(D) asserts

**138.** (A) Please give us your honest opinion of its appeal.
(B) You will not have to come by my office in person after all.
(C) We would like you to use it as the basis for your logo design.
(D) I hope you can figure out what the problem is.

**Questions 139–142** refer to the following Web page.

http://www.russontmining.com/careers/tp

Trainee Program

The Trainee Program is ------- an exciting career opportunity for recent university graduates
**139.**
and an important way for Russont Mining Co. to cultivate our future leaders. We choose promising young people from a variety of fields and give them the tools and knowledge they need to become valuable members of the Russont team. Over the twelve-month program, trainees travel to Russont sites across Canada and speak with employees and executives at all levels. -------. Room, board, and a generous living stipend are provided. Successful
**140.**
completion of the program entitles trainees to a full-time position at Russont in the area to which their qualifications and interests are best -------.
**141.**

Would you like to find out how to become a trainee? Click here to learn about the -------
**142.**
process.

**139.** (A) both
(B) what
(C) either
(D) intended

**140.** (A) In particular, they should have excellent communication skills.
(B) They are even given opportunities to work on major projects.
(C) For example, our current vice president of operations is a graduate.
(D) We will review submissions on a rolling basis throughout this time.

**141.** (A) to suit
(B) suits
(C) suited
(D) suitable

**142.** (A) development
(B) appraisal
(C) application
(D) procurement

*GO ON TO THE NEXT PAGE*

**Questions 143–146** refer to the following notice.

**Notice to Online Banking Customers:**

Starting from January 1, Meypt Bank will provide account statements electronically by default. After that date, you will no longer receive paper statements in the mail ------- you specifically inform us that you wish to. You can do this by logging in to your online banking account, opening the "Settings" tab, and selecting "Continue to receive paper statements."
**143.**

Electronic statements are available under the "Statements" tab on your account page. We will send you an e-mail ------- upon the release of your statement each month. -------. It will only mention your name and the last four digits of your account number. Please keep the e-mail address associated with your account updated at all times. This will ensure the ------- of these and other important messages from Meypt Bank.
**144.** **145.** **146.**

**143.** (A) wherever
(B) unless
(C) besides
(D) once

**144.** (A) notification
(B) notifying
(C) notified
(D) notifiable

**145.** (A) This message is designed to protect customer privacy.
(B) The process is the same for joint account holders.
(C) The statement lists all of your recent transactions.
(D) At present, this date cannot be changed online.

**146.** (A) clarity
(B) deletion
(C) relevance
(D) delivery

## PART 7

**Directions:** In this part you will read a selection of texts, such as magazine and newspaper articles, e-mails, and instant messages. Each text or set of texts is followed by several questions. Select the best answer for each question and mark the letter (A), (B), (C), or (D) on your answer sheet.

**Questions 147–148** refer to the following coupon.

**Hones Hill Nursery**

**Bring this coupon to Hones Hill Nursery between April 14 and April 23 to get 25% off all plants and 15% off all pottery. Celebrate the first warm weather of the new year by buying beautiful flowers, bushes, and even trees for your home or business at amazing prices. Delivery and planting assistance for our everyday low fees will be available for all purchases.**

**147.** What is indicated about the promotion?
(A) It involves giving out free plants.
(B) It applies to multiple types of items.
(C) It rewards the nursery's long-time customers.
(D) It requires shoppers to spend a certain amount of money.

**148.** What is suggested about Hones Hill Nursery?
(A) It also stocks outdoor furniture.
(B) It is closed one day per week.
(C) It offers some off-site services.
(D) It mainly serves other businesses.

**Questions 149–150** refer to the following text-message chain.

**Jamar Richardson [6:14 P.M.]**
Hi, Amina. I just got approved to attend the University Financial Aid Professionals conference this year, and I saw that you're presenting. Why don't we meet up while we're there?

**Amina Ndiaye [6:28 P.M.]**
Hi, Jamar. Sure, I'd love to catch up. It's been two years since you left, right? I can't believe it. It seems like only yesterday that you were our newest student counselor.

**Jamar Richardson [6:31 P.M.]**
I know! So, my plane will arrive on Thursday at around 7. Could we get together for a late dinner?

**Amina Ndiaye [6:33 P.M.]**
Hmm. How about lunch on Saturday? I'd like to use Thursday evening to prepare for my presentation.

**Jamar Richardson [6:34 P.M.]**
That should work.

**Amina Ndiaye [6:35 P.M.]**
Great. If we don't run into each other before then, let's text again on Friday to figure out the details.

**149.** Who most likely is Mr. Richardson?
(A) Ms. Ndiaye's former coworker
(B) Ms. Ndiaye's co-presenter
(C) A university student
(D) A conference organizer

**150.** At 6:34 P.M., what does Mr. Richardson mean when he writes, "That should work"?
(A) He thinks some preparations will be useful.
(B) He believes some equipment is reliable.
(C) He does not mind providing some assistance.
(D) He can probably meet at a suggested time.

**Questions 151–152** refer to the following e-mail.

E-Mail message

From: <lester.knight@eorp.com>

To: <benita.garza@niy-mail.com>

Subject: Upcoming appointment

Date: January 2

Attachment: Information

Dear Ms. Garza,

Thank you for making an appointment to meet with me on **January 17 at 2 P.M.** I am excited to have the chance to help you achieve your goals—whether they are buying a house, sending children to university, or something else—through careful money management and smart investing.

In order to make our first meeting as productive as possible, there is some information about your income, assets, debts, and so on that you will need to have at hand. Please review the attachment to this e-mail to see the full range of paperwork that will be necessary. It is also a good idea to think of and write down any questions that you may have for me before coming to my office.

I look forward to meeting you.

Sincerely,

Lester Knight

**151.** What most likely is Mr. Knight's job?

(A) Real estate agent

(B) Private tutor

(C) Financial advisor

(D) Job recruiter

**152.** According to Mr. Knight, what is the purpose of the attachment?

(A) To describe the location of an office

(B) To justify a request for payment

(C) To summarize the details of an offer

(D) To provide a list of required documents



GO ON TO THE NEXT PAGE

**Questions 153–155** refer to the following notice.

## PUBLIC NOTICE

March 6: The City of Donnerly proposes the upgrading of a portion of its water distribution system starting in April. —[1]—. Steel pipes of insufficient size for the city's current needs will be replaced with high-density plastic pipes. —[2]—. A city assessment has determined that this project may have an impact on local wetlands. Therefore, this notice is being given in order to provide residents with an opportunity to express their environmental and safety concerns. —[3]—. The project file, which includes the results of the assessment, is available for public viewing at the Water Services Department in City Hall. Comments on the project may be submitted at the same place until March 27. —[4]—.

**153.** Why was the notice written?
(A) To announce a business opportunity
(B) To seek feedback on a proposal
(C) To caution residents about service interruptions
(D) To correct a misunderstanding about a project

**154.** What is suggested about Donnerly?
(A) Its water usage has increased.
(B) It is located in a relatively dry region.
(C) Its officials will hold a public meeting.
(D) It evaluated the quality of its drinking water.

**155.** In which of the positions marked [1], [2], [3], and [4] does the following sentence best belong?
"Valves will also be added to the remaining pipes to limit water loss from line breaks."
(A) [1]
(B) [2]
(C) [3]
(D) [4]

**Questions 156–157** refer to the following sign.

*Nabors Associates*

**Please read before using the microwave!**

1. Do not use the microwave to heat any foods that are likely to give off a strong smell (e.g., fish).
2. Cover your dish with a lid or paper towel to prevent food from splattering inside the microwave.
3. If your food does splatter or drip in the microwave, clean it up immediately. Cleaning products can be found under the sink.
4. Any problems with the microwave should now be reported to Tony Mitchell in Maintenance (ext. 32), not an office administrator.

**156.** What is the purpose of the sign?
(A) To publicize the features of an amenity
(B) To warn about some dangers
(C) To explain a process
(D) To issue a set of rules

**157.** What is most likely true about Mr. Mitchell's job duties?
(A) They are specified in a handbook.
(B) They have recently grown.
(C) They mainly consist of cleaning tasks.
(D) They include communicating with office administrators.

**Questions 158–160** refer to the following e-mail.

| | |
|---|---|
| **From:** | Scott Pham |
| **To:** | Volunteer List |
| **Subject:** | Munseck Book Fair |
| **Date:** | August 7 |

Hello, Volunteers!

On behalf of the Munseck Book Fair Organizing Committee, I'd like to welcome you all to the team responsible for putting on this wonderful event.

You'll receive an e-mail later this month from the supervisor of your particular area (e.g., exhibitor assistance, transportation, etc.) that specifies details such as where to report for your shift, but I have some general tips and information to share first.

We recommend that all volunteers wear comfortable shoes, as well as bring sunscreen just in case it is needed. Also, because the Hondina Convention Center is a large venue, you should plan to arrive 15 minutes early to ensure that you make it to your shift on time.

No matter what you do at the fair, your priority once you put on your "Volunteer" badge will be to assist the guests. Please take a look at the "Fairgoers Guide" booklet that you will be given at the entrance so that you can help them find convenience facilities. If you're asked a question that you can't answer, direct the asker to the nearest information booth.

See you at the fair!

Regards,

Scott Pham
Head Volunteer Coordinator

**158.** What information does Mr. Pham mention will be provided in a future e-mail?

(A) Some training session dates
(B) Some uniform requirements
(C) Some transportation costs
(D) Some work sites

**159.** What is suggested about the volunteers?

(A) Some of them will be stationed outside.
(B) There will be 15 of them in each activity area.
(C) They will receive a badge at the entrance to the fair.
(D) They will be entitled to free lodging.

**160.** How are volunteers encouraged to learn about the fair?

(A) By asking their supervisors
(B) By exploring it on foot
(C) By reading a publication
(D) By visiting an information booth

**Questions 161–163** refer to the following article.

# Excitement, Controversy Surround Tourism Board Contest

The Haspanton Tourism Board has caused a stir with its latest event, the "#MyHaspanton Contest." The contest offers $1,000 to the person who creates a short video that best embodies Haspanton. Videos must be posted to the social media platform Shoutster and tagged with "#MyHaspanton." The winner will be determined by a combination of the number of "Likes" that each video receives and votes to be submitted by members of the tourism board.

The contest was dreamed up by Ella Forte, the board's newest member as well as its only one under 35. In a phone call yesterday, Ms. Forte said the contest "makes use of both technology and Haspanton's greatest resource—its people." It has certainly been met with enthusiasm from Shoutster users. Nearly 80 videos have been posted so far, and they have garnered more than 10,000 "Likes" in total.

However, not everyone is pleased with the contest. At last week's city council meeting, local restaurant owner Ernest Mathews complained that the board was essentially ignoring the ideas of anyone who does not use Shoutster. "Most of my customers are seniors, and none of them are on Shoutster," he said. "The side of Haspanton that is represented in this contest is too narrow." In response, Council Member Juanita Padilla said she would urge the board to consider multiple participation methods for future promotions.

**161.** What phase is the contest currently in?
(A) It has not yet begun.
(B) Entries are being submitted.
(C) The tourism board is voting.
(D) The winner has been chosen.

**162.** What is stated about Ms. Forte?
(A) She was present at a city council meeting.
(B) She has a personal Shoutster account.
(C) She appeared in a short promotional video.
(D) She is the youngest member of an organization.

**163.** What does Mr. Mathews dislike about the contest?
(A) That the tourism board can influence its results
(B) That it excludes some residents' perspectives
(C) That it has been unsuccessful in the past
(D) That it is expensive for the city

*GO ON TO THE NEXT PAGE*

**Questions 164–167** refer to the following online chat discussion.

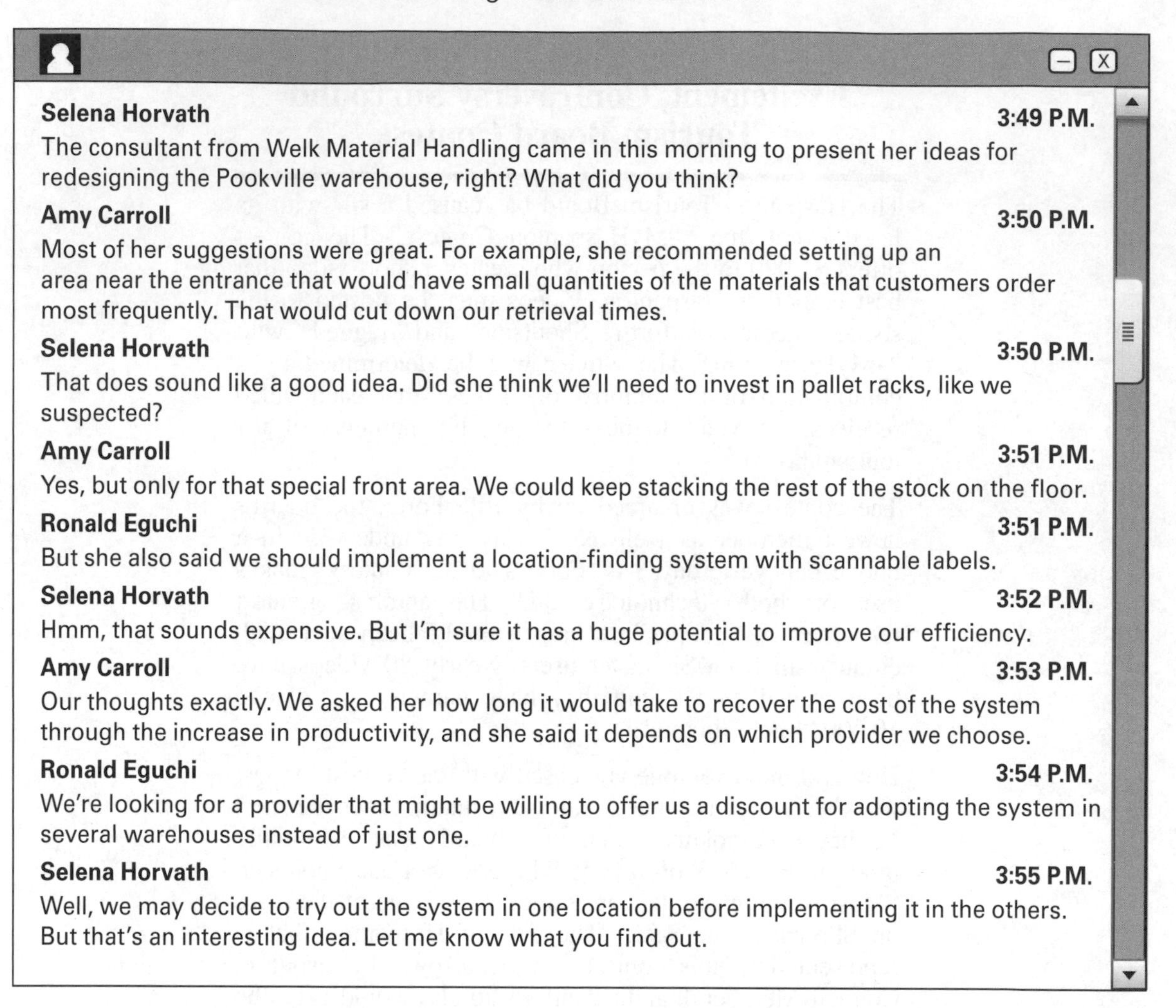

**Selena Horvath** 3:49 P.M.
The consultant from Welk Material Handling came in this morning to present her ideas for redesigning the Pookville warehouse, right? What did you think?

**Amy Carroll** 3:50 P.M.
Most of her suggestions were great. For example, she recommended setting up an area near the entrance that would have small quantities of the materials that customers order most frequently. That would cut down our retrieval times.

**Selena Horvath** 3:50 P.M.
That does sound like a good idea. Did she think we'll need to invest in pallet racks, like we suspected?

**Amy Carroll** 3:51 P.M.
Yes, but only for that special front area. We could keep stacking the rest of the stock on the floor.

**Ronald Eguchi** 3:51 P.M.
But she also said we should implement a location-finding system with scannable labels.

**Selena Horvath** 3:52 P.M.
Hmm, that sounds expensive. But I'm sure it has a huge potential to improve our efficiency.

**Amy Carroll** 3:53 P.M.
Our thoughts exactly. We asked her how long it would take to recover the cost of the system through the increase in productivity, and she said it depends on which provider we choose.

**Ronald Eguchi** 3:54 P.M.
We're looking for a provider that might be willing to offer us a discount for adopting the system in several warehouses instead of just one.

**Selena Horvath** 3:55 P.M.
Well, we may decide to try out the system in one location before implementing it in the others. But that's an interesting idea. Let me know what you find out.

**164.** Why did Ms. Horvath begin the online chat discussion?

(A) To learn about the outcome of a meeting
(B) To clarify the contents of a document
(C) To discuss arrangements for an inspection
(D) To share her opinions on a presentation

**165.** What is NOT a recommendation that a consultant made?

(A) Installing racks in one part of a facility
(B) Painting lines on a floor to mark aisle sizes
(C) Using stickers that can be read electronically
(D) Making popular types of stock more accessible

**166.** At 3:53 P.M., what does Ms. Carroll most likely mean when she writes, "Our thoughts exactly"?

(A) She and Mr. Eguchi have mixed feelings about an idea.
(B) She and Mr. Eguchi are confused by some findings.
(C) A warehouse's output is disappointingly low.
(D) The budget for a project should not be increased.

**167.** According to Ms. Horvath, what might the chat participants' company choose to do?

(A) Open a new location in Pookville
(B) Customize some features of a system
(C) Conduct a small-scale test of a scheme
(D) Discount some older merchandise

**Questions 168–171** refer to the following Web page.

http://www.allstons.com/corporate

Allston's >> Corporate Inquiries

For over 40 years, Allston's has been committed to giving our customers the best selection of quality apparel and footwear for every athletic activity. —[1]—. Today, we maintain business relationships with hundreds of vendors who represent some of the country's most popular and exciting products. Still, we are always seeking new brands and styles to sell under the "Allston's" banner. We boast a large, loyal customer base and fast, dependable payment schedules. In return, we merely ask vendors to follow our reasonable standards for merchandise packing and truck deliveries. —[2]—. To inquire about establishing a vendor relationship with us, please call us at (809) 555-0162 or e-mail us at vendors@allstons.com. —[3]—. We will be happy to provide testimonials from select existing vendors.

In addition, Allston's is constantly reviewing potential locations for opening new stores throughout the Midwestern region of the U.S. —[4]—. If you own a suitable commercial property and would like to discuss leasing it to us, please call our Chicago head office at (809) 555-0160.

**168.** What kind of business mostly likely is Allston's?

(A) A health food supplier
(B) A sports clothing store
(C) A chain of fitness centers
(D) An event planning firm

**169.** What is suggested about Allston's?

(A) It recently moved its headquarters.
(B) It will soon change its name.
(C) It is attempting to expand.
(D) It attends regional trade shows.

**170.** According to the Web page, what are all existing vendors required to do?

(A) Pack items according to company policies
(B) Give a testimonial upon request
(C) Display the Allston's logo on their trucks
(D) Prove that their operations are environmentally-friendly

**171.** In which of the positions marked [1], [2], [3], and [4] does the following sentence best belong?

"Our minimum requirement for floor space is generally 15,000 square feet."

(A) [1]
(B) [2]
(C) [3]
(D) [4]



GO ON TO THE NEXT PAGE

**Questions 172–175** refer to the following memo.

To: Managers
From: Joon-Tae Shin
Re: Employee treatment
Date: July 20

As you all know, Ms. Noolan hired me earlier this year to be Noolan Software's first full-time human resources employee. One of my duties is looking at our overall situation from a personnel perspective, and now that I have been here for a few months, I have developed some suggestions for improvements. As a small business that hopes to grow into a larger one, it is important that we provide working conditions that attract and keep talented employees.

One important consideration is workload. We should be checking in with employees regularly to ensure that their tasks can be completed in a standard workweek. If your department's workload becomes too heavy, please set up a meeting with Ms. Noolan and me to discuss adding more personnel.

Similarly, employees should feel comfortable taking sick time when needed and using their full allotment of vacation days. This is an important way of protecting their health and morale.

Finally, please allow employees some flexibility in their hours as long as they meet their performance targets. While we are not yet able to support remote work, we can at least empower our employees to manage their own schedules within reason.

All of you, Ms. Noolan, and I will meet on Thursday at 10 A.M. to talk about the contents of this memo. Please note that Ms. Noolan has already given her approval to my recommendations, so the meeting will not be an opportunity to debate them. Instead, we will focus on how best to achieve them. Thank you.

**172.** What is indicated about Noolan Software?

(A) It recently opened a new office.

(B) It was founded less than a year ago.

(C) It does not have many employees.

(D) It must satisfy its shareholders.

**173.** What is NOT mentioned as a way to improve treatment of employees?

(A) Adjustable working hours

(B) A reasonable workload

(C) Easy usage of leave time

(D) An on-site health program

**174.** According to the memo, why should recipients schedule a meeting with Mr. Shin?

(A) To express opposition to his ideas

(B) To propose hiring more workers

(C) To recommend a performance-based bonus

(D) To secure permission for a staff member to work remotely

**175.** What does Mr. Shin suggest about the recommendations in the memo?

(A) They will also be announced to the entire staff.

(B) They are supported by scientific research.

(C) They are endorsed by the business's owner.

(D) They have been adopted by a competitor.



*GO ON TO THE NEXT PAGE*

**Questions 176–180** refer to the following Web page and e-mail.

www.orosco-pac.org/fscs

# Orosco Performing Arts Center

**Free Autumn Concert Series**

Every Thursday evening from September through November, the center offers a free concert in the Ervin Amphitheater, its most intimate performance space. The series, which is carefully planned to represent a variety of genres, is an excellent chance to see established musicians and discover exciting new ones.

Performances begin at 7 P.M. Reservations are only allowed for bookings of more than 10 people. All other attendees are encouraged to line up at the box office well before the concert in order to secure their tickets.

**Upcoming Concerts** (Full Schedule)

| | |
|---|---|
| October 19 | **Emilia Bernauer:** Ms. Bernauer, called "the next big star in classical piano" by renowned concert pianist Roman Huff, will give a recital of works by French composers. |
| October 26 | **The Green Cliff Trio:** Enjoy the smooth blending of piano, double bass, and drums that earned the group its prestigious "Album of the Year" honor from the Academy of Jazz Music. |
| November 2 | **Johnny and The Farmers:** The legendary folk band makes its first visit to Helmsped in over a decade! Come and listen to "Broken Banjo" and other hits from its bestselling records. |
| November 9 | **Orosco Opera Company:** Talented singers from right here in Helmsped will perform famous arias and duets from various operas in Italian and English. |

Call 555-0180 for more information, or follow us on social media to see photos of past concerts and receive reminders of upcoming ones.

**From:** Eloise Flynn
**To:** Trina McGee
**Subject:** Re: Free Autumn Concert
**Date:** October 10

Dear Trina,

Sure, I would love to go to the concert with you. I can't believe we'll be able to see opera singing in the Orosco Performing Arts Center for free! I've never been there before, and I've heard that it's really nice. You always seem to know about the most interesting events around the city—someday you'll have to tell me how you do that! And no, I wouldn't mind handling the tickets, since you work on Thursdays. It will just be the two of us, right?

–Eloise

**176.** What is indicated about the Orosco Performing Arts Center?

(A) It has more than one stage.
(B) It displays various architectural styles.
(C) It posts interviews on its social media accounts.
(D) It allows children under age 10 to attend some events.

**177.** On the Web page, what is NOT mentioned as an accomplishment of the listed performers?

(A) Selling many albums
(B) Winning a major award
(C) Performing around the world
(D) Receiving acclaim from a famous musician

**178.** Why was the e-mail written?

(A) To request a change to some plans
(B) To answer a question about a completed booking
(C) To confirm that a reservation has been made
(D) To accept a friendly invitation

**179.** On which date does Ms. Flynn probably want to see a concert?

(A) October 19
(B) October 26
(C) November 2
(D) November 9

**180.** What will Ms. Flynn most likely do?

(A) Arrive early on the day of the performance
(B) Call the performing arts center's box office
(C) Go through an online process on a certain date
(D) Download a tourism-related mobile app

GO ON TO THE NEXT PAGE

**Questions 181–185** refer to the following article and letter to the editor.

(February 7)—A Waymarr convenience store is coming to Denold City.

The city's Economic Development Committee (EDC) unanimously approved Waymarr's plans to construct a 4,600-square-foot convenience store, which will feature a tiled canopy above its 12 gas pumps. It will be built on a plot of vacant land on Milden Drive, near Route 7, and remain open 24 hours a day, 7 days a week.

To operate the store, the company will have to comply with the city's noise and traffic reduction regulations. Among other things, it will not be allowed to accept deliveries via heavy trucks between 1:00 A.M. and 5:00 A.M., with the exception of gasoline. Trucks will also be unable to access the store from Milden Drive, so Waymarr will build a private road leading to the store's receiving area.

Approval came after a public meeting that included presentations by the company's own traffic engineers. The residents in attendance voiced a mixture of support and opposition. Betty Timpano, who lives on the 400 block of Milden Drive, said she liked the idea of a convenience store in the neighborhood but had concerns about increased traffic along nearby Ramona Way. As evidence, she showed a digital video she had shot from her car window during rush hour. It showed heavy vehicle congestion on Ramona Way near Brook Street.

On the other hand, resident Steve Grossick said he would welcome the store because it would provide a "quick, warm bite to eat" after work. Currently, the nearest convenience store is a Weisbold Plus Shop on Laurel Street, about three kilometers away.

Dear Editor,

As a lifelong resident of Denold City, I was grateful for your February 7 report on the planned Waymarr convenience store. However, the article contained some incorrect information. The digital video I presented at the public meeting was a recording of congested traffic on my street of residence.

Also, I would like to remind you that two citizens voiced concerns about the modern design of the store. I agree with them that we must try to retain our city's distinctive architectural character. New buildings should, if possible, blend in with our historical structures.

Again, thank you for your reporting.

Sincerely,

Betty Timpano

**181.** What is NOT true about the planned convenience store?

(A) It will have a covered fueling area.

(B) It will not sell gas in the early mornings.

(C) It will offer cooked food selections.

(D) It will be constructed on empty land.

**182.** What is mentioned about Denold City?

(A) It is known for its large warehouse district.

(B) It is the site of an annual engineering conference.

(C) It has three other convenience stores.

(D) It has implemented policies to decrease traffic.

**183.** Where did Ms. Timpano most likely film a video for a public meeting?

(A) On Milden Drive

(B) On Ramona Way

(C) On Brook Street

(D) On Laurel Street

**184.** What does the letter to the editor indicate about Ms. Timpano?

(A) She is a local historian.

(B) She prefers modern architecture.

(C) She has never lived outside of Denold City.

(D) She has been to a Waymarr convenience store.

**185.** In the letter to the editor, the word "retain" in paragraph 2, line 2, is closest in meaning to

(A) appoint

(B) conceal

(C) preserve

(D) confine



GO ON TO THE NEXT PAGE

**Questions 186–190** refer to the following proposal, advertisement, and customer review.

Mintana Spa

## Proposal for a Sales Promotion

Submitted by Joseph Barham, Sales Assistant

September 2

Form of Promotion: A 15% discount on any service

Target Customer: Nurses

Dates/Duration: Ongoing, starting as soon as possible

Advantages:

- New group of customers. As holders of a job that is high stress but not always well paid, nurses could benefit greatly from our services but may feel that they are not affordable at full price.
- Improvement of our corporate image among the general public.

Challenges:

- Logistical issues. Our staff would have to carefully check the credentials of participants and remember that only services are included in the discount.

## *Mintana Spa Supports Medical Personnel!*

Mintana Spa knows that saving lives and providing day-to-day medical care is difficult work. That is why, starting November 1, we will offer a 15% discount on all of our services to nurses, paramedics, and emergency medical technicians.* These include relaxing massages, refreshing facial and body treatments, and cleansing sauna time—even in our new infrared sauna pods, which use infrared light to induce detoxifying sweat and improve circulation! This is our small way of thanking the heroes who keep our community healthy.

Mintana Spa is located at 1200 Whitcomb Road in Bruner. Walk-ins are accepted, but we recommend making an appointment, as our schedule does frequently fill up. Call 555-0122 for more information.

**Proof of eligible employment is required. Note that the discount cannot be used toward spa gift certificates or merchandise.*

http://www.brunerbusinessreviews.com/mintanaspa

**Bruner Business Reviews**

Latest reviews for Mintana Spa:

"I had a day off yesterday, so I visited in the early afternoon to take advantage of their new discount for nurses. They were quite busy for a weekday, and I was lucky that I didn't get turned away for not having an appointment. Still, I never felt hurried by the staff. Everyone was very attentive and treated me like I was the only customer that day. That's what I appreciated the most. In contrast, the benefits of the blueberry extract facial faded by this morning, and the sauna pod, while relaxing, wasn't much better than a hot bath. I will probably go to this spa again but try some different services next time."

By Teisha Coyne, November 12

**186.** What does the proposal mention as a potential difficulty of a promotion?
(A) Making potential participants aware of it
(B) Serving large numbers of new patrons
(C) Maintaining sufficient profit margins
(D) Evaluating participants' qualifications

**187.** What is different about the promotion in the proposal and the advertisement?
(A) The size of its discount
(B) The duration it is available
(C) The people eligible for it
(D) The purchases to which it can be applied

**188.** In the customer review, the phrase "turned away" in paragraph 1, line 3, is closest in meaning to
(A) dismissed
(B) rejected
(C) avoided
(D) abandoned

**189.** What is implied about Ms. Coyne?
(A) She visited on the first day of the promotion.
(B) She received a light-based treatment.
(C) She tried Mintana Spa's most popular offering.
(D) She called the phone number listed in the advertisement.

**190.** What did Ms. Coyne especially like about Mintana Spa?
(A) Its considerate customer service
(B) Its luxurious interior decoration
(C) The effectiveness of its procedures
(D) The privacy afforded by its layout



GO ON TO THE NEXT PAGE

**Questions 191–195** refer to the following article, e-mail, and excerpt from a report.

## Arabic Language Exam To Be Administered in Cobshaw

By Sheila Ridenour

COBSHAW (May 13)—The National Foreign Language Association (NFLA), a non-profit organization committed to advancing Americans' competency in languages other than English, will begin offering its Arabic language proficiency test in Cobshaw. The Test of Competency in Arabic (TOCIA) will be administered twice a year starting this July.

Ken Reed, an NFLA official, says the decision was an easy one to reach. "We noticed that there have been a lot of test-takers coming from the Cobshaw region." He believes that this is thanks to the University of Cobshaw's Arabic language program. The program also, he says, supplies local people qualified to administer the test, as such work requires some knowledge of the language.

The TOCIA consists of a 50-minute listening section and a 70-minute reading section. The first exam will be held in the university's Duckett Auditorium, though Mr. Reed says other venues may be added if there are over 150 test-takers. Registration, which costs $40, must be completed online at www.nfla.org/tocia by 5 P.M. on June 4.

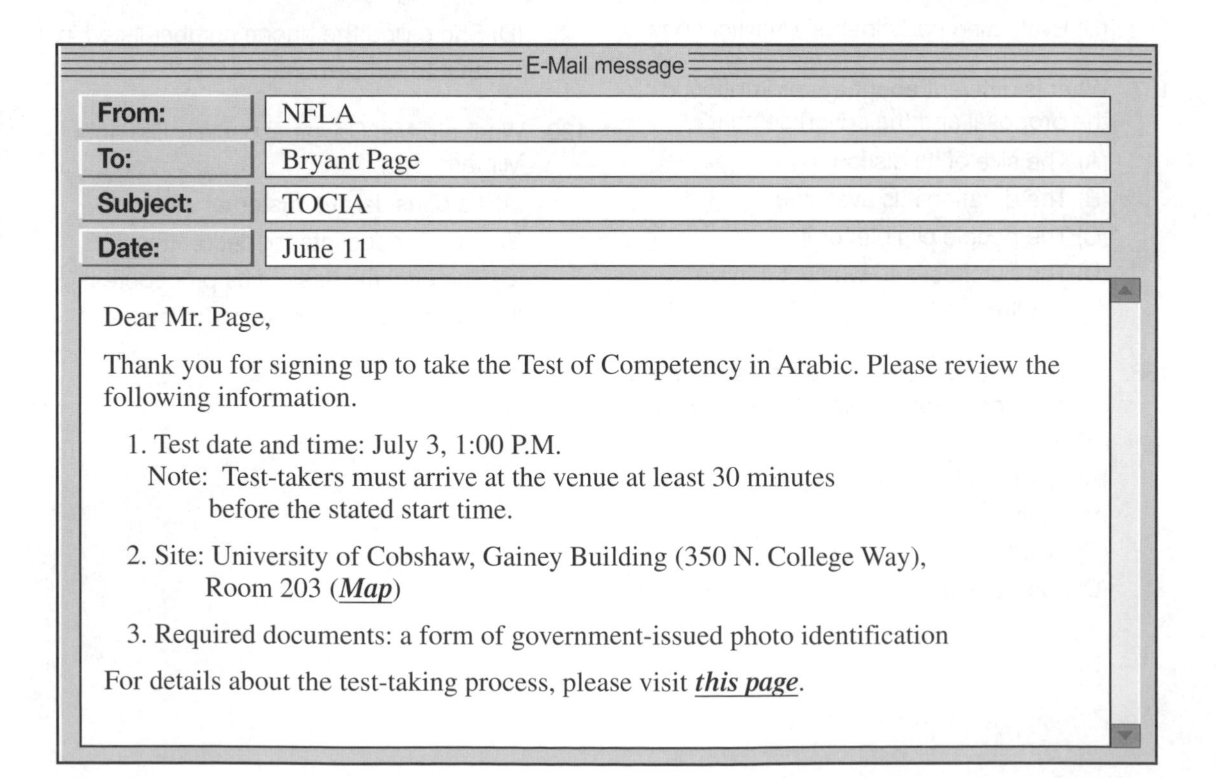
E-Mail message

| | |
|---|---|
| From: | NFLA |
| To: | Bryant Page |
| Subject: | TOCIA |
| Date: | June 11 |

Dear Mr. Page,

Thank you for signing up to take the Test of Competency in Arabic. Please review the following information.

1. Test date and time: July 3, 1:00 P.M.
   Note: Test-takers must arrive at the venue at least 30 minutes before the stated start time.
2. Site: University of Cobshaw, Gainey Building (350 N. College Way), Room 203 (***Map***)
3. Required documents: a form of government-issued photo identification

For details about the test-taking process, please visit ***this page***.

## Test of Competency in Arabic (TOCIA)
### Report on the Observance of Testing Procedures

Test Site: University of Cobshaw, Duckett Auditorium
Test Date: July 3
Test Administrator: Savanna Keenan

Please check the box next to each item to indicate that the relevant procedure was executed. If any box is left unmarked, a full explanation of the reason must be appended to this report.

- No test-takers were admitted to the site fewer than 30 minutes before the start of the test. ☑
- The identity of each test-taker was verified. ☑
- All personal electronics brought by test-takers were stored away from the site. ☐
- Test-takers filled out all of the required pre-test forms. ☑

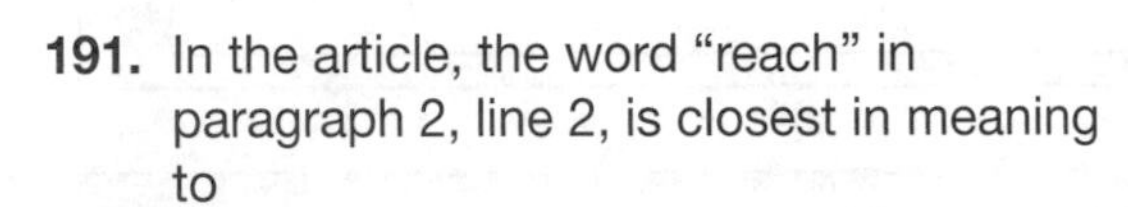

**191.** In the article, the word "reach" in paragraph 2, line 2, is closest in meaning to
(A) stretch
(B) accomplish
(C) contact
(D) make

**192.** Why was the e-mail sent to Mr. Page?
(A) To prepare him for the test
(B) To ask him to finalize his registration
(C) To advertise a study service
(D) To respond to an inquiry

**193.** What is suggested about the TOCIA?
(A) More than 150 people signed up to take it in Cobshaw.
(B) There is a 30-minute break between its sections.
(C) It is usually administered on a weekend day.
(D) There are practice versions of it on the NFLA Web site.

**194.** What will most likely be explained in an attachment to the report?
(A) When the last test-taker arrived
(B) How test-takers proved their identities
(C) What paperwork test-takers completed before the test
(D) Where test-takers' belongings were kept during the test

**195.** What is most likely true about Ms. Keenan?
(A) She participated in a training session in June.
(B) She has some Arabic language skills.
(C) She was interviewed by Ms. Ridenour.
(D) She is a professor at the University of Cobshaw.



GO ON TO THE NEXT PAGE

**Questions 196–200** refer to the following e-mails and Web page.

| | |
|---|---|
| **To:** | Nick Borrows <nickborrows1@renseed.com> |
| **From:** | Vanessa Castle <vanessacastle@renseed.com> |
| **Date:** | April 20 |
| **Subject:** | San Diego |
| **Attachment:** | Revised presentation |

Hi Nick,

I just wanted to give you an update on the slides for our presentation in San Diego next week. I've left the graphs and balance sheet as they are, but I've made the pictures of our products a little bigger and sharper. I also have some notes about the text of the slides, but I didn't want to alter it without talking to you first. I'll send my ideas in a separate file.

Also, we need to book a flight. For the way there, there are four options available on our preferred carrier. I don't know about you, but I'd like to take the one that gets us there in the evening. It would allow us to prepare here in the office for most of the day but also arrive in time to relax a bit. If you agree, I'll book it before I leave today.

Let me know.

–Vanessa

www.lightningair.com/departures/april28/query83789

**Lightning Air—Operating Budget Flights Daily Across the US!**

**Departure Date:** April 28

**Departure Airport:** San Francisco

**Arrival Airport:** San Diego

| | | |
|---|---|---|
| O Flight No: L106 | Departure: 4:30 A.M. | Arrival: 6:00 A.M. |
| O Flight No: L982 | Departure: 11:00 A.M. | Arrival: 12:30 P.M. |
| O Flight No: L392 | Departure: 1:00 P.M. | Arrival: 2:30 P.M. |
| O Flight No: L720 | Departure: 5:45 P.M. | Arrival: 7:15 P.M. |

**Important note:** We have eliminated our complimentary meal service for economy class passengers on flights shorter than three hours. These passengers may purchase a meal for an additional cost. Business class passengers are still entitled to this meal free of charge. Club class passengers receive the meal and their choice of unlimited beverages. Premium class passengers get the same as club class, as well as entry to our exclusive Lightning Air lounge.

NEXT PAGE ▶

| | |
|---|---|
| **To:** | Vanessa Castle <vanessacastle@renseed.com> |
| **From:** | Nick Borrows <nickborrows1@renseed.com> |
| **Subject:** | Re: San Diego |
| **Date:** | April 22 |

Hi Vanessa,

Thank you for your e-mail and your hard work on the presentation slides.

I've got the company credit card with me right now, so I went ahead and got tickets for the flight that you wanted, plus another one coming back on the thirtieth. The prices were quite reasonable, although I had to pay a little extra to get in-flight meals for us.

If you don't mind, I'll make reservations now at the hotel I usually use in the city center. We won't have to book transportation from the airport, because the hotel has a free shuttle bus. It also has a nice business center where we can print our presentation slides. Does that sound all right?

Nick

**196.** What did Ms. Castle do to some images?
(A) She made them more visible.
(B) She put them in a different file.
(C) She added text to them.
(D) She removed flaws from them.

**197.** What does Ms. Castle promise to send to Mr. Borrows?
(A) Verification of a reservation
(B) Details about some travel options
(C) An audio recording of a presentation
(D) Suggestions for revising some writing

**198.** Which flight does Ms. Castle prefer?
(A) L982
(B) L106
(C) L720
(D) L392

**199.** What class of flight ticket did Mr. Borrows most likely purchase?
(A) Economy class
(B) Club class
(C) Business class
(D) Premium class

**200.** What does Mr. Borrows indicate he will do next?
(A) Apply for reimbursement for an expense
(B) Arrange ground transportation
(C) Book some accommodations
(D) Print some computer screenshots

**Stop! This is the end of the test. If you finish before time is called, you may go back to Parts 5, 6, and 7 and check your work.**

# ACTUAL TEST 

## READING TEST

In the Reading test, you will read a variety of texts and answer several different types of reading comprehension questions. The entire Reading test will last 75 minutes. There are three parts, and directions are given for each part. You are encouraged to answer as many questions as possible within the time allowed. You must mark your answers on the separate answer sheet. Do not write your answers in your test book.

## PART 5

**Directions:** A word or phrase is missing in each of the sentences below. Four answer choices are given below each sentence. Select the best answer to complete the sentence. Then mark the letter (A), (B), (C), or (D) on your answer sheet.

**101.** The amount of each employee's ------- is based on his or her performance review.

(A) workstation
(B) bonus
(C) uniform
(D) promotion

**102.** Gillis Mining Group issued a firm ------- of rumors that it plans to replace its CEO.

(A) deny
(B) denies
(C) denied
(D) denial

**103.** ------- a minimal additional charge, our design professionals can produce eye-catching illustrations you can add to your promotional pieces.

(A) For
(B) As
(C) With
(D) To

**104.** Fellant Inn ------- a considerable amount of effort into maintaining its reputation for style and comfort.

(A) shows
(B) spends
(C) puts
(D) needs

**105.** One way to shorten the preparation time of this dish is by buying cabbage that has ------- been cut into strips.

(A) sometimes
(B) already
(C) finally
(D) since

**106.** The warehouse manager praised the members of the sprinkler installation team for ------- skilled and careful work.

(A) they
(B) them
(C) theirs
(D) their

**107.** The Galaxxania Plus navigation device for drivers ------- automatically as soon as the vehicle is started.

(A) activation
(B) activator
(C) activates
(D) activated

**108.** The responses to the recent student survey on the university's health services vary -------.

(A) wide
(B) widened
(C) widening
(D) widely

**109.** Ms. Dudley's article calls on the authorities to increase ------- of some sectors of the telecommunications industry.

(A) supervision
(B) supervised
(C) supervisors
(D) supervises

**110.** Mr. Flores, the assistant manager, is in charge of the store ------- Ms. Weaver is gone.

(A) during
(B) if not
(C) so that
(D) when

**111.** Our consistently high customer satisfaction ratings ------- the excellent quality of our product line.

(A) transmit
(B) reflect
(C) deliver
(D) arrange

**112.** Handdahar Chemicals, Inc. has 12 research laboratories spread ------- the major regions of the world.

(A) between
(B) out
(C) upon
(D) across

**113.** Nishioka Industrial's leadership is ------- supportive of staff efforts to develop environmentally-friendly detergents.

(A) enthusiastically
(B) enthusiasm
(C) enthusiastic
(D) enthusiast

**114.** According to the janitor, ------- has been leaving unwashed dishes in the break room sink.

(A) who
(B) whoever
(C) someone
(D) one another

**115.** Mastery of a foreign language is not a fast process, and it is normal for skills to develop ------ over a long period of time.

(A) hurriedly
(B) affirmatively
(C) gradually
(D) reluctantly

**116.** In some small companies, the person ------- for ordering supplies may work in the accounting or finance department.

(A) responsibly
(B) responsible
(C) responsibility
(D) responsibilities

**117.** The casting director conducted an ------- search to find the perfect performer for the film's starring role.

(A) absolute
(B) eligible
(C) exhausted
(D) extensive

**118.** An extraordinary number of citizens participated ------- in the city's campaign to reduce water usage.

(A) voluntarily
(B) voluntary
(C) volunteers
(D) volunteering

**119.** ------- its materials' delicacy and high value, access to the rare books collection is limited to library staff only.

(A) Because of
(B) Along with
(C) In spite of
(D) Regardless of

**120.** This week's issue includes a review of jogging accessories that ------- in detail the differences in functionality, price, and durability.

(A) have analyzed
(B) analyzes
(C) analyze
(D) is analyzed



GO ON TO THE NEXT PAGE

**121.** Casey Street has become famous for having a high ------- of technology start-ups.

(A) position
(B) standard
(C) concentration
(D) attendance

**122.** Please reserve Conference Room 3 so that we can practice our sales ------- in advance of the client visit.

(A) presentation
(B) presentable
(C) presenter
(D) presented

**123.** Submitting this application does not ------- you to accept a loan from Masple Bank.

(A) ensure
(B) relieve
(C) obligate
(D) expedite

**124.** ------- construction of the condominiums is complete, they may be exhibited to prospective buyers.

(A) Now that
(B) Throughout
(C) Whatever
(D) In order that

**125.** All ------- to the logo design should be discussed in advance with a copyright expert and approved by Mr. Wang.

(A) proposals
(B) concepts
(C) modifications
(D) necessities

**126.** For the sake of its patients, Morrol Hospital urges medical personnel ------- sick leave as needed.

(A) have taken
(B) to take
(C) took
(D) taking

**127.** Boasting scenic views of the ocean, Raynor Highway was ------- the only route between the coastal cities of Autry and Lambort.

(A) what
(B) among
(C) far
(D) once

**128.** Several times in the past year, production at the Nettsald factory ------- by easily preventable machine breakdowns.

(A) was delaying
(B) has been delayed
(C) would have delayed
(D) can be delayed

**129.** Investors in Balters Incorporated are requesting that the company undergo an audit to prove that it is financially -------.

(A) sound
(B) equivalent
(C) feasible
(D) detailed

**130.** After the meal, Harkon Catering's servers will clear tables ------- to avoid distracting guests' attention from speeches or other events.

(A) accurately
(B) discreetly
(C) persistently
(D) luxuriously

# PART 6

**Directions:** Read the texts that follow. A word, phrase, or sentence is missing in parts of each text. Four answer choices for each question are given below the text. Select the best answer to complete the text. Then mark the letter (A), (B), (C), or (D) on your answer sheet.

**Questions 131–134** refer to the following notice.

***Important Customer Notice***

Deldunne's Bargain Store will be closed for inventory and computer updates on Monday, January 13. We apologize for any inconvenience this may cause, and we thank you in advance for your patience. On occasion, it is not possible for our staff to handle every task ------- (**131.**) to inventory processing during normal opening hours. ------- (**132.**). We chose to take care of these important business functions on this day because we have ------- (**133.**) few shoppers on Mondays. It is usually the ------- (**134.**) day of the week. Our store will open again promptly at 9 A.M. on Tuesday, January 14. Thank you.

**131.** (A) relates
(B) related
(C) relation
(D) relatively

**132.** (A) Therefore, closing for one day is our only option.
(B) The software program is a new addition.
(C) However, most of them are still available online.
(D) Please ask the customer service desk for assistance.

**133.** (A) solely
(B) considerably
(C) comparatively
(D) regularly

**134.** (A) shortest
(B) slowest
(C) earliest
(D) busiest



GO ON TO THE NEXT PAGE

**Questions 135–138** refer to the following e-mail.

From: Douglas Bailey
To: <totycontest@inspiriteach.com>
Subject: Recommendation for Kerri Wilkinson
Date: November 26

To Whom It May Concern:

I would like to endorse Kerri Wilkinson's nomination for InspiriTeach's "Teacher of the Year" award. -------. **135.** Ms. Wilkinson has been my coworker at Winkfield Middle School for five years, and I cannot imagine ------- **136.** more representative of these qualities.

Ms. Wilkinson demonstrates endless creativity in her lesson plans for her sixth grade class. For example, she recently made excellent use of the school's technological capabilities for a unit on -------. **137.** Her students planned, filmed, and edited a newscast about the school.

Ms. Wilkinson is also very compassionate. She shows nothing but understanding toward even our most difficult students. -------, **138.** she is able to handle disruptive behavior with patience and kindness that are an inspiration to her coworkers.

In closing, I recommend you strongly consider Ms. Wilkinson for Teacher of the Year.

Sincerely,

Douglas Bailey

**135.** (A) She deserves recognition for her dedication to the campaign.
(B) I am a wholehearted supporter of InspiriTeach's activities.
(C) Please route my e-mail to the appropriate person or committee.
(D) Your Web site says you seek to reward innovation and caring.

**136.** (A) educating that
(B) an educator
(C) she educates
(D) whose education

**137.** (A) journalism
(B) geography
(C) economics
(D) government

**138.** (A) At first
(B) In fact
(C) Otherwise
(D) Nevertheless

**Questions 139–142** refer to the following information.

**Requirements for VieraGo Hotels**

Being listed on VieraGo is a privilege that comes with a variety of responsibilities. ------- **139.** the key one is to provide guests with a pleasant stay, we also expect our member hotels to assist in upholding VieraGo's good reputation through the following actions.

First, respond quickly to any inquiries made through VieraGo about your hotel—even those from guests you are not able to accept. Next, after a booking has been made through VieraGo, do not cancel it unless it is absolutely necessary. ------- **140.**. Finally, please try to achieve a high rating on VieraGo by both taking good care of your property and ------- **141.** issues that are mentioned in guest reviews.

VieraGo tracks the performance of each member hotel in these areas (responsiveness, cancelation rate, and guest ratings) and may impose penalties on hotels that drop below certain levels. To avoid this, we recommend ------- **142.** this data yourself through your account page.

**139.** (A) While
(B) Regarding
(C) Whether
(D) Besides

**140.** (A) You can also provide a physical copy at your front desk.
(B) Some hotels may not benefit from advertising on VieraGo.
(C) For most reservations, these would be toiletries and towels.
(D) Remember, your guests' travel plans depend on you.

**141.** (A) resolve
(B) resolved
(C) resolving
(D) resolution

**142.** (A) supplying
(B) revising
(C) monitoring
(D) saving



GO ON TO THE NEXT PAGE

**Questions 143–146** refer to the following press release.

FOR IMMEDIATE RELEASE

Contact: publicrelations@pearron.com

TORONTO (October 22)—Pharmaceutical firm Pearron, Inc. has announced the signing of a deal with Wompler Capital. Under the terms of the agreement, Wompler Capital has purchased a minority stake in Pearron for C$72 million, ------- (143.) providing funding to realize Pearron's growth strategy.

Pearron's shareholders support ------- (144.) landmark deal. They firmly believe that it ------- (145.) the company to expand significantly in the coming years.

Pearron develops and commercializes medications for a variety of skin, hair, and nail conditions. ------- (146.). In the future, it will focus on refining its rigorous development process that prioritizes the needs and safety of patients. It will also build up the dedicated sales force that markets its drugs to medical providers throughout Canada.

**143.** (A) yet
(B) instead
(C) thereby
(D) quite

**144.** (A) this
(B) every
(C) most
(D) our

**145.** (A) allows
(B) will allow
(C) has allowed
(D) allowing

**146.** (A) Many patients still prefer conventional medicine to alternative remedies.
(B) Its machines can be found in hospital rooms around the country.
(C) Its products include Travarin, a cream used to treat nail infections.
(D) The early results of an ongoing clinical trial have been promising.

## PART 7

**Directions:** In this part you will read a selection of texts, such as magazine and newspaper articles, e-mails, and instant messages. Each text or set of texts is followed by several questions. Select the best answer for each question and mark the letter (A), (B), (C), or (D) on your answer sheet.

**Questions 147–148** refer to the following advertisement.

### Swann Space

Swann Space provides a comfortable, high-tech working environment for individuals and small businesses. Our facility offers options ranging from flexible coworking lounges to private offices with dedicated conference space. Amenities available to all members include:

- Free, high-speed wireless Internet and access to printers, scanners, and shredders
- A kitchen and break lounge with free beverages and well-stocked vending machines
- Package receiving services and use of our building's impressive Highlands District address (3100 Barney Street) for business mailings

Want to know more? Join our next Swann Space Open Reception on May 3 to connect with us, our current members, and other leaders of the Linkley business community. Alternatively, you can visit us between 8 A.M. and 6 P.M. on weekdays for a personal tour or simply go to www.swannspace.com.

**147.** What is indicated about Swann Space?
(A) It caters mainly to workers in creative industries.
(B) It provides technical support to its members.
(C) It is located in a prestigious neighborhood.
(D) Its members have access to exercise machines.

**148.** What will Swann Space do on May 3 ?
(A) Raise a monthly rate
(B) Lead a tour of a facility
(C) Welcome a new executive
(D) Host a networking event



GO ON TO THE NEXT PAGE

**Questions 149–150** refer to the following e-mail.

E-Mail message

| | |
|---|---|
| From: | Eiji Furuta |
| To: | Jill Bennett |
| Subject: | Delivery packaging |
| Date: | April 3 |

Hi Jill,

Customer Service has let me know that several of our grocery delivery customers have contacted us about our meat packaging. Apparently, they are concerned that the meat is only packed in our normal packaging (a foam tray covered with stretchable film). They would like another layer to be added to protect the other products from bacteria in case this packaging fails and the meat's juices leak.

Now, we haven't received any reports of the normal packaging actually failing, so I'm not convinced that it has to be upgraded. However, I think we should at least look into ways to accommodate these customers' wishes. Could you research additional packaging options and the cost and environmental impact involved in using them? I'd like a short report on your findings by the end of the month.

Thanks,

Eiji

**149.** What are customers concerned about?

(A) The use of non-recyclable packaging materials

(B) The temperature of meat rising to an unsafe level

(C) Staff not handling delivery containers gently

(D) Foods becoming cross-contaminated

**150.** What does Mr. Eiji suggest about a potential change to some packaging?

(A) It may not be necessary.

(B) It must be introduced slowly.

(C) It requires Ms. Bennett's approval.

(D) It will be unpopular with employees.

**Questions 151–152** refer to the following information.

*Hadnar City Community Newsletter*

## Hadnar City Garden Club (HCGC)

Come and join us as we begin our new season! Our first meeting of the year will be held on Monday, March 13 at 7:00 P.M. at our usual venue, the Hadnar Community Center. Patrick Lett and Gina Lu will give a lecture and demonstration about "How Honeybees Help Gardeners." As members of the Hadnar City Beekeepers Association, they are committed to educating the public on the environmental benefits of honeybees. Their lecture will include valuable advice on designing gardens that will attract bees. This program will be interactive, so please bring your questions.

We hope to see a lot of new faces next Monday. An individual membership to the HCGC costs $20 per year, and membership registration forms will be available at the meeting. A complete calendar of our upcoming field trips, plant sales, and volunteer activities can be found online at www.hcgc.org.

**151.** What is one purpose of the information?
(A) To announce a change in venue
(B) To recruit new members for a club
(C) To seek feedback about a previous lecture
(D) To highlight a local environmental problem

**152.** According to the information, what is available on the HCGC Web site?
(A) A schedule of events
(B) A membership application
(C) A map of the city
(D) A discussion forum



GO ON TO THE NEXT PAGE

**Questions 153–154** refer to the following text-message chain.

**Jeff Kriess, 3:22 P.M.**
Amy, one of the labeling machines has an issue. The labels are coming out crooked.

**Amy Mora, 3:23 P.M.**
Try cleaning the feeder section. It may be dirty. Are you still down on the factory floor?

**Jeff Kriess, 3:24 P.M.**
Yes, I'm down here now. Do you know who the service technician is for this equipment? It was just cleaned, actually.

**Amy Mora, 3:24 P.M.**
Good question. Let me get back to you.

**Jeff Kriess, 3:25 P.M.**
Oh, no need, in that case. I'll try the manufacturer's technical support hotline.

**153.** Where most likely is Mr. Kriess?
(A) In a production plant
(B) In a printing shop
(C) In a building's lobby
(D) In a computer store

**154.** At 3:24 P.M., what does Ms. Mora most likely mean when she writes, "Good question"?
(A) Mr. Kriess has pointed out an important problem.
(B) She is unsure of whom to contact about a repair.
(C) She does not know why a machine is malfunctioning.
(D) Mr. Kriess has reminded her about an urgent task.

**Questions 155–157** refer to the following excerpt from an agreement.

## 8. Code of Conduct

As the exposition is primarily intended as a venue for the sharing of knowledge, the exhibitor and its representatives will not engage in selling, order-taking, etc., on the expo floor. Similarly, no prices may be displayed in the contracted exhibition space.

In order to encourage the free flow of visitors throughout the venue, exhibitors will not place any representatives or materials outside of the contracted exhibition space. Similarly, the placement of representatives and materials within the space must be arranged so that they draw attendees in instead of filling the aisles.

Like all attendees, exhibitor representatives must wear their official expo credentials and be appropriately dressed in business or business casual attire at all times.

Any demonstrations or other activities engaged in by the exhibitor will not generate a noise of greater than 85 decibels.

Exhibitors will not be allowed to dismantle their exhibits or begin packing before the official end of the expo.

**155.** What is stated about the exposition?
(A) Its purpose is educational.
(B) It will occupy several buildings.
(C) It has been held before.
(D) It is free for members of the press.

**156.** The word "flow" in paragraph 2, line 1, is closest in meaning to
(A) sequence
(B) direction
(C) quantity
(D) circulation

**157.** What does the excerpt specify about exhibitors?
(A) The amount of electricity they can use
(B) The kind of handouts they can distribute
(C) The loudness of the sounds they can make
(D) The number of representatives they can send



GO ON TO THE NEXT PAGE

**Questions 158–161** refer to the following article.

## Local Business

(September 13)—With the opening of a Cainlen Superstore just two weeks away, the Bakert Merchants Association (BMA) has begun an initiative that encourages consumers to support local businesses. At least thirty stores have hung "Buy from Bakert" signs in their front windows.

Like other Cainlen locations across the nation, the new Bakert store stretches over 180,000 square feet of land and will sell groceries, clothing, and electronics and boast a garden supply center and a photo developing lab. The massiveness of its floor plan meant that its construction was subject to public review regarding potential harm to plants and wildlife near its site on Todd Road.

At that time, the BMA almost succeeded in blocking the development by pressing the city council to consider its effects in another area—that of local commerce. The BMA argued that Cainlen would put smaller retailers out of business and thus weaken the community in the long term.

However, the council was more persuaded by Cainlen representatives' claims that the store would ultimately benefit Bakert by creating new jobs for its citizens and allowing them to enjoy the chain's famously low prices.

BMA president and Bakert Sporting Goods owner Laura Comstock says the Buy from Bakert campaign "just asks people to think before they shop" and adds that it will continue "for as long as it feels necessary."

**158.** Why was the article written?
- (A) To publicize a campaign led by local retailers
- (B) To explain the history of a nationwide company
- (C) To describe the opening celebration of a new store
- (D) To invite citizens to a city council meeting

**159.** According to the article, what can visitors to a Cainlen Superstore do?
- (A) Have a portrait photograph taken
- (B) Fill a prescription for medication
- (C) Buy landscaping goods
- (D) Eat at a restaurant

**160.** The word "area" in paragraph 3, line 3, is closest in meaning to
- (A) size
- (B) field
- (C) distance
- (D) region

**161.** What is NOT mentioned as a possible effect of a new Cainlen Superstore?
- (A) An increase in employment opportunities
- (B) New types of products becoming available
- (C) The closing of other businesses
- (D) Damage to the environment

**Questions 162–164** refer to the following letter.

**Molsher University**

*Department of Music*

*Ottawa, ON K1A 4H9*

Dear Alumni and Friends:

Molsher University has had the use of new pianos for the past year thanks to the "Giving Music" program operated by the Tynor Arts Foundation (TAF). —[1]—. Now, as part of the program, we are offering a selection of the pianos to the public for purchase.

The instruments available will include grand pianos, upright pianos, and digital pianos from leading manufacturers. Most of them are still under warranty, and delivery arrangements can be made on site upon purchase. —[2]—.

To view and purchase an instrument, please visit the Center for the Arts on Saturday, February 10 between 2:00 P.M. and 6:00 P.M. No appointment is needed. —[3]—. The center is located on Canby Road, between First and Second Street. A $2-per-hour rate applies to all street parking in the vicinity. Alternatively, paid parking is available in the center's garage. For directions, please visit www.arts-center.org. —[4]—.

A portion of the proceeds from each instrument is returned to the TAF to maintain Giving Music, which plays an important part in our department's ability to give quality music instruction.

Regards,

Paul Lembke
Interim Chair, Department of Music
Molsher University

**162.** What is the main purpose of the letter?
(A) To welcome new staff to a department
(B) To give details about a fund-raising sale
(C) To thank donors for their contributions
(D) To announce a program's expansion

**163.** What is suggested about the Center for the Arts?
(A) It is usually closed on weekends.
(B) It has more than one entrance.
(C) It does not have free parking nearby.
(D) It is operated by volunteers from the TAF.

**164.** In which of the positions marked [1], [2], [3], and [4] does the following sentence best belong?
"It generously supplies our department with high-quality instruments at no cost every year."
(A) [1]
(B) [2]
(C) [3]
(D) [4]



GO ON TO THE NEXT PAGE

**Questions 165–167** refer to the following summary of a report.

## Padgino Employee Satisfaction Survey Report

### Executive Summary

Tayona Consulting Services conducted a survey to measure the job satisfaction of employees of Padgino. Data was primarily collected with the use of the survey platform ZestSurvey. Employees were asked to numerically rate their satisfaction with factors such as company management, job duties, and employee benefits. The list of questions and a detailed analysis of the collected data are included in this report's appendices. Four supplementary interviews were conducted with employees who indicated willingness to further discuss their answers. To protect these employees' privacy, these interviews are not described in detail in this report.

The findings indicate that employees are satisfied with most aspects of their jobs and particularly their pay. The only part of the survey with a significant number of negative ratings is that of employee support. It appears that when employees encounter a problem during a call, they are often directed to connect the customer to a manager. In such cases, the employee does not learn how the problem can be resolved in the future. Employees expressed frustration with this situation. Therefore, this report proposes that regular training sessions be held to teach employees how to successfully deal with recurring problems.

**165.** Who most likely were the survey participants?
(A) Retail store clerks
(B) Bank tellers
(C) Flight attendants
(D) Call center representatives

**166.** How was the survey data mainly obtained?
(A) Through specialized software
(B) Through individual interviews
(C) Through paper questionnaires
(D) Through focus group discussions

**167.** What does the report recommend doing?
(A) Discontinuing service to difficult customers
(B) Increasing employee compensation
(C) Providing ongoing instruction to staff
(D) Directing supervisors to manage less strictly

**Questions 168–171** refer to the following online chat discussion.

**Danica Fay [11:02 A.M.]**
In-Tak, a law firm just ordered six Ivy desks through our Web site. I know our stock of the walnut wood is low, so I wanted to check with you before I gave them an estimated ship date.

**In-Tak Lee [11:03 A.M.]**
We don't have enough walnut left for that. Three of the desks would be delayed by an extra month.

**Danica Fay [11:04 A.M.]**
Well, I'd hate to lose this client. What if we offered them Ivy desks in another type of wood?

**In-Tak Lee [11:04 A.M.]**
Hmm. Let me bring Bente in. Her team builds them.

**In-Tak Lee [11:05 A.M.]**
Bente, are there any alternative woods that you could use to make the Ivy desk? We're almost out of walnut.

**Bente Dahl [11:07 A.M.]**
Oak would work. It's also a hard wood, and it's got a similar color.

**Danica Fay [11:08 A.M.]**
If we use that, could the order be shipped within the usual four weeks?

**In-Tak Lee [11:08 A.M.]**
Yes. We have plenty of oak.

**Danica Fay [11:09 A.M.]**
That's much better. I'll ask whether the law firm is interested.

**In-Tak Lee [11:10 A.M.]**
OK, but you should probably add "backordered" banners to the pages of our larger walnut products. We can't do custom orders for every client.

**168.** What does the chat participants' company manufacture?
(A) Packaging
(B) Car parts
(C) Clothing
(D) Furniture

**169.** What does Ms. Dahl confirm?
(A) A color scheme has been decided.
(B) A product could be made with another material.
(C) Her team understands a manufacturing process.
(D) Her schedule for the next month is not yet full.

**170.** At 11:09 A.M., what does Ms. Fay most likely mean when she writes, "That's much better"?
(A) A new sample item is more attractive.
(B) A shorter production time is preferable.
(C) A client will appreciate a price reduction.
(D) An order should be shipped over land.

**171.** What does Mr. Lee recommend that Ms. Fay do?
(A) Update a company Web site
(B) Withdraw from a negotiation
(C) Display an advertisement in a store
(D) Add a feature to the design of some goods



GO ON TO THE NEXT PAGE

**Questions 172–175** refer to the following article.

# Galtwood Native to Open Restored Antrell Theater

GALTWOOD (June 22)—After much painstaking restoration work, Galtwood native Jude Raglan says that the Antrell Theater will reopen in the fall with a performance of *A Faraway Year*.

During an interview at a Lockett Street café, Mr. Raglan says that the idea of restoring the theater drew him back to Galtwood after twenty years away. —[1]—. He was working as an administrator at a Latimev theater when he learned during a family visit two years ago that Antrell Theater was about to close.

"I was shocked," he says. The old theater, which sits at the corner of Fourth Street and Nichols Boulevard, had been a beloved part of his youth. He recalls, "We used to walk over from our house on Carden Lane. Seeing *The Glass Flag* there even inspired me to work in theater."

Antrell Theater's owners, however, said that it was no longer profitable. —[2]—. So Mr. Raglan bought it for the low price they were asking, quit his job, and set about restoring it with the help of a grant from the Galtwood city council.

The work, he explains, has focused on revealing and replicating the beauty of its original design. —[3]—. At the same time, some modernizing improvements, such as better accessibility for wheelchairs, have also been made.

Mr. Raglan says he chose *A Faraway Year*, the story of a group of friends' journey through a fantastical land of witches and giants, for the theater's first show because "it's a production that people of all ages can enjoy." —[4]—. He encourages those interested in being part of its cast or crew to visit www.antrelltheater.com for more information.

**172.** What does the article mention about Mr. Raglan?

(A) He is a friend of the theater's previous owners.

(B) He was a professional actor for two decades.

(C) He received funding from the city of Galtwood.

(D) The first play he attended was *The Glass Flag*.

**173.** Where did Mr. Raglan live when he was young?

(A) On Lockett Street

(B) On Fourth Street

(C) On Nichols Boulevard

(D) On Carden Lane

**174.** What is stated about *A Faraway Year*?

(A) Its plot includes magical elements.

(B) It is based on a popular film.

(C) Some of its characters are children.

(D) Mr. Raglan will modernize its setting.

**175.** In which of the positions marked [1], [2], [3], and [4] does the following sentence best belong?

"Work crews used old photographs of the theater for reference."

(A) [1]

(B) [2]

(C) [3]

(D) [4]



GO ON TO THE NEXT PAGE

**Questions 176–180** refer to the following e-mail and press release.

| | |
|---|---|
| **From** | Rodolfo Escorza <r.escorza@oqui-mail.com> |
| **To** | Marcella Perry <anb-recruiting.com> |
| **Subject** | Re: Opportunity at Osborne Rental Cars |
| **Date** | August 7 |
| **Attachment** | Résumé |

Dear Ms. Perry,

Thank you for contacting me. I am familiar with Osborne Rental Cars and interested in this opening. Please see my attached résumé. It will give you a fuller understanding of my career than what you saw on my profile page on Exec-Link.

However, I should tell you up front that I am content at Panella and wouldn't consider leaving for anything less than a very good opportunity. This means a situation where I have both the support of global management and the autonomy to make the best decisions for the U.S. market. If Osborne is willing to meet these conditions, I would be happy to discuss this position further.

If you do decide to move forward with my candidacy, please let me know what the next steps will be. I will be away from Atlanta on a business trip for the next few days, but I will make sure to keep up with my correspondence.

Sincerely,

Rodolfo Escorza

Senior Vice President of Operations
Panella Airlines

## Osborne Rental Cars Appoints New U.S. Executive

(October 22)—Osborne Rental Cars has hired Rodolfo Escorza as the director of its operations in the United States. Mr. Escorza will replace Jeanette Huff, who is retiring.

Mr. Escorza has worked in many sectors of the travel and airline industries over his 23-year career. As a senior product officer for Globastic, an online seller of consumer travel products, he oversaw the creation of its popular rental car booking service. Most recently, he served as the senior vice president of operations for Panella Airlines. In that position, he built up the airline's safety ratings without increasing its operational costs.

Osborne Rental Cars is a British company that entered the U.S. market just four years ago. It now has 18 locations and over 500 vehicles in the states of Florida and Georgia. From its national headquarters in Atlanta, Mr. Escorza is expected to lead its continued growth throughout the southeastern United States and beyond.

**176.** How does Mr. Escorza suggest that Ms. Perry became aware of him?

(A) Through a Web site
(B) Through a magazine article
(C) Through a mutual acquaintance
(D) Through a conference

**177.** In the e-mail, the word "meet" in paragraph 2, line 4, is closest in meaning to

(A) gather
(B) perform
(C) border
(D) fulfill

**178.** What is implied about Mr. Escorza?

(A) Osborne Rental Cars agreed to raise his salary.
(B) His hiring process took less than two months.
(C) He spoke to Ms. Perry on the phone.
(D) He will not have to relocate.

**179.** According to the press release, what did Mr. Escorza accomplish at Panella Airlines?

(A) A reduction in spending
(B) Improvements in safety
(C) The implementation of a new offering
(D) Higher passenger satisfaction ratings

**180.** What is mentioned about Osborne Rental Cars?

(A) It has branches in many countries.
(B) It is attempting to expand.
(C) Its founder is leaving the workforce.
(D) It was acquired by another company.



GO ON TO THE NEXT PAGE

**Questions 181–185** refer to the following Web page and e-mail.

www.nationalbaseballfederation.com/llions/tickets/groups

## Group and Corporate Options for Single Games

Attending a Lanchner Lions game is a fun way to celebrate events with family or friends, entertain clients, or show appreciation for employees. Lanchner Field boasts an array of amenities to suit the needs of groups and corporations, and all options include discounts on stadium parking.

| The Dugout Section | Lions Patios |
|---|---|
| - Regular outdoor seating<br>- $15 in "Lions Bucks," which can be used at Lanchner Field shops<br>- Pay per ticket; available for groups of 10 to 200 | - Outdoor seating at tables with excellent sight lines<br>- Unlimited ballpark fare (hot dogs, popcorn, etc.) from admission through the 7th inning<br>- Pay per ticket; best for groups of 2 to 6 |
| **The Fastball Deck** | **Diamond Lounges** |
| - Indoor, non-private seating<br>- Unlimited ballpark fare from admission through the last inning<br>- Pay per ticket; best for groups of 2 to 10 | - Indoor, private seating<br>- "Classic" catering package<br>- 25 tickets |
| **Home Run Suites** | |
| - Indoor, private seating in one of two premium locations behind home plate<br>- "Premium" catering package<br>- 50 tickets | |

For more information, call the hospitality department at (708) 555-0186 or click here to access its live chat service.

From: Andre Delgado
To: Keith Holt
Subject: Request
Date: July 15

Keith,

I'd like you to look into purchasing tickets for the Lions baseball game on the evening of August 4. I was just speaking with Ms. Walsh, the head of the group visiting us from Rioso Electronics that week, and she mentioned that she loves the sport. I feel confident about the proposal we're putting together for marketing their tablet computers, but we should also make sure the delegation enjoys their time in Lanchner.

As for the type of seats, please choose a climate-controlled option so that we can avoid the summer heat. And of course, it will need to accommodate between 15 and 20 people, since the group will also include members of our staff.

Please research the options and send me your recommendation.

Thanks,

Andre

**181.** What is indicated about the Lanchner Lions hospitality department?

(A) Its office overlooks Lanchner Field.
(B) It operates an online messaging platform.
(C) It offers service in multiple languages.
(D) It is seeking new employees.

**182.** What is NOT a benefit of Lions Patios?

(A) Complimentary food
(B) A lower parking fee
(C) Early admission to the stadium
(D) A clear view of the game

**183.** Where does Mr. Delgado most likely work?

(A) At a sports television network
(B) At an industrial supply company
(C) At an electronics manufacturer
(D) At an advertising agency

**184.** What is indicated about Ms. Walsh?

(A) She is a baseball fan.
(B) She will lead a presentation.
(C) She used to live in Lanchner.
(D) Her birthday is August 4.

**185.** Which option will Mr. Holt most likely recommend?

(A) The Dugout Section
(B) The Fastball Deck
(C) A Diamond Lounge
(D) A Home Run Suite



*GO ON TO THE NEXT PAGE*

**Questions 186–190** refer to the following Web page, work schedule, and client reviews.

http://www.jackfogelphotography.com 

## Jack Fogel Photography

Jack Fogel Photography is the county's top real estate photography company. Whether you are a real estate agent or a private homeowner seeking to sell a property quickly, we will provide the highest quality photos possible. Unlike other local real estate photography companies, we offer the following:

- Guaranteed next-day turnaround – you will get your images by the next day, or you pay nothing* (**two-day turnaround for Saturday visits)*
- Easy payment options – pay by credit card or company check on the day of the photo shoot
- Fixed pricing, regardless of the property's size – visit our rates page for details

Our founder, Jack Fogel, still conducts many photo shoots himself, and every photographer in our network has at least 10 years of experience. They will choose the best angles and lighting to help you sell your property faster. To read reviews about our services, visit our testimonials page.

**Today's Photo Sessions** **Date:** *August 23*

| Photographer | Time | Address | # of photos | Payment | Notes |
|---|---|---|---|---|---|
| Jack Fogel | 11:00 A.M. | 177 Dunn Street | 25 | Credit card | External flash needed |
| Jack Fogel | 2:00 P.M. | 865 Reyes Avenue | 15 | Credit card | |
| Brad Mull | 3:00 P.M. | 262 Fir Drive | 10 | Check | |
| Ellen Sato | 1:00 P.M. | 190 Moy Road | 35 | Credit card | Repeat client |

http://www.jackfogelphotography.com/testimonials

***Most recent client reviews***

"As a real estate agent, I highly recommend this company. I booked a photo shoot with little notice a few weeks ago, and the photographer, Ms. Sato, arrived early and worked hard. I got the high-quality images back in only two days, and I was even allowed to pay with a company check."

— Lisa Tobias, Tuesday, August 26

"They are professional yet affordable. I originally booked the 10-photo package, but at the last minute I decided to have 15 pictures taken. I'm glad I did. Mr. Mull, the photographer, was excellent. I just received my photos today, two days after the shoot. They look great."

— Larry Hodges, Monday, August 25

**186.** What is NOT listed as a unique feature of Mr. Fogel's company?
(A) Its guaranteed delivery times
(B) The payment methods it accepts
(C) Its use of sophisticated equipment
(D) The price structure of its services

**187.** In the work schedule, what is implied about the 11:00 A.M. photo session?
(A) It is the largest session of the day.
(B) It will mainly take place indoors.
(C) It is for a regular client.
(D) It will last less than three hours.

**188.** In the client reviews, the word "notice" in paragraph 1, line 2, is closest in meaning to
(A) warning
(B) attention
(C) resignation announcement
(D) public posting

**189.** What do the clients who posted the recent reviews have in common?
(A) Their photos required special editing.
(B) Their shoots happened on a Saturday.
(C) They work for real estate agencies.
(D) They paid deposits in advance.

**190.** Which property did Mr. Hodges most likely have photographed?
(A) 177 Dunn Street
(B) 865 Reyes Avenue
(C) 262 Fir Drive
(D) 190 Moy Road



GO ON TO THE NEXT PAGE

**Questions 191–195** refer to the following instructions and e-mails.

*Telges Hotel*

## Morning Sun Four-Cup Coffee Maker Instructions for Use

1. Remove the pot from the hotplate.
2. Open the cover of the pot and use the pot's indicator lines to fill it with the desired amount of water. Close the pot.
3. Pour the water from the pot into the water reservoir in the top of the coffee maker.
4. Return the pot to the hotplate.
5. Insert a paper filter into the filter basket in the top of the coffee maker.
6. Put the desired amount of ground coffee into the filter. We recommend 1 to 1.5 tablespoons of ground coffee per cup.
7. Close the top of the coffee maker securely.
8. Push the "On" button to begin brewing. Do not remove the pot from the hotplate until the power light shuts off.

---

The machine must be cleaned between uses, but we ask that you do not attempt to do it yourself. The cleaning staff will do it during their daily visit to your room.

| | |
|---|---|
| **From:** | Vicky Schmidt |
| **To:** | Travis Peters |
| **Subject:** | Coffee maker issue |
| **Date:** | January 11 |

Hi Travis,

We've received some minor guest complaints about the Lywen "Morning Sun" coffee makers that we bought through Bruggins Limited. Guests are saying that you can't actually put the filter into the filter basket without taking it out of the coffee maker first. But the instructions we've provided don't specify that, and the filter is a little hard to remove, so people aren't sure if it's the right thing to do or not.

I checked the instructions for the Jares Home coffee makers in our business suites and the Qualcedo in the breakfast room, and the results were mixed—the Qualcedo model mentions removing the basket and the Jares doesn't. But we've never had complaints about the Jares.

Could you look into the issue?

Thanks,

Vicky

| From: | Travis Peters |
| --- | --- |
| To: | Vicky Schmidt |
| Subject: | Re: Coffee maker issue |
| Date: | January 12 |

Hi Vicky,

I called the manufacturer, and they confirmed that the instructions should have specified that extra step. They were very apologetic and said they're planning to revise the product manual. So, I will replace the current instructions in our guest rooms with a corrected version.

You know, this happened because I just copied the instructions in the manual without actually trying them out. That had been fine for our other machines. But now I see that it is risky. I'm sorry, and I won't make that mistake again.

Best,

Travis

**191.** In the instructions, what is suggested about the Morning Sun coffeemaker?
(A) It allows users to adjust a brewing duration.
(B) Telges Hotel supplies a special type of water for it.
(C) Its indicator light comes on to signal that it must be cleaned.
(D) Telges Hotel expects it to be needed only once per day.

**192.** Which step does Ms. Schmidt indicate users are unsure about?
(A) Step 2
(B) Step 3
(C) Step 5
(D) Step 6

**193.** According to the first e-mail, what does Telges Hotel have?
(A) A clothes-washing service
(B) A dedicated place for morning meals
(C) A computerized system for analyzing guest complaints
(D) A loyalty program for business travelers

**194.** Which company did Mr. Peters most likely contact?
(A) Lywen
(B) Bruggins Limited
(C) Jares Home
(D) Qualcedo

**195.** What does Mr. Peters apologize for?
(A) Not testing the instructions himself
(B) Copying a manual's contents incorrectly
(C) Not buying a different coffee machine instead
(D) Dismissing a coworker's concerns



GO ON TO THE NEXT PAGE

**Questions 196–200** refer to the following Web page, form, and e-mail.

http://www.cityofrowder.gov/business/signs

## Sign Regulations

Rowder's Department of Planning and Development Services (DPDS) oversees the enforcement of city regulations relating to commercial uses of signs. Its staff is committed to providing a favorable atmosphere for businesses while also maintaining a pleasant living space for citizens.

The city's comprehensive sign ordinances are listed here, but for your convenience, information on the most common types of temporary commercial signs is provided below in a simplified form.

**Grand opening signs:** With the approval of the DPDS, a new business can display signs advertising its opening for up to 30 days. This is the only circumstance in which free-standing outdoor signs are permitted.

**Holiday promotional signs**: Businesses do not need the DPDS's approval to display promotional signs related to Christmas or New Years for up to 15 days, and signs related to six other specified holidays for up to 5 days.

**Other large promotional banners:** The DPDS's approval is required for all other promotional banners over 20 square feet in surface area. These banners may be displayed for up to 14 days at a time, three times per year.

Do you disagree with a DPDS decision? Click here to find out how to file an appeal with the city council.

City of Rowder
Department of Planning and Development Services

## Commercial Sign Permit Application

**Applicant:** Gail Brock

**Address:** 922 Ellis Drive, Rowder, MI 48097

**Phone:** (810) 555-0124 **E-mail:** gail.brock@ubi-mail.com

**Business:** Radiant Gem Salon

**Address:** 640 Main Street, Rowder, MI 48097 **Site ID:** 0943-886

**Project description:**

I would like to hang a 24-square-foot banner to advertise the fifth anniversary of the salon's opening and a related sales event. The banner would display "Radiant Gem Salon Celebrates 5 Years in Business" in large text and "15% Off All Services June 6–8" in smaller text. It would have a pink background and black writing. Please see the attachment for a mock-up image of the design. I would hang it over the top half of one of the salon's windows until June 8.

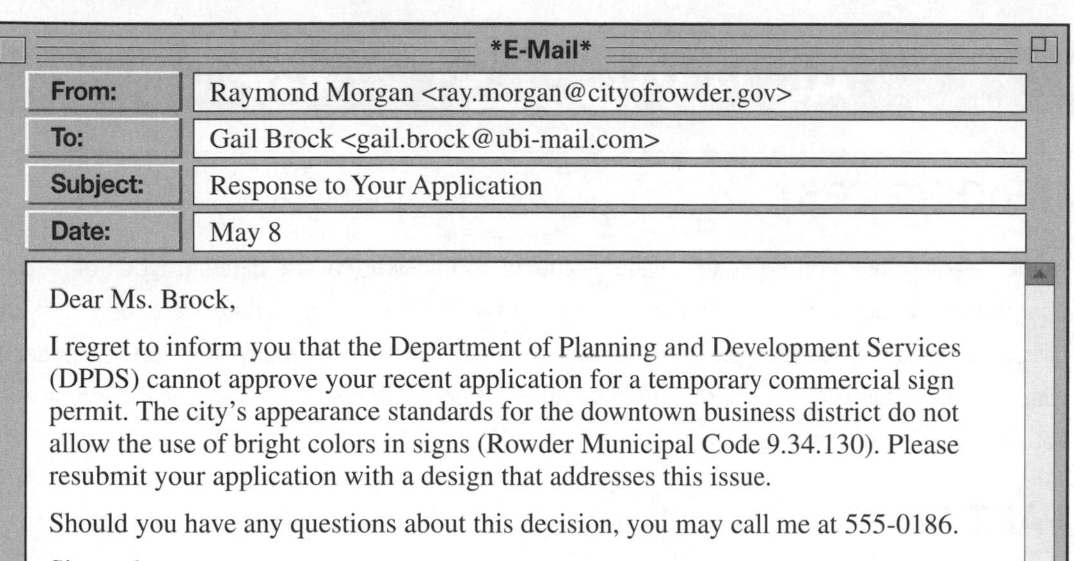
*E-Mail*

From: Raymond Morgan <ray.morgan@cityofrowder.gov>
To: Gail Brock <gail.brock@ubi-mail.com>
Subject: Response to Your Application
Date: May 8

Dear Ms. Brock,

I regret to inform you that the Department of Planning and Development Services (DPDS) cannot approve your recent application for a temporary commercial sign permit. The city's appearance standards for the downtown business district do not allow the use of bright colors in signs (Rowder Municipal Code 9.34.130). Please resubmit your application with a design that addresses this issue.

Should you have any questions about this decision, you may call me at 555-0186.

Sincerely,

Raymond Morgan
Associate Director
Department of Planning and Development Services

**196.** What does the Web page state about the DPDS?

(A) Its employees are highly qualified.
(B) It is the result of a departmental merger.
(C) It tries to serve the needs of two groups.
(D) It recently created new sign-related ordinances.

**197.** How long could Ms. Brock potentially display her sign?

(A) For up to 5 days
(B) For up to 14 days
(C) For up to 15 days
(D) For up to 30 days

**198.** What does Ms. Brock suggest about her business?

(A) It appears in a photograph attached to the form.
(B) It is located at an intersection.
(C) It used to have another owner.
(D) It will offer customers a temporary discount.

**199.** Why does Mr. Morgan reject Ms. Brock's application?

(A) A required piece of text is missing from a design.
(B) Her sign's color would not conform to a regulation.
(C) A city district does not allow certain advertising methods.
(D) The placement of her sign would not obey safety standards.

**200.** What is NOT mentioned as an action Ms. Brock could take?

(A) Contacting Mr. Morgan
(B) Altering the plan for the sign
(C) Asking the city council to review a decision
(D) Submitting an application for a different permit

**Stop! This is the end of the test. If you finish before time is called, you may go back to Parts 5, 6, and 7 and check your work.**

# ACTUAL TEST 6

## READING TEST

In the Reading test, you will read a variety of texts and answer several different types of reading comprehension questions. The entire Reading test will last 75 minutes. There are three parts, and directions are given for each part. You are encouraged to answer as many questions as possible within the time allowed. You must mark your answers on the separate answer sheet. Do not write your answers in your test book.

## PART 5

**Directions:** A word or phrase is missing in each of the sentences below. Four answer choices are given below each sentence. Select the best answer to complete the sentence. Then mark the letter (A), (B), (C), or (D) on your answer sheet.

**101.** Penelope Styles is proud of the artwork ------- created for the lobby of the Andrews Plaza Building.

(A) hers
(B) her
(C) she
(D) herself

**102.** Call Klinter Associates today to schedule an initial ------- with one of our experienced attorneys.

(A) consultant
(B) consultation
(C) consulted
(D) consults

**103.** Peltzer Real Estate's Web site provides an ------- of the monthly energy expenses for each of its listed properties.

(A) advice
(B) estimate
(C) evidence
(D) advantage

**104.** Thanks to the new television commercials, enrollment in carpentry classes is up 22% ------- last semester.

(A) than
(B) above
(C) throughout
(D) from

**105.** Lina Oakes will be ------- employee productivity this month at Deerford Cosmetics' main warehouse.

(A) assessing
(B) presenting
(C) disciplining
(D) resuming

**106.** Redesigning our Web site might help us attract a broader range of clients and ------- boost profits.

(A) closely
(B) rarely
(C) typically
(D) consequently

**107.** The emergency exit row seats are the only ------- equipped with a fold-out table that is stored in the armrest.

(A) some
(B) these
(C) whose
(D) ones

**108.** The employee handbook provides guidance on acceptable apparel and footwear, ------- not on hairstyles.

(A) but
(B) for
(C) or
(D) even

**109.** Situated at the foot of Emerald Mountain, Selway Valley ------- the cleanest natural spring water in the country.

(A) excels
(B) emphasizes
(C) distinguishes
(D) boasts

**110.** Now that the bank has switched to electronic billing, its stationery expenses are ------- lower.

(A) highly
(B) heavily
(C) considerately
(D) noticeably

**111.** Lost property is kept at the gym's reception desk for a maximum of two months, after which the item -------.

(A) is discarded
(B) has been discarded
(C) will be discarding
(D) discards

**112.** All employees ------- for any reason must submit an official letter to Human Resources for recordkeeping purposes.

(A) resign
(B) resigned
(C) resigning
(D) resignation

**113.** The hotel manager says there are ------- ten complaints about the noise from the poolside renovations.

(A) all
(B) already
(C) other than
(D) as many

**114.** The school board will debate a ------- educational proposal to change the way that the region's history is taught.

(A) controversy
(B) controversially
(C) controversial
(D) controversies

**115.** The new ward was named after Dr. Suzuki in ------- of his valuable contributions to the hospital.

(A) association
(B) obligation
(C) recognition
(D) occasion

**116.** Before he steps down as CFO of Hardin Furniture in July, Mr. Grady will play an active role in choosing his -------.

(A) successor
(B) succeeds
(C) succeeding
(D) success

**117.** In the summer, Colfax Public Library will be showing animated movies ------- for children as young as three.

(A) appropriate
(B) equivalent
(C) cautious
(D) tentative

**118.** To ensure a fun and effortless trip, book your summer vacation ------- Royes Travel Agency.

(A) to
(B) with
(C) around
(D) by

**119.** Caroba Manufacturing ------- strict safety policies to prevent accidents in its factories.

(A) entails
(B) produces
(C) presumes
(D) enforces

**120.** By the time the workers arrived to repair the store's roof, a large amount of merchandise -------.

(A) has damaged
(B) had been damaged
(C) will be damaged
(D) is damaged

*GO ON TO THE NEXT PAGE*

**121.** The museum's south wing is temporarily off-limits to visitors ------- the new prehistoric fossil exhibits are being set up.

(A) touring
(B) as
(C) so that
(D) who

**122.** The first customer ------- the café's reward book with one hundred stickers will receive a year's supply of free coffee.

(A) fills
(B) is filling
(C) to fill
(D) filled

**123.** Mr. Sulaiman prefers training new hires in customer service etiquette ------- after they join his company.

(A) personally
(B) more personal
(C) personal
(D) personalizes

**124.** Individuals caught littering ------- 50 meters of a body of water are subject to a $250 fine.

(A) nearby
(B) during
(C) within
(D) anywhere

**125.** Mr. Menzel is doubtful that an expansion will truly make the CEO's annual sales target ------- by the end of the year.

(A) attain
(B) attainable
(C) attained
(D) attainment

**126.** Some government offices ------- avoid providing a contact phone number in an effort to cut down on the volume of public inquiries.

(A) adequately
(B) formerly
(C) proficiently
(D) intentionally

**127.** Many fast food outlets have significantly changed their menus in response to a ------- in demand for vegan-friendly products.

(A) pace
(B) flow
(C) surge
(D) phase

**128.** If we do not clearly determine our objectives ------- the commencement of negotiations, we will be unable to bargain effectively.

(A) before
(B) on behalf of
(C) according to
(D) against

**129.** The Owenberg Fresh Air Society uses sensors placed around the city to carry out pollution ------- in real time.

(A) monitor
(B) monitors
(C) monitored
(D) monitoring

**130.** On the weekend of the music festival, the city council will ------- the charges for parking along Main Street.

(A) contend
(B) waive
(C) delegate
(D) redeem

## PART 6

**Directions:** Read the texts that follow. A word, phrase, or sentence is missing in parts of each text. Four answer choices for each question are given below the text. Select the best answer to complete the text. Then mark the letter (A), (B), (C), or (D) on your answer sheet.

**Questions 131–134** refer to the following notice.

Attention Fairfax Public Library Members:

When using the library's hold system, please bear in mind that items are only held at the circulation desk for 24 hours. ------- **131.** you fail to collect an on-hold item within that timeframe, it will be put back into circulation.

------- **132.**. First, you can speak with an employee at the circulation desk. When the item you desire becomes available, it will be set aside for you. You may also request a hold on items using the database terminals ------- **133.** throughout the library, or through our Web site.

Please keep the above time limit in mind when ------- **134.** items. It is one of the policies that support our goal of ensuring that our members have a wide selection of books, magazines, and multimedia materials to enjoy.

**131.** (A) Should
(B) Although
(C) Yet
(D) Until

**132.** (A) Applying for a membership could not be easier.
(B) Our collections can be browsed in person or online.
(C) There are several ways to put a hold on library items.
(D) Please follow these steps to file a complaint.

**133.** (A) to install
(B) install
(C) installing
(D) installed

**134.** (A) purchasing
(B) reserving
(C) returning
(D) reading

GO ON TO THE NEXT PAGE

**Questions 135–138** refer to the following e-mail.

From: Mina Wang
To: All staff members
Subject: Customer Service Workshops
Date: January 21

Dear employees,

I am writing to remind you all about our first Positive Customer Interaction (PCI) workshop on February 5. It ------- **135.** by Tim Ellison, a renowned motivational speaker and the author of *Key Factors for Customer Satisfaction*.

We have asked Mr. Ellison to discuss the attitudes and practices that are most ------- **136.** to attracting, satisfying, and retaining customers. As the first in our series, this session will also be ------- **137.** by an introductory talk by our president, Howard Botting, who will discuss the overall aims of the workshops. There is space for no more than 100 participants at each workshop, and registrations will be accepted on a first-come, first-served basis. ------- **138.**.

Regards,
Mina Wang
Personnel Manager

**135.** (A) was led
(B) leads
(C) is leading
(D) will be led

**136.** (A) critics
(B) critical
(C) critically
(D) criticisms

**137.** (A) preceded
(B) officiated
(C) combined
(D) recorded

**138.** (A) Rest assured that these fees will be used to enhance your experience.
(B) A makeup session for the canceled seminars will be held at later dates.
(C) Requests for a full refund can be made by phone or e-mail.
(D) Please visit the personnel office if you are interested in attending.

**Questions 139–142** refer to the following letter.

May 22
Gabriella Heron
4827 Dayton Avenue
Bakersfield, CA 93311

Dear Ms. Heron,

Please be advised that Hercules Fitness Center is scheduled to undergo renovations in order to expand. -------, **139.** we will be shut down from June 3 to June 9. We have acquired the adjacent commercial unit recently vacated by Rantillo Apparel and will be converting it into an additional space mainly containing fitness studios of various specifications. -------. **140.** The currently available areas of the center will reopen for business as usual at 7 A.M. on June 10, and the new space will be brought into ------- **141.** the next month.

We apologize for this temporary ------- **142.** and appreciate your understanding. Also, we encourage you to check our July schedule, available at our front desk and online at www.herc-fitness.com/schedule from June 15, to see the new offerings.

Best wishes,
Gary Salinger
Hercules Fitness Center

**139.** (A) Occasionally
(B) After that time
(C) Accordingly
(D) Even so

**140.** (A) This will allow us to offer a wider range of exercise classes.
(B) An increasing number of people are shifting to a healthier lifestyle.
(C) There is no longer sufficient room in the existing parking lot.
(D) Our facilities have been highly praised by local publications.

**141.** (A) used
(B) use
(C) using
(D) users

**142.** (A) relocation
(B) negligence
(C) congestion
(D) closure

*GO ON TO THE NEXT PAGE*

**Questions 143–146** refer to the following article.

**Midlands Biosciences Names New R&D Director**

Midlands Biosciences ------- (143.) Clifford Maxwell of its R&D department to be the company's new research and development director. The biofuel maker announced Mr. Maxwell's ------- (144.) in a post on its Web site yesterday. Midlands CEO Ellen Stern is quoted as saying, "It is my pleasure to welcome Mr. Maxwell to our executive team. His expertise will enable us to succeed ------- (145.) our research goals."

According to the Web post, Mr. Maxwell joined Midlands soon after earning a doctoral degree in biotechnology. ------- (146.). He rose steadily through the company's ranks thanks to his diligence and innovative ideas. In his new role, which he will assume on December 10, Mr. Maxwell will determine and implement Midlands' research and development objectives.

**143.** (A) to choose
(B) has chosen
(C) was chosen
(D) choose

**144.** (A) retirement
(B) candidacy
(C) initiative
(D) appointment

**145.** (A) that reaches
(B) reached by
(C) in reaching
(D) the reaching of

**146.** (A) The move reflects the company's goal of becoming more streamlined.
(B) While he began as a junior researcher, he did not hold that position for long.
(C) The board of directors is conducting an extensive search to find his replacement.
(D) His latest research project received a lot of attention within the industry.

# PART 7

**Directions:** In this part you will read a selection of texts, such as magazine and newspaper articles, e-mails, and instant messages. Each text or set of texts is followed by several questions. Select the best answer for each question and mark the letter (A), (B), (C), or (D) on your answer sheet.

**Questions 147–148** refer to the following invitation.

*You are invited to enjoy an exclusive demonstration here at Salisbury Culinary Institute!*

Visiting Guest Chef:

**Gustav Perot**

Owner of the five-star restaurant
The Partridge Bistro in New York City

Chef Perot will demonstrate how to expertly prepare a variety of Mediterranean dishes in Instruction Kitchen 3 on June 14 from 9:15 to 11:45 A.M.

This demonstration has been specifically arranged for those currently enrolled in the institute's advanced cooking courses. Space is limited to 250 people, and you must confirm your intention to attend by speaking with Ms. Ibrahim in the administration office before June 8.

**147.** For whom is the invitation most likely intended?

(A) Culinary instructors
(B) Food critics
(C) Aspiring cooks
(D) Restaurant diners

**148.** What is indicated about the event?

(A) It happens every year.
(B) Attendees will take part in the activity.
(C) It will finish in the afternoon.
(D) Admission is restricted.

GO ON TO THE NEXT PAGE

**Questions 149–150** refer to the following voucher.

# RIALTO PET MART

Rialto Pet Mart would like to reward our loyal customers as part of our tenth anniversary celebrations. From March 1 to March 14, you may hand over this voucher to any checkout operator to receive $15 off any purchase valued at $50 or more. This voucher may not be exchanged for cash, cannot be used at our automated checkout kiosks, and will expire at 9 P.M. on March 14. Please visit www.rialtopetmart.ca/voucher for full terms and conditions.

**149.** What is mentioned about Rialto Pet Mart?

(A) It recently launched a new branch.

(B) It is currently hiring checkout operators.

(C) It runs a membership reward program.

(D) It has self-checkout machines.

**150.** What must shoppers do in order to use the voucher?

(A) Spend a minimum amount

(B) Visit the store twice

(C) Present it to a store manager

(D) Activate it on a Web page

**Questions 151–152** refer to the following text-message chain.

**Susie Levy** **2:04 P.M.**
Hideo, are you still down on the third floor?

**Hideo Fujita** **2:05 P.M.**
Yes, the meeting just finished. Do you need something?

**Susie Levy** **2:06 P.M.**
I'm trying to set up that new graphic design suite on my computer, but I'm having problems. I was hoping you could find the person who recommended it to me.

**Hideo Fujita** **2:07 P.M.**
Was it someone from here in our company?

**Susie Levy** **2:08 P.M.**
Yes, the tall guy on the Web design team.

**Hideo Fujita** **2:10 P.M.**
Our Web design team is rather large.

**Susie Levy** **2:11 P.M.**
Oh, sorry. He's the one who has short blonde hair. He might be new.

**Hideo Fujita** **2:13 P.M.**
I think I know who you're talking about. His name is Chris, right?

**Susie Levy** **2:14 P.M.**
Yes, that sounds right! Please ask him to stop by my office whenever he's free. Thanks, Hideo.

**151.** What's Ms. Levy's problem?
(A) She is running late for a meeting.
(B) An electronic device will not turn on.
(C) She cannot install some software.
(D) Some graphics are confusing.

**152.** At 2:10 P.M., what does Mr. Fujita mean when he writes, "Our Web design team is rather large"?
(A) It is unnecessary to hire new workers.
(B) He needs a more detailed description.
(C) He is worried about the size of a space.
(D) Someone on the team probably has a certain skill.

GO ON TO THE NEXT PAGE

**Questions 153–154** refer to the following advertisement.

# Glow Car Wash

3476 Kingsman Street, Lansing 48213

***Try our new Deluxe Wash & Premium Detailing services!***

**Deluxe Wash**

$25 per car, approximately 15 minutes required
- Pre-wash, undercarriage wash, exterior wash
- Machine air dry plus manual soft towel dry

**Premium Detailing**

$35 per car, approximately 45 minutes required
- Full interior cleaning (X-Press Air technology to remove dust and dirt from all crevices and cracks)
- Conditioning of all upholstery and shampooing of carpeted areas
- Hand-applied "X-polymer" wax for supreme paint protection and shine

Deluxe Wash + Premium Detailing Package Deal available on request for only $50!

**153.** What is indicated about Glow Car Wash?
(A) Its Deluxe Wash takes over half an hour.
(B) It offers a discount for combined services.
(C) It specializes in a certain type of automobile.
(D) It sells some cleaning products.

**154.** What is the X-polymer product used for?
(A) Conditioning a vehicle's interior
(B) Repelling water from a vehicle's windows
(C) Protecting a vehicle's paint job
(D) Removing dirt from a vehicle's exterior

**Questions 155–157** refer to the following notice.

Dear Martino Health Foods Customers,

Our owner, Dino Martino, and the rest of the Martino Health Foods team have enjoyed serving you at our location on Harrison Street for the past five years, but it is now time for a change. Ever since we expanded our range of stock to include organic groceries, we have been struggling to keep up with demand. You may have noticed that checkout lines continue to get longer, and we can barely cope with the number of downtown orders we receive per day.

Therefore, we will move to a larger building in the downtown core on July 1 so that we can increase our stock volume and serve our customers more efficiently. The new and improved Martino Health Foods will be situated at 411 Thrush Drive.

Rest assured that all customer memberships and rewards will remain valid and unchanged. Further details regarding the move will be provided via our monthly newsletter. If you do not already receive the newsletter, please visit the customer service desk to subscribe.

Thank you!

**155.** What is the main purpose of the notice?
(A) To publicize a new type of merchandise
(B) To announce the store's relocation
(C) To introduce a new business owner
(D) To provide details of upcoming renovations

**156.** What is most likely true about Martino Health Foods?
(A) It solicits feedback from employees.
(B) It is a family-operated business.
(C) It is experiencing financial difficulties.
(D) It is becoming increasingly popular.

**157.** What are some readers of the notice encouraged to do?
(A) Sign up for a regular mailing
(B) Recommend a friend for a membership
(C) Attend a grand opening event
(D) Make use of rewards points quickly

GO ON TO THE NEXT PAGE

**Questions 158–160** refer to the following press release.

# PLAYSMART TOYS, INC.
# OFFICIAL PRESS RELEASE

Playsmart has become aware of recent reports and rumors that one of our toy ranges is made using low-quality materials and workmanship. These stories have understandably led to many customers contacting us to ask whether the toys are truly of inferior quality, and in some cases, demanding a refund.
—[1]—. The range in question is our recently-launched Galaxy Pirate toy line, which includes action figures and vehicles from the animated television show of the same name. Rumors have been circulating online that the toys are manufactured abroad and break very easily as a result of poor construction and cheap plastic. This has resulted in a noticeable drop in sales, and several Web sites have even removed our advertisements for the range. —[2]—.

While it is true that the toys are produced at a plant overseas, Playsmart works in close collaboration with the plant operators to ensure that high-grade materials are being used and proper manufacturing steps are being adhered to. —[3]—. We can unequivocally state that the toys are professionally assembled and highly durable. This morning, we have posted a video on our Web site that shows the entire manufacturing process for the Galaxy Pirate toys. —[4]—. We guarantee all customers that Playsmart remains fully committed to producing the best toys on the market.

**158.** What is the purpose of the press release?
(A) To launch a new line of toys
(B) To issue a product recall
(C) To describe how to obtain a refund
(D) To address customer concerns

**159.** What is NOT stated about the Galaxy Pirate toys?
(A) They are manufactured in a different country.
(B) They have been discontinued.
(C) They have been advertised online.
(D) They are based on some entertainment media.

**160.** In which of the positions marked [1], [2], [3], and [4] does the following sentence best belong?
"In fact, we carry out weekly quality assurance checks on the assembly line."
(A) [1]
(B) [2]
(C) [3]
(D) [4]

**Questions 161–163** refer to the following e-mail.

E-Mail message

| | |
|---|---|
| **From:** | Chinenye Umeh |
| **To:** | All Employees |
| **Subject:** | Employee referral bonus |
| **Date:** | June 29 |

Hi everyone,

Now that we have to quickly expand our workforce as a condition of the funding we received from Ribdins Group, it seems like a good time to remind all of you about our employee referral bonus program. This entitles employees to a $500 bonus for a successful referral for an open position. If you are interested in participating, please regularly check the "Jobs" page on our Web site.

Note that it is very important that you only recommend candidates that have all of the qualifications required for the position. We instituted the new tiered payment system at the beginning of this year to cut down on the number of unhelpful recommendations. As you might remember, it entails issuing the bonus to the referrer in stages:

- First 20% when the referred person is chosen for an in-person interview
- Additional 30% when the candidate is hired
- Remaining 50% when the new hire is still an employee after 90 days

See page 28 of the employee handbook for more details on the program, including instructions on how to submit your referral. For any issues not covered in the handbook, you may call (ext. 233) or e-mail me.

Thanks,

Chinenye Umeh
Director of Human Resources
Patondo Technology

**161.** What is indicated about Patondo Technology?
(A) It recently attracted outside investment.
(B) A new page has been added to its Web site.
(C) Its employee handbook is distributed electronically.
(D) It implemented referral bonuses for the first time this year.

**162.** What does Ms. Umeh suggest has been a problem with the program in the past?
(A) Submission of referrals through incorrect channels
(B) Lack of diversity among referred people
(C) Endorsement of unsuitable candidates
(D) Late payment of bonuses

**163.** At what point will a referrer have received exactly half of the bonus?
(A) After an application has been completed
(B) After a face-to-face interview has been proposed
(C) After a job offer has been accepted
(D) After a probationary period has passed



GO ON TO THE NEXT PAGE

**Questions 164–167** refer to the following online chat discussion.

**Leah Young [1:04 P.M.]**
Do you have a moment, Wade and Ursula? Management just told me about two new destinations they have chosen for us to cover in our next European Explorer travel books—one country and one city.

**Wade Corbin [1:08 P.M.]**
Great! What are they?

**Leah Young [1:10 P.M.]**
They want a full extensive guide for Luxembourg and a pocket-sized city guide for Venice.

**Ursula Eriksson [1:11 P.M.]**
Oh, I've spent a lot of time in Luxembourg, and it's an amazing place.

**Leah Young [1:14 P.M.]**
Definitely. So, we'll be sending two field researchers to Luxembourg from May 1 to June 29, and one to Venice from June 1 to June 30. We'll receive all of their notes in the first week of July, and then we'll have approximately one month to edit the information before the scheduled publication and launch dates.

**Ursula Eriksson [1:16 P.M.]**
That gives us plenty of time. And I can start designing the layout for each publication this week so that we're all prepared for the editing stage.

**Wade Corbin [1:22 P.M.]**
I'm not sure that's wise, Ursula. Remember the Bulgaria book?

**Ursula Eriksson [1:23 P.M.]**
Good point, Wade. I'll wait to see exactly what Management wants to be included this time.

**Leah Young [1:25 P.M.]**
That sounds good. All right, I'll give you more information after my meeting with Management tomorrow.

**164.** Why did Ms. Young send the first message to her colleagues?
(A) To ask for their opinions on competing proposals
(B) To recommend some changes to their publications
(C) To thank them for their work on a project
(D) To let them know about upcoming assignments

**165.** What is suggested about the Venice book?
(A) It will be published in July.
(B) It will be compact.
(C) It is a revised edition.
(D) It is Mr. Corbin's responsibility.

**166.** What information does Ms. Young provide?
(A) The qualifications for some researchers
(B) The maximum length of some writings
(C) The durations of some trips
(D) The reasons for some edits

**167.** At 1:22 P.M., what does Mr. Corbin most likely mean when he writes, "Remember the Bulgaria book"?
(A) Ms. Eriksson has another task that must be finished soon.
(B) Ms. Eriksson's expectations for a new book's success are too high.
(C) Ms. Eriksson could use an existing layout template for reference.
(D) Ms. Eriksson should not begin a process too early again.

**Questions 168–171** refer to the following article.

## Winners Announced for This Year's British Architecture Awards

LONDON (15 December)—Fifty extraordinary structures chosen from around 250 shortlisted candidates have won the prestigious British Architecture Awards this year for the most innovative architecture by British architects or foreign architects with offices in Britain. Now in their twenty-second year, the British Architecture Awards are jointly presented by the London Museum of Architecture & Design and the British Centre for Urban Planning & Art. They recognize the architects of exceptional contemporary structures that shape our lives in a wide variety of ways, including skyscrapers, corporate headquarters, bridges, park pavilions, hospitals, private residences, and academic institutions.

Among this year's biggest winners were Simon Thorpe for Maitland Street Car Park, a stunning 9-level, 768-space car park with various eco-friendly features in Central Manchester; Marcus Fryer for Horizon Bridge, a breathtaking 195-meter-long pedestrian bridge uniquely equipped with 4,500 blinking LED stars synchronized with music; and Isobel McDuff for The Spire, an elegant 28-floor apartment building with a heated rooftop swimming pool that is located near Edinburgh's busy shopping areas.

As in previous years, because of the sheer number of winners, the awards were given out over the course of three evenings and three ceremonies from Friday, 12 December to Sunday, 14 December. The opening night saw the awards presented in the Corporate and Commercial categories, Saturday's awards were for the Residential and Urban Planning categories, and the final night recognized those in the Institutional category. Maitland Street Car Park made history by being the first structure to win its architect two awards in the same year: one in the Urban Planning category and the top honour, Most Innovative Design of the Year.

**168.** What is stated about the British Architecture Awards?
(A) Two organizations collaborate to issue them.
(B) They come with various amounts of prize money.
(C) Their list of categories recently increased.
(D) Only British citizens are eligible for them.

**169.** According to the article, what is special about Mr. Fryer's design?
(A) Its integration with a commercial area
(B) Its environmentally-friendly features
(C) Its combination of light and sound
(D) Its impressive height

**170.** When most likely did Ms. McDuff accept her award?
(A) On December 12
(B) On December 13
(C) On December 14
(D) On December 15

**171.** What is suggested about Mr. Thorpe?
(A) He has won awards in the past.
(B) He presented an award on Saturday.
(C) He was given a lifetime achievement award.
(D) He received two awards this year.

GO ON TO THE NEXT PAGE

**Questions 172–175** refer to the following e-mail.

| To: | Len Goldman <lgoldman@whizzomail.net> |
|---|---|
| From: | Mi-Kyung Choi <mkchoi@summitsc.com> |
| Subject: | SparkLite Fire Pit |
| Date: | September 6 |

Dear Mr. Goldman,

I was very excited to receive the information pack for your latest patented invention. The SparkLite Fire Pit seems fantastic and is certainly a product that we would be highly interested in making available in Summit Sports & Camping Stores. We love its portability and solar charging option. —[1]—. However, I do have a few questions about its design. First, would you mind clarifying how the air jets pump oxygen into the wood fire? —[2]—. Also, the information pack outlines how the fire intensity can be controlled via smartphone app. Which operating systems is the app compatible with?

—[3]—. While I would very much like for you to answer those quick questions at your earliest convenience, I would also like you to visit our headquarters in person with one of the fire pits. As I am sure you know, our executives prefer to see new products in use firsthand before approving a contract to purchase and sell them. We would be grateful if you could attend a meeting at 2 P.M. on September 13 at which you would be allotted one hour to showcase the device's functions and capabilities.

Based on the product specifications and photographs you sent me, not to mention the popularity of your camping stove and multifunctional cooler, which are still among our top sellers, I am confident that we will choose to stock the SparkLite Fire Pit. —[4]—. I look forward to hearing from you.

Sincerely,

Mi-Kyung Choi
Head of Purchasing
Summit Sports & Camping

172. What is NOT true about the SparkLite Fire Pit?
(A) It can use renewable energy.
(B) It is easy to transport.
(C) It connects to mobile devices.
(D) It is awaiting a patent confirmation.

173. What does Ms. Choi ask Mr. Goldman to do?
(A) Give a live demonstration
(B) Send over a prototype
(C) Suggest contract terms
(D) Visit a manufacturing site

174. What can be inferred about Summit Sports & Camping?
(A) It is planning to expand its selection of sportswear.
(B) It is Mr. Goldman's former employer.
(C) It stocks other products created by Mr. Goldman.
(D) It has placed an initial order for SparkLite Fire Pits.

175. In which of the positions marked [1], [2], [3], and [4] does the following sentence best belong?
"We have some minor concerns regarding the safety of such a mechanism."
(A) [1]
(B) [2]
(C) [3]
(D) [4]



GO ON TO THE NEXT PAGE

**Questions 176–180** refer to the following advertisement and registration form.

## Growth Strategies for Newly Founded Companies

Do you want to grow and improve your new company, but you are unsure where to start? Fulbridge Growth Strategies is the place for you. We offer seminars on an array of subjects that are useful to novice business owners. Each one is taught with a combination of wisdom earned through decades of hands-on professional work and cutting-edge understanding of the latest management techniques and trends. Below is a sample of what we will be offering this fall:

**Coming Together** (Seminar Code #1809) - Price: $48

This seminar provides a variety of strategies for encouraging your employees to work together effectively.

➥Wednesday, September 3, 10:00 A.M.–12:00 P.M.; Main Building, Room 204

**Tomorrow's Market** (Seminar Code #3487) - Price: $95

This seminar offers advice on how to attract a wider range of clients to your products or services.

➥Wednesday, September 24, 10:00 A.M.–3:00 P.M.; Training Center, Room 3

**Broaden Your Horizons** (Seminar Code #2276) - Price: $149

This seminar gives business owners essential tips on what to consider when planning to open a new branch.

➥Wednesday, October 15, 10:00 A.M.–4:00 P.M.; Main Building, Room 206

**Keeping the Pace** (Seminar Code #3785) - Price: $109

This seminar introduces popular employee perks, such as flexible working hours, and explains how to implement them.

➥Wednesday, November 5, 10:00 A.M.–4:00 P.M.; Training Center, Room 4

*Visit www.fulbridge-gs.com for more information.*

**Fulbridge Growth Strategies - Seminar Registration**

Name: Robin Booky
Address: 84 Ballack Avenue, Seattle, WA 98121
Phone: 555-0139
E-mail: r.booky@globenet.com
Seminar Code: #3487
Payment Method: Bank Transfer
Comments: I am really looking forward to attending my first Fulbridge seminar at your training center in September. As requested, I have sent the $59 registration fee to your corporate account. My only concern is that I might not make it to the center by 10 A.M., as I live very far away. I would appreciate it if someone could let me know via e-mail whether this would be a major problem. Thank you.

176. What is implied about Fulbridge Growth Strategies?
(A) It provides sample teaching materials on its Web site.
(B) Its instructors have practical business experience.
(C) Its offerings can be customized upon request.
(D) It holds the same set of seminars every season.

177. What topic is NOT covered by the listed seminars?
(A) Advising customers on purchasing decisions
(B) Fostering teamwork between employees
(C) Adding new work sites to a company
(D) Granting certain benefits to staff

178. In the advertisement, the word "flexible" in paragraph 5, line 2, is closest in meaning to
(A) gradual
(B) obedient
(C) bendable
(D) variable

179. What information has Mr. Booky most likely read incorrectly?
(A) The location of the seminar
(B) The fee for the seminar
(C) The month of the seminar
(D) The start time of the seminar

180. What does Mr. Booky ask Fulbridge Growth Strategies to do?
(A) Determine the seriousness of a risk
(B) Make an exception to a policy
(C) Compile some alternative options
(D) Give regular updates on a situation



GO ON TO THE NEXT PAGE

**Questions 181–185** refer to the following information from a brochure and customer review.

## Castellente Storage Company
## Residential Storage Units

Castellente's residential storage units come in a variety of sizes and can be rented for as little as two weeks or as long as you like. Each one is on the ground floor for convenient packing and unpacking, and has its own security alarm and camera. You keep the key to your unit's lock so that you can access your belongings at any time, on any day of the week. What's more, our built-in heating and cooling systems ensure that it never becomes dangerously hot or cold in your unit.

| Unit Type | Size | Weekly / Monthly Price* | Suitable for: |
|---|---|---|---|
| A | 13.6m² | £52 / £208 | The contents of a three-bedroom house |
| B | 6.7m² | £32 / £128 | The contents of a one-bedroom apartment |
| C | 3.4m² | £18 / £72 | Several items of furniture |
| D | 1.6m² | £10 / £40 | A few boxes |

*A deposit of £50.00 is also required. Castellente Storage Company may keep all or part of this if the rental unit is found to be dirty or damaged at the end of the rental period.

http://www.birminghamsmartreviews.com/storage/0421

### Castellente Storage Company Reviews

I rented a unit from Castellente to store my belongings in when I had to move to Germany for a six-month study program. My experience couldn't have been better. First, I wasn't sure how much space I needed, so their representative kindly explained the options without pressuring me. She also made sure I understood the terms of the rental contract before I signed it. And when I brought over my stuff—a bed, a dresser, some small appliances—the worker on duty offered to help me unload it and organise it all efficiently. Six months later, everything was right where I'd left it, safe and dry. Castellente is an excellent self-storage facility.

By Kiera Ritz, 2 December

181. What is NOT mentioned as a feature of each storage unit?
(A) Temperature control
(B) 24-hour accessibility
(C) A security system
(D) An electric power outlet

182. According to the information, for what is there an additional charge?
(A) Choosing a rental period of less than two weeks
(B) Renting a unit on the ground floor
(C) Leaving a unit in poor condition
(D) Replacing the key to a unit

183. Which type of storage unit did Ms. Ritz most likely rent?
(A) Type A
(B) Type B
(C) Type C
(D) Type D

184. Why did Ms. Ritz need to store some items?
(A) She went to live abroad temporarily.
(B) She relocated to a smaller home.
(C) She was remodeling her residence.
(D) She bought supplies for a new hobby.

185. What does Ms. Ritz indicate about Castellente Storage Company?
(A) Its facilities are spacious.
(B) Its staff are helpful.
(C) Its reputation is excellent.
(D) Its contracts are easy to understand.



GO ON TO THE NEXT PAGE

**Questions 186–190** refer to the following Web pages and e-mail.

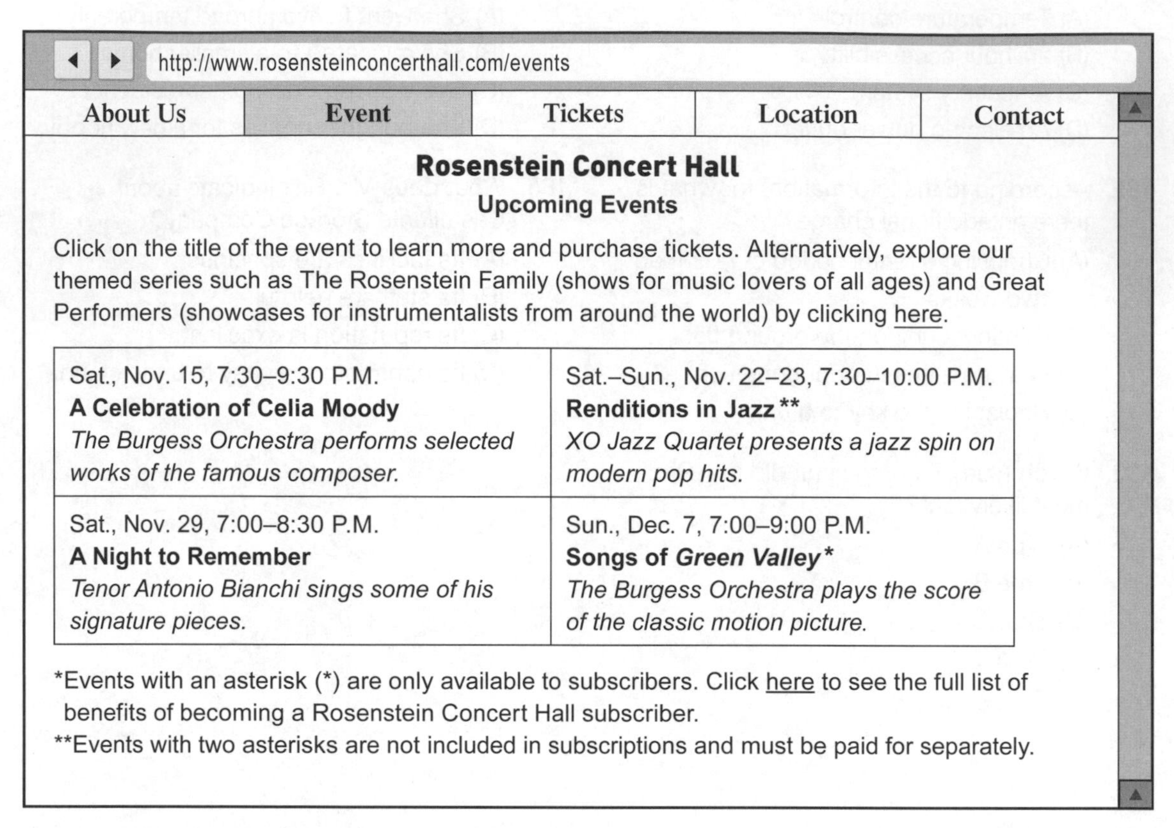

http://www.rosensteinconcerthall.com/events

About Us | Event | Tickets | Location | Contact

**Rosenstein Concert Hall**

**Upcoming Events**

Click on the title of the event to learn more and purchase tickets. Alternatively, explore our themed series such as The Rosenstein Family (shows for music lovers of all ages) and Great Performers (showcases for instrumentalists from around the world) by clicking here.

| | |
|---|---|
| Sat., Nov. 15, 7:30–9:30 P.M.<br>**A Celebration of Celia Moody**<br>*The Burgess Orchestra performs selected works of the famous composer.* | Sat.–Sun., Nov. 22–23, 7:30–10:00 P.M.<br>**Renditions in Jazz****<br>*XO Jazz Quartet presents a jazz spin on modern pop hits.* |
| Sat., Nov. 29, 7:00–8:30 P.M.<br>**A Night to Remember**<br>*Tenor Antonio Bianchi sings some of his signature pieces.* | Sun., Dec. 7, 7:00–9:00 P.M.<br>**Songs of *Green Valley****<br>*The Burgess Orchestra plays the score of the classic motion picture.* |

*Events with an asterisk (*) are only available to subscribers. Click here to see the full list of benefits of becoming a Rosenstein Concert Hall subscriber.

**Events with two asterisks are not included in subscriptions and must be paid for separately.

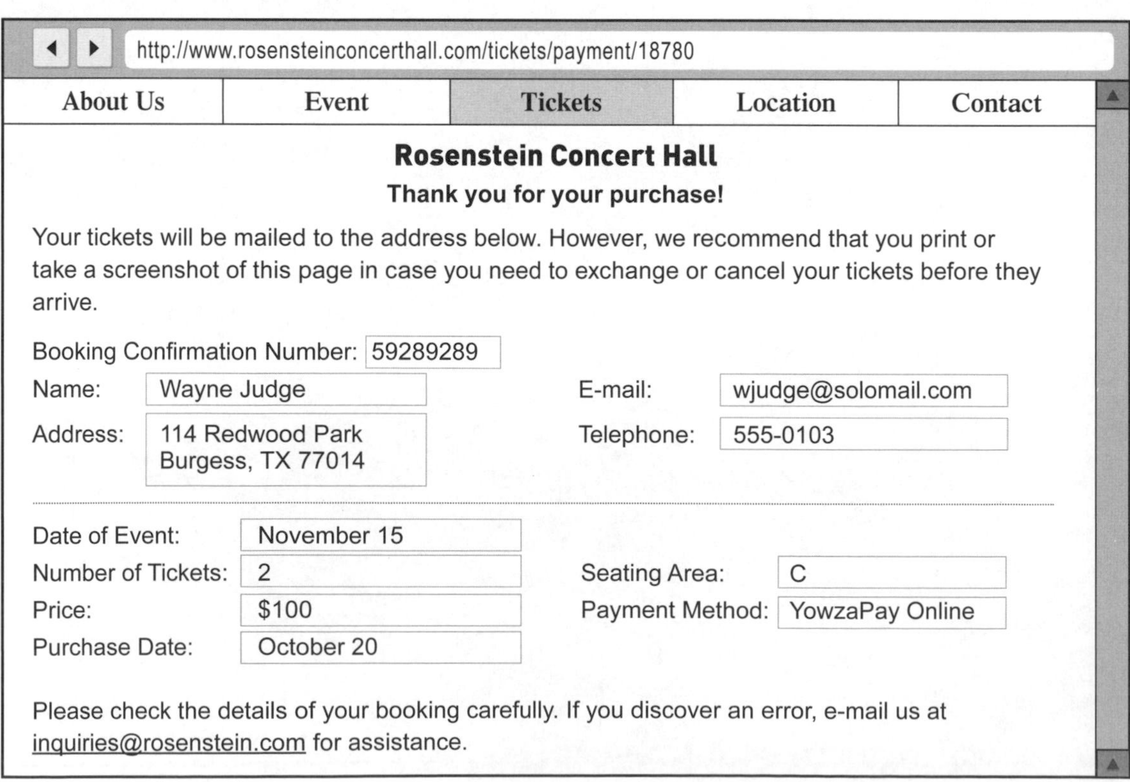

http://www.rosensteinconcerthall.com/tickets/payment/18780

About Us | Event | Tickets | Location | Contact

**Rosenstein Concert Hall**

**Thank you for your purchase!**

Your tickets will be mailed to the address below. However, we recommend that you print or take a screenshot of this page in case you need to exchange or cancel your tickets before they arrive.

Booking Confirmation Number: 59289289

Name: Wayne Judge

E-mail: wjudge@solomail.com

Address: 114 Redwood Park<br>Burgess, TX 77014

Telephone: 555-0103

Date of Event: November 15

Number of Tickets: 2

Seating Area: C

Price: $100

Payment Method: YowzaPay Online

Purchase Date: October 20

Please check the details of your booking carefully. If you discover an error, e-mail us at inquiries@rosenstein.com for assistance.

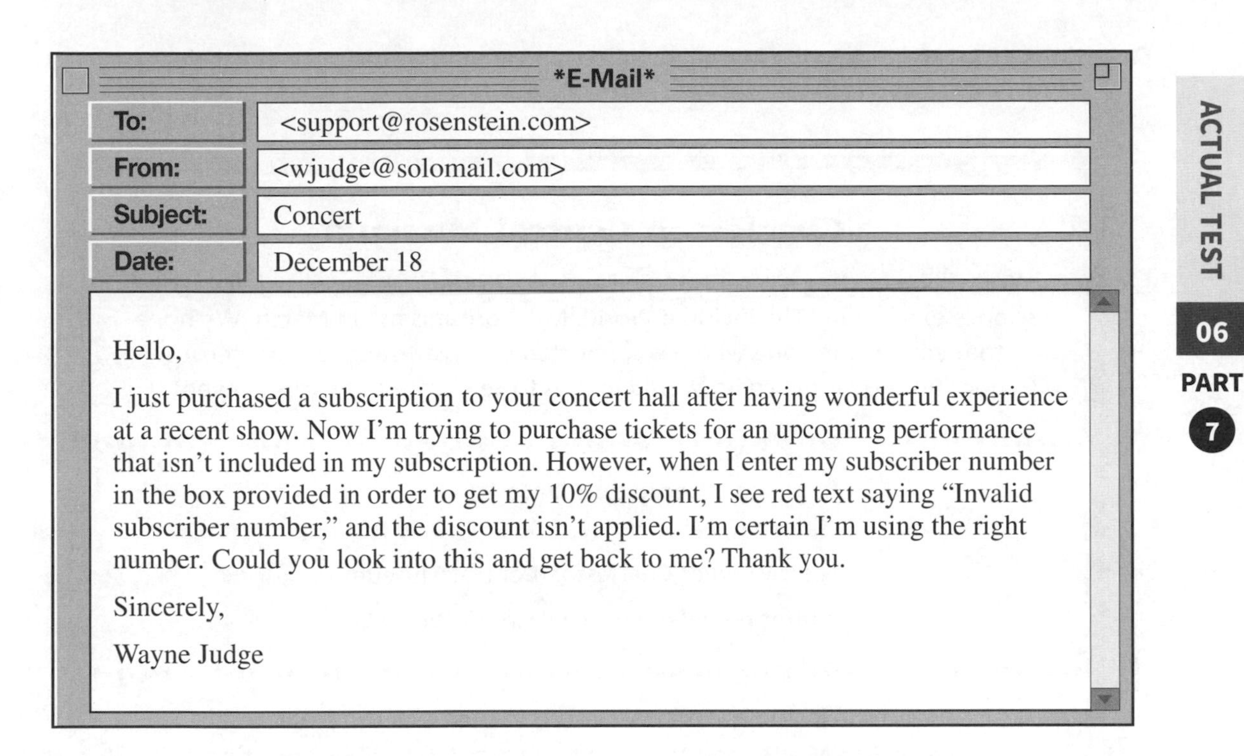
*E-Mail*

To: <support@rosenstein.com>
From: <wjudge@solomail.com>
Subject: Concert
Date: December 18

Hello,

I just purchased a subscription to your concert hall after having wonderful experience at a recent show. Now I'm trying to purchase tickets for an upcoming performance that isn't included in my subscription. However, when I enter my subscriber number in the box provided in order to get my 10% discount, I see red text saying "Invalid subscriber number," and the discount isn't applied. I'm certain I'm using the right number. Could you look into this and get back to me? Thank you.

Sincerely,

Wayne Judge

**186.** What do the events listed in the first Web page have in common?
(A) They take place on the weekend.
(B) They last the same amount of time.
(C) They involve groups of performers.
(D) They are each only offered on a single day.

**187.** What does the second Web page instruct Mr. Judge to do?
(A) Check his e-mail inbox
(B) Save his booking information
(C) Print his tickets at home
(D) Note a cancellation deadline

**188.** What did Mr. Judge hear at the concert he attended?
(A) A vocal performance
(B) Music created for a film
(C) Songs converted into a different genre
(D) Musical pieces written by one person

**189.** Why did Mr. Judge write the e-mail?
(A) To express appreciation for a service
(B) To report a technical problem
(C) To seek confirmation of a purchase
(D) To inquire about the terms of an agreement

**190.** What is most likely true about Mr. Judge?
(A) He is entitled to attend exclusive performances.
(B) He will begin receiving a regular publication.
(C) He has misunderstood a benefit of a special status.
(D) He is interested in child-friendly entertainment.



GO ON TO THE NEXT PAGE

**Questions 191–195** refer to the following notice, article, and e-mail.

## Charleston Central Museum

We will be hosting a reception on February 26 to mark the opening of the science exhibition "The Invisible World: Microorganisms" in March. We hope that you, as someone who has supported our institution with generous donations over the years, would join us to celebrate this exciting event.

**Reception Details:**

Saturday, February 26, 6:00 P.M.–9:30 P.M.

East Wing of Charleston Central Museum

Buffet provided by Silver Star Catering Co.

"The Invisible World: Microorganisms" will run from March 3 to May 31 and feature more than 250 exhibits depicting the wonders of the smallest forms of life.

*The Midwestern Gazette*

## Charleston Central Museum Claims Prestigious Honor

*by Jill Bradford*

MERRITT (April 20)—Charleston Central Museum was awarded the Scientific Literature Award at the first-ever Midwestern Arts & Science Awards ceremony on April 18. Put on by the Midwestern Knowledge Foundation, the event took place at Washington Convention Hall in front of an audience of around 6,000 members of the arts and science communities.

Charleston Central Museum won the prize for the detailed and entertaining information pack that supplements its exhibition "The Invisible World: Microorganisms." Lead designer Yui Takahashi accepted the award and thanked graphic designer Raymond Schlupp, who provided many of the pack's illustrations. She also promised that the pack would be publically available on the new version of the museum's Web site, which is currently under construction.

"The Invisible World: Microorganisms" was conceptualized by scientist Thomas Ellson, who enlisted the knowledge and expertise of architect Fiona Watson to construct the exhibits. The exhibition has been a tremendous success for the museum, with ticket sales topping those of all previous exhibitions. After its run there comes to an end, it will be transported to neighboring Georgetown to be displayed at Georgetown Science Institute for approximately two months.

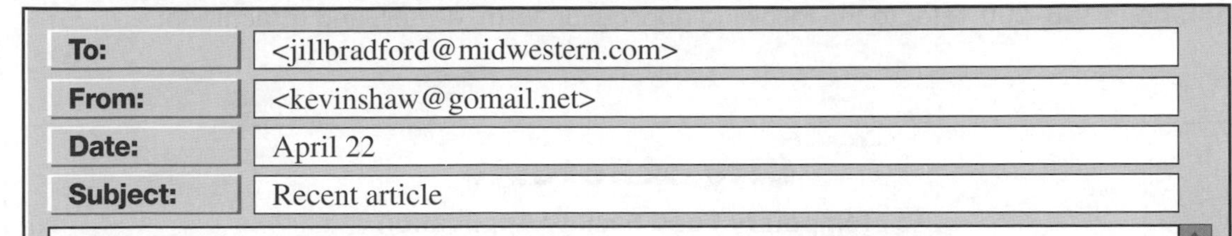

| | |
|---|---|
| **To:** | <jillbradford@midwestern.com> |
| **From:** | <kevinshaw@gomail.net> |
| **Date:** | April 22 |
| **Subject:** | Recent article |

Dear Ms. Bradford,

I was initially happy to see your recent coverage of Charleston Central Museum's success at the Midwestern Art & Science Awards. However, as I read through the article, excitedly waiting to see my name in print, I found that my work had been mistakenly attributed to Fiona Watson, who merely served as an advisor to me during the process. This was very disappointing. I encourage you to carry out more thorough research for future articles.

Sincerely,

Kevin Shaw

**191.** Who is the notice intended for?
(A) Museum employees
(B) Potential exhibitors
(C) Financial donors
(D) University students

**192.** In the notice, the word "mark" in paragraph 1, line 1, is closest in meaning to
(A) characterize
(B) evaluate
(C) acknowledge
(D) brand

**193.** What is indicated about the Midwestern Art & Science Awards ceremony?
(A) It had not been held previously.
(B) It took place at Charleston Central Museum.
(C) It was hosted by Ms. Takahashi.
(D) It was broadcast to a live audience.

**194.** What most likely will happen on June 1?
(A) The nomination period for an honor will begin.
(B) Some educational materials will be released online.
(C) A talk will be sponsored by a funding organization.
(D) An exhibition will move to a different town.

**195.** What did Mr. Shaw probably do?
(A) Provided artwork for an information pack
(B) Accepted an award on behalf of an institution
(C) Developed the concept for an exhibition
(D) Constructed some museum displays

GO ON TO THE NEXT PAGE

**Questions 196–200** refer to the following application form, e-mail, and attachment.

# City of Sotorik

## Temporary Food Facility Application

Please submit this application to receive permission to operate a temporary food and/or drink facility within Sotorik city limits during a special event.

Applicant: Lynne McKinley
Business: Lynne's Tacos
Address: 32 West Road, Sotorik, NY 47372
Phone: 555-0153

Event Name: Global Crafts Festival
Organizer: Sotorik Tourism Board
Date(s): May 8–10
Location: Sotorik Grand Park

Supplementary materials (required unless specified otherwise):

(a) Photographs of all facilities and equipment to be used on-site for food/drink preparation and service
(b) A list of all food/drink items to be sold and the ingredients of all of the non-prepackaged items
(c) A check payable to Sotorik City Hall for $50 OR, if the application is being submitted fewer than 10 days before the event, for $100
(d) A certificate of inspection from the Sotorik Department of Health (only required for vendors intending to use gas-powered appliances in their facility)

Signature of applicant: *Lynne McKinley*

Date: *April 19*

| | |
|---|---|
| **To** | Angel Munoz and 3 others |
| **From** | Lynne McKinley |
| **Date** | May 3 |
| **Subject** | Global Craft Festival booth |
| **Attachment** | Schedule, Festival Map |

Hi all,

Thanks for agreeing to represent Lynne's Tacos at the Global Crafts Festival this weekend. In addition to following the instructions on the attached schedule, please note that there will be a city-issued food safety checklist that the early shift workers must fill out, and that the late shift workers on Friday and Saturday must carefully store the food and lock up our booth. The actual food sale period will start a half hour later and end a half hour earlier than the shifts, so we should have plenty of time for these tasks.

If we start to run low on supplies before the dinner rush, if the gas grill stops working (which has happened before), or if another problem comes up, please contact me or Grady, who will be managing the restaurant all weekend.

Thanks,
Lynne

***Lynne's Tacos***

**Global Crafts Festival Schedule**

| | Friday | Saturday | Sunday |
|---|---|---|---|
| **Early shift** (9:30 A.M.–2:00 P.M.) | Lynne<br>Kwang-Sun | Lynne<br>Ron | Dallas<br>Kwang-Sun |
| **Late shift** (2:00 P.M.–6:00 P.M.) | Angel<br>Dallas | Angel<br>Ken | Dallas<br>Lynne |

- Use the vendors' parking area and entrance on Fourth Street.
- Bring a form of ID (your name will be checked against a vendor list).
- Arrive at least 15 minutes early so that you have time to get to the booth.

**196.** What was Ms. McKinley required to provide with the form?
(A) A list of staff members
(B) A blueprint of a temporary facility
(C) A photocopy of a business license
(D) A payment to a government office

**197.** In the e-mail, the word "following" in paragraph 1, line 2, is closest in meaning to
(A) complying with
(B) comprehending
(C) accompanying
(D) subsequent

**198.** What is implied about Ms. McKinley?
(A) Her application had to be expedited.
(B) Her equipment passed an inspection.
(C) She hired a professional food photographer.
(D) She chose to rent a cooking appliance.

**199.** What will Ron most likely do with a coworker?
(A) Complete some paperwork
(B) Carpool to the festival site
(C) Secure some company property
(D) Pick up some supplies

**200.** In the attachment, what is suggested about vendors at the Global Crafts Festival?
(A) They are grouped by merchandise type.
(B) They are given identification badges.
(C) They may enter before 9:30 A.M. each day.
(D) They can disassemble their booths on Monday.

**Stop! This is the end of the test. If you finish before time is called, you may go back to Parts 5, 6, and 7 and check your work.**

# ACTUAL TEST 

## READING TEST

In the Reading test, you will read a variety of texts and answer several different types of reading comprehension questions. The entire Reading test will last 75 minutes. There are three parts, and directions are given for each part. You are encouraged to answer as many questions as possible within the time allowed. You must mark your answers on the separate answer sheet. Do not write your answers in your test book.

## PART 5

**Directions:** A word or phrase is missing in each of the sentences below. Four answer choices are given below each sentence. Select the best answer to complete the sentence. Then mark the letter (A), (B), (C), or (D) on your answer sheet.

**101.** As Ms. Roy's parking space is far from the entrance, Mr. Ezra has kindly agreed to let her park in ------- until her injury heals.
(A) he
(B) his
(C) him
(D) himself

**102.** The powerful ------- provided by the Yarov-A coat's fabric will make sure you stay warm in the world's coldest places.
(A) protected
(B) protects
(C) protectively
(D) protection

**103.** Designed to offer as much ------- as possible, the Lorene Convention Center is an ideal venue for a wide variety of events.
(A) flexibility
(B) enthusiasm
(C) financing
(D) accuracy

**104.** Pattison Bank has been providing entry-level career opportunities to recent university graduates ------- years.
(A) in
(B) following
(C) for
(D) during

**105.** Restaurant owners ------- face new challenges, especially in today's competitive business environment.
(A) heavily
(B) constantly
(C) diversely
(D) variably

**106.** When it runs updates, antivirus software may temporarily affect the ------- of your computer.
(A) innovation
(B) measurement
(C) performance
(D) representation

**107.** A market report indicated that social media marketing reaches young consumers ------- than television advertising.
(A) effective
(B) effectively
(C) more effectively
(D) effectiveness

**108.** At Klevaratix Supply, we aim to ------- the highest quality kitchen equipment for professional chefs.
(A) commit
(B) earn
(C) remain
(D) produce

109. ------- learning to play the guitar, practice with a durable model like the Franmawr-5.
(A) Whether
(B) Since
(C) From
(D) When

110. To prevent ------- of records, a notification appears if the same client number is entered in the database more than once.
(A) transportation
(B) duplication
(C) organization
(D) differentiation

111. Sales of signs and banners have continued to ------- decline as more businesses move online.
(A) steady
(B) steadied
(C) steadily
(D) steadying

112. The safety consultant recommended treating the flooring ------- non-slip finish in order to prevent workplace accidents.
(A) with
(B) of
(C) to
(D) until

113. At the next Town Hall meeting, officials will give a progress report on the construction of the ------- community center.
(A) planned
(B) nominated
(C) acquainted
(D) relieved

114. Smart-Tekk, Inc. makes educational toys that help young children gain ------- with scientific concepts.
(A) familiarly
(B) familiarity
(C) familiarized
(D) more familiar

115. Though some managers may think -------, using off-site storage for old paper documents is a very affordable solution.
(A) particularly
(B) otherwise
(C) moreover
(D) formerly

116. Many entrepreneurs, ------- experience, may make the mistake of expanding their businesses too quickly.
(A) regardless of
(B) instead of
(C) nevertheless
(D) as much as

117. Next time that we buy office furniture, I propose selecting chairs and desks that can ------- to a variety of heights.
(A) raising
(B) raise
(C) be raised
(D) being raised

118. Sunara Food Market ------- all of its produce from local organic farms.
(A) proceeds
(B) succeeds
(C) intends
(D) obtains

119. Keeping your customers fully ------- depends largely on the ability to resolve complaints in a professional manner.
(A) satisfies
(B) satisfied
(C) satisfying
(D) satisfaction

120. Researchers at Novarraic Tech, Inc. have been developing a robot that can teach ------- basic new tasks.
(A) themselves
(B) yourself
(C) itself
(D) ourselves



GO ON TO THE NEXT PAGE

**121.** Digital videos ------- larger amounts of data than most other applications, especially when they are viewed in high definition.

(A) requiring
(B) to require
(C) having required
(D) require

**122.** The road improvement project has faced several delays, and sources say that the work may extend ------- June.

(A) along
(B) above
(C) plus
(D) past

**123.** The recent drop in the value of the dollar has made importing goods from the United States more ------- for us.

(A) profitable
(B) profitability
(C) profiting
(D) profit

**124.** The new Web site is expected to be launched ------- the developers complete usability testing.

(A) once
(B) ever
(C) whereas
(D) upon

**125.** The museum's staff and a team of IT experts will work ------- to design a virtual reality exhibit.

(A) relatively
(B) unusually
(C) collaboratively
(D) absently

**126.** Although the merger discussions have progressed slowly, company negotiators are ------- that a deal will be reached.

(A) ongoing
(B) probable
(C) dedicated
(D) optimistic

**127.** The new policy allows selected staff to work from home, ------- regular deadlines are met.

(A) as for
(B) provided that
(C) concerning
(D) in case of

**128.** Rosemary is one of the most commonly used herbs in Italian cooking because the plant ------- in the region's warm, dry climate.

(A) thrives
(B) flatters
(C) characterizes
(D) absorbs

**129.** If ------- incorrectly, the software program will display an error message on the start-up menu.

(A) installation
(B) installer
(C) installed
(D) installs

**130.** Ms. Cho has made a detailed transcript of ------- was discussed in the last department meeting.

(A) that
(B) what
(C) everything
(D) it

# PART 6

**Directions:** Read the texts that follow. A word, phrase, or sentence is missing in parts of each text. Four answer choices for each question are given below the text. Select the best answer to complete the text. Then mark the letter (A), (B), (C), or (D) on your answer sheet.

**Questions 131–134** refer to the following e-mail.

To: Don Chen <don-chen@mail.org>
From: Brundy Storage <brundy-storage@mail.com>
Date: January 30
Subject: Update on Space 1032

Dear Mr. Chen,

Please know that we at Brundy Storage appreciate your business and loyalty.

Recently, rental rates have increased due to greater ------- **131.** for storage space in this area. Based on these market conditions, the new monthly rent for Space 1032 ------- **132.** $208 starting on Sunday, March 1.

This ------- **133.** represents less than a 2% increase in your rental rate. -------. **134.** Your new rate is still lower than the current rate for first-time customers renting a storage unit the same size as yours.

Again, we are grateful for your business as a longtime customer of Brundy Storage.

Regards,
The Management at Brundy Storage

**131.** (A) range
(B) sales
(C) demand
(D) renovation

**132.** (A) was to be
(B) will be
(C) has been
(D) would have been

**133.** (A) adjusts
(B) adjuster
(C) adjustable
(D) adjustment

**134.** (A) We would like to thank all of our customers for their input in this matter.
(B) We wish to emphasize that, with fewer tenants, we are now downsizing.
(C) Be aware that the terms and conditions of rental agreements can vary greatly.
(D) Rest assured that, even at that price, you are still receiving a good value.

*GO ON TO THE NEXT PAGE*

**Questions 135–138** refer to the following Web page.

> Petralla Publishing is a leading publisher of instructional books ------- (135.) to readers who enjoy hands-on arts and crafts hobbies. Supporting fresh talent and ideas is a key part of our business. ------- (136.), we actively seek book proposals from people who would like to make a useful addition to the body of writing in our field. ------- (137.). For many of our authors, writing a book was only a ------- (138.) dream, something they had hoped to do someday. With our encouragement and guidance, they went on to create a beautiful new work for publication.
>
> Please click here to see our submission guidelines.

**135.** (A) caters
(B) catering
(C) is to cater
(D) are catered

**136.** (A) For that reason
(B) By comparison
(C) Afterward
(D) Alternatively

**137.** (A) On certain days, educators may request copies of recent titles for review.
(B) We will set up a phone appointment to speak with you further about this.
(C) Our team of editors can make a promising concept for a book into a reality.
(D) Research shows that fairy tales still appeal more to younger readers.

**138.** (A) distant
(B) vacant
(C) subtle
(D) deep

**Questions 139–142** refer to the following article.

DORTLUND (19 March)—The 25th annual Dortlund Folk Music Festival drew a record crowd of over 6,000 people last Saturday and Sunday. According to organizers, this impressive ------- (139.) can be credited to the new features of this year's event. ------- (140.). For the first time ever, the performance lineup included not only popular folk groups but also Cuban mambo bands, Polish dance ensembles, and ------- (141.) jazz soloists. There were also chances for attendees to take part in hands-on workshops ------- (142.) to show them techniques for playing various traditional instruments. Organizers say both of these popular changes will be carried over to next year's festival.

**139.** (A) prize
(B) funding
(C) turnout
(D) rating

**140.** (A) They noted that traditional culture may continue to change in the future.
(B) All volunteers received free meals and specially-made festival T-shirts.
(C) In fact, a background in music is not necessary for greater appreciation.
(D) For example, a more diverse array of musical styles was represented.

**141.** (A) yet
(B) very
(C) even
(D) much

**142.** (A) designer
(B) designed
(C) to design
(D) designs

ACTUAL TEST 07 PART 6

GO ON TO THE NEXT PAGE

**Questions 143–146** refer to the following information.

*The HGA's annual Household Goods Trade Show in Dallas Texas—Why you should attend*

For more than 60 years, the Household Goods Association (HGA) ------- **143.** the industry's largest trade show featuring household goods from the world's leading manufacturers. Purchasing managers for retail stores attend every year to meet with wholesale suppliers and seize opportunities to form business partnerships. Are you looking for original merchandise to distinguish your business from competitors and gain a market advantage? ------- **144.** walk the trade floor and explore the displays. You are certain to ------- **145.** innovative new household products. -------. **146.** By attending the HGA trade show, you are assured of staying up to date on the latest trends in household goods.

**143.** (A) has hosted
(B) was hosted
(C) is being hosted
(D) would have hosted

**144.** (A) Simply
(B) Lately
(C) Closely
(D) Shortly

**145.** (A) utilize
(B) navigate
(C) demonstrate
(D) discover

**146.** (A) There are several other important ways to care for a home.
(B) In addition, there are talks and workshops on current industry issues.
(C) A few of the vintage items on display are over 50 years old.
(D) When your business is finished, enjoy our complimentary lunch buffet.

# PART 7

**Directions:** In this part you will read a selection of texts, such as magazine and newspaper articles, e-mails, and instant messages. Each text or set of texts is followed by several questions. Select the best answer for each question and mark the letter (A), (B), (C), or (D) on your answer sheet.



**Questions 147–148** refer to the following notice.

## Meeting Room Policy

The Cleary City Public Library's meeting rooms are available at no charge to community groups under the following conditions. All community meetings held in the rooms must be free of charge and open to the public. Meeting rooms are available only during the library's normal opening hours. Requests to reserve a meeting room must be made via the library's online reservation system. Groups may reserve a room for the current month or the following month. Under no circumstances may any group reserve a room for more than one meeting within a 14-day period. Reservations are accepted on a first-come, first-served basis.

Please note that all rooms are equipped with chairs and conference tables. Library-owned audiovisual equipment may be requested on the meeting room application and must be checked out with a library card.

**147.** What is suggested about the library's meeting rooms?
(A) Their seating may be rearranged by patrons.
(B) They have different maximum capacities.
(C) They do not have audiovisual equipment.
(D) They may be used outside of the library's regular hours.

**148.** According to the notice, what is true about meeting room reservations?
(A) They will be taken in the order they are received.
(B) There is a penalty for canceling them after a certain point.
(C) They must be requested via an in-person visit.
(D) They must be made one month in advance.

GO ON TO THE NEXT PAGE

**Questions 149–150** refer to the following job advertisement.

**Wanted: Graphic Designer (Digital Media)**

**Company/Location:** Strobbels, Inc. Headquarters, Hamilton, Ontario

---

Strobbels, Inc. is seeking a creative individual to design graphics for our digital marketing initiatives. These include the company Web site, online advertising, social media, and mobile phone apps. The successful candidate will also attend industry trade shows on the company's behalf and acquire in-house training to stay current on digital communication trends. Qualifications include a minimum of 2 years' experience as a graphic designer in an advertising agency and proficiency in digital design software.

Strobbels, Inc. is a family-owned chain of convenience stores that provide snacks and quick meals for customers on the go. We have earned recognition from the media as one of the province's five best companies for employees. We are also well known for our strong commitment to the communities in which we are located. Each year, the company sponsors fundraising activities for several charitable organizations.

**149.** What is mentioned as a requirement for the job?

(A) An educational background in computer programming
(B) Previous employment with an advertising agency
(C) Proven ability to design in-house training courses
(D) Experience with organizing trade show events

**150.** What is indicated about Strobbels, Inc.?

(A) It has various staff recognition programs.
(B) It recently relocated its headquarters.
(C) It runs a delivery service.
(D) It supports local charities.

**Questions 151-152** refer to the following ticket.

**City Railways** Ticket Coupon 01 of 01 Retain During Trip

**Name of passenger:** Steven Rigby
**Reservation #:** 834253
19 March
**Place of issue:** Dover
**Issued:** In-person
**Class of Seating:** Business Class
**Train Number:** 192
**From:** Dover
**To:** Vernon Heights
**Departs:** 1:45 P.M.
**Arrives:** 3:44 P.M.

Photo ID required on board
*Refund/exchange penalties apply

Total charge: $53*
*Change fee applies

*Join our Frequent Rider Program and get discounted upgrades from Coach to Premium Class seating. Visit www.city-railways.com for more details.*

**151.** What is implied about Mr. Rigby?
(A) He will eat a meal while on board.
(B) He is a frequent rider on City Railways.
(C) He changed an itinerary at no charge.
(D) He must present identification during his trip.

**152.** What is suggested about City Railways?
(A) It accepts reservations by telephone.
(B) Its Web site was recently upgraded.
(C) Its trains have multiple classes of seating.
(D) It offers discounts for tickets booked online.

GO ON TO THE NEXT PAGE

**Questions 153–154** refer to the following text-message chain.

**Todd Miele (1:23 P.M.)**
Hi, Marissa. Do you know if the meeting room downstairs is available this afternoon?

**Marissa Kozlowski (1:24 P.M.)**
Yes, it's open. Are you meeting with a client today?

**Todd Miele (1:24 P.M.)**
No, I just need to practice the presentation I'll give at the landscape architecture conference. I added a slide showing my latest garden design project.

**Marissa Kozlowski (1:25 P.M.)**
Great. Oh, the projector in that meeting room uses a different remote control unit. It's in the storage cabinet. I can bring it down for you.

**Todd Miele (1:26 P.M.)**
I'm good. I have to get some other materials from the office anyway.

**Marissa Kozlowski (1:27 P.M.)**
All right. Good luck with the rehearsal.

**153.** Who most likely is Mr. Miele?
(A) A building superintendent
(B) A conference organizer
(C) A landscape architect
(D) An information technology expert

**154.** At 1:26 P.M., what does Mr. Miele mean when he writes, "I'm good"?
(A) He is skilled at making presentations.
(B) He does not need further assistance.
(C) He has a suitable amount of storage space.
(D) He has a strong working relationship with a client.

**Questions 155–157** refer to the following online article.

http://www.keys-to-success.com/articles/023421

# Some common advice that experts share

Showing homes well requires preparation. Clients need to feel confident in your expertise in local neighborhoods and properties for sale. —[1]—. When you drive a prospective buyer to a home for viewing, be sure you have memorized the directions ahead of time. You may even want to practice driving to the home the day before the showing. —[2]—. Getting lost en route to a property will suggest a lack of knowledge about the community. When you are giving house tours to prospective buyers, it is a good idea to bring several copies of a buyers' packet with information about the home and the surrounding district. —[3]—. Even a paper map of the local area can be helpful. Also, confirm you have the correct key to access the home. —[4]—. Having the wrong key, or no key, will not make a good impression.

ACTUAL TEST 07

PART 7

**155.** Who is the article most likely intended for?
(A) Real estate salespeople
(B) Residential renovation specialists
(C) Volunteer tour guides
(D) First-time home buyers

**156.** What does the writer of the article suggest doing?
(A) Having extra sets of door keys made
(B) Mastering travel routes in advance
(C) Stopping briefly at scenic viewpoints
(D) Researching community service opportunities

**157.** In which of the positions marked [1], [2], [3], and [4] does the following sentence best belong?
"Any recipients will appreciate it, and you will be able to refer to the material to answer questions if needed."
(A) [1]
(B) [2]
(C) [3]
(D) [4]

GO ON TO THE NEXT PAGE

**Questions 158–160** refer to the following letter.

Yvonne Clark
803 Bates Street
Bowen City, IL 60419

Dear Ms. Clark,

As one of the coaches of Bowen City's Youth Soccer League, you should be aware of an upcoming special meeting of Bowen City's Parks and Recreation Committee. It will take place on Tuesday, February 4 at 6:30 P.M. in Room 5 of City Hall.

The topic will be Parks Department director Fiorello Sauro's proposal to allocate a portion of the Parks Department's budget to upgrade Hohman Park's recreational amenities. Specifically, photos taken of the Youth Soccer Stadium's equipment storage buildings show exposed nails, holes in the siding, and cracked windows that must be taken care of.

Director Sauro will also discuss installing modern electric lighting on the stadium's scoreboard. He has secured an estimate from Seiffert Electric, Inc. of the overall cost of these endeavors. At the meeting, the committee will seek the public's input on this plan.

The Youth Soccer League Board urges you to attend to share your valuable opinion as one of the people who would be affected by the project.

Sincerely,

Calvin Waters
President of the Board, Bowen City Youth Soccer League

**158.** What most likely is the purpose of the upcoming meeting?

(A) To provide updates on a park's event schedule

(B) To discuss financing for park improvements

(C) To announce the results of a public contest

(D) To introduce a newly-appointed parks official

**159.** What is suggested about a stadium's storage buildings?

(A) They serve additional functions.

(B) They will be moved to a new location.

(C) They may be rented for a fee.

(D) They are in need of repair.

**160.** According to the letter, what has Mr. Sauro done recently?

(A) Received a cost estimate

(B) Photographed other city parks

(C) Attended a local sporting event

(D) Revised a park brochure

**Questions 161–163** refer to the following online review.

**Book-bargains.com *"The most trusted Web-based seller of secondhand books"***

**Customer review of**: ***Logo Design Inspirations*** | soft-cover, 148 pages

**Review number**: 1 of 7 for items purchased from Book-bargains.com
click here to see other reviews

**Date of review**: May 26

**Customer name**: Jeff Starks ✓ Verified purchase

**Overall rating**: Excellent

**Comments**:

This compact, easy-to-carry book presents 55 examples of famous, highly-effective logo designs. All of the logos are shown in full color against a white background, and the accompanying text outlines the history of their creation and analyzes their design elements. In addition to the main text, the publisher has thoughtfully provided about ten empty pages for taking notes—a nice feature. The logos have been selected from a wide range of companies, from software developers to package delivery services. The latter was covered in what was for me the most interesting chapter of the book: "Patterns Showing Movement." This section also features my favorite piece of design—the dynamic logo for Zlatariax, a maker of exercise machines that is known for its innovation. The book is a valuable resource for any commercial designer.

**161.** What most likely is true about Mr. Starks?
(A) He has purchased several used books online.
(B) He is a professional buyer for a bookstore.
(C) He recently joined a book discussion group.
(D) He has created logos for a variety of companies.

**162.** What is mentioned about *Logo Design Inspirations*?
(A) It includes a section of blank pages.
(B) It is also available in an electronic edition.
(C) A friend of Mr. Starks did research for it.
(D) It is currently out of print.

**163.** What kind of company is Zlatariax?
(A) A computer software developer
(B) A fitness equipment manufacturer
(C) A package delivery service
(D) A graphic design firm



*GO ON TO THE NEXT PAGE*

**Questions 164–167** refer to the following announcement on a Web page.

www.curiosom.com/news/0111

***January 11 - Official announcement regarding Curiosom.com's change of payment processors—what it means for our subscribers***

Since its inception nearly 15 years ago, Curiosom.com has grown to become the premier venue for photographers to share their pictures with the entire global community. When we started offering paid subscriptions for unlimited photo uploading privileges, our management chose the Brainard-Plus payment processing service to handle our billing for subscriptions. —[1]—. We based our decision primarily upon Brainard-Plus's ability to automatically renew our 1-year and 2-year subscription plans.

However, when we became a subsidiary of Panamat.com last June, we began the process of switching to their payment processing firm, Digitexx-D, in order to unify our billing systems. —[2]—. Unfortunately, we have been notified by Digitexx-D that they cannot renew any Curiosom.com subscriptions that originated on our prior payment processor. This affects all Curiosom.com members who began their subscription on or before June 30 of last year. To get around this problem, we are encouraging these members to take advantage of a 20% discount on early subscription renewals. —[3]—. If you do so, your subscription will continue uninterrupted until its end date and can be renewed automatically. If you take no action, you will have to update your subscriber profile and billing information at the end of your current subscription. —[4]—. We therefore urge all of our affected subscribers to renew early.

**164.** What type of business most likely is Curiosom.com?

(A) A digital magazine for visual artists
(B) An advertising analytics service
(C) An online accounting app
(D) A photo sharing platform

**165.** According to the announcement, what happened the previous year?

(A) An anniversary celebration
(B) A business acquisition
(C) A new product release
(D) An increase in subscription fees

**166.** Who is currently eligible for a discount?

(A) Subscribers who started their service within the past week
(B) Subscribers who select a renewal period of three or more years
(C) Subscribers who were initially billed by Brainard-Plus
(D) Subscribers who are also members of Panamat.com

**167.** In which of the following positions marked [1], [2], [3], and [4] does the following sentence best belong?

"The regular fee for your chosen subscription plan will then be charged."

(A) [1]
(B) [2]
(C) [3]
(D) [4]

**Questions 168–171** refer to the following online chat discussion.

| | | |
|---|---|---|
| **Aurelia Ramos** | **[2:04 P.M.]** | Hi, all. I'm just checking in. How is it going with the brainstorming for our customer forum page? Any article ideas? |
| **Peter Xiu** | **[2:05 P.M.]** | Yes — I'd like to write a how-to guide for lighting a warehouse properly. |
| **Aurella Ramos** | **[2:06 P.M.]** | Good. We do have many commercial clients that purchase lighting supplies from us, so our forum's content should reflect their needs. Other ideas? |
| **Linda Melo** | **[2:07 P.M.]** | For our consumer clients, I was thinking of writing tips on how to select the best lighting fixtures for recreation rooms. There are so many options. |
| **Aurelia Ramos** | **[2:07 P.M.]** | For sure. |
| **Linda Melo** | **[2:08 P.M.]** | I could also write a profile on Moishe Wietz, the artisan who makes wall lamps from recycled industrial pipes. |
| **Aurelia Ramos** | **[2:09 P.M.]** | Great. You used to work with him, right? |
| **Linda Melo** | **[2:10 P.M.]** | Yes, I was his apprentice. |
| **Peter Xiu** | **[2:11 P.M.]** | That reminds me. I have another idea. We should create a post that clarifies some common technical terms, and make them easier to understand. |
| **Aurelia Ramos** | **[2:12 P.M.]** | That would be very helpful. Could you do that? |
| **Peter Xiu** | **[2:13 P.M.]** | Sure thing. |
| **Aurelia Ramos** | **[2:14 P.M.]** | Great. Thank you, both, for your input. I'll check on your progress later this week. |

**168.** What kind of company do the participants most likely work for?
(A) A maker of gardening tools
(B) A seller of lighting supplies
(C) A chain of storage facilities
(D) A trade publication for electricians

**169.** At 2:07 P.M., what does Ms. Melo most likely mean when she writes, "There are so many options"?
(A) A coworker may need more time for a decision.
(B) She is not sure how to begin a piece of writing.
(C) Customers may be overwhelmed by a selection.
(D) She is impressed by a list of suggestions.

**170.** What is indicated about Ms. Melo?
(A) She worked under Mr. Wietz's guidance.
(B) She organizes recycling initiatives.
(C) She is currently remodeling her home.
(D) She used to be a magazine journalist.

**171.** What does Mr. Xiu agree to do?
(A) Collect data to measure customer satisfaction
(B) Develop content that explains some expressions
(C) Post reminder notes on a shared calendar
(D) Supervise a new internship program

GO ON TO THE NEXT PAGE

**Questions 172–175** refer to the following article.

*Entrepreneur News-Times* *April 23*

**What Café Owners Should Know . . .**

By Kayla Leitch

➢ Those who run an independent café will soon find that their decision on how much to charge for their offerings will have a major effect on profits. Because there is much competition among cafés, it is important to determine the optimal prices for products and services.

➢ When I first opened Café Connective nearly 10 years ago, I aimed to charge the same prices as the major coffee shop chains while providing superior service. This strategy succeeded in attracting customers, but it did not result in decent earnings. After my first year in business, I commissioned a market research study and found that most customers already perceive independent coffee shops as offering higher levels of service and product quality. With this in mind, I began to serve higher-quality, more expensive gourmet coffee products.

➢ To further justify my higher prices, I have made efforts to carve out a niche for my café as a neighborhood meeting place. Every month, I hold fun special events, such as brewing workshops or coffee tasting sessions, for customers. These gatherings have had a positive impact on my establishment's image.

➢ It is, of course, possible to charge lower prices than the competition, but this may not bring in enough additional sales to ensure profitability. Independent café owners have, after all, invested a good amount of money in equipment and inventory, so they must maximize their returns.

---

**About the writer:** A native of Dee City, Ms. Leitch runs a successful café there, and just last week her online resource for café and tea shop owners worldwide, www.cafe-owners.com, went operational.

**172.** Why most likely was the article written?

(A) To explain why many cafés fail to make profits

(B) To give tips for managing a café's staff

(C) To offer pricing advice for café owners

(D) To outline recent trends in the café industry

**173.** What is indicated about Café Connective?

(A) It has been in business for over a decade.

(B) It hosts biweekly special events.

(C) It was profiled in a marketing book.

(D) It is located in Ms. Leitch's hometown.

**174.** What is one reason changes were implemented in Café Connective?

(A) To differentiate it from its competitors

(B) To shorten the wait time for customers

(C) To reduce its impact on the environment

(D) To make it a more enjoyable place to work

**175.** The word "good" in paragraph 4, line 3, is closest in meaning to

(A) satisfactory

(B) dependable

(C) substantial

(D) useful



GO ON TO THE NEXT PAGE

**Questions 176–180** refer to the following article and notice on a Web page.

## Colway City Theater Group to Present *Cagen Street*

COLWAY CITY (June 3)—The Colway City Theater Group (CCTG) will kick off its summer season with Donna Mason's delightfully comical play *Cagen Street*, running from Friday, June 10 through Sunday, June 26. Friday and Saturday performances will be at 7:00 P.M. and Sunday performances will be at 2:00 P.M.

The play centers around a day in the life of Brad and Mary, a young married couple who invite their new neighbors, Ken and Janice, over for a barbecue dinner. During the cookout, the two couples learn that they went on the same tour company's overland journey across Africa just a few weeks apart. As the characters share anecdotes about the funny, adventurous, and inspirational aspects of international travel, the play carries audiences toward a sense of wonder.

The cast includes Eric Griffey, of West Town; Amy Yoon, of Hillside City; Kevin Braddock, of East Valley; and Betsy Maliki, of West Town. After the performance on June 10, audience members can meet and take photos with the performers. The director, George Mulway, will be on hand to answer audience questions as well.

For more information about the CCTG, visit www.colway-theater.org. Tickets may be purchased via its Web site or at the box office.

http://www.colway-theater.org/home 

### The Colway City Theater Group (CCTG)

Update for June 6: The management of the CCTG is happy to announce that we will offer extra performances, at 2:00 P.M. each Saturday, for *Cagen Street*, the first play of our summer season. Evening performances for Friday and Saturday are at 7:00 P.M., and the Sunday matinee is at 2:00 P.M.

The play, directed by Colway City native George Mulway, will feature the talented Kevin Braddock, making his stage debut with our group, in the role of Brad. He is joined by Amy Yoon, as Mary; Eric Griffey, as Ken; and Betsy Maliki, as Janice.

**176.** What is *Cagen Street* mainly about?
(A) Neighbors with a common experience
(B) A family's humorous cooking mistakes
(C) Immigrants adapting to a new culture
(D) The challenges of moving house frequently

**177.** In the article, the word "carries" in paragraph 2, line 11, is closest in meaning to
(A) propels
(B) maintains
(C) communicates
(D) captures

**178.** What will audiences at *Cagen Street*'s premiere receive?
(A) A preview of a future CCTG production
(B) The opportunity to interact with the cast
(C) Entry into a drawing for a theater tour
(D) A small gift related to the play's theme

**179.** What most likely is the main purpose of the notice?
(A) To encourage early ticket purchases
(B) To honor the director of a stage play
(C) To announce the retirement of an actor
(D) To publicize an expanded performance schedule

**180.** What is implied about Mr. Braddock?
(A) He appears in a video on the CCTG's Web site.
(B) He will perform at 7:00 P.M. on June 26.
(C) He will play the husband of Ms. Yoon's character.
(D) He is from the same city as Mr. Mulway.



GO ON TO THE NEXT PAGE

**Questions 181–185** refer to the following summary and e-mail.

*Goalmarkk Research*

## Summary of market research study on four milkshake drinks

**Name of client**: Montroy's Spot

**Description**: Goalmarkk Research was hired by Montroy's Spot, a large chain of casual dining restaurants, to assess consumer reactions to four of its milkshake drinks. The study took place between mid-August and mid-September at the company's restaurant locations in Cleveland, Ohio and Pittsburgh, Pennsylvania. Participants were instructed to visit a restaurant in their local region, where they were randomly assigned one of the four flavors of milkshake drinks to sample. They then had to access a link via their mobile phone and take a survey consisting of multiple-choice and open-ended questions.

**Overall findings**:

| | |
|---|---|
| Sample #1 | ***Banana and cherry flavor***<br>Percent of respondents who indicated "*tasted great*" — 79%<br>Most frequent comments: "too much banana flavor," "couldn't taste much cherry" |
| Sample #2 | ***Pineapple and mango flavor***<br>Percent of respondents who indicated "*tasted great*" — 82%<br>Most frequent comments: "refreshing flavor," "not enough pineapple taste" |
| Sample #3 | ***Salted caramel flavor***<br>Percent of respondents who indicated "*tasted great*" — 84%<br>Most frequent comments: "Strong flavor," "attractive color" |
| Sample #4 | ***Coconut and vanilla flavor***<br>Percent of respondents who indicated "*tasted great*" — 87%<br>Most frequent comments: "thick texture," "just sweet enough" |

| | |
|---|---|
| To: | Barbara Milligan <b.milligan@goalmarkkresearch.com> |
| From: | Carl Pella <c.pella@goalmarkkresearch.com> |
| Date: | October 2 |
| Subject: | Results of Montroy's Spot research study |
| Attachment: | Graphs_and_tables |

Hi, Barbara,

As per your request, I have attached the graphs and tables for the report for Montroy's Spot. The electronic questionnaire you designed was quite effective in eliciting feedback. I'm pleased the survey process went so smoothly, especially considering our firm had never used the online format before.

Based on our previous studies for this client, most of the results were consistent with what I had projected. One finding, however, did stand out. What I had thought would be the least popular flavor ended up being the second most popular. I really hadn't anticipated this.

Let me know if you need any more information to support our recommendations for the client.

Thanks,

Carl

**181.** What is NOT stated about the market research study?
(A) It was conducted in two cities.
(B) It required the use of a mobile device.
(C) It had multiple-choice survey questions.
(D) Each of its participants sampled four drinks.

**182.** What feedback did two of the drink samples receive in common?
(A) The texture was too thick.
(B) The taste was refreshing.
(C) The flavor mix was uneven.
(D) The color was appealing.

**183.** What most likely is true about Montroy's Spot?
(A) It plans to expand into other regions.
(B) It is based in Pittsburgh.
(C) It offers a range of bottled beverages.
(D) It has consulted Goalmarkk Research in the past.

**184.** Which sample received more positive feedback than Mr. Pella had expected?
(A) Sample #1
(B) Sample #2
(C) Sample #3
(D) Sample #4

**185.** What is indicated about Ms. Milligan?
(A) She used to work for a food manufacturer.
(B) She created a firm's first electronic survey.
(C) She will meet with a client in October.
(D) She revised graphs for a market report.



GO ON TO THE NEXT PAGE

**Questions 186–190** refer to the following newsletter article, flyer, and e-mail.

## *Altarr Properties Newsletter*

***August Issue***

**Chicago**—At Altarr Properties, residents' comfort and convenience are important to us. That is why we are pleased to announce that we have formed a partnership with Laundry Flash, an on-demand service that will pick up a tenant's laundry and deliver the cleaned garments back to a convenient storage locker.

The service will be available in both of our apartment buildings. Installation of the lockers will take place on August 20 in the tenant lounge of the Menworth Building and August 27 across from the fitness center in the Courtway Building. Each tenant will receive a key for an assigned locker from the building manager. The front desk attendant in each building's lobby will be entrusted with signing in the Laundry Flash personnel.

Laundry pick-ups are easy to schedule via the company's Web site, www.laundry-flash.com. Turnaround time is two days, with a same-day express option available. Cleaning fees are $3 per shirt, $5 per pair of pants, and $15 per suit or dress. A discount coupon is provided on the company's flyer, available in the lobby.

## Laundry Flash

***We pick up, clean, and deliver your laundry back in 2 days—guaranteed!***

**Attention Residents of Altarr Properties' Buildings**
—we're all set to do business with you!

***Special Coupon (mention code 166)***
For residents of the Menworth Building and the Courtway Building, we are offering *10 percent off* any service totaling $20 or more.

- **How to Make a Service Request**
  Visit our Web site at www.laundry-flash.com and go to the online scheduling section. We are also available via phone at 555-0129.

- **Pickup Schedule**
  -NORTH ZONE (includes the Menworth Building at 5320 Avery Street)
  Monday, Wednesday, Friday.
  -SOUTH ZONE (includes the Courtway Building at 1811 Dixon Drive)
  Tuesday, Thursday, Saturday

- **Pricing** (standard 2-day service, includes pick-up and delivery)
  Shirt $3, Pair of Pants $5, Dress $8, Suit $15, Wash and Fold $1.60 per pound; same-day express service available for a $10 surcharge

- **Laundry Bags**
  Each customer will receive one complimentary laundry bag upon their first delivery—it is yours to keep for future service requests. Additional laundry bags can be purchased for $14 each.

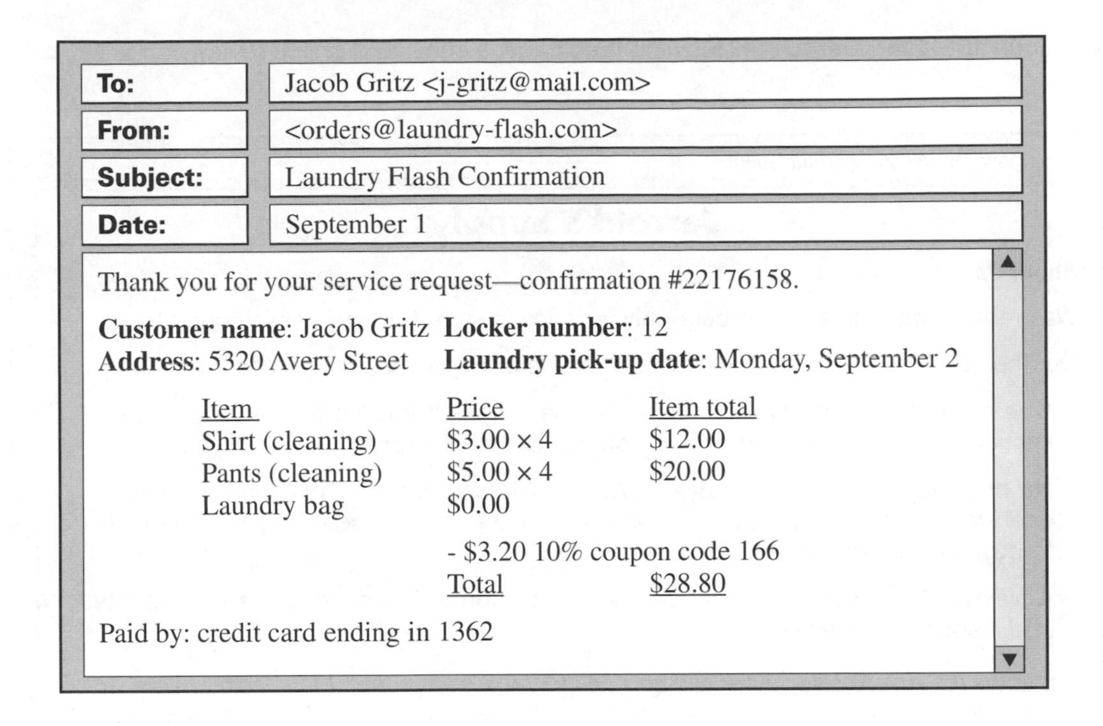

| To: | Jacob Gritz <j-gritz@mail.com> |
|---|---|
| From: | <orders@laundry-flash.com> |
| Subject: | Laundry Flash Confirmation |
| Date: | September 1 |

Thank you for your service request—confirmation #22176158.

**Customer name**: Jacob Gritz **Locker number**: 12
**Address**: 5320 Avery Street **Laundry pick-up date**: Monday, September 2

| Item | Price | Item total |
|---|---|---|
| Shirt (cleaning) | $3.00 × 4 | $12.00 |
| Pants (cleaning) | $5.00 × 4 | $20.00 |
| Laundry bag | $0.00 | |
| | - $3.20 10% coupon code 166 | |
| | Total | $28.80 |

Paid by: credit card ending in 1362

**186.** What is main purpose of the newsletter article?
(A) To solicit opinions from readers
(B) To thank tenants for their loyalty
(C) To give a progress report on renovations
(D) To give details about a new service

**187.** According to the newsletter article, what do the Menworth and the Courtway Buildings have in common?
(A) They have exercise facilities for residents.
(B) They will have lockers installed on the same day.
(C) They have the same number of rental units.
(D) They have attended front desks.

**188.** In the flyer, the word "set" in paragraph 1, line 2, is closest in meaning to
(A) estimated
(B) restored
(C) ready
(D) fixed

**189.** What information in the article may NOT be accurate?
(A) An expedited turnaround option
(B) A garment cleaning fee
(C) A Web address
(D) A coupon's availability

**190.** What most likely is true about Mr. Gritz?
(A) He requested an additional laundry bag.
(B) He lives in the Menworth Building.
(C) His clothing will be returned on a Tuesday.
(D) He will receive a discount for using a credit card.



GO ON TO THE NEXT PAGE

**Questions 191–195** refer to the following Web page, e-mail, and online review.

www.jerroldssupply.com/about

# Jerrold's Supply

About Us

We are the area's largest members-only warehouse store for food service operators.

Our membership is free for any qualified* business. Enjoy these great benefits:

- **One-stop shopping**—We stock food and beverages from all major brands, plus kitchen equipment and even chef's apparel. Get all of your supplies in just one trip.
- **No minimum purchase required**—We are different from Bascor Club and other open-to-the-public warehouse stores in the most important sense—you never have to buy items in bulk at Jerrold's Supply.
- **Advertised specials**—We keep our members informed with monthly e-mail updates about special sale events.

*Note: *We are a wholesale market and not open to the general public. Membership cards are issued only to those who own or manage a restaurant. On your first store visit, you must present a valid document showing you are licensed as a food service business. You will then be issued a card that is not transferable. You may, however, bring one guest shopper with you per month, as long as that person presents a photo ID upon entering.*

E-Mail message

**To:** Stella Adelson

**From:** Tina Rawley

**Date:** October 9

**Subject:** Tomorrow's errand - of interest?

Hi Stella,

I have to run over to Jerrold's Supply tomorrow morning to stock up on napkins and carry-out containers for the restaurant. You had once expressed interest in seeing the warehouse store, so I was wondering if you'd like to come along. I can pick you up in front of your apartment at 9 A.M. sharp. Please text or e-mail me back and let me know if you can make it.

For the visit, be sure to bring ID and wear comfortable shoes. The warehouse store has a large floor area, so there is a lot of walking. Also, if you'd like to look around the freezer section, bring some kind of outerwear. It's quite cold.

Hope to see you tomorrow,

Tina

**Reviewed by:** Stella Adelson **Reviewed on:** October 11

I visited Jerrold's Supply for the first time yesterday. Like Bascor Club, it is a warehouse store that sells goods at impressively low prices. But, unlike that store, it does not sell flat-screen TVs or computer equipment. Instead, it offers everything needed to keep a restaurant up and running. I saw paper napkins in huge packages of 6,000! Even more amazing was the vast selection of frozen seafood. I spent much longer in that area than I'd intended, and it made me wish I'd brought a sweater. The store is crowded and the checkout lines are long, but they move quickly. I am lucky that I know someone with a membership, so I was able to come as a guest while she was picking up supplies.



**191.** In the Web page, what is indicated about Jerrold's Supply?
(A) Its memberships may not be transferred.
(B) It is open every day of the week.
(C) It holds cooking classes for chefs.
(D) It has automated checkout stations.

**192.** What is required for a Jerrold's Supply membership card?
(A) An e-mailed invitation
(B) A minimum monthly purchase
(C) A valid business license
(D) Two forms of photo identification

**193.** What is NOT suggested about Bascor Club?
(A) It sells consumer electronics.
(B) The general public can shop there.
(C) Its goods are only available in large quantities.
(D) It shares a parent company with Jerrold's Supply.

**194.** In the e-mail, what is one thing Ms. Rawley mentions buying?
(A) Cookware
(B) Eating utensils
(C) Food packaging
(D) Raw ingredients

**195.** What is most likely true about Ms. Adelson?
(A) She did not follow some of Ms. Rawley's advice.
(B) Her trip to Jerrold's Supply was postponed.
(C) She did not end up traveling with Ms. Rawley.
(D) She visited Jerrold's Supply on an unusually busy day.

*GO ON TO THE NEXT PAGE*

**Questions 196–200** refer to the following presentation handout, agenda, and text message.

### *How To Improve Your Business's Web Site*

**Presented by:** Greg Wu, Web site consultant
**For:** Brexby Cycle Co. **Date:** May 2

***Strengths*** **of company's Web site:**

- Attractive color schemes—comfortable to look at while browsing the site
- Appealing photos of all product lines—size and spacing are appropriate
- Section titled "Why Take Up Cycling?" persuasively outlines health benefits of cycling

***Weaknesses*** **of company's Web site:**

- Too much text and information on each page—can be confusing
- Takes too much time to load—some customers may leave the site because of this
- Complicated checkout process for purchases—too many forms to fill out

***Action plan*****—at company's approval, will improve Web site by:**

- Removing a digital video that plays when the site is launched, which will greatly reduce the time needed for loading
- Streamlining the checkout process, while presenting the payment options (e.g., credit card, gift card, e-commerce accounts, etc.) with more prominent graphics
- Creating a separate section on the site for company's newest line of electric bikes, which would include a short explanation on how the bicycles are charged

**Brexby Cycle Co.**

### Proposed Agenda for May 30 Strategy Meeting*

| | |
|---|---|
| 2:00 P.M. | **Overview of topic**—Ongoing efforts to upgrade company Web site |
| 2:15 P.M. | **Item 1**—Walk-through of current site, with explanation of implemented (faster loading time, more visible payment options, added section for latest products) and rejected (shorter checkout process) suggestions from consultant |
| 3:00 P.M. | **Item 2**—Presentation by Digital Marketing Director Troy Vaden of additional, smaller modifications to site suggested during consultant's visit |
| 4:00 P.M. | **Item 3**—Discussion of pros and cons of offering online chat support; to be led by our in-house Web developer, Fred Calloway |
| 4:30 P.M. | **Item 4**—Brainstorming of potential interactive features for site |
| 5:00 P.M. | **Adjournment** |

**To be led by Sales Manager Allison Hull; attendees should bring laptop computers*

**From:** Fred Calloway [10:17 A.M. on May 30]

Hi, Allison. I just researched a competitor's Web site and found something interesting. One section provides a digital image of a bicycle that can be 'customized' by manipulating a computer mouse or touch screen. I'll show this to everyone at the meeting, so I'd like to allot 15 more minutes to our discussion on potential interactive features. Thanks.

**196.** What is NOT mentioned as a strong point of Brexby Cycle Co.'s Web site?
(A) The images of merchandise
(B) The choice of colors
(C) The size of text
(D) The content on cycling and health

**197.** What will attendees at the May 30 meeting most likely do?
(A) Debate the merits of a proposal
(B) Use borrowed laptop computers
(C) Listen to a consultant's presentation
(D) Decide on some deadlines for a project

**198.** What change most likely was made recently to Brexby Cycle Co.'s Web site?
(A) An explanation page was shortened.
(B) A digital video was eliminated.
(C) A payment process was simplified.
(D) A product category was modified.

**199.** In the text message, the word "manipulating" in line 4 is closest in meaning to
(A) tricking
(B) operating
(C) altering
(D) installing

**200.** What item on the agenda does Mr. Calloway want to schedule more time for?
(A) Item 1
(B) Item 2
(C) Item 3
(D) Item 4

**Stop! This is the end of the test. If you finish before time is called, you may go back to Parts 5, 6, and 7 and check your work.**

# ACTUAL TEST 

## READING TEST

In the Reading test, you will read a variety of texts and answer several different types of reading comprehension questions. The entire Reading test will last 75 minutes. There are three parts, and directions are given for each part. You are encouraged to answer as many questions as possible within the time allowed. You must mark your answers on the separate answer sheet. Do not write your answers in your test book.

## PART 5

**Directions:** A word or phrase is missing in each of the sentences below. Four answer choices are given below each sentence. Select the best answer to complete the sentence. Then mark the letter (A), (B), (C), or (D) on your answer sheet.

**101.** At the end of each group tour, participants will receive a souvenir photo that is ------- to keep.

(A) they
(B) them
(C) theirs
(D) themselves

**102.** The key to success in running an ethnic food restaurant is -------.

(A) authenticity
(B) authentic
(C) authenticate
(D) authentically

**103.** The city's landscape architects are working to ------- how more trees can be included in the Spencer Canal project.

(A) reflect
(B) encourage
(C) strengthen
(D) determine

**104.** A printed catalog with descriptions and images of our products can be mailed to customers ------- request.

(A) after
(B) on
(C) for
(D) along

**105.** Schandrax Ltd.'s mining machinery is designed to perform ------- even under the harshest conditions.

(A) successively
(B) reliably
(C) spaciously
(D) thoughtfully

**106.** It is recommended that novice hikers walk at a relaxed ------- and avoid going too fast, especially on steep trails.

(A) level
(B) stretch
(C) approach
(D) pace

**107.** Your home's heating system should be checked every six months to ensure that it is operating as ------- as possible.

(A) efficiency
(B) efficient
(C) efficiently
(D) more efficient

**108.** There are plans to build a new R&D center in East Hills City, but its exact location is ------- to be decided.

(A) enough
(B) once
(C) yet
(D) later

**109.** The Xtelia X10 mobile phone is so durable that it will not ------- any damage even if it is dropped onto a hard surface.

(A) terminate
(B) sustain
(C) diminish
(D) commit

**110.** Lahxmitech Ltd. develops ------- personal and business Web sites at affordable prices.

(A) impressive
(B) impress
(C) impressively
(D) impression

**111.** Fairview City's new recycling containers are free for residents and available ------- supplies last.

(A) toward
(B) during
(C) while
(D) within

**112.** The company's vision and objectives are summarized briefly ------- its mission statement.

(A) of
(B) to
(C) in
(D) about

**113.** The VT-5 exercise bike is ------- for small apartments because it occupies very little space.

(A) ideal
(B) deliberate
(C) convincing
(D) capable

**114.** Renarc Co.'s model building kits feature ------- labeled pieces that can be assembled with minimum effort.

(A) extremely
(B) remotely
(C) promptly
(D) explicitly

**115.** The winner of the photo contest, Mark Murdo, says he finds ------- in empty desert scenery.

(A) inspired
(B) to inspire
(C) inspirational
(D) inspiration

**116.** Thanks to new educational applications, mobile phones can ------- as learning tools in the classroom.

(A) be used
(B) be using
(C) have used
(D) use

**117.** Greenveld Park does not allow any vehicle traffic on its scenic road ------- its own tour buses that run on bio-fuels.

(A) throughout
(B) except for
(C) regardless of
(D) out of

**118.** A highly ------- interior designer, Alfonso Grieco provides design solutions for a wide variety of clients.

(A) accomplishing
(B) accomplished
(C) accomplishes
(D) accomplishment

**119.** The Mangim Career Fair is open to ------- who is seeking a new job, without regard to current employment status.

(A) every
(B) all
(C) those
(D) anyone

**120.** Recent research has found that social media posts have a limited ------- on people's buying decisions.

(A) value
(B) function
(C) association
(D) impact



*GO ON TO THE NEXT PAGE*

**121.** Jenebec Catering Co. allows clients to ------- their meal options to suit their exact tastes.

(A) fasten
(B) monitor
(C) customize
(D) patronize

**122.** Candidates will be asked for the names of three people who can provide ------- professional references for them.

(A) positives
(B) positivity
(C) positively
(D) positive

**123.** Members of the marketing team are contributing articles to online news outlets to attract ------- for our brand.

(A) publicity
(B) publically
(C) publicizes
(D) public

**124.** Ms. Booth plans to transfer to an overseas office ------- her replacement is properly trained.

(A) beginning from
(B) as soon as
(C) no earlier
(D) up to

**125.** When salespeople exceed their quarterly sales goals, the company rewards them ------- in the form of bonuses.

(A) financial
(B) financially
(C) finances
(D) financed

**126.** If the package had been lost in transit, the shipping company ------- to compensate for the loss.

(A) would have been offered
(B) will have offered
(C) had been offered
(D) would have offered

**127.** ------- you are traveling for leisure or business, it is important to choose a hotel with a convenient location.

(A) Notwithstanding
(B) Either
(C) Whether
(D) No matter

**128.** Unfortunately, the ------- wording of the contract led to there being multiple interpretations of its meaning.

(A) ambiguous
(B) forceful
(C) widespread
(D) skeptical

**129.** FNR Metals has earned ample recognition, including ------- the first local manufacturer to receive an "eco-friendly factory" certification.

(A) that is
(B) to be
(C) being
(D) is to be

**130.** Alarax Graphics can print all types of signs, in ------- shape and size may be required.

(A) whatever
(B) particular
(C) contrast
(D) any

## PART 6

**Directions:** Read the texts that follow. A word, phrase, or sentence is missing in parts of each text. Four answer choices for each question are given below the text. Select the best answer to complete the text. Then mark the letter (A), (B), (C), or (D) on your answer sheet.

**Questions 131–134** refer to the following e-mail.

To: Current clients
From: Saffler Shipping Co.
Subject: Update
Date: November 30

**UPDATE** for e-commerce businesses—*a solution for making return shipping labels*

The ongoing rise in online sales transactions means that e-commerce businesses may also need to handle more requests from customers who wish to return ------- **131.** merchandise that they purchased recently. Including a return label with each outbound package makes the process of sending items back ------- **132.** for the customer. A return label is a sticker stating the address of the company ------- **133.** the goods were purchased. ------- **134.** Saffler Shipping's label solution software makes elegant and functional return shipping labels. To try it out and create a sample label in just minutes, click here. You can then choose whether or not to purchase the software for your business.

**131.** (A) canceled
(B) unwanted
(C) unintended
(D) expired

**132.** (A) ease
(B) easily
(C) easier
(D) eased

**133.** (A) where
(B) whose
(C) that
(D) which

**134.** (A) It also has a barcode for tracking the package that is being returned.
(B) You may exchange merchandise that you are not completely satisfied with.
(C) For better results, we recommend that customers ship it at a later date.
(D) As an online business, you can sell goods from the comfort of your home.

GO ON TO THE NEXT PAGE

**Questions 135–138** refer to the following Web page.

**Longmont Real Estate, Inc.—virtual home tours**

Thanks to today's digital technology, homebuyers can now take virtual tours of homes and look at properties ------- (**135.**) leaving their own residence. By providing such tours for most of our properties, Longmont Real Estate is at the forefront of this industry revolution.

------- (**136.**). The tours ------- (**137.**) using a camera that provides three-dimensional images of all the spaces in each home. These images allow the viewer to "move" around the home digitally in the same manner they would in person.

Once virtual tours have been uploaded to our site, our clients can use a computer or mobile device to review a virtual tour from ------- (**138.**) anywhere. The technology is guaranteed to save prospective homebuyers hours of travel time and tens of dollars in gas.

To view our current properties for sale that offer virtual tours, click here.

**135.** (A) until
(B) inside
(C) without
(D) behind

**136.** (A) Home prices are increasing in some regions but staying steady in others.
(B) Surveyed shoppers also indicated that they prefer to visit homes in person.
(C) All of our virtual tours include photos and interactive videos of each property.
(D) If you have questions about this residence, one of our experts can help you.

**137.** (A) were being created
(B) are created
(C) would have been created
(D) will be created

**138.** (A) even
(B) not
(C) hardly
(D) almost

**Questions 139–142** refer to the following flyer.

***Explore Florham City's nature trails—with upgraded amenities!***

The Florham Parks and Recreation Department is proud to announce that its six-month trail improvement project has been completed in time for summer. -------. We thank you for your patience during the construction process.
**139.**

The upgrades include a new boardwalk that extends across Florham Park's pond, ------- providing access to wetland areas. -------, the well-traveled Blue Trail, a favorite for both local residents and out-of-town visitors, has been widened to accommodate more hikers. Many more small improvements have been made to other trails as well.
**140.** **141.**

From challenging climbs up steep hillsides to leisurely walks along flat meadows, the improved nature trails offer hikes for people of all -------. Interactive trail maps can be found by visiting www.florham-trails.org.
**142.**

**139.** (A) The park department's staff works closely with volunteers.
(B) Organized hiking clubs are becoming more and more popular.
(C) Our entire network of trails is now once again open to visitors.
(D) The city's park system has a long and interesting history.

**140.** (A) safe
(B) safety
(C) safest
(D) safely

**141.** (A) Still
(B) Instead
(C) For example
(D) In addition

**142.** (A) abilities
(B) holidays
(C) landscapes
(D) benefits



GO ON TO THE NEXT PAGE

**Questions 143–146** refer to the following information.

***Locally Grown Food—A Quick Overview***

There is no specific definition for locally grown food. However, it is generally understood to be food that is grown relatively close to its ------- (143.) of sale. Purchasing locally grown food can help regional economies ------- (144.) more money goes directly to the food growers. Local farmers almost never require the services of an outside distributor to get their products to market. -------. (145.) During much of the year, locally grown food ------- (146.) at farmers' markets and outdoor farm stands. Produce items are sold only when they are in season, so they are fresh and full of flavor. This means that buying locally grown food also has advantages for individual consumers.

**143.** (A) date
(B) point
(C) volume
(D) manner

**144.** (A) in that
(B) based on
(C) owing to
(D) in case

**145.** (A) Moreover, farmers may give gardening tips to visitors.
(B) In fact, eating a lot of processed foods may be less healthy.
(C) Therefore, the food transportation industry continues to grow.
(D) Thus, their earnings are more likely to stay within the region.

**146.** (A) available
(B) is available
(C) had been available
(D) to be available

# PART 7

**Directions:** In this part you will read a selection of texts, such as magazine and newspaper articles, e-mails, and instant messages. Each text or set of texts is followed by several questions. Select the best answer for each question and mark the letter (A), (B), (C), or (D) on your answer sheet.

**Questions 147–148** refer to the following receipt.

**Ayali Supermarket**
North Weaver City Branch
12 Devon Road
Store telephone: 555-0163

May 03 02:28 P.M.

| | |
|---|---|
| Blueberry muffins (5-pack) | $3.70 |
| Bottled water (12-pack) | $4.90 |
| Vegetable soup (small can) | $2.20 |
| Dried fruit snack (large bag) | $5.80 |
| ***TOTAL | $16.60 |
| CASH | $20.00 |
| CHANGE | $ 3.40 |

Thank you for shopping at our
North Weaver City location!

Store manager: Dave Soto
Your cashier: SELF-CHECKOUT, Station #3

Sign up at the customer service desk for a preferred shopper card and start saving money!

*********************************************

How are we doing? Visit www.ayali-survey.com and give us your feedback for the chance to win $500.* Use PIN number **334 05081** to log in and complete the survey.
**Inquire at the customer service counter for more details on the prize drawing*

**147.** What is NOT suggested about Ayali Supermarket?
(A) Its baked goods are made on the premises.
(B) It issues loyalty cards to some shoppers.
(C) It has more than one store location.
(D) Its customers can process their own purchases.

**148.** How are customers instructed to participate in a survey?
(A) By obtaining a form at a service counter
(B) By supplying a current phone number
(C) By accessing a designated Web site
(D) By speaking directly to management

GO ON TO THE NEXT PAGE

**Questions 149–150** refer to the following Web page.

**Customer reviews for: Dennward Co.**

**Latest posting:** June 9

**Posted by:** Jeff Andersen, District Manager, Standard Paper Company

Dennward Co. offers outstanding service. Owing to our recent expansion, I had to order extra uniforms for our newly hired production and warehouse staff on short notice. Dennward Co. provided us with what we needed and their delivery driver, Stan, was punctual and courteous. The quality of their clothing is excellent, and they can easily add a company logo. They are always responsive to a client's needs.

---

➥ **Company response:** Thanks, Mr. Andersen! Customer satisfaction has always been of utmost importance to Dennward Co. We were the first company in our region to employ ACPS (Advanced Client Processing System), an order management program that has won awards from the Business Software Developers Association. This cutting-edge solution enables us to track and sort orders faster and more accurately, giving us an on-time delivery rate of 99.6%.

**149.** What kind of business most likely is Dennward Co.?

(A) A food delivery service

(B) A manufacturer of paper products

(C) A building maintenance company

(D) A supplier of work apparel

**150.** What is indicated about ACPS?

(A) It has achieved industry recognition.

(B) It was tailored to suit Mr. Andersen's needs.

(C) It has been released in several versions.

(D) It is considered to be easy to use.

**Questions 151-152** refer to the following text-message chain.

**Brad Iqbal** **[10:40 A.M.]**
Maria, I just came down here to the computer room to install the new software. Did you know that the cooling system is acting strange again? It's pretty warm in here.

**Maria Dee** **[10:41 A.M.]**
Yes, we're aware of the problem. I just called the HVAC company to have a repair person come by.

**Brad Iqbal** **[10:42 A.M.]**
Really? Then I'll wait to finish this assignment until after they've fixed it. This temperature is uncomfortable.

**Maria Dee** **[10:43 A.M.]**
Are you sure? They're coming in tomorrow.

**Brad Iqbal** **[10:44 A.M.]**
Oh, I see. I guess there's no choice but to work in the heat.

**151.** Who most likely is Mr. Iqbal?
(A) An air conditioning repair person
(B) An office furniture installer
(C) A computer technician
(D) A building superintendent

**152.** At 10:43 A.M., what most likely does Ms. Dee mean when she writes, "They're coming in tomorrow"?
(A) She does not yet have some information.
(B) She will not be available to provide assistance.
(C) Mr. Iqbal should hurry to complete a task.
(D) A delay might be longer than Mr. Iqbal expected.

GO ON TO THE NEXT PAGE

**Questions 153–154** refer to the following e-mail.

| **To:** | Constance Baylor <constance-baylor@mail.com> |
|---|---|
| **From:** | <greenbrandtbooks@green-brandt.com> |
| **Subject:** | Your purchase |
| **Date:** | August 1 |

Dear Ms. Baylor,

Thank you for shopping with us. We would like to inform you that the book you ordered, *Carpentry for Novices*, was damaged during processing due to an unexpected malfunction with our mailing machine. However, we do have a used copy of this same book, with a slightly faded back cover and a small moisture stain on the bottom edge. Its pages are clean, with no folds or markings of any kind.

If you are interested in ordering this replacement book, we will credit $7.00 to your customer account to reflect its price difference with a new copy.

Please reply to this e-mail by Monday (August 4) to let us know how you would like to proceed. Otherwise, we will automatically cancel your order and return the full amount of the purchase price to you.

Thank you for your understanding,

All of us at Greenbrandt Books

**153.** Why most likely was the e-mail written?

(A) To give information about a new discount program

(B) To notify Ms. Baylor about a problem with her order

(C) To provide an explanation for a price increase

(D) To clarify guidelines for purchasing collectible books

**154.** What most likely will happen if Ms. Baylor does not respond to the e-mail by Monday?

(A) She will not earn a bonus credit.

(B) She will be given a substitute item.

(C) She will receive a full refund.

(D) She will lose an opportunity to upgrade her account.

**Questions 155–157** refer to the following press release.

## Storeymoore Theater Company Debuts Online Programming

**For Immediate Release (June 22)**—The Storeymoore Theater Company (STC) concluded its last season with a successful run of its highly-praised stage comedy *The Big Family Reunion*. The production, which brought in the biggest crowds in the company's history, included post-performance panel discussions on the play's topic—the joyful aspects of family gatherings. These lively conversations led the STC's public relations director, Gloria Chatham, to come up with the idea of developing an audio podcast in which the company's crew members talk about the creative processes in theater. —[1]—. The first episode, titled "Why Design Matters," was posted on June 19. It features an engaging conversation between Hal Brady, the costume designer for *The Big Family Reunion*, and Michelle Lindley, the play's stage designer. —[2]—. The second episode will go up on June 26 and will include a conversation with the play's director. —[3]—. Chatham plans to continue posting 30-minute episodes each week, or perhaps twice a week. —[4]—. The public can listen to the podcast for free by visiting www.stc-theater.org/podcast.

**155.** What is indicated about *The Big Family Reunion*?

(A) Its cast included Gloria Chatham.
(B) It had two different directors.
(C) It set an attendance record.
(D) It had high production costs.

**156.** What is stated about the STC's podcast?

(A) It was inspired by panel discussions.
(B) It will be funded by audience donations.
(C) It requires listeners to have a paid subscription.
(D) It was developed especially for journalists.

**157.** In which of the positions marked [1], [2], [3], and [4] does the following sentence best belong?

"She noted, however, that it can take a few days to produce just one half-hour program."

(A) [1]
(B) [2]
(C) [3]
(D) [4]



GO ON TO THE NEXT PAGE

**Questions 158–160** refer to the following online list.

*Nigerian Sources—West Africa's most trusted business journal* *Online Edition*

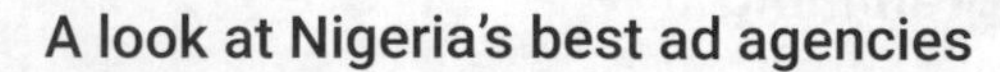
A look at Nigeria's best ad agencies

**Posted**: 1 day ago **by** Madalina Ikande 1242 views

In recent months, many of our subscribers have suggested that we publish a list of the top advertising agencies in Nigeria. The agencies listed below have been recommended enthusiastically by the business leaders I've interviewed in the past for this publication.

**Marketing Reach**—Founded 20 years ago, Marketing Reach is one of the largest ad agencies in Nigeria, with branches in the cities of Lagos and Abuja. To meet the needs of Dangoumie Food Manufacturing, a major client, the firm recently opened a field office in Senegal to conduct market research studies.

**Fusiontekk**—In its four years of operation, this domestic agency, with offices in Lagos and Abuja, has become highly respected for its digital marketing campaigns. Last year it added Sunmurru Brands, a maker of instant noodle products, to its client base. It was for this company that the agency created an award-winning series of online advertisements.

**Olouwaa Solutions**—This decade-old specialty agency has offices in Nigeria, Ghana, and Kenya. Unlike many other agencies, it focuses mainly on helping client companies develop and introduce new brands. Recently, it was tasked with ensuring a successful launch for BCC Industries' line of packaged snacks. The agency is also known for having partnered with Prospectar Tech to develop Infomatt-Plus, a software program that enables businesses to create online customer surveys in service of improving their brand image.

**158.** Who most likely is Ms. Ikande?

(A) The owner of an advertising agency
(B) The manager of a bookstore
(C) A software developer
(D) A business reporter

**159.** What do the listed advertising agencies have in common?

(A) They have offices in more than one country.
(B) They have been in business for over five years.
(C) They work with clients in the food industry.
(D) They are headquartered in the same city.

**160.** What is Infomatt-Plus most likely used to do?

(A) Track public mentions of brands
(B) Collect customer feedback
(C) Analyze market research data
(D) Manage social media accounts

**Questions 161–163** refer to the following information.

**Rohnart Properties**

*RENTING SOON > The Dunmawr Building, an amenity-rich rental complex at 2 Snyder Street*

The Dunmawr Building stretches across nearly an entire city block and combines comfortable apartment living with an abundance of amenities, including a ground-floor fitness center with an indoor pool. The spacious lobby acts as a co-working space for tenants, and the building is just steps away from neighborhood shops and restaurants. Built originally as a garment production facility, the Dunmawr Building possesses a vintage look and beautifully preserved architectural details. Its 38 units consist of one-bedroom and two-bedroom apartments in a variety of layouts.

Available for occupancy starting July 1. Apply before June 5 and Rohnart Properties will waive its customary $50 fee to process new applications.

**161.** What is the information mainly about?
(A) An opening ceremony
(B) City neighborhoods
(C) Residential vacancies
(D) A business opportunity

**162.** What is indicated about the Dunmawr Building?
(A) It has entrances on two streets.
(B) It has outdoor recreation facilities.
(C) It was previously a factory.
(D) It is in a historic district.

**163.** What is suggested about Rohnart Properties?
(A) It usually charges a fee to rental applicants.
(B) It specializes in commercial properties.
(C) It offers short-term leases to renters.
(D) It plans to hire additional staff members.



GO ON TO THE NEXT PAGE

**Questions 164–167** refer to the following e-mail.

| | |
|---|---|
| **From:** | Nutrition Newsletter <healthnutrition-newsletter@maynard.edu> |
| **To:** | Janet Lee <j.lee@mail.com> |
| **Subject:** | MU Nutrition Newsletter |
| **Date:** | March 1 |

**Maynard University Nutrition Newsletter** 

Dear Ms. Lee,

These days, we have become overloaded with information about healthy eating. A vast number of sources, from TV shows to online cooking forums, dispense conflicting nutritional advice of questionable scientific authority. —[1]—. This leads me to bring up the primary reason you can trust everything you read in each monthly Maynard University Nutrition Newsletter.

Each article has been researched by the editorial staff and by leading nutrition experts at the Maynard University School of Nutritional Science, and gives science-based health advice that is easy to follow. —[2]—. What's more, the newsletter carries no advertising, giving us the freedom to discuss the nutritional quality of popular foods without any obligation to please corporate advertisers in the food industry.

Our current newsletter, for example, contains an impartial guide to the healthiest types of pasta. We invite you to sample the online version of this issue, in its entirety, by visiting www.mu-health.com and entering the code "A12." We are doing so in the hopes that you will want to subscribe to our extraordinary publication. —[3]—. With our introductory discount, you can subscribe to the print or digital edition for one year for $32—a savings of 35% from our regular rate.

We are reaching out to you because our records indicate you currently receive free "health update" e-mails from our university's alumni Web site. —[4]—. Our monthly newsletter provides even more detailed health guidance, so we urge you to take advantage of this special offer.

Sincerely,

David Ahmed
Editorial Director, Maynard University Nutrition Newsletter

**164.** What is the main purpose of the e-mail?
(A) To give an update on a newsletter's new editorial policies
(B) To compare health recommendations made by various experts
(C) To outline the benefits of a subscription-based publication
(D) To propose a collaboration on a series of articles

**165.** What most likely is true about the newsletter?
(A) It is no longer sold in a print edition.
(B) It does not have advertisements.
(C) It is aimed primarily at scientists.
(D) It is associated with a television show.

**166.** What is suggested about Ms. Lee?
(A) She graduated from Maynard University.
(B) She teaches an online cooking class.
(C) She used to work with Mr. Ahmed.
(D) She attempted to cancel a free service.

**167.** In which of the positions marked [1], [2], [3], and [4] does the following sentence best belong?
"The newsletter is always written in simple language, not full of complex medical terminology."
(A) [1]
(B) [2]
(C) [3]
(D) [4]

**Questions 168–171** refer to the following online chat discussion.

**Live chat**

| | | |
|---|---|---|
| **Amir Nazari** | **[9:22 A.M.]** | Hi, all. I'm here in the conference room practicing the presentation for our team. I just reviewed the slides with side-by-side comparisons of the original and new logos, with descriptions of the changes we made. They look good. |
| **Nadia Ghosn** | **[9:23 A.M.]** | Did you add my slides showing the reasons for our selection of graphics? |
| **Amir Nazari** | **[9:24 A.M.]** | Yes, they were very helpful. |
| **Nadia Ghosn** | **[9:25 A.M.]** | How does the video look on screen? |
| **Amir Nazari** | **[9:26 A.M.]** | That's our problem. It's not playing. |
| **Linda Wade** | **[9:27 A.M.]** | Try changing its format. |
| **Amir Nazari** | **[9:28 A.M.]** | OK. Just a minute. |
| **Nadia Ghosn** | **[9:37 A.M.]** | Any luck? |
| **Amir Nazari** | **[9:38 A.M.]** | Got it. It's working now. |
| **Linda Wade** | **[9:39 A.M.]** | Did the suggestion help? |
| **Amir Nazari** | **[9:40 A.M.]** | As always. |
| **Dale Kang** | **[9:41 A.M.]** | Remember too that you can pause the video with the remote control unit. You may want to try it out a few times. The buttons can be tricky. |
| **Amir Nazari** | **[9:42 A.M.]** | Good idea—thanks. |

**168.** What most likely is the topic of the team's presentation?

(A) Revisions to the design of a logo
(B) Present and future sales forecasts
(C) An overview of competing brands
(D) How to describe a product's features

**169.** What is suggested about Mr. Nazari?

(A) He has not seen a promotional film yet.
(B) He gives workshops on presentation strategies.
(C) He hired all the graphic designers on the work team.
(D) He incorporated Ms. Ghosn's content into a presentation.

**170.** At 9:40 A.M., what does Mr. Nazari most likely mean when he writes, "As always"?

(A) The team regularly has to make changes on short notice.
(B) A colleague gives dependable troubleshooting advice.
(C) A problem occurs repeatedly on a computer.
(D) He often assists with converting the format of videos.

**171.** What does Mr. Kang suggest Mr. Nazari do?

(A) Memorize an introduction
(B) Brainstorm potential audience questions
(C) Schedule a break between sections
(D) Practice using an accessory



*GO ON TO THE NEXT PAGE*

**Questions 172–175** refer to the following article.

## Heritage museum showcases memorabilia from everyday life

HAZLETT VIEW—The Keeler Heritage Museum has been called "a hidden gem" by visitors who have explored its huge collection of vintage treasures. The museum is home to more than 30,000 items, displayed in four massive buildings on a repurposed farm complex. The exhibits represent the personal collection of Marvin Keeler, a lifelong resident of Hazlett View who has been gathering up local memorabilia since his childhood. Today, he is often seen relaxing in the museum's garden pavilion, where visitors can try their hand at operating the antique farm equipment on display. "It was Mr. Keeler's dream to start a museum," said facility manager Julia Halstead, who now leads tours for small groups.

The museum's exhibits and historical timelines cover a variety of aspects of daily life in the region. Part of the museum shows off memorabilia from local industries, including an intact seating booth and service counter from Centralia Diner, which Mr. Keeler owned and operated until his retirement. A wide range of other historical items are on exhibit, from antique printing presses to old school uniforms. Exploring the museum, many visitors connect the exhibits with their own memories of past times.

The museum is located at 1100 Ridge Road, just outside the small town of Hazlett View. It is open seven days a week, from 8 A.M. to 5 P.M. Admission is $8 for adults and $5 for students. Visitors should set aside three or more hours to view all of the museum's objects in a leisurely manner. The museum also offers a membership program that allows access to a range of special events. For more information on the museum, visit www.keeler-mus.org.

**172.** What is NOT mentioned about the museum's collection?
(A) It features interactive exhibits.
(B) It is housed in multiple buildings.
(C) It displays sections of Mr. Keeler's former business.
(D) It includes objects donated by past visitors.

**173.** The word "cover" in paragraph 2, line 2 is closest in meaning to
(A) fill in for
(B) relate to
(C) enclose
(D) guarantee

**174.** What is implied about Mr. Keeler?
(A) He also operates a local jewelry store.
(B) He purchased a farm from Ms. Halstead.
(C) He grew up near the site of his museum.
(D) He has taken up gardening as a hobby.

**175.** What does the writer of the article recommend doing?
(A) Allowing several hours to look around a facility
(B) Buying single tickets through a Web site
(C) Enrolling in a new membership program
(D) Participating in a special group tour

GO ON TO THE NEXT PAGE

**Questions 176–180** refer to the following online review and response.

*Reviews Plus* —The area's top online review site

Review of Alerro's Bistro by: Matt Browski

**Matt Browski's** profile → Reviews Plus member for: 5 years 7 months

Total reviews posted: 32 Photos posted: 11

The quality of the food at Alerro's Bistro is good, but it could be better considering the prices that are charged. I ordered a tofu burger ($13.00), a bowl of mushroom soup ($7.00), cross-cut fries ($8.00), and a "farm special" salad plate ($9.00). Everything was reasonably tasty. There are several healthy salad options, but for some reason the taco salad was removed from the menu. I've had it here before and wish it would be brought back. In general, the food here would appeal to health-conscious diners who are not concerned with fancy artisanal food preparation. The most positive part of my visit was the responsiveness of the staff. Even though the small dining room was busy when I visited, I waited less than a minute for a server to arrive at my table.

↪ Response from: Lisa Trapani, General Manager, Alerro's Bistro

Hi Matt,

Thank you for your feedback. We pride ourselves on our hospitality and, above all, our high standards for sourcing food ingredients. In particular, all of our fries are made from organically grown potatoes. As supplies have been tight this season, we recently had to source some potatoes from a different grower. Accordingly, the charge for that dish was not applied to your bill. We hope that you noticed this gesture; if not, you can confirm it by checking your receipt.

We are certain we can offer you a better experience than the most recent one you had, so we would like to invite you back to our restaurant. Could you send me a message through this site and provide your e-mail address? Our customer service supervisor would like to know more about your visit.

Thank you again,

Lisa Trapani, www.alerro-bistro.com

**176.** What does Mr. Browski imply about the food at Alerro's Bistro?

(A) It is served in large portions.

(B) It is prepared in a simple way.

(C) Its prices are surprisingly low.

(D) It does not match the dining room's décor.

**177.** What most likely is true about Mr. Browski?

(A) He has eaten at Alerro's Bistro previously.

(B) He is an employee of a local health food store.

(C) He posts pictures with each of his online reviews.

(D) He went to Alerro's Bistro on a weekday.

**178.** In the response, the word "tight" in paragraph 1, line 3, is closest in meaning to

(A) strict

(B) lacking

(C) closely packed

(D) strongly fixed

**179.** Which amount was most likely removed from Mr. Browski's bill?

(A) $7.00

(B) $8.00

(C) $9.00

(D) $13.00

**180.** What does Ms. Trapani suggest that she will do if Mr. Browski responds?

(A) Refund the full cost of his meal

(B) Share his complaints with a business owner

(C) Send him an electronic coupon

(D) Pass on his contact details



GO ON TO THE NEXT PAGE

**Questions 181–185** refer to the following Web page and e-mail.

**Welcome to Brightlane Publishing!**

Brightlane Publishing is a publisher of cutting-edge guidebooks on marketing strategy. Since our founding nearly 15 years ago, we have put out hundreds of popular and useful titles. Here are our newest releases:

***Write Better Product Descriptions*** In this illustrated volume, noted advertising copy-writer Jack Schoeffel gives practical advice on writing product descriptions that generate sales. This is Mr. Schoeffel's debut book, and we are confident it will become a classic in its field. *Paperback - $27 + $5 shipping, Electronic edition $13*

***Start a Hotel Business*** This inspiring book focuses on entrepreneurship, making it different from any of our previous releases. The lively text, written by hospitality expert Hugh Tsangaras, lays down key principles for getting a hotel business off the ground, even in regions without a strong tourism base. *Paperback - $22 + $4 shipping*

***Boost Your E-Commerce Sales*** This book's author, Lois Mazza, holds the view that marketing skills are even more important than technical expertise in building a profitable online business. She supplies tips for increasing your online sales, and lists contact information for top e-commerce consultants. *Paperback - $29 + $6 shipping, Electronic edition $14*

***Selling via Social Media*** Written by *Online Age* magazine editor Amy Kang, this comprehensive volume provides detailed direction on effective selling via social media sites, and includes a bonus 24-page pocket book listing words that are proven to increase sales. *Hardcover - $37 + $7 shipping*

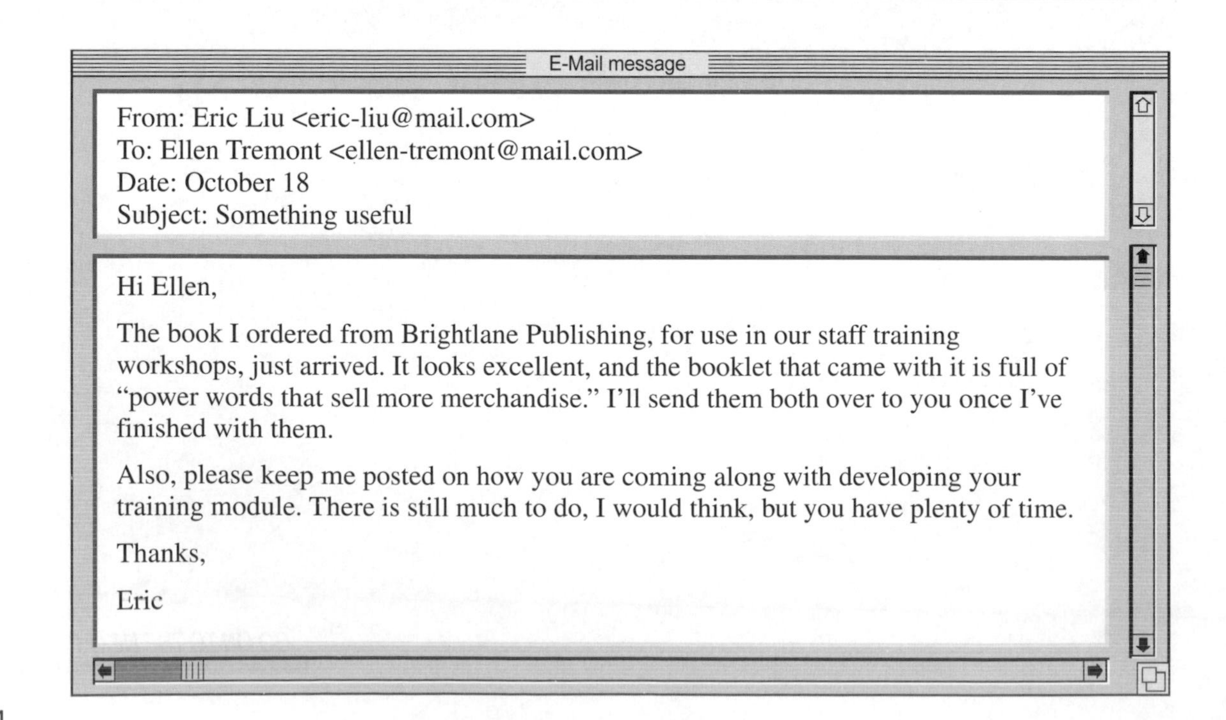

E-Mail message

From: Eric Liu <eric-liu@mail.com>
To: Ellen Tremont <ellen-tremont@mail.com>
Date: October 18
Subject: Something useful

Hi Ellen,

The book I ordered from Brightlane Publishing, for use in our staff training workshops, just arrived. It looks excellent, and the booklet that came with it is full of "power words that sell more merchandise." I'll send them both over to you once I've finished with them.

Also, please keep me posted on how you are coming along with developing your training module. There is still much to do, I would think, but you have plenty of time.

Thanks,

Eric

**181.** What most likely is NOT true about Brightlane Publishing?

(A) It published a work by a first-time author.

(B) It imposes a separate charge for delivery.

(C) It offers digital editions for some titles.

(D) It was founded by a magazine editor.

**182.** What is suggested about *Start a Hotel Business*?

(A) It cannot be shipped to some regions.

(B) It is the first book of its type for the publisher.

(C) It is recommended by experts in the tourism industry.

(D) It took longer to write than the other new titles.

**183.** In the Web page, the word "holds" in paragraph 4 line 1, is closest in meaning to

(A) contains

(B) secures

(C) adheres to

(D) suspends

**184.** Which book did Mr. Liu most likely purchase recently?

(A) *Write Better Product Descriptions*

(B) *Start a Hotel Business*

(C) *Boost Your E-commerce Sales*

(D) *Selling via Social Media*

**185.** What does Mr. Liu ask Ms. Tremont to do?

(A) Provide him with a progress report on a project

(B) Find a replacement leader for a training session

(C) Proofread the content of a staff presentation

(D) Reimburse him for a business expense

**Questions 186–190** refer to the following Web page, meeting summary, and online registration form.

http://www.cityofstenley.gov/services/recycling-waste

**Stenley City** >> *Recycling and Waste Removal Services for Residents*

➢ Stenley City contracts with Grunby Industries Co. (GIC) to collect waste from all parts of the city. Non-recyclable waste is first taken to the Stenley City Transfer Facility (SCTF) on the city's north side, and then transported to a landfill. All recyclable material is sent to the GIC-managed recycling facility for on-site processing. Recyclable waste must be placed by the curb before 6:00 A.M. on your designated recycling pick-up day each week. The city provides every home and business with one (1) of each type of bin for recyclables:

➢ Blue—for household recyclables, including cans and bottles

➢ Red—for compostable yard waste, such as weeds and leaves*

➢ Green—for all other yard waste, including branches and tree limbs

➢ Yellow—for electronic waste, including computers and peripherals, mobile phones, and electrical accessories

*Pick-up available from mid-March to mid-December

**Summary of Stenley City regular weekly meeting for Tuesday, April 28**

**Attending:** Mayor Ray Conley, Director of Waste Management Drew Morro, All Members of the Budget Committee, GIC representative Eunice Woo

**New mobile application:** Mr. Morro announced that the *Recycling Reminder* mobile phone app, created by GIC (Grunby Industries Co.) specifically for city residents, will go live on Friday, May 1. Ms. Woo, the lead developer of the app, gave a demonstration on navigating its features. Mr. Morro confirmed that the weekly recycling pick-up schedule will be divided into the following sectors: Zone 1 (residences with "North" addresses) — every Tuesday; Zone 2 (businesses with "North" addresses) — every Wednesday; Zone 3 (residences with "South" addresses) — every Thursday; Zone 4 (businesses with "South" addresses) — every Friday. The first pick-up dates for the month will be May 5, 6, 7, and 8 for Zones 1, 2, 3, and 4 respectively.

***Recycling Reminder***
**Registration Screen**

**Complete the fields below and press "submit" to register for reminders.**

**Today's date** May 1

**Name of resident** Debbie Guarini **E-mail** Debbie@mail.com

**Address** 1736 Bradley Street North

**Type of property:** [V] **residential** [ ] **commercial**

**(Optional) Ask the *Recycling Helper* your question.**

**How do I dispose of** *computer keyboards and speakers, power cables* **?**

submit

*You will receive a reminder text message one day before your pick-up day each week.*
*Recycling Helper is available to advise you on which container to use.*

**186.** What is mentioned about the GIC?
(A) It is expanding its information technology department.
(B) It operates its own recycling facility.
(C) It manufactures recycling containers.
(D) It is located next to the SCTF.

**187.** What is most likely true about Stenley City?
(A) Many of its residential properties include outdoor land.
(B) Its non-recyclable waste is transported overseas.
(C) It does not pick up some recyclables in November.
(D) It asks citizens to dispose of glass separately from metal.

**188.** What is stated about Ms. Woo?
(A) She is a member of a financial committee.
(B) She is currently a resident of Stenley City.
(C) She illustrated how to use a mobile app on April 28.
(D) She used to work in Mr. Conley's office.

**189.** When most likely will Ms. Guarini receive a reminder message?
(A) On May 4
(B) On May 5
(C) On May 6
(D) On May 7

**190.** What container will Ms. Guarini need to use for the waste she inquired about?
(A) A blue bin
(B) A red bin
(C) A green bin
(D) A yellow bin



GO ON TO THE NEXT PAGE

**Questions 191–195** refer to the following announcement, entry form, and e-mail.

## Enter *Barbados Life* magazine's photo contest!

Your winning photograph could be seen by our magazine's more than 70,000 readers living in Barbados and internationally. Our photo contest is open to all amateur photographers—that is, anyone who does not earn any income as a photographer. All entrants must be residents of Barbados. Each entrant may submit up to 10 images in any one category.

Please ensure that your entry form—available via www.magazine-contest.com—and your photos are submitted electronically no later than February 15.

The top three photos will appear in our June special issue, *Best of Barbados*, and Honorable Mention entrants will be mentioned by name. Our editors will also review Honorable Mention photos for inclusion in future monthly issues. If we wish to run your photo in the magazine, we will contact you to arrange for its one-time use.

**Prizes in each category:**

**First Place — $300 cash** | **Third Place — a two-year subscription to Barbados Life**
**Second Place — $150 cash** | **Honorable Mention — A *Barbados Life* T-shirt**

Questions? E-mail us at editor@barbados-mag.com

## Barbados Life Photo Contest

### Entry Form

**Category of photo(s):**

_________ Festivals (taken at an event)
____v____ Wildlife (animals, insects, or plants)
_________ Scenery (views and vistas)

**Name:** Ida Serrano  **E-mail address:** serrano@mail.com

**Please attach a title and description to each photo, specifying where and when it was taken. In the space below, explain any unique circumstances surrounding the photo(s):**

I captured these images while I was leading tours as a volunteer guide.

**Signature:** *Ida Serrano*

E-Mail message

| | |
|---|---|
| **From:** | James Marlin <marlin@barbados-mag.com> |
| **To:** | Ida Serrano <serrano@mail.com> |
| **Date:** | April 17 |
| **Subject:** | Congratulations! |

Dear Ms. Serrano,

Congratulations—*Barbados Life* magazine has recognized one of your photographs (Butterfly #2), taken at the Tropical Butterfly Garden on January 24, as an Honorable Mention photo. We have confirmed that you have met all entry requirements. To claim your prize, please e-mail me back within five days. In your e-mail, please confirm that it is OK for us to include your name in our special issue.

Please e-mail me if you have any questions as well.

Regards,

James Marlin, Photo Editor

**191.** What does the announcement indicate about *Barbados Life* magazine?

(A) It comes out every other month.
(B) It has readers outside of Barbados.
(C) It has photo contests for each issue.
(D) It sponsors Barbadian festivals.

**192.** In the announcement, the word "run" in paragraph 3, line 4, is closest in meaning to

(A) edit
(B) oversee
(C) evaluate
(D) print

**193.** What most likely is NOT true about Ida Serrano?

(A) She submitted 10 or fewer images.
(B) Her income does not come from photography.
(C) Her entry was received after February 15.
(D) She is a current resident of Barbados.

**194.** What is suggested about one of Ms. Serrano's photos?

(A) It will be featured on a T-shirt design.
(B) It was taken during a tour of a garden.
(C) It was entered in two different categories.
(D) It will be recognized with a cash award.

**195.** What does Mr. Marlin ask Ms. Serrano to do?

(A) Give permission for her name to be published
(B) Create a list of other suitable prizes as substitutes
(C) Direct future inquiries to another department
(D) Confirm her home address for a mailing



GO ON TO THE NEXT PAGE

**Questions 196–200** refer to the following article, column, and Web page.

**Birley City News** **March 20**

## *New manager has new marketing plans for Birley Hotel*

*By Sarah Cozzi, Business Writer*

Located on Frontage Road, which separates Dahlman and Henley Counties, the 200-year-old Birley Hotel is surrounded by shaded gardens and offers a relaxing stay for guests.

During my visit, facility manager Monica Hu told me she has ambitious marketing plans for the hotel, which is owned by local entrepreneur Dan Crosby. Mr. Crosby hired her late last year to allow him to focus more on his growing, three-year-old café business.

As we talked, I mentioned that the hotel's Web site did not fully represent the facility's luxurious amenities. She smiled as she picked up a tablet device and pointed out a page on the newly-redesigned site showcasing images of each beautifully-decorated guest room. She then discussed her efforts to promote the hotel as a launch point for exploring Henley County, which boasts many attractions but receives far fewer visitors than Dahlman County. She says the hotel's new brochures encourage visitors to "experience Henley County."

Ms. Hu said she also plans to rework the Birley's dinner menu to include options to "match every budget." Currently, its gift shop sells artisanal herbs and spices created by Mr. Crosby.

**Birley City News** March 24

## *Exploring Henley County*

*By Jim Skandar, Travel Columnist*

Birley City—Recently, I stayed at the Birley Hotel and explored the charming attractions of Henley County. The hotel's manager put me in contact with Brian Kuzo, president of the Henley County Tourist Association (HCTA), and he guided my daylong tour of the county. It began with a delicious breakfast at Lite Bistro, one of several highly-rated restaurants located near the hotel. We then stopped at Grayley Town, a famous arts community, and toured Paxton Park historical village. The highlight of the trip was a narrated cruise down Paxton Canal in an open-air barge. Mr. Kuzo showed great enthusiasm for the region, and I highly recommend seeing its many sights.

www.birleyhotel.com/home

***Stay at the Birley Hotel—and experience Henley County***

| **Relax**<br>*Learn about our services* | **Stay**<br>*View our rooms* |
| --- | --- |
| **Eat**<br>*See our meal menus* | **Discover**<br>*Explore nearby attractions* |

* The Birley Hotel welcomes group events. A large conference room, with a projector and speaker system, is available for rental. The hotel also features charging stations for electric bikes and cars, which are free to guests and $15 for non-guests.

**196.** What most likely is true about the Birley Hotel?
(A) It has recently increased its occupancy rates.
(B) It is decorated with vintage furniture.
(C) It offered a discounted stay to a columnist.
(D) It sells food-related products made by its owner.

**197.** Which section of the Web site did Ms. Hu show Ms. Cozzi?
(A) Relax
(B) Stay
(C) Eat
(D) Discover

**198.** What is implied about Mr. Kuzo?
(A) He was referred by Ms. Hu to a columnist.
(B) He hosted a meal at one of Mr. Crosby's cafés.
(C) He spoke to Ms. Cozzi during a sightseeing trip.
(D) He designed a brochure for the Birley Hotel.

**199.** What is indicated about Henley County?
(A) It receives more tourists than Dahlman County.
(B) It was settled before Dahlman County.
(C) Its visitors can take boat tours.
(D) Its parks were expanded recently.

**200.** What does the hotel offer guests at no charge?
(A) Use of audiovisual equipment
(B) Workshops on plant care techniques
(C) Charging facilities for electric vehicles
(D) Laundering of some types of clothing

**Stop! This is the end of the test. If you finish before time is called, you may go back to Parts 5, 6, and 7 and check your work.**

# ACTUAL TEST 

## READING TEST

In the Reading test, you will read a variety of texts and answer several different types of reading comprehension questions. The entire Reading test will last 75 minutes. There are three parts, and directions are given for each part. You are encouraged to answer as many questions as possible within the time allowed. You must mark your answers on the separate answer sheet. Do not write your answers in your test book.

## PART 5

**Directions:** A word or phrase is missing in each of the sentences below. Four answer choices are given below each sentence. Select the best answer to complete the sentence. Then mark the letter (A), (B), (C), or (D) on your answer sheet.

**101.** Providing excellent support to customers is ------- with Woshett's online chat platform.
(A) simply
(B) simple
(C) simplify
(D) simplifying

**102.** With its affordability and straightforward design, the Cruiser 10 sewing machine is a great choice for ------- sewers.
(A) durable
(B) wealthy
(C) casual
(D) fresh

**103.** Meese, Inc. expects sales of its hair care products to improve when it ------- their prices next month.
(A) will lower
(B) lowers
(C) had lowered
(D) is lowered

**104.** The candidate said it was the prospect of frequent international travel that caused him to ------- the promotion to manager.
(A) retreat
(B) withhold
(C) enroll
(D) decline

**105.** While it represented a personal record, Ms. Polk's score was not high ------- to qualify her for the national competition.
(A) anyway
(B) enough
(C) much
(D) up

**106.** All of the department's fall courses will take place as initially scheduled ------- "Ethics in Nursing," which has been moved to Tuesday evenings.
(A) except
(B) on
(C) for
(D) during

**107.** Mr. Wellington has requested a hotel adjacent to the conference center for ------- and two coworkers.
(A) he
(B) his own
(C) himself
(D) his

**108.** Because of the office's open floor plan, employees must use unoccupied meeting rooms to hold ------- phone conversations.
(A) privately
(B) privacy
(C) private
(D) privatized

**109.** In order to maintain your wooden furniture, Hilge Home recommends ------- rubbing coconut oil into its surface.

(A) carelessly
(B) occasionally
(C) unexpectedly
(D) recently

**110.** The studio reluctantly allowed the director to cast Mel Frazier, ------- is better known for his television work, as the star of her film.

(A) someone
(B) whoever
(C) who
(D) that

**111.** Company regulations state that shift supervisors have the ------- to assign tasks to employees.

(A) amenity
(B) adjustment
(C) intention
(D) authority

**112.** Apontle's poorly designed mobile app requires users to ------- enter their log-in information each time they open it.

(A) repeatedly
(B) repetition
(C) repetitive
(D) repeat

**113.** Many participants in Pittman Group's survey of urban consumers preferred name-brand products ------- generic ones.

(A) just as
(B) down to
(C) over
(D) toward

**114.** After several years of operating under restricted budgets, we have become accustomed to ------- unnecessary expenses.

(A) avoid
(B) avoided
(C) avoidance
(D) avoiding

**115.** Because of rumors that it has security issues, passengers are ------- to use the metro system's payment card.

(A) critical
(B) sensitive
(C) unsuitable
(D) hesitant

**116.** Mr. Bailey's latest book offers readers interested in real estate investment practical ------- on entering the field.

(A) guide
(B) guidance
(C) guidable
(D) guiding

**117.** Corporate policies must be easy for staff to understand and ------- enforced by management.

(A) consistently
(B) relatively
(C) shortly
(D) supposedly

**118.** ------- her session drew almost 30 people, Ms. Sato endeavored to speak individually with each at least once.

(A) Nevertheless
(B) Although
(C) Prior to
(D) Apart from

**119.** Building ample bike parking facilities is just one of the ------- Stounville has taken to promote cycling among the public.

(A) indicators
(B) objectives
(C) measures
(D) terms

**120.** Members of the Osborne Opera Supporters Club receive ------- access to discounts on tickets and merchandise.

(A) exclusive
(B) excludes
(C) exclude
(D) exclusively



*GO ON TO THE NEXT PAGE*

**121.** Ever since we began advertising in *Enterprising Now*, business travelers ------- our hotel in large numbers.

(A) visited

(B) were visiting

(C) would have visited

(D) have been visiting

**122.** Ms. Philips has built a strong relationship with her team at the Beijing branch ------- their cultural differences.

(A) on behalf of

(B) in addition to

(C) notwithstanding

(D) in exchange for

**123.** The ------- of workshops to a full day will enable each one to cover significantly more information.

(A) lengthening

(B) lengthiest

(C) lengthen

(D) length

**124.** Choosing to specialize in wedding planning may ------- to be one of the best decisions Vohan Events has made.

(A) unite

(B) prove

(C) envision

(D) strive

**125.** ------- Zinte Apparel decides not to have us run its marketing campaign, this quarter is still on track to be one of our most successful ever.

(A) Upon

(B) As soon as

(C) In order that

(D) Even if

**126.** It is actually easier to reach Caswell Waterfall by Summers Road than by the ------- traveled Highway 24.

(A) more frequent

(B) most frequent

(C) most frequently

(D) more frequently

**127.** Patrons of Mason Café are ------- to connect to our wireless Internet service using the password on their receipt.

(A) possible

(B) welcome

(C) suggested

(D) beneficial

**128.** Consultants have recommended that the store's loyalty program ------- to offer more immediate and tangible rewards.

(A) be redesigned

(B) was to redesign

(C) was redesigned

(D) will be redesigning

**129.** The electronic time tracking system notifies supervisors when workers are ------- reach their weekly limit of working hours.

(A) nearly

(B) close to

(C) about to

(D) within

**130.** Frigigo's refrigerated trucks ensure that food items do not undergo dangerous ------- in temperature during delivery.

(A) fluctuations

(B) boundaries

(C) sensations

(D) standards

## PART 6

**Directions:** Read the texts that follow. A word, phrase, or sentence is missing in parts of each text. Four answer choices for each question are given below the text. Select the best answer to complete the text. Then mark the letter (A), (B), (C), or (D) on your answer sheet.

**Questions 131–134** refer to the following e-mail.

From: <accounts@final-tally.com>
To: Tonya Bell
Subject: End of Free Trial
Date: February 7

Dear Ms. Bell,

Your free trial of Final Tally ------- (131.) to end on February 10. That means that you have just 3 days left of comprehensive cloud-based accounting solutions. We hope that Final Tally has helped you not just organize your small business's day-to-day finances but also understand its ------- (132.) financial situation. If you would like to keep using Final Tally, please log in to your account and become a paid subscriber.

If you do not buy a subscription, you will have 60 days to retrieve any materials you are storing in Final Tally. ------- (133.), all data associated with your account will be deleted. Also, if there is a particular reason you end up deciding not to subscribe, please let us know.

------- (134.).

Thanks,

The Final Tally Team

**131.** (A) is scheduled
(B) was scheduled
(C) has scheduled
(D) scheduled

**132.** (A) preliminary
(B) assorted
(C) overall
(D) foremost

**133.** (A) Meanwhile
(B) However
(C) Therefore
(D) Afterward

**134.** (A) We have been eagerly awaiting your reply.
(B) We are always looking for ways to improve.
(C) We have several options that may be appropriate.
(D) We love to share praise with the rest of our team.

GO ON TO THE NEXT PAGE

**Questions 135–138** refer to the following instructions.

**Instructions for Fingerprinting**

Clear impressions of your fingers and thumbs are necessary in order to confirm that you are eligible for a long-term visa. ------- (**135.**) your own fingerprints, you will need a black ink pad. Roll a single finger on the ink pad so that it becomes evenly coated in ink. Find the box on the background check form that ------- (**136.**) to that finger. Press one side of the finger into it and roll toward the other side of the finger, maintaining an even amount of pressure. Repeat the procedure for all other fingers. You may attempt to retake unclear impressions only if there is sufficient space ------- (**137.**) in the appropriate box. ------- (**138.**).

**135.** (A) Take
(B) To take
(C) Having taken
(D) The taking of

**136.** (A) devotes
(B) designates
(C) corresponds
(D) consents

**137.** (A) remained
(B) remaining
(C) remainder
(D) remains

**138.** (A) Doing so would cause serious imperfections in the fingerprint.
(B) You will not need to be fingerprinted again until shortly before that date.
(C) Finally, allow the participant to thoroughly wipe his or her hands off.
(D) Otherwise, please start the process over with a new copy of the form.

**Questions 139–142** refer to the following memo.

From: Jerry Moore
To: All employees
Re: Accounting area

Hi everyone,

Following the recent remodel, many employees have been choosing to pass through the accountants' area in order to go from the front entrance to the break room or vice versa. I understand that this way is the ------- (139.), but this practice cannot be allowed to continue. The accountants have reported that they find it very distracting. ------- (140.). On my advice, they have tried locking the door and directly asking the employees who do this to stop, but ------- (141.) effort has succeeded. Therefore, building maintenance has given its permission to block off the door between the accounting area and the break room with heavy furniture. This memo is intended to notify you all that from tomorrow, the door will be absolutely unusable. Please adjust your ------- (142.) accordingly.

Jerry Moore
Head of Human Resources

**139.** (A) convenient
(B) convenience
(C) most convenient
(D) more conveniently

**140.** (A) If you are having a similar problem, we can speak to management together.
(B) The break room would be a better place for such a conversation anyway.
(C) Please knock first to give them some warning that you are approaching.
(D) More importantly, they need to be able to work on confidential materials freely.

**141.** (A) this
(B) any
(C) their
(D) neither

**142.** (A) routes
(B) priorities
(C) estimates
(D) greetings



*GO ON TO THE NEXT PAGE*

**Questions 143–146** refer to the following article.

**Lewitts Episode of *On The Case* To Air**

LEWITTS (October 2)—An episode of the television drama *On The Case* that was shot ------- (143.) in Lewitts will be broadcast on NBO tonight at nine.

The show stars Farida Abboud and Henry Bryant as detectives who travel around the country solving crimes. In tonight's episode, they visit the ------- (144.) town of Marndale to investigate a disappearance.

Several locations around Lewitts, including the courthouse, Kelley Park, and Butler General Store, were chosen to embody the places imagined by the show's staff. ------- (145.). As usual, though, the beginning and end of the episode were shot on sets in Dromery City.

Town official Albert Cheong said he hopes that the broadcast attracts the ------- (146.) of other productions: "We would welcome more film and television projects."

**143.** (A) primarily
(B) highly
(C) overly
(D) exclusively

**144.** (A) authentic
(B) fictional
(C) adjacent
(D) diverse

**145.** (A) All other sites require a permit from Lewitts's government.
(B) Residents should expect traffic disruptions in these areas.
(C) The scenes were filmed over a one-week period in August.
(D) So far, the episode has been well-received by critics and viewers.

**146.** (A) attendant
(B) most attentive
(C) attention
(D) attending

## PART 7

**Directions:** In this part you will read a selection of texts, such as magazine and newspaper articles, e-mails, and instant messages. Each text or set of texts is followed by several questions. Select the best answer for each question and mark the letter (A), (B), (C), or (D) on your answer sheet.

**Questions 147–148** refer to the following Web page.

www.leampter.com/order

**The Leampter Company**

**Order Summary**

Please review your order before completing it.

Ship to: c/o Derrick McGuire
University of Bowmoss
Maintenance Department
1660 University Ave.
Bowmoss, MS 38637

Payment method: Credit card ending in 0455
Billing address: *Same as shipping*
Shipping preference: Standard Ground Shipping

| Product | Quantity | Unit Price | Total |
|---|---|---|---|
| Medium-strength trash bags (box of 200) | 5 | $25.00 | $125.00 |
| 13-watt fluorescent light bulbs (box of 12) | 1 | $4.20 | $4.20 |
| 12-volt cordless drill | 1 | $129.00 | $129.00 |
| Chemical-resistant rubber gloves (box of 10) | 2 | $10.40 | $20.80 |
| | | Shipping | $24.99 |
| | | **Total** | $303.99 |

Promotional code: ____________

**Place Order**

**147.** What kind of business most likely is the Leampter Company?
(A) A furniture store
(B) A hardware retailer
(C) An office supplies distributor
(D) An auto parts manufacturer

**148.** What information has Mr. McGuire NOT provided?
(A) Where the order should be sent
(B) How the goods should be shipped
(C) What he will use to make a payment
(D) Why he is eligible for a discount

GO ON TO THE NEXT PAGE

**Questions 149–150** refer to the following online chat discussion.

**Judy Klein [2:14 P.M.]**
Eric, I'm glad I caught you online. I ran into a problem processing your travel reimbursement request this morning.

**Eric Holland [2:15 P.M.]**
Hi, Judy. What was the issue?

**Judy Klein [2:16 P.M.]**
Sorry, but could you give me a second? I thought I had the form right here, but I've been working on a few other files since then.

**Eric Holland [2:16 P.M.]**
Sure.

**Judy Klein [2:19 P.M.]**
OK, here we are. In the "Miscellaneous" section, you listed a $24.38 charge on May 25, but I can't read your handwriting in the description box. Do you remember what you wrote there? It looks like it starts with an "h."

**Eric Holland [2:20 P.M.]**
Hmm. I'll come over to your desk.

**Judy Klein [2:21 P.M.]**
Oh, that would be great. See you in a minute.

**149.** What is suggested about Ms. Klein?
(A) She is often interrupted by questions from colleagues.
(B) She sometimes has trouble opening a software program.
(C) She retrieved some pages from a printer before the chat.
(D) She is searching for some paperwork during part of the chat.

**150.** At 2:20 P.M., what does Mr. Holland imply when he writes, "I'll come over to your desk"?
(A) He needs a request to be processed quickly.
(B) He prefers to submit a physical copy of a form.
(C) He cannot recall how he spent some funds.
(D) He is offering to demonstrate a procedure.

**Questions 151–152** refer to the following article.

## A New Way to Get News

(October 15)—For more than 70 years, the *Boldwin Times* has been Boldwin citizens' preferred source of daily news. These days, however, people want to learn about news events as they happen, not once a day. For this reason, we released the Boldwin Times app this morning as an even more convenient alternative to our Web site.

With our app, readers can get the same in-depth local coverage and insightful analyses of regional and national news that they have come to expect from our print and online editions. However, they can also use its customizable notifications feature to receive alerts about breaking news stories that are of interest to them. The app's content is free for the first month and just $4.99 per month after that. Visit any major app store today to download it.

**151.** What is the purpose of the article?
(A) To advertise a digital product
(B) To inform about a local trend
(C) To summarize a company's history
(D) To announce the launch of a new column

**152.** What is indicated about the *Boldwin Times?*
(A) It used to be the most popular publication in the region.
(B) It is famous for its business news coverage.
(C) There is more than one way to access its content.
(D) Many of its readers live outside of Boldwin.



*GO ON TO THE NEXT PAGE*

**Questions 153–155** refer to the following advertisement.

## *Enjoy both dinner and a movie at Hasley Cinema!*

Funfare Hall, Hasley Cinema's new dine-in theater, is open for business! Ticketholders to all screenings in the hall can enjoy not just popcorn but also less traditional movie fare like hamburgers and pizza. —[1]—. Our waiters will take your order and serve the food at your seat, which is extra-wide and equipped with a retractable tray table. Funfare Hall's unique dining-and-viewing experience is an exciting addition to the cinema that the *Billegant Herald* has already called "the top choice for film enthusiasts in Billegant." —[2]—.

### *Special events at Hasley Cinema in March:*

Director's Screening of *Southerland*: Come to Funfare Hall on March 19 to see the thoughtful new drama before its wide release. —[3]—. After the screening, director Tanesha Robson will discuss the film and take questions from the audience.

Kids Tuesdays: Every Tuesday morning in March, parents can bring kids under six years old to screenings of child-friendly movies for just $5 per adult and $2 per child. —[4]—.

**153.** What is NOT mentioned about Funfare Hall?

(A) It is the site of an upcoming preview screening.

(B) Its patrons can order a variety of foods.

(C) It was reviewed in a magazine.

(D) Its seating is spacious.

**154.** What is indicated about a weekly event in March?

(A) It is intended for groups of schoolchildren.

(B) Its ticket prices are lower for some viewers.

(C) Its schedule includes an interactive discussion.

(D) It offers an opportunity to see older films.

**155.** In which of the positions marked [1], [2], [3], and [4] does the following sentence best belong?

"And all of this is available at the touch of a button—even while the film is playing!"

(A) [1]

(B) [2]

(C) [3]

(D) [4]

**Questions 156–158** refer to the following customer review.

www.tradespeoplereview.com

**Home >> Cities >> Omaha >> Plumbers >> Fulton Plumbing**

**Reviewed by: Harper Quintero** Posted: March 22

My friend had a bathroom renovation done by Chad Fulton and his team, and she recommended the business to me. When I discovered that water was dripping from my kitchen faucet even when it was turned all the way off, I contacted Fulton Plumbing to resolve the issue. The representative I spoke to was able to provide an estimate over the phone, and it was an affordable price. But what I want to emphasize is how quickly the workers arrived—just twenty minutes after I made the call! This is definitely the best thing about the service, even though it wasn't really necessary in my case because my issue was unlikely to cause water damage. But I can see how those in emergency situations would really appreciate it. Anyway, Mr. Fulton and the employee accompanying him carried out the work quickly and professionally. I certainly recommend Fulton Plumbing.

**156.** Why did Ms. Quintero hire Fulton Plumbing?
(A) To improve a home's water pressure
(B) To have a faulty tap repaired
(C) To renovate a bathroom
(D) To hook up a kitchen appliance

**157.** What aspect of Fulton Plumbing does Ms. Quintero provide the most detail on?
(A) Its variety of service options
(B) Its employees' attitudes
(C) Its work fees
(D) Its response time

**158.** What is implied about the service Fulton Plumbing provided?
(A) It is the company's specialty.
(B) Ms. Quintero did not regard it as urgently needed.
(C) Ms. Quintero had obtained it from another provider before.
(D) It included a consultation visit.



GO ON TO THE NEXT PAGE

**Questions 159–160** refer to the following advertisement.

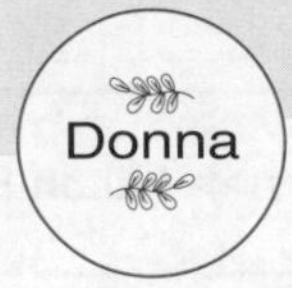


# Master of Greenery

Does your office use plants to create a nurturing work environment? Or is there only a potted fern sitting at the foot of the receptionist's desk, with the rest of the decorations composed of boring paintings?

Unfortunately, most offices miss out on the joys of a vibrant assortment of flora because they are concerned that it will not be easy to keep the plants alive. Did you know that there are many plant species that are extremely resilient and don't need fancy soil or frequent watering, though?

Let Donna recommend which plants to buy and how to arrange them to maximize the desired effects. When she redesigns your office with a thoughtful selection of plants that require little upkeep, you'll be amazed at the resulting improvements in staff morale and productivity. Call Donna today at (990) 555-0107 to get started.

**159.** According to the advertisement, why do most offices choose not to have many plants?

(A) They are expensive to buy.
(B) They give off strong smells.
(C) They create a low-energy atmosphere.
(D) They seem difficult to care for properly.

**160.** What type of service is being advertised?

(A) Regular on-site plant tending
(B) Advice on decorating with plants
(C) Lessons on how to grow plants
(D) Disposal of unwanted plants

**Questions 161–164** refer to the following e-mail.

E-Mail message

| | |
|---|---|
| From: | Douglas McCoy |
| To: | Itsumi Wakimoto |
| Subject: | Trial results |
| Date: | January 28 |
| Attachment: | Report |

Hi Ms. Wakimoto,

I just received the report on the trial of our new safety measure, and the results are clear: conducting a job hazard analysis (JHA) before construction begins has a positive effect on keeping projects on track and reducing cost. The full report is attached, but I'll summarize the key points here.

We implemented the measure on three projects—Robinson Tower, Sparks Apartments, and Bryant Market—over the past two years, and had Broseley Consulting analyze and compare those projects to our other projects that took place in the same period. Because of the injuries and other problems that the JHA prevented, Robinson Tower and Bryant Market were completed 8% and 11% faster and cost 6% and 10% less than similar projects, respectively. Sparks Apartments was merely average in both categories, but considering that it faced major problems due to unseasonable regional weather, this is excellent. For comparison, the Hubert Building, which ran into similar issues, was 15% more behind schedule and cost 13% more than average.

Remember, the initial time and money spent to conduct the JHA is *already* factored into this data. It seems pretty clear to me that we should implement this process on all projects as soon as possible. When you're ready, why don't we meet to talk about how to present this idea to the other departments? Let me know.

Sincerely,

Doug

**161.** What measure was most likely tested in the trial?
(A) Immediately investigating incidents of injury
(B) Studying potential dangers to workers ahead of time
(C) Encouraging workers to suggest safety improvements
(D) Requiring additional qualifications for certain positions

**162.** What is indicated about the trial?
(A) It lasted longer than initially planned.
(B) It involved an external company.
(C) Its findings were unexpected.
(D) Its data will be released publicly.

**163.** Which project was completed the most successfully?
(A) Robinson Tower
(B) Sparks Apartments
(C) Bryant Market
(D) The Hubert Building

**164.** What does Mr. McCoy suggest doing?
(A) Creating a promotional strategy
(B) Researching service providers
(C) Double-checking some calculations
(D) Streamlining an implementation process

GO ON TO THE NEXT PAGE

**Questions 165–167** refer to the following memo.

## MEMO

To: Jem Fashion Directors
From: Larry May, Supply and Control Manager
Date: October 2
Re: Operational updates

As you know, it has been a busy year for us in the Jem Fashion operations department. We have overseen the opening of five new manufacturing hubs, and I am pleased to announce that all five are now fully operational. Goods are being produced at a rapid rate in line with the targets we set last year.

However, I have concerns about one particular area of our business. After liaising with the customer services team, it became clear to me that our goods are not being delivered within the timeframe promised to our customers. I personally conducted investigations into this and discovered the delivery company we currently use has an insufficient number of vehicles to meet our demands. This has led to a backlog of orders and many customer complaints.

Therefore, I propose meeting with the head of the delivery firm to discuss the terms of our contract with them. We need to hold them accountable for this problem and demand changes to the document as necessary. If you have any concerns about or suggestions for taking this step, please call me at extension 553 or e-mail me at larry.may@jem-fashion.com.

Larry

**165.** What is stated about Jem Fashion?
(A) It achieved record profits last year.
(B) It has reorganized a department.
(C) It has launched a new product line.
(D) It recently underwent an expansion.

**166.** What problem does Mr. May mention?
(A) Orders are not being completed on time.
(B) A manufacturing facility is not yet operational.
(C) Merchandise has been found to be defective.
(D) Delivery vehicles are frequently breaking down.

**167.** What does Mr. May propose that Jem Fashion do?
(A) Replace an account manager
(B) Revise a complaints procedure
(C) Renegotiate an agreement
(D) Make a public apology



GO ON TO THE NEXT PAGE

**Questions 168–171** refer to the following letter.

**Goodwin Place Condominium Association**

9070 Bradley Street
Abentel, ON N0G 1Y0

18 August

Julio Salazar
Unit 503

Dear Mr. Salazar,

Greetings from the Goodwin Place Condominium Association. We are writing to officially inform you of an addition to our condominium bylaws. From 1 September, unit owners will no longer be allowed to let any part of their unit for short-term rental (less than six months). —[1]—. You may be familiar with this practice as "using Owillo.com," but this ban applies to short-term rentals set up through any channels, even offline ones.

As you are likely aware, this addition is the result of a formal vote among association members following months of discussion. As such, it is legally binding for all members, and violating the rule even a single time will result in a substantial fine. —[2]—. For details, see the full text of the rule (Article 9, Section B, Clause 12), which is enclosed.

We hope that those among you who voted against the ban will keep in mind the considerable benefits of not allowing short-term rental. First, it will eliminate the security issues created by a constant stream of non-residents coming and going from our grounds. —[3]—. Moreover, it will preserve the spirit of Goodwin Place as a community of friendly neighbors.

To confirm that you understand this change, please sign the enclosed form and return it to the association office by 31 August. —[4]—. Note that refusal to sign does not exempt you from the rule.

Sincerely,

*Courtney Graham*

President
Goodwin Place Condominium Association

Encl.

**168.** What most likely can people use Owillo.com to do?

(A) Arrange paid stays on their property

(B) Communicate with their neighbors

(C) Report issues with common spaces

(D) View estimated values of homes in their area

**169.** What does the letter come with?

(A) A form for casting a vote

(B) A timeline for some maintenance work

(C) A collection of statistics

(D) An excerpt from a set of regulations

**170.** What is suggested about some residents of Goodwin Place?

(A) They requested a safety inspection.

(B) They expressed opposition to a proposal.

(C) They have incurred some financial penalties.

(D) They would like to make alterations to their units.

**171.** In which of the positions marked [1], [2], [3], and [4] does the following sentence best belong?

"Multiple violations will provoke legal action by the association."

(A) [1]

(B) [2]

(C) [3]

(D) [4]

ACTUAL TEST 09 PART 7

GO ON TO THE NEXT PAGE

**Questions 172–175** refer to the following online chat discussion.

Brather Public Library | Staff Chat

**Clifton Sanders** [10:19 a.m.]
Hey, Amanda and Jeffrey. I'm going through the comment cards that we got from book club participants this past week, and there's an issue I think you should know about.

**Amanda Thomas** [10:20 a.m.]
What is it, Clifton?

**Clifton Sanders** [10:22 a.m.]
More than half of the participants of the Classics Club wrote something like, "The leader isn't doing a good job of moderating the discussion." It seems that Sabrina—the leader of that group—lets one of the participants talk too much.

**Amanda Thomas** [10:23 a.m.]
Ah, yes, that's the group that Doyle is in this year. He's one of the library's regular book club participants, and he tends to dominate the conversation if the leader isn't assertive.

**Jeffrey Shim** [10:24 a.m.]
Oh, Doyle! It's too bad that Sabrina has to deal with him her first time leading a club.

**Clifton Sanders** [10:25 a.m.]
Should I just give her a summary of the feedback as usual, or does this require some kind of special response?

**Amanda Thomas** [10:26 a.m.]
We should do something about it. I'll sit down with her and give her some tips for balancing the participants' contributions better. But I need to run to a meeting right now. Is there anything else, Clifton?

**Jeffrey Shim** [10:27 a.m.]
I have a pretty good relationship with Sabrina, and I've had to lead a group with Doyle in it before. Maybe I should be the one to speak with her.

**Amanda Thomas** [10:28 a.m.]
Sure, Jeffrey. That sounds good.

**Clifton Sanders** [10:29 a.m.]
Thanks, Jeffrey. OK, talk to you both later.

**172.** What are the writers discussing?
(A) Advertisements for an upcoming event
(B) Book selections for a reading club
(C) Evaluations of a library program
(D) Inefficiencies in an automated process

**173.** What is indicated about Sabrina?
(A) She is new to a role.
(B) She is an aspiring author.
(C) She is an unpaid volunteer.
(D) She is free to take on an assignment.

**174.** At 10:26 A.M., what does Ms. Thomas mean when she writes, "Is there anything else, Clifton?"
(A) She hopes there is an alternative way to resolve a problem.
(B) She does not have enough information to make a decision.
(C) She is concerned that she has forgotten about a task.
(D) She wants to know if it is acceptable to end the chat.

**175.** What does Mr. Shim state that he has experience with?
(A) Handling a difficult patron
(B) Providing training on a skill
(C) Giving tours of a building
(D) Editing a type of writing



*GO ON TO THE NEXT PAGE*

**Questions 176–180** refer to the following information and e-mail.

## Montara Campground

### Information on Camping Facilities

Montara Campground is an excellent lodging option for visitors to Montara National Park. Its team of rangers is always ready to recommend hiking trails, fishing spots, and fun activities—and even answer questions about their iconic flat hats! Restroom and shower facilities at the campground are shared among all campers, and the following campsites are available for rent (fire pit included with all sites):

-Pioneer ($15/night): Space for one tent and one vehicle
-Adventurer ($20/night): Space for one tent and one vehicle (picnic table included)
-Explorer ($18/night): Space for one motor home
-Pathfinder ($26/night): Space for one motor home (water and electricity included)

Please note that demand is high in early March, when the park first opens for the season, and on national holidays, so advance booking is strongly advised.

To make a booking at Montara Campground, visit www.campingmontara.gov.

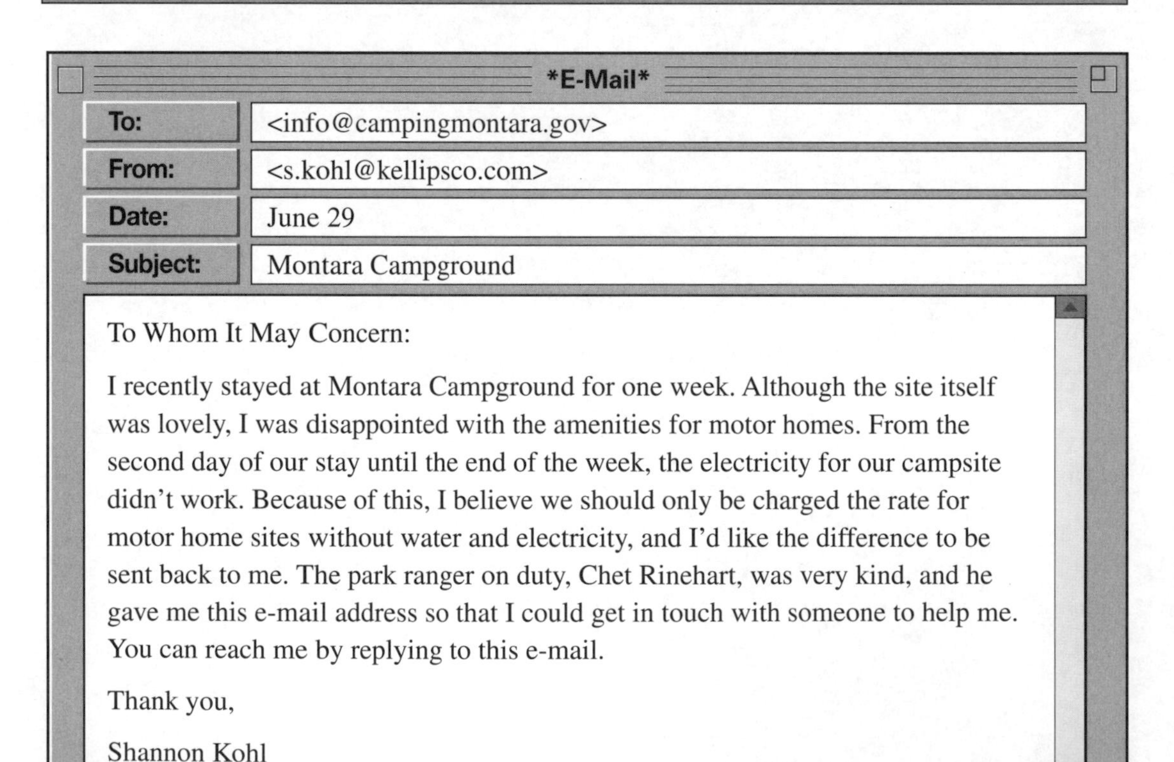

*E-Mail*

**To:** <info@campingmontara.gov>
**From:** <s.kohl@kellipsco.com>
**Date:** June 29
**Subject:** Montara Campground

To Whom It May Concern:

I recently stayed at Montara Campground for one week. Although the site itself was lovely, I was disappointed with the amenities for motor homes. From the second day of our stay until the end of the week, the electricity for our campsite didn't work. Because of this, I believe we should only be charged the rate for motor home sites without water and electricity, and I'd like the difference to be sent back to me. The park ranger on duty, Chet Rinehart, was very kind, and he gave me this e-mail address so that I could get in touch with someone to help me. You can reach me by replying to this e-mail.

Thank you,

Shannon Kohl

**176.** In the information, the word "shared" in paragraph 1, line 4, is closest in meaning to
(A) divided
(B) discussed
(C) made known
(D) used in common

**177.** What is implied about Montara National Park?
(A) It is located in a region with a wet climate.
(B) It receives more visitors than any other national park.
(C) It is closed for part of the year.
(D) It has recently hired more park rangers.

**178.** Why did Ms. Kohl write the e-mail?
(A) To suggest revising a description
(B) To request a partial refund
(C) To explain a negative review
(D) To check the status of a complaint

**179.** What type of campsite did Ms. Kohl most likely reserve?
(A) Pioneer
(B) Adventurer
(C) Explorer
(D) Pathfinder

**180.** What is indicated about Mr. Rinehart?
(A) He wears a special type of headgear at work.
(B) He recommended moving to a different campsite.
(C) He had temporary access to a fire pit.
(D) He leads hikes on a famous mountain.



GO ON TO THE NEXT PAGE

**Questions 181–185** refer to the following conference schedule and notice.

## Association of Retail Pharmacy Managers (ARPM) 11th Annual Conference

**Schedule for: Day 2 — December 4**

| | | |
|---|---|---|
| 8:00–9:00 A.M. | Shuttle service from designated hotels | |
| 9:15–9:30 A.M. | Remarks by Anita Morrison, ARPM Executive Vice President | Main Auditorium |
| 9:30 – 10:45 A.M. | Morning Session 1<br>"Refining Your Sales and Marketing Strategy"<br>*Drew Espino, Consultant, Caruso Pharmaceutical Solutions* | Main Auditorium |
| 11:00 A.M.– 12:15 P.M. | Morning Session 2<br>"Is It Time to Upgrade Your Point-of-Sale Technology?"<br>*Kelly Powell, Editor, 'Retail Pharmacy Today' Web site* | Main Auditorium |
| 12:30–2:00 P.M. | Lunch Buffet | South Hall |
| 2:00–3:15 P.M. | Afternoon Session 1<br>"Effective Staff Training on Patient Care"<br>*Marshall Holloway, Manager, Allsworth Pharmacy* | Main Auditorium |
| 3:30–4:45 P.M. | Afternoon Session 2<br>"Get Ready: Future Trends in Retail Pharmacy"<br>*Radka Bielik, Professor, Paxon University College of Pharmacy* | Main Auditorium |
| 5:00–8:00 P.M. | Closing Banquet | Grand Ballroom |

- See www.arpm-conf.com for information about each speaker and their session.
- The last half hour of each session will be reserved for audience Q&A.
- Refreshments will be available outside the auditorium during the morning and afternoon breaks.

## Notice

For personal reasons, Marshall Holloway will be unable to join us today to give his scheduled session, "Effective Staff Training on Patient Care." Sarah Hughes, our standby speaker and the ARPM's chief operating officer, will lead a replacement session. In a presentation entitled "How to Find and Eliminate Inefficiency," she will describe her five-step system for identifying and addressing issues that waste pharmacies' time and money. Attendees who feel strongly inconvenienced by this change and would prefer financial compensation over attending Ms. Hughes's presentation must make this request at the registration desk before the session begins.

In addition, conference center management has informed us that the South Hall's catering fridge failed last night, spoiling much of the food that would have been served at lunch today. Please use the attached voucher to purchase lunch at a nearby restaurant instead. Tonight's dinner event will go forward as planned.

We apologize deeply for these inconveniences and ask for your understanding.

—Organizers of the ARPM 11th Annual Conference

181. What is most likely true about the conference?

(A) It takes place over a two-day period.

(B) Its venue has accommodations on site.

(C) It will be recorded and broadcast online.

(D) It is mainly attended by academics.

182. According to the conference schedule, what can conference attendees do?

(A) Bring certain beverages into the auditorium

(B) Test new types of retail equipment

(C) Ask questions at the end of each session

(D) Reveal their reactions to conference content electronically

183. By what time must attendees ask to be reimbursed for an inconvenience?

(A) 9:30 A.M.

(B) 11:00 A.M.

(C) 12:30 P.M.

(D) 2:00 P.M.

184. What is suggested about Ms. Hughes?

(A) She prepared a talk in case of an emergency.

(B) She will use another speaker's materials.

(C) She will finish at a later time than scheduled.

(D) She spoke at a previous ARPM conference.

185. What caused the second problem mentioned in the notice?

(A) A mistake in a catering order

(B) A malfunctioning appliance

(C) Poor behavior by ARPM members

(D) Unplanned road work on a nearby street

GO ON TO THE NEXT PAGE

**Questions 186–190** refer to the following e-mails and advertisement.

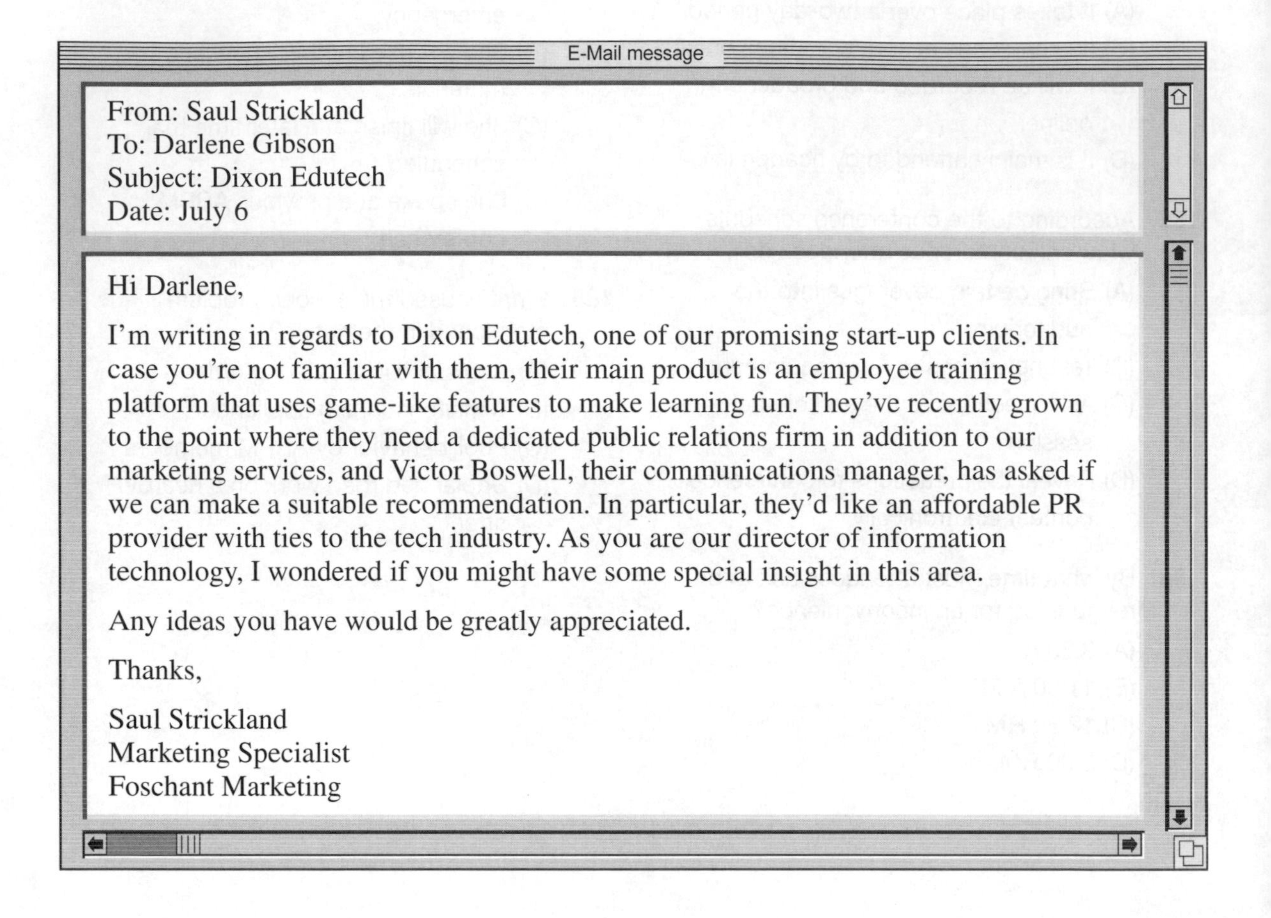

E-Mail message

From: Saul Strickland
To: Darlene Gibson
Subject: Dixon Edutech
Date: July 6

Hi Darlene,

I'm writing in regards to Dixon Edutech, one of our promising start-up clients. In case you're not familiar with them, their main product is an employee training platform that uses game-like features to make learning fun. They've recently grown to the point where they need a dedicated public relations firm in addition to our marketing services, and Victor Boswell, their communications manager, has asked if we can make a suitable recommendation. In particular, they'd like an affordable PR provider with ties to the tech industry. As you are our director of information technology, I wondered if you might have some special insight in this area.

Any ideas you have would be greatly appreciated.

Thanks,

Saul Strickland
Marketing Specialist
Foschant Marketing

## Luneday Partners

*Public Relations Services*

Whether your company is just starting out or is an established business, Luneday Partners is ready to provide you with smart, cutting-edge service. We will take the time to understand your brand, challenges, and goals in order to craft a unique and effective public relations strategy for you.

Here are a few more reasons to choose Luneday Partners:

- Our wide range of services include everything from copywriting to event support.
- We use advanced digital tools to give you valuable data about how your brand is perceived.
- We have special connections in several fields, including real estate, technology, and finance.

Visit us at www.luneday.com to see testimonials from our many satisfied clients.

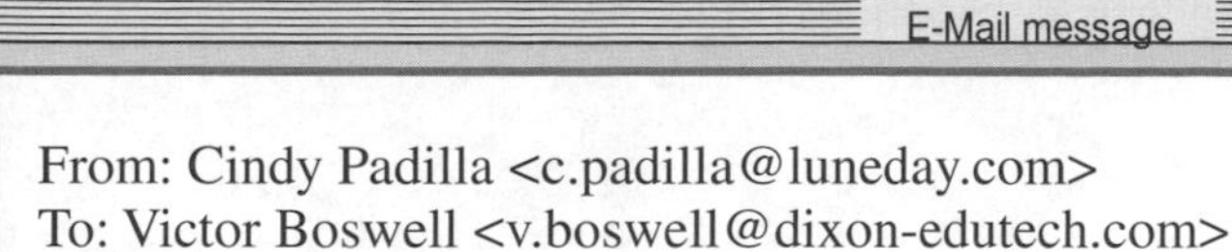

E-Mail message

From: Cindy Padilla <c.padilla@luneday.com>
To: Victor Boswell <v.boswell@dixon-edutech.com>
Subject: Meeting follow-up
Date: August 2

Dear Mr. Boswell,

It was a pleasure to speak with you at your office yesterday. As I said then, I will now assemble a crew of appropriate specialists, based on the information I gained about your situation and goals, to handle your account. We will then schedule another meeting in two-to-three weeks to present our proposed strategy for your approval. If needed, we will coordinate with your account manager at Foschant Marketing as you suggested.

Please contact me by phone or e-mail if you have any questions about this process. And thank you again for choosing Luneday Partners for your public relations needs.

Sincerely,

Cindy Padilla
Account Representative
Luneday Partners



**186.** What is the purpose of the first e-mail?
(A) To ask for assistance with a client inquiry
(B) To introduce a staff training resource
(C) To report a difficulty with a contractor
(D) To express concern about the scope of an endeavor

**187.** Why most likely would Ms. Gibson recommend Luneday Partners to Mr. Strickland?
(A) Its price range
(B) Its technological tools
(C) Its connections in another industry
(D) Its services for live events

**188.** According to the advertisement, what is available on Luneday Partners' Web site?
(A) Appointment reservation forms
(B) Data on current trends in its field
(C) Positive feedback about its work
(D) Profiles of its top executives

**189.** Whom did Ms. Padilla meet with on August 1?
(A) A sales representative at Dixon Edutech
(B) The communications manager at Dixon Edutech
(C) The director of information technology at Foschant Marketing
(D) A marketing specialist at Foschant Marketing

**190.** What does Ms. Padilla indicate she will do next?
(A) Schedule a presentation meeting
(B) Update a strategy proposal
(C) Set a project budget
(D) Form an account team

GO ON TO THE NEXT PAGE

**Questions 191–195** refer to the following article, brochure page, and e-mail.

## Arts in Rellsdale

By Shane Weller

RELLSDALE (September 10)—Just weeks after its children's summer classes came to an end, the Rellsdale Community Center has begun planning another exciting activity. The 32nd Annual Rellsdale Community Art Show will be held in its auditorium during the week of October 22–28.

The event began 32 years ago when Grant Lindsey, a local watercolor painter, invited his friends to join him in exhibiting their paintings in a small show. It has since grown into a chance for all of Rellsdale's professional and amateur visual artists to display their talents.

In its current form, the art show features a contest judged by a committee led by Tina Jordan, the community center's director, and including Adnan Khalif, an art historian at Malker University. Also, most of the artwork in the show is for sale. Twenty-five percent of the proceeds of each sale goes toward funding the upkeep of the center's buildings and grounds.

Hye-Ran Kyeong, the center's vice director of recreation and the show's organizer, urges citizens of all ages, backgrounds, and artistic disciplines to consider exhibiting. Those interested should visit www.rellsdaleart.com for instructions.

## 32nd Annual Rellsdale Community Art Show

Welcome to the Rellsdale Community Art Show!
The Rellsdale Community Center is glad you have joined us to celebrate the artistic gifts of our community.

**Schedule of the Opening Night Reception**

5 P.M.– Doors open
6 P.M.– Provision of refreshments donated by Rellsdale Supermarket
7 P.M.– Welcoming remarks and announcement of contest results by the head of the judging committee
9 P.M.– Doors close

**Other helpful information:**

- To locate a certain work of art, see the full list of entries ordered alphabetically by artist on pages 3 and 4.
- To inquire about purchasing a piece, please speak promptly with a member of our staff. Remember, sales are first come, first served!

Page 1

E-Mail message

| | |
|---|---|
| From: | Samuel Mayhew |
| To: | Eulalia Prosser |
| Subject: | Inquiry |
| Date: | November 4 |

Dear Ms. Prosser,

Hello. My friend Anne Watson bought the wooden sculpture you exhibited in the Rellsdale Community Arts Show. I think it's gorgeous, and I would love to have one like it for my office. So I got your e-mail address from the business card that came with Anne's purchase. Could you write me back and let me know whether you have other pieces for sale? Thank you.

Sincerely,

Samuel Mayhew

**191.** What is one purpose of the article?
(A) To describe the success of a fund-raising effort
(B) To publicize the accomplishments of local artists
(C) To invite people to participate in a community event
(D) To announce a new offering at a community center

**192.** How will some collected funds be used?
(A) To maintain a facility
(B) To hold classes for youth
(C) To publish a history book
(D) To reward a contest winner

**193.** According to the brochure page, how is a list of artwork organized?
(A) By the type of art
(B) By the title of the artwork
(C) By the location of the artwork
(D) By the name of the creator

**194.** Who spoke publicly on October 22?
(A) Mr. Lindsey
(B) Ms. Jordan
(C) Mr. Khalif
(D) Ms. Kyeong

**195.** What is most likely true about Ms. Prosser?
(A) She was mentioned on another page of the brochure.
(B) She contributed refreshments to a gathering.
(C) She received an e-mail from Ms. Watson.
(D) She is an amateur visual artist living in Rellsdale.



GO ON TO THE NEXT PAGE

**Questions 196–200** refer to the following job advertisement, meeting notes, and article.

# Summer Legal Intern

Huane Associates, a growing presence in the field of commercial law in the Gilvey area, is offering a legal internship from June 1 through July 31. The intern will perform legal research and analysis, draft a variety of legal documents, attend client meetings, and complete special projects, all with the benefit of direction and feedback from seasoned attorneys.

**Requirements**

- Current law student who has completed at least one year of law school
- Able to work 30 hours per week at firm's office in Waterfront District

**Preferred qualifications**

- Familiarity with local, state, and federal commercial law
- Proficiency in legal research platforms such as Rolento

To apply, e-mail the following documents to marlon.terry@huanelegal.com by March 31: a one-page cover letter, your résumé, your law school transcript, and a writing sample of between three and five pages.

| **Internship Documentation—Biweekly Meeting Notes** | |
|---|---|
| **Date:** Wed., July 8<br>**Intern:** Renée Walters<br>**Supervisor:** Marlon Terry | |
| **Reflections on previous projects/ experiences** | • Analysis of online retailer tax laws: Marlon gave general feedback and suggestions for improving "Summary" section<br>• Meeting with Sovaughn Shoes: In response to Renée's question, Marlon discussed options for handling surprising requests from clients |
| **Updates on ongoing projects** | • Blog post on history of non-disclosure agreements: Renée reported difficulty working with Rolento; Marlon scheduled training session for July 10 at 1 P.M.<br>• Drafting of employment contract for Marquitta Café: Renée has been unable to schedule necessary meeting with Jeannie Wilkerson; Marlon will contact Jeannie about this |
| **New assignments** | • Drafting of operating agreement for Blair-Logue, LLC: Tentatively due July 15; Renée should refer to resources in internal network's "Operating Agreements" file |

http://www.huanelegal.com/blog 

## Saying Goodbye to Huane Associates' First Intern

By Akira Chinen | Posted Tuesday, July 28

Renée Walters' internship at our firm will be coming to a close at the end of this week. Ms. Walters has spent the past two months working on a variety of tasks under the supervision of associate Marlon Terry. You may have seen Ms. Walters attending meetings with Mr. Terry or read her blog post on non-disclosure agreements.

As she finished up a draft of an operating agreement yesterday, Ms. Walters told me that the practical experience she has gotten here has been very valuable. She also said she was especially thankful to Mr. Terry for his thoughtful mentorship.

For his part, Mr. Terry said that he has really enjoyed supervising Ms. Walters because he has "seen her grow so much even in this short time." He expressed hopes that the internship program would take place again next summer with even more student participants.

All members of the firm are invited to a goodbye party for Ms. Walters at 4 P.M. on Friday in Conference Room A.

**196.** What does the job advertisement NOT ask applicants to submit?
(A) A record of school performance
(B) A letter of professional reference
(C) A list of career experiences
(D) Evidence of writing skills

**197.** What do the meeting notes indicate Ms. Walters had trouble with?
(A) Arranging a meeting with an executive
(B) Understanding some printed feedback
(C) Commuting to a certain neighborhood
(D) Using an electronic research tool

**198.** In the article, the word "under" in paragraph 1, line 2, is closest in meaning to
(A) having as her title
(B) concealed by
(C) subject to
(D) less than

**199.** What is suggested about Ms. Walters?
(A) She uploaded a document to a network folder.
(B) She took Mr. Terry's advice for dealing with a client.
(C) The deadline for one of her projects was postponed.
(D) A special training session for her did not take place.

**200.** According to the article, how does Mr. Terry want to change the internship program?
(A) By increasing the number of positions
(B) By extending its duration
(C) By having more employees involved
(D) By giving participants more responsibilities

**Stop! This is the end of the test. If you finish before time is called, you may go back to Parts 5, 6, and 7 and check your work.**

# ACTUAL TEST 

## READING TEST

In the Reading test, you will read a variety of texts and answer several different types of reading comprehension questions. The entire Reading test will last 75 minutes. There are three parts, and directions are given for each part. You are encouraged to answer as many questions as possible within the time allowed. You must mark your answers on the separate answer sheet. Do not write your answers in your test book.

## PART 5

**Directions:** A word or phrase is missing in each of the sentences below. Four answer choices are given below each sentence. Select the best answer to complete the sentence. Then mark the letter (A), (B), (C), or (D) on your answer sheet.

**101.** The caterers have been instructed to serve additional ------- of the dessert upon request only.

(A) guests
(B) menus
(C) recipes
(D) portions

**102.** Mr. Hayes has been using tax software to prepare ------- income tax report for years.

(A) he
(B) him
(C) his own
(D) himself

**103.** All entries must be signed and submitted on or ------- February 11 to be considered.

(A) within
(B) until
(C) before
(D) from

**104.** ------- more graduates would apply for its specialist positions, Colep Farms agreed to host field trips for university agricultural classes.

(A) If
(B) Even
(C) In order that
(D) As soon as

**105.** One way that grocery chains are addressing the environmental problems ------- with delivery services is by using reusable packaging.

(A) associated
(B) associate
(C) associating
(D) associations

**106.** The construction noise from the building next door was so loud that we could ------- hear our coworkers speak.

(A) still
(B) hardly
(C) finally
(D) ever

**107.** The enthusiastic ------- of the band's new album by audiences has been a surprise to critics.

(A) receipt
(B) received
(C) recipient
(D) reception

**108.** Several candidates interviewed for the receptionist position, ------- of whom impressed the hiring committee.

(A) none
(B) nobody
(C) those
(D) both

**109.** The project leader is responsible for ------- the members of the team of any updates to the plan.

(A) coordinating
(B) notifying
(C) recruiting
(D) crediting

**110.** Yarroll Bank provides loans to ------- small business owners at attractive interest rates.

(A) relative
(B) aspiring
(C) unprecedented
(D) customary

**111.** Once the air conditioning units -------, one employee on each floor should be assigned to monitor their use.

(A) were installed
(B) installed
(C) install
(D) are installed

**112.** The laboratory may have been contaminated with a hazardous chemical substance and has ------- been sterilized.

(A) since
(B) so
(C) yet
(D) enough

**113.** The panel's moderator was praised for ------- maneuvering the discussion through some difficult topics.

(A) skills
(B) skilled
(C) skillful
(D) skillfully

**114.** Sales representatives at Bigor Communications earn a flat commission ------- $100 for each cable package sold.

(A) about
(B) of
(C) over
(D) toward

**115.** Travel ------- will only be processed upon return from a trip and are contingent on managerial approval.

(A) reimbursing
(B) reimbursement
(C) reimbursements
(D) reimbursed

**116.** ------- our longstanding relationship with Garston Tech, it is no surprise that it will play an important part in developing our new apps.

(A) Given
(B) Notwithstanding
(C) Beyond
(D) In place of

**117.** Bunod Hotel patrons are encouraged to call the front desk ------- they require service.

(A) that
(B) whether
(C) anytime
(D) as though

**118.** Clinical trials have shown that the drug can treat symptoms that have proven ------- to other medications.

(A) resistant
(B) resisting
(C) resistibly
(D) resistible

**119.** Although it was not popular during her lifetime, Ms. Chang's unique style of design ------- considerable influence over later generations of architects.

(A) invested
(B) conferred
(C) dominated
(D) exerted



GO ON TO THE NEXT PAGE

**120.** In general, customers struggle with making decisions when ------- too many options to choose from.

(A) offers
(B) offered
(C) offering
(D) offer

**121.** Sorgan latex paint should be used only ------- a coat of Sorgan-brand primer has been applied to the bare surface.

(A) as much as
(B) after
(C) over
(D) in case

**122.** Specialty Health and Cosmetics Mart presents a satisfying ------- of wellness products in a small, well-organized space.

(A) array
(B) substitute
(C) expectation
(D) outcome

**123.** ------- among the reasons Franklin Bookstore purchased this software was its effectiveness at keeping data secure.

(A) Primary
(B) Informative
(C) Productive
(D) Selective

**124.** Ms. Nakano is ------- the hardest-working executive at Shibata Engineering.

(A) reputation
(B) reputable
(C) reputing
(D) reputedly

**125.** The popularity of the outdoor summer exhibition "Rock Art" has led the park's department to look into whether it can be made -------.

(A) feasible
(B) mandatory
(C) permanent
(D) abundant

**126.** If the prototype for our newest V2 coffee maker had received high marks from product testers, Techmart ------- to enter into a long-term contract with us.

(A) decided
(B) can decide
(C) would have decided
(D) would have been decided

**127.** Wait times at Skyspear Airlines' service counters have been cut in half ------- the self-check-in kiosks it recently introduced.

(A) wherever
(B) together with
(C) while
(D) thanks to

**128.** Some conference participants were displeased that organizers scheduled the only two workshops on statistics to take place -------.

(A) identically
(B) simultaneously
(C) intentionally
(D) adversely

**129.** The photographers whose pictures are used on the blog are not named, ------- do they receive compensation for their contributions.

(A) nor
(B) rather
(C) except
(D) although

**130.** The next task assigned to the interim accountant is to ------- the system by which research projects are funded.

(A) grant
(B) overhaul
(C) deduct
(D) experiment

# PART 6

**Directions:** Read the texts that follow. A word, phrase, or sentence is missing in parts of each text. Four answer choices for each question are given below the text. Select the best answer to complete the text. Then mark the letter (A), (B), (C), or (D) on your answer sheet.

**Questions 131–134** refer to the following e-mail.

From: Theresa Yates
To: Irma Sims
Subject: Gryell Toys Project Team
Date: September 2

Hi Irma,

As you requested, I thought about which of the senior engineers should replace me as head of the Gryell Toys team when I retire. While Karen could probably do the job if needed, Trevor is my recommendation. Karen's grasp of engineering may be -------, but she doesn't **131.** always communicate clearly, and communication is very important in managing. In contrast, Trevor ------- his decent engineering know-how with outstanding interpersonal skills. In my **132.** opinion, he ------- an excellent project team leader. **133.**

Please let me know if you need any more information to make your decision, or if you would like to discuss my recommendation in person. -------. **134.**

—Theresa

**131.** (A) superior
(B) urgent
(C) maximum
(D) eager

**132.** (A) prioritizes
(B) amplifies
(C) assesses
(D) designates

**133.** (A) is
(B) would be
(C) has been
(D) would have been

**134.** (A) And thank you again for this exciting opportunity.
(B) I have no particular preference, so choose whichever you like.
(C) I will be in-office all week, wrapping up my assignments.
(D) There are only a few more minor points to cover.

GO ON TO THE NEXT PAGE

**Questions 135–138** refer to the following press release.

**Melapin Symphony**
**Media Relations Office**

Beginning in May, the Melapin Symphony will play and livestream a monthly special concert in a program called *Share the Music*.

The program has been made possible by a grant from the Okafor Foundation, an organization dedicated to increasing access to music. -------. (135.) *Share the Music* is mainly intended for people with mobility issues, but it will be open to all members of the public.

The concerts will be viewable for free through a page on the symphony's Web site, www.melapinsymphony.com, ------- (136.) they take place. -------, (137.) visitors may be required to create and log in through a member account in order to access the page.

Symphony members and officials are pleased to be collaborating with the Okafor Foundation. Daiki Sano, its director, said, "The opportunity to share our music with more people is -------. (138.) We are very grateful."

**135.** (A) Its other activities include music camps for children with disabilities.
(B) The funding will even enable the concerts to be streamed over the Internet.
(C) Later, wheelchair spaces were also added to Melapin Symphony Hall.
(D) Before now, no patrons were permitted backstage during performances.

**136.** (A) meanwhile
(B) unless
(C) as
(D) then

**137.** (A) Namely
(B) However
(C) Likewise
(D) Instead

**138.** (A) honored
(B) to honor
(C) an honor
(D) honoring

**Questions 139–142** refer to the following letter.

11 May

Shaheena Singh
83 Bowfield Street
Benningham, UK
BN4 7DA

Dear Ms. Singh,

I recently received your letter in which you described the poor condition of the pavement on your street and the flat tyre you suffered ------- **139.** the uneven paving slabs. As you pointed out in your letter, the roads and pavements in your neighbourhood have been in desperate need of repair for quite some time. -------. **140.**

Beginning on 18 May, work crews will remove and reinstall all paving slabs on Bowfield Street and several other streets in the area. They will also fix the potholes in the roads that many motorists complained about at the community meeting in March. I hope this will come as good news to you and your fellow constituents ------- **141.** in the area.

Please accept my apologies for the incident with your car. I am confident that the planned work will prevent any similar ------- **142.** from occurring in the future.

Sincerely,

Mike Duke
City Councillor

**139.** (A) by
(B) following
(C) during
(D) due to

**140.** (A) I am proud to announce that the work is finally complete.
(B) Unfortunately, street repairs are not within our budget this year.
(C) Please know that I am committed to rectifying the situation.
(D) We will consider your proposal and attempt to find a solution.

**141.** (A) reside
(B) residing
(C) residents
(D) residential

**142.** (A) inaccuracies
(B) misunderstandings
(C) cancelations
(D) accidents



GO ON TO THE NEXT PAGE

**Questions 143–146** refer to the following advertisement.

**Diamond Sewing**

308 Third Street, Lawrence, 555-0184
www.diamondsewing.com

Diamond Sewing has been helping the people of Lawrence look ------- **143.** in their clothes for over 10 years. Whether it is because your size has changed or a new purchase doesn't quite fit right, our sewing specialists are always ready to make the alterations you need. ------- **144.**.

We ------- **145.** specialize in wedding gowns, tuxedoes, and other formalwear. Hundreds of brides and grooms have walked down the aisle in clothing altered by Diamond Sewing.

Do you have clothing that is frayed, worn or ripped? We also provide expert ------- **146.** services! Come see us for a free consultation before you throw away that beloved pair of jeans or vintage jacket. We are open Monday through Friday, from 9 A.M. to 5 P.M., and from 9 A.M. to 12 P.M. on Saturdays.

**143.** (A) stuns
(B) stunned
(C) stunning
(D) stunningly

**144.** (A) A well-fitting suit is essential for today's business professional.
(B) Orders can even be placed entirely online through our Web site.
(C) Simply choose from among our collection of design templates.
(D) We can shorten pants, put darts in shirts, and much more.

**145.** (A) ideally
(B) recently
(C) exceedingly
(D) particularly

**146.** (A) mending
(B) manufacturing
(C) laundering
(D) styling

## PART 7

**Directions:** In this part you will read a selection of texts, such as magazine and newspaper articles, e-mails, and instant messages. Each text or set of texts is followed by several questions. Select the best answer for each question and mark the letter (A), (B), (C), or (D) on your answer sheet.

**Questions 147–148** refer to the following notice.

### NOTICE

We believe the monitor on this stationary bicycle was shattered by a person who used it while also holding hand weights. We cannot be sure, because our security cameras only show that the person who likely did it was a non-member that followed a member into our center. Please do not allow other people to enter the building with you. If someone asks you to do this, claiming they have lost or forgotten their card, tell them to wait outside while you alert the front desk. Thank you.

—Hounsler Fitness Center Management

**147.** Where would the notice most likely appear?

(A) On some damaged machinery
(B) Outside of a building entrance
(C) Next to some training weights
(D) Behind a reception area

**148.** What are readers of the notice asked to do?

(A) Avoid blocking security cameras
(B) Use one type of equipment at a time
(C) Report the loss of their cards immediately
(D) Refrain from letting others into a facility

**Questions 149–150** refer to the following text-message chain.

**Alex White, 3:09 P.M.**
Bratislava, I'm sorry to bother you on your day off, but I have a quick question. We're almost out of gloves. Didn't you order some last week?

**Bratislava Kovac, 3:11 P.M.**
Oh yes, they came in yesterday, but I didn't have the chance to unpack them. They're in a box on my desk.

**Alex White, 3:13 P.M.**
Yes, I see them. Thanks! We had a couple of extra walk-in patients today, so we've gone through gloves faster than expected.

**Bratislava Kovac, 3:14 P.M.**
Got it. I'm going to need a record of how many you take and who they're for, though.

**Alex White, 3:16 P.M.**
Oh, can I just tell you on Monday? I'm already back at Reception.

**Bratislava Kovac, 3:17 P.M.**
Sorry, but that's a bit too far off. Could you just write it on a sticky note and put it on my door? I'd rather not risk either of us forgetting.

**Alex White, 3:18 P.M.**
Sure, I'll do that. Thanks again, Bratislava.

**149.** What is probably true about Ms. Kovac?
(A) She used up some supplies.
(B) She does not have a private office.
(C) She has gone out on an errand.
(D) She is not currently on duty.

**150.** At 3:17 P.M., what does Ms. Kovac mean when she writes, "that's a bit too far off"?
(A) She is arguing that a figure has been miscalculated.
(B) She is criticizing a modification to a document.
(C) She is refusing to seek out a location.
(D) She is opposing a suggestion to delay a task.

**Questions 151–153** refer to the following consent form.

**Ticard, Inc.**

## Market Research Participation Consent Form

Thank you for agreeing to participate in this study of men aged 18 to 34. You will be shown two versions of a television advertisement for a facial razor and asked for your opinions on each. The entire process will take approximately 30 minutes.

Please read the items below and write your initials in the adjacent boxes to indicate your agreement to each.

- I consent to the audio recording of my responses during the study and the use of these recordings, with my identifying information removed, internally by Ticard. ☐
- I understand that I may stop my participation in the study at any time by informing the researchers of my wish to do so. ☐
- Afterward, I will not speak about or create any physical or digital materials about the contents of this study. ☐
- I have asked the researchers any questions I have about this study. ☐

**Participant name:** ____________ **Signature:** ____________

**Date:** ____________

**151.** What will participants do for the study?
(A) Try out a product
(B) Compare two designs
(C) Describe their habits
(D) Watch some video clips

**152.** According to the form, what will happen after the study?
(A) The data will be anonymized.
(B) Some recordings will be destroyed.
(C) A follow-up questionnaire will be sent out.
(D) The researchers will answer participants' questions.

**153.** What must the participants agree to do?
(A) Speak honestly about their opinions
(B) Keep information about the study confidential
(C) Disclose their participation in any previous studies
(D) Retain a copy of the form for a period of time



GO ON TO THE NEXT PAGE

**Questions 154–155** refer to the following e-mail.

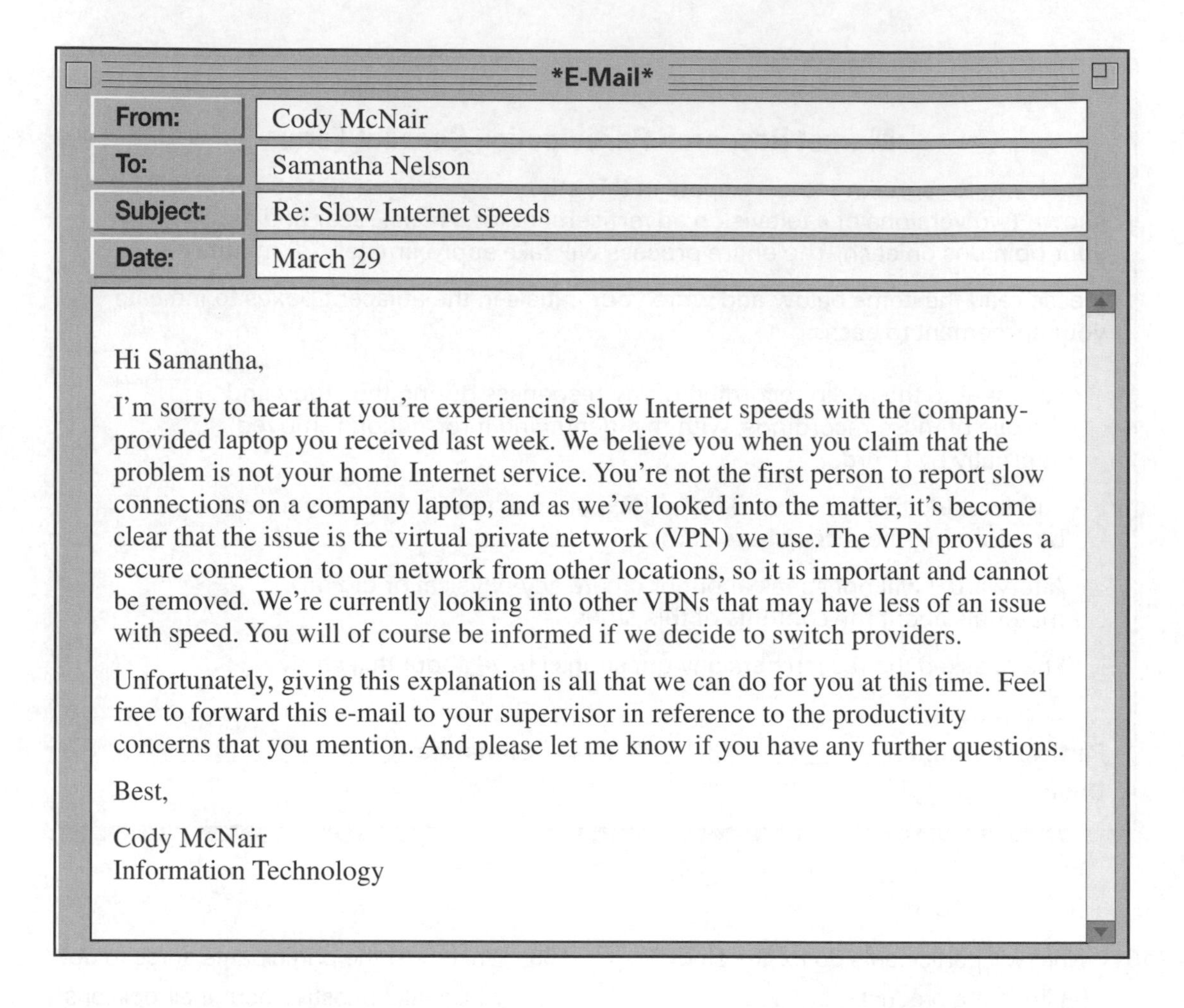

*E-Mail*

| | |
|---|---|
| **From:** | Cody McNair |
| **To:** | Samantha Nelson |
| **Subject:** | Re: Slow Internet speeds |
| **Date:** | March 29 |

Hi Samantha,

I'm sorry to hear that you're experiencing slow Internet speeds with the company-provided laptop you received last week. We believe you when you claim that the problem is not your home Internet service. You're not the first person to report slow connections on a company laptop, and as we've looked into the matter, it's become clear that the issue is the virtual private network (VPN) we use. The VPN provides a secure connection to our network from other locations, so it is important and cannot be removed. We're currently looking into other VPNs that may have less of an issue with speed. You will of course be informed if we decide to switch providers.

Unfortunately, giving this explanation is all that we can do for you at this time. Feel free to forward this e-mail to your supervisor in reference to the productivity concerns that you mention. And please let me know if you have any further questions.

Best,

Cody McNair
Information Technology

**154.** What is most likely true about Ms. Nelson?
(A) She is not authorized to access part of a network.
(B) She asked to have some equipment replaced.
(C) She did not read an instruction manual.
(D) She is currently working remotely.

**155.** What does Mr. McNair give Ms. Nelson permission to do?
(A) Uninstall a program from a laptop
(B) Share his message with another person
(C) Contact him at home if an issue reoccurs
(D) Use an alternative to an approved provider

**Questions 156–157** refer to the following announcement.

**Blizzard Hockey**

## Press Conference

Blizzard management is excited to offer you the opportunity to meet the person tasked with leading the team to victory in their new home. Dolores Ikeda, owner of the Blizzard, is hosting a press conference to introduce the team's new general manager. The press conference will consist of a speech by Ms. Ikeda, a speech by the new general manager, a question-and-answer session, and a photo opportunity.

**WHERE:** Shallard Arena Press Room (1st floor, near North Entrance)
*Space will be limited, so bring press credentials to ensure entry.*

**WHEN:** Wednesday, June 8, at 11 A.M.
*Please be present and seated by 10:45.*

**CONTACT:** Rex Welch, Blizzard Media Relations Manager
rex.welch@blizzard-hockey.com

**156.** What will be announced at the press conference?
(A) The relocation of a hockey team
(B) The appointment of a sports executive
(C) A contract with a professional athlete
(D) Plans for building a new playing space

**157.** What is suggested about the press conference?
(A) Priority admission will be given to journalists.
(B) There will be a chance to tour a facility.
(C) Mr. Welch will speak after Ms. Ikeda.
(D) Promotional gifts will be handed out.

GO ON TO THE NEXT PAGE

**Questions 158–160** refer to the following letter.

December 7

Dixonette Hotel
1520 Sunset Street
Vancouver, BC V54 1R9

Dear sir or madam,

I stayed at your hotel during my visit to Vancouver on December 2–4, and I would like to share with you a memorable experience that I had. —[1]—.

On the last day of my stay, I was about to drive my rental car to the airport when I found that its battery had died. I contacted the rental car company, but their representative said that they would not be able to send assistance for two hours. —[2]—. Fortunately, I had this conversation on my mobile phone in the lobby, and Delray Scott, a member of your front desk staff, overheard it. He offered to jump-start my rental car using his own vehicle and cables. —[3]—. I gratefully accepted, and his cheerful and efficient work allowed me to arrive at the airport on time.

While I was satisfied with many aspects of your establishment, it was this act of kindness that I found most impressive. Mr. Scott deserves to be rewarded for being willing to use his valuable supplementary abilities to help out a guest in need. —[4]—. I hope that you have some kind of policy in place for this.

Sincerely,

*Travis Quinn*

**158.** What is the main purpose of the letter?

(A) To suggest an additional service
(B) To complain about a facility
(C) To convey praise for a worker
(D) To ask about the details of a policy

**159.** What did Mr. Scott most likely do on December 4 ?

(A) Left his assigned work station for a short time
(B) Charged a mobile device in a private area
(C) Asked a guest to move a parked vehicle
(D) Looked up some information on an airport Web site

**160.** In which of the positions marked [1], [2], [3], and [4] does the following sentence best belong?

"This could have caused me to miss my flight."

(A) [1]
(B) [2]
(C) [3]
(D) [4]

**Questions 161–163** refer to the following job posting.

**Job title**: Route Salesperson (part-time) **Company name**: Rotunno's, Inc.

**Job location**: Stockton area, California **Job posted**: 10 days ago

**Details**: Rotunno's is a family-owned food manufacturer specializing in snacks aimed at health-conscious consumers. All of our products are made from at least 80% natural ingredients. We are committed to making our business a healthy and enjoyable place to work for our more than 1,100 employees. Last year, Rotunno's, Inc. was presented with a "Workplace Well-being" award from the Stockton Business Association (SBA).

The route salesperson is responsible for delivering Rotunno's products to grocery stores in a specific area. Other essential duties include conducting inventory checks and monitoring the stocking of store shelves with the company's products. Strong communication skills are a must, as regular interaction with store managers is necessary to provide the most suitable mix of Rotunno's products.

The successful candidate will drive a 22-foot delivery truck over the assigned route. While on duty, the employee will also use a tablet computer to input inventory data. The assigned work hours are from 4 P.M. to 10 P.M., Thursday to Sunday (24 hours per week).

To apply for the position, visit www.rotunnos.com/jobs and follow the instructions to upload your résumé. In order to qualify for an interview, candidates must achieve a certain score in a basic computer proficiency test that requires about 20 minutes to take.

**161.** What is NOT stated about Rotunno's, Inc.?
(A) Its products are made from mostly natural ingredients.
(B) It has been recognized by a business group.
(C) It regularly posts multiple job openings.
(D) It employs over 1,100 people.

**162.** What is mentioned as a duty of the advertised position?
(A) Acquiring new business clients
(B) Setting up displays at trade shows
(C) Entering data into a portable device
(D) Providing updates to the holder's supervisor

**163.** What are job candidates required to do?
(A) Promise to protect confidential information
(B) Submit copies of professional licenses
(C) Perform well in a phone interview
(D) Demonstrate technical skills



GO ON TO THE NEXT PAGE

**Questions 164–167** refer to the following advertisement.

# Harris & Kwon Group

Harris & Kwon Group provides high-quality language services in English and Korean for reasonable prices. Located in the heart of Seoul, we have assisted domestic, overseas, and international companies of all sizes in bridging gaps in communication.

Our services include translation of printed and digital materials, transcription of video and audio clips, and interpretation for in-person meetings and large events. We also rent out audio systems that can ensure the smooth transmission of interpretations to up to 300 participants.

Automated translation and interpretation software still regularly makes errors that can cause serious confusion, while the expertise of professional translators/interpreters is unreliable, even among those with a degree in the field. That is why Harris & Kwon Group only employs language specialists who grew up using both English and Korean with native fluency. We guarantee that our output will not just be error-free, but also capture and sensitively convey cultural nuances.

Visit our Web site, www.hkgroup.co.kr, to learn more about our process and read testimonials from satisfied clients. If you would then like to discuss hiring Harris & Kwon Group for a project, use the convenient form in the "Contact" section. We are happy to provide a reliable quote for the cost of our services up front. Also, if you are inquiring on behalf of an organization that serves the public good, ask about our special rates for nonprofits.

**164.** What is NOT listed as a service that Harris & Kwon Group provides?

(A) Lending of specialized equipment
(B) Conversion of the language of a text
(C) Making a written copy of audio materials
(D) Advising on cultural differences in business

**165.** What is mentioned as a characteristic of Harris & Kwon Group's employees?

(A) Substantial career experience
(B) A completely bilingual upbringing
(C) Serious academic study of a subject
(D) Extensive training on a technology

**166.** What is implied about Harris & Kwon Group?

(A) It has branches in more than one country.
(B) It specializes in serving companies in a certain field.
(C) It gives a discount to clients whose work benefits society.
(D) It recently increased its number of employees.

**167.** According to the advertisement, what can Harris & Kwon Group do for its new customers?

(A) Supply a price estimate in advance
(B) Research the terminology of their industry
(C) Provide personal references from executives
(D) Create a customized work process



GO ON TO THE NEXT PAGE

**Questions 168–171** refer to the following online chat discussion.

| | |
|---|---|
| Guy Wallace, 11:24 A.M. | Hi, everyone. I'm sorry to bother you, but I was wondering where to get images to post on our Web site. I need some for the latest post I'm putting on our blog. |
| Jerry Grant, 11:25 A.M. | Sorry, I don't know. |
| Sania Najjar, 11:26 A.M. | I think Mark used Photofield to download stock photos. Didn't he give you the log-in information for that site? |
| Guy Wallace, 11:26 A.M. | Let me check. |
| Guy Wallace, 11:28 A.M. | Ah, yes, I see it! Thank you, Sania. |
| Peter Chen, 11:29 A.M. | How are you finding it filling in for Mark, Guy? |
| Guy Wallace, 11:30 A.M. | It's tough. There have been a lot of experiences like this, where the information needed to do his work isn't available or isn't labeled clearly. |
| Peter Chen, 11:31 A.M. | I had the same issues when I took over Robin's position last year. We really should be documenting our job processes more clearly. It's in the company handbook, after all. |
| Guy Wallace, 11:32 A.M. | Oh, really? I had no idea. |
| Peter Chen, 11:33 A.M. | Most employees aren't aware of it. I'm going to speak to Amy about encouraging everyone to set aside time to create documentation. |
| Jerry Grant, 11:34 A.M. | That's a great idea. And please don't feel hesitant to ask us questions, Guy. It's better than guessing and making a mistake. |
| Guy Wallace, 11:35 A.M. | Thank you. I appreciate that. |

**168.** At 11:28 A.M., what does Mr. Wallace report finding?

(A) A file of digital images

(B) A draft of an online article

(C) A user name and password

(D) A comment under a blog post

**169.** What is suggested about Mr. Wallace?

(A) He is temporarily handling a colleague's duties.

(B) He is a newly hired employee.

(C) He recently returned from a leave of absence.

(D) He was not previously aware of an internal Web site.

**170.** At 11:31 A.M., what does Mr. Chen mean when he writes, "It's in the company handbook, after all"?

(A) He is instructing Mr. Wallace to seek out some information.

(B) He is explaining why he is not allowed to assist Mr. Wallace with a task.

(C) He is emphasizing the importance of a work responsibility.

(D) He is suggesting that a company policy is outdated.

**171.** What does Mr. Wallace thank Mr. Grant for?

(A) Confirming the accuracy of some directions

(B) Sharing the location of some documentation

(C) Forgiving him for misunderstanding an assignment

(D) Reassuring him about potentially causing inconvenience



*GO ON TO THE NEXT PAGE*

**Questions 172–175** refer to the following newsletter article.

***District News Tribune*** *October 22*

Three businesses in the Vine Heights District—Barksdale Bakery, Triollo Grill, and Raley's Laundromat—have closed recently. Barksdale Bakery, a regional chain that also has a location in Balboa Shopping Mall, closed its Vine Heights location on October 9. Company spokesperson Brenda Chiu said it "had become difficult to compete" in the area, as a number of neighborhood coffee shops have been expanding their offerings of baked goods. —[1]—.

Triollo Grill, a Mexican-Japanese fusion restaurant, has been closed for two weeks, and a "space available" sign now hangs on its door. The popular eatery had been operating at 56 Dew Street. —[2]—. Its owner, Antonio Cruz, said he will reopen his establishment in a larger space near Alvin Park.

Raley's Laundromat closed last week. It offered customers self-service, coin-operated laundry machines, along with laundry soap vending machines. "With all the recent development, the neighborhood is changing," said owner Dolores Raley. "The new apartment buildings, such as the Deltonne, are equipped with in-unit washers and dryers. So demand for our services is decreasing." She added that, as part of a trend, several local laundromats are being converted into restaurants. —[3]—.

Ms. Raley moved her business to 17 Butler Avenue, where she has also started to offer commercial laundry services. —[4]—. Only one self-service laundry establishment, Laundry Breeze, still exists in the Vine Heights District.

The district is also left with only one eatery, Tampico Burrito, that serves Mexican food, while a food truck, Ivy's Quick Bites, offers its only Japanese food.

**172.** What is NOT suggested about the Vine Heights District?

(A) It is a competitive market for bakeries.

(B) It now has several coin-operated laundry services.

(C) It has newly-built housing.

(D) It is served by mobile food facilities.

**173.** What is indicated about Triollo Grill?

(A) It had recently changed ownership.

(B) It was famous for its coffee drinks.

(C) It has not gone completely out of business.

(D) It was a district's first fusion restaurant.

**174.** Which establishment is outside of the Vine Heights District?

(A) Balboa Shopping Mall

(B) Deltonne

(C) Laundry Breeze

(D) Tampico Burrito

**175.** In which of the positions marked [1], [2], [3], and [4] does the following sentence best belong?

"Indeed, an Italian bistro will soon move into her facility's empty space."

(A) [1]

(B) [2]

(C) [3]

(D) [4]



GO ON TO THE NEXT PAGE

**Questions 176–180** refer to the following information and e-mail.

## *Autumn Classes at the Artesia Institute*

Classes begin the week of September 25. Each class will meet on the same day each week for eight sessions. Class fees include all necessary materials. Students are charged 80% of the class fee for second/third/fourth classes within the autumn term.

| Class/Price | Description | Day/Time of Sessions |
|---|---|---|
| Room Life Drawing ($285) | Recommended for intermediate artists, this class will have a different live model each week. | Tuesdays/6:30 P.M.–7:30 P.M.<br>Wednesdays/7:00 P.M.–8:00 P.M.<br>Thursdays/6:30 P.M.–7:30 P.M. |
| Pottery ($300) | Students will learn wheel-throwing techniques to make bowls, vases, and more. All levels welcome. | Mondays/6:30 P.M.–8:30 P.M.<br>Thursdays/6:30 P.M.–8:30 P.M. |
| Watercolor Painting ($260) | Intended for beginners, this class teaches basic watercolor techniques with a focus on landscape painting. | Mondays/6:00 P.M.–7:00 P.M.<br>Wednesdays/6:00 P.M.–7:00 P.M.<br>Thursdays/7:00 P.M.–8:00 P.M. |
| Screen Printing ($280) | Learn the steps of screen printing to make your own T-shirts. Designed for beginners, this class has never been offered before. | Tuesdays/6:30 P.M.–8:00 P.M. |

To register for classes, or for more detailed information, visit www.artesiainst.com/autumn. The registration deadline is September 12. Early registration is highly recommended.

**To:** Cynthia Lopez <c.lopez@artesiainst.com>
**From:** Tae-Woo Park <t.park@artesiainst.com>
**Date:** November 22
**Subject:** Feedback survey

Dear Cynthia,

I have finished compiling the answers from the feedback survey we distributed to students on the last day of class. We had overwhelmingly positive reviews for your class, and all of the students stated that they would recommend it to others. Because of the popularity of your teaching, I don't think two classes per term is enough. If possible, I'd like you to teach an additional class for the winter term, a matter we can discuss further at the staff dinner this Friday. It will be somewhere within walking distance to the institute, and it's tentatively scheduled for 7 P.M. Pablo is making the arrangements, so please let him know if you will attend alone or with your spouse.

Thanks for your hard work!

Tae-Woo

**176.** How can students get a discount?

(A) By recommending the institute to friends
(B) By paying the full fee in advance
(C) By meeting an early registration deadline
(D) By enrolling in more than one class

**177.** What is true about the autumn classes?

(A) Two are suitable for students with a moderate level of ability.
(B) Two are being held for the first time.
(C) One is taught by a different instructor each week.
(D) One has shorter single-day sessions than all of the others.

**178.** Which class does Ms. Lopez most likely teach?

(A) Room Life Drawing
(B) Pottery
(C) Watercolor Painting
(D) Screen Printing

**179.** What does Mr. Park want Ms. Lopez to do?

(A) Train a newly hired instructor
(B) Review some survey results
(C) Increase her working hours
(D) Request supplies for the next term

**180.** What information does Pablo need regarding a dinner?

(A) Whether attendees have food allergies
(B) Which time is most convenient
(C) Which restaurant is preferred
(D) Whether a guest will be brought



GO ON TO THE NEXT PAGE

**Questions 181–185** refer to the following mobile device screenshot and online article.

## EyeChat

*Mobile Version 3.0*

Top User Reviews

**Kerry Lucas** ★★★★☆ (4.5 stars)

Eyechat is great for keeping in touch with family and friends from anywhere. I've tried several of the video chat apps available on Allivanta, and this is the best one. I just wish that it would let you customize or hide the menu—its color hurts my eyes.

**Dominick Frazier** ★★★★☆ (4 stars)

I'm glad that Eyechat is offering "invisible" status again, but the range of stickers is still really limited. It should allow other companies to make stickers for its platform, like Spangler does.

**Chien Nguyen** ★☆☆☆☆ (1 star)

It doesn't let you use Mooth to add money to your account, even though that's much safer than handing over your credit card information. I will be uninstalling.

**Yolanda Castillo** ★★★★☆ (4 stars)

Please let users stop this app from starting automatically! My Titus phone doesn't have great battery life, and EyeChat makes it run out even more quickly. Otherwise, I have no complaints. Reliable video and sound quality.

### Platformula Releases EyeChat Version 3.1 for Mobile

*By Adriana Russell, April 8, 10:35 A.M.*

Earlier this week, Platformula launched the newest version of video chat app EyeChat for mobile devices. Version 3.1 features a simplified menu that can be hidden to allow more space for video. It also supports greater integration, allowing users to charge their account through Mooth and import contacts from StarMail. The update notice from Platformula even boasts that Eyechat now allows users to buy stickers from third-party developers, though these do not seem to exist yet. In addition, one popular feature from the desktop version of EyeChat, screen-sharing, has finally been made available in the mobile version.

Platformula bought EyeChat's developer from its founder, Gus Danielson, three years ago. The first update that the company spearheaded, 2.0, was met with strong criticism from users. Several of the preexisting features that were removed from that version, such as the ability to set the user status to "invisible," were restored in 3.0.

Online reviews of version 3.1 have been positive so far. Platformula is expected to update the mobile version of EyeChat Business next.

**181.** What does Mr. Nguyen indicate that he is concerned about?

(A) The security of his financial information
(B) The unhealthfulness of an online activity
(C) The increasing cost of a chat service
(D) The difficulty of deleting a mobile app

**182.** What is mentioned as a competitor of EyeChat?

(A) Allivanta
(B) Spangler
(C) Mooth
(D) Titus

**183.** What is implied about Mr. Frazier?

(A) Part of his review refers to the desktop version of EyeChat.
(B) He has experience with version 2.0 of EyeChat.
(C) His work is the primary reason that he uses EyeChat.
(D) He paid to download EyeChat.

**184.** Whose suggestion was NOT adopted in the updated version of EyeChat?

(A) Ms. Lucas's
(B) Ms. Russell's
(C) Mr. Ngyuen's
(D) Ms. Castillo's

**185.** What is mentioned about Platformula?

(A) It was founded three years ago.
(B) It used to be headed by Mr. Danielson.
(C) It is not the original creator of EyeChat.
(D) It outsourced some development work.



GO ON TO THE NEXT PAGE

**Questions 186–190** refer to the following e-mails and property listing.

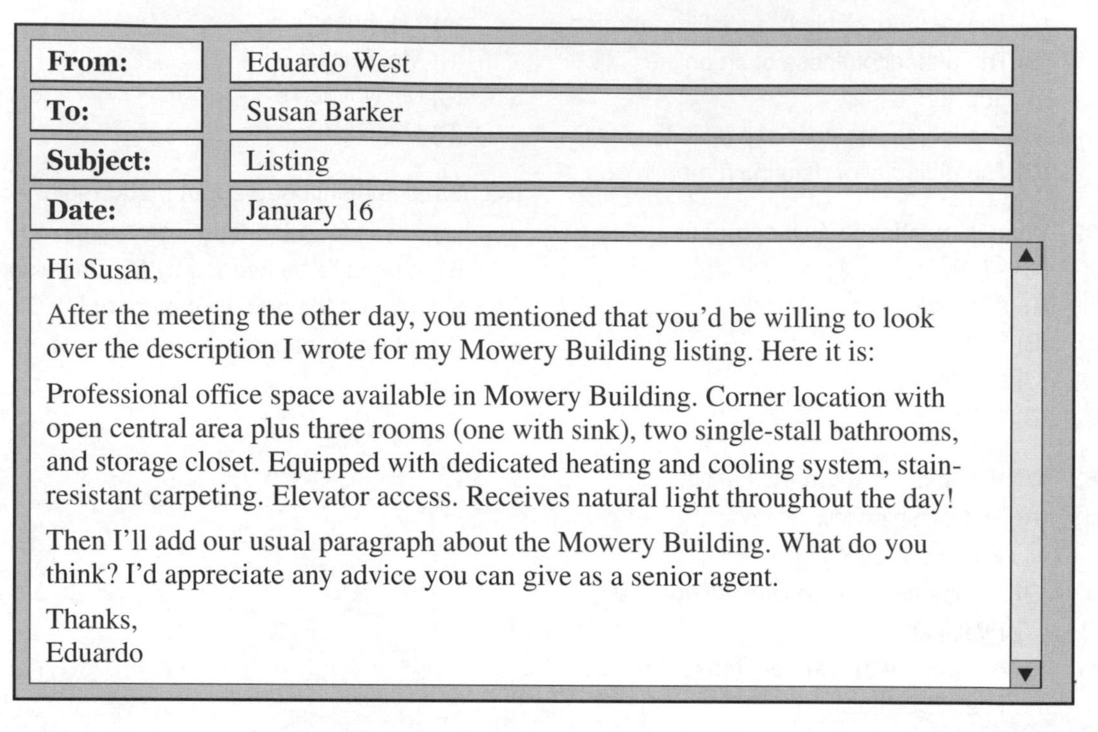

| | |
|---|---|
| **From:** | Eduardo West |
| **To:** | Susan Barker |
| **Subject:** | Listing |
| **Date:** | January 16 |

Hi Susan,

After the meeting the other day, you mentioned that you'd be willing to look over the description I wrote for my Mowery Building listing. Here it is:

Professional office space available in Mowery Building. Corner location with open central area plus three rooms (one with sink), two single-stall bathrooms, and storage closet. Equipped with dedicated heating and cooling system, stain-resistant carpeting. Elevator access. Receives natural light throughout the day!

Then I'll add our usual paragraph about the Mowery Building. What do you think? I'd appreciate any advice you can give as a senior agent.

Thanks,
Eduardo

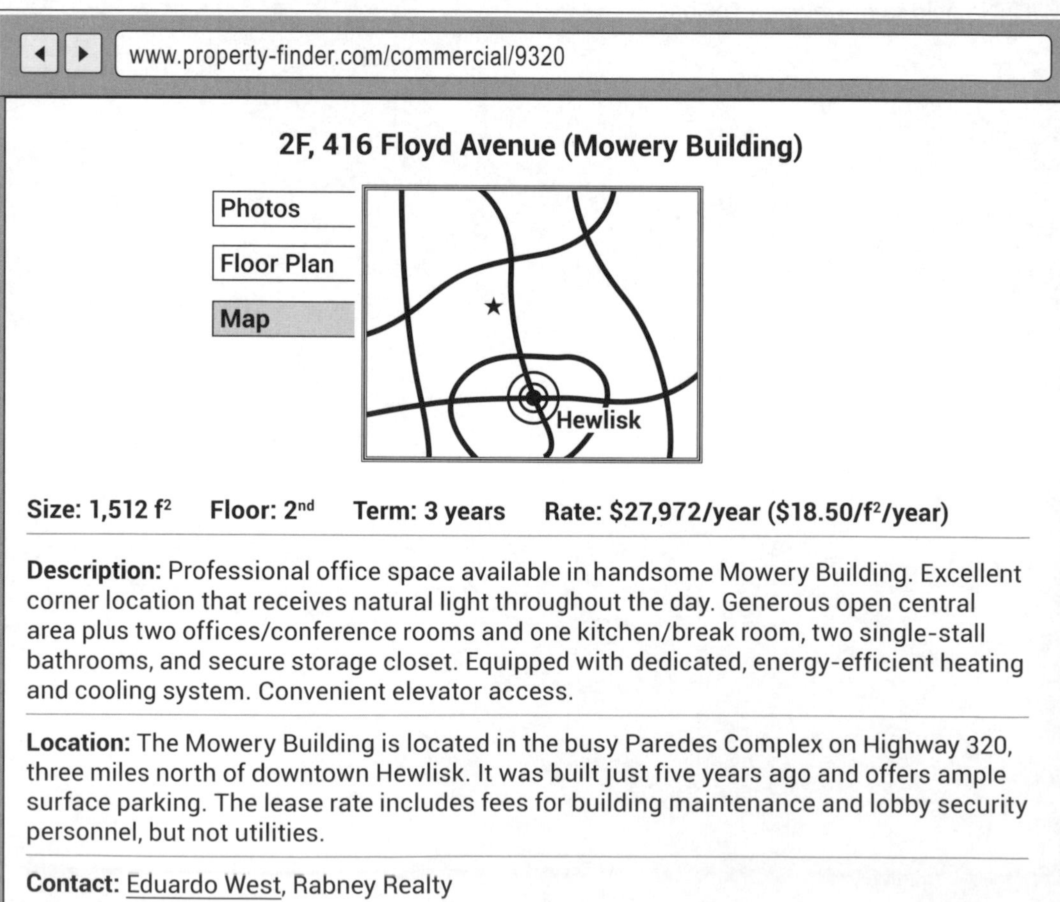

www.property-finder.com/commercial/9320

**2F, 416 Floyd Avenue (Mowery Building)**

Photos
Floor Plan
Map



**Size:** **1,512 $f^2$** **Floor:** **2nd** **Term:** **3 years** **Rate:** **\$27,972/year (\$18.50/$f^2$/year)**

**Description:** Professional office space available in handsome Mowery Building. Excellent corner location that receives natural light throughout the day. Generous open central area plus two offices/conference rooms and one kitchen/break room, two single-stall bathrooms, and secure storage closet. Equipped with dedicated, energy-efficient heating and cooling system. Convenient elevator access.

**Location:** The Mowery Building is located in the busy Paredes Complex on Highway 320, three miles north of downtown Hewlisk. It was built just five years ago and offers ample surface parking. The lease rate includes fees for building maintenance and lobby security personnel, but not utilities.

**Contact:** Eduardo West, Rabney Realty

| From: | Darlene Bullard |
|---|---|
| To: | Amir Ramdani |
| Subject: | Potential office space |
| Date: | January 19 |

Hi Amir,

I know that you liked the Gilbardo Street office that I showed you on Monday, but I've just learned about a new space that might be an even better fit for your business. It's a second-floor corner space in the Mowery Building that gets a lot of light. It's larger than the Gilbardo Street office, but the price per square foot is the same. The Gilbardo Street office is a little closer to downtown, but since the Mowery Building is right next to the highway, there won't be a big difference in convenience. And the Mowery office has a shorter lease term, so if you don't like it, you won't have to stay there long.

I really think you should take a look at this new space. Let me know if you're interested, and I can schedule a viewing.

Regards,

Darlene

**186.** What is suggested about Ms. Barker?
(A) She is Mr. West's current supervisor.
(B) She has more work experience than Mr. West.
(C) She wrote a description of an office building.
(D) She gave an assignment at a meeting.

**187.** What is mentioned in the first email but NOT in the published description of the space?
(A) A third enclosed space
(B) The type of flooring
(C) The security system
(D) Exposure to some light

**188.** What would a tenant in the Mowery Building most likely need to pay extra for?
(A) Usage of water infrastructure
(B) Repairs to a temperature control system
(C) Access to an outdoor parking area
(D) Security services at the building entrance

**189.** Who most likely is Ms. Bullard?
(A) Mr. Ramdani's business partner
(B) Mr. Ramdani's legal advisor
(C) Mr. Ramdani's real estate agent
(D) Mr. Ramdani's administrative assistant

**190.** What can be concluded about the Gilbardo Street office?
(A) It has more than 1,500 square feet of space.
(B) It is more than 3 miles from central Hewlisk.
(C) It requires a lease term of over 5 years.
(D) It costs less than $28,000 per year.

**Questions 191–195** refer to the following brochure, e-mail, and notice.

# Corlingdale History Museum

**Major Exhibitions**

| ***Wood, Steel, and Concrete*** | ***Ms. Collins's Library*** |
|---|---|
| Find out the fascinating stories behind Corlingdale buildings ranging from small houses and storefronts to factories and skyscrapers. | This look into the life of Deanna Collins, Corlingdale native and writer of the *Kiera Smith* series, is sure to delight her fans—even the ones who have grown up. |
| ***50 Years of Fur*** | ***Over the Mountains*** |
| Created for the recent fiftieth anniversary of the Corlingdale Zoo, this exhibition traces the history of the facility and its amazing creatures. | You may not have heard of Nicolas Vicario, but you'll never forget his name once you see his beautiful paintings of the nearby Trueheart Mountains. |

**Notes**

- We welcome groups, but please make a reservation 24 hours in advance if you plan to bring more than eight people. This can be done with our online reservation system at www.corlingdalehistory.com.
- Guided tours are only available in English, but self-guided audio tours are available in several other languages.

E-Mail message

| | |
|---|---|
| From: | <verag@corlingdalehistory.com> |
| To: | <chiranjeevi.somchai@ben-mail.net> |
| Subject: | RE: A visit today? |
| Date: | July 15 |

Dear Mr. Somchai,

Thank you for letting us know about your visit this afternoon. While we do usually require groups like yours to give us at least one day's notice before arrival, we will luckily be able to accommodate you this time.

Since you mentioned the *Over the Mountains* exhibition that is normally located on our third floor, I have to warn you it is currently on loan to the Meehan Museum in the United Kingdom. There is related merchandise available in our first-floor gift shop, but if the exhibition is the main attraction for your group, you should consider rescheduling your visit for August, when it will be on display here again.

If you decide to come anyway, we will look forward to seeing you this afternoon.

Best,

Vera Gordan
Operations Manager
Corlingdale History Museum

# Sorry!

The exhibition normally housed in this space is currently on loan to London's Meehan Museum. It is scheduled to reopen here on August 1. Ask our information desk how your party can get free admission if you would like to return to see it then. We apologize for the inconvenience.

— Corlingdale History Museum staff

**191.** According to the brochure, what is the subject of a major exhibit?
(A) Textile manufacturing
(B) A children's book author
(C) Paintings of a city
(D) Local wildlife

**192.** What is probably true about Mr. Somchai's group?
(A) It consists of more than eight individuals.
(B) Some of its members are relatives of an artist.
(C) Some of its members do not speak English.
(D) It will receive a personal guided tour.

**193.** What does Ms. Gordan recommend to Mr. Somchai?
(A) Making a reservation for a performance
(B) Buying some limited-edition goods
(C) Contacting an overseas organization
(D) Touring the museum on a later date

**194.** On what floor of Corlingdale History Museum is the notice most likely posted?
(A) The first floor
(B) The second floor
(C) The third floor
(D) The fourth floor

**195.** In the notice, the word "party" in paragraph 1, line 4, is closest in meaning to
(A) celebration
(B) collection of people
(C) participation
(D) time off



GO ON TO THE NEXT PAGE

**Questions 196–200** refer to the following Web page, e-mail, and article.

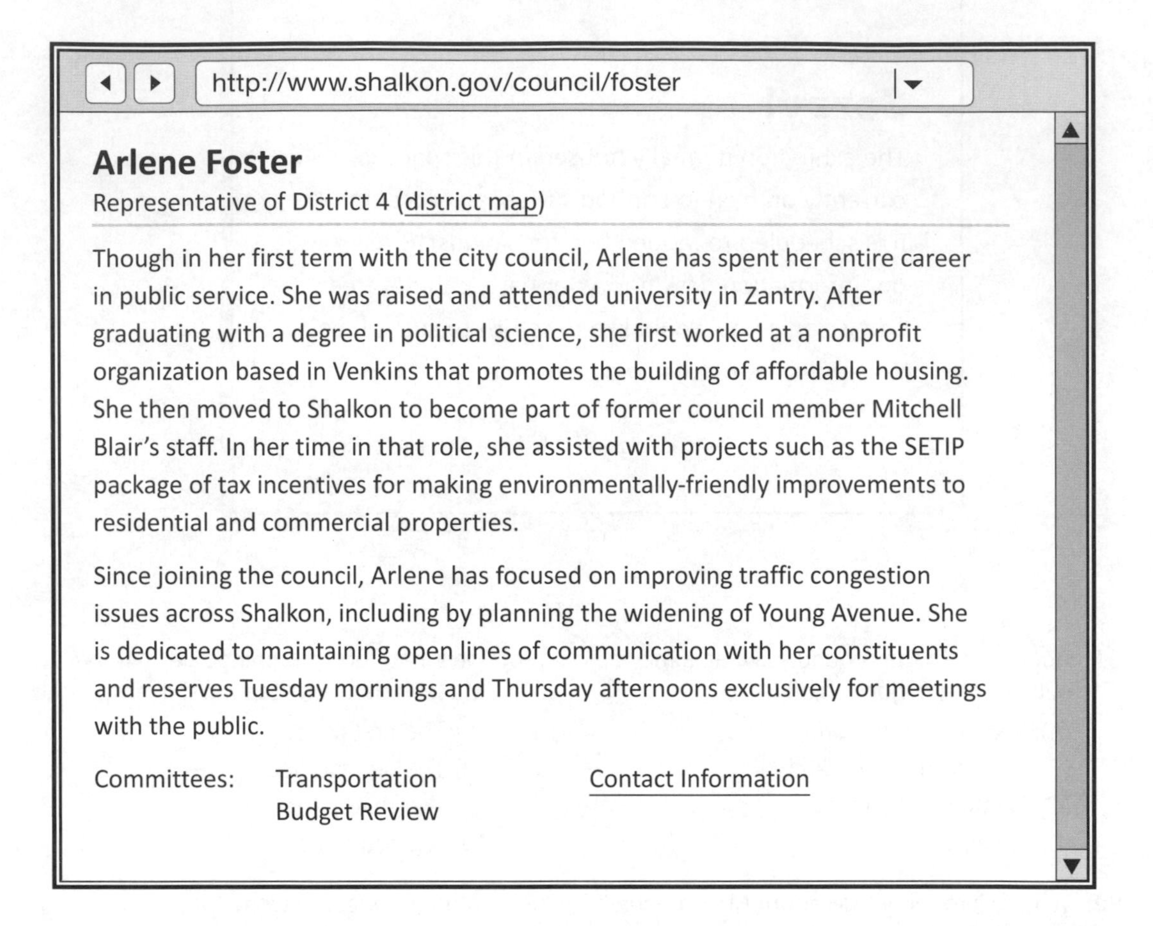

http://www.shalkon.gov/council/foster

**Arlene Foster**

Representative of District 4 (district map)

Though in her first term with the city council, Arlene has spent her entire career in public service. She was raised and attended university in Zantry. After graduating with a degree in political science, she first worked at a nonprofit organization based in Venkins that promotes the building of affordable housing. She then moved to Shalkon to become part of former council member Mitchell Blair's staff. In her time in that role, she assisted with projects such as the SETIP package of tax incentives for making environmentally-friendly improvements to residential and commercial properties.

Since joining the council, Arlene has focused on improving traffic congestion issues across Shalkon, including by planning the widening of Young Avenue. She is dedicated to maintaining open lines of communication with her constituents and reserves Tuesday mornings and Thursday afternoons exclusively for meetings with the public.

Committees: Transportation
Budget Review

Contact Information

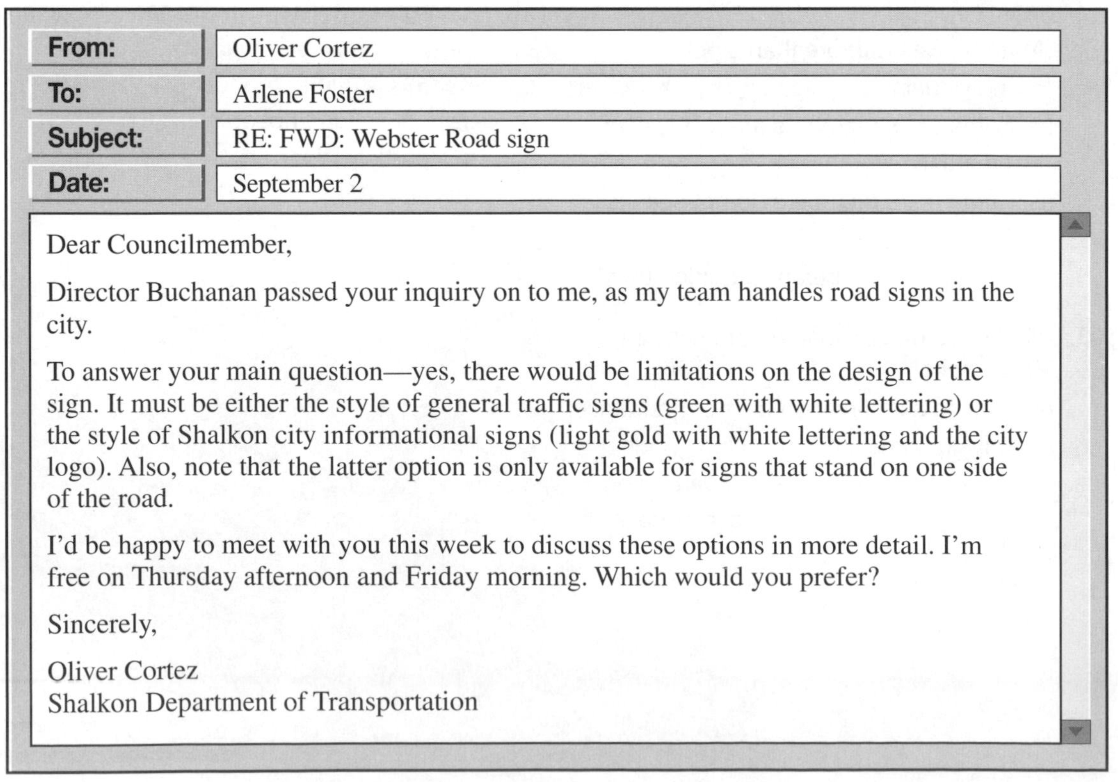

**From:** Oliver Cortez
**To:** Arlene Foster
**Subject:** RE: FWD: Webster Road sign
**Date:** September 2

Dear Councilmember,

Director Buchanan passed your inquiry on to me, as my team handles road signs in the city.

To answer your main question—yes, there would be limitations on the design of the sign. It must be either the style of general traffic signs (green with white lettering) or the style of Shalkon city informational signs (light gold with white lettering and the city logo). Also, note that the latter option is only available for signs that stand on one side of the road.

I'd be happy to meet with you this week to discuss these options in more detail. I'm free on Thursday afternoon and Friday morning. Which would you prefer?

Sincerely,

Oliver Cortez
Shalkon Department of Transportation

## City Names Stretch of Webster Road after Cummings

(September 29)—A section of Webster Road between Coleman Street and Young Avenue has been co-named in honor of Frances Cummings, Shalkon's first female mayor.

Shalkon city council member Arlene Foster, who proposed the tribute, gathered with members of the late Mayor Cummings's family and others near the intersection of Webster Road and Coleman Street yesterday for a small unveiling ceremony.

The crowd cheered as a tarp was pulled off a new sign bridge that spans Webster Road and proclaims the subsequent half-mile of road to be "Frances Cummings Way." This section of road was chosen because of its proximity to Talmage Park, which Mayor Cummings famously revitalized during her tenure in office.

Council member Foster and Edmund Cummings, Mayor Cummings's son, gave speeches highlighting the mayor's positive impact on Shalkon.

**196.** What does the Web page state about Ms. Foster?
(A) She is not a native of Shalkon.
(B) She has been elected multiple times.
(C) She owns property on Young Avenue.
(D) She does not work in the field her degree is in.

**197.** When did Mr. Cortez and Ms. Foster most likely meet?
(A) On a Thursday morning
(B) On a Thursday afternoon
(C) On a Friday morning
(D) On a Friday afternoon

**198.** In the e-mail, the word "passed" in paragraph 1, line 1, is closest in meaning to
(A) relayed
(B) enacted
(C) declined
(D) surpassed

**199.** What is most likely true about the finished sign?
(A) It features a city symbol.
(B) It is visible from the entrance to a park.
(C) It is located outside of a city's limits.
(D) Its background is green.

**200.** What did Ms. Foster speak about on September 28?
(A) The future of a scientific endeavor
(B) The accomplishments of a local politician
(C) The importance of environmental conservation
(D) The unique characteristics of a neighborhood

**Stop! This is the end of the test. If you finish before time is called, you may go back to Parts 5, 6, and 7 and check your work.**

# Translation

# ACTUAL TEST 1

## PART 5 P. 8–10

### 101. 動詞詞彙題 難

阿德瑞先生對於受推薦的候選人缺乏必須的組織技巧表達擔憂。

(A) 失敗　**(C) 缺乏**
(B) 掙扎　(D) 限制

- proposed (adj.) 被推薦的　candidate (n.) 候選人
  organizational (adj.) 組織的

---

### 102. 名詞詞彙題——動詞的受詞

雷維爾的公共工程部門聘僱當地的承包商來清理湖邊。

(A) 合約　(C) 承包商
(B) 收縮的　**(D) 承包商**

- lakeside (n.) 湖邊

---

### 103. 相關連接詞 

提交的翻譯作品必須包括原文和你的翻譯。

(A) 沿著……　(C) 全部
**(B) 和……**　(D) 也

- submission (n.) 提交

---

### 104. 介系詞詞彙題

除了喇叭系統暫時出現問題外，產品發表會皆按計畫進行。

**(A) 除了……外**　(C) 代替
(B) 畢竟　(D) 不只……

- product launch (n.) 產品上市

---

### 105. 代名詞詞彙題

請在指定日期前將書籍歸還圖書館，讓其他讀者能自由借閱。

(A) 它　**(C) 它們**
(B) 它自己　(D) 它們自己

- patron (n.) 老主顧；常客

---

### 106. 動詞詞彙題

將此藥物暴露在強光或高溫下會降低其效用。

(A) 攝取　(C) 允許
(B) 處理　**(D) 暴露**

- effectiveness (n.) 效能；有效性
  consume (v.) 攝取；消耗

---

### 107. 副詞詞彙題 難

當機器缺紙或無法運作時，顯示螢幕上會出現通知。

**(A) 在其他方面**　(C) 萬一
(B) 然而　(D) 再也（不）

- function (v.) 運作；起作用
  notification (n.) 通知

---

### 108. 名詞詞彙題

可以透過填寫線上表格來延長 MimEx 智慧型手機的保固期。

**(A) 保固**　(C) 設計
(B) 生命週期　(D) 小販

- lifespan (n.) 生命週期

---

### 109. 代名詞詞彙題——主詞動詞單複數一致性

為了提高參與意願，每位參加攝影比賽的人都會收到一份小禮物。

(A) 那些　(C) 他們
**(B) 每個人**　(D) 許多

- boost (v.) 提升；提高
  participation (n.) 參與　receive (v.) 獲得

---

### 110. 介系詞詞彙題 

艾爾提斯汽車的大部分財務資源都用於開發新車。

(A) 藉由　**(C) 為了**
(B) 除……之外　(D) 到……之上

- bulk (n.) 大部分　direct (v.) 指派給……
  vehicle (n.) 汽車

---

### 111. 形容詞詞彙題——修飾名詞

即使是多山地帶，無線電塔將為保育巡查員提供可靠的通訊方式。

**(A) 可靠的**　(C) 可靠性
(B) 可靠地　(D) 依靠的

- radio tower (n.) 電波塔
  park ranger (n.) 保育巡查員
  mountainous (adj.) 多山的
  terrain (n.) 地帶；地域

**112. 副詞詞彙題——修飾動詞**

將植物盡可能密集地排列在水族箱的地板上，好為您的魚創造理想的環境。

(A) 最密集的　(C) 密度
**(B) 密集地**　(D) 較密集的

- density (n.) 密度

**113. 形容詞詞彙題** 難

繆爾女士認為，製造業的技術進步為消費者帶來了更好的價格。

(A) 可比較的　(C) 市場
(B) 充滿的　**(D) 較好的**

- advancement (n.) 進步
  manufacturing (n.) 製造業
  consumer (n.) 消費者
  comparable (adj.) 可比較的；比得上的
  market price (n.) 市場價格

**114. 動詞詞類變化題——分詞構句**

古雷夫公司昨天舉行記者會宣布了擴張的計畫，令其在採礦業的競爭對手感到驚訝。

(A) 感到驚訝的　(C) 使……驚訝
**(B) 使……驚訝**　(D) 驚喜

- press conference (n.) 記者會
  expand (v.) 拓展；擴張　rival (n.) 競爭對手
  mining industry (n.) 採礦業

**115. 副詞詞彙題** 難

柯琳娜辣味起司漢堡作為布倫福特燒烤餐廳最受歡迎的品項，在該餐廳的廣告中是主打焦點。

**(A) 顯著地；突出地**　(C) 快速地
(B) 不經意地　(D) 各自地

- feature (v.) 作為主要角色
  inadvertently (adv.) 不慎地；非故意地
  respectively (adv.) 各自地；分別地

**116. 名詞詞彙題**

嗨歐健康公司關於其芳香精油好處的說法，並未經過科學驗證。

(A) 結果　(C) 實驗
**(B) 認證**　(D) 藉口

- claim (v.) 宣稱；主張　benefit (n.) 好處；利益
  experiment (n.) 實驗　excuse (n.) 藉口；理由

**117. 副詞子句連接詞詞彙題**

電視廣告適用於目標市場廣泛的產品，而行動廣告更適用於小眾產品。

(A) 儘管　**(C) 然而**
(B) 與……相反　(D) 除非……

- appropriate for 對……合適的
  target market (n.) 目標市場
  niche product (n.) 利基產品
  contrary to 與……相反

**118. 不定詞 to V——當形容詞的用法**

這份備忘錄詳細說明了我們將二級儲藏室改造成小型會議空間的提議。

(A) 將會轉變　(C) 被轉變
(B) 轉變　**(D) 轉變**

- storage closet (n.) 儲物櫃
  convert A into B 將 A 轉換成 B

**119. 動詞詞彙題**

只要不妨礙工作，生產線工人可以蓄鬍。

(A) 影響　**(C) 妨礙；干預**
(B) 使中斷　(D) 妥協

- assembly line (n.) 生產線　facial hair (n.) 鬍子

**120. 形容詞詞彙題——受詞補語**

調查數據顯示，實習生發現書面培訓資料比影片內容資訊更豐富。

(A) 通知　(C) 資訊豐富地
(B) 資訊　**(D) 資訊豐富的**

- material (n.) 資料　inform (v.) 通知

**121. 副詞子句連接詞詞彙題**

新員工將被要求佩戴臨時識別證，直到他們的正式識別證被發下來為止。

(A) 是否　(C) 彷彿
(B) 而不是　**(D) 直到**

- official (adj.) 正式的；官方的
  identification card (n.) 識別證　issue (v.) 核發

**122. 動詞詞類題——語態** 

由於佩里女士持續不懈地發起行動，教育現在成為市議會選舉的核心議題。

(A) 浮現　**(C) 正在浮現**
(B) 將被浮現　(D) 已被浮現

- thanks to 幸虧；由於　tireless (adj.) 不懈怠的
  council (n.) 議會　election (n.) 選舉

**123. 名詞詞彙題**

佣金制度為銷售人員提供了努力工作的強烈動機。

**(A) 動機；激勵**　(C) 監督
(B) 滿足　(D) 方法

- commission (n.) 佣金
  sales associate (n.) 銷售專員
  supervision (n.) 監督　approach (n.) 方法

**124. 副詞詞彙題——修飾介系詞片語** 難

顧名思義，「初學者繪畫」專門針對那些以前從未學習過這門工藝的人。

(A) 明確說明　(C) 明確說明的
(B) 明確的　**(D) 明確地**

- suggest (v.) 指出　cater to 為……服務
  craft (n.) 技藝　specify (v.) 明確指出
  specific (adj.) 明確的

**125. 形容詞詞彙題** 

技術支援部門的預算已不足以支付其人員開支。

(A) 必不可少的　(C) 習慣的
(B) 豐富的　**(D) 足夠的**

- budget (n.) 預算
  staffing expense (n.) 人事費用
  vital (adj.) 必不可少的
  accustomed (adj.) 習慣的

**126. 副詞詞彙題**

塔斯科軟體可幫助管理人員確保在團隊成員之間平均分配任務。

(A) 簡要地　**(C) 平均地**
(B) 寬鬆地　(D) 最近

- ensure (v.) 確保　distribute (v.) 分發

**127. 名詞詞彙題——動詞的受詞**

我們的服務包括提供任何所需的進出口文件。

(A) 提供　**(C) 提供**
(B) 供應商　(D) 提供的

- required (adj.) 必要的　import (n.) 進口
  export (n.) 出口　supplier (n.) 供應商

**128. 介系詞詞彙題**

Hogan & Partners 的實習計畫，讓法學院的學生有機會在經驗豐富的律師指導下學習。

(A) 在……之中　(C) 在……之後
**(B) 在……之下**　(D) 在……之間

- guidance (n.) 指導；輔導
  seasoned (adj.) 經驗豐富的　attorney (n.) 律師

**129. 動詞詞類變化題——時態——與過去事實相反的假設語氣**

如果馬丁先生從馬德里起飛的航班有準時到達，他當時就可以參加這場會議的歡迎會了。

(A) 正在參加　(C) 可以參加
**(B) 可以參加**　(D) 已參加

- attend (v.) 參加　conference (n.) 會議
  reception (n.) 接待會；歡迎會

**130. 名詞詞彙題**

琴瓦新飲料系列的成功，減少了其對旗艦能量棒收益的依賴。

(A) 專業知識　(C) 觀點
**(B) 依賴**　(D) 短缺

- flagship (n.) 旗艦　revenue (n.) 收入
  expertise (n.) 專門知識
  perspective (n.) 觀點；角度

## PART 6 P. 11–14

**131–134 網頁**

www.vegashift.com

**VegaShift**

VegaShift 是一款行動應用程式，可為餐廳、商店和其他輪班制的企業提供一種快速、簡單的方法來讓排班更便利。員工 [131] **直接**給同事多的輪班時間，同事可以自己選擇是否接受輪班。這讓員工能夠在不給主管帶來不便的情況下，增加工作時間的彈性。[132] **同時，** VegaShift 讓管理階層能保有對時程的控制。主管可以要求所有輪班交換都需獲得批准，這樣任何人的工作時間都不會超過其 [133] **被允許的**工作時間。該應用程式還可以提醒管理階層，注意可能因員工時薪差異而增加的成本。

我們對 VegaShift 的品質非常有信心，因此提供企業免費使用整整一個月。[134] **在以下輸入您的資料，立即開始免費試用。**

- shift (n.) 輪班　facilitate (v.) 促進
  supervisor (n.) 監督人；管理人
  management (n.) 管理　retain (v.) 保留
  approve (v.) 核准；同意
  alert A to B 警告 A 注意 B

**131. 副詞詞彙題——修飾動詞**

(A) 領導　(C) 正領導
**(B) 直接地**　(D) 方向

- direct 將……導向

---

**132. 連接副詞** 難

(A) 因此　(C) 相反地
(B) 也就是說　**(D) 同時**

---

**133. 形容詞詞彙題**

**(A) 被允許的**　(C) 偏好的
(B) 被縮短的　(D) 多餘的

---

**134. 句子插入題** 難

(A) 了解《Tech Z》為何將我們評為業界最佳雇主之一。
**(B) 在以下輸入您的資料，立即開始免費試用。**
(C) 如需完整的產品列表，請點選「產品」。
(D) 可撥打 1-800-555-0184 以獲得其他技術支援。

- employer (n.) 雇主　trial (n.) 試用期
  offering (n.) 出售物

---

**135–138 報導**

**雷諾將舉辦國家科學節**

雷諾　訊（12 月 11 日）——國家科技部（NDST）宣布，雷諾市將於六月舉辦第二屆的年度國家科學節。

NDST 發言人艾薩克．霍奇斯表示，這項榮譽的 135 **競爭**非常激烈，但選擇雷諾是因其「快速發展的農業科學和生物技術產業」。他還提到了該市最近為科技新創企業所建立的雷諾 300 大樓。136 **在那裡的租戶公司可以獲得特別的資金和建議。**

國家科學節是一個為期一週的活動，展示國家的科學成就和專案計畫。它的特點包括向大眾介紹最新概念的講座、適合所有年齡層的展覽和 137 **吸引人的**演示。第一屆是在奧格斯比 138 **舉辦**。

- announce (v.) 宣布；公告
  agricultural (adj.) 農業的
  biotechnology (n.) 生物科技　industry (n.) 產業
  establishment (n.) 建立；創建
  start-up (n.) 剛起步的小企業
  achievement (n.) 成就
  cutting-edge (adj.) 尖端的；領先的
  exhibition (n.) 展覽
  demonstration (n.) 展示；示範操作

**135. 名詞詞彙題**

(A) 選擇　**(C) 競爭**
(B) 機會　(D) 推薦

---

**136. 句子插入題** 

(A) 希望住宿的遊客應儘快預訂。
(B) 他在市府任職期間發起了數個同樣的專案計畫。
**(C) 在那裡的租戶公司可以獲得特別的資金和建議。**
(D) 擔心施工會在活動期間造成交通問題。

- initiate (v.) 開始；創始　tenant (n.) 租客；租戶

---

**137. 形容詞詞彙題——修飾名詞**

**(A) 吸引人的**　(C) 著迷的
(B) 迷人地　(D) 使迷住

- fascinate (v.) 使……迷住

---

**138. 動詞詞類變化題——時態**

(A) 曾正被舉辦　(C) 被舉辦
**(B) 被舉辦**　(D) 將被舉辦

---

**139–142 電子郵件**

寄件人：派翠克．霍爾布魯克
收件人：圖書館服務人員
主旨：同儕評價
日期：11 月 15 日
附件：評估表

大家好：

年度員工績效評估將於下個月進行。和以前一樣，評估將由我進行，但會包括 139 **來自**圖書館服務部同仁的意見。為了收集這些反饋意見，我需要你們每個人都填寫附件中的評估表並寄回。請為部門的每位成員都填寫一份。141 **問卷的格式沒有改變。**和上次一樣，你需要先評價你的同事在一系列領域中的表現，然後寫一段來解釋並詳細說明你的回答。但是，我呼籲大家，今年要特別注意後半部分。請記住，深思熟慮的意見回饋可以讓你的同事受益匪淺。

圖書館服務部副主任
派翠克．霍爾布魯克

- performance evaluation (n.) 表現評估
  conduct (v.) 執行 peer (n.) 同儕 rate (v.) 評價
  a range of 一系列 expand on 闡述；詳述
  urge (v.) 力勸

**139. 介系詞詞彙題**

| | |
|---|---|
| **(A) 來自……** | (C) 像…… |
| (B) 在……之上 | (D) 在……之上 |

**140. 動詞詞彙題**

| | |
|---|---|
| (A) 同意 | **(C) 完成** |
| (B) 匯編 | (D) 參加 |

- grant (v.) 給予；授與 compile (v.) 彙編

**141. 句子插入題** 

(A) 問卷也會發送給圖書館常客。
**(B) 問卷的格式沒有改變。**
(C) 湯主任將出席每次審查。
(D) 你似乎有一些格子沒有填。

- survey (n.) 調查 distribute (v.) 發送；分發
  patron (n.) 老主顧；常客
  questionnaire (n.) 問卷

**142. 副詞詞彙題——修飾動詞**

| | |
|---|---|
| (A) 考量 | (C) 相當大的 |
| (B) 考量 | **(D) 相當大地** |

- considerable (adj.) 相當大的；相當多的

**143–146 公告**

顧客須知

由於紙張和墨水等原物料成本增加，惠勒印刷廠決定自 2 月 1 日起調漲印刷服務價格。[143] **我們的平面設計服務價格將維持不變。**

這是我們五年多來第一次進行這種 [144] **調整**。出於對客戶的尊重，我們已延後調漲，但由於上述經濟因素，調漲現在已是勢在必行。為了讓我們能夠在未來繼續提供一流的服務，[145] **提高**價格是必要的。

我們將於 2 月 1 日更新價目表以反映上述變更，我們並鼓勵員工清楚說明所有印刷服務的成本以避免誤會。關於漲價的疑問可以向我們的經理露西亞．賽瑟 [146] **反應**。感謝您的理解。

- due to 因為；由於 raw material (n.) 原物料
  abovementioned (adj.) 上述的 factor (n.) 因素
  top-notch (adj.) 一流的 upfront (adj.) 坦率的

**143. 句子插入題** 

(A) 我們將無法再接受任何其他格式的電子檔。
(B) 我們將自 2 月 8 日起恢復固定營業時間。
(C) 若要印刷包裝材料，請造訪我們的霍洛威分廠。
**(D) 我們的平面設計服務價格將維持不變。**

- resume (v.) 恢復；重新開始

**144. 名詞詞彙題**

| | |
|---|---|
| **(A) 調整** | (C) 離開 |
| (B) 支出 | (D) 錯誤 |

- expenditure (n.) 消費；支出

**145. 動名詞詞彙題——主詞**

| | |
|---|---|
| (A) 已調漲 | (C) 要被調漲 |
| (B) 調漲 | **(D) 調漲** |

**146. 動詞詞類變化題——時態**

| | |
|---|---|
| (A) 已被反應 | (C) 正在反應 |
| **(B) 可以被反應** | (D) 將會被反應 |

**PART 7** P. 15–35

**147–148 資訊**

《豪威爾航空》

**豪威爾「空中貴賓休息室」賓客政策**

「空中貴賓休息室」會員可以攜帶持有豪威爾航空當日航班機票的旅客以賓客身分進入休息室。[147] **白金會員可以免費攜帶兩名賓客或配偶，和任何 21 歲以下子女進入「空中貴賓休息室」；黃金會員也可以支付每人 25 美元的費用，即享可有同樣的權利。**[148] **在到訪期間，賓客須由獲准進入的會員陪同**，也必須遵守「空中貴賓休息室」在服裝、舉止和設施使用上的相關規定。

- holder (n.) 持有者 spouse (n.) 配偶
  at no cost 免費 accompany (v.) 陪同
  admit (v.) 准許進入 duration (n.) 持續期間
  be subject to 服從於……；受……支配
  attire (n.) 服裝 amenities (n.) 便利設施

**147. 相關細節**

根據本則資訊，會員類型有什麼不同？

(A) 賓客可以停留的時間
(B) 允許入內的賓客人數
**(C) 攜帶賓客入內的費用**
(D) 賓客所需具備的資歷

- amount (n.) 量　qualification (n.) 資格

**148. 相關細節**

賓客進入「空中貴賓休息室」後，必須做什麼事情？

**(A) 與陪同者待在一起**
(B) 佩戴身分證明
(C) 將行李寄放在指定區域
(D) 支付設施的費用

- identification (n.) 身分證明文件
  designated (adj.) 指定的；特定的

**換句話說**
be accompanied by the admitted member（由獲准進入的會員陪同）
→ (A) Remain with an escort（與陪同者待在一起）

**149–150 電子郵件**

**寄件人：**娜塔莎．阿克斯
**收件人：**薩切爾頓跑步俱樂部
**主旨：**三月的活動
**日期：**2 月 28 日

嗨跑者們！天氣開始變暖是不是很好呢？很快地，我們將在聚會時欣賞到許多綠意盎然的美景。

以下是三月分俱樂部規劃的活動：

- 近期活動提醒：斯普拉特市馬拉松。詳情如下。[149] **如果您想在前一天晚上一起搭車到該市，請在比賽報名截止日前與我聯繫。**
  - 日期：3 月 30 日
  - 地點：斯普拉特
  - 路線長度：26.2 英里
  - [149] **報名截止日期：3 月 16 日**
  - 網站：www.sprattcitymarathon.com
- 我們將持續在每週日上午 10 點（7 英里路線）和週三晚上 7 點（5 英里路線）於科斯蒙公園舉行團跑。[150] **請記得在俱樂部網站事先報名，好讓我知道要寄關於活動取消或其他變更的簡訊通知給你。**

期望能在課程中見到你！
娜塔莎

- greenery (n.) 青枝綠葉；綠色植物
  outing (n.) 遠足；郊遊　registration (n.) 登記報名
  in advance 事先　notification (n.) 通知
  cancellation (n.) 取消

**149. 相關細節**

應該要在哪天之前聯繫阿克斯女士有關共乘到斯普拉特的事情？

(A) 2 月 28 日　(C) 3 月 29 日
**(B) 3 月 16 日**　(D) 3 月 30 日

**換句話說**
carpooling（共乘）
→ sharing transportation（共乘）

**150. 相關細節**

阿克斯女士提醒收件人要做什麼？

(A) 每個星期天發簡訊給她
(B) 在團跑前熱身
**(C) 報名以收到活動相關的最新消息**
(D) 事先研究跑步路線

**換句話說**
sign up（登記報名）→ (C) Register（登記註冊）
text message notifications about cancellations or other changes（關於活動取消或其他變更的簡訊通知）→ (C) updates about events（活動相關的最新消息）

**151–153 電子郵件**

**寄件人：**<service@hildytea.com>
**收件人：**羅莎琳德．伯克 <roz.burke@pow-mail.com>
**主旨：**提醒
**日期：**12 月 8 日

親愛的伯克女士：

「希爾迪茶盒」希望您在過去一年中，對我們服務的禮品訂閱感到滿意。[151] **若欲於 12 月之後繼續收到每月的優質散裝茶葉包，請造訪此頁面並輸入您的帳單資訊。**商品含運費只要每月 14 美元，您可以選擇為期三個月、六個月或一年的訂閱方案。此外，[152] **作為現有訂戶，您有資格獲得一份特別的續訂禮物：一個普雷亞品牌的旅行杯**，一次可保溫長達 12 小時。請注意，一旦您目前的訂閱到期，此份優惠將失效。

[153] **如果您有任何問題，請直接回覆此電子郵件即可。**我或其他代表將在 24 小時內回覆。

希爾迪茶盒
客服部　埃爾莫・史坦利　謹啟

- subscription (v.) 訂閱
  loose leaf tea (n.) 散茶；原葉茶葉
  billing (n.) 開具發票　existing (adj.) 現行的
  be eligible for 有資格……　renewal (n.) 更新
  invalid (adj.) 無效的　current (adj.) 目前的
  run out 到期；失效

**151. 主旨或目的**

為什麼會寄這封電子郵件給伯克女士？

(A) 她抱怨有關「希爾迪茶盒」的事情。
(B) 她向一位朋友介紹了「希爾迪茶盒」。
(C) 一項新產品上市了。
**(D) 她的訂閱即將到期。**

- refer A to B 將 A 送交給 B；向 A 轉介 B

**152. 相關細節**

史坦利先生向伯克女士提供了什麼？

**(A) 一個飲用容器**
(B) 一些寒冷天氣穿的服飾
(C) 一年免運費
(D) 一項促銷的提前通知

- apparel (n.) 服飾　sales promotion (n.) 促銷

換句話說
travel mug（旅行杯）
→ (A) drinking container（飲用容器）

**153. 句子插入題**

「我或其他代表將在 24 小時內回覆。」最適合放在 [1]、[2]、[3]、[4] 哪個位置？

(A) [1]　(C) [3]
(B) [2]　**(D) [4]**

- representative (n.) 代表；代理人

**154–155 線上聊天室**

艾力克斯・柯林斯〔上午 9:02〕
梅賽德斯，我有一個小問題。[154] **我購買新筆記型電腦的申請是怎麼回事？**我以為現在就可以處理了。

梅賽德斯・伯奇〔上午 9:03〕
嗨，艾力克斯。[154] **你沒有收到我的電子郵件嗎？**資訊科技部推薦不同的型號。[154] **只要你同意變更，我們就可以完成處理你的申請。**

艾力克斯・柯林斯〔上午 9:07〕
原來如此。嗯，看起來他們推薦的機種比我申請的還重。但 [155] **我經常必須攜帶筆記型電腦到工地現場附近**，因此有台輕量型機種很重要。

梅賽德斯・伯奇〔上午 9:08〕
在這種情況下，你可以反對變更。只要寫一個簡短的段落解釋情況，然後我會把它附在申請後面。

艾力克斯・柯林斯〔上午 9:08〕
我很高興有這樣的選擇。我會照做的，謝謝。

- purchase (n.) 購買　request (n.) 需求
  process (v.) 處理　approve (v.) 核准；同意
  construction site (n.) 工地現場
  lightweight (adj.) 輕便的　oppose (v.) 反對
  append A to B 將 A 附加在 B 之後

**154. 掌握意圖**

上午 9:03，伯奇女士寫道：「你沒有收到我的電子郵件嗎？」是什麼意思？

**(A) 她的電子郵件解釋了為何延遲。**
(B) 她的電子郵件通知某項流程結束。
(C) 她的電子郵件描述了一項政策變更。
(D) 她的電子郵件宣布了一項員工調動。

- transfer (v.) 轉移；調動

**155. 相關細節**

柯林斯先生說他的工作常常需要什麼？

(A) 執行培訓
**(B) 造訪工地**
(C) 進行具有說服力的寫作
(D) 研究個人電子產品

- carry out 執行

換句話說
construction site（工地現場）
→ (B) work sites（工地現場）

**156–157 通知**

**桑德林公寓住戶須知**

在過去的幾個月裡，寄到公寓管理辦公室的租戶包裹數量已經超出了我們所能處理的範圍。這導致了我們員工的工作量過大、設施的空間減少，並且發生了幾起包裹遺失事件。因此，[156] **自 10 月 1 日星期一開始，辦公室將不再為租戶收包裹**。請利用這則提前通知，為可能在該日或之後寄達的任何包裹做其他的安排。[157] **可以安排送到您的大樓門口**或寄到第三方地點（如郵政信箱或您的工作場所）。

桑德林公寓管理處

- tenant (n.) 租戶；租客　capacity (n.) 容量；能力
  excessive (adj.) 過多的　facility (n.) 場所
  incident (n.) 事件　take advantage of 利用
  ample (adj.) 足夠的；充裕的
  advance notice 事先告知

**156. 主旨或目的**

公寓住戶主要收到了什麼通知？

(A) 召開租戶會議
**(B) 取消收件服務**
(C) 安裝便利設施
(D) 某些商品送錯地方

- elimination (n.) 淘汰；排除
  misplacement (n.) 錯置

換句話說
no longer accept delivery of packages（不再收包裹）
→ (B) The elimination of a receiving service（取消收件服務）

**157. 推論或暗示** 難

文中提到關於桑德林公寓的什麼事？

(A) 它的辦公室週末休息。
(B) 它很快將由新的管理方接手。
(C) 它近期縮減了員工人數。
**(D) 它占據了多棟建築。**

- occupy (v.) 占領；占據
  multiple (adj.) 由許多部分組成的；複合的

**158–160 備忘錄**

寄件人：尚恩．麥克斯維爾
收件人：全體員工
關於：公告
日期：5 月 8 日

到了每年高德溫出版社讓所有員工有機會展現創造力的時候了。[158/159] **我們再次徵求新增西班牙語言教育解決方案系列的創新提案。**我們歡迎任何發行過的商品類型（書籍、閃示卡、桌遊等）或與它們相似的產品。我們相信有價值的貢獻可能來自非常規的來源，因此我們鼓勵各個領域的員工參與。[159] **去年，會計部的露易絲．愛德華茲推薦了一本書，該書不僅出版了**，而且銷量也很好。如果你有新的想法，我們鼓勵你暫時擱置慣常的工作，並為其撰寫提案。

每個員工最多可以提交兩個提案。提案沒有特定的格式，但 [160] **應包括對產品及其目標市場的詳細描述**。然而，為了使提交的文件易於管理，我們要求長度不超過一頁。請在 5 月 19 日星期五之前寄到 ivan@goldwinpublishing.com 給我的助理伊凡．布里格茲。

- innovative (adj.) 創新的
  reasonably (adv.) 合理地；相當地
  unconventional (adj.) 非常規的；不依慣例的
  participate (v.) 參加　put aside 擱置
  submit (v.) 提交　submission (n.) 提交
  manageable (adj.) 可管理的

**158. 相關細節**

麥克斯維爾要求備忘錄的收件人提交什麼？

(A) 針對現有產品的評論
**(B) 潛在新產品的想法**
(C) 加入產品開發團隊的申請
(D) 改善產品開發過程的提案

- potential (adj.) 可能的；潛在的
  improve (v.) 改善；改進

換句話說
proposals for innovative additions（新增創新提案）
→ (B) Ideas for potential new products（潛在新商品的想法）

**159. 推論或暗示** 

愛德華茲女士的書最有可能是要給誰看的？

(A) 桌遊迷　**(C) 語言學習者**
(B) 業餘廚師　(D) 會計系學生

**160. 確認事實與否**

文中提到關於提交文件的什麼事？

(A) 應該要寄給兩個人。
(B) 一年收件兩次。
(C) 最多可長達兩頁。
**(D) 必須包含兩種資訊。**

**換句話說**

a detailed description of the product and its target market（對產品與其目標市場的詳細描述）
→ (B) two pieces of information（兩種資訊）

## 161–164 網頁

www.shopslam.com/hiring/faq

**有關 Shopslam 招聘的常見問題**

[161] **由於我們令人振奮的工作環境和出色的員工福利，每年都有許多人表示有興趣成為 Shopslam 團隊的一員**。我們的招聘人員無法回覆收到的所有詢問，因此我們在這個網頁上集結了一些常見問題及回答。

1. 我可以應徵一份以上的工作嗎？
   可以的。但是，[163] **我們強烈建議您專注於您最適合的職位**。
2. 你們在招聘過程中是否提供身心障礙者調整服務？
   [162] **我們很樂意為來自外地的面試者提供手語翻譯、輪椅無障礙飯店等服務**。只需填寫選填的「無障礙申請表」並將其附在您的其他應徵資料中。
3. [164] **如果我的應徵被拒絕，你們會通知我嗎？**
   由於我們收到大量的應徵，意味著 [164] **我們只能向成功應徵的求職者寄送有關招聘流程的最新資訊**。
4. 被拒絕後，我可以重新應徵同一份工作嗎？
   可以的，但如果是技術職位，我們會要求您在此之前獲得豐富的額外經歷。

- **employee benefits (n.)** 員工福利
  **inquiry (n.)** 詢問 **permit (v.)** 允許；准許
  **qualified (adj.)** 有資格的 **disability (n.)** 身障
  **accommodation (n.)** 便利設施
  **sign language interpreter (n.)** 手語譯者
  **wheelchair-accessible (adj.)** 輪椅可通行的
  **accessibility (n.)** 易到達；易接近
  **candidate (n.)** 應徵者 **substantial (adj.)** 大量的

### 161. 推論或暗示

關於 Shopslam，下列何者最可能為真？

(A) 它每年僱用數千人。
(B) 它派遣招聘人員至大學校園。
(C) 它對於部分技術職位的要求較低。
**(D) 它以身為好雇主而聞名。**

- **annually (adv.)** 一年一度地
  **reputation (n.)** 名譽；名聲

### 162. 確認事實與否 難

本文提到了何種身心障礙人士的適應服務？

**(A) 協助面對面溝通**
(B) 有大字體的表格
(C) 容易抵達的面試地點
(D) 額外填寫文件的時間

- **in-person** 親自

### 163. 相關細節

根據網頁，求職者應該做什麼？

(A) 確認網頁上的招聘更新資訊
**(B) 集中精力在一個職缺上**
(C) 在申請資料裡附上工作樣本
(D) 查看常見面試問題清單

- **concentrate (v.)** 集中；全神貫注

**換句話說**

focus on the position for which you are best qualified（專注於您最適合的職位）
→ (B) Concentrate their efforts on a single opening（集中精力在一個職缺上）

### 164. 確認事實與否 難

哪一個問題沒有得到肯定的答覆？

(A) 1 **(C) 3**
(B) 2 (D) 4

- **affirmative (adj.)** 肯定的

## 165–168 簡訊串

琳恩・弗萊明〔下午 1:45〕
強尼，你還在超市嗎？

約翰・里維拉〔下午 1:47〕
不，我在回去的路上了。我把車停在路邊回覆妳的簡訊。怎麼了嗎？

琳恩・弗萊明〔下午 1:48〕
[165] **我剛剛為五點要到的客人打掃了玫瑰房**，我們的一些清潔用品用完了。[166] **你介意回去買一些嗎？**我知道這很不方便。

約翰・里維拉〔下午 1:49〕
嗯，[166] **我就在奈許商場旁邊**。

琳恩・弗萊明〔下午 1:50〕
哦，[166] **那可以！**我們需要紙巾和窗戶清潔劑。

約翰・里維拉〔下午 1:51〕
真的嗎？[167] **我們的紙巾用完了？我上週剛買了一個 12 入的。**

琳恩・弗萊明〔下午 1:52〕
對，上週末住在丁香套房那個有小孩的家庭，用了很多來清理打翻的東西。這次何不買 24 入的呢？這應該可以讓我們用一段時間。

約翰・里維拉〔下午 1:53〕
好的。我應該半小時後回去。

琳恩・弗萊明〔下午 1:53〕
太棒了。[168] **別忘了也要索取這次購物的收據。**

- **pull over** 停靠路邊　**run out of** 用完；耗盡
  **spill (n.)** 溢出的東西

**165. 暗示或推論**

打字的人最可能在哪裡工作？

**(A) 小型旅館**　(C) 清潔公司
(B) 造景公司　(D) 教育機構

**166. 掌握意圖**

下午 1:49，里維拉先生寫道：「我就在奈許商場旁邊」，是什麼意思？

(A) 他的旅程進展快速。
**(B) 他可能可以在奈許商場買東西。**
(C) 他想要弗萊明女士來接他。
(D) 弗萊明女士從她的所在位置應該可以看見他。

**167. 推論或暗示**

什麼事最可能讓里維拉先生感到驚訝？

(A) 他被選中要做一項任務
(B) 弗萊明女士知道一項問題
(C) 一個事件發生後已過了一週了
**(D) 某些生活用品已經用完了**

- **use up** 用完；耗盡

**換句話說**
out of paper towels（紙巾用完了）
→ (D) some supplies have been used up（某些生活用品已經用完了）

**168. 相關細節**

弗萊明女士提醒里維拉先生做什麼事？

(A) 給汽車加油　**(C) 收取購買證明**
(B) 避免灑出液體　(D) 向同事發送通知

**換句話說**
get a receipt for this purchase（索取這次購物的收據）
→ (C) Receive proof of a payment（收取購買證明）

**169–171 電子郵件**

**寄件人：**瓦力・巴恩斯 <w.barnes@mclerdon.com>
**收件人：**阿拉薩莉・迪亞茲 <araceli@hevneymanufacturing.com>
**主旨：**請求
**日期：**4 月 28 日

親愛的迪亞茲女士：

我的名字是瓦力・巴恩斯，我是麥克萊登企業的行銷專員。[169] **敝部門在今年稍早得以成立，係多虧赫夫尼製造公司等客戶的忠實支持推動成長。**您的客戶經理奎因先生告訴我，[170] **麥克萊登的員工有幸守衛赫夫尼的工廠近五年了。**

除了自我介紹之外，[171] **寫此信也是為了提出一項請求。我目前正在為麥克萊登的網站增添客戶商標，並且希望也納入貴公司的標誌。**這通常會由貴公司與我們之間的服務協議授權，但我們在簽訂合約時尚未有那麼多的行銷技能，這意味著這項合約不包括這項條款。如果您同意此項請求，我們只需要您目前商標的清晰圖像，大小為 150×150 像素。但是，如果您希望我們不顯示您的商標，請隨時告訴我。

麥克萊登再次感謝您的惠顧。我們希望儘快收到您的來信。

麥克萊登企業
瓦力・巴恩斯　謹啟

- **fuel (v.)** 激起；刺激　**loyal (adj.)** 忠誠的
  **patronage (n.)** 贊助
  **account manager (n.)** 客戶經理
  **premises (n.)** 生產場所；經營場址
  **normally (adv.)** 通常；按慣例
  **authorize (v.)** 授權；批准
  **agreement (n.)** 同意；協定
  **expertise (n.)** 專業技能
  **provision (n.)** 規定；條款

**169. 推論或暗示**

文中提到關於巴恩斯先生的什麼事？

(A) 奎因先生是他的主管。
(B) 他協助草擬了一份協議。
**(C) 他擔任一個剛設立的職位。**
(D) 他瀏覽了赫夫尼製造公司的網站。

- draft (v.) 草擬

**換句話說**
My department was established earlier this year（敝部門於今年稍早成立）
→ (C) He holds a newly-created position（他擔任一個剛設立的職位）

---

**170. 推論或暗示** 

麥克萊登企業最可能為其客戶做什麼？

(A) 執行行銷活動
**(B) 提供保全人員**
(C) 修理工廠設備
(D) 提供法律建議

- equipment (n.) 設備

**換句話說**
guarding Hevney's factory premises（守衛赫夫尼的工廠場址）
→ (B) security（保全）

---

**171. 相關細節**

巴恩斯先生要求迪亞茲女士做什麼事？

(A) 客戶見證
(B) 已簽署的合約影本
(C) 確認機器尺寸
**(D) 使用圖像的許可**

- testimonial (n.) 推薦；見證
  confirmation (n.) 確認　dimension (n.) 尺寸
  permission (n.) 允許；批准

**換句話說**
include your company's [logo]（納入貴公司的〔商標〕）
→ (D) use an image（使用一張圖像）

---

**172–175 報導**

**《多雷塔》在播客界引起轟動**
文／菲利普．克努森

《多雷塔》這部八集的播客記錄了小說家多雷塔．沃斯的生平。《多雷塔》的粉絲很快就會有許多類似的節目可以聆聽。《多雷塔》的成功激發了其製作公司艾爾佳傳媒和其他幾家播客界鉅子的靈感，他們開發了描述歷史上有趣事件與人物的腳本化播客。

根據播客業界分析公司「廣播之眼」宣稱，[172] **十大最受歡迎的播客中，通常絕大多數是時事或採訪節目**。正因如此，《多雷塔》在主流中大受歡迎的成就才給人留下如此深刻的印象。[172] **作為歷史小說播客**，該節目以專業演員的腳本對話、音效及配樂為特色。然而，在播出的第二個月，它在「廣播之眼」的排行榜就上升到第四名。[173] **該節目在艾爾佳的網站上還有一個熱烈的討論區**，演員們在節目結束後不久就舉行了五場刪節版的現場表演，門票場場售罄。

有人推測，《多雷塔》的獨特性與其說是阻礙，倒不如說是它受歡迎的原因。然而，「廣播之眼」分析師辛西雅．邁爾斯不同意這種看法。「畢竟《多雷塔》不是第一個歷史小說播客，」她說。[174] **「我們的研究顯示，是這齣節目的出色寫作和表演吸引了聽眾。」**

儘管如此，業界認為現在有類似企劃的受眾。[175] **艾爾佳向《多雷塔》的創作者肯特．穆里根提供了一項利潤豐厚的交易，將在明年開發另一個歷史小說播客**。該公司的一位發言人表示，它將與科比特大橋的建設有關。與此同時，蘭斯頓工作室將在下個月公開《1955》，一個詳細介紹馬查德黑豹冠軍賽季的播客，而隨你聽廣播表示它目前正在製作一個描述穆雷爾與塔爾伯特訴訟案的節目。

- stir (n.) 騷動；轟動
  chronicle (v.) 按事件發生先後順序記錄
  scripted (adj.) 照稿子唸的
  depict (v.) 描述；描寫
  majority (n.) 大多數　achievement (n.) 成就
  mainstream (n.) 主流　popularity (n.) 流行
  make an impression 使人印象深刻
  score (n.)（電影、歌舞等的）配樂
  abridged (adj.) 刪節的　speculate (v.) 推測
  barrier (n.) 阻礙　indicate (v.) 指出
  lucrative (adj.) 獲利豐厚的
  court case (n.) 法庭案件

**172. 確認事實與否**

文中提到關於《多雷塔》的什麼事？

(A) 是以一本暢銷書為基礎。
(B) 預計會播出更多集。
**(C) 它和其他熱門播客屬於不同類型。**
(D) 是其製作公司所製作的第一個節目。

**173. 推論或暗示**

《多雷塔》的粉絲在艾爾佳傳媒的網站上最有可能做什麼？

(A) 購買主題商品
**(B) 互相留言**
(C) 閱讀一些生平事蹟
(D) 查看一場表演的照片

**換句話說**
an active discussion board（熱烈的討論區）
→ (B) Post messages to each other（互相留言）

**174. 相關細節**

邁爾斯女士針對什麼提供了專業意見？

**(A) 《多雷塔》成功的原因**
(B) 《多雷塔》的歷史正確性
(C) 「廣播之眼」排名的可靠性
(D) 艾爾佳傳媒的未來前景

- accuracy (n.) 正確性　reliability (n.) 可信度
  prospect (n.) 前途

**175. 句子插入題** 

「該公司的一位發言人表示，它將與科比特大橋的建設有關。」最適合放在 [1]、[2]、[3]、[4] 哪個位置？

(A) [1]　　(C) [3]
(B) [2]　　**(D) [4]**

**176–180 電子郵件與網頁**

**寄件人：**南妍熙
**收件人：**研發團隊
**主旨：**工作坊
**日期：**1 月 30 日

大家好：

我相信你們大多數人都聽說過新的資料視覺化軟體 Slinview。下個月，其製造商威盛科技將在這裡舉辦一個教育工作坊，八小時的教學，[178] **每人只需 40 美元**。這將是我們在投入大量資金購買 Slinview 之前，熟悉它的絕佳機會。[176/178] **我想派兩名團隊成員參加工作坊，並確認採用 Slinview 對范儂農業諮詢公司是否有益。**

你們可以在此頁面上找到有關工作坊的資訊。請注意，我們將支付你們在附近餐廳的午餐費用，但你們需要自行安排前往格諾瑞飯店的交通工具，並在上午八點前抵達。

如果你們有興趣，[176/177] **請在今天結束前回覆此電子郵件，並簡述徵求參加的理由。**[179] **我明天會通知被選中的人，並請我的助理致電幫他們報名。**

妍熙

- visualization (n.) 視覺化
  agricultural (adj.) 農業的　adopt (v.) 採用
  coordinate (v.) 協調
  transportation (n.) 交通工具

http://www.vazenttech.com

| 關於 | 商品 | 最新消息 | 聯絡我們 |
|---|---|---|---|

**在安大略省舉行的**
**Slinveiw 一日工作坊**

威盛科技邀請有興趣學習 Slinview 基礎知識的安大略省企業及個人，參加將於二月在全省各地舉行的四場介紹工作坊其中之一場。[180] **我們的專業講師將示範 Slinview 的許多功能，然後讓參與者有機會透過實際操作試用該軟體。**請注意，[180] **參加人數上限為 20 人，以符合此活動可用的電腦數量。**

工作坊將從上午 8 點持續至下午 5 點，中間有一小時的午休時間。[178] **費用為每人 55 美元，而具有安大略商業協會公司或個人會員資格者，費用則為 40 美元。**現場將提供點心和水，但參與者必須自備午餐或在該地區購買。

地點與日期：

| 地點 | 日期 |
|---|---|
| 西多倫多（辛德利會議中心） | 2 月 17 日 |
| 東多倫多（赫諾特廣場） | 2 月 19 日 |
| 渥太華（格諾瑞飯店） | 2 月 21 日 |
| 漢密爾頓（布萊恩斯大學） | 2 月 24 日 |

[179] **點擊這裡註冊。**

- individual (n.) 個人　introductory (adj.) 介紹的
  province (n.) 省　expert (adj.) 專業的
  instructor (n.) 講師　demonstrate (v.) 示範
  participant (n.) 參加者
  hands-on exercise (n.) 實際操作練習
  cap (n.) 限額　corporate (adj.) 企業的

**176. 暗示或推論**

南女士最有可能是什麼身分？

**(A) 團隊經理**　　(C) 行政助理
(B) 軟體開發商　　(D) 自由活動協調員

**177. 同義詞考題**

在電子郵件中，第三段第二行的「arguments」，意思最接近何者？

(A) 程序　　(C) 爭吵
(B) 態度　　**(D) 理由**

---

**178. 整合題**　難

關於范儂農業諮詢公司，可由文中得知什麼？

(A) 它位於多倫多的西部。
(B) 它會定期支付員工技能培訓的費用。
**(C) 它屬於安大略商業協會。**
(D) 它最近採用了一種新的資料收集技術。

---

**179. 整合題** 

南女士提供關於工作坊的細節，與網頁上哪一項資訊不同？

(A) 她建議抵達的時間
**(B) 她描述的註冊方法**
(C) 她希望參與者用餐的地方
(D) 她認為教學部分持續的時間

- attribute (v.) 將……歸於

---

**180. 相關細節**

根據網頁，為什麼限制工作坊的參與人數？

**(A) 確保參與者可以練習使用軟體**
(B) 防止活動場地變得難以進入
(C) 讓參與者能與講師交談
(D) 激發對於獨家體驗的興趣

- venue (n.) 場地　access (v.) 通行；進入
  exclusive (adj.) 獨有的

**換句話說**

capped（限額）→ limited（有限制的）
try out the software through hands-on exercises（透過實際操作試用該軟體）
→ (A) practice using the software（練習使用軟體）

---

**181–185 報導與電子郵件**

**施雷德進修部將提供**
**遠距工作證書**

施雷德市　訊（12 月 1 日）——施雷德大學進修部宣布將開始提供「遠距工作能力證書」。

施雷德進修部由該大學營運，是一個以施雷德為範圍的辦公室網絡，負責透過持續的教育課程和其他學程分享知識。[185] **進修部院長厄爾文．平野博士**提到，[181] **該學程的目標是為郊區低度就業的人提供機會**：「我們希望他們能夠謀生，同時仍然待在所屬的社區，而不是被迫搬到一個都市。」

為了學生的方便，該學程將完全由線上管理。平野博士解釋道：「人們所需要的只是一台電腦、中等的電腦素養和良好的網路連線。」他指出在行銷或平面設計等領域的背景很有幫助，但表示「還是有些遠距工作，例如客戶服務代表，幾乎不需要先前的工作經驗。」

這門為期五週的學程，對特定郊區居民不收取任何費用，課程主要教授遠距工作所需的技術工具和工作技能。[182] **課程結束後，證書持有者將可以在開始求職時獲得生涯導師的幫助。**

有意願報名的學生必須在 12 月 26 日之前註冊 [184] **1 月 2 日開課的初階課程**，並在 2 月 24 日之前註冊 3 月 3 日開始的課程。有關該學程的更多資訊，請上 www.extension.shrader.edu/rwpc。

- extension (n.) 進修部　certificate (n.) 證書
  remote (adj.) 遠距的　proficiency (n.) 精通；熟練
  be charged with 負責
  dean (n.) 學院長；系主任
  underemployed (adj.) 低度就業的
  rural (adj.) 郊區的
  make a living 維生　administer (v.) 管理
  moderate (adj.) 中等的
  computer literacy (n.) 電腦素養
  representative (n.) 代表人員
  have access to 能使用　potential (adj.) 潛在的
  inaugural (adj.) 首次的

**寄件人：**翠西．伯恩
<tracy.byrne@obr-mail.com>
**收件人：**<editor@shraderherald.com>
**主旨：**施雷德的遠距工作能力證書
**日期：**11 月 7 日

親愛的編輯：

大約在一年前，貴報報導了施萊德大學推廣部培訓人們進行遠距工作的學程。[184] **我報名了首次課程**，而就在獲得證書後的兩週內，我找到了一份遠距工作，直到今天我仍在職。跟我同期的大多數同學也都有類似的經歷。

這就是為什麼我最近很驚訝地發現該學程似乎再也無法報名了。它的網頁已被撤下。[185] **平野博士已離開該大學，而當我寄了一封關於該計畫的電子郵件給他的繼任者**，我並沒有收到回信。[183] **可以請你們的一位記者調查一下這個問題嗎？**我認為我們這區的居民有權知道為什麼這麼成功的計畫被中止了。

感謝您對此事的關注。

翠西・伯恩　謹啟

- take down 撤除　successor (n.) 接任者
  initiative (n.) 新計畫　discontinue (v.) 中斷

**181. 相關細節**

這個學程的受眾是誰？

**(A) 居住在低人口密度地區的人**
(B) 有家庭照顧責任的人
(C) 沒有大學學歷的人
(D) 之前在特定產業工作的人

- density (n.) 密度　industry (n.) 產業

**換句話說**
people in rural areas（郊區的人）
→ (A) People . . . in areas with low population density（在低人口密度區的人）

---

**182. 確認事實與否**

關於這個學程的課程，文中提到什麼事？

(A) 內容包含一個期末考。
(B) 某些學生被減免了費用。
(C) 有些課程在大學進修部的辦公室上課。
**(D) 畢業生可以獲得求職協助。**

**換句話說**
have access to a career coach as they launch their job search（在開始求職時可以獲得生涯導師的幫助）→ (D) get job seeking assistance（獲得求職協助）

---

**183. 主旨或目的**

這封電子郵件的目的為何？

**(A) 要求調查該學程的狀況**
(B) 抱怨該學程設計的改變
(C) 推薦該學程給其他有報名意願的學生
(D) 感謝刊物宣傳該學程

- investigation (n.) 調查　status (n.) 狀況；狀態
  publication (n.) 發表；出版

**換句話說** look into this issue（調查一下這個問題）→ (A) an investigation into the program's status（調查該學程的狀況）

---

**184. 整合題**

伯恩女士最可能在 1 月 2 日時做什麼事？

(A) 注意到一篇文章　**(C) 開始上課**
(B) 完成註冊　(D) 獲得證書

- enrollment (n.) 入學；註冊

**換句話說**
begin classes（開始課程）
→ (C) Started her course（開始上課）

---

**185. 整合題** 

文中提到關於施雷德大學進修部的什麼事？

(A) 它是伯恩女士的現任雇主。
(B) 它沒有做到對伯恩女士所做的承諾。
(C) 它已經沒有出現在網路上了。
**(D) 它有了新院長。**

- fulfill (v.) 履行　presence (n.) 存在

---

**186–190 網頁與電子郵件**

www.locetopumpkinfair.com/participate/music/

[186] **音樂表演徵才！**

現場表演的音樂是洛杉多南瓜節非常重要的一部分。雖然 [186] **我們每年都會透過聯繫經紀人預約一些主要的表演者**，[187] **但我們喜歡為較小的、即將嶄露頭角的表演者保留大部分的位置**。如果您會演奏適合闔家聆賞的流行樂、搖滾樂或節奏藍調音樂，這可能是您在數百、甚至數千名觀眾面前表演的機會。如欲申請，請寄信至 music@locetopumpkinfair.com，提交一份簡短的藝術家／樂團傳記（50–100 字）和兩個表演影片檔案。我們不接受音檔，我們建議您繳交在觀眾面前表演的影片。繳交截止日期是 7 月 31 日下午 5 點。[189] **可能會要求在洛杉多郡活動的被選定表演者親自甄選**。我們將在 8 月底做出最終決定。

- act (n.) 節目　vital (adj.) 非常重要的
  fair (n.) 展覽會
  up-and-coming (adj.) 很有前途的；嶄露頭角的
  family-friendly (adj.) 適合闔家老少的
  biography (n.) 自傳　submission (n.) 提交

www.locetopumpkinfair.com/music/lineups/sat

[190] **10 月 19 日星期六的表演陣容**

點擊表演者名稱以獲得更多資訊。

[190] **下午 4:30–5:10** 行家們
下午 5:30–6:10 銀色海星
晚上 6:30–7:10 珍娜與詹莫斯
晚上 7:30–8:30 搖滾開局

◀ 10 月 18 日 星期五 | 10 月 20 日 星期日 ▶

**寄件人：**<music@From: locetopumpkinfair.com>
**收件人：**蘿拉．高登 <lora.g@pmt-mail.com>
**主旨：**洛杉多南瓜節
**日期：**9 月 23 日

親愛的高登女士：

[188] **其中一個計劃於 10 月 19 日在洛杉多南瓜節演出的樂團意外退出，我們想將替補此位置的機會給您的樂團。**正如我在先前的電子郵件中提到的，[189] **音樂委員會的其他成員和我都對髮夾樂團的甄選印象非常深刻**，很抱歉我們最初無法提供您這個機會。您是我們對於此缺額第一個聯繫的樂團。

[190] **您將會從下午 4:30 開始 40 分鐘的表演**，報酬為 300 美元。我們知道髮夾樂團當天可能已經有另外的行程了，所以請與您的樂團成員討論我們的提議，並讓我們知道您的決定。我們需要在明天結束前收到您的回音。

謝謝您。

洛杉多南瓜節音樂委員會
溫德爾．福克斯

- drop out 退出 committee (n.) 委員會
  initially (adv.) 起初 engagement (n.) 約會；約定

**186. 確認事實與否**

第一個網頁提到了關於申請流程的什麼事？

(A) 比前一年簡單。
(B) 有一個解說的導覽影片。
**(C) 有些樂團不會通過。**
(D) 會要求申請人付款。

**187. 同義詞考題** 難

在第一個網頁中，第一段第二行的「reserve」，意思最接近何者？

(A) 擁有 (C) 接管
**(B) 留出（時間或金錢）** (D) 施加

**188. 主旨或目的**

這封電子郵件的目的為何？

**(A) 提醒高登小姐一個機會**
(B) 修訂一項提議的條款
(C) 給予準備的指示
(D) 警告高登女士一個問題

**換句話說**
chance（機會）→ (A) opportunity（機會）

**189. 整合題**

關於髮夾樂團，下列何者最可能為真？

(A) 他們演奏節奏藍調音樂。
(B) 他們在 7 月 31 日出席了一場表演。
(C) 他們由一個專業的經紀人所代表。
**(D) 他們的成員住在洛杉多郡。**

**190. 整合題**

哪一個樂團將不會在 10 月 19 日演出？

**(A) 行家們** (C) 珍娜與詹莫斯
(B) 銀色海星 (D) 搖滾開局

**191–195 廣告、電子郵件與帳單**

**貝爾克科學的高效通風櫥**

幾乎所有類型的實驗室都需要通風櫥，這樣科學家才可以安全使用會釋放有害氣體的化學品。不幸的是，通風櫥也是最吃能源的實驗室設備之一。這就是貝爾克科學創造高效通風櫥系列的原因。[191] **每個通風櫥都有一個精密的控制器和三段速鼓風機，它們一起可以減少通風櫥使用的氣流，進而減少其能源需求。**此外，[191] **特殊馬達比傳統馬達消耗更少的能源。**[193] **通風櫥有 2 英尺、4 英尺、6 英尺和 8 英尺型號可供選擇，**還具有垂直安全玻璃窗框，可實現最大的安全性和可用性。

立即瀏覽 www.belkerscience.com，了解更多關於這些和其他創新產品的資訊。

- efficiency (n.) 效率 fume hood (n.) 通風櫥

hazardous (adj.) 有害的
sophisticated (adj.) 精密的
blower (n.) 風箱；送風機　airflow (n.) 氣流
requirement (n.) 要求　vertical (adj.) 垂直的
sash (n.) 窗框　usability (n.) 合用；可用性

**寄件人：** 琳達．墨菲 <l.murphy@simonroylabs.com>
**收件人：** 賈比爾．奈瑟 <j.nasser@simonroylabs.com>
**日期：** 2月2日
**主旨：** 替換通風櫥

嗨，賈比爾：

按照你的要求，[192] **我在上週的貿易展覽會上為實驗室尋找節省資金的方法**，而我在貝爾克科學展攤位上看到的東西給我留下了最深刻的印象。他們的高效通風櫥似乎就是我們正在尋找的東西。我們的通風櫥都有十幾年的歷史，所以我確信更換它們會明顯降低能源費用。另外，銷售人員提到，我們的能源供應商 [194] **威森威整個五月都有「EE」（能源效率）折扣**，所以如果我們快點的話，我們可以因為升級設備而獲得最多 500 元的折扣。

你可以在 www.belkerscience.com/fumehoods/he 上查看一系列的機型。[193] **我認為我們應該利用這次改變，將通風櫃從目前的 4 英尺升級一個尺寸**，但我知道這取決於我們的預算。

我希望這個建議有幫助！

琳達

- trade fair (n.) 貿易展
  noticeably (adv.) 顯著地；明顯地
  rebate (n.) 折扣　take advantage of 利用
  depend on 依……而定　budget (n.) 預算

**威森威能源**

80022
科羅拉多州克羅芬德
柯爾巷 540 號
西蒙羅伊實驗室

帳戶編號：4018532
**應付帳款：648.86 元**
**截止日期：7 月 22 日**

**能源帳單**

[194] **計費週期：6 月 1 日至 6 月 30 日**
**能源使用量：7,348 度**
電錶編號：8231004248
抄表日期：6 月 30 日
費率類型：商業型

歷史使用量：
- 前期 8,011 度
- [195] **去年同期：** 8,104 度

| 費用類型 | 費率 | 總費用 |
|---|---|---|
| 能源 | 0.120 元／度 | 881.76 元 |
| 配電 | 0.032 元／度 | 235.14 元 |
| 系統存取 | 7.00 元／度 | 7.00 元 |
| [194] **EE 折扣** | −500.00 元（一次性） | −500.00 元 |
| | 小計 | 623.90 元 |
| | 稅金（4.0%） | 24.96 元 |
| | **總計** | **648.86 元** |

付款方式請見背面 →

- distribution (n.) 配送

**191. 確認事實與否**

通風櫥的哪個部分沒有被描述為提高能源效率？

(A) 控制器
(B) 鼓風機
**(C) 窗框**
(D) 馬達

**換句話說**

reduce . . . its energy requirements / uses less energy（減少能源需求／消耗更少的能源）
→ increasing energy efficiency（提高能源效率）

**192. 同義詞考題**

在電子郵件中，第一段第一行的「spent」，意思最接近何者？

(A) 貢獻
**(B) 度過**
(C) 付款
(D) 闡明

**193. 整合題**

墨菲女士建議購買哪個尺寸的通風櫥？

(A) 2 英尺
(B) 4 英尺
**(C) 6 英尺**
(D) 8 英尺

**194. 整合題**

關於折扣方案，可由文中得知了什麼？

**(A) 已被展期。**
(B) 提高了最高限額。
(C) 現在由兩個組織提供。
(D) 其名稱已改變。

- extend (v.) 延長　organization (n.) 組織

**195. 確認事實與否**

帳單指出了有關西蒙羅伊實驗室的什麼事？

(A) 本期帳單會在下個計費週期結束時到期。
**(B) 他們已經當威森威能源的顧客至少一年了。**
(C) 其能源費用自動從銀行帳戶扣款。
(D) 一般能源費用會根據能源使用量而有所不同。

- due (adj.) 到期的　withdraw (v.) 提款

## 196–200 廣告與電子郵件

**費利金傑企業餐飲服務**

www.delicious-fcds.com

費利金傑企業餐飲服務（FCDS）因致力於提供卓越和彈性的服務，已成為伯明翰地區首屈一指的企業自助餐廳營運商。[197] **我們可以規劃打造新的自助餐廳**或從內部供應商手中接管現有設施的營運，以提高效率。[197] **如果需要的話，我們可以從早上 6 點到晚上 10 點供應餐點。**對於有環境考量的企業，[197] **我們提供菜餚僅由當地供應的食材製成的菜單方案**。最重要的是，我們保證提供美味、營養的餐點和點心。[196] **瀏覽我們的網站以獲取更多資訊和資源，包括我們廚師工作時的影片片段。**

- corporate dining (n.) 企業餐飲
  operator (n.) 經營者　dedication (n.) 貢獻
  range (n.) 類別；種類　take over 接管
  existing (adj.) 現存的　in-house (adj.) 內部的
  efficiency (n.) 效率
  environmental (adj.) 環境的；環保的
  regional (adj.) 地區的　supplier (n.) 供應商
  nutritious (adj.) 有營養的　footage (n.) 一段影片

**寄件人：**羅納德．謝爾巴 <r.scherba@wibbenslogistics.com>
**收件人：**<inquiries@delicious-fcds.com>
**主旨：**詢問
**日期：**1 月 14 日

您好：

我叫作羅納德．謝爾巴，是「威本斯物流」行政服務部的主管。我們是一家位於市中心、[199] **約 60 人的小公司**。我寫這封信是因為我們正在尋找一家新的服務供應商來經營我們的員工自助餐廳，而您近期的一則廣告令我印象深刻。[197] **我們目前的供應商不提供環保的菜單方案或深夜服務**，而我們特別需要後者，因為我們的員工為了與海外聯絡人溝通而有著與他人不同的作息。

儘管如此，我們主要關注的是基本問題，如餐點品質和顧客服務。為此，[198] **我想參觀貴公司目前管理的其中一間自助餐廳**。這將幫助我在我們開始商談合約之前，確定您的服務適合我們企業。不知是否能做這樣的安排呢？請回覆此電子郵件讓我知道。

威本斯物流
行政服務處處長
羅納德．謝爾巴　謹啟

- administrative services department (n.) 行政服務部門
  operate (v.) 營運；經營　negotiate (v.) 協商

**寄件人：**<inquiries@delicious-fcds.com>
**收件人：**桃樂絲．海根 <dorothy.hagen@delicious-fcds.com>
**主旨：**轉寄：詢問
**日期：**1 月 14 日

嗨，桃樂絲：

下面轉發的訊息是今天早上「威本斯物流」的謝爾巴先生寄來的，是則很有希望的詢問。[199] **由於該公司的規模與妳管理的其他客戶規模相似**，因此我想分配給妳。但是，妳會看到 [200] **謝爾巴先生在電子郵件中提出了一個不尋常的要求。**

[200] **妳能在下午兩點到我辦公室來，一起討論最好的處理方式嗎？**如果我在 1:30 之前沒有收到妳的回覆，我會透過公司的訊息服務跟妳聯繫。

謝謝。

文森．波特

- promising (adj.) 有希望的

**196. 相關細節**

根據廣告，瀏覽 FCDS 網站的訪客可以做什麼？

(A) 閱讀現有顧客的評論
(B) 得到各種菜單方案樣本
(C) 看到公司的供應商名單
**(D) 觀看準備餐點的影片**

**換句話說**

footage of our chefs at work（我們廚師工作時的影片片段）
→ (D) videos of meals being prepared（準備餐點的影片）

**197. 整合題** 

謝爾巴先生沒有詢問廣告中的哪一項服務？

(A) 特殊場合的餐飲供應
**(B) 自助餐廳的建設計畫**
(C) 一個使用當地生產的食物計畫
(D) 延長的服務時間

- occasion (n.) 場合

**換句話說**
menu plans with dishes made only with foods from regional suppliers（僅由當地供應商製作的餐點菜單計畫）
→ (C) A locally-sourced food program（當地生產的食物計畫）
serve meals from 6 A.M. to 10 P.M.（從早上 6 點至晚上 10 點供餐）
→ (D) Extended serving hours（延長的服務時間）

**198. 相關細節**

夏爾巴先生希望安排什麼？

**(A) 造訪一個餐飲服務地點**
(B) 與 FCDS 的員工開視訊會議
(C) 寄送資訊豐富的資料
(D) 兩家餐飲服務供應商的合作

- conference call (n.) 視訊會議
  collaboration (n.) 合作

**換句話說**
tour one of the cafeterias（參觀其中一間自助餐廳）→ (A) A visit to a food service facility（造訪一個餐飲服務地點）

**199. 整合題** 

關於海根女士，下列何者最可能為真？

(A) 她管理一個特定城市區域的所有客戶。
(B) 她在一個社交場合中遇到謝爾巴先生。
**(C) 她有和小公司合作的經驗。**
(D) 她專攻海外客戶。

- district (n.) 區域
  specialize in 專攻；專門從事

**200. 相關細節**

為什麼謝爾巴先生要求海根女士去他的辦公室？

(A) 展示一些研究成果
(B) 協助分配任務給其他員工
**(C) 討論回覆一項要求的策略**
(D) 解決某個軟體的問題

- present (v.) 展示　strategy (n.) 策略
  resolve (v.) 解決

**換句話說**
talk about the best way to handle it [=an unusual request]（討論處理它〔一個不尋常的要求〕最佳方案）→ (C) discuss strategies for responding to a request（討論回應一項要求的策略）

# ACTUAL TEST 2

## PART 5 P. 36–38

**101. 動詞詞類變化題——主詞動詞單複數一致性－主動語態**

當局已向用路人發出警告，提醒注意近期因暴風雨造成的惡劣路況。

(A) 正在發布　　(C) 將被發布
(B) 被發布　　**(D) 已發布**

- **authorities (n.)** 當權者；管理機構
  **issue (v.)** 發布；發行

---

**102. 副詞詞彙題——最高級強調用法** 難

班．強森無疑是當年最有影響力的攝影師之一。

(A) 簡單的　　**(C) 無疑**
(B) 簡單　　(D) 最簡單的

- **influential (adj.)** 有影響力的

---

**103. 介系詞詞彙題**

該城市正在考慮將空地變成小遊樂場或社區園藝用地。

**(A) 成為⋯⋯**　　(C) 橫越
(B) 分開　　(D) 只有

- **vacant (adj.)** 空著的；未被佔用的
  **plot (n.)** 小塊土地

---

**104. 人稱代名詞題——受格**

由於赫夫女士的演講涉及極具爭議性的話題，因此聽眾的大部分問題都是針對她。

(A) 她自己　　**(C) 她**
(B) 她的（東西）　　(D) 她

- **lecture (n.)** 演講　**deal with** 與⋯⋯相關
  **controversial (adj.)** 具有爭議的
  **direct (v.)** 將⋯⋯指向　**majority (n.)** 大多數

---

**105. 介系詞詞彙題**

柯林斯集團經常出現在客戶滿意度最高的銀行名單上。

(A) 在⋯⋯　　(C) ⋯⋯的
**(B) 在⋯⋯上**　　(D) 到⋯⋯

- **customer satisfaction (n.)** 顧客滿意度

---

**106. 副詞詞彙題** 難

在嘗試操作印表機之前，請確認已牢固闔上紙匣。

**(A) 牢固地**　　(C) 幾乎不
(B) 廣泛地　　(D) 嚴厲地

---

**107. 副詞詞彙題——修飾動詞**

SwiftPlay 遊戲機被策略性地安排在假期購物季開始之際發售。

(A) 策略　　(C) 策略上的
(B) 被策略規劃的　　**(D) 策略性地**

- **release (v.)** 上市；發售
  **time (adj.)** 安排⋯⋯的時間
  **strategy (n,)** 策略
  **holiday shopping season (n.)** 假期購物季（在歐洲地區指聖誕節至新年期間的購物季，而在美加兩國則是指從感恩節至翌年新年的購物季。）

---

**108. 副詞詞彙題** 

彈性的工作安排，越來越受到全職和兼職員工的青睞。

(A) 皆不　　(C) 兩者都
**(B) 同樣地**　　(D) 一樣的

---

**109. 名詞詞彙題——複合名詞** 

經慎重考慮，馬許先生要求延後截止日的理由被認定為不充分。

**(A) 延長**　　(C) 可延長的
(B) 被延長的　　(D) 延長

- **insufficient (adj.)** 不足的
  **extendable (adj.)** 可延長的

---

**110. 名詞詞彙題** 

應徵者可能會被要求以文憑、證書等形式提供資格證明。

(A) 管道　　**(C) 證明**
(B) 更新　　(D) 賠償

- **diploma (n.)** 學位　**certificate (n.)** 證書
  **access (n.)** 管道　**renewal (n.)** 更新
  **compensation (n.)** 補償；彌補

### 111. 動詞詞彙題

阿隆塔企業要求其員工通知公司其住家地址的變更。

(A) 注意　(C) 教育
(B) 揭露　**(D) 通知**

- note (v.) 注意　reveal (v.) 揭露

### 112. 名詞子句連接詞題 難

《威拉德每日新聞》吸引讀者的是我們對公平和誠實報導的承諾。

(A) 有些事物　(C) 誰
**(B) ……的事物**　(D) 任何人

### 113. 副詞詞彙題——比較級的強調用法

貝里工作室的新喜劇在票房上的表現，比電影界分析師預測的要好得多。

**(A) 遠遠；極**　(C) 非常
(B) 如此　(D) 在……之上

- box office (n.) 票房　analyst (n.) 分析師

### 114. 動名詞——動詞的主詞

準備施工許可證申請的時間，比承包商預期的還長。

(A) 準備　(C) 準備
**(B) 準備**　(D) 準備了

- application (n.) 申請　contractor (n.) 承包商
  anticipate (v.) 預期；預料

### 115. 動詞詞類變化題——時態

在新人培訓會上，總部代表講述我們的企業價值觀時，受訓者們應認真聆聽。

(A) 講述　(C) 講述
(B) 已講述　**(D) 正在講述**

- attentively (adv.) 專心地；聚精會神地
  headquarters (n.) 總部
  corporate (adj.) 公司的；企業的

### 116. 介系詞詞彙題

包夫特軟體公司的展位雖然被安排在展廳後方角落不方便的位置，還是擠滿了參觀者。

**(A) 儘管**　(C) 除了……
(B) 在……之間　(D) 不像……

- placement (n.) 安排位置　exhibition (n.) 展覽

### 117. 副詞詞彙題——修飾過去分詞

我們的數據中心頻繁升級最新的硬體，提供安全、可靠的數據儲存服務。

(A) 頻繁的　(C) 頻率
(B) 常去　**(D) 頻繁地**

- frequency (n.) 頻率　frequent (v.) 常去

### 118. 形容詞詞彙題

你的部門要製作的年終報告，必須包括已結案和正在進行的專案摘要。

(A) 多種的　(C) 客製的
(B) 有野心的　**(D) 進行中的**

- summary (n.) 摘要；大綱　multiple (adj.) 多個的
  ambitious (adj.) 有野心的；有企圖心的
  tailored (adj.) 客製的

### 119. 形容詞詞彙題——修飾名詞——最高級

由於天氣和煦，這似乎是詹寧斯冬季遊樂區過去 15 年來最短的一個旺季。

(A) 使縮短　(C) 較短的
**(B) 最短的**　(D) 短地

### 120. 名詞詞彙題

夜間關閉閒置電子產品的活動，成功地降低了辦公室的能源消耗。

(A) 轉換　**(C) 消耗**
(B) 效率　(D) 意識

- idle (adj.) 閒置的　transition (n.) 轉換
  efficiency (n.) 效率
  awareness (n.) 意識；察覺

### 121. 名詞詞彙題——介系詞的受詞 難

關於即將舉行的一系列訓練課程的電子郵件通知，已經寄給新進人員。

(A) 招聘人員　(C) 聘僱
**(B) 新進人員**　(D) 聘僱

- notification (n.) 通知
  upcoming (adj.) 即將到來的
  session (n.) 講習會　recruiter (n.) 雇主
  recruit (v.) 聘僱

**122. 形容詞詞彙題**

這份食譜需要一磅碎牛肉，但這可以用等量的素食替代品取代，例如煮熟的扁豆。

(A) 存在的　　**(C) 等量的**
(B) 應負責任的　　(D) 整體的

- **ground (adj.)** 切碎的　**substitute (n.)** 替代品
  **accountable (adj.)** 可數的

**123. 代名詞詞彙題**

必須鼓勵商界和學術界相互合作，投入實際的研究。

(A) 其他的　　(C) 它自己
(B) 哪個　　**(D) 彼此**

- **collaborate with** 與……合作
  **engage in** 從事；參與　**practical (adj.)** 實務的

**124. 動詞詞彙題**

莫克西斯汽車公司致力於為運輸業者提供經濟、省油的商用車。

**(A) 致力**　　(C) 中斷
(B) 遵從　　(D) 專精

- **transportation provider (n.)** 運輸服務業者
  **fuel-efficient (adj.)** 高效使用燃料的
  **commercial (adj.)** 商業的　**conform (v.)** 遵從
  **specialize (v.)** 專精於；專攻

**125. 名詞詞彙題**

認證流程的最後一步是實務考試，驗證申請者在造型髮型藝術方面的熟練程度。

(A) 洞見　　**(C) 熟練**
(B) 特權　　(D) 順從

- **licensing (n.)** 許可；核准　**verify (v.)** 證實
  **applicant (n.)** 申請者　**insight (n.)** 遠見
  **privilege (n.)** 特權　**compliance (n.)** 順從；屈從

**126. 介系詞詞彙題**

在加入凱勒福克斯公司之前，姜女士是柯蒂斯飯店的銷售副總裁。

**(A) 在……之前**　　(C) 自從
(B) 跟……相比　　(D) 根據

**127. 動詞詞類變化題——時態** 難

IT 主管向我們保證，技術人員將在明天這個時候完成系統維修。

**(A) 將會完成**　　(C) 正在完成
(B) 已完成　　(D) 正在完成

**128. 介系詞詞彙題**

伊斯頓先生透過他的發言人發表了一份聲明，而不是直接對媒體發表談話。

(A) 甚至　　(C) 宣布
(B) 正式地　　**(D) 透過**

- **press (n.)** 媒體　**announce (v.)** 宣布

**129. 動詞詞彙題** 

委員會提議將史巴克斯和柯根法院合併到位於柯根西部的新大樓中。

(A) 迅速執行　　(C) 委任
**(B) 合併**　　(D) 免除

- **committee (n.)** 委員會
  **expedite (v.)** 加速；迅速執行
  **delegate (v.)** 委任　**waive (v.)** 免除；放棄

**130. 對等連接詞**

旺奇顧問公司的策略規畫服務，將幫助您確定商業目標，並評估達成這些目標的進度。

(A) 尚未　　**(C) 和**
(B) 在……旁邊　　(D) 關於

- **objective (n.)** 目標　**evaluate (v.)** 評估
  **in regard to** 有關；關於

## PART 6 P. 39–42

**131–134 信件**

2 月 25 日
戴安娜・湯森
04007 緬因州伯克特市
羅賓路 407 號

湯森女士：

特此邀請您參加社區會議，討論建設一條與金線平行的特快列車線提案。會議將在 3 月 18 日星期四下午 6 點至 8 點於波樂社區中心的禮堂舉行。[131] **該中心位於伯克特市第二街 150 號。**

[132] **如**附件中所詳述，特快線將從伯克特行駛至格林罕中央車站，中間只有兩站。因此，它將讓往返市中心的旅程 [133] **更加便捷**。

本次會議將是伯克特居民就提案提供意見的機會。議程包括由交通官員 [134] **進行**的簡報與問答時間。

我們希望您能參加。

格林罕地區交通管理局局長

加里．墨菲　謹啟
附件

- hereby (adv.) 特此；以此方式
paralleling (adj.) 平行的　enclosure (n.) 附件
agenda (n.) 會議議程　input (n.) 輸入；投入
transit (n.) 公共交通運輸系統
official (n.) 官方人員

**131. 句子插入題**

(A) 不巧的是，這個日期與我的日程安排衝突。
**(B) 該中心位於伯克特市第二街 150 號。**
(C) 我們預期屆時將近完工。
(D) 過來時請準備提案的修正草案。

- revised (adj.) 經過修訂的；已校正的
draft (n.) 草稿；草圖

**132. 副詞子句連接詞詞彙題**

(A) 在……之上　(C) 直到
(B) 為了　**(D) 如同**

**133. 形容詞詞彙題** 

**(A) 更快捷的**　(C) 景色更秀麗的
(B) 更舒適的　(D) 更便宜的

- swift (adj.) 快速的　cozy (adj.) 舒適的
scenic (adj.) 景色秀麗的

**134. 動詞詞類變化題——過去分詞**

(A) 將進行　(C) 要進行
(B) 被進行　**(D) 被進行**

- conduct (v.) 執行

**135–138 電子郵件**

寄件人：格溫多琳．拉姆齊
收件人：所有志工
主旨：政策
日期：12 月 16 日

親愛的林迪時尚博物館志工們：

我最近無意中聽到一位志工導遊在導覽我們的展品時，提供了不正確的訊息。請不要這樣做。我知道被問到回答不出來的問題可能會很尷尬。136 **但是**，在這種情況下，正確的回應是將遊客引導至我們的教育工作人員。137 **如果他們沒空，遊客可以稍後寄電子郵件至 info@lfm.org.nz 給他們。**自己記住答案以防止問題再次發生也是明智之舉。

我想向你們所有人說明這項政策，因為目前尚不清楚我目睹的事件是一次性錯誤還是普遍問題的一部分。請簡短回覆，確認你已閱讀並理解此電子郵件。

謝謝。

林迪時尚博物館
志工協調員　格溫多琳．拉姆齊

- overhear (v.) 偶然聽到　incorrect (adj.) 不正確的
direct A to B 將 A 派給 B
recur (v.) 再發生；復發　spell out 詳細說明
policy (n.) 政策　witness (v.) 目睹
widespread (adj.) 普遍的；廣泛的

**135. 介系詞詞彙題**

(A) 像　(C) 雖然
**(B) 在……期間**　(D) 然而

**136. 連接副詞** 

(A) 同樣地　(C) 更重要地
(B) 相反地　**(D) 然而；但是**

- likewise (adv.) 同樣地　on the contrary 相反地

**137. 句子插入題**

(A) 他們將會概述我們的活動日程。
(B) 博物館開放時間是星期二至星期日的上午 10 點至下午 6 點。
**(C) 如果他們沒空，遊客可以稍後寄電子郵件至 info@lfm.org.nz 給他們。**
(D) 我們一直在尋求更多志工來帶導覽。

- overview (n.) 大綱　unavailable (adj.) 沒空的

**138. 名詞子句連接詞**

**(A) 是否**　(C) 畢竟
(B) 基於　(D) 當……的時候

**139–142 資訊**

**感謝您向莎琳塔工作室訂購！**

附上的蠟燭是採用優質原料手工製成。139 **保持**燈芯修剪成 1/8 英寸的長度，以獲得最佳效果。我們還建議每次燃燒蠟燭至頂層的蠟完全融化為止，以防頂部變得凹凸不平。

如果您因任何原因對您購買的東西不滿意，請隨時與我們聯繫。[140] **除了退換貨，我們也能提供有用的建議。**我們數十年的香水專業知識可隨時為您服務。我們很樂意為您推薦另一種 [1341] **香味**，甚至能夠客製。您可以透過電子郵件 sarinta@pexo-market.com，或於一般營業時間致電 (864) 555-0192 與我們聯繫。

另一方面，如果您對莎琳塔蠟燭感到滿意，請讓 [142] **其他人**知道！您可以在 www.pexo-market.com/sarinta 留下對我們工作室的正面評價。我們非常感謝您的支持。

- wick (n.)（蠟燭、油燈等的）芯　trim (v.) 修剪
  be displeased with 對……感到不悅
  hesitate (v.) 遲疑　fragrance (n.) 香氣
  expertise (n.) 專業知識；專門技術
  at one's disposal 可供……使用
  customized (adj.) 客製的　reach (v.) 取得聯繫

**139. 動詞詞類變化題——祈使句**

(A) 為了保持　(C) 保持
(B) 已保持　**(D) 保持**

---

**140. 句子插入題**

(A) 目前，莎琳塔工作室沒有經營任何實體商店。
(B) 我們的社群媒體帳號經常更新新產品的照片。
(C) 使用優惠碼「MYSARINTA」，下一筆訂單可享 85 折折扣。
**(D) 除了退換貨，我們也能提供有用的建議。**

- at present 目前　operate (v.) 營運

---

**141. 名詞詞彙題**

**(A) 香味**　(C) 材質
(B) 形狀　(D) 圖樣

- texture (n.) 組織；紋理；質地

---

**142. 代名詞詞彙題**

(A) 她　**(C) 其他人**
(B) 一些　(D) 他們

---

**143–146 備忘錄**

收件人：所有鵬樂員工
關於：勞斯商業服務

我之所以撰寫此信，是為了與大家分享我們公司最近的成功故事。

勞斯商業服務是一家維護和維修供應商，過去常常遇到文書工作的問題。他們的服務訪問報告書很長而且容易弄丟。客戶抱怨每次訪問後都要為技術人員手動 [143] **完成**報告所花費的時間付費，而丟失的報告通常使該公司難以為其提供的服務正確開立帳單。

幸運的是，勞斯選擇購買平板電腦並開始使用鵬樂商業的服務。他們的技術人員 [144] **現在**填寫的電子表格會自動儲存在一個共享且井井有條的資料夾中。

勞斯的服務業務主管告訴我們：「您們使我們的技術人員更具生產力。[145] **同樣重要的是，我們不再因少開款項金額而蒙受損失。**」多虧這些好處，該公司在短短一年內就 [146] **回收**了投資成本。

我們都應該為鵬樂提供勞斯商業服務的幫助感到自豪。讓我們繼續保持吧。

首席執行長
韓建宇

- maintenance (n.) 維修　repair (n.) 修理
  paperwork (n.) 文書工作
  misplace (v.) 誤置；錯放
  well-organized (adj.) 井然有序的
  supervisor (n.) 監督人；管理人
  productive (adj.) 有生產力的　benefit (n.) 好處
  investment (n.) 投資

**143. 動詞詞類變化題——動名詞** 難

(A) 一完成　**(C) 完成**
(B) 完成　(D) 完成了

---

**144. 副詞詞彙題**

**(A) 現在**　(C) 鮮少
(B) 然後　(D) 仍然

- rarely (adv.) 鮮少地

---

**145. 句子插入題** 

(A) 我們聘請管線、電力與建築維修方面的專家。
**(B) 同樣重要的是，我們不再因少開款項金額而蒙受損失。**
(C) 我們想讓顧客知道，我們一直都保護著他們的資料。
(D) 事實上，我們現在正在探索這種可能性。

- underbilling (n.) 少開款項

**146. 動詞詞彙題** 難

(A) 保留　(C) 維持
**(B) 收回**　(D) 鼓勵

- reserve (v.) 保留　maintain (v.) 維持

## PART 7 P. 43–63

### 147–148 電子郵件

**寄件人：**羅威爾．道森
**收件人：**安德莉雅．希科斯
**主旨：**房地產
**日期：**9 月 9 日

嗨，安德莉雅：

我一直在思考昨天的會面，我想分享一下我的發現。還記得我不喜歡妳給我看的房產，即使它們符合我的預算和空間要求嗎？好吧，問題是他們沒有足夠的自然光。[148] **我會在我選擇開設律師事務所的辦公室裡待上很長的時間**，而陽光會幫助我保持積極正向的心情。所以 [147] **在我們下次見面時，請讓我看看有窗戶讓大片陽光灑進來的地方。**

謝謝。

羅威爾

- appointment (n.) 會面　realization (n.) 理解
  property (n.) 房地產　budget (n.) 預算

**147. 主旨或目的**

道森先生為何寄這封電子郵件？

(A) 告知一個選擇
(B) 詢問預算
**(C) 提供具體規格**
(D) 預約會面

- specification (n.) 規格

**148. 推論或暗示**

可由文中得知關於道森先生的什麼事？

(A) 他即將會花很多時間待在戶外。
(B) 他想要更新一些燈具。
(C) 他在擔憂有關財產法的事情。
**(D) 他打算開創自己的事業。**

**換句話說**
open my law firm（開設我的律師事務所）
→ (D) start his own business（開創自己的事業）

### 149–150 資訊

**狐頭岩**

[149] **狐頭岩是在此處對面的斜坡上可見的大型岩層。**因其形似狐狸的頭部而得名，是公園內最著名的地質特徵之一。這座 27 英尺的結構由砂岩構成，經過侵蝕等數百萬年的自然過程形塑而成。

雖然從步道上的其他地點可以看到狐頭岩，但 [150] **這個地方為健行者提供了最佳的拍照機會。**請不要離開步道嘗試接近狐頭岩，因為它周圍的地面陡峭且有很多岩石。謝謝。

隆德斯國家公園

- rise (n.) 斜坡　opposite (adj.) 對面的
  resemblance (n.) 相像；相似
  geological (adj.) 地質的　erosion (n.) 侵蝕；腐蝕
  trail (n.) 步道；小徑　steep (adj.) 陡峭的

**149. 推論或暗示** 

這則資訊最有可能出現在哪裡？

(A) 博物館展間　(C) 商品標籤上
(B) 公園導覽手冊上　**(D) 戶外指示牌上**

**150. 相關細節**

這則資訊告訴讀者可以做什麼？

**(A) 拍照**　(C) 購買紀念品
(B) 碰觸展覽品　(D) 報名導覽

**換句話說**
the best photo opportunity（最佳的拍照機會）
→ (A) Take photographs（拍照）

### 151–152 文字訊息串

**赫爾曼．阿德羅姆〔下午 3:02〕**
瑞恩女士，[151] **您帶來的應徵者沒有回應我的視訊要求。**

**埃利諾．瑞恩〔下午 3:03〕**
馬修．卡斯帕？應徵資料輸入員的那位？

**赫爾曼．阿德羅姆〔下午 3:03〕**
沒錯。

**埃利諾．瑞恩〔下午 3:04〕**
很抱歉，讓我跟他確認看看。

**埃利諾．瑞恩〔下午 3:05〕**
我想一定是有誤會，他說他在線上。

**赫爾曼．阿德羅姆〔下午 3:06〕**
我們來確認一下資訊吧。我用 Chatrich 這個程式打給他，而 [152] **他的使用者名稱是 matthew_kasper，對吧？**

**埃利諾．瑞恩〔下午 3:07〕**
事實上，[152] **是 matthew.kasper，我的資料是這麼寫的，試試看那個**。

**赫爾曼．阿德羅姆〔下午 3:09〕**
好，現在通話接通了。謝謝妳。我之後會再打給妳，讓妳知道面試如何。

- candidate (n.) 應徵者　confirm (v.) 確認　material (n.) 資料

**151. 推論或暗示**

瑞恩女士最有可能是什麼身分？

(A) 電腦資訊人員　(C) 活動策畫人
(B) 政治線記者　**(D) 招聘人員**

---

**152. 掌握意圖**

下午 3:07，瑞恩女士寫道「試試看那個」，她建議做什麼？

**(A) 使用不同的聯絡資訊**
(B) 重開一個軟體程式
(C) 閱讀教學指示資料
(D) 更改電腦顯示設定

---

## 153–154 網頁

http://www.scheelerexpress.com/rail

**席勒快捷鐵路服務**

鐵路是運輸大量貨物的絕佳方式。與卡車運輸——另一種主要的陸上運輸方式——相比，鐵路運輸速度較慢且不太方便，但安全性更高，對環境的危害更小。[153] **它最適合需要定期長距離運輸大量貨物的企業**。

[153] **席勒快捷的運輸專家可以為您提供建議，了解鐵路運輸是否適合您的公司**。如果您決定適合，我們可以協助貴公司在您的路線上引導至不同鐵路公司的複雜系統。[154] **我們與所有主要營運商保持關係，使我們能夠及時了解他們不斷進步的技術**。

今天就聯繫我們開始吧。

- freight (n.) 貨物　on a regular basis 定期地　transportation (n.) 交通運輸　navigate (v.) 引導　operator (n.) 經營者　stay up-to-date on 在……方面保持最新資訊

**153. 推論或暗示**

這個網頁是要給誰看的？

(A) 通勤上班的員工
**(B) 運送貨物的公司**
(C) 造訪特定地區的旅客
(D) 尋求維修服務的列車營運商

- commute (v.) 通勤　cargo (n.) 貨物

**換句話說**
businesses that need to transport large amounts of freight（需要運輸大量貨物的企業）
→ (B) Companies shipping cargo（運送貨物的公司）

---

**154. 相關細節** 

根據網頁，席勒快捷的優點之一為何？

(A) 它提供長時間的營運。
(B) 它採用先進的技術。
**(C) 它與其他公司有聯繫。**
(D) 它擁有一條鐵路的專屬使用權。

- employ (v.) 利用；使用　advanced (adj.) 先進的　exclusive (adj.) 獨占的；專用的

**換句話說**
maintain relationships with all major operators（與所有主要營運商保持關係）
→ (C) has connections with other companies（與其他公司有聯繫）

---

## 155–157 電子郵件

**寄件人：**札特斯硬體公司
**收件人：**瓦勒斯．古羅佛
**主旨：**通知
**日期：**11 月 1 日

親愛的貴客：

[155] **札特斯硬體公司很遺憾地宣布終止我們的札特斯點數計畫**。在過去的八年裡，札特斯點數一直是我們客戶獲得產品折扣的好方法。不幸的是，[156] **營運程式的成本已經增長到一個繼續提供點數計畫不再是合乎理性的地步**。從今天開始，本計畫將不再接受新的申請。但是，我們將允許現有參與者能繼續累積札特斯點數至 11 月 30 日，並在 1 月 31 日之前使用這些點數。在決定如何使用剩餘點數時，[157] **請記住後面的截止日期**。我們也將定期寄送相關情況的電子郵件提醒通知。

我們一如既往感謝您身為札特斯硬體公司的忠實客戶。

札特斯硬體公司

執行長　達里爾．哈蒙　謹啟

- hardware (n.) 硬體　discontinuation (n.) 終止
  accrue (v.) 累積　periodic (adj.) 定期的
  reminder (n.) 提醒

**155. 主旨或目的** 難

電子郵件主要要通知收件人什麼事？

(A) 一間零售店倒閉
**(B) 結束一項忠誠度計畫**
(C) 更換一位行政主管
(D) 召回一項硬體商品

- replacement (n.) 替換　recall (n.) 召回

**換句話說**

the discontinuation of our Zaters Points program（終止我們札特斯點數計畫）
→ (B) The end of a loyalty program（結束一項忠誠度計畫）

---

**156. 相關細節**

根據電子郵件，做出該項決策的原因為何？

(A) 安全問題　**(C) 財務考量**
(B) 法律糾紛　(D) 企業重組

- dispute (n.) 爭論；爭執

**換句話說**

the cost of running the program has grown（營運程式的成本已經增長）
→ (C) Financial considerations（財務考量）

---

**157. 相關細節**

收件人被要求做什麼？

(A) 填寫表格
(B) 等待之後的電子郵件
(C) 在兩個選擇中做決定
**(D) 記住一個日期**

**換句話說**

keep the latter deadline in mind（記住後面的截止日）→ (D) Remember a date（記住一個日期）

## 158–160 網頁

http://www.olimmer.com/purchase/step2

**步驟 2：選擇您的訂閱方案**

加爾薩女士，感謝您建立 Olimmer 帳戶。現在是時候 [158] **決定您希望能使用我們龐大的模板、主題和圖片收藏庫多久，好為您的客戶製作一流的線上內容**。請查看以下資訊，並在頁面底部的下拉選項中選擇您想要的訂閱方案。

價格：

- 3 個月訂閱方案（90 美元）
- 6 個月訂閱方案（160 美元）
- 1 年訂閱方案（270 美元）
- 2 年訂閱方案（410 美元）

如您所見，我們為長期訂閱提供超值優惠。我們的 2 年訂閱方案費用每天只有 0.56 美元，幾乎是我們 3 個月訂閱方案費用的一半，而 3 個月訂閱方案每天 0.98 美元的費用仍是合理的價格。[159] **我們的 6 個月和 1 年訂閱方案也是不錯的選擇，每天分別為 0.88 美元和 0.73 美元**。

付款：

[160] **可以按月或按年付款**。您應立即支付第一筆款項。我們接受信用卡和簽帳金融卡付款。將於下一頁要求您提供付款的詳細資料。

[160] 更改訂閱期限：

[160] **可以隨時免費完成更改**。開始一個新的計費周期時，您的第一張請款單將包含您之前訂閱中未使用時間的餘額。

[159] **訂閱方案：** 1 年 ▼　下一步 ▶

- subscription (n.) 訂閱　template (n.) 模板
  first-rate (adj.) 一流的；最佳的
  barely (adv.) 幾乎沒有；僅僅
  respectively (adv.) 各自地
  debit card (n.) 簽帳金融卡　at no charge 免費
  credit (n.) 餘額

**158. 推論或暗示**

Olimmer 最有可能是給誰使用的？

(A) 自由會計師　(C) 圖書館員
**(B) 網站設計師**　(D) 記者

---

**159. 相關細節**

加爾薩女士將為她的方案每日支付多少元？

(A) 0.56 美元　(C) 0.88 美元
**(B) 0.73 美元**　(D) 0.98 美元

**160. 確認事實與否**

文中提到關於 Olimmer 訂閱方案的什麼事？

(A) 可隨時取消。
(B) 價格反映了允許使用的服務。
**(C) 轉換方案不收費。**
(D) 必須按月支付。

- access (n.) 管道　on a monthly basis 每月一次

**換句話說**
changing your subscription term（更改訂閱期限）
→ (C) switching from one to another（轉換至另一個方案）
no charge（免費）→ (C) no fee（不收費）

---

### 161–163 備忘錄

收件人：全體員工
寄件人：黛安．埃里克森
關於：彈性工作時間

最近我注意到，員工對普拉斯克的彈性工時政策有些疑惑。我已改寫員工手冊如下，以澄清問題：

「普拉斯克要求所有全職員工每週在辦公室工作 40 小時。但是，獲准採取彈性工時的員工可於週一至週五上午 7 點至晚上 8 點之間的任意組合工作時間來達到此一要求。[161] **彈性工時僅適用於工作職責未要求他們於特定時間待在辦公室的員工。**員工必須獲得管理階層的批准才能採取彈性工時。[163] **由於業務需要或員工績效問題，可以隨時撤銷彈性工時的特權。**在任何一種情況下，員工的主管應清楚說明情況，並提前告知員工變更。」

如果你認為自己有資格採取彈性工時並有意願這麼做，[162] **你應先制定一個建議的時間表**，然後與你的主管會面討論。請不要將彈性工作時間的要求直接帶到人力資源部。不過，你可以透過聯繫約翰．布洛斯（分機 72，john.burrows@prask.com）向我們部門提出有關該政策的一般查詢。

人力資源部總監
黛安．埃里克森

- come to one's attention 引起……注意
  with regard to 有關
  employee handbook (n.) 員工手冊
  requirement (n.) 要求　specific (adj.) 特定的
  managerial (adj.) 管理人的；經理的
  privilege (n.) 特權
  revoke (v.) 撤回；消除　eligible (adj.) 有資格的

**161. 確認事實與否** 難

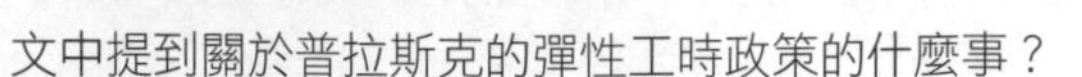
文中提到關於普拉斯克的彈性工時政策的什麼事？

(A) 允許週末工作。
(B) 最近才開始實施。
**(C) 部分員工除外。**
(D) 在員工之間很受歡迎。

- implement (v.) 執行；實施

---

**162. 相關細節** 

根據備忘錄，對彈性工時有興趣的員工應該先做什麼？

**(A) 決定他們想要的工作時間**
(B) 向主管請求准許
(C) 向人力資源部提出請求
(D) 獲得正向的績效評分

- evaluation (n.) 評估

**換句話說**
creating a proposed schedule
（制定一個建議的時間表）
→ (A) Determine their desired working hours
（決定他們想要的工作時間）

---

**163. 句子插入題**

「在任何一種情況下，員工的主管應清楚說明情況，並提前告知員工變更。」最適合放在[1]、[2]、[3]、[4] 的哪個位置？

(A) [1]　　**(C) [3]**
(B) [2]　　(D) [4]

---

### 164–167 線上聊天室

拉娜．諾頓〔上午 11:54〕
嗨大家。我正在看醫生，但時間拖很久，所以我今天可能沒辦法教我下午一點的有氧課。景模請我傳訊息問你們大家，[164/165] **看是否有人能幫我代課。**

亨利．羅梭〔上午 11:54〕
我是願意，但那時剛好卡到我的皮拉提斯課。

肯亞．亨特〔上午 11:55〕
我結束今天的課了，妳可以給我更多細節嗎？

拉娜．諾頓〔上午 11:55〕
[166] **這是一堂低強度、以舞蹈為主的課程，從 1:00 到 1:50**，地點在第三教室。不需要任何器材，學生通常是年長女性。

肯亞・亨特〔上午 11:56〕
[165] **好，聽起來可行。我可以接**。妳通常都播放哪種音樂？

全景模〔上午 11:57〕
謝謝妳，肯亞。[166] **我會發一則簡訊給固定會來上這堂課的學生，讓他們知道**會由不同的老師來上。

拉娜・諾頓〔上午 11:58〕
[167] **其實我有一個幾週前錄的課程影片**。這應該可以給妳播放音樂和我們通常會做哪種動作的點子。[167] **妳的電子郵件地址是什麼？**

肯亞・亨特〔上午 11:58〕
kenya.hunt@pnb-mail.com，謝啦！這幫了大忙。

拉娜・諾頓〔上午 11:59〕
不，謝謝妳自願代課！如果妳有其他問題，請再告訴我。在我接下來的看診期間應該可以定期確認手機。

- **appointment (n.)** 預約看診　**intensity (n.)** 強度
  **doable (adj.)** 可行的　**attendee (n.)** 參與者
  **substitute (v.)** 代替　**periodically (adv.)** 定期地

**164. 相關細節**

諾頓女士為什麼傳訊息給其他人？

**(A) 請求幫忙**
(B) 宣傳某個活動
(C) 為一個情況致歉
(D) 宣布一個行程表

**165. 掌握意圖**

上午 11:56，亨特女士寫道：「我可以接」，她最可能的意思是？

**(A) 她接受一個教學機會。**
(B) 她自願去搬一個物品。
(C) 她想保留一些設備。
(D) 她對學得新技能感興趣。

**166. 確認事實與否**

關於下午一點的課，沒有提到什麼？

(A) 上課時間不到一小時。
**(B) 需要事前報名。**
(C) 包含相對簡單的運動。
(D) 固定由某些人參加。

- **relatively (adv.)** 相對地　**routinely (adv.)** 定期地

**換句話說**
runs from 1:00 to 1:50（從 1:00 到 1:50）
→ (A) lasts for less than an hour（不到一個小時）
low-intensity（低強度）→ (C) relatively easy（相對簡單）
the regular attendees（固定會來上這堂課的學生）
→ (D) attended routinely by some people（固定由某些人參加）

**167. 推論或暗示**

諾頓女士最有可能用電子郵件寄給亨特女士什麼？

**(A) 一個短片**　(C) 一份報名表單
(B) 一份歌單　(D) 一份鄰近地區地圖

**換句話說**
a video of the class that I recorded（一個我錄的課程影片）→ (A) A video clip（一個短片）

**168–171 信件**

克萊兒・菲爾茲
4C24+8G 橋鎮
霍爾特路 390 號

3 月 18 日

露絲之家
3CV4+9Q 橋鎮
菲利普路 2090 號

敬啟者您好：

我的名字是克萊兒・菲爾茲，我是貴店的常客。[168] **我喜歡你們的冰摩卡咖啡**，我認為你們的服務非常好。但是，[169] **身為輪椅使用者，我想提醒你們注意一個無障礙問題。你們的服務台相當高**，似乎離地面大約有 150 公分。我看不到上面的東西，很難將手伸到它的上面，而且它甚至擋到我看菜單。

更換櫃檯可能會非常昂貴，所以我不要求你們這樣做。相反地，我寫信是因為 [170] **我聽說你們正在橋鎮的其他地區開設新分店**。請考慮為他們配備更多適合輪椅使用的設施。另外，[171] **我建議聯繫巴巴多斯身障人士管理局（BDA）以獲得更多有關無障礙設計的實用資訊**。它的網站是 www.bda.bb。

感謝你們花時間閱讀我的信，祝你們好運！看到本地企業蓬勃發展總是令人興奮的。

克萊兒・菲爾茲　謹啟

- **frequent customer (n.)** 常客
  **accessibility (n.)** 容易到達　**obstruct (v.)** 阻礙
  **replace (v.)** 替換　**authority (n.)** 官方；當局

**168. 推論或暗示**

露絲之家是做什麼的公司？

**(A) 咖啡廳** (C) 花店
(B) 髮型沙龍 (D) 服飾店

**169. 相關細節**

菲爾茲女士描述了什麼問題？

(A) 門口太窄。
(B) 標誌上的文字太小。
(C) 有些地板材料不太平整。
**(D) 一個家具太高了。**

換句話說
Your service counter is quite high
（你們的服務櫃台相當高）
→ (D) A piece of furniture is too tall.
（一個家具太高了。）

**170. 確認事實與否**

文中提到關於露絲之家的什麼事？

**(A) 目前正在拓展業務。**
(B) 提供一項特別的服務。
(C) 僱用身障人士。
(D) 是一家國際連鎖店。

換句話說
opening new locations（開設新分店）
→ (A) expanding（拓展）

**171. 相關細節**

菲爾茲女士為什麼建議聯繫巴巴多斯身障人士管理局？

(A) 規劃一項檢查
**(B) 獲得更多資訊**
(C) 申請財務支援
(D) 報告一項困難

換句話說
for more tips（獲得更多實用資訊）
→ (B) To receive further information（為了獲得更多資訊）

**172–175 報導**

## 埃瓦森農民在州議會提出請願書

斯卡維爾　訊（9月8日）——今天，[174] **州議會議員娜歐密．布萊克提交了一份由埃瓦森地區農民簽署的請願書**，抗議政府計劃減少他們的用水許可證。

用水許可證授權持有人使用特定且大量的地下水。[172] **政府的減水計畫將在未來五年內，將農業許可證持有者有權獲得的用水量緩慢縮減 10%。這項計畫是由埃瓦森用水與農業專案小組（EWAT）開發**，作為對抗該地區日益嚴重的乾旱的一種方式。

「每個人都必須做出調整，」EWAT 的主席艾爾文．布魯克斯說道。「州政府已透過如用石礫取代公園中的草地等行動來減少公家的用水量。許可證計畫將會鼓勵農民更有效地用水。」

然而，農民們抱怨說，減少用水量將會不公平地降低他們的土地價值並危害當地經濟。埃瓦森農民協會（EFA）負責人也是請願書的發起人之一科特尼．格蘭特表示：「我們早就在有效利用水資源了。減少用水量只會降低我們的產量。」

[173] **EWAT 代表和 EFA 成員在上個月宣布該計畫後不久，在一次公開會議上討論了該計畫，但未能找到雙方都能接受的和解方案。**協會隨後撰寫並傳閱「負責任水資源管理請願書」。

[175] **請願書建議州政府投資尋找或開發額外的水源，**在兩週內獲得了超過一千份連署。請願書現在已正式提交給州議會，將交給適當的議會委員會進行審查。

- petition (n.) 請願書　introduce (v.) 提出；制定
  parliament (n.) 議會　protest (v.) 抗議
  authorize (v.) 批准；許可
  groundwater (n.) 地下水　shrink (v.) 使變少
  agricultural (adj.) 農業的
  be entitled to 有資格的　combat (v.) 對抗
  gravel (n.) 砂礫；碎石　devalue (v.) 使……貶值
  output (n.) 產量　compromise (n.) 妥協；讓步
  circulate (v.) 傳閱；傳送
  water resources (n.) 水資源
  refer (v.) 將……提交；交付

**172. 相關細節** 難

EWAT 建議做什麼？

(A) 補貼省水技術
**(B) 減少農業用水量**
(C) 提高用水許可證的條件
(D) 在公有財產使用省水造景

- subsidize (v.) 補助　allocate (v.) 分派；分配
  qualification (n.) 資格；條件　conserve (v.) 節省
  property (n.) 財產；資產

**換句話說**
shrink the amount of water that licence-holders in the agricultural industry are entitled to（減少農業許可證持有者有權獲得的水量）
→ (B) Allocating less water to farming efforts（減少農業用水量）

**173. 推論或暗示** 難

關於 EWAT 的計畫，文中提到了什麼？

**(A) 在缺少 EFA 參與的情況下制定。**
(B) 將會延後幾年實施。
(C) 類似於其他州提出的計畫。
(D) 將需要大量的政府資金。

- input (n.) 投入（意見等）
  implement (v.) 執行；實施

**174. 推論或暗示**

布萊克女士最有可能是什麼身分？

(A) 大學教授　　**(C) 地區政治家**
(B) 農產品種植者　　(D) 環保運動人士

- produce (n.) 農產品

**換句話說**
member of State Parliament（州議會議員）
→ (C) regional politician（地區政治家）

**175. 句子插入題**

「在兩週內獲得了超過一千份連署。」最適合放在 [1]、[2]、[3]、[4] 哪個位置？

(A) [1]　　(C) [3]
(B) [2]　　**(D) [4]**

- garner (v.) 獲得

**176–180 圖表與電子郵件**

**活動準備與總結計畫**

4月1日　4月8日　4月15日　4月22日　4月29日　5月6日　5月13日　5月20日　5月27日　6月3日　6月10日　6月17日　6月24日　7月1日　7月8日

176 **預訂場地（魯弗斯）**
募集拍賣捐贈（卡拉、路易斯）
176/179 **聘請外燴業者（格雷格）**
聘請現場音樂演奏者（格雷格）
176 **宣傳活動（魯弗斯）**
收集拍賣物品（路易斯）
176 **設置和參加活動（所有人）**
178 **完成會計工作（卡拉）**
評估結果（所有人）
176 **宣傳結果（魯弗斯）**

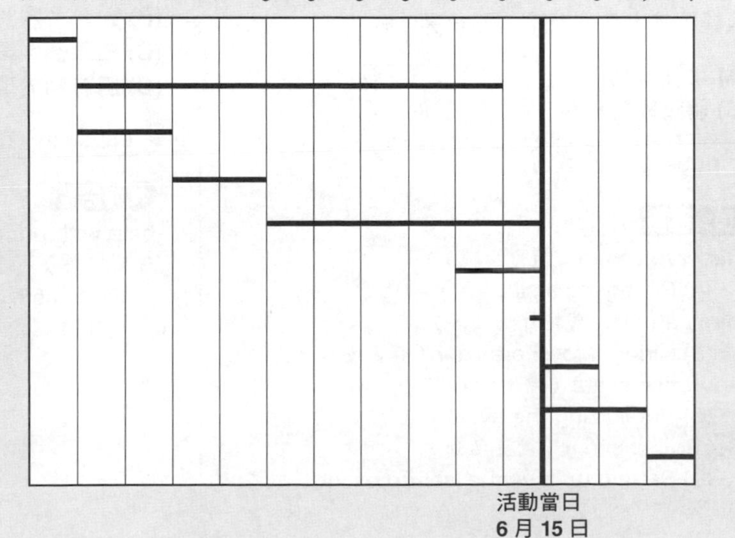

活動當日
6月15日

- venue (n.) 場地　solicit (v.) 懇求；徵集　caterer (n.) 外燴業者

**寄件人：**卡拉．葛林芬
**收件人：**路易斯．羅德里格斯
**主旨：**好消息
**日期：**4 月 24 日

嗨，路易斯：

[177] **我今天早上在獵鷹畫廊和博布羅夫先生見面時有一個好消息——他同意捐贈一幅加布葉爾．塞西的畫作**！它的價值將近 500 美元，因此它可能會帶來相當高的出價。原來 [180] **博布羅夫先生很喜歡菲利克斯森林，所以他很樂意幫助我們的保育工作**。

不過，你應該提前和他談談如何領取和運送這件作品，因為我認為這可能會很困難。如果你確實需要使用打包或運送服務，請確定 [178] **你有留著收據和任何其他的文件。活動結束後，會計作業將會需要用到它們**。

你的努力進展如何？有收到遊樂園的回覆了嗎？他們的入場券對於家庭來說會是一個很有吸引力的東西。

另外，我注意到 [179] **格雷格尚未達到他的第一個截止日期**。你知道為什麼嗎？我想你可能已經聽到了什麼，因為你的辦公桌就在他的旁邊。

卡拉

- bid (n.) 出價　conservation (n.) 保育
  in advance 事先；預先　transport (v.) 運輸
  admission (n.) 准許入場

**176. 確認事實與否**

根據圖表，魯弗斯不需要負責什麼？

(A) 預訂場地　　(C) 宣傳活動
**(B) 聘請餐飲業者**　　(D) 設置場地

- publicize (v.) 宣傳

**換句話說**
Reserve venue（預訂場地）
→ (A) Reserving a site（預訂場地）
Hire caterer（聘請外燴業者）
→ (B) Hiring a food provider（聘僱餐飲業者）
Advertise event（宣傳活動）
→ (C) Publicizing the event（宣傳活動）
Set up . . . event（設置活動）
→ (D) Setting up a venue (set up event)（設置場地）

**177. 相關細節**

葛林芬女士獲得了什麼捐贈品？

**(A) 藝術品**
(B) 藝廊導覽
(C) 一系列的繪畫課程
(D) 與一位藝術家一同用餐

**換句話說**
painting（畫作）→ (A) artwork（藝術品）

**178. 整合題** 

誰最可能需要電子郵件中提到的文件？

(A) 魯弗斯　　(C) 格雷格
**(B) 葛林芬女士**　　(D) 塞西女士

**179. 整合題**

格雷格沒有達成哪個截止日？

(A) 4 月 8 日　　**(C) 4 月 22 日**
(B) 4 月 15 日　　(D) 5 月 6 日

**換句話說**
hasn't met（尚未達到）→ fail to meet（沒有達成）

**180. 推論或暗示**

在電子郵件中，關於正在規劃的活動提到了什麼？

(A) 需要重新安排時程。
(B) 與會者需要特殊的交通工具。
(C) 由某個娛樂企業所贊助。
**(D) 將有利於環境目標。**

- cause (n.) 目標；事業

**換句話說**
help with our conservation efforts（幫助我們的保育工作）
→ (D) benefit an environmental cause（有利於環境目標）

**181–185 請款單與電子郵件**

## 請款單

**布倫丹艾切瓦利亞服務**

M4N 3P6 安大略省
多倫多市
郵政信箱 10392
647-555-0129
www.
brendanechevarria.com

請款單編號：62 號
施工期間：
1 月 1 日至
1 月 31 日
核發日：
2 月 1 日
**到期日：**
**3 月 2 日**

客戶：巴爾多拉線上網站
經辦人：亞曼達．青木
M6J 1B9 安大略省多倫多市
瑞奇蒙街 780 號
416-555-0105

| 服務 | 費用 | 總額 |
|---|---|---|
| [181] **關於委拉企業擴展的 300 字新聞文章** | 0.3 美元／字 | 90 美元 |
| [181] **關於管理技巧的 450 字報導性文章** | 0.5 美元／字 | 225 美元 |
| 與客戶通話 30 分鐘 | 5 美元／ 15 分鐘 | 10 美元 |
| [183] **修改 450 字的文章** | [183] **0.1 美元／字** | 45 美元 |
| | **總額** | 370 美元 |

可將支票寄至上述實體地址付款，
或是透過 WeisPay 付款至
payment@brendanechevarria.com。

謝謝您的惠顧！

- **date due (n.)** 到期日　**expansion (n.)** 擴張
  **informative (adj.)** 提供資訊的
  **revision (n.)** 修訂
  **physical (adj.)** 實體的

**寄件人：**布蘭登．艾切瓦利亞
<contact@brendanechevarria.com>
**收件人：**亞曼達．青木
<amanda.aoki@baldora.com>
**主旨：**關於：問題
**日期：**2 月 5 日

親愛的阿曼達：

我很高興回答 [182] **您關於本月請款單的問題**。首先，您說對了，[183] **我今年的改寫費用提高了**。如果讓您感到意外，我很抱歉，但我在 12 月寄給您的前任業務的費率表中已註明新費率，而他同意了。[184] **我會單獨將往返的電子郵件轉寄給您**，方便您確認。我猜他忘了更新我在貴公司檔案中的資訊。

至於 [182] **您請求推薦其他潛在撰稿人**，我確實認識某人您可能會感興趣。[185] **她的名字是梅樂蒂．索普，她是我在《約克維爾先驅報》的前同事，近期成為一名自由科學作家**。她有一種簡單、引人入勝的風格，您可以在《先驅報》網站上的舊報導中看到她的這種風格。如果您決定要聯繫她，她的電子郵件地址是 m.thorpe@vct-mail.com。

如果您有任何其他問題或疑慮，請告訴我。除非您另有說明，否則我將繼續撰寫我目前的 250 字新聞文章。

布蘭登　謹啟

- **predecessor (n.)** 前任
  **potential (adj.)** 潛在的；可能的
  **contributor (n.)** 投稿人

**181. 相關細節**

艾切瓦利亞先生在一月為巴爾多拉線上網站撰寫了關於什麼的文章？

(A) 運動
(B) 政治
**(C) 企業**
(D) 娛樂

**182. 主旨或目的**

這封電子郵件的目的為何？

**(A) 回答客戶的疑問**
(B) 報告某項付款的問題
(C) 討論計畫的更動
(D) 為請款錯誤致歉

**183. 整合題**

艾切瓦利亞先生提到最近改變了哪項費率？

(A) 每個字 0.3 美元
(B) 每個字 0.5 美元
(C) 每 15 分鐘 5 美元
**(D) 每個字 0.1 美元**

---

**184. 同義詞考題** 難

在電子郵件中，第一段第四行的「exchange」，意思最接近何者？

(A) 交易　　(C) 轉換
(B) 市場　　**(D) 通信**

---

**185. 確認事實與否** 

電子郵件中提到關於索普女士的什麼事？

(A) 她是艾切瓦利亞先生的一位客戶。
(B) 她擁有科學領域的學位。
**(C) 她不再有全職雇主。**
(D) 她回應了網站上的一個廣告。

- degree (n.) 學位　field (n.) 領域

**換句話說**

became a freelance science writer
（成為一名自由科學作家）
→ (C) no longer has a full-time employer
（不再有全職雇主）

---

**186–190 電子郵件、表格與便條**

**寄件人：**艾德．派傑特
**收件人：**蘿絲．泰特
**主旨：**辦公室裝修
**日期：**9 月 30 日
**附件：**辦公室_裝修_要求

親愛的泰特女士：

歡迎來到倫斯福德企業！我的名字是艾德．派傑特，我是您所在樓層的辦公室管理員。由於您開始工作後會非常忙碌，您可能想要現在就開始為您的新辦公室進行採買。我們的辦公室裝修政策如下：

- 擁有私人辦公室的員工（以下簡稱「辦公人員」）應在一個月內進行裝修，以給客戶留下良好的印象。
- [188] **在聘用或升職時，新辦公人員可在辦公室裝修上花費最多 1000 美元。**
- 可以向辦公室管理員提交辦公室裝修電子申請表來申請購買。
- [188] **本次或往後花費任何額外款項的請求，必須得到辦公人員的經理批准。**
- [187] **裝飾品必須兼具品味和專業。**
- [190] **裝修活動應提前通知附近的辦公人員，**以免影響他們的工作。

作為參考，[186] **您的辦公室大約長 10 英尺、寬 10 英尺**。此外，您可能還記得，上次您造訪時，[186] **辦公室有灰色的大理石地板，已經有一張書桌、一個小沙發和一個書櫃**——當然，如果您願意，您可以更換這些物品。

我已在這封電子郵件中附上了必要的表格。如果您對此資訊有任何疑問，請告訴我。

艾德　謹啟

- administrator (n.) 管理人　hereafter (adv.) 此後　disturb (v.) 干擾　for reference 提供參考

**辦公室裝修申請**

姓名：蘿絲．泰特　　僱用／升遷生效日期：10 月 4 日
職稱：資深會計師　　辦公室號碼：305 號

| 物品描述 | 賣家 | [189] 網頁連結 | 數量 | 估計總價* |
|---|---|---|---|---|
| 書桌椅 | 瑪羅琳 | www.mallorin.com/4024 | 1 | 235 美元 |
| [189] **藝術複製畫** | 妮可．潘 | [189] **無** | 1 | 175 美元 |
| 扶手椅 | 伯恩家居 | www.bohnhomes.com/3421 | 2 | 210 美元 |
| 茶几 | 伯恩家居 | www.bohnhomes.com/0257 | 1 | 65 美元 |
| 掛衣架 | 伯恩家居 | www.bohnhomes.com/6369 | 1 | 40 美元 |
| | | [188] **預計總額** | | [188] **725 美元** |

提交日：10 月 6 日　　收件人：艾德．派傑特

* 估價必須包含任何可能的運費／快遞費／安裝費。

- effective date (n.) 生效日　quantity (n.) 數量　approx. (= approximate) (adj.) 大約的　estimated (adj.) 預估的

嗨，奧黛麗：

[190] **我只是想讓妳知道，我今天早上需要在我的辦公室做一些裝修**。請告訴我是否有任何時間對妳來說特別不方便，因為我可以彈性調整。

謝謝。

蘿絲

**186. 確認事實與否**

關於泰特女士的辦公室，派傑特先生沒有提供什麼資訊？

(A) 尺寸大小　(C) 地板材質
(B) 既有物品　**(D) 位置**

**換句話說**
roughly 10 feet long by 10 feet wide（大約 10 英尺長、10 英尺寬）
→ (A) dimensions（尺寸大小）
already contains a desk, a small sofa, and a bookcase（已包含一張書桌、一個小沙發和一個書櫃）
→ (B) existing contents（既有物品）
grey marble floors（灰色的大理石地板）
→ (C) flooring material（地板材質）

**187. 同義詞考題**

在電子郵件中，第六段第一行的「professional」，意思最接近何者？

(A) 獲得金錢　**(C) 適用於企業**
(B) 耐用的　(D) 有禮貌的

**188. 整合題** 難

關於泰特女士的要求，文中提到了什麼？

**(A) 不需要管理階層的批准。**
(B) 包含一些舊家具的替換。
(C) 比建議時間還晚提交。
(D) 已經修改過一次。

**189. 確認事實與否** 

關於表格上列出的產品，文中提到了什麼？

(A) 其中一項將會客製化。
**(B) 不全是在網路上販售。**
(C) 有一些是二手物品。
(D) 都是由同一家製造商製造。

- customized (adj.) 客製化的

**190. 整合題**

文中暗示了什麼關於奧黛麗的事？

(A) 她不在早上工作。
**(B) 她的辦公室在泰特女士的附近。**
(C) 她是一位維修主管。
(D) 她的職稱與派傑特先生相同。

- maintenance (n.) 維修

**191–195 報導與網頁**

## 哈梅爾於維隆斯普林斯獲最佳男演員獎

維隆斯普林斯　訊（5 月 17 日）——在週日晚上的頒獎典禮上，維隆斯普林斯電影節的評審團將最佳男演員獎頒予資深演員克里斯多福．哈梅爾。在本電影節中競爭的 22 部獨立電影和無數演員中，其他的大贏家包括《風中吶喊》（最佳影片）和西爾維婭．馬蒂斯（因在《前進》中的角色而獲獎的最佳女演員）。

哈梅爾先生因在《我們的柵欄》中的絕佳表現而獲獎。由維多米爾．霍姆伍德執導、與菲莉希亞．卡爾森共同主演的 [193] **《我們的柵欄》講述了一位退休的西雅圖卡車司機（哈梅爾飾）的故事，當一位藝術家（卡爾森飾）和她的小女兒搬進隔壁的房子時，他發現自己平靜的生活被打斷了**。這部感人的電影深受觀眾喜愛，並已被 RTY 影視選中於美國夏末發行。

該獎項可能代表哈梅爾先生的職業生涯捲土重來。約十年前，在一連串令人失望的票房成績之後，他不再出現在主要工作室製作的電影中。[192] **從那時起，他一直在戲劇作品和小型電影中穩定工作，但《我們的柵欄》是第一個獲得多方認可的作品**。

[191] **哈梅爾先生在維隆劇院的舞台上發表獲獎感言時，感謝霍姆伍德先生、卡爾森女士和電影節評審團**，最後表示：「感覺就像我得到了第二次機會，我不敢置信。」

- costar (v.) 共同出演　interrupt (v.) 打斷
  distribution (n.) 發行　box-office (n.) 票房
  widespread (adj.) 廣泛的
  recognition (n.) 認可

http://www.all-about-movies.com/053809

| 首頁 | 近期上映 | 編輯推薦 | 聯絡我們 |
| --- | --- | --- | --- |

**電影資訊**

**《我們的柵欄》**

**種類：**戲劇、喜劇、家庭
**上映日期：**8 月 31 日（全國）
**影片總長：**125 分鐘
**執導：**維多米爾・霍姆伍德
[195] **編劇：艾波尼・法蘭西斯**
**音樂：**柯瑞・吉卜森

**簡介：**一位老人因新鄰居而體驗前所未有的人生教訓

[193] **細節：在多倫多拍攝。**看更多

**主要陣容：**

克里斯多福・哈梅爾 .......... 特倫斯・瓊斯
伊芳・派克 ...................... 伊娃・韋伯
菲莉希亞・卡爾森 ........... 凡妮莎・韋伯
勞爾・阿爾維佐 .............. 馬可

看更多卡司與工作人員名單

- **release (v.)** 釋出；推出 **trivia (n.)** 細節

http://www.all-about-movies.com/053809/reviews

| 首頁 | 近期上映 | 編輯推薦 | 聯絡我們 |
| --- | --- | --- | --- |

**電影資訊**

評論：《我們的柵欄》

**「比喜劇更有戲劇性」★★★☆☆**
[194] **我去看這部電影是因為它的電視廣告看起來很有趣**，但結果卻在某些地方很悲傷。不過，我仍然會給它正面的評價。演員陣容很棒。

西爾維婭・弗洛雷斯，9 月 3 日

**「整體都很傑出！」★★★★☆**
克里斯多福・哈梅爾獲得電影節獎項肯定實至名歸，但 [195] **我認為艾波尼・法蘭西斯是這部電影中真正的天才**。我肯定會尋找更多她的作品。

柯特・史都華，9 月 1 日

**191. 相關細節**

報導中提到關於電影節的什麼資訊？

(A) 評審團的主席
(B) 為期多久的時間
(C) 舉辦過的次數
**(D) 頒獎典禮的地點**

**192. 推論或暗示** 

報導中提到哈梅爾先生近幾年做了什麼？

**(A) 出演獨立電影**
(B) 擔任電影製作人
(C) 在戲劇課程中教導學生
(D) 參加某個募款活動

**193. 整合題**

關於《我們的柵欄》，下列何者最可能為真？

(A) 全國上映時間延後。
(B) 在電影節之後被縮短了。
**(C) 不是在故事發生的地點拍攝的。**
(D) 電影的海報未被 RTY 影視批准。

**194. 相關細節**

弗洛雷斯女士為何決定要看《我們的柵欄》？

(A) 她閱讀了一則對於該片的正面觀眾評價。
(B) 她是其中一名卡司的粉絲。
(C) 她想更了解這個主題。
**(D) 她喜歡該片的宣傳資料。**

- **promotional materials (n.)** 宣傳資料

**換句話說**
**TV commercials for it**（它的電視廣告）
→ **(D) its promotional materials**（該片的宣傳資料）

**195. 整合題** 

史都華先生最喜歡《我們的柵欄》哪一點？

(A) 演出
(B) 執導
**(C) 編劇**
(D) 音樂

- **appreciate (v.)** 欣賞

**196–200 網頁、保證書與電子郵件**

http://www.gwi-insulation.com/services/sprayfoaminsulation

| 首頁 | 服務 | 顧客見證 | 關於我們 |
| --- | --- | --- | --- |

## 聚氨酯泡沫隔熱層

聚氨酯泡沫隔熱層是價格最高的家庭絕緣材料，但它也形成了最強大的隔熱及防寒屏障。[196] **我們的客戶告訴我們，他們的家用能源帳單費用在安裝後降低了 50% 或更多**。泡沫有兩種類型：開孔和閉孔。開孔泡沫較便宜，更適合填充難以觸及的角落，而閉孔泡沫可提供更多針對抵抗極端溫度的保護。在馬丁縣，這兩種類型的泡沫都必須由擁有執照的專家施工，但 [197] **只有在佛菲特才需要申請市政府許可證**。申請流程很少需要超過一天的時間。

致電 555-0173 或寄電子郵件至 services@gwi-insulation.com，了解更多有關 GWI 聚氨酯泡沫隔熱層服務的資訊。

- testimonial (n.) 證言推薦　insulation (n.) 隔離
  barrier (n.) 障礙物　installation (n.) 安裝
  extreme (adj.) 極端的
  licensed (adj.) 得到許可的；經認證的
  rarely (adv.) 鮮少地

GWI 隔熱層

### 保證書

工程資訊

[197] **GWI 隔熱層應業主艾伯特．馬奇的要求，在位於佛菲特市布魯爾街 450 號的房屋閣樓上安裝了開孔絕緣泡沫。**

保障範圍

GWI 隔熱層將免費提供工人和商品，以修復安裝時因瑕疵產品或不正確施工而引起的任何絕緣問題。

[198] **本保固在建築的壽命之內有效，並且可與建築的所有權一起轉移。**

例外事項

GWI 隔熱層不對以下情況的絕緣問題負責：

1. 絕緣體本身或周圍區域已被業主或其他公司更改或更換。
2. 因狂風、暴雨或其他自然災害而損壞。
3. 附著的表面因結構基礎或牆壁的倒塌或移位而損壞。
4. [199] **附著的表面發生白色霉斑、霉菌或自然老化。**

GWI 隔熱層 總裁
莉莉蓮．蒂爾

- warranty (n.) 保固證書　attic (n.) 閣樓
  at no charge 免費　defective (adj.) 有缺陷的
  valid (adj.) 有效的　transfer (v.) 轉移
  alter (v.) 改變　occurrence (n.) 發生；出現
  collapse (n.) 崩塌　mildew (n.) 發霉；黴菌
  mold (n.) 發霉；黴菌

寄件人：艾伯特．馬奇
收件人：德瑞克．蘇利文
主旨：關於：保證書索賠
日期：2 月 24 日
附件：保證書＿馬奇

親愛的馬奇先生：

[200] **我們 GWI 隔熱層很遺憾地得知，**[199] **由於發霉問題，您需要更換閣樓中的一些橫樑和木板。**很遺憾，[199] **這種情況是明確排除在您的保固範圍之外的情況之一**，因此我們需要就我們對您的閣樓絕緣所做的任何工程向您收費。我已附上我們的保證書掃描副本供您參考。

如果您想聘請我們維修或更換您的安裝，請告訴我們。雖然這項工程不是免費的，但我們仍然可以為您提供優惠的價格。

GWI 隔熱層
德瑞克．蘇利文　謹啟

- beam (n.) 樑　explicitly (adv.) 明確地
  exclude (v.) 排除；除外

**196. 相關細節**

根據網頁，GWI 隔熱層的顧客回報了什麼？

**(A) 較低的能源支出**
(B) 較好的室內空氣品質
(C) 降低噪音污染
(D) 增加結構強度

- structural (adj.) 結構的

換句話說

their home energy bills dropped 50% or more（他們的家用能源帳單費用減少了 50% 或更多）
→ (A) lower energy costs（較低的能源支出）

**197. 整合題**

關於馬奇先生的房屋工程，文中提到了什麼？

(A) 在地下的空間進行。
**(B) 在市政府的核准下進行。**
(C) 包括更昂貴的噴霧泡沫類型。
(D) 需要超過一天來完成。

**換句話說**

a city permit（市政府許可證）
→ (B) a city government's permission（市政府的核准）

---

### 198. 確認事實與否 難

文中提到關於保證書的什麼事？

(A) 有終止日期。
(B) 馬奇先生付了額外的費用而得到的。
**(C) 即使馬奇先生賣掉房子，依然有效。**
(D) 不包括維修所需的產品費用。

- expiration (n.) 到期

**換句話說**

can be transferred along with the ownership of the structure（可與建築的所有權一起轉移）
→ (C) still be valid even if Mr. Mackle sells the house（即使馬奇先生賣掉房子，依然有效）

---

### 199. 整合題

蘇利文先生提到保證書裡的哪一條例外事項？

(A) 例外事項 1
(B) 例外事項 2
(C) 例外事項 3
**(D) 例外事項 4**

**換句話說**

one of those explicitly excluded from your warranty
（明確排除在您的保固範圍之外的其中一項）
→ exclusion in the warranty
（保證書裡的例外事項）

---

### 200. 同義詞考題

在電子郵件中，第一段第一行的「learn」與下列何者意義最接近？

(A) 精通
**(B) 發現**
(C) 記住
(D) 經歷

# ACTUAL TEST 3

## PART 5 P. 64–66

**101. 副詞詞彙題**

伊迪絲．史丹利說，她從未後悔將大學主修科系從財經轉為工程。

**(A) 從未** (C) 非常
(B) 足夠的 (D) 較少的

- regret (v.) 懊悔 switch (v.) 改變
  major (n.)（大學的）主修科目

---

**102. 副詞詞彙題——修飾動名詞**

使用者應避免以不必要的暴力關上影印機的蓋子。

(A) 猛力的 (C) 強迫
**(B) 猛力地** (D) 力氣

- lid (n.) 蓋子

---

**103. 人稱代名詞考題——受格** 難

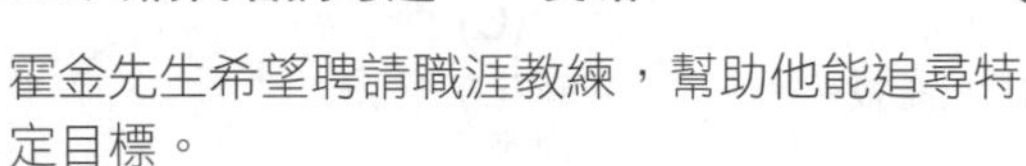

霍金先生希望聘請職涯教練，幫助他能追尋特定目標。

(A) 他自己 (C) 他的
**(B) 他** (D) 他

- career coach (n.) 職涯教練；就業顧問
  pursue (v.) 追求

---

**104. 介系詞詞彙題**

奎沙達燒烤提供距離該店五英里內免費外送，但超過後的收費相對很高。

(A) 大約 **(C) 在……範圍內**
(B) 在……上 (D) 至多

- delivery (n.) 遞送
  charge (v.)（尤指對某一服務或活動）收費
  relatively (adv.) 相對地

---

**105. 動詞詞類變化題——語態**

季節性的運動設備和其他不常用到的東西，可以存放在公寓大樓的地下室。

**(A) 可以被存放** (C) 正在存放
(B) 應該存放 (D) 存放

- equipment 設備 (n.) infrequently (adv.) 不常
  complex (n.) 綜合大樓 basement (n.) 地下室
  store (v.) 存放

---

**106. 動詞詞類變化題——動名詞**

擔任工廠營運職務僅幾星期，詹寧斯女士就開始進行改革以提升效率。

(A) 擔任 (C) 擔任
**(B) 擔任** (D) 擔任

- operation (n.) 營運 increase (v.) 增加
  efficiency (n.) 效率 assume (v.) 擔任

---

**107. 副詞詞彙題——修飾介系詞片語** 

除了早上尖鋒時間外，研究發現市區公車通常整天都很準時。

(A) 通常的 **(C) 通常地**
(B) 普遍的 (D) 概括

- be on time 準時 generalize (v.) 概括；歸納

---

**108. 形容詞詞彙題**

雖然無法確切證明這一點，但考古學家相信，這個物品很有可能用於準備食物。

(A) 事實上的 (C) 通常的
(B) 機能的 **(D) 很有可能的**

- conclusively (adv.) 不容置疑地 prove (v.) 證明
  archaeologist (n.) 考古學家
  functional (adj.) 機能的

---

**109. 人稱代名詞考題——受格**

蒙塔諾先生的現代書迷可能會驚訝地發現，他的書在出版時幾乎沒有一本得到評論家的青睞。

(A) 他們的（東西） **(C) 他們**
(B) 他們的 (D) 他們自己

- critic (n.)（尤指書籍、電影、音樂等的）評論家
  release (n.) 發行

---

**110. 形容詞詞彙題——主詞補語** 

儘管最近的果汁吧專門店失敗，但迪亞茲女士仍因她早期開設迪亞茲咖啡的成功，而備受投資者尊敬。

(A) 恭敬的 (C) 可敬地
(B) 關於 **(D) 備受尊敬的**

- in spite of 儘管 recent (adj.) 最近的
  franchise (n.) 專門店
  investor (n.) 投資者；出資者
  respectful (adj.) 表示尊敬的

**111. 副詞詞彙題** 難

羅斯坦大樓以前從來沒有這麼受歡迎過，雖然多年來，它一直被視為亨特維爾的地標。

**(A) 這麼**　(C) 如何
(B) 高　(D) 非常

- consider (v.) 把……視為　landmark (n.) 地標

---

**112. 名詞詞彙題——介系詞的受詞**

重鋪楓樹街路面的工程人員，將從它和希格斯路的交叉路口開始，然後繼續朝萊斯科特大道的方向進行。

(A) 指導者　(C) 指導
(B) 最直接的　**(D) 方向**

- resurface (v.) 重鋪路面
  intersection (n.) 十字路口　proceed (v.) 繼續做
  director (n.) 指導者　direct (v.) 管理；指揮

---

**113. 副詞子句連接詞詞彙題**

儘管鮑伊斯老鷹隊曾屢次進入威克斯盃最後一輪的賽事，但他們至今尚未贏得獎盃。

**(A) 當……的時候**　(C) 無論何時
(B) 即使　(D) 儘管

- reach (v.) 達到　manage (v.) 設法做到

---

**114. 形容詞詞彙題** 難

朴博士在《組織心理學》中的文章解釋了，積極回應強而有力的領導風格的人，如何在水平結構的工作場域中遇到困難。

(A) 回應　(C) 反應熱烈地
**(B) 反應熱烈的**　(D) 反應

- organizational (adj.) 組織的
  psychology (n.) 心理學
  horizontally (adv.) 水平地
  responsively (adv.) 反應熱烈地

---

**115. 不定詞——「to ＋原形動詞」**

你簽名就表示同意遵守這份合約的條款。

(A) 和……一起　(C) 關於
(B) 通過　**(D)（不定詞，用於動詞前）**

- indicate (v.) 表明　abide by 遵守
  terms (n.) 條款　contract (n.) 合約

---

**116. 動詞詞類變化題—主詞動詞單複數一致性**

從今天開始，所有市立圖書館前都已放置了丟棄用過電池的特殊垃圾箱。

**(A) 已被放置**　(C) 將放置
(B) 放置了　(D) 正被放置

- as of . . . 自……起　bin (n.) 垃圾箱；箱子
  disposal (n.) 拋棄

---

**117. 介系詞詞彙題**

根據最新的市場報告，由於收入增加，化妝品業仍將持續發展。

(A) 除了……以外　(C) 除了……尚有
(B) 透過　**(D) 根據**

- industry (n.) 行業　thanks to 由於
  income (n.) 收入　except for . . . 除了……以外
  in addition to 除了……尚有

---

**118. 動詞詞彙題**

我們的談判員說服席爾蒙軟體公司將服務費打折，以換取顧客的正面推薦。

(A) 爭論　(C) 使安心
**(B) 說服**　(D) 安頓

- negotiator (n.) 談判者；談判專家
  in exchange for 作為……的交換
  testimonial (n.) 推薦；顧客見證
  argue (v.) 爭論　assure (v.) 使安心
  settle (v.) 安頓

---

**119. 主詞補語考題——過去分詞**

傑洛特公司的員工感謝獲准遠距工作，而且很容易透過線上排班系統做安排。

(A) 允許　(C) 允許
(B) 允許　**(D) 允許**

- appreciate (v.) 感謝
  telecommuting (n.) 遠距工作
  via (prep.) 透過；經由

---

**120. 名詞詞彙題**

有某些證據顯示，常喝茶的人罹患心臟病的風險會降低。

(A) 治療　**(C) 風險**
(B) 進步　(D) 診斷

- regular (adj.) 經常的；習慣性的
  diagnosis (n.) 診斷

**121. 副詞詞彙題** 難

當我們的員工抱怨這個問題時，飯店經理迅速提議將她升等到一個更好的房間。

(A) 非常　　(C) 隨機地
(B) 共同地　　**(D) 迅速地**

- collectively (adv.) 共同地；集體地
  randomly (adv.) 隨機地；任意地

---

**122. 名詞詞彙題——不定詞 to V 的受詞** 難

樸美拉航空將開始提供加大伸腿空間的航班，以確保乘客的舒適。

(A) 令人安慰的　　**(C) 舒適**
(B) 舒適的　　(D) 舒適地

- leg room (n.)（與前排座位間的）伸腿空間
  comfort (n.) 舒適

---

**123. 形容詞詞彙題** 難

要求線上公開醫院費用的法律，旨在讓醫藥界的定價對病人更公開透明。

**(A) 透明的**　　(C) 足夠的
(B) 相等的　　(D) 知識淵博的

- be intended to 打算做……
  equivalent (adj.) 相等的；等值的
  adequate (adj.) 足夠的
  knowledgeable (adj.) 知識淵博的；有見識的

---

**124. 名詞詞彙題**

宴會上將介紹瑞爾特獎的得獎者，並讓他們有機會發表得獎感言。

(A) 反應　　(C) 感謝
**(B) 接受**　　(D) 分析

- recipient (n.) 接受者　opportunity (n.) 機會
  make remarks 談話；評論
  gratitude (n.) 感謝　analysis (n.) 分析

---

**125. 動詞詞彙題** 

我們的訓練課程經常更新，以確保它們與人力需求一致。

(A) 合作　　(C) 配備
(B) 實施　　**(D) 一致**

- constantly (adv.) 經常；不斷地
  requirement (n.) 需要；要求
  workforce (n.) 勞動力　collaborate (v.) 合作
  implement (v.) 實施　equip (v.) 配備

---

**126. 關係代名詞——主格**

普羅斯特農業的攤位最顯眼的是一個螢幕，播放由貿易展的參加者拍攝的照片。

(A) 那些人的　　**(C) ……的（事物）**
(B) 只是　　(D) 屬於

- agriculture (n.) 農業
  attendee (n.) 參加者；出席者

---

**127. 名詞詞彙題** 

人力資源部人員在處理他們同事的個人資料時必須謹慎。

(A) 繁榮　　(C) 共識
**(B) 謹慎**　　(D) 抱負

- demonstrate (v.) 顯示；表現
  prosperity (n.) 繁榮　consensus (n.) 共識
  aspiration (n.) 抱負

---

**128. 名詞詞彙題——介系詞的受詞**

為了他們停留日本期間做準備，JFLT 節目提供參賽者 50 小時的日語教學。

**(A) 教學**　　(C) 有啟發性的
(B) 指示　　(D) 教師

- participant (n.) 參加者；參與者
  instructive (adj.) 有啟發性的；有教育意義的
  instructor (n.) 教師；教練

---

**129. 動詞詞彙題** 

等獲得所有必要的許可後，高恩斯公司就會開始大樓的興建工程。

(A) 補救　　**(C) 開始**
(B) 練習　　(D) 操縱

- approval (n.) 核准；許可　obtain (v.) 獲得
  redeem (v.) 補救；贖回　exercise (v.) 練習
  maneuver (v.) 操縱

---

**130. 形容詞詞彙題** 

史貝隆公司的收益減少，是它的主力產品數位相機需求下滑的必然結果。

(A) 稀少的　　(C) 能幹的
**(B) 必然的**　　(D) 合作的

- revenue (n.) 收益；收入　scarce (adj.) 稀少的
  competent (adj.) 能幹的；稱職的
  cooperative (adj.) 合作的；配合的

## PART 6 P. 67–70

### 131–134 報導

**葛朗茲沃克將舉行第一千次每週公園淨地活動**

非營利組織「葛朗茲沃克」將在這個星期六9月8日，於舒樂公園舉行它的第一千次每週公園淨地活動。

從由一群本地保育人士 [131] **創立**開始，葛朗茲沃克就努力對梅林郡居民推廣對大自然的愛。那些它幾乎每週 [132] **派去**舒樂公園的熱心志工，是這些努力的重要部分。在公園的工作人員監督下，他們撿拾垃圾、協助照顧植物，前後已超過 19 個年頭。該組織也定期舉辦適合所有年齡層的居民參加的健行活動以及與大自然相關主題課程。

葛朗茲沃克計劃在星期六的淨地活動後，舉行派對慶祝這個 [133] **里程碑**。[134] **派對將以音樂、適合全家參與的遊戲以及茶點為特色。**有興趣參加的人，可以瀏覽它的網站 www.groundswork.org，了解更多詳情。

- **nonprofit (adj.)** 非營利的
  **conservationist (n.)** 保育人士
  **strive to** 努力；奮鬥 **promote (v.)** 推廣
  **oversee (v.)** 監督 **attend (v.)** 參加

**131. 動名詞詞彙題**

(A) 同意 **(C) 創立**
(B) 完成 (D) 加入

- **grant (v.)** （通常指官方）同意；准予
  **achieve (v.)** 完成；實現

---

**132. 關係代名詞的省略** 

(A) 已被派去 (C) 派去的
**(B) 它派去** (D) 正派去

---

**133. 名詞詞彙題** 

**(A) 里程碑** (C) 改進
(B) 獲得 (D) 決定

- **acquisition (n.)** 獲得 **improvement (n.)** 改進

**134. 句子插入題**

(A) 全年都歡迎申請加入會員。
(B) 事實上，所有公園的活動都必須提出淨地計畫。
**(C) 派對將以音樂、適合全家參與的遊戲以及茶點為特色。**
(D) 詹市長甚至在社群媒體上發布道賀訊息。

- **application (adj.)** 申請 **submit (v.)** 提出
  **refreshments (n.)** 茶點
  **congratulatory (adj.)** 祝賀的

---

### 135–138 電子郵件

**寄件者：**伊瑪妮．傑克森
**收件者：**托比．奧特嘉
**主旨：**接待員工作應徵者
**日期：**4月2日
**附件：**應徵者電子試算表

嗨，托比：

你可能還記得，接待員工作的應徵期限到上星期五截止。在此開心報告：我們收到 50 多份履歷！[135] **在那個求職網站登廣告的確大有幫助。**

總之，我已根據你具體說明的條件，篩選應徵者，在附件的電子試算表中 [136] **描述**了前十名的可能人選。等你有時間，請 [137] **看一下**檔案並選出你想要面談的人。[138] **可能的話**，我們應該按照廣告中所列的時間表，這個星期開始打電話給他們。

如果你還有其他需求，請告訴我。

伊瑪妮　敬上

- **job candidate (n.)** 求職者
  **narrow down** 縮減 **in accordance with** 根據
  **requirement (n.)** 要求；必要條件
  **specify (v.)** 具體說明；明確指出
  **prospect (n.)** 有希望的人選

**135. 句子插入題**

**(A) 在那個求職網站登廣告的確大有幫助。**
(B) 然而，那正是我們無法立刻回覆你的應徵的原因。
(C) 在四月底前把十個空缺全都補滿，可能畢竟不是那麼困難。
(D) 幸運的是，馬克下個星期有空協助我檢視每個應徵者。

- **make a difference** 改善；有影響
  **promptly (adv.)** 立即地；迅速地

**136. 動詞詞類變化題——語態**

(A) 已描述 (C) 正被描述
(B) 正已描述 **(D) 被描述**

**137. 動詞詞彙題**

(A) 放棄 **(C) 查看**
(B) 要求 (D) 翻轉

- pass up 放棄；錯過 call for 要求
  turn around 翻轉；轉身

**138. 連接副詞**

**(A) 可能的話** (C) 因此
(B) 反而 (D) 尤其是

- instead (adv.) 反而；卻 therefore (adv.) 因此
  in particular 尤其是；特別是

**139–142 信件**

**洛羅郡道路收費局**

22432 維吉尼亞州卡爾森市緬因街 430 號

4 月 10 日

梅爾芭．葛雷維斯

22433 維吉尼亞州卡爾森市

富蘭克林街 108 號

親愛的葛雷維斯女士：

您會收到這封信是因為一輛登記在您名下的車輛，於 4 月 2 日行經奈普收費道路。由於該車輛未在洛羅郡的電子收費系統（ETCS）註冊，這種行為違反郡法令。請見附件的 139 **費用清單**。上面所須繳的金額必須於 5 月 2 日前支付。請注意，如果 140 **屆時**還未收到您的款項，將向您收取額外費用。

此外，如果您未來有可能再度行經收費道路，我們強力建議您註冊 ETCS。141 **這可以到我們位於上述地址的辦公室來辦理**。註冊免費且能避免 142 **更多**這類的問題。

如果您認為這封信是誤寄給您的，請遵照本頁背面的指示提出異議。

附件

- toll road (n.) 收費道路 register (v.) 登記；註冊
  enroll (v.) 註冊 violation (n.) 違反
  enclosed (adj.) 隨函附上的 in error 錯誤地
  instruction (n.) 指示 dispute (v.) 對……有異議

**139. 名詞詞彙題**

**(A) 費用清單** (C) 手冊
(B) 照片 (D) 執照

- license (n.) 執照；牌照；許可證

**140. 代名詞詞彙題** 難

(A) 許多 (C) 你自己
**(B) 那時** (D) 明天

**141. 句子插入題**

(A) 收取的道路通行費會用於道路保養工程。
(B) 它也減緩了其他鄰近地區的塞車狀況。
**(C) 這可以到我們位於上述地址的辦公室來辦理。**
(D) 您車上的一個裝置會每次傳送一個電子信號。

- upkeep (n.) 維修（費）；保養（費）
  congestion (n.) 壅塞 transmit (v.) 傳送（信號）

**142. 形容詞詞彙題** 

(A) 總計的 (C) 貴重的
(B) 完全相同的 **(D) 更多的**

- identical (adj.) 完全相同的

**143–146 資訊**

**資料的驗證**

作為開源線上百科全書，科爾宏科學百科全書的撰稿者可能不是專家，因此 143 **嚴肅**看待資料的驗證。撰稿者必須明確指出他們加進百科全書文章裡的 144 **任何**內容來源。要達到這個目標，請在正文的相關部分加上注腳的連結，並在所連結的注腳裡提供所有必要的資料。（注腳的格式請見這一頁。）來源必須可靠並經專業出版。145 **理想的例子是學術期刊文章和教科書。**未附上引用這種來源的注腳內容會被 146 **刪除**。移除的理由應在該篇文章的討論頁中說明，以便其他人能檢閱。最後，在可信來源內容各異的情況下，撰稿者應提供各方立場的中立說明。

- verification (n.) 驗證
  open-source (adj.) 開放原始碼的
  encyclopedia (n.) 百科全書
  contributor (n.) 撰稿者；投稿者
  specify (v.) 明確指出 append (v.) 附加
  cite (v.) 引用 trustworthy (adj.) 值得信賴的
  neutral (adj.) 中立的 account (n.) 說明

**143. 副詞詞彙題——修飾動詞**

(A) 嚴肅的 (C) 嚴肅
**(B) 嚴肅地** (D) 更嚴肅的

**144. 形容詞詞彙題**

**(A) 任何** (C) 那一些
(B)（兩者中）任一個 (D) 另一個

**145. 句子插入題** 

(A) 後者的這種主張需要額外的驗證。
**(B) 理想的例子是學術期刊文章和教科書。**
(C) 否則，引用的句子可能違反著作權。
(D) 這包括作品的標題、作者、出版社和日期。

- **quotation (n.)** 引用；引文

**146. 動詞詞彙題**

(A) 強調 (C) 濃縮
(B) 重組 **(D) 刪除**

- **condense (v.)** 濃縮；壓縮

## PART 7 P. 71–91

**147–148 通知**

> **行道樹修剪通知**
>
> 您所在街道的行道樹將在 6 月 28 至 29 日，上午 8 點到下午 5 點間進行修剪。街道上空 13 英尺內，或人行道上 8 英尺內的樹枝將予以修剪或移除。
>
> [147] **道斯頓公園處定期在市立公園及鄰近街道進行這項工作，以改善樹木的結構穩定性並保護它們**不因折斷而受損。[148] **一位認證的樹木照護專業人員將監督我們的工作人員，確保修剪工作確實無誤。**
>
> 在這幾天裡，請保持街道淨空，將車輛停放在私人車道或其他街道上。此外，我們請您諒解修剪機器所發出的巨大噪音。

- **perform (v.)** 執行 **adjacent (adj.)** 鄰接的
  **certified (adj.)** 認證的；獲得資格的
  **automobile (n.)** 汽車
  **driveway (n.)**（住宅通往大路的）私人車道

**147. 相關細節**

為什麼要修剪樹木？

(A) 保護居民的汽車 (C) 改善它們的外觀
(B) 預防電線受損 **(D) 維護它們的健康**

> **換句話說**
> **improve the trees' structural stability and protect them from damage**（改善樹木的結構穩定性並保護它們免於受損）→ **(D) maintain their well-being**（維護它們的健康）

**148. 相關細節**

根據這則通知，市政府如何確保做好修剪工作？

**(A) 請專家監督**
(B) 納入市民的回饋意見
(C) 派遣數組工作人員
(D) 使用特殊機器

- **incorporate (v.)** 納入；吸收

> **換句話說**
> **make certain that the work is done properly**（確保修剪工作確實無誤）
> → **ensure the work is done well**（確保做好修剪工作）
> **A certified tree care professional supervises our crew**（一位認證的樹木照護專業人員將監督我們的工作人員）
> → **(A) having an expert monitor it**（請專家監督）

**149–150 收據**

> **巴瑞書店 四號店**
> 61087 伊利諾州中央市
> 費爾街 47 號
> 555-0161
>
> [149] **店號：4** 收銀機：3 收銀員：凱特．G.
> [149] **卡片：巴瑞忠誠會員** 到期日：5 月 11 日
>
> 書籍：《孟買遺產》 26.00 美元
> 會員卡 9 折（−2.60） →23.40 美元
> 雜誌：《電影月刊》 7.00 美元
> 會員卡 9 折（−0.70） →6.30 美元
> 小計 29.70 美元

顧客特別訂單 #1127　　* 到店取貨
* 通知方式：簡訊

[150] **書籍：《大膽的建築風格》**　34.00 美元

[150] **促銷 2848 — 5 折**（－17.00）17.00 美元

會員卡 9 折（－1.70）　15.30 美元

特別訂單小計　15.30 美元

**總計　45.00 美元**

現金　50.00 美元

找零　5.00 美元

[149] **歡迎光臨店內咖啡館**——書店一般營業時間內開放

購買日期／時間：3 月 7 日下午 4:09

- register (=cash register) (n.) 收銀機
  architecture (n.) 建築學；建築風格
  purchase (n.) 購買

**149. 確認事實與否**

關於巴瑞書店，收據上未顯示什麼？

**(A) 只在限定期間內接受退貨。**
(B) 有忠誠會員方案。
(C) 不只一家店。
(D) 也經營咖啡館。

換句話說

Barry's Loyalty Club Member（巴瑞忠誠會員）
→ (B) a customer loyalty program（忠誠會員方案）
Store number: 4（店號：4）
→ (C) It has more than one store.（不只一家店。）
our in-store café（我們店內的咖啡館）
→ (D) It . . . operates a café.（……經營咖啡館。）

**150. 確認事實與否**

根據收據，關於《大膽的建築風格》，下列何者為真？

(A) 只能在線上購買。
**(B) 為促銷活動的一部分。**
(C) 為打電話訂購的。
(D) 為店員推薦。

- recommendation (n.) 推薦

換句話說

Promotion 2848 — 50% off（促銷 2848 — 5 折）
→ (B) a sales promotion（促銷活動）

**151–152 文字訊息串**

**裘蒂．羅德里格茲〔下午 1:43〕**
葛雷迪，你現在人在工地嗎？

**葛雷迪．韋伯〔下午 1:44〕**
對，我在北側和電工組講話。怎麼了？

**裘蒂．羅德里格茲〔下午 1:44〕**
我想問你，可以讓 RBX80 飛上去吧。

**葛雷迪．韋伯〔下午 1:45〕**
RBX80？抱歉，但 [151] **我不知道那是什麼。**

**裘蒂．羅德里格茲〔下午 1:46〕**
噢，[151] **那是新科技**，是架配有相機的無人機。我們要讓它繞著大樓外面飛，確定到目前為止蓋好的牆面沒有問題。

**葛雷迪．韋伯〔下午 1:47〕**
啊，了解。應該沒問題。不過，[152] **請事先通知那些在你要查看的樓層上工作的團隊——尤其是在高樓層的人**。嚇到他們可能會有危險。

**裘蒂．羅德里格茲〔下午 1:48〕**
我現在發群組簡訊給各小組長。

- construction site (n.) 工地

**151. 掌握意圖**

下午 1:46，羅德里格茲女士寫道：「那是新科技」，她意指什麼？

(A) 她無法保證 RBX80 會正常運作。
**(B) 韋伯先生不熟悉 RBX80 是可理解的。**
(C) 以前發生過的某個問題，現今可以避免。
(D) 她的團隊需要時間準備工作流程。

**152. 推論或暗示**

關於正在建造的大樓，可由文中得知什麼？

(A) 它的形狀是圓的。
(B) 它有磚牆。
(C) 它位於機場裡。
**(D) 它將會變得很高。**

## 153–154 廣告

### 佛倫斯公司

宣布：藍天系列賀卡

[153] **當路弗斯・佛倫斯在 70 多年前創辦佛倫斯公司，出版一本生活風格雜誌時**，他並沒有想像到它未來的樣子。路弗斯只是開始利用他的印刷機印製賀卡以賺取額外收入。然而，[153] **這些由雜誌社美編所設計的賀卡立刻大賣，路弗斯不久就決定專賣卡片**。從那之後，佛倫斯公司成了全國最值得信賴的美麗又貼心賀卡的來源之一。

現在，佛倫斯公司很榮幸在我們的目錄中增加一個新系列卡片：藍天系列。[154] **藍天卡片用來在日常生活中寄送誠摯的愛、支持與友誼的訊息。簡單而迷人的風格是為了將焦點放在寄件者的文字上而設計。不用等待生日或節日，現在就讓人們知道你關心他們**。今天就去各大文具行瀏覽藍天系列吧。

- printing press (n.) 印刷機
  exclusively (adv.) 專門地
  heartfelt (adj.) 衷心的；誠摯的
  stationery (n.) 文具

**153. 確認事實與否** 難

關於佛倫斯公司，文中提到什麼？

(A) 公司仍是佛倫斯家族所有。
(B) 它創立時有 70 名員工。
(C) 它透過印刷廣告而成功。
**(D) 它以前生產不同的產品。**

---

**154. 相關細節**

藍天系列想要讓顧客能夠做什麼事？

(A) 客製化賀卡的設計
**(B) 在特殊節日之外表達善意**
(C) 以電子方式寄送正向訊息
(D) 以購買支持當地藝術家

- customize (v.) 客製化；訂做
  occasion (n.) 特殊場合；重大活動
  electronically (adv.) 以電子方式

**換句話說**

let people know you care about them
（讓人們知道你關心他們）
→ (B) Express goodwill（表達善意）
Instead of waiting for a birthday or holiday
（不用等待生日或節日）
→ (B) outside of special occasions
（在特殊節日以外）

## 155–157 電子郵件

**寄件人**：賽門・柏吉斯
**收件人**：薇歐拉・麥唐諾
**主旨**：關於：詢問
**日期**：7 月 30 日

親愛的麥唐諾女士：

感謝您來信詢問羅倫特智慧玻璃。從您的來信內容來看，我想我們的 RC-2 玻璃會非常適合您的工程案。[155] **在設定成透明模式時，可以消除所有您形容的大樓陰暗、狹小感，而設定成不透光的「霧面」模式時，它能為您的會議室、影印室等**提供您目前享有的隱私感。

我也可以解決您擔心的費用問題。[156] **雖然智慧玻璃在轉換設定時的確需要電力，但並不需要電力來維持任一種設定模式**。我們許多感到滿意的客戶中，沒有一位發現他們的電費帳單受到明顯的影響。

[157] **我很樂意去現場提供更多關於 RC-2 玻璃的資訊，以及在您的工程中發揮最佳效用的建議**。如果您有興趣，請回覆這封電子郵件，或撥打 555-0196 給我。

羅倫特公司銷售人員
賽門・柏吉斯　謹啟

- fit (n.) 適合　transparent (adj.) 透明的
  eliminate (v.) 消除　cramped (adj.) 狹小的
  opaque (adj.) 不透明的；不透光的
  frosted (adj.)（玻璃等）霧面的
  address (v.) 處理；設法解決　concern (v.) 擔心
  utility bill (n.) 水電帳單

**155. 推論或暗示**

麥唐諾女士最可能計劃做什麼？

(A) 蓋一棟大樓
(B) 改善車輛設計
**(C) 整修辦公室**
(D) 設計一個戶外展覽

---

**156. 相關細節** 難

柏吉斯先生寫了什麼消除麥唐諾女士對智慧玻璃的疑慮？

**(A) 它不會用到太多能源。**
(B) 安裝費不貴。
(C) 保持清潔不難。
(D) 不會很容易破裂。

### 157. 相關細節 難

柏吉斯先生提議給麥唐諾女士什麼？

(A) 一份推薦函　　(C) 一場示範
**(B) 一次諮詢**　　(D) 一項折扣

換句話說
visit your site to provide more information . . . and suggestions on its best use in your project（去現場提供更多……的資訊，以及在您的工程中發揮最佳效用的建議）
→ (B) consultation（諮詢）

## 158–160 公告

松頓漢堡湖濱分店

**通知**

[158] **我們的員工工作坊預計在下星期二上午 9 點到 12 點舉行。**所有員工無論年資深淺都必須參加，因此，餐廳在那段時間將休息。如果你有其他事要辦，請與直屬經理聯絡，好做適當安排。

工作坊將由凱倫．道寧主持。[159] **她要談維持我們餐廳的衛生標準。道寧女士已在全國各地分店主持過這個工作坊，而且知道最新的法規與研究。**我確信你們會發現是資訊豐富的一天。

你們都已自動預先登記這個活動。[160] **這一天不一定要穿制服。**然而，我們期望你們穿著公司認可的商務休閒套裝。請見員工手冊的相關章節。

- be due to 預期
  mandatory (adj.) 義務的；強制的
  regardless of 不管；不顧
  seniority level (n.) 年資
  prior (adj.) 在先的；在前的
  commitment (n.) 必須做（或處理）的事情
  line manager (n.) 直屬經理
  appropriate (adj.) 適當的
  arrangement (n.) 安排　hygiene (n.) 衛生
  up to date (adj.) 最新的
  regulation (n.) 規定；規章
  informative (adj.) 資訊豐富的
  employee handbook (n.) 員工手冊

### 158. 主旨或目的

通知裡宣布什麼事？

**(A) 一場訓練活動**　(C) 一次工廠檢查
(B) 一個職缺　　(D) 一項新的服裝儀容規定

- inspection (n.) 檢查

換句話說
Our staff workshop（我們的員工工作坊）
→ (A) A training event（一場訓練活動）

### 159. 確認事實與否

文中提到關於道寧女士的什麼事？

(A) 她最近剛晉升為管理階級。
(B) 她將觀察餐廳的營運。
(C) 她提出一些公司的規章。
**(D) 她是食品衛生專家。**

### 160. 句子插入題

「然而，我們期望你們穿著公司認可的商務休閒套裝。」最適合放在 [1]、[2]、[3]、[4] 的哪個位置？

(A) [1]　　(C) [3]
(B) [2]　　**(D) [4]**

## 161–163 合約

**花豹汽車**

在任職期間，我可能會接觸到花豹汽車的機密資料。[162] **這包括但不限於汽車與生產設備的詳細規格、商業行為、公司計畫、市場調查資料、銷售與收益資料，以及安全程序的細節。**我了解這個範圍也包括我自己任職於花豹汽車期間所開發的情報資料和材料。

[161] **在任職花豹汽車期間或離職後，我不會將這些資料透露給第三方，包括競爭對手、記者和大眾。**

[163] **在我離職時，我會立刻將所有實體安全憑證以及公司發的裝置歸還公司，並將所有密碼提供給公司系統。**

我已拿到本文件的副本供自我保存。

簽名：傑瑞米．富頓
職稱：製造經理
日期：11 月 19 日

- employment (n.) 受僱；工作
  be exposed to 接觸……
  confidential (adj.) 機密的
  specification (n.) 規格
  manufacturing (adj.) 製造的；生產的
  practice (n.) 實行　revenue (n.) 收益
  disclose (v.) 透露；揭露
  competitor (n.) 競爭對手　credential (n.) 憑證
  device (n.) 裝置

### 161. 推論或暗示 難

關於這份合約，可由文中得知什麼？

(A) 它也必須有公司代表的簽名。
**(B) 它的效期延伸到富頓先生離職之後。**
(C) 它無法從公司的營業場所移除。
(D) 已在富頓先生的要求下修改。

- representative (n.) 代表人
  extend (v.) 延長；延伸 premise (n.) 營業場所

**換句話說**
following my employment（在我離職後）
→ (B) past Mr. Fulton's period of employment（延伸到富頓先生離職後）

### 162. 確認事實與否

哪一項不是文中提及的機密資料？

(A) 消費者研究的結果
(B) 公司盈收
**(C) 供應商的名字**
(D) 車輛規格

**換句話說**
data from market research（市場調查資料）
→ (A) Results of consumer studies（消費者研究的結果）
revenue（收益）→ (B) earnings（盈收）
automobiles（汽車）→ (D) Vehicle（車輛）

### 163. 相關細節

協議明確說明什麼？

**(A) 富頓先生離職時應該做什麼事**
(B) 違反的話，富頓先生可能面對的處罰
(C) 富頓先生可以分享某些資料的對象
(D) 富頓先生可以如何使用公司發的裝置

- violate (v.) 違反

**換句話說**
At the end of my employment period（在我離職時）→ (A) upon leaving his job（在離職時）

### 164–167 電子郵件

**收件人：**露易絲・安德森
**寄件人：**傑西・里德
**主旨：**小組討論邀請函
**日期：**6 月 18 日

親愛的安德森女士：

哈囉，我是傑西・里德，是「IT 健康連結」的籌辦人之一。[167] **IT 健康連結已成為英國最令人興奮的醫療資訊科技研討會之一**，每年聚集了上百名醫療照護提供者、企業家、投資者、政府代表與其他人士。在三天的活動中，與會者建立人脈、分享實用的祕訣並討論遠大的理想。我們目前正在尋找今年研討會的演講人和討論小組參與者，研討會將於 10 月 5 日至 7 日在倫敦的費奧爾會議廳舉行。

我是為了一項特別活動而聯絡您，那是個長達一小時、名稱為「下一代的醫療科技」的討論小組。我們已經邀請到克萊夫・米納摩爾、科瓦米・歐本、羅根・諾威克和安德魯・厄爾，四位業界最富有創新精神的青年才俊參加。然而，如同您可能已發現的，[164] **這個團體裡少了什麼——女性的觀點**。因此，[165] **我在我的交友圈中四處打聽推薦人選，而哈洛德・科比說，您去年在「利物浦健康」活動上的演講讓他留下深刻的印象**。在網路上看完那場演講的影片後，我也同樣感到讚賞。如果您願意加入我們的小組，和我們的與會者分享您創新的想法，將會是我們的榮幸。

[166] **如果您有興趣，目前只要以肯定的答案回覆這封電子郵件，並附上要放在我們網站上的一張專業大頭照和您的正式職稱**。我會在月底前，寄一份含有活動所有詳情的演講同意書給您。或者，如果您有任何問題或疑慮，您可以回覆這封電子郵件，或在上班時間撥打 020-7043-5214 給我。

希望很快能得到您的回音。

傑西・里德 謹啟

- entrepreneur (n.) 企業家
  annually (adv.) 每年；每年一次
  engage (v.) 聘用
  innovative (adj.) 富有創新精神的；新穎的
  mind (n.) 有才智的人 participate (v.) 參加
  perspective (n.) 觀點 attendee (n.) 出席者
  affirmative (adj.) 肯定的
  professional headshot (n.) 專業大頭照
  alternatively (adv.)（用以建議其他可能）或者

### 164. 確認事實與否

文中提到關於討論小組的什麼事？

(A) 將於 10 月 7 日舉行。
(B) 將由科比先生主持。
**(C) 目前排定的人選不包含女性。**
(D) 是之前研討會的一部分。

- moderate (v.) 當主持人

換句話說

missing from that group—a female perspective（這個團體裡少了什麼——女性的觀點）
→ (C) not currently scheduled to include any women（目前排定的人選不包含女性）

### 165. 相關細節

里德先生如何找到安德森女士？

(A) 參加演講　　(C) 上網搜尋
(B) 看報紙　　**(D) 別人介紹**

- referral (n.) 推薦；介紹

換句話說

recommendations（推薦）→ (D) referral（介紹）

### 166. 相關細節

如果安德森女士想要參加，她首先要提供什麼？

**(A) 一張她自己的照片**　　(C) 一份報價單
(B) 一份簽了名的合約　　(D) 一個建議的主題

換句話說

If you are interested（如果您有興趣）
→ If she wants to participate（如果她想參加）
a professional headshot（一張專業大頭照）
→ (A) A photograph of herself（一張她自己的照片）

### 167. 句子插入題

「在三天的活動中，參加者建立人脈、分享實用的祕訣並討論遠大的理想。」最適合放在標示 [1]、[2]、[3]、[4] 的何處？

**(A) [1]**　　(C) [3]
(B) [2]　　(D) [4]

### 168–171 線上報導

**奧克蘭商業新聞**

（2 月 19 日）——克莉絲汀．瑞德曼最近發現，即使她帶了很多現金，也無法在她最愛的咖啡店付她所點的冰拿鐵。「他們幾個星期前轉為電子支付了，」瑞德曼女士解釋道：「但那天，我忘了帶我的簽帳金融卡，真是尷尬。」

168/169 **這家咖啡店「喜利咖啡豆」是幾家店內已不再接受現金付款的紐西蘭零售商店之一。**支持這個趨勢的人表示，電子支付有一些優點，像交易更快速、交易紀錄無誤和比較不會觸摸到可能不乾淨的帳單與硬幣。喜利咖啡豆的發言人雪倫．瑞特說：「坦白說，這是很自然的選擇。」

然而，消費者並無法信服。雖然一直有持續改用卡片與應用程式而不是紙鈔的行動，但很多人仍偏好使用現金，或至少有能夠使用現金的選擇。「對我來說，這事關隱私。169 **我不會去無現金商店，因為我不喜歡信用卡公司知道我買的所有東西，**」奧克蘭市民查德．威廉斯說。

170 **類似的消費者抵制已使美國有些市政府禁止商家不收現金。零售分析家鄭相旭相信，這裡也可能發生這種事，但不是現在。**「目前只有幾家無現金的商店，因此不是太不方便。但如果很多商店開始轉變，我們可能也會看到強烈反彈。」

171 **你去過無現金商店嗎？留言告訴我們你的經驗！**（請注意，留言者需建立奧克蘭論壇報的帳號。）

- electronic payment (n.) 電子支付
  debit card (n.) 簽帳金融卡
  retailer (n.) 零售商；零售店
  transaction (n.) 交易；買賣
  potentially (adv.) 可能地；潛在地
  unsanitary (adj.) 不衛生的
  convinced (adj.) 確信的；信服的
  steady (adj.) 穩定的；持續的
  cashless (adj.) 無現金的；不透過現金的
  resistance (n.) 抵抗；抵制　prohibit (v.) 禁止
  inconvenience (n.) 不便　backlash (n.) 強烈反彈

### 168. 主旨或目的

這篇報導的主題是什麼？

**(A) 零售付款方式的趨勢**
(B) 一家咖啡連鎖店的擴張
(C) 一條市府法規的提案
(D) 顧客與店家間的爭執

- ordinance (n.) 法令；法規；條例
  dispute (n.) 爭執；爭論

**169. 推論或暗示**

關於威廉斯先生，可由文中得知什麼？

(A) 他在金融界工作。
**(B) 他不會光顧像喜利咖啡豆這樣的咖啡館。**
(C) 他在二月初和瑞德曼女士談過話。
(D) 他希望成為地方政治人物。

- patronize (v.) 經常光顧（商店、餐廳等）

---

**170. 確認事實與否** 難

這篇文章為什麼提到另一個國家？

(A) 為了解釋一種管理方法的來源
(B) 為了強調一家公司的結構
**(C) 為了帶出某種情況的可能結果**
(D) 為了表達對一個地區成就的自豪

- outcome (n.) 結果　achievement (n.) 成就

---

**171. 相關細節**

這篇文章鼓勵讀者做什麼？

(A) 註冊以收到一則新聞的最新發展
**(B) 討論任何相關經驗**
(C) 查看一系列類似的文章
(D) 報告任何事實錯誤

- relevant (adj.) 相關聯的；有關的
  factual (adj.) 事實的

**換句話說**
Tell us about it（告訴我們你的經驗）
→ (B) Discuss any relevant experiences（討論任何相關經驗）

---

**172–175 線上聊天室**

莫妮卡・迪翠克〔下午 2:11〕
好消息！[172] **拉蒙納企業的代表終於同意接受我的訪問！**

侯道〔下午 2:12〕
太棒了！[173] **我們的讀者**一定會很興奮能深入看到業界成長最快的軟體公司之一。妳什麼時候要去？

莫妮卡・迪翠克〔下午 2:14〕
下星期一下午兩點。我沒有多少時間準備，而且他們只給我一個小時的空檔，但我能問到什麼就寫什麼。

羅珊・托羅〔下午 2:16〕
賈克，[174] **你有空和莫妮卡一起去拍照嗎？**

莫妮卡・迪翠克〔下午 2:17〕
其實，[174] **只有我一個人獲准進去辦公室**。公司說，他們比較喜歡提供他們自己的照片。

賈克・費佛侯〔下午 2:18〕
真可惜。我很想看看他們辦公室。我聽說，員工可以打造自己的工作空間，所以你會看到從帶著跑步機的站立式辦公桌到躺椅，什麼都有。

莫妮卡・迪翠克〔下午 2:19〕
我一定會告訴你是不是真的！

羅珊・托羅〔下午 2:22〕
[173/175] **妳的文章趕得上這個月這一期嗎？** [175] **截稿日是 3 月 18 日，就在妳去拉蒙納企業的兩天後。**

莫妮卡・迪翠克〔下午 2:23〕
[175] **我想，那不是個好主意。**

侯道〔下午 2:24〕
我同意。要以品質為最優先考慮。

- insight (n.) 深刻的理解
  fastest-growing (adj.) 成長最快速的
  personalize (v.) 使個性化；使具個人特色
  treadmill (n.) 跑步機
  recliner chair (n.)（可調整椅背的）躺椅
  priority (n.) 優先考慮的事

**172. 推論或暗示** 難

文中提到關於迪翠克女士的什麼事？

(A) 她以前是拉蒙納企業的員工。
**(B) 她多次對拉蒙納企業提出要求。**
(C) 她定期查看拉蒙納企業的網站。
(D) 她敲定一筆和拉蒙納企業的交易。

---

**173. 推論或暗示**

這些記者最可能在哪裡工作？

(A) 科技公司　(C) 人力銀行
(B) 新聞台　**(D) 雜誌社**

---

**174. 相關細節**

費佛侯先生為什麼不能陪同迪翠克女士一起去？

(A) 他離太遠而無法及時抵達。
**(B) 他未獲准進去。**
(C) 他在忙其他工作。
(D) 他無法勝任一項任務。

- grant (v.) 准予　qualified (adj.) 勝任的

換句話說

go with（和……一起去）→ accompany（陪同）
be allowed in the offices（獲准進去辦公室）
→ (B) been granted access（獲准進去）

### 175. 掌握意圖

下午 2:23，迪翠克女士寫道：「我想，那不是個好主意」，她意指什麼？

(A) 她打算監督過程。
(B) 她比較喜歡親自會面。
**(C) 她想要有更多作業時間。**
(D) 她認為有項工作場所的政策考慮不周。

- in-person 親自

### 176–180 電子郵件與報導

**寄件人：**梅根．戴娜
**收件人：**楊麗玲
**主旨：**請求
**日期：**9 月 3 日
**附件：**七個檔案

親愛的楊教授：

哈囉！收信平安。我寫這封信是想接受您在我去年夏天畢業時所給的提議。尤其是，我已決定參加昆士蘭年輕設計師競賽，[176] **我希望您可以在我寄出參賽作品之前先看一下。**

我猜您對這項比賽很熟悉，但為了以防萬一，還是讓我為您概述一下。這是由昆士蘭時裝協會所籌辦的比賽，以支持有才華的年輕設計師。頭獎得主將在協會的年鑑中特別介紹，但我只希望能拿到前五名，[178] **因為前五名會受邀參加協會的年度時裝秀。**至於參賽作品，參加者必須交出三套作品，每一套包含三張服裝設計的素描，由參賽者自己選擇的創作概念所連貫。

因此，[177] **我在此寄給您我的素描以及我所選的創作概念的附帶說明。**[177] **我也附上一份列有評選標準的文件**給您參考。我知道您很忙，但如果您能在 9 月 10 日前抽空看看這些資料並告訴我您想到的任何意見，我將不勝感激。先謝謝您的幫忙。

梅根　敬上

- submission (n.) 交出；呈遞　organize (v.) 籌辦
  council (n.) 委員會　entry (n.) 參賽作品
  contestant (n.) 參賽者　applicant (n.) 申請人
  accompany (v.) 伴隨；和……一起
  criteria (n.)（評判、決定等的）標準
  for reference 以供參考

**昆士蘭年輕設計師競賽**
**得主出爐**

布里斯本　訊（12 月 12 日）—— [179] **昆士蘭時裝協會（QFC）昨天公布第四屆年度年輕時裝設計師競賽得主。**[179] **山培思服裝的助理採購員**，同時也是最近才從威爾伯特大學畢業的 [179] **賈桂琳．艾波特**，在將近 500 位參賽者中摘冠。

[179] **QFC 有超過三千位會員**，包括設計師、其他行業的從業人員和投資者，而昆士蘭年輕設計師競賽的評審委員會包含東澳洲時裝界的一些頂尖人物。

艾波特女士的參賽作品具體展現「新穎」、「反射」和「飛行」的概念，經典風格的原創詮釋讓評審耳目一新。[179] **評審委員會主席暨 QFC 董事會成員蓋瑞．歐德爾**說：「艾波特女士的服裝與配件非常迷人，你盯著它們看得越久，就變得更加複雜難解。我們認為，[180] **她在這一行前途光明。**」

[178] **艾波特女士以及前幾名得主潔達．雷恩、海登．諾伊、梅根．戴娜和凱文．奈勒**，將得到協會提供的一系列支援。

- assistant buyer (n.) 助理採購員
  apparel (n.) 服裝；衣著
  consist of 包含；由……組成
  embody (v.) 具體展現
  interpretation (n.) 闡釋；詮釋
  a range of 一系列

### 176. 主旨或目的

為什麼寄這封電子郵件？

(A) 要求說明某項規定
(B) 回應參加比賽的建議
**(C) 請求提供參賽資料的回饋意見**
(D) 提醒某個截止日期

- clarification (n.) 說明；澄清
  requirement (n.) 規定
  reminder (n.) 提示；提醒物

換句話說

my submission（我的參賽作品）
→ (C) some entry materials（參賽資料）

**177. 確認事實與否**

電子郵件未附什麼？

**(A) 文件範本的樣板**
(B) 一份評選標準的清單
(C) 設計概念的描述
(D) 服裝的素描

- template (n.) 範本　evaluation (n.) 評估；評價

**換句話說**

a document listing the judging criteria（一份列有評選標準的文件）
→ (B) A list of some evaluation standards（一份評選標準的清單）
the accompanying explanations of the creative concepts（我所選的創作概念的附帶說明）
→ (C) Descriptions of design concepts（設計概念的描述）
sketches（素描）→ (D) Drawings of fashion items（服裝的素描）

**178. 整合題** 難

文中提到關於戴娜女士的什麼事？

(A) 她在 QFC 完成實習。
(B) 一份年度出版品會宣傳她。
(C) 她寫了一封電子郵件給一位威爾伯特大學的教授。
**(D) 她將得到參加一場時裝活動的通行證。**

**換句話說**

come with（配有）→ (D) receive（得到）
an invitation to the council's yearly fashion show（協會年度時裝秀的邀請函）
→ (D) a pass to a fashion event（時裝活動的通行證）

**179. 確認事實與否** 

根據報導，關於 QFC，下列何者為真？

(A) 它有約 500 位會員。
(B) 它的董事會主席是歐德爾先生。
**(C) 它以前舉辦過三次競賽。**
(D) 它是山培思服裝的附屬機構。

**180. 同義詞考題**

報導中，第三段第九行的「bright」，意義最接近何者？

(A) 陽光普照的　**(C) 有前途的**
(B) 歡樂的　(D) 聰明的

**181–185 議程與電子郵件**

**松伍德市議會月會**
松伍德社區中心 105 室
2 月 10 日星期二下午 7 點

[181] **出席人數：12 位市議員中的 10 位**　**缺席者：**派翠克．周、塔瑪拉．華頓
朗讀一月議事錄並通過。

| **部門報告：** |
| --- |
| [181] **財政部：通過三月營運費用需求**<br>公園與休閒部：說明公園改善補助金 |
| **公開簡報：** |
| 藍道爾公園補助金使用建議<br>- 理查．迪金，前議員：蓋一座天幕野餐亭，放置數張野餐桌<br>- [183] **羅瑞娜．帕勒摩，松伍德居民：在公園內增設一條柏油路供慢跑者使用**<br>- 維爾．卡邁斯，松伍德居民：在足球場附近蓋一座有圍籬的籃球場<br>- [181] **海瑟．鮑林，「此刻自然」慈善團體主席：**栽植一座花園以改善公園外觀 |
| **審議：** |
| 市議員就數個提案的優點進行辯論。 |
| **下次會議（3 月 13 日）：** |
| [182] **市議會將就公園改善補助金進行表決。會議將在大禮堂舉行，因為出席人數預期會超乎尋常的多。** |

- attendance (n.) 出席人數　absent (adj.) 缺席的
  minutes (n.) 會議紀錄　approve (v.) 批准
  operating expense (n.) 營運費用
  grant (n.) 補助金　shelter (n.) 躲避處
  enhance (v.) 提升；改善　debate (v.) 辯論
  merit (n.) 優點　auditorium (n.) 禮堂

**收件人：**路易斯．努森 <lknutson@thornwood.gov>
**寄件人：**維多莉亞．皮卡德 <vpickard@thornwood.gov>
**日期：**3 月 15 日
**主旨：**藍道爾公園專案

嗨，路易斯：

既然我們已選出藍道爾公園的專案內容，我們必須開始執行計畫。這星期找個時間，[184] **我想和公園與休閒部的主任及副主任坐下來好好談談，可以請你安排嗎？** [183] **對於慢跑道要設在哪裡，我們必須有精確的地圖。**

一旦定下初步計畫，我們就可以開始宣傳這個專案並接受營造公司的投標。我相信，這個專案會是我們收到的補助款的最佳運用。不過，[185] **我擔心過程會比市民預期得更久**。如果我們想要它在夏天結束時完成的話，我們必須加快腳步。

請隨時讓我知道你的進度。

謝謝！

維多莉亞

- **accurate (adj.)** 精確的　**tentative (adj.)** 暫定的
  **bid (n.)** 投標　**lengthy (adj.)** 漫長的

**181. 確認事實與否** 難

關於二月的會議，文中未提及什麼？

(A) 通過每月預算。
(B) 一位慈善團體的代表做了簡報。
(C) 議會的大多數成員都出席了。
**(D) 對於下次會議的地點有一番辯論。**

- **majority (n.)** 大多數，大部分
  **debate (n.)** 辯論　**venue (n.)** 場地

**換句話說**
March's operating expenses（三月的營運費用）→ (A) A monthly budget（每月預算）
president of the . . . charity（慈善團體的主席）→ (B) A charity representative（一位慈善團體的代表）
Attendance: 10 out of 12 council members（出席人數：12 位市議員中的 10 位）
→ (C) The majority of council members were present.（議會的大多數成員都出席了。）

**182. 推論或暗示** 

關於公園改善補助金的投票，可由會議的議程看出什麼？

(A) 有些議會成員沒有參加。
(B) 應該在二月舉行。
(C) 會播送給當地觀眾看。
**(D) 預期會吸引大眾極大的關注。**

**換句話說**
unusually large attendance is predicted（出席人數預料會超乎尋常的多）
→ (D) It was expected to attract a lot of public interest.（預期會吸引大眾極大的關注。）

**183. 整合題**

誰的提案成功了？

(A) 迪金先生　(C) 卡邁斯先生
**(B) 帕勒摩女士**　(D) 鮑林女士

**184. 相關細節**

文中要求努森先生這星期做什麼？

(A) 訓練一些志工　(C) 聯絡營造公司
**(B) 安排會議**　(D) 刊登廣告

**換句話說**
arrange that（安排）→ (B) Set up a meeting（安排會議）

**185. 確認事實與否**

皮卡德女士提及關於公園改善專案的什麼事？

(A) 補助單位可能不會批准計畫。
(B) 不會使用所有的現有資金。
**(C) 她擔心計畫持續的時間。**
(D) 專案可能中斷一個季節性慶典。

- **duration (n.)** 持續期間　**disrupt (v.)** 中斷

**換句話說**
worried that the process will be much lengthier（擔心過程會更久）
→ (C) concerned about its duration（擔心計畫持續的時間）

**186–190 網頁與電子郵件**

www.bernlakeoutfitters.com

| 首頁 | 人員 | 船隻 | 證言 | 聯絡 |
| --- | --- | --- | --- | --- |

**伯恩湖上運動用品店**

歡迎光臨伯恩湖上運動用品網路商店！保羅．加士伯十年前開了伯恩湖上運動用品店，當時他開始把 [188] **他的私人獨木舟「小奔號」**租給朋友度週末。現在，[186/188] **有了今年稍早買下的 50 公尺長遊艇「湖上妖精號」，我們成了這地區擁有最多船隻的公司**。我們可以滿足任何顧客的需求，不論是想駕駛 [188] **我們其中一艘「金色火焰快艇」參加高速水上運動**，或是和一群朋友 [188] **划著「平靜漣漪號」垂釣一個下午的魚**。

*** 如果您要住在這區，讓我們幫您解決住宿問題。[190] **我們可以為您取得與我們長期合作的旅館「拉古拿旅舍」的折扣房價**。

- outfitter (n.)（從事某種活動的）專用設備（或服裝）商店
  watercraft (n.)（總稱）船隻
  aquatic (adj.) 水上的　lodging (n.) 寄宿的地方

寄件人：<chloeblosser@sod.ch>
收件人：<paolo@bernlakeoutfitters.com>
主旨：詢問
日期：1 月 15 日

哈囉：

我代表瑞士牙醫組織寫這封信。[187] **我們的年會將於六月在伯恩湖附近舉行，我負責籌備閉幕晚餐會。**[188] **這是一個非正式的活動，讓我們可以一起放鬆玩玩**，所以，我覺得在湖上舉行應該不錯。[188] **我們大約有 40 個人**。你有夠大的船可以容納那麼多人嗎？

我也歡迎你提供任何關於住宿的情報。

謝謝你。

瑞士牙醫組織
克蘿伊．布勞瑟

- accommodation (n.) 住宿處

寄件人：<paolo@bernlakeoutfitters.com>
收件人：<chloeblosser@sod.ch>
主旨：關於：詢問
日期：1 月 15 日

親愛的布勞瑟女士：

感謝您與我們聯絡！

我們公司當然有能夠符合您需求的船隻。您可以告訴我，您在六月需要用船的確切日期嗎？

[189] **至於您所詢問的住宿問題，**[190] **我知道「拉古拿旅舍」在那段時間有一些空房間**，而「全新日落飯店」如果還沒訂滿的話，則可能是較低價的選擇。請告訴我您的決定，因為根據您選哪一家，我們也許能幫您以折扣價訂到房間。

保羅．加士伯　謹啟

- opening (n.) 空缺　pricey (adj.) 高價的

**186. 確認事實與否**

文中提到伯恩湖上運動用品店的什麼特色？

(A) 悠久歷史
(B) 船隻的租金
(C) 地點的便利性
**(D) 擁有的船隻數量**

**換句話說**
we have the most watercraft
（我們擁有最多船隻）
→ (D) The number of boats it owns（擁有的船隻數量）

---

**187. 相關細節**

布勞瑟女士為何將造訪伯恩湖地區？

**(A) 參加一場專業聚會**
(B) 出國度假
(C) 看一系列的運動比賽
(D) 進行科學研究

- gathering (n.) 集會

**換句話說**
conference（會議）→ (A) gathering（聚會）

---

**188. 整合題**

最有可能推薦哪一艘船給布勞瑟女士？

(A) 小奔號　　(C) 金色火焰號
**(B) 湖上妖精號**　　(D) 平靜漣漪號

---

**189. 同義詞考題** 難

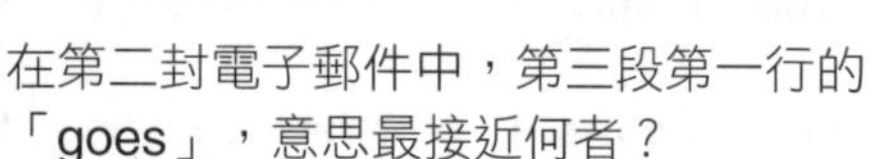
在第二封電子郵件中，第三段第一行的「goes」，意思最接近何者？

(A) 可用的　　(C) 作用
**(B) 關於**　　(D) 離開

---

**190. 整合題** 

關於伯恩湖上運動用品店的合作飯店，加士伯先生暗示什麼？

(A) 相對較便宜。
(B) 最近重新開幕。
**(C) 目前六月還有空房。**
(D) 附設餐廳。

**換句話說**
the Laguna Lodge has some openings for that time frame
（拉古拿旅舍在那段時間有一些空房間）
→ (C) It currently has vacancies for June.（目前六月還有空房。）

## 191–195 報導、電子郵件與訂單

### 讓世界變得更好

（8 月 4 日）——雖然，對世界各地的消費者來說，企業的社會責任越來越重要，但有些公司發現回饋可能很棘手。

去年，當一份「慈善監督」公司的報告因為它的主要慈善夥伴沒有發揮影響力，而把它評為「D」等時，平佛萊許公司感到很尷尬。同樣地，[193] **杜恩蓋洛威最近終止了與一個藝術非營利組織的合作關係，因為他們對會計流程的意見不同。**

正因如此，彼得．岡迪才成立了 [191] **「給樂」，這是一家努力讓企業的回饋付出盡可能簡單、有效的營利公司。**

「我們一手包辦所有事，」岡迪先生說：[191] **「我們幫助企業選擇一個贊助標的，以一個信譽良好的慈善機構或非營利組織連結兩者，處理捐款流程，並提供宣傳工具。」**

在它營運的這兩年裡，給樂服務過的公司超過一百家，預估它的客戶已捐出大約三百萬元給各式各樣的目標。

在這些成功案例中，岡迪先生說，他最以利卡德紙業為榮：「我們定了一個計畫，他們差不多每賣出一個文具產品，就種一棵樹。不但到目前為止已種了五萬六千棵樹，而且 [192] **這個計畫所帶來的宣傳已使利卡德的銷售額增加了一成**。那正是我們想要帶給我們所有的客戶和他們的合作組織的互惠關係。」

- corporate (adj.) 公司的
  nonprofit (adj.) 非營利的
  disagreement (n.) 意見不合
  for-profit (adj.) 營利的
  cause (n.) （某些人強烈支持的）原則、目標
  reputable (adj.) 聲譽良好的
  logistics (n.) 運籌；物流
  publicity (n.) 宣傳　estimate (v.) 估計
  stationery (n.) 文具
  mutually beneficial (adj.) 互惠的

**寄件人：**山繆．阿卡基 <samuel.akagi@giveler.com>
**收件人：**珍妮兒．霍恩 <janelle.hawn@weatherfordpro.com>
**主旨：**可能的合作夥伴
**日期：**8 月 24 日
**附件：**非營利評論

親愛的珍妮兒：

很高興昨天與您見面。正如我當時答應的，我現在寄一份我們連結企業與合作的慈善機構和非營利組織流程的概述給您。我相信這能消除 [193] **您提到經歷過與杜恩蓋洛威相同挫折的憂慮**。

此外，這是一些我們認為可能適合威勒福德專業公司的組織：

- 克許納基金會：經營免費兒童鄉間夏令營
- 現在就要綠！：遊說政府擴大國家公園
- [195] **衛希洛協會：保護許多棲地的瀕危動物**
- 清潔任務：清除海灘與海洋的垃圾

每一個組織的名稱可連結到他們的網站，因此您可以多了解他們一點。如果您想到什麼問題，或您準備好要做選擇了，就寄電子郵件或撥打 555-0186 給我。

客戶部經理
山繆．阿卡基　謹啟

- overview (n.) 概述　relieve (v.) 緩和
  setback (n.) 挫折　rural (adj.) 鄉下的
  endangered (adj.) 瀕臨絕種的
  habitat (n.) （動物的）棲息地；（植物的）產地

http://www.weatherfordpro.com

| 首頁 | 產品 | 促銷 | 關於我們 |
|---|---|---|---|

### 威勒福專業

| 送貨資料： | 帳單地址： |
|---|---|
| 維多利亞．科爾 | 同送貨地址 ☑ |
| 81008 科羅拉多州 | 付款方式：付無誤 |
| 帕布羅市葛里芬街 | 帳號： |
| 340 號 | vicky100@efr-mail.com |

| 產品編號 | 內容 | 數量 | 價格 |
|---|---|---|---|
| H2420 | [194] 追蹤大師背包—海軍藍 | 1 | 59.99 美元 |
| R4371 | [194] 歐尼文登山鞋—10 號 | 1 | 89.99 美元 |
| | | 小計 | 149.98 美元 |
| | | 稅金 | 10.50 美元 |
| | | 總計 | 160.48 美元 |

**您知道嗎？[195] 威勒福專業將每一筆交易稅前金額的 5% 捐給衛希洛協會！**現在就點擊「完成訂單」幫我們捐出 7.50 美元。

**完成訂單**

- pre-tax (adj.) 稅前的

**191. 主旨或目的**

這篇報導的目的為何？

(A) 調查某些企業的錯誤
(B) 簡要介紹一位本地企業家
**(C) 宣傳某家公司的服務**
(D) 鼓勵消費者做出特定的選擇

- profile (v.) 簡要介紹　entrepreneur (n.) 企業家

---

**192. 同義詞考題**

在報導中，第六段第七行的「bump」，意思最接近何者？

(A) 困難　(C) 機會
(B) 碰撞　**(D) 增加**

---

**193. 整合題** 

文中提到關於霍恩女士的什麼事？

(A) 她認為宣傳方式要簡單。
**(B) 她希望不要涉入財務糾紛。**
(C) 她擔心有可能合作的組織的效益。
(D) 她擔心會不小心觸法。

- publicity (n.) 宣傳　be engaged in 從事；涉入
  effectiveness (n.) 效果
  potential (adj.) 可能的；潛在的

換句話說
experiencing（經歷）
→ (B) becoming engaged in（涉入）
a disagreement over accounting processes（對會計流程意見不合）
→ (B) a financial dispute（財務糾紛）

---

**194. 相關細節**

科爾女士向威勒福專業訂購了什麼？

(A) 單車裝備　(C) 釣魚用具
(B) 露營用品　**(D) 健行配件**

---

**195. 整合題**

威勒福專業選擇支持什麼理想標的？

**(A) 拯救珍稀動物免於滅絕**
(B) 讓兒童能在戶外活動
(C) 影響政府針對自然區域的政策
(D) 清除沿海棲地的廢棄物

- extinction (n.) 滅絕

換句話說
Protects endangered animals（保護瀕危動物）
→ (A) Saving rare animals from extinction（拯救珍稀動物免於滅絕）

---

**196–200 網頁與電子郵件**

http://www.kurgess.com/packages

| 首頁 | 關於 | 方案 | 聯絡 |
|---|---|---|---|

[196]**「科格斯物業管理」提供各種對您的房屋、出租公寓或公寓大樓投入不同管理程度的方案**。不論您選哪一種，您都能確信，所有的服務都是由盡職的專家執行，保證照顧好您的房產。

- 黃銅：服務包含帶看房屋、辦理租賃申請、查核信用與背景、簽訂租約以及收取押金。
  費用：一個月租金（乙次）。
- 白銀：所有黃銅方案的服務，加上每月收租。
  費用：月租金的 4%（每月）。
- [198] **黃金**：所有白銀方案的服務，加上維護與修理服務。
  [198] **費用：月租金的 6%**（每月）。
- 黃金＋：所有黃金方案的服務，但僱用科格斯管理三間以上物業者享有折扣。
  費用：每個物業收取月租金的 5%（每月）。

- property management (n.) 物業管理
  a range of 各種；一系列
  involvement (n.) 參與　perform (v.) 執行
  dedicated (adj.) 盡職的
  tenancy agreement (n.) 租約　deposit (n.) 押金
  maintenance (n.) 維護

**寄件人：**雷克斯．康貝爾 <rex@kurgess.com>
**收件人：**朵拉．麥克洛林 <d.mclaughlin@rui-mail.com>
**主旨：**好消息
**日期：**3 月 21 日
**附件：**申請書、背景查核、信用查核、合約

親愛的麥克洛林女士：

我很高興通知您，我們已為您位於漢尼斯柏格市派瑞路 682 號的房產找到合適的房客。我們已對他的信用與背景進行完整查核，結果如附件供您詳閱。您可以看到，[197] **艾賽亞．普利查德有一份穩定的中學教職工作，還有他過往的財務責任狀況**。此外，當然，他也願意同意您明確說明的所有物業使用條款。

普利查德先生想要他的一年租約從 4 月 14 日星期六開始。如果您滿意我們提供的資料，[200] **請印出合約並簽名，然後盡快以掛號信寄到我的辦公室**。感謝您。

敬祝　安康

科格斯物業管理 [200] **漢尼斯柏格分公司**
會計經理　雷克斯・康貝爾　謹啟

- background check (n.) 背景查核
  tenant (n.) 房客　carry out 進行；執行
  thoroughness (n.) 完全；徹底
  perusal (n.) 細讀　history (n.) 經歷
  financial responsibility (n.) 財務責任；支付能力
  terms (n.) 條款　specify (v.) 明確說明
  certified mail (n.) 掛號信

**寄件人**：朵拉・麥克洛林
<d.mclaughlin@rui-mail.com>
**收件人**：雷克斯・康貝爾
<rex@kurgess.com>
**主旨**：關於：好消息
**日期**：3 月 22 日

親愛的康貝爾先生：

我想普利查德先生會是很好的房客。[200] **我會按照你的要求去做。**[199] **一旦簽了合約，在普利查德先生能搬進去之前，還需要做什麼呢？**

還有，非常謝謝你辛苦帶看房子並篩選房客。你知道，當我搬到希勒南時，我對要把我的老房子交到物業管理公司手上，感到很緊張不安。我差點決定要賣掉房子。不過，到目前為止，你們的服務讓我覺得很高興沒有這麼做。[198] **我非常樂意為了得到的心靈上的平靜，付給貴公司承諾的普利查德先生月租金的 6%**。

謝謝。

朵拉・麥克洛林

- screen (v.) 篩選；審查　afford (v.) 提供

**196. 推論或暗示**

關於「科格斯物業管理」，可由文中得知什麼？

(A) 它將一些維修服務外包。
**(B) 它只處理住宅房產。**
(C) 它需要先付訂金。
(D) 合作超過三年的客戶享有折扣。

- outsource (v.) 外包

**換句話說**
your house, apartment, or condominium（您的房屋、出租公寓或公寓大樓）
→ (B) residential properties（住宅房產）

**197. 確認事實與否**

文中提到普利查德先生的什麼正面特質？

(A) 曾擁有自用住宅
(B) 彈性的遷入日期
**(C) 一份穩定的工作**
(D) 沒有寵物

**換句話說**
a steady job as a high school teacher（一份穩定的中學教職工作）
→ (C) A stable career（一份穩定的工作）

**198. 整合題**

麥克洛林女士最可能選擇哪一種服務方案？

(A) 黃銅
(B) 白銀
**(C) 黃金**
(D) 黃金＋

**199. 相關細節**

麥克格林女士詢問什麼事？

**(A) 流程中的一些步驟**
(B) 合約中的一些變更
(C) 推薦的理由
(D) 某項工作的負責人

**200. 整合題** 

關於麥克洛林女士，可由文中得知什麼？

(A) 她將造訪科格斯物業管理公司。
(B) 她將在 4 月 14 日之前搬出她現在住的房子。
(C) 她將撥打康貝爾先生的公務電話。
**(D) 她將會寄一些文件到漢尼斯柏格市。**

# ACTUAL TEST 4

## PART 5 P. 92–94

**101. 副詞詞彙題——修飾介系詞片語**

在她的電子郵件中，執行長向股東保證，情勢完全都在她掌握中。

(A) 填充物 (C) 更滿的
(B) 充滿的 **(D) 完全地**

- assure (v.) 向……保證 shareholder (n.) 股東
  fill in 填寫

**102. 人稱代名詞考題——主格**

摩斯先生和我參加了研討會，並在回來後立即和團隊其他成員分享我們在會中所學。

**(A) 我們** (C) 我們的
(B) 我們 (D) 我們自己

- attend (v.) 參加 conference (n.) 研討會
  upon ＋ Ving 在……後立即

**103. 動詞詞彙題**

列車長受到指示，在大雨期間將火車減速。

(A) 檢查 (C) 談到
**(B) 指示** (D) 修理

- conductor (n.) 列車長

**104. 形容詞詞彙題——修飾名詞**

前田先生呼籲讀者不要忽略使用社群媒體的有利影響。

(A) 受惠的 **(C) 有利的**
(B) 利益 (D) 有利地

- overlook (v.) 忽略 benefit (v.) 有利於

**105. 名詞詞彙題**

我們課程的註冊期間總共會持續十個工作天。

(A) 要求 **(C) 期間**
(B) 行政人員 (D) 表格

- registration (n.) 註冊

**106. 動詞詞類變化題——主詞動詞單複數一致性——語態**

華頓宴會廳最近改裝後，已讓它成為一個漸受歡迎的正式活動場地。

(A) 增加 (C) 被增加
**(B) 已增加** (D) 增加

- ballroom (n.) 宴會廳；舞廳 venue (n.) 會場
  enhance (v.) 增加

**107. 介系詞詞彙題** 難

想要使用免費停車場的顧客，應在經過植物園咖啡館後，在榆樹街左轉。

(A) 在……之間 **(C) 經過**
(B) 在……之上 (D) 穿過

- botanic (adj.) 植物的

**108. 名詞詞彙題——不定詞的受詞**

葉慈女士同意為一份全國性報紙，拍攝恩柏格舞蹈比賽整日賽事的照片。

(A) 比賽 (C) 競爭者
(B) 競爭者 **(D) 比賽**

- photograph (v.) 為……拍照
  compete (v.) 比賽
  competitor (n.) 競爭者；對手

**109. 形容詞詞彙題**

身為經理，史丹利先生要為大樓建案的結果負責。

(A) 有信心的 (C) 明智的
**(B) 應負責任的** (D) 被迫的

- outcome (n.) 結果

**110. 代名詞詞彙題——主詞動詞單複數一致性** 難

雖然很多人使用沃倫的試算表軟體，但幾乎沒人知道它的專業功能。

**(A) 幾乎沒有** (C) 每一個
(B) 那個 (D) 很多

**111. 連接詞詞彙題**

卡伯自助餐廳 12 月的位子都訂滿了，所以你必須找別的地點辦尾牙。

(A) 直到 (C) 但是
(B) 那時 **(D) 所以**

- booked solid 訂滿了 banquet (n.) 宴會

**112. 形容詞詞彙題——主詞補語**

安古鐘錶要拍攝一系列動畫廣告，試圖展現行銷創意。

(A) 有創造力地　　(C) 創作者
**(B) 有創造力的**　　(D) 創作

- timepiece (n.) 鐘、錶等各種計時器
  in an attempt to 試圖

**113. 副詞子句連接詞詞彙題——複合關係副詞** 難

不論可能有多忙，接待人員都必須立刻接起電話。

(A) 非常　　(C) 同樣地
(B) 即使　　**(D) 不論如何**

- receptionist (n.) 接待人員
  promptly (adv.) 立即地；迅速地
  likewise (adv.) 同樣地

**114. 副詞詞彙題——修飾不定詞**

伍德先生將要求協助，好在最後期限前順利完成預算報告。

**(A) 順利地**　　(C) 順利的
(B) 成功　　(D) 成功

- require (v.) 要求　assistance (n.) 協助
  budget (n.) 預算

**115. 名詞詞彙題**

興建佛蘭克林倉庫，是為了讓我們的產品在該地區的配送更快速。

(A) 接近　　**(C) 配送**
(B) 目的地　　(D) 完成

- region (n.) 地區　proximity (n.) 接近
  destination (n.) 目的地　fulfillment (n.) 完成

**116. 動詞詞彙題** 

既然喬卡比亞市集的主辦單位已經和市政府解決了市集的營業執照糾紛，市集現在將重新開張。

**(A) 解決**　　(C) 傳達
(B) 辭職　　(D) 選舉

- organizer (n.) 組織幹部；組織者
  dispute (n.) 糾紛；爭執　resign (v.) 辭職
  convey (v.) 傳達　elect (v.) 選舉

**117. 關係代名詞考題——關係代名詞所有格**

路易奇．曼西尼的球員成就包括贏得「最有價值球員」獎，其現已受僱擔任阿德夏烏鴉隊的教練。

(A) 無論哪個　　(C) 某人
**(B) 某人的……**　　(D) 他的

- achievement (n.) 成就　coach (v.) 指導；訓練

**118. 形容詞詞彙題**

有些公司偏愛賀萊增空氣清淨機，因為它體積小巧輕便。

(A) 簡短的　　(C) 費力的
**(B) 小巧的**　　(D) 真實的

- air purifier (n.) 空氣清淨機
  portability (n.) 輕便
  demanding (adj.) 吃力的；要求高的
  authentic (adj.) 真實的

**119. 動詞詞類變化題——不定詞——副詞用法** 

為符合忙碌旅客的需求，塞法特飯店提供的服務包括數位登記入住。

(A) 符合　　(C) 正符合
(B) 符合　　**(D) 為符合**

- on the go 忙碌的　accommodate (v.) 使符合

**120. 名詞詞彙題——動詞的受詞** 

「贊巴地 -Z」背包的側袋，讓你可以輕鬆拿取必要物品，例如水瓶和零食。

(A) 拿取　　**(C) 拿取**
(B) 正拿取　　(D) 拿取

- essential (adj.) 必要的

**121. 名詞詞彙題** 

雖然員工手冊禁止上班時使用智慧型手機，但它並未明確說明違規的結果。

(A) 違法者　　(C) 選擇
**(B) 結果**　　(D) 目標

- staff handbook (n.) 員工手冊
  prohibit (v.) 禁止　on the job 工作期間
  specify (v.) 明確說明　offender (n.) 違法者
  alternative (n.) 可供選擇的事物
  objective (n.) 目標

**122. 副詞詞彙題**

「伍里歐」利用它的手機應用程式所收集的資料來改善它自己的服務，但它並未把顧客資料分享出去。

**(A) 在外部地** (C) 周密地
(B) 不精確地 (D) 原先

- inaccurately (adv.) 不精確地
  meticulously (adv.) 周密地

**123. 介系詞詞彙題** 難

市長出席聚會，是他將近一個月來首度公開露面。

**(A) 在……之內** (C) 自從
(B) 在……期間 (D) 大約

- attendance (n.) 出席 gathering (n.) 聚會
  mark (v.) 標記

**124. 動詞詞彙題——動名詞**

斯鐸根教育的語言課程，教出能適應新環境的自動自發學習者。

(A) 合作 (C) 處理
(B) 轉變 **(D) 適應**

- self-motivated (adj.) 自動自發的
  cooperate (v.) 合作 address (v.) 處理

**125. 動詞詞類變化題——分詞——修飾名詞**

倉管人員的職責之一，就是確保所有店內販售的商品都擺放在正確的貨架上。

(A) 正在販售 **(C) 正被販售**
(B) 將要販售 (D) 已售出

- merchandise (n.) 商品

**126. 副詞詞彙題**

自從安裝了新的溫度控制系統後，我們每個月的電費帳單大幅降低。

(A) 深深地 **(C) 大幅地**
(B) 猛力地 (D) 極端地

- utility bill (n.) 水電帳單 install (v.) 安裝

**127. 名詞子句連接詞考題**

歐科女士接到調查是否正確遵照標準程序的任務。

(A) 進入 (C) 在……之前
**(B) 是否** (D) 任何

- task (v.) 派給……任務 investigate (v.) 調查
  procedure (n.) 程序；步驟
  properly (adv.) 正確地

**128. 形容詞詞彙題——受詞補語** 

興建綜合電話服務中心，將使布朗戴爾的經濟狀況較少依賴製造業。

(A) 依賴 **(C) 依賴的**
(B) 依賴 (D) 可靠的

- establishment (n.) 建立 manufacturing (n.) 製造業

**129. 動詞詞彙題** 

儘管仔細做好準備，派對的外燴業者在冷藏設備突然故障時，仍只好臨機應變。

**(A) 臨機應變** (C) 濃縮
(B) 指定 (D) 獲得

- caterer (n.) 外燴業者 refrigeration (n.) 冷藏
  improvise (v.) 臨機應變 designate (v.) 指定
  condense (v.) 濃縮

**130. 名詞詞彙題——複合名詞** 

摩特爾諮商的領導力研討會中，最受歡迎的是教導經理人如何促進團隊合作，同時尊重員工的個人特質。

(A) 個人的 (C) 具有個性的
(B) 單獨地 **(D) 個人的特質**

- foster (v.) 促進 individual (adj.) 個人的；個別的
  individually (adv.) 單獨地
  individualized (adj.) 具有個性的；針對個人的

## PART 6 P. 95–98

**131–134 報導**

《城市新聞時報》 3 月 3 日當週

眾所期待的 [131] **知名**主廚大衛・友的新餐廳「無國界創意料理」的盛大開幕日，已訂於 3 月 13 日星期四下午五時舉行。活動的重點將是剪綵儀式及免費佳餚招待。

在他 24 年的職業生涯中，友先生已成為這個地區最傑出且受歡迎的主廚。[133] **「無國界創意料理」是他的第二間餐廳。**他的第一間餐廳「西 24 咖啡館」去年稍早開幕，廣受好評，一直是受本市食客歡迎的選擇。[134] **在**經營自己的餐廳**之前**，友先生在第三街的吉安馬提小酒館當了十年主廚。

「無國界創意料理」位於喬丹街 3402 號。從 3 月 14 日起，它將從星期二營業至星期日，供應午晚餐。菜單已在線上公開：www.fusion-food.com。

- highly anticipated (adj.) 備受期待
  reception (n.) 接待

complimentary (adj.) 免費贈送的
delicacy (n.) (尤指稀有昂貴的)佳餚
prominent (adj.) 著名的;傑出的
eatery (n.) 餐館

**131. 形容詞詞彙題** 難

(A) 有抱負的 (C) 退休的
(B) 訪問的 **(D) 知名的**

- aspiring (adj.) 有抱負的 retired (adj.) 退休的

---

**132. 動詞詞類變化題——時態——be + 不定詞**

(A) 以……為特色 **(C) 將以……為特色**
(B) 已以……為特色 (D) 將以……為特色

- feature (v.) 以……為特色

---

**133. 句子插入題**

(A) 他目前在那裡教授烹飪藝術課。
**(B)「無國界創意料理」是他的第二間餐廳。**
(C)「無國界創意料理」可能很快就要易主。
(D) 他也計劃延長營業時間。

- culinary (adj.) 烹飪的

---

**134. 介系詞詞彙題**

(A) 一……就…… (C) 之後
**(B) 在……之前** (D) 除……之外還

- afterward (adv.) 之後;後來

---

**135–138 電子郵件**

**收件者:**<customerservice@romerouniforms.com>
**寄件者:**<natasha.maxwell@odn-mail.com>
**主旨:**球衣標誌
**日期:**11 月 25 日
**附件:**獅子_圖樣

哈囉:

我正試著要用你們的網站,為我擔任教練的青少年籃球隊訂做球衣,但似乎無法 [135] **正確**運作。我們是獅隊,我們一位隊員的家長設計了一個獅子圖樣,我們打算用來當我們的標誌。[136] **不巧的是**,當我們把圖樣上傳到你們的網站後,在球衣預覽圖中看起來是扭曲的。我們試過不同的圖像大小和所有可能的檔案格式,但問題還是一樣。因此,我把圖樣附加在這封電子郵件中寄給你們。[138] **我希望你們能找出問題所在。**我不確定這有沒有關係,但我們選了「贏家鑽石灌籃」球衣款,底色是翡翠綠並附有白色鑽石。

謝謝。

娜塔莎.麥克斯威爾

- attachment (n.) 附件 customized (v.) 訂做的
distorted (adj.) 扭曲的 preview (n.) 預覽

**135. 副詞詞彙題——修飾現在分詞**

(A) 更正 **(C) 正確地**
(B) 正確的 (D) 修改

- correction (n.) 修改

---

**136. 連接副詞**

(A) 反而 (C) 同樣地
(B) 也就是說 **(D) 不幸地**

- namely (adv.) 也就是說;即

---

**137. 動詞詞彙題**

**(A) 持續** (C) 決定
(B) 定居 (D) 聲稱

- reside (v.) 定居 determine (v.) 決定
assert (v.) 聲稱

---

**138. 句子插入題** 難

(A) 請就它的吸引力,說出你最真實的看法。
(B) 你畢竟不需要親自來我辦公室。
(C) 我們想要你們以它為基礎來設計標誌。
**(D) 我希望你們能找出問題所在。**

- in person 親自 after all 終究 figure out 想出

---

**139–142 網頁**

http://www.russontmining.com/careers/tp

**實習生計畫**

實習生計畫 [139] **既**對大學剛畢業的學生是個令人興奮的工作機會,**也**是盧松特礦業公司培養未來領導人的一個重要方式。我們從各種領域中選出前途看好的年輕人,給予他們成為盧松特團隊有價值成員所需的工具與知識。在 12 個月的計畫期間,受訓的實習生走遍盧松特在加拿大各地的礦場,和各層級的員工及行政主管交談。[140] **他們甚至有機會參與重大專案。**公司提供住宿、伙食和豐厚的生活津貼。順利完成計畫的實習生有資格在最 [141] **適合**他們的資歷與興趣的領域中,獲得盧松特的正職工作。

想知道如何成為實習生嗎？點擊這裡以了解 [142] **申請**程序。

- career opportunity (n.) 工作機會
  university graduate (n.) 大學畢業生
  cultivate (v.) 培養　promising (adj.) 有前途的
  field (n.)（知識）領域
  executive (n.) 行政主管；經理
  generous (adj.) 豐富的
  living stipend (n.) 生活津貼
  completion (n.) 完成　entitle (v.) 使符合資格
  qualification (n.) 資格；資歷

**139. 相關連接詞**

**(A) 既……且……**　(C) 不是……就是……
(B) 凡是……的事物　(D) 打算中的

---

**140. 句子插入題** 難

(A) 他們尤其應具備優異的溝通技巧。
**(B) 他們甚至有機會參與重大專案。**
(C) 例如，我們現在的營運副總裁是大學畢業生。
(D) 我們會在這段時間裡，採取「隨來隨審」的方式審核繳交的文件。

- in particular 尤其是
  graduate (n.)（大學）畢業生
  submission (n.) 繳交的文件
  on a rolling basis 隨來隨審；（錄取）先到先得

---

**141. 形容詞詞彙題——主詞補語** 難

(A) 適合　**(C) 適合**
(B) 適合　(D) 適合的

---

**142. 名詞詞彙題**

(A) 發展　**(C) 申請**
(B) 評價　(D) 採購

- appraisal (n.) 評價　procurement (n.) 採購

---

**143–146 公告**

**給網路銀行客戶的通知：**

從 1 月 1 日起，梅波特銀行將預設提供電子對帳單。在此日之後，您將不會再收到紙本對帳單，[143] **除非**您特別通知我們想收到紙本。您可以透過登入您的網路銀行帳號，點開「設定」標籤，選擇「繼續收到紙本對帳單」來通知我們。

電子對帳單可以在您的帳號頁面的「對帳單」標籤下看到。每個月在您的對帳單公布後，我們會寄給您一封電子郵件 [144] **通知**。[145] **這個訊息被設計用於保護客戶隱私。**它只會提到您的大名以及帳號的末四碼。請隨時更新與您的帳號連結的電子郵件地址。這樣可以確保這些對帳單以及梅波特銀行的其他重要訊息的傳送。

- account statement (n.) 對帳單　by default 預設
  specifically (adv.) 特別地；明確地
  associated with 和……有關連

**143. 副詞子句連接詞詞彙題**

(A) 無論在哪裡　(C) 此外
**(B) 除非**　(D) 一旦

---

**144. 名詞詞彙題—動詞的間接受詞—複合名詞** 難

**(A) 通知**　(C) 通知
(B) 通知　(D) 需通報的

---

**145. 句子插入題** 

**(A) 這個訊息被設計用於保護客戶隱私。**
(B) 流程和加入帳號持有人一樣。
(C) 對帳單列出您近期所有的交易。
(D) 這個日期目前無法在網路上更改。

- transaction (n.) 交易

---

**146. 名詞詞彙題**

(A) 澄清　(C) 關聯
(B) 刪除　**(D) 傳送**

- clarity (n.) 澄清　relevance (n.) 關聯

## PART 7 P. 99–119

**147–148 優惠券**

**洪斯丘苗圃**
春季特賣會

在 4 月 14 日到 4 月 23 日間，帶這張優惠券到洪斯丘苗圃來，[147] **所有植物都打 75 折，以及全部陶製盆栽都打 85 折**。用令人驚喜的價格為您的住家或商店添購美麗的花卉、灌木，甚至是樹木，來慶祝新年的第一個溫暖天氣。凡購買 [148] **皆能享有天天低價的運費和協助種植服務**。

- nursery (n.) 苗圃

### 147. 確認事實與否

文中提到關於這項促銷的什麼事？

(A) 包括免費贈送植物。
**(B) 適用於多種商品。**
(C) 苗圃酬謝長期客戶。
(D) 要求顧客消費一定金額。

- multiple (adj.) 多樣的　reward (v.) 酬謝

換句話說

all plants and . . . off all pottery
（所有的植物……，以及全部陶製盆栽）
→ (B) multiple types of items（多種商品）

### 148. 推論或暗示 難

文中提到關於洪斯丘苗圃的什麼事？

(A) 它也有戶外家具庫存。
(B) 它每星期休息一天。
**(C) 它提供某些異地服務。**
(D) 它主要服務其他企業。

- stock (v.)（商店或工廠）有庫存
  off-site (adj.) 工作場地以外的；異地的

換句話說

Delivery and planting assistance
（運費和協助種植服務）
→ (C) some off-site services（某些異地服務）

### 149–150 文字訊息串

**賈邁爾・理查森〔下午 6:14〕**
嗨，亞米娜。我剛剛獲准參加今年的大學助學補助人員研討會，我看到妳要發表簡報，我們何不趁我們在那裡時碰個面？

**亞米娜・恩迪亞耶〔下午 6:28〕**
嗨，賈邁爾。當然，我很樂意敘敘舊。
[149] **你已經離職兩年了，對嗎？**真不敢相信。
[149] **你是我們最新的學生顧問好像才昨天的事。**

**賈邁爾・理查森〔下午 6:31〕**
我知道！那麼，我的飛機會在星期四大約七點抵達。我們可以一起吃個晚一些的晚餐嗎？

**亞米娜・恩迪亞耶〔下午 6:33〕**
嗯，[150] **星期六吃午餐如何？**我想要利用星期四晚上準備我的簡報。

**賈邁爾・理查森〔下午 6:34〕**
[150] **應該可以。**

**亞米娜・恩迪亞耶〔下午 6:35〕**
好。如果在那之前我們沒有遇到的話，我們就星期五再傳簡訊討論出細節。

- approve (v.) 批准　catch up 了解最新情況
  run into 偶然碰到

### 149. 推論或暗示

理查森先生最有可能是什麼身分？

**(A) 恩迪亞耶女士的前同事**
(B) 恩迪亞耶女士的簡報共同主講人
(C) 大學生
(D) 研討會籌備人員

### 150. 掌握意圖

下午 6:34，理查森先生寫道：「應該可以」，他意指什麼？

(A) 他認為做些準備是有用的。
(B) 他相信某些設備是可靠的。
(C) 他不介意提供一些協助。
**(D) 他很可能可以在建議的時間碰面。**

### 151–152 電子郵件

**寄件人：**<lester.knight@eorp.com>
**收件人：**<benita.garza@niy-mail.com>
**主旨：**即將來臨的會面
**日期：**1 月 2 日
**附件：**資料

親愛的戈爾札女士：

謝謝您和我約定 1 月 17 日下午兩點會面。我很高興有機會 [151] **透過謹慎的財務管理和聰明投資，協助您達成目標——不論是要買房子、送小孩上大學或其他事情。**

為了讓我們的第一次會面盡可能有所收穫，您手邊必須準備一些關於您的收入、資產、債務等資料。[152] **請檢閱這封電子郵件的附件，看看所有的必要文件。**在來我的辦公室之前，思考並寫下您可能想問我的任何問題也是個好主意。

期待與您見面。

萊斯特・奈特　謹啟

- achieve (v.) 達到；實現
  money management (n.) 財務管理
  productive (adj.) 有收穫的　asset (n.) 資產
  debt (n.) 債務
  full range of 全部的；各種的
  paperwork (n.)（與某一工作、交易等有關的）書面資料

**151. 暗示或推論**

萊斯特先生的工作最可能是什麼？

(A) 不動產經紀人　**(C) 財務顧問**
(B) 私人家教　(D) 招募人員

---

**152. 相關細節**

根據奈特先生，此附件的目的為何？

(A) 描述辦公室的地點
(B) 解釋要求付款的正當理由
(C) 概述一個提議的細節
**(D) 提供一份必要文件的清單**

- describe (v.) 描述
  justify (v.) 證明……是正當的
  summarize (v.) 概述　required (adj.) 必要的

> **換句話說**
> the full range of paperwork that will be necessary（所有的必要文件）
> → (D) a list of required documents（一份必要文件的清單）

---

**153–155 公告**

> **公告**
>
> 3 月 6 日：唐納利市提議從四月起，升級部分供水系統。[154/155] **尺寸不符合本市目前所需的鋼管將更換為高密度的塑膠管**，其餘的水管也會加裝閥門，以減少管線的漏水。市府評估的結果發現，這個工程專案可能對當地的濕地造成衝擊，因此發出這則公告，[153] **提供居民一個機會，表達他們對環境與安全的疑慮**。民眾可至市政府自來水事業處查看包括評估結果在內的工程檔案。對於此項工程的意見也可於 3 月 27 日前，在同一地點提出。

- propose (v.) 提議　portion (n.) 部分
  distribution (n.) 分配；分發
  steel pipe (n.) 鋼管
  insufficient (adj.) 不足的　density (n.) 密度
  assessment (n.) 評估
  environmental (adj.) 環境的

**153. 主旨或目的**

撰寫這則公告的原因為何？

(A) 宣布一個商機
**(B) 尋求對於提案的意見回饋**
(C) 警示居民服務中止
(D) 糾正對一項工程的誤解

- caution (v.) 警示；警告　interruption (n.) 中止

> **換句話說**
> in order to provide residents with an opportunity to express their environmental and safety concerns（提供居民一個機會，表達他們對環境與安全的疑慮）
> → (B) To seek feedback on a proposal（尋求對於提案的意見回饋）

---

**154. 推論或暗示** 難

文中提到關於唐納利市的什麼事情？

**(A) 用水量增加。**
(B) 位於相對乾燥的地區。
(C) 官員將舉行公開會議。
(D) 對飲用水品質進行過檢測。

---

**155. 句子插入題** 

「其餘的水管也會加裝閥門，以減少管線的漏水。」最適合放在 [1]、[2]、[3]、[4] 的哪個位置？

(A) [1]　(C) [3]
**(B) [2]**　(D) [4]

- remaining (adj.) 其餘的；剩餘的

---

**156–157 說明**

> 納博斯企業
>
> **[156] 使用微波爐前，請先閱讀！**
>
> 1. 請勿使用微波爐加熱任何可能發出強烈氣味的食物（例如：魚肉）。
> 2. 將你的菜用蓋子或紙巾覆蓋，以防止食物在微波爐內濺開。
> 3. 如果你的食物真的在微波爐內濺開或滴落，請立刻清理乾淨。清潔劑可以在水槽下找到。
> 4. [157] **任何微波爐的問題，現在應匯報給維修部的東尼．米契（分機 32），而不是辦公室的行政人員。**

- prevent A from Ving
  阻止 A 做……；使 A 無法做……
  splatter (v.)（液體）潑濺
  administrator (n.) 行政人員

### 156. 主旨或目的

這份說明的目的為何？

(A) 宣傳一個便利設施的功能
(B) 警告某些危險
(C) 解釋一個流程
**(D) 頒布一套規定**

- feature (n.) 功能；特色　amenity (n.) 便利設施
  issue (v.) 頒布；發布

### 157. 推論或暗示 難

關於米契先生的工作職責，下列何者最可能為真？

(A) 明確規定在一本手冊裡。
**(B) 最近增加了。**
(C) 主要是清潔工作。
(D) 包括和辦公室的行政人員溝通。

- specify (v.) 明確說明
  consist of . . . 由……組成

### 158–160 電子郵件

**寄件人：**史考特．范
**收件人：**志工名單
**主旨：**穆薩克書展
**日期：**8 月 7 日

哈囉，志工們！

我代表穆薩克書展籌備委員會，歡迎大家加入負責舉辦這場美好活動的團隊。

[158] **本月稍晚時，你們會收到一封來自你們特定工作範圍（例如協助參展廠商、交通等）主管的電子郵件，裡面會詳細說明諸如當你輪值時要去哪裡報到的細節**，但我有些一般性的提示與資訊要先分享。

[159] **我們建議所有志工穿著舒適的鞋子，並帶著防曬乳，以防萬一需要**。此外，因為宏第納會議中心很大，你應該安排好提早 15 分鐘到達，確保你可以準時上工。

不管你在書展的工作是什麼，一旦你戴上「志工」的徽章後，你的優先工作就是協助來賓。[160] **請看一下會在入口發給你們的〈參觀者指南〉小冊子，以便你們可以幫助他們找到便利設施**。如果有人問了你答不出來的問題，請指引提問者到最近的服務台去。

書展見！

祝　安康

志工協調主任　史考特．范

- on behalf of . . . 代表……
  organizing committee (n.) 籌備委員會
  supervisor (n.) 主管；監督人
  exhibitor (n.) 參展者　report (v.) 報到
  shift (n.) 輪班　venue (n.) 會場
  priority (n.) 優先事項
  convenience facility (n.) 便利設施

### 158. 相關細節

范先生提及在之後的電子郵件中會提供什麼資訊？

(A) 一些訓練課程的日期
(B) 一些制服的規定
(C) 一些交通費用
**(D) 一些工作場地**

**換句話說**
an e-mail later this month（本月稍晚的電子郵件）→ future e-mail（之後的電子郵件）
where to report for your shift（輪值時要去哪裡報到）→ (D) Some work sites（一些工作場地）

### 159. 推論或暗示 

文中提到關於志工的什麼事？

**(A) 其中有些人會被分派到戶外。**
(B) 每個活動工作範圍裡會有 15 個人。
(C) 他們會在書展入口拿到一個徽章。
(D) 他們將享有免費住宿。

- be entitled to 有資格

### 160. 相關細節

文中鼓勵志工如何了解書展？

(A) 詢問他們的主管
(B) 徒步探索會場
**(C) 閱讀一本刊物**
(D) 去服務台

- publication (n.) 刊物；出版品

**換句話說**
take a look at the "Fairgoers Guide" booklet（看一下〈參觀者指南〉小冊子）
→ (C) reading a publication（閱讀一本刊物）

## 161–163 報導

### 被興奮與爭議環繞的
### 觀光局競賽

赫斯本頓觀光局的最新活動「# 我的赫斯本頓競賽」已引發騷動。拍出最能展現赫斯本頓的短片的人可以得到比賽提供的一千元獎金。影片必須發布在社群媒體平台「蕭茲特」上，並加上「# 我的赫斯本頓」標籤。優勝者將視每支影片得到的按讚數和觀光局成員所投的票數相加結果來決定。

比賽是由觀光局剛到職且是 [162] **局內唯一一位 35 歲以下的成員艾拉・佛特**憑空想出來的。在昨天的電話訪問中，佛特女士表示，比賽「使用了科技和赫斯本頓的最棒資源——居民」。比賽無疑受到蕭茲特使用者的熱烈響應。[161] **目前為止已發布了將近 80 支影片**，它們總共已獲得超過一萬個「讚」。

然而，不是所有人都滿意這次競賽。在上週的市議會上，[163] **當地的餐廳業者恩尼斯特・馬修抱怨，觀光局根本就忽略了所有不使用蕭茲特的人的想法**。「我的顧客大部分是年長者，他們沒有人在用蕭茲特，」他說：「這個比賽所呈現的赫斯本頓範圍太狹隘。」為回應這項不滿，市議員璜妮塔・帕迪拉表示，她會敦促觀光局未來的宣傳活動要考慮更多元的參與方式。

- controversy (n.) 爭議　stir (n.) 騷動
  embody (v.) 具體呈現
  dream up 憑空想出（尤指不切實際的想法）
  resource (n.) 資源　enthusiasm (n.) 熱情
  garner (v.) 獲得
  essentially (adv.) 根本上；本質上
  participation (n.) 參加

### 161. 相關細節

比賽目前在哪個階段？

(A) 比賽還沒有開始。
**(B) 遞交參賽作品。**
(C) 觀光局正在投票。
(D) 已選出優勝者。

**換句話說**

have been . . . so far（到目前為止已……）
→ currently（目前）
Nearly 80 videos have been posted
（已發布了將近 80 支影片）
→ (B) Entries are being submitted
（遞交參賽作品）

### 162. 確認事實與否

文中提到關於佛特女士的什麼事？

(A) 她出席了市議會。
(B) 她個人有蕭茲特的帳號。
(C) 她出現在宣傳短片中。
**(D) 她是某個機構中最年輕的成員。**

**換句話說**

its only one under 35
（唯一一位 35 歲以下的成員）
→ (D) the youngest member of an organization
（某個機構中最年輕的成員）

### 163. 相關細節

馬修先生不喜歡比賽的什麼事？

(A) 觀光局可以影響比賽結果
**(B) 比賽把某些居民的觀點排除在外**
(C) 以前的比賽失敗了
(D) 對本市來說，比賽太昂貴了

- exclude (v.) 把……排除在外
  perspective (n.) 觀點；看法

**換句話說**

the board was essentially ignoring the ideas of anyone who does not use Shoutster（觀光局根本就忽略了所有不使用蕭茲特的人的想法）
→ (B) it excludes some residents' perspectives
（比賽把某些居民的觀點排除在外）

## 164–167 線上聊天室

薩琳娜・霍瓦特〔下午 3:49〕
[164] **「威爾克原料處理」的顧問今年早上來做簡報，呈現她對重新設計普克維爾倉儲的想法，對嗎？**你們覺得呢？

艾美・卡羅〔下午 3:50〕
她的大部分建議都很棒。例如 [165] **她建議在靠入口的地方設一個區域，放少量顧客最常訂購的材料**。那可以縮短我們撿貨的時間。

薩琳娜・霍瓦特〔下午 3:50〕
那的確聽起來是個好主意。[165] **她是否認為我們要如原先設想的，需要投資在托板式貨架上？**

艾美・卡羅〔下午 3:51〕
[165] **是的，但只有那個前面的特別區域**。我們仍可以把剩下的存貨堆放在地板上。

羅納德・江口〔下午 3:51〕
但 [165] **她也說，我們應該開始採用可掃描標籤的位置搜尋系統**。

薩琳娜．霍瓦特〔下午 3:52〕
嗯，[166] **那聽起來很貴。但我確定，它很有可能大大提升我們的效率。**

艾美．卡羅〔下午 3:53〕
[166] **我們也這麼想。**我們問她，生產力增加後，多久才能讓系統的費用回本，她說要看我們選擇哪個廠商。

羅納德．江口〔下午 3:54〕
因為我們在好幾間倉儲而不是只有一間採用這套系統，我們正在尋找可能願意給我們折扣的廠商。

薩琳娜．霍瓦特〔下午 3:55〕
嗯，[167] **我們可能決定先在一個據點試用這套系統，再安裝到其他地方**，但那是個不錯的建議。告訴我你們搜尋的結果。

- **quantity (n.)** 數量 **frequently (adv.)** 經常地
  **retrieval (n.)** 檢索 **pallet rack (n.)** 托板式貨架
  **stack (v.)** 堆放 **implement (v.)** 實施
  **potential (adj.)** 可能的 **efficiency (n.)** 效率
  **productivity (n.)** 生產力

**164. 主旨或目的**

霍瓦特女士為何開啟了線上聊天討論？

**(A) 為了得知某個會議的結果**
(B) 為了釐清某份文件的內容
(C) 為了討論一項檢查的準備工作
(D) 為了分享她對一場簡報的看法。

- **arrangement (n.)** 準備工作；安排
  **inspection (n.)** 檢查

**165. 確認事實與否**

下列何者不是顧問的建議？

(A) 在工廠的某個區域安裝貨架
**(B) 在地板上畫線以標示走道大小**
(C) 使用能以電子方式讀取的標籤
(D) 讓受歡迎的貨品種類更容易拿取

- **install (v.)** 安裝 **aisle (n.)** 走道
  **accessible (adj.)** 可得到的；易取得的

**換句話說**

invest in pallet racks（投資托板式貨架）
→ (A) Installing racks（安裝貨架）
for that special front area
（在那個前面的特別區域）
→ (A) in one part of a facility
（在工廠的某個區域）
scannable labels（可掃描的標籤）
→ (C) stickers that can be read electronically
（能以電子方式讀取的標籤）
setting up an area near the entrance
（在靠入口的地方設一個區域）
→ (D) Make . . . more accessible
（讓……更容易拿取）
the materials that customers order most frequently（顧客最常訂購的材料）
→ (D) popular types of stock（受歡迎的貨品種類）

**166. 掌握意圖**

下午 3:53，當卡羅女士寫道：「我們也這麼想」，她最可能的意思是？

**(A) 她和江口先生對某個主意抱持矛盾的看法。**
(B) 她和江口先生對某些結果感到不解。
(C) 有間倉儲的輸出量令人失望地低。
(D) 某個專案的預算不應該增加。

**167. 相關細節**

根據霍瓦特女士，參與聊天者的公司可能選擇做什麼？

(A) 在普克維爾開設一間新的倉儲
(B) 客製化一個系統的某些功能
**(C) 進行某個計畫的小規模測試**
(D) 將一些較舊的商品打折

- **customize (v.)** 客製化；訂製
  **scheme (n.)** 計畫 **merchandise (n.)** 商品；貨物

**換句話說**

try out the system in one location
（在一個據點試用這套系統）
→ (C) Conduct a small-scale test of a scheme
（進行某個計畫的小規模測試）

**168–171 網頁**

http://www.allstons.com/corporate

歐斯頓 >> 詢問公司業務

40 多年來，[168] **歐斯頓一直致力於提供顧客每項體育活動所需的最佳品質運動服裝與鞋款。**今天，我們與上百家供應商維持商業關係，他們代表某些國內最受歡迎與令人興奮的產品。儘管如此，我們仍一直尋找能放在「歐斯頓」旗下販售的新品牌與款式。我們以擁有廣大的忠實顧客群，以及快速、可靠的付款時程而自豪。[170] **而我們只反過來要求供應商遵照我們合理的商品包裝與卡車運送標準。**若欲詢問與我們建立供應商關係，請撥打 (809) 555-0162，或寄電子郵件到 vendors@allstons.com 給我們。我們很樂意提供最優秀的現有供應商的推薦證言。

此外，[169/171] **歐斯頓經常檢視在美國中西部開設新店面的可能地點**。我們樓地板面積的最低要求是 1.5 萬平方英尺。[171] **如果您擁有合適的商業地產，想要討論把店面租給我們**，請打到我們的芝加哥總公司 (809) 555-0160。

- committed (adj.) 盡心盡力的　apparel (n.) 服裝
  vendor (n.) 供應商
  boast (v.) 擁有（感到自豪的事物）
  dependable (adj.) 可靠的　merchandise (n.) 商品
  testimonial (n.) 推薦證言
  commercial (adj.) 商業的　property (n.) 房地產

**168. 暗示或推論**

歐斯頓最可能是哪一種公司？

(A) 健康食品供應商　(C) 連鎖健身中心
**(B) 運動服飾店**　(D) 活動規畫公司

**換句話說**
quality apparel . . . for every athletic activity（每項體育活動所需的高品質服飾）
→ (B) sports clothing（運動服飾）

---

**169. 推論或暗示**

關於歐斯頓，可由文中得知什麼事情？

(A) 它的總公司最近搬遷。
(B) 它很快會更改公司名稱。
**(C) 它正試圖擴張。**
(D) 它參加地區貿易展。

- expand (v.) 擴張

**換句話說**
opening new stores（開設新店面）
→ (C) expand（擴張）

---

**170. 相關細節**

根據網頁，所有現有的供應商必須做什麼事？

**(A) 根據公司政策包裝商品**
(B) 依照要求做推薦
(C) 在他們的卡車上顯示歐斯頓的商標
(D) 證明他們的營運符合環保

**換句話說**
follow our reasonable standards for merchandise packing（遵照我們合理的商品包裝標準）→ (A) Pack items according to company policies（根據公司政策包裝商品）

**171. 句子插入題**

「我們樓地板面積的最低要求是 1.5 萬平方英尺。」最適合放在標示 [1]、[2]、[3]、[4] 的何處？

(A) [1]　(C) [3]
(B) [2]　**(D) [4]**

---

**172–175 備忘錄**

**收件人**：各級經理
**寄件人**：申俊泰
**關於**：員工待遇
**日期**：7 月 20 日

如你們大家所知，努蘭女士今年稍早聘請我擔任努蘭軟體公司的首位全職人力資源人員。我的工作之一就是從人事的角度來看我們的整體狀況，而現在既然我已經來了好幾個月，我有些改善的建議。[172] **作為一個希望能成長為較大公司的小企業**，很重要的是，我們能提供吸引並留住人才的工作條件。

一個重要的考量是工作量。我們應該定期和員工談談，[173] **確保他們的工作可以在標準的一週工作時間內完成**。如果你部門的工作量變得太重，[174] **請安排時間與努蘭女士和我開會，討論增加更多人手**。

同樣地，[173] **員工在需要請病假和利用他們分配到的所有休假天數時，應能自由請假**。這是保護他們的健康與士氣的重要方式。

最後，只要員工達到他們的工作目標，請 [173] **讓他們保有時間上的彈性**。雖然我們還無法支援遠距工作，但我們至少可以准許我們的員工合理管理他們自己的時間表。

你們所有人、努蘭女士和我將在星期四上午十點開會，討論這份備忘錄的內容。請注意，[175] **努蘭女士已認可我的建議**，因此這場會議並不是一個討論這些建議的機會。相反地，我們會把焦點放在如何最有效達成它們。謝謝你們。

- perspective (n.)（思考問題的）角度；觀點
  workweek (n.) 一週工作時間
  allotment (n.) 分配額
  morale (n.) 士氣　flexibility (n.) 彈性
  remote work (n.) 遠距工作
  empower (v.) 給（某人）做⋯⋯的權力；准許
  within reason 合情合理　debate (v.) 辯論

**172. 確認事實與否**

文中提到關於努蘭軟體公司的什麼事？

(A) 最近開了新辦公室。
(B) 成立不到一年。
**(C) 沒有很多員工。**
(D) 必須讓它的股東滿意。

- shareholder (n.) 股東

換句話說
a small business（一個小企業）
→ (C) It does not have many employees.（沒有很多員工。）

---

**173. 確認事實與否** 難

文中未提及什麼樣的改善員工待遇的方式？

(A) 可調整的工作時間
(B) 合理的工作量
(C) 輕鬆使用假期時間
**(D) 設於公司內的健康中心**

- adjustable (adj.) 可調整的
  reasonable (adj.) 合理的

換句話說
allow employees some flexibility in their hours
（讓員工保有時間上的彈性）
→ (A) Adjustable working hours
（可調整的工作時間）
their tasks can be completed in a standard workweek
（他們的工作可以在標準的一週工作時間內完成）
→ (B) A reasonable workload（合理的工作量）
feel comfortable taking sick time . . . vacation days
（在有需要請病假……休假天數時，應能自由請假）
→ (C) Easy usage of leave time
（輕鬆使用假期時間）

---

**174. 相關細節** 

根據備忘錄，為何收到的人要安排和申先生開會？

(A) 表達對他想法的反對
**(B) 提議僱用更多人手**
(C) 推薦績效獎金制
(D) 得到對一名員工遠距工作的許可

- opposition (n.) 反對
  performance-based bonus (n.) 績效獎金

換句話說
set up a meeting（安排會議）
→ schedule a meeting（安排開會）
to discuss adding more personnel
（討論增加更多人手）
→ (B) To propose hiring more workers
（提議僱用更多人手）

---

**175. 推論或暗示**

關於備忘錄中的建議，申先生有什麼暗示？

(A) 它們也會對所有員工宣布。
(B) 它們有科學研究的支持。
**(C) 它們得到公司老闆的背書。**
(D) 它們已被一名競爭對手採用。

- endorse (v.) 背書　adopt (v.) 採用
  competitor (n.) 競爭對手

換句話說
Ms. Noolan has already given her approval
（努蘭女士已認可）
→ (C) endorsed by the business's owner
（得到公司老闆的背書）

---

**176–180 網頁與電子郵件**

www.orosco-pac.org/fscs

歐洛斯可表演藝術中心

免費秋季音樂會系列
從九月到十一月的每個星期四晚上，[176] **本中心在最舒適怡人的表演空間「爾文圓形露天劇場」推出免費音樂會。**這個系列經過仔細規劃，演出各種音樂類型，是個見到著名音樂家以及發現令人驚艷新星的絕佳機會。

表演從晚上七點開始。十人以上才能預訂座位。[180] **我們鼓勵其他的來賓在音樂會開始前早早到售票處排隊，確保拿到票。**

即將舉行的音樂會（完整節目表）

| | |
|---|---|
| 10 月 19 日 | **艾蜜莉亞．布瑙爾：**[177] **被知名鋼琴演奏家羅曼．霍夫稱為「古典鋼琴界的下一位巨星」的布瑙爾女士**，將舉行法國作曲家的作品獨奏會。 |
| 10 月 26 日 | **綠色懸崖三重奏：**欣賞為這個團體贏得 [177] **聲譽卓著的爵士音樂學院「年度專輯」殊榮**的鋼琴、低音提琴與鼓的流暢融合。 |

| 11 月 2 日 | 強尼與農夫：這個傳奇民謠樂團逾十年來，首度造訪赫姆斯培德！來 [177] 聽「破碎的斑鳩琴」和樂團暢銷專輯中的其他暢銷歌曲。 |
|---|---|
| [179] 11 月 9 日 | 歐洛斯可歌劇團：[179] 來自赫姆斯培德當地的天才歌唱家將以義大利文和英文演唱出自許多歌劇的著名詠嘆調和二重唱。 |

更多資訊請撥打 555-0180，或追蹤我們的社群媒體觀看過去音樂會的照片，並接收即將舉行活動的提醒通知。

- amphitheater (n.) 圓形露天劇場
  intimate (adj.) 怡人的；舒適的
  represent (v.) 演出　established (adj.) 著名的
  renowned (adj.) 有名的
  recital (n.) 獨奏會　prestigious (adj.) 有聲譽的
  aria (n.) 獨唱曲；詠嘆調

**寄件人**：艾洛伊絲．佛林
**收件人**：翠娜．麥克吉
**主旨**：關於：免費秋季音樂會
**日期**：10 月 10 日

親愛的翠娜：

[178] **沒問題，我很樂意和妳去聽音樂會。**[179] **我不敢相信，我們可以去歐洛斯可表演藝術中心觀賞免費的歌劇演出**！我以前從來沒去過那裡，我聽說那裡真的很棒。妳好像總是知道這個城市裡最有趣的活動，改天妳得告訴我，妳是怎麼辦到的！還有，不會，既然妳星期四要上班，[180] **我不介意負責票券的事。只有我們兩個，對嗎？**

艾洛伊絲

- wouldn't mind + V-ing 不介意做……

**176. 確認事實與否** 難

文中提到關於歐洛斯可表演藝術中心的什麼事？

**(A) 有不止一個舞台。**
(B) 呈現多種建築風格。
(C) 在社群媒體帳號發布訪談。
(D) 允許十歲以下的兒童參加某些活動。

**177. 確認事實與否** 難

在網頁上，未提及所列表演者的什麼成就？

(A) 賣出許多專輯
(B) 贏得重大獎項
**(C) 於世界各地演出**
(D) 得到知名音樂家的讚譽

- acclaim (n.) 讚譽

**換句話說**

its bestselling records（它的暢銷專輯）
→ (A) Selling many albums（賣出許多專輯）
its prestigious "Album of the Year" honor（它聲譽卓著的「年度專輯」殊榮）
→ (B) a major award（重大獎項）
called "the next big star in classical piano" by renowned concert pianist（被知名音樂家鋼琴家羅曼．霍夫稱為「古典鋼琴界的下一位巨星」）
→ (D) Receiving acclaim from a famous musician（得到知名音樂家的讚譽）

**178. 主旨或目的**

為何撰寫這封電子郵件？

(A) 要求更改某些計畫
(B) 回答一筆已完成預訂的問題
(C) 確認預訂已完成
**(D) 接受朋友的邀請**

**179. 整合題**

佛林女士可能想在哪一天聽音樂會？

(A) 10 月 19 日　(C) 11 月 2 日
(B) 10 月 26 日　**(D) 11 月 9 日**

**180. 整合題**

佛林女士最可能做什麼？

**(A) 在表演當天提早到達**
(B) 打電話到表演藝術中心的售票處
(C) 在特定的日子完成線上處理程序
(D) 下載一個與旅遊有關的行動應用程式

**換句話說**

line up at the box office well before the concert（在音樂會開始前早早到售票處排隊）
→ (A) Arrive early on the day of the performance（在表演當天提早到達）

## 181–185 報導與信件

（2 月 7 日）——威瑪便利商店要來迪諾市了。

本市經濟發展委員會（EDC）一致通過威瑪興建一間 4,600 平方英尺便利商店的計畫，[181] **該店的特色是在它 12 座加油機上有個磚瓦屋頂。**[181] **該店將建於米爾登路的一塊空地上**，鄰近 7 號公路，全年無休 24 小時營業。

為了讓商店營運，[182] **公司必須遵守市政府的噪音與交通減量規定**。除此之外，在上午 1 點到 5 點之間，除了汽油外，重型卡車不得運送貨物過來。卡車也無法從米爾登路開進店裡，因此，威瑪會蓋一條私有道路通往商店的卸貨區。

在包含該公司自己的交通工程師簡報的公開說明會後，計畫獲得了市府的核准。參加的民眾發出正反意見的不同聲音。[183] **住在米爾登路 400 號大樓的貝蒂·提姆帕挪**表示，她喜歡住處附近有便利商店的想法，但擔心附近的拉蒙納路車流增加。為了證明所言，她放了一段她在尖峰時間從車窗拍的影片。影片顯示大批車輛塞在靠近布魯克街的拉蒙納路上。

另一方面，居民史提夫·葛羅席克表示，他歡迎這家店，因為 [181] **它會提供下班後「快速、溫暖的便餐」**。目前，最近的便利商店是月桂街上的威斯博德加商店，大約有三公里遠。

- unanimously (adv.) 一致同意地；無異議地
  comply with 遵守；服從
  regulation (n.) 規定；規則
  attendance (n.) 出席　voice (v.) 表達
  opposition (n.) 反對　congestion (n.) 擁塞

親愛的編輯：

[184] **身為一輩子住在迪諾市的居民**，很感謝您 2 月 7 日關於威瑪便利商店計畫的報導。然而，文章中有一些資訊不正確。[183] **我在公開說明會上播放的數位影片，是我所住的街道上塞車情形的錄影**。

還有，我想要提醒您，有兩位市民表達了關於商店現代化設計的擔憂。我認同他們的看法，[185] **我們必須努力保持我們這個城市獨有的建築特徵**。如果可能的話，新建築應該和我們的歷史建物融合在一起。

再次謝謝您的報導。

貝蒂·提姆帕挪　謹啟

- lifelong (adj.) 一輩子的；終身的　retain (v.) 保持
  distinctive (adj.) 獨特的；與眾不同的
  architectural (adj.) 建築的　blend in with 融入

### 181. 確認事實與否 難

關於已規劃的便利商店，下列何者不正確？

(A) 加油區會有屋頂。
**(B) 清晨不會賣汽油。**
(C) 將提供熟食的選擇。
(D) 將建在空地上。

**換句話說**
feature a tiled canopy above its 12 gas pumps
（特色是在它 12 座加油機上有個磚瓦屋頂）
→ (A) have a covered fueling area
（加油區會有屋頂）
provide a "quick, warm bite to eat"
（提供「快速、溫暖的便餐」）
→ (C) offer cooked food selections
（提供熟食的選擇）
built on a plot of vacant land（建於一塊空地上）
→ (D) constructed on empty land（建在空地上）

### 182. 確認事實與否

關於迪諾市，文中提及什麼？

(A) 以大片倉儲區而聞名。
(B) 是年度工程師研討會的地點。
(C) 另有三間便利商店。
**(D) 已執行減少車流量的政策。**

- implement (v.) 執行；實施　decrease (v.) 減少

**換句話說**
traffic reduction regulations（交通減量規定）
→ (D) policies to decrease traffic（減少車流量的政策）

### 183. 整合題 

提姆帕挪女士最可能在哪裡拍攝公開說明會上的影片？

**(A) 米爾登路**　(C) 布魯克街
(B) 拉蒙納路　(D) 月桂街

### 184. 確認事實與否

關於提姆帕挪女士，可由給編輯的信中看出什麼？

(A) 她是當地的歷史學家。
(B) 她偏好現代建築。
**(C) 她從來沒住過迪諾市以外的地方。**
(D) 她曾去過威瑪便利商店。

換句話說

a lifelong resident of Denold City
（一輩子住在迪諾市的居民）
→ (C) She has never lived outside of Denold City.（她從來沒住過迪諾市以外的地方。）

**185. 同義詞考題**

在給編輯的信中，第二段第二行的「retain」，意思最接近何者？

(A) 指派
(B) 隱藏
**(C) 保存**
(D) 限制

**186–190 提案、廣告與顧客評論**

明塔納礦泉浴場

**促銷提案**

提案人：業務助理約瑟夫．巴漢
9 月 2 日

促銷方式：任何服務均 85 折

[187] **目標客群：護理師**

日期／期間：不間斷，儘快開始

優點：

—新客群。身為從事高壓但不一定待遇優沃的工作者，護理師可以從我們的服務中受惠良多，但可能覺得他們無法負擔得起完整價格。
—改善我們在一般大眾之間的企業形象。

[186] **挑戰：**

—後勤問題。[186] **我們的員工必須仔細核對參加者的證件**，並記住只有服務費打折。

- **sales assistance (n.)** 業務助理
  **logistical (adj.)** 後勤的
  **credential (n.)** 證件；資格

**明塔納按摩會館**
**挺醫護人員！**

明塔納按摩會館了解，拯救生命和提供每日醫療照護是困難的工作。因此，從 11 月 1 日開始，[187] **我們將對護理師、輔助醫護人員和緊急救護技術員 *，提供所有服務 85 折優惠**。這包括放鬆按摩、消除疲勞的臉部與身體護理，和淨化桑拿時間——甚至 [189] **包含進入我們的新紅外線桑拿小屋內，利用紅外線光**引起出汗排毒，並增進循環！這是我們對維持我們社區健康的英雄的小小感謝方式。



明塔納按摩會館位於布魯內的惠特康路 1200 號。我們接受未預約的顧客，但建議要預約，因為我們的時間經常滿檔。更多詳情請撥打 555-0122。

* 需有合格的工作證明。請注意，折扣優惠不適用於按摩禮券或商品。

- **paramedic (n.)** 輔助醫護人員
  **refreshing (adj.)** 消除疲勞的
  **treatment (n.)** 治療　**cleansing (adj.)** 淨化的
  **infrared (adj.)** 紅外線的　**induce (v.)** 引起；導致
  **detoxify (v.)** 排毒　**circulation (n.)** 循環
  **walk-in (n.)** 未經預約而來的人
  **eligible (adj.)** 合格的；有資格的
  **employment (n.)** 工作；受僱
  **gift certificate (n.)** 禮券　**merchandise (n.)** 商品

http://www.brunerbusinessreviews.com/mintanaspa

**布魯內商業評論**

明塔納按摩會館的最新評價：

「我昨天休假，因此我在中午之後去造訪，趁機利用他們給護理師的新折扣優惠。以平時上班日來說，他們相當忙碌，而 [188] **我很幸運，沒有因為未預約而吃閉門羹**。然而，我一點也不覺得員工一直趕我。[190] **每個人都很專注周到，把我當那天唯一的顧客一樣款待。那是我最欣賞的地方**。相較之下，藍莓精華液的臉部護理效果今天早上消退了，而 [189] **桑拿小屋雖然令人放鬆，但效果沒有比熱水澡好**。我很可能會再去，但下次會試試不同的服務。」

泰莎．柯恩 於 11 月 12 日評論

- **take advantage of** 利用
  **attentive (adj.)** 照顧周到的
  **appreciate (v.)** 欣賞
  **extract (n.)**（尤指食物或藥物的）萃取物；精華

**186. 確認事實與否**

提案中提及促銷活動可能有的困難是什麼？

(A) 讓可能參加的人知道此活動
(B) 服務大量的新客戶
(C) 維持足夠的淨利率
**(D) 評估參加者的資格**

- **patron (n.)** 主顧（尤指老顧客）
  **sufficient (adj.)** 足夠的　**evaluate (v.)** 評估
  **qualification (n.)** 資格

換句話說

Challenges（挑戰）
→ a potential difficulty（可能有的困難）
carefully check the credentials of participants（仔細核對參加促銷者的資格）
→ (D) Evaluating participants' qualifications（評估參加者的資格）

---

**187. 整合題**

提案中的促銷活動和廣告裡的有什麼不同？

(A) 折扣的高低
(B) 促銷期間
**(C) 符合資格的人**
(D) 適用的商品

---

**188. 同義詞考題** 

在顧客評論中，第一段第三行「turned away」，意思最接近何者？

(A) 把……打發走　(C) 避免
**(B) 拒絕**　(D) 放棄

---

**189. 整合題** 

關於柯恩女士，可由文中得知什麼？

(A) 她在促銷活動首日造訪。
**(B) 她接受了光照治療。**
(C) 她試用了明塔納按摩會館最受歡迎的服務。
(D) 她撥打了廣告上的電話號碼。

---

**190. 相關細節**

柯恩女士特別喜歡明塔納按摩會館的什麼？

**(A) 體貼的顧客服務**
(B) 奢華的室內裝潢
(C) 療程的治療效果
(D) 格局所提供的隱私性

- considerate (adj.) 體貼的
  effectiveness (n.) 療效

換句話說

appreciated the most（最欣賞）
→ especially like（特別喜歡）
very attentive and treated me like I was the only customer that day（很專注周到，把我當那天唯一的顧客一樣款待）
→ (A) considerate customer service（體貼的顧客服務）

## 191–195 文章、電子郵件與報導摘要

### 阿拉伯語測驗將在柯伯修施行

文／席拉．瑞德諾

柯伯修　訊（5 月 13 日）——致力於促進美國人英語以外語言能力的非營利組織「全美外語學會」（NFLA），將開始在柯伯修提供阿拉伯語能力測驗。從今年 7 月起，阿拉伯語言能力測驗（TOCIA）將每年舉行兩次。

NFLA 高級職員肯．里德表示，[191] **這個決定很自然就達成了**。「我們注意到，有很多應試者來自柯伯修地區。」他相信，這是由於柯伯修大學的阿拉伯語學程之故。他指出，該學程也使當地人 [195] **具有執行這項測驗的資格，因為這樣的工作需要一些這種語言的知識**。

TOCIA 包含 50 分鐘的聽力測驗和 70 分鐘的閱讀測驗。[193] **第一次測驗將在大學的杜凱特大禮堂舉行，不過，里德先生表示，如果應試者超過 150 人，可能會增加其他的考場。**報名必須在 6 月 4 日下午 5 點前，至 www.nfla.org/tocia 網站完成，費用 40 美元。

- non-profit (adj.) 非營利的
  commit (v.)（使）致力於
  proficiency (n.) 精通；熟練
  administer (v.) 執行；實施
  qualified to 合格的；勝任的
  consist of 包含；由……構成　venue (n.) 會場
  registration (n.) 報名

寄件人：NFLA
收件人：布萊恩特．佩吉
主旨：TOCIA
日期：6 月 11 日

---

親愛的佩吉先生：

[192] **感謝您報名參加阿拉伯語言能力測驗。請看以下的資訊。**

1. 測驗日期與時間：7 月 3 日下午 1 點。
   注意：應試者必須於指定的開始時間前，提早至少 30 分鐘抵達。
2. [193] **地點：柯伯修大學，甘寧大樓**（北大學路 350 號）203 室。（<u>地圖</u>）
3. 所需文件：政府機關核發附有照片的證件。

關於應試過程的細節，請上<u>這個網頁</u>。

- stated (adj.) 指定的
  photo identification (n.) 附有照片的身分證件

阿拉伯語言能力測驗（TOCIA）
測驗程序遵行報告

測驗地點：柯伯修大學杜凱特大禮堂
測驗日期：7 月 3 日
[195] **監考人員：莎凡娜．基內**

請在每個項目旁的空格打勾，表示相關程序已執行。[194] **如果有任何空格未打勾，必須在此份報告後附上完整的說明理由。**

- 在測驗開始之前的 30 分鐘內，沒有應試者獲准進入考場。☑
- 已驗明每位應試者的身分。☑
- [194] **所有應試者帶來的個人電子產品已存放在遠離考場的地方。**☐
- 考生填寫所有測驗前需填寫的表格。☑

- observance (n.) 遵行　append (v.) 附加　verify (v.) 證明

**191. 同義詞考題**

文章中第二段第二行的「reach」，意思最接近何者？

(A) 伸長　(C) 接觸
(B) 完成　**(D) 達成**

**192. 主旨或目的**

為何寄電子郵件給佩吉先生？

**(A) 讓他為考試做好準備**
(B) 要求他完成報名
(C) 宣傳課程服務
(D) 回覆詢問

**193. 整合題** 難

文中提到關於 TOCIA 的什麼事？

**(A) 超過 150 人報名參加在柯伯修的測驗。**
(B) 在兩個測驗之間有 30 分鐘的休息時間。
(C) 通常在週末舉行。
(D) 在 NFLA 的網站上，有可供練習的版本。

**194. 推論或暗示**

報告的附件中，最可能解釋什麼事情？

(A) 最後一位應試者抵達的時間
(B) 應試者如何證明他們的身分
(C) 應試者在考試前填完什麼文件
**(D) 應試者的物品在考試時存放於何處**

換句話說

a full explanation of the reason must be appended（必須附上完整的說明理由）
→ be explained in an attachment（在附件中解釋）
All personal electronics brought by test-takers were stored（所有應試者帶來的個人電子產品已存放）
→ (D) test-takers' belongings were kept（應試者的物品存放）

**195. 整合題** 

關於基內女士，下列何者最可能為真？

(A) 她六月時參加了一個訓練課程。
**(B) 她擁有一些阿拉伯語的技能。**
(C) 她是由瑞德諾女士面試的。
(D) 她是柯伯修大學的教授。

換句話說

some knowledge of the language
（一些這種語言的知識）
→ (B) some Arabic language skills
（一些阿拉伯語的技能）

**196–200 電子郵件與網頁**

**收件人**：尼克．包洛斯
<nickborrows1@renseed.com>
**寄件人**：凡妮莎．凱梭
<vanessacastle@renseed.com>
**日期**：4 月 20 日
**主旨**：聖地牙哥
**附件**：修正後的簡報

嗨，尼克：

我只是想告訴你，我們下週在聖地牙哥簡報的最新投影片內容。我沒有改圖表和財務狀況表，但 [196] **我把產品的照片改得稍微大一點和清楚一點**。我也有一些關於投影片內容的註解，但 [197] **在和你談過之前，我不想改它。我把我的想法用另一個檔案寄給你。**

還有，我們需要訂機票。以前往那裡的航班而言，我們偏好的航空公司裡有四種選擇。我不知道你的想法，但 [198] **我想要搭傍晚抵達的那班**。這讓我們白天大部分的時間可以在這裡的辦公室做準備，但也能及時抵達，稍做休息。如果你同意，在我今天下班前，我會訂好機票。

告訴我你的決定。

凡妮莎

- sharp (adj.) 清晰的　alter (v.) 修改
  separate (adj.) 不同的
  preferred (adj.) 偏好的；更合意的
  carrier (n.) 航空公司

www.lightningair.com/departures/april28/query83789

**閃電航空——經營每日飛往全美各地的廉價航班！**

**起飛日期：**4 月 28 日
**出境機場：**舊金山
**入境機場：**聖地牙哥

- 航班號碼：L106　起飛：上午 4:30　抵達：上午 6:00
- 航班號碼：L982　起飛：上午 11:00　抵達：下午 12:30
- 航班號碼：L392　起飛：下午 1:00　抵達：下午 2:30
- [198] **航班號碼：L720　起飛：下午 5:45　抵達：下午 7:15**

**重要事項：**[199] **少於三小時的航班，我們已取消經濟艙旅客的機上免費供餐服務。這些旅客可能須額外付費購買餐點。**商務艙旅客仍可享有此項免費餐點。俱樂部商務艙旅客享有餐點與飲料無限暢飲。頭等艙旅客的餐飲和俱樂部商務艙相同，同時還能進入我們的閃電航空專屬休息室。

下一頁 ▶

- eliminate (v.) 排除
  complimentary (adj.) 免費贈送的
  purchase (v.) 購買　entitled to 有資格
  exclusive (adj.) 專有的

**收件人：**凡妮莎．凱梭 <vanessacastle@renseed.com>
**寄件人：**尼克．包洛斯 <nickborrows1@renseed.com>
**主旨：**關於：聖地牙哥
**日期：**4 月 22 日

嗨，凡妮莎：

謝謝妳的電子郵件和妳對簡報投影片的投入。我現在手上有公司的信用卡，所以就直接訂了妳想要的航班機票，加上另一張 30 日回程的票。票價很公道，雖然 [199] **我得多付點錢幫我們點飛機餐**。

如果妳不介意的話，[200] **我現在就預訂我通常在市中心住的飯店**。我們不需要預訂從機場接送的車，因為飯店有免費接駁車。飯店也有個不錯的商務中心，我們可以在那裡印出我們簡報的投影片。聽起來很棒吧？

尼克

- reasonable (adj.)（價錢）公道的
  reservation (n.) 預訂
  transportation (n.) 交通工具

**196. 相關細節**

凱梭女士對一些影像做了什麼？

**(A) 她讓它們更顯眼。**
(B) 她把它們放在不同的檔案夾。
(C) 她在上面加了文字。
(D) 她修補了上面的缺失。

- visible (adj.) 顯眼的　flaw (n.) 缺點

**換句話說**
made the pictures of our products a little bigger and sharper
（把產品的照片改得稍微大一點和清楚一點）
→ (A) made them more visible（讓它們更顯眼）

**197. 相關細節**

凱梭女士答應要寄什麼給包洛斯先生？

(A) 預訂的確認信
(B) 一些旅行選擇的細節
(C) 簡報的錄音檔
**(D) 修改一些文字的建議**

**換句話說**
ideas（想法）→ (D) Suggestions（建議）
alter（改）→ (D) revising（修改）

**198. 整合題**

凱梭女士偏好哪一班飛機？

(A) L982　　**(C) L720**
(B) L106　　(D) L392

**199. 整合題**

包洛斯先生最可能購買哪個艙等的機票？

**(A) 經濟艙** (C) 商務艙
(B) 俱樂部商務艙 (D) 頭等艙

**200. 確認事實與否**

包洛斯先生表示他接下來會做什麼？

(A) 報銷一筆費用
(B) 安排路上交通
**(C) 預訂一些住宿**
(D) 列印一些電腦螢幕截圖

- **reimbursement (n.)** 報銷 **expense (n.)** 費用
  **accommodation (n.)** 住處

**換句話說**

**make reservations . . . at the hotel**
（預訂……飯店）
→ **(C) Book some accommodations**
（預訂一些住宿）

# ACTUAL TEST 5

## PART 5 P. 120–122

**101. 名詞詞彙題**

每個員工的紅利獎金，是以他或她的績效考核為準。

(A) 工作站　(C) 制服
**(B) 紅利**　(D) 升遷

- workstation (n.) 工作站　promotion (n.) 升遷

---

**102. 名詞詞彙題——動詞的受詞** 

吉利斯礦業集團發布聲明，堅決否認公司計劃更換執行長的謠傳。

(A) 否認　(C) 否認
(B) 否認　**(D) 否認**

- issue (v.) 發布　firm (adj.) 堅決的

---

**103. 介系詞詞彙題** 

只要額外支付最低費用，我們的專業設計人員就能做出吸睛的插圖，讓你能加進宣傳文件中。

**(A) 以……為交換**　(C) 用
(B) 如同　(D) 到

- minimal (adj.) 最小的
  eye-catching (adj.) 引人注目的
  promotional (adj.) 促銷的

---

**104. 動詞詞彙題**

費蘭特飯店投入很多心力維持它具有格調與舒適的名聲。

(A) 顯示　**(C) 投入**
(B) 花費　(D) 需要

- considerable (adj.) 相當多的
  maintain (v.) 維持　reputation (n.) 名聲

---

**105. 副詞詞彙題**

要縮短這道菜的準備時間的方法之一，是購買已經切成條的高麗菜。

(A) 有時候　(C) 終於
**(B) 已經**　(D) 自……以來

- strip (n.) 條

---

**106. 人稱代名詞考題——所有格**

倉庫經理稱讚消防灑水頭安裝團隊人員的純熟與細心作業。

(A) 他們　(C) 他們的（東西）
(B) 他們　**(D) 他們的**

- praise A for B 讚揚 A 做的 B
  installation (n.) 安裝　skilled (adj.) 熟練的

---

**107. 動詞詞類變化題——時態**

車輛一發動，駕駛人使用的「星團加導航裝置」就會自動啟動。

(A) 啟動　**(C) 啟動**
(B) 活化劑　(D) 啟動

- vehicle (n.) 車輛　activation (n.) 啟動
  activator (n.) 活化劑

---

**108. 副詞詞彙題——修飾動詞**

學生對大學醫療服務近期調查的回應差異很大。

(A) 寬闊的　(C) 加寬
(B) 加寬　**(D) 廣泛地**

---

**109. 名詞詞彙題——不定詞的受詞**

杜德利女士的文章呼籲當局加強對電信業中某些部分的管理。

**(A) 管理**　(C) 管理人
(B) 管理　(D) 管理

- call on (v.) 號召；要求
  authority (n.)〔複〕當局；官方
  supervise (v.) 管理　supervisor (n.) 管理人

---

**110. 副詞子句連接詞詞彙題**

當威佛女士不在時，副理佛羅瑞斯先生負責管理店鋪。

(A) 在……期間　(C) 以便
(B) 如果沒有　**(D) 當……時**

- be in charge of 負責

**111. 動詞詞彙題**

我們的顧客滿意度評價始終很高，反應出我們系列產品的優異品質。

(A) 傳送　　(C) 遞送
**(B) 反應**　　(D) 安排

- consistently (adv.) 始終如一地
  customer satisfaction (n.) 顧客滿意度
  transmit (v.) 傳送

**112. 介系詞詞彙題**

亨達哈化學公司有 12 座研究實驗室，遍布在世界主要地區。

(A) 在……之間　　(C) 在……之上
(B) 向外　　**(D) 遍及……各處**

- chemical (n.) 化學製品；化學藥品
  laboratory (n.) 實驗室　spread (v.) 分布
  region (n.) 地區

**113. 副詞詞彙題——修飾形容詞**

西岡工業的領導階層熱烈支持員工努力發展環保清潔劑。

**(A) 熱烈地**　　(C) 熱烈的
(B) 熱情　　(D) 對……熱衷的人

- industrial (n.) 工業公司
  leadership (n.) 領導階層
  detergent (n.) 清潔劑　enthusiasm (n.) 熱情
  enthusiastic (adj.) 熱烈的
  enthusiast (v.) 對……熱衷的人

**114. 代名詞詞彙題——主詞**

根據工友指出，有人把沒洗的盤子留在茶水間的水槽裡。

(A) ……的人　　**(C) 某人**
(B) 無論誰　　(D) 彼此

- janitor (n.) 工友　break room (n.) 茶水間

**115. 副詞詞彙題**

精通一種外語的過程並非快速可達，而且技能要經過一長段時間才能逐漸發展出來是很正常的。

(A) 匆忙地　　**(C) 逐漸地**
(B) 肯定地　　(D) 不情願地

- hurriedly (adv.) 匆忙地
  affirmatively (adv.) 肯定地
  reluctantly (adv.) 不情願地；勉強地

**116. 形容詞詞彙題——修飾名詞**

在某些小公司裡，負責訂購辦公用品的人可能在會計或財務部工作。

(A) 負責地　　(C) 責任
**(B) 負責的**　　(D) 責任

- supplies (n.) 日用品　accounting (n.) 會計

**117. 形容詞詞彙題** 難

選角指導進行大規模的搜尋以找到最適合擔任電影主角的演員。

(A) 完全的　　(C) 精疲力竭的
(B) 有資格的　　**(D) 大規模的**

- conduct (v.) 實施　starring role (n.) 主角
  eligible (adj.) 有資格的

**118. 副詞詞彙題——修飾動詞**

出乎意料有許多的市民自願加入本市減少用水的運動。

**(A) 自願地**　　(C) 志願者
(B) 自願的　　(D) 自願做

- extraordinary (adj.) 意想不到的
  participate (v.) 參加　voluntary (adj.) 自願的

**119. 介系詞詞彙題**

由於材質脆弱且價值高昂，珍本書典藏只限圖書館館員閱覽。

**(A) 由於**　　(C) 儘管
(B) 和……一起　　(D) 不論

- delicacy (n.) 易碎；脆弱
  access (n.)（使用某物的）權利
  along with 和……一起　in spite of 儘管
  regardless of 不管

**120. 動詞詞類變化題——主詞動詞單複數一致性** 難

本週這一期的內容包括一篇對慢跑配件的評論，內容詳細分析功能、價格和耐用度的不同。

(A) 已分析　　(C) 分析
**(B) 分析**　　(D) 被分析

- functionality (n.) 功能　durability (n.) 耐用

**121. 名詞詞彙題** 

凱西街因為有許多新創科技公司集中在此而出名。

(A) 位置　　**(C) 集中**
(B) 標準　　(D) 出席

- start-up (n.) 新創公司　attendance (n.) 出席

**122. 名詞詞彙題——動詞的受詞——複合名詞**

請預約三號會議室，以便我們在客戶來訪前練習我們的銷售簡報。

**(A) 簡報**　　(C) 演講人
(B) 像樣的　　(D) 提出

- reserve (v.) 預約　in advance of 在……之前
  presentable (adj.)（尤指穿著）像樣的；體面的
  presenter (n.) 演講人　present (v.) 提出

**123. 動詞詞彙題** 

提出這份申請，並不保證你能得到梅思波銀行的貸款。

(A) 保證　　**(C) 迫使**
(B) 緩和　　(D) 迅速完成

- application (n.) 申請　relieve (v.) 緩和
  expedite (v.) 迅速完成

**124. 副詞子句連接詞詞彙題**

既然大廈工程已完工，也許要展示給潛在買家看了。

**(A) 既然**　　(C) 不論如何
(B) 遍布　　(D) 為了……

- exhibit (v.) 展示　prospective (adj.) 有希望的
  throughout (v.) 遍布

**125. 名詞詞彙題** 

所有關於商標設計的修改，都應該先和著作權專家討論，並得到王先生的同意。

(A) 提案　　**(C) 修改**
(B) 概念　　(D) 必要性

**126. 動詞詞類變化題——不定詞——受詞補語**

為了病人著想，莫若醫院鼓勵醫護人員有需要就請病假。

(A) 已請（假）　　(C) 請（假）
**(B) 請（假）**　　(D) 請（假）

- for the sake of . . . 為了……
  sick leave (n.) 病假

**127. 副詞詞彙題** 

擁有美麗海景的雷諾公路，曾是奧特瑞和蘭博特這兩個濱海城市間的唯一道路。

(A) 凡是……的事物　　(C) 遠的
(B) 在……之中　　**(D) 曾經**

- boast (v.) 擁有（值得自豪的東西）
  scenic view (n.) 優美的風景
  coastal (adj.) 海岸的；濱海的

**128. 動詞詞類變化題——時態和語態**

去年有好幾次，奈索德工廠的生產因為可輕易預防的機械故障而延誤了。

(A) 正延誤　　(C) 原本會延誤
**(B) 已被延誤**　　(D) 可能被延誤

- preventable (adj.) 可預防的
  breakdown (n.) 故障

**129. 形容詞詞彙題** 

巴特斯公司的出資者要求公司接受查帳，證明它財務健全。

**(A) 健全的**　　(C) 可行的
(B) 相等的　　(D) 詳細的

- investor (n.) 出資者；投資者　undergo (v.) 接受
  audit (n.) 查帳　equivalent (adj.) 相等的
  feasible (adj.) 可實行的

**130. 副詞詞彙題** 

用完餐後，哈肯餐飲的服務人員會低調地清理桌面，以避免讓客人從談話或其他活動中分神。

(A) 精確地　　(C) 持續地
**(B) 不張揚地**　　(D) 豪華地

- distract one's attention 分散某人的注意力
  discreetly (adv.) 不引人注目地

## PART 6　P. 123–126

**131–134 公告**

### 給顧客的重要公告

德爾登平價商店將在 1 月 13 日星期一公休，進行存貨盤點與電腦升級作業。若造成不便，謹此致歉，並先感謝您的耐心。有時候，我們的員工無法在正常營業時間裡處理與盤點存貨 131 **有關的**所有工作。132 **因此，休息一天是我們唯一的選擇**。我們還在這一天處理這些重要的商業活動，因為 133 **相對**來說，星期一客人很少。那通常是一星期中 134 **生意最清淡的**一天。敝店將於 1 月 14 日星期二上午九點再次準時開門營業。謝謝您。

- inventory (n.) 存貨；盤點存貨
  apologize for . . . 為……道歉
  promptly (adv.) 準時地

TEST 5　PART 5 / 6

**131. 形容詞詞彙題——分詞**

(A) 有關　　(C) 關係
**(B) 有關的**　　(D) 相對地

- **relate (v.)** 有關　**relation (n.)** 關係
  **relatively (adv.)** 相對地

**132. 句子插入題**

**(A) 因此，休息一天是我們唯一的選擇。**
(B) 那個軟體程式是新加的。
(C) 然而，大部分仍可在網路上買到。
(D) 請客戶服務處協助。

- **addition (n.)** 附加　**assistance (n.)** 幫助

**133. 副詞詞彙題** 

(A) 單獨地　　**(C) 相對地**
(B) 相當地　　(D) 有規律地

- **considerably (adv.)** 相當地

**134. 形容詞詞彙題**

(A) 最短的　　(C) 最早的
**(B) 最不忙碌的**　　(D) 最忙的

**135–138 電子郵件**

寄件者：道格拉斯．貝利
收件者：<totycontest@inspiriteach.com>
主旨：推薦凱莉．威金森
日期：11 月 26 日

敬啟者：

我想要為凱莉．威金森獲得啟發教育的「年度教師」獎的提名背書。[135] **你們的網站說，你們嘗試獎勵創新和關懷。**威金森女士和我在溫克菲爾中學已共事五年，我想像不出更能代表這些特質的 [136] **教師**。

威金森女士在為她的六年級學生所編寫的教案上展現了無窮的創意。例如她最近在一個關於 [137] **新聞業**的單元上，善加利用學校的科技能力。她的學生規劃、拍攝並剪輯了一則關於學校的新聞節目。

威金森女士也非常富有同情心。就連對最難相處的學生，她只是表達理解。[138] **事實上**，她能以耐心與仁慈處理搗亂行為，這對同事們是一種啟發。

最後，我建議你們慎重考慮選擇威金森女士為年度教師。

道格拉斯．貝利　謹啟

- **endorse (v.)** 背書；支持　**nomination (n.)** 提名
  **representative (adj.)** 代表性的
  **compassionate (adj.)** 富有同情心的
  **disruptive (adj.)** 引起混亂的；破壞性的
  **inspiration (n.)** 啟發；鼓舞

**135. 句子插入題** 難

(A) 她在這項活動的貢獻值得表揚。
(B) 我全心全意支持啟發教育的活動。
(C) 請將我的電子郵件傳給適當的人或委員會。
**(D) 你們的網站說，你們嘗試獎勵創新和關懷。**

- **recognition (n.)** 表揚
  **dedication (n.)** 貢獻；奉獻
  **wholehearted (adj.)** 全心全意的
  **appropriate (adj.)** 適當的

**136. 名詞詞彙題——動詞的受詞** 

(A) ……的教育　　(C) 她教育
**(B) 一個教師**　　(D) 那些人的教育

**137. 名詞詞彙題**

**(A) 新聞業**　　(C) 經濟
(B) 地理　　(D) 政府

- **geography (n.)** 地理　**economics (n.)** 經濟學
  **government (n.)** 政府

**138. 連接副詞**

(A) 起初　　(C) 否則
**(B) 事實上**　　(D) 儘管如此

**139–142 資訊**

**薇艾拉啟程飯店的規定**

被列在「薇艾拉啟程」的名單上是一項殊榮，也伴隨著許多責任。[139] **雖然**關鍵是提供旅客舒適的住宿，但我們也希望我們的會員飯店透過以下行動，幫忙維持薇艾拉啟程的好名聲。

首先，迅速回覆任何透過薇艾拉啟程所提出關於你飯店的詢問——即使是來自你無法接待的客人。其次，除非絕對必要，否則不要取消透過薇艾拉啟程完成的預訂。[140] **記得，客人的旅行計畫取決於你。**最後，請藉由好好維護你的飯店，以及 [141] **解決**客人於評價中提及的問題，努力在薇艾拉啟程上獲得高評價。

薇艾拉啟程會追蹤會員飯店在這些方面（回應迅速、取消率和顧客評價）的表現，而且可能處罰掉到某些等級以下的飯店。為了避免這種情況，我們建議你自己透過你的帳號頁面 [142] **密切注意**這些資料。

- **requirement (n.)** 規定；要求
  **privilege (n.)** 殊榮 **uphold (v.)** 維護
  **reputation (n.)** 名譽
  **responsiveness (n.)** 反應迅速
  **impose (v.)** 施行

**139. 副詞子句連接詞詞彙題**

**(A) 雖然** (C) 是否
(B) 關於 (D) 此外

**140. 句子插入題**

(A) 你也可以在櫃檯提供實體影本。
(B) 有些飯店也許無法從在薇艾拉啟程上打廣告而受惠。
(C) 對大部分的訂房而言，會是盥洗用具和毛巾。
**(D) 記得，客人的旅行計畫取決於你。**

- **toiletry (n.)** 盥洗用具

**141. 動詞詞類變化題——動名詞——介系詞的受詞**

(A) 解決 **(C) 解決**
(B) 解決 (D) 決心

**142. 動詞詞彙題——動名詞**

(A) 供應 **(C) 密切注意**
(B) 修改 (D) 挽救

**143–146 新聞稿**

立即發布

聯絡人：publicrelations@pearron.com

多倫多 訊（10 月 22 日）——培倫製藥公司宣布與溫培樂投資公司簽訂一項交易。根據協議的條款，溫培樂投資以加幣七千兩百萬元買下培倫的少數股權，[143] **以此**提供資金讓培倫能實現成長策略。

培倫的股東支持 [144] **這**項重大的交易。他們堅信，這將讓該公司在未來幾年大幅擴張。

培倫開發並供應市場許多皮膚、頭髮和指甲疾病的藥物。[146] **它的產品包括崔瓦寧，一種用來治療指甲感染的乳膏。**未來，它將專注於讓嚴謹的開發過程更完善，以病人的需求與安全為優先。它也會建立專屬的業務團隊，將它的藥品賣給全加拿大的醫事人員與機構。

- **pharmaceutical (adj.)** 製藥的 **stake (n.)** 股份
  **shareholder (n.)** 股東
  **landmark (n.)** 重大事件；里程碑
  **firmly (adv.)** 堅定地 **expand (v.)** 擴張
  **significantly (adv.)** 顯著地
  **commercialize (v.)** 商品化 **medication (n.)** 藥物
  **condition (n.)** 疾病 **refine (v.)** 改善
  **rigorous (adj.)** 嚴格的
  **prioritize (v.)** 給予……優先權
  **build up** 建立 **dedicated (adj.)** 專門的

**143. 副詞詞彙題** 

(A) 然而 **(C) 以此**
(B) 相反地 (D) 相當

**144. 限定詞——指示形容詞**

**(A) 這** (C) 大部分
(B) 每一個 (D) 我們的

**145. 動詞詞類變化題——時態**

(A) 使有可能 (C) 已可能
**(B) 將有可能** (D) 使有可能

**146. 句子插入題**

(A) 許多病人仍偏愛常規醫藥，而不是另類療法。
(B) 可以在全國的醫院病房中看到它的機器。
**(C) 它的產品包括崔瓦寧，一種用來治療指甲感染的乳膏。**
(D) 正在進行的一項臨床試驗的初期結果看來很好。

- **conventional (adj.)** 傳統的
  **alternative (adj.)** 另類的
  **remedy (n.)** 療法；治療
  **infection (n.)** 感染
  **clinical trial (n.)** 臨床試驗
  **promising (adj.)** 前景看好的

## PART 7 P. 127–147

### 147–148 廣告

**史旺空間**

史旺空間提供舒適、高科技的工作環境給個人與小型企業使用。我們公司提供的選項從可靈活使用的共同工作休憩區，到附有專屬會議空間的私人辦公室都有。所有會員皆可使用的便利設施包含：

- 免費高速無線網路，並可使用印表機、掃描機和碎紙機
- 廚房與休息區，附有免費飲料與裝滿的自動販賣機
- 收包裹服務，以及使用 [147] **我們大樓令人印象深刻的「高地區」地址**（巴尼街 3100 號）作為商業郵寄之用

想知道更多嗎？ [148] **來參加我們下次在 5 月 3 日的史旺空間開放參觀日，和我們、我們的現有會員，以及其他林克利商務界領導人交流**。或者，您可以在上班日的上午 8 點到下午 6 點之間來趟私人參訪，或直接上網站 www.swannspace.com。

- facility (n.) （有特定用途的）場所
  range from A to B 範圍從 A 到 B
  dedicated (adj.) 專用的
  amenity (n.) 便利設施　shredder (n.) 碎紙機
  well-stocked (adj.) 儲藏量多的
  alternatively (adv.) 或者

**147. 確認事實與否**

文中提到關於史旺空間的什麼事？

(A) 它主要滿足文化創意產業人士的需求。
(B) 它為會員提供科技支援。
**(C) 它位於一個頗具聲望的地區。**
(D) 它的會員可以使用運動器材。

- cater (v.) 滿足或提供（個人或團體的）願望或需求
  prestigious (adj.) 頗具聲望的

**換句話說**
impressive Highlands District address（令人印象深刻的「高地區」地址）
→ (C) located in a prestigious neighborhood（位於一個頗具聲望的地區）

**148. 相關細節**

史旺空間在 5 月 3 日會做什麼事？

(A) 調漲月租費
(B) 帶領大家參觀公司
(C) 歡迎新的行政主管
**(D) 主辦社交活動**

- executive (n.) 行政主管

**換句話說**
to connect with us, our current members, and other leaders of the Linkley business community（和我們、我們的現有會員，以及其他林克利商務界領導人交流）
→ (D) networking（建立人脈）
Swann Space Open Reception（史旺空間開放參觀日）→ (D) event（活動）

### 149–150 電子郵件

**寄件人：**古田英司
**收件人：**吉兒．班奈特
**主旨：**貨物包裝
**日期：**4 月 3 日

嗨，吉兒：

客戶服務部告訴我，好幾位食品雜貨配送的顧客因為肉品包裝的事聯絡我們。顯然，肉品僅以我們的普通包裝材料包裝（以伸縮膜覆蓋著發泡托盤），令他們很擔心。[149] **他們想再加一層包裝，以防萬一這個包裝材料破損，肉汁流出時，其他產品不會被細菌污染。**

目前，我們還沒有收到任何普通包裝材料真的破損的報告，因此，[150] **我不確定包裝材料必須升級**。然而，我認為我們至少應該研究一下能顧及這些顧客期望的方法。妳可以搜尋其他的包裝材料選擇，以及使用它們的費用和對環境的影響嗎？我希望妳在月底前給我一份調查結果的簡短報告。

謝謝。

英司

- apparently (adv.) 顯然　foam tray (n.) 發泡托盤
  stretchable film (n.) 伸縮膜
  layer (n.) 層　leak (v.) （液體或氣體）外漏
  convinced (adj.) 確信的
  accommodate (v.) 顧及
  impact (v.) 對……產生影響　involved in 涉及
  finding (n.) 調查（或研究的）結果

**149. 相關細節** 難

顧客擔心什麼？

(A) 使用不可回收的包裝材料
(B) 肉品的溫度上升到不安全的程度
(C) 員工沒有小心拿取配送貨物的容器
**(D) 食物會交叉污染**

- temperature (n.) 溫度　contaminate (v.) 污染

**150. 推論或暗示** 難

關於可能改變某些包裝，英司先生建議什麼？

**(A) 可能不需要。**
(B) 必須慢慢引進。
(C) 需要班奈特女士同意。
(D) 員工不會喜歡。

**換句話說**
be upgraded（升級）→ (A) change（改變）
I'm not convinced（我不確定）
→ (A) It may not be necessary.（可能不需要。）

**151–152 資訊**

《哈德納市社區通訊》

**哈德納市園藝俱樂部（HCGC）**

在我們新一季開始時，加入我們吧！我們今年的第一場集會將在 3 月 13 日星期一晚上七點，在我們的老地方「哈德納社區中心」舉行。派崔克．雷特和吉娜．呂將開設講座並示範「蜜蜂如何幫助園丁」。身為哈德納市養蜂人協會的會員，他們致力於教育大眾關於蜜蜂帶給環境的好處。他們的演講包含設計吸引蜜蜂的花園的有用建議。這個講座是互動式的，因此請提出你們的問題。

**[151] 我們希望下星期一能看到許多新面孔。HCGC 個人會員一年的會費是 20 美元，集會時可以拿到會員報名表。[152] 我們未來完整的實地考察、植物拍賣和志工活動日曆，可於 www.hcgc.org 線上閱覽。**

- venue (n.) 會場；舉行活動的地點
  demonstration (n.) 實地示範
  beekeeper (n.) 養蜂人
  be committed to . . . 致力於……
  interactive (adj.) 互動的

**151. 主旨或目的**

這則資訊的目的之一為何？

(A) 宣布改地點
**(B) 為俱樂部召募新會員**
(C) 尋求先前講座的意見回饋
(D) 突顯一個當地的環境問題

- recruit (v.) 召募　previous (adj.) 先前的；以前的
  highlight (v.) 突顯；強調

**換句話說**
a lot of new faces（許多新面孔）
→ (B) new members（新會員）

**152. 相關細節**

根據這則訊息，在 HCGC 網站上可看到什麼？

**(A) 活動的時程表**　(C) 城市地圖
(B) 會員申請書　(D) 論壇討論區

**換句話說**
can be found online（可於線上閱覽）
→ available on the HCGC Web site（在 HCGC 網站上可看到）
A complete calendar of our upcoming field trips, plant sales, and volunteer activities（我們未來完整的實地考察、植物拍賣和志工活動日曆）
→ (A) A schedule of events（活動的時程表）

**153–154 文字訊息串**

傑夫．克萊斯〔下午 3:22〕
艾美，有一台貼標機有問題。打出來的標籤是歪的。

艾美．摩拉〔下午 3:23〕
試試清一下送紙區，可能髒了。**[153] 你還在下面的工廠樓層嗎？**

傑夫．克萊斯〔下午 3:24〕
**[153] 是的，我現在在這下面。[154] 妳知道這台機器的服務技師是誰嗎？**其實機器才剛清理過。

艾美．摩拉〔下午 3:24〕
**[154] 好問題。我等一下回你話。**

傑夫．克萊斯〔下午 3:25〕
喔，那樣的話，不用了。我打廠商的技術支援熱線試試。

- issue (n.) 問題　crooked (adj.) 歪的；扭曲的
  feeder (n.) 送紙器；（機器的）供給裝置
  manufacturer (n.) 廠商；製造公司

### 153. 推論或暗示

克萊斯先生最可能在哪裡？

**(A) 生產工廠**　　(C) 大樓的大廳
(B) 印刷行　　(D) 電腦專門店

**換句話說**

on the factory floor（在工廠樓層）
→ (A) In a production plant（在生產工廠）

### 154. 掌握意圖 難

下午 3:24，當摩拉女士寫道：「好問題」時，她最可能的意思是什麼？

(A) 克萊斯先生指出了一個重要的問題。
**(B) 她不確定要聯絡誰來修理。**
(C) 她不知道機器為何故障。
(D) 克萊斯先生提醒她有個緊急工作。

- malfunction (n.) 故障

## 155–157 合約摘錄

### 8. 行為準則

由於 [155] **博覽會主要是作為分享知識的場地，**因此參展者和它的代表人員不得在博覽會場從事銷售、接單等活動。同樣地，在合約所訂的展覽空間裡，不可以標示價格。

[156] **為了有助展場各處的參觀人潮流動順暢，**參展者不能在合約簽訂的展覽空間外安排任何公司代表或放置資料。同樣地，在展覽空間裡的人員或資料配置必須經過安排，以便吸引參觀者入內而不是塞在走道上。

就如同所有參觀者一樣，參展公司的代表必須佩戴他們的官方博覽會參展證，並一直穿著合宜的商務或商務休閒服裝。

[157] **任何參展者所進行的示範說明或其他活動，不得產生高於 85 分貝的噪音。**

參展者不得在博覽會正式結束之前就拆除他們的展示品或開始打包。

- code (n.) 規範；規則　conduct (n.) 行為
exposition (n.) 博覽會　primarily (adv.) 主要地
representative (n.) 代表　engage in 從事於
contracted (adj.) 合約簽訂的；商定的
encourage (v.) 助長；促進　exhibitor (n.) 參展者
placement (n.) 放置　credential (n.) 資格證明
generate (v.) 產生　dismantle (v.) 拆除

### 155. 確認事實與否

關於博覽會，文中說明了什麼？

**(A) 它的目的具有教育意義。**
(B) 它會占據數棟大樓。
(C) 以前曾舉辦過。
(D) 媒體從業人員免費。

**換句話說**

the exposition is primarily intended（博覽會主要作為）→ (A) Its purpose（它的目的）
the sharing of knowledge（分享知識）
→ (A) educational（具有教育意義）

### 156. 同義詞考題 

第二段第一行的「flow」，意思最接近下列何者？

(A) 順序　　(C) 數量
(B) 方向　　**(D) 循環**

### 157. 確認事實與否

關於參展者，摘錄文字中明確說明了什麼事？

(A) 他們可以使用的電量
(B) 他們可以分發的傳單種類
**(C) 他們可以發出的音量**
(D) 他們可以派出的代表人員人數

- handout (n.) 傳單　distribute (v.) 分發

**換句話說**

will not generate a noise of greater than 85 decibels（不得產生高於 85 分貝的噪音）
→ (C) The loudness of the sounds they can make（他們可以發出的音量）

## 158–161 報導

### 地方商業

（9 月 13 日）——離肯林超級賣場開幕只剩兩個星期，[158] **貝克爾特商會（BMA）已展開行動，鼓勵消費者支持本地商家。**至少有 30 家商店已在店面櫥窗掛出「跟貝克爾特買」的標誌。

[159] **就與全國各地的其他肯林據點一樣，新的貝克爾特分店占地達 18 萬平方英尺，將販售食品雜貨、衣服和電子產品，而且擁有園藝用品中心和照片沖印室。**它廣大的建築平面圖意味著，[161] **它的工程可能對陶德路施工現場附近的植物與野生動物造成傷害，而容易受到大眾的檢視。**

當時，BMA 極力勸說市議會仔細考量 [160] **肯林對另一個領域的影響——本地商業活動，差點成功阻擋開發案**。BMA 表明 [161] **肯林會造成較小的零售商店倒閉**，從長遠來看，因此使得社區難以發展。

然而，市議會比較相信肯林代表的主張，[161] **賣場會為居民創造新工作**，並讓他們享受連鎖店出名的低價，最終會讓貝克爾特受惠。

BMA 會長暨貝克爾特運動用品店老闆蘿拉．康姆斯多克表示，「跟貝克爾特買」活動「只是要求人們在購物之前想一想」，並補充道：「只要覺得有必要」就會持續下去。

- initiative (n.) 行動；計畫　location (n.) 據點
  boast (v.) 擁有（值得自豪的東西）
  photo developing (n.) 照片沖印
  be subject to 遭受　press (v.)（極力）勸說
  commerce (n.) 商業；商業活動
  retailer (n.) 零售商
  out of business 倒閉
  in the long term 從長遠來看
  ultimately (adv.) 最終

**158. 主旨或目的** 難

為何撰寫這篇報導？

**(A) 宣傳一個由本地零售商發起的活動**
(B) 說明一家全國性公司的歷史
(C) 描述一家新商店的開幕慶祝活動
(D) 邀請市民去市議會的會議

換句話說
an initiative（一個行動）→ (A) a campaign（一個活動）
the Bakert Merchants Association (BMA)（貝克爾特商會〔BMA〕）
→ (A) local retailers（本地零售商）

**159. 相關細節**

根據報導，顧客去肯林超級賣場可以做什麼？

(A) 拍一張人像照片
(B) 拿處方藥
**(C) 買造景用品**
(D) 在餐廳吃飯

- portrait (n.) 人像照片　prescription (n.) 處方

換句話說
garden supply（園藝用品）
→ (C) landscaping goods（造景用品）

**160. 同義詞考題**

第三段第三行的「area」，意思最接近下列何者？

(A) 尺寸　(C) 距離
**(B) 領域**　(D) 區域

**161. 確認事實與否** 難

文中並未提及哪個新肯林超級賣場可能造成的影響？

(A) 增加就業機會
**(B) 可買到新產品**
(C) 其他商家倒閉
(D) 對環境的傷害

換句話說
creating new jobs for its citizens
（為居民創造新工作）
→ (A) An increase in employment opportunities
（增加就業機會）
put smaller retailers out of business
（造成較小的零售商店倒閉）
→ (C) The closing of other businesses
（其他商家倒閉）
potential harm to plants and wildlife
（對植物和野生動物的可能傷害）
→ (D) Damage to the environment
（對環境的傷害）

**162–164 信件**

**摩修大學**

音樂系
K1A 4H9 安大略省渥太華市

親愛的校友與朋友們：

[164] **由於泰諾藝術基金會（TAF）所施行的「分送音樂」計畫，摩修大學過去這一年才能有新鋼琴可用。**它每年慷慨地免費提供高品質的樂器給我們學系。現在，身為參與計畫的一分子，[162] **我們要提供一些鋼琴給大眾購買。**

可供購買的鋼琴包括主要品牌製造的平臺鋼琴、直立式鋼琴和數位鋼琴。大部分都還在保固期內，而且可以在購買時當場安排運送。

欲查看並購買樂器，請在 2 月 10 日星期六下午 2 點到 6 點之間抵達藝術中心。不需預約。本中心位在肯比路，第一街和第二街中間那段。[163] **周圍的路邊停車位，費用都是每小時 2 元。或者，中心的停車場也可以付費停車。**欲知交通指南請上 www.arts-center.org。

[162] **每台鋼琴的部分收入將回捐給 TAF，用來持續「分送音樂」計畫**扮演的重要角色，讓我們得以教授高品質課程。

敬祝　安康

摩修大學
音樂學系代理主任　保羅．藍博基

- a selection of 一些　purchase (n.) 購買
  manufacturer (n.) 製造商　warranty (n.) 保固
  arrangement (n.) 安排　vicinity (n.) 附近地區
  directions (n.) 指示路徑　proceeds (n.) 收入
  instruction (n.) 教授；指導
  interim (adj.) 臨時的

**162. 主旨或目的**

這封信的主要目的是什麼？

(A) 歡迎新教職員加入一個學系
**(B) 提供一項募款義賣的細節**
(C) 感謝捐款人的贊助
(D) 宣布擴大一項計畫

---

**163. 推論或暗示**

文中提到關於藝術中心的什麼事？

(A) 週末通常閉館。
(B) 有不只一個入口。
**(C) 附近沒有免費停車位。**
(D) 由 TAF 的志工經營。

**換句話說**
in the vicinity（在周圍地區）→ nearby（附近）

---

**164. 句子插入題**

「它每年慷慨地免費提供高品質的樂器給我們學系。」最適合放在標示 [1]、[2]、[3]、[4] 的何處？

**(A) [1]**　(C) [3]
(B) [2]　(D) [4]

---

**165–167 報告摘要**

**帕德吉諾員工滿意度調查報告**

**執行摘要**

「塔優納諮詢服務」進行一項調查以評量帕德吉諾員工的工作滿意度。[166] **資料主要利用調查平台「贊斯特調查」收集而來**。調查要求員工對於諸如公司管理、工作職務和員工福利等因素的滿意度打分數。問題清單和所收集資料的詳細分析包含在這份報告的附件中。對於表示願意進一步討論他們的答案的員工，進行了四次額外訪談。為了保護這些員工的隱私，這份報告並未詳細描述這些訪談。

調查結果指出，員工對工作的大部分層面都很滿意，尤其是他們的薪水。調查中唯一有顯著負面評價的部分是對員工的支持協助。看起來 [165] **當員工在電話中遇到問題時，他們常被指示把顧客轉給經理**。在這種情況下，員工沒有學會以後要如何解決該項問題。對於這種情況，員工表示很沮喪。因此 [167] **本報告提議，定期舉行訓練課程，教導員工如何順利處理重覆發生的問題**。

- numerically (adv.) 用數字表示地
  employee benefits (n.) 員工福利
  appendix (複數 appendices) (n.) 附件；附錄
  supplementary (adj.) 額外的
  conduct (v.) 實施　aspect (n.) 方面；層面
  encounter (v.) 遇到（困難、危險等）
  recurring (adj.) 重複出現的；再次發生的

**165. 推論或暗示**

誰最有可能參與調查？

(A) 零售商店的店員
(B) 銀行行員
(C) 空服員
**(D) 電話客服中心的服務代表**

---

**166. 相關細節**

調查的資料主要如何取得？

**(A) 透過專門的軟體**
(B) 透過個別訪問
(C) 透過紙本問卷
(D) 透過焦點集團的討論

- questionnaire (n.) 問卷
  focus group (n.) 焦點團體（為聽取對某一問題、產品或政策之意見而召集來的一群人）

**換句話說**
primarily collected（主要收集）
→ mainly obtained（主要取得）
with the use of the survey platform ZestSurvey（利用調查平台「贊斯特調查」）
→ (A) Through specialized software（透過專門的軟體）

**167. 相關細節**

報告建議做什麼事？

(A) 不再服務難搞的顧客
(B) 增加員工的津貼
**(C) 持續為員工上課**
(D) 指示主管較為放鬆管理

- discontinue (v.) 停止；中斷
  compensation (n.) 津貼

換句話說
proposes（提議）→ recommend（建議）
regular training sessions be held to teach employees（定期舉行訓練課程教導員工）
→ (C) Providing ongoing instruction to staff（持續為員工上課）

**168–171 線上聊天室**

丹妮卡．費依〔上午 11:02〕
仁卓，[168] **有家律師事務所剛在我們的網站上訂了六張常春藤書桌**。我知道我們的胡桃木存貨很少，所以我想先問你一下，再告訴他們預計的送貨日。

李仁卓〔上午 11:03〕
我們剩下的胡桃木不夠做六張。[170] **有三張書桌要延後一個月出貨**。

丹妮卡．費依〔上午 11:04〕
呃，我很怕失去這個客戶。如果，我們報給他們用另一種木頭做的常春藤書桌呢？

李仁卓〔上午 11:04〕
嗯。讓我把斑塔加進來，書桌是她的團隊做的。

李仁卓〔上午 11:05〕
斑塔，[169] **還有任何其他木頭妳可以用來做常春藤書桌嗎？**我們的胡桃木幾乎用完了。

斑塔．達爾〔上午 11:07〕
[169] **橡木可以**。它也是一種硬木，而且顏色類似。

丹妮卡．費依〔上午 11:08〕
[170] **如果我們用那個，訂的貨可以像平常那樣四星期內交貨嗎？**

李仁卓〔上午 11:08〕
可以。我們的橡木很多。

丹妮卡．費依〔上午 11:09〕
[170] **那樣更好**。我會問一下，律師事務所有沒有興趣。

李仁卓〔上午 11:10〕
好，但 [171] **妳可能應該在我們的較大型胡桃木產品頁面加上「延期交貨」橫幅**。我們無法為每個客戶都客製化。

- law firm (n.) 律師事務所
  alternative (adj.) 替代的
  backordered (adj.) 延期交貨的
  custom order (n.) 訂製；客製化

**168. 相關細節**

參與聊天者的公司製造什麼？

(A) 包裝材料
(B) 汽車零件
(C) 衣服
**(D) 家具**

**169. 相關細節**

達爾女士確認了什麼？

(A) 決定配色。
**(B) 某個產品可以用另一種材料來做。**
(C) 她的團隊了解製造過程。
(D) 她下個月的時間表還有空。

- color scheme (n.) 配色

換句話說
any alternative woods（任何其他木頭）
→ (B) another material（另一種材料）

**170. 掌握意圖**

上午 11:09，當費依女士寫道：「那樣更好」，她最可能的意思是什麼？

(A) 新的樣本更有吸引力。
**(B) 生產時間較短會更好。**
(C) 有個客戶會感謝減價。
(D) 有張訂單的貨應該走陸路。

- preferable (adj.) 更好的

**171. 相關細節**

李先生建議費依女士做什麼？

**(A) 更新公司的網站**
(B) 退出談判
(C) 在商店貼出廣告
(D) 在某些商品的設計上加入一個新功能

- withdraw (v.) 退出　feature (n.) 功能

換句話說

add "backordered" banners to the pages
（在頁面加上「延期交貨」橫幅）
→ (A) Update a company Web site
（更新公司的網站）

## 172–175 報導

### 高特伍德居民將開放修復的安卓爾劇院

高特伍德　訊（6 月 22 日）——在耗費許多精力的修復工作後，高特伍德當地居民裘德．瑞格蘭表示，安卓爾劇院將在秋天重新開放，演出《遙遠的一年》。

在拉克特街一家咖啡館接受訪問時，瑞格蘭先生表示，修復劇院的想法吸引他在離開 20 年後又回到高特伍德。當他兩年前來探親時，得知安卓爾劇院即將關閉，當時他在拉提梅夫劇院擔任管理人。

「我很震驚。」他說道。這家坐落於第四街與尼可斯大道轉角的老劇院，曾是他青春歲月中深愛的地方。他回憶：「[173] **我們以前常常從位於卡爾登街的家走路過來**。在那裡觀賞《玻璃旗》那齣劇，甚至激勵了我進劇院工作。」

然而，安卓爾劇院的老闆卻指出，它已不再賺錢。因此，[172] **瑞格蘭先生以他們要求的低價買下劇院，辭去工作，然後在高特伍德市議會提供的補助款資助下，開始整修劇院。**

[175] **這項工作，他解釋道，聚焦於展現與複製它原有的設計之美。**工作人員參考劇院的舊照片。同時，也進行一些現代化的改善工程，例如：讓輪椅更容易進入。

瑞格蘭先生指出，他選擇 [174] **《遙遠的一年》，這個關於一群朋友穿越一個女巫與巨人的奇幻國度之旅的故事**，作為劇院的開幕戲是因為「它是一齣不分老少都會喜歡的戲」。他鼓勵那些有興趣參與演出或劇組工作的人，瀏覽 www.antrelltheater.com 了解更多細節。

- restore (v.) 修復（受損文物等）
  beloved (adj.) 深愛的；心愛的
  profitable (adj.) 獲利的　replicate (v.) 複製
  accessibility (n.) 容易到達
  production (n.)（戲劇）演出

### 172. 確認事實與否

關於瑞格蘭先生，報導中提到什麼？

(A) 他是劇院前老闆的朋友。
(B) 他當了 20 年的職業演員。
**(C) 他得到高特伍德市政府的資金。**
(D) 他觀賞的第一齣戲是《玻璃旗》。

- decade (n.) 十年

換句話說

a grant from the Galtwood city council
（高特伍德市議會提供的補助款）
→ (C) funding from the city of Galtwood
（高特伍德市政府的資金）

### 173. 相關細節

瑞格蘭先生年輕時住在哪裡？

(A) 拉克特街　　(C) 尼可斯大道
(B) 第四街　　**(D) 卡爾登街**

### 174. 確認事實與否

關於《遙遠的一年》，文中陳述了什麼事？

**(A) 它的劇情包含魔法元素。**
(B) 它改編自一部受歡迎的電影。
(C) 它有些角色是小孩。
(D) 瑞格蘭先生將把它的布景現代化。

換句話說

story（故事）→ (A) plot（劇情）
a fantastical land of witches and giants
（女巫與巨人的奇幻國度）
→ (A) magical elements（魔法元素）

### 175. 句子插入題

「工作人員參考劇院的舊照片。」最適合放在標示 [1]、[2]、[3]、[4] 的何處？

(A) [1]　　**(C) [3]**
(B) [2]　　(D) [4]

## 176–180 電子郵件與新聞稿

寄件人：羅多弗．艾斯科薩 <r.escorza@oqui-mail.com>
收件人：瑪賽拉．培瑞 <anb-recruiting.com>
主旨：關於：奧斯朋租車的工作機會
日期：8 月 7 日
附件：履歷表

親愛的培瑞女士：

謝謝您聯絡我。我熟知奧斯朋租車，對這個職缺很有興趣。請見我隨信附上的履歷表。這會讓您對我的職業生涯有比 [176] **您在 Exec-Link 上我的簡介裡所見**更完整的了解。

然而，我要先告訴您，我對潘尼拉的工作很滿意，如果不是非常好的機會，我不會考慮離職。這表示，它是一個我既有全球管理部門的支援，也有為美國市場做出最好決定的自主權的工作。如果 [177] **奧斯朋願意滿足這些條件**，我很樂意進一步討論這個工作。

如果您真的決定繼續考慮我的候選資格，請告訴我下一步是什麼。接下來幾天，[178] **我要離開亞特蘭大去出差**，但我會確保一直收信。

潘尼拉航空
資深營運副總裁　羅多弗・艾斯科薩　謹啟

- **opening (n.)** 職缺　**up front** 事先；預先
  **content (adj.)** 滿意的　**autonomy (n.)** 自主權
  **position (n.)** 職務；職位
  **candidacy (n.)** 候選資格
  **correspondence (n.)** （總稱）信件
  **operation (n.)** 營運

## 奧斯朋租車任命新的美國行政主管

（10 月 22 日）——奧斯朋租車已聘請羅多弗・艾斯科薩為美國的營運總監。艾斯科薩先生將接替即將退休的珍妮特・赫夫。

艾斯科薩先生在 23 年的職業生涯中，曾於許多旅遊與航空業的公司任職。在銷售消費性旅遊產品的網路公司「格洛巴斯提克」擔任資深產品經理時，他負責推出該公司受歡迎的租車預訂服務。他最近期的工作是擔任潘尼拉航空的資深營運副總裁。在這個職位上，[179] **他在不增加營運成本之下，提升了航空公司的安全等級**。

奧斯朋租車是家英國公司，四年前才打入美國市場。它現在在佛羅里達州和喬治亞州擁有 18 個據點和超過 500 輛車。[178/180] **艾斯科薩先生預期將從該公司位於亞特蘭大的總部，帶領它在美國東南部各州繼續成長並拓展到其他地區。**

- **sector (n.)** 領域；行業　**oversee (v.)** 監督
  **build up** 增強　**operational cost (n.)** 營運成本
  **headquarters (n.)** 總公司

**176. 推論或暗示**　難

艾斯科薩先生暗指培瑞女士是如何認識他的？

**(A) 透過一個網站**
(B) 透過一篇雜誌的文章
(C) 透過共同的朋友
(D) 透過研討會

- **mutual (adj.)** 共有的；共同的
  **acquaintance (n.)** 熟人；相識的人

**換句話說**
on my profile page on Exec-Link
（在 Exec-Link 上我的簡介）
→ (A) Through a Web site（透過一個網站）

**177. 同義詞考題**

在電子郵件中，第二段第四行的「meet」，意思最接近何者？

(A) 收集　(C) 圍住
(B) 表現　**(D) 實現**

**178. 整合題** 

可從文中得知關於艾斯科薩先生的什麼事？

(A) 奧斯朋租車同意為他加薪。
(B) 他的聘用過程不到兩個月。
(C) 他和培瑞女士通電話。
**(D) 他不需要搬家。**

**179. 相關細節** 

根據新聞稿，艾斯科薩先生在潘尼拉航空完成了什麼事？

(A) 減少開銷　(C) 完成新的提案
**(B) 改善安全**　(D) 乘客滿意度評等更高

**換句話說**
built up the airline's safety ratings
（提升航空公司的安全等級）
→ (B) Improvements in safety（改善安全）

**180. 確認事實與否**

關於奧斯朋租車，文中提到什麼事？

(A) 它在很多國家都有分公司。
**(B) 它企圖擴張業務。**
(C) 它的創辦人要離職。
(D) 它被另一家公司收購。

- **attempt (v.)** 企圖；嘗試　**acquire (v.)** 取得；購得

換句話說

continued growth throughout the southeastern United States and beyond（在美國東南部各州繼續成長並拓展到其他地區）
→ (B) expand（擴張業務）

## 181–185 網頁與電子郵件

www.nationalbaseballfederation.com/llions/tickets/groups

### 團體和企業的單場比賽票券方案

觀賞藍契諾獅隊的比賽，是和家人或朋友慶祝重大事件、招待客戶或對員工表達感謝的愉快方式。藍契諾球場有許多滿足團體和企業需求的便利設施，[182] **所有的方案都包含球場的停車折扣優惠**。

| 選手休息區 | 獅隊露台 |
| --- | --- |
| - 一般戶外座位區<br>- 15 元「獅幣」，可以在藍契諾球場商店使用<br>- 按票券數量收費，適用於 10 到 200 人的團體 | - [182] **戶外座位區，有桌子，視野良好**<br>- [182] **從入場到第七局享有球場內的無限飲食（熱狗、爆米花等）**<br>- 按票券數量收費，最適合 2 到 6 人的團體 |
| **快速球甲板** | [185] **鑽石休息區** |
| - 室內，非私人座位區<br>- 從入場到最後一局享有球場內的無限飲食<br>- 按票券數量收費，最適合 2 到 10 人的團體 | - [185] **室內，私人座位區**<br>-「經典」外燴套餐<br>- [185] **25 張票** |
| **全壘打套房** | |
| - 室內，本壘板後面兩個頂級位置之一的私人座位區<br>-「頂級」外燴套餐<br>- 50 張票 | |

[181] **更多資訊，請撥打接待部門的電話 (708) 555-0186，或點擊這裡進入線上聊天服務。**

- attend (v.) 出席；到場　appreciation (n.) 感謝
  an array of 一系列　amenity (n.) 便利設施
  fare (n.) 食物；飲食　admission (n.) 准許進入
  catering (n.) 外燴服務　hospitality (n.) 招待

**寄件人：**安德烈・迪加多
**收件人：**濟斯・霍特
**主旨：**要求
**日期：**7 月 15 日

濟斯：

[185] **我想要你查一下購買 8 月 4 日晚上獅隊棒球賽入場券的事**。我剛和威爾許女士通過電話，就是那一週要來訪的里歐索電器訪問團的領隊，[184] **她提到她喜歡棒球**。[183] **我對我們要行銷他們平板電腦的整合提案很有信心**，但我們也應該確保代表團在藍契諾過得愉快。

[185] **至於座位的種類，請選一個有空調的選項**，以便我們可以避開夏季的高溫。還有，[185] **當然要能容納 15 到 20 人**，因為看球的人也包括我們的員工。

請查一下有哪些方案，然後把你的建議寄給我。

謝謝。

安德烈

- delegation (n.) 代表團
  climate-controlled (adj.) 有空調的
  accommodate (v.) 能容納

### 181. 確認事實與否

關於藍契諾獅隊的接待部門，可由文中得知什麼事？

(A) 它的辦公室俯瞰藍契諾球場。
**(B) 它有提供一個線上通訊平台。**
(C) 它提供數種語言的服務。
(D) 它正在找新員工。

換句話說

its live chat service（線上聊天服務）
→ (B) an online messaging platform（線上通訊平台）

### 182. 確認事實與否

下列何者不是「獅隊露台」的好處？

(A) 免費食物
(B) 較低的停車費
**(C) 提早進入球場**
(D) 觀看球賽視野清晰

- complimentary (adj.) 贈送的

換句話說

Unlimited ballpark fare（球場內的無限飲食）
→ (A) Complimentary food（免費食物）
discounts on stadium parking（球場的停車折扣優惠）
→ (B) A lower parking fee（較低的停車費）
excellent sight lines（視野良好）
→ (C) A clear view（視野清晰）

**183. 推論或暗示**

迪加多先生最可能在哪裡工作？

(A) 體育電視台
(B) 工業用品公司
(C) 電子產品製造商
**(D) 廣告公司**

**184. 確認事實與否**

關於威爾許女士，可由文中得知什麼事？

**(A) 她是棒球迷。**
(B) 她會主持簡報。
(C) 她以前住在藍契諾。
(D) 她的生日是 8 月 4 日。

**185. 整合題**

霍特先生最可能推薦哪一種方案？

(A) 選手休息區
(B) 快速球甲板
**(C) 鑽石休息區**
(D) 全壘打套房

**186–190 網頁、工作日程表與顧客評論**

http://www.jackfogelphotography.com

**傑克．佛格攝影**

傑克．佛格攝影是郡內首屈一指的不動產攝影公司。無論您是不動產經紀人或是試圖要快快賣掉房子的私人屋主，我們都盡可能提供最高品質的照片。我們與其他地方性的不動產攝影公司不同，以下是我們所提供的服務：

- [186] **保證隔天交件**：您會在第二天收到您的照片，否則不用付費 *（[189] * **星期六來店，兩天交件**）
- [186] **便利的付款選擇**：拍照當天以信用卡或公司支票付款
- [186] **無論不動產的大小，價格固定**：詳情請上我們的價格網頁

我們的創辦人傑克．佛格仍親自執行許多拍攝工作，而我們合作的每一位攝影師都有至少十年的經驗。他們會選擇最好的角度和光線，幫助您更快賣掉房產。要看關於我們服務的評價，請上我們的推薦證言網頁。

- county (n.) 郡（美國僅次於州的行政區）
  real estate (n.) 不動產　property (n.) 房地產
  turnaround (n.) 處理時間　regardless of 不論
  testimonial (n.) 推薦；證言

**今天的拍照工作表**　　日期：[190] **8 月 23 日**

| 攝影師 | 時間 | 地址 | 照片數 | 付款方式 | 備註 |
|---|---|---|---|---|---|
| [187] **傑克．佛格** | [187] **上午 11 點** | 鄧恩街 177 號 | 25 | 信用卡 | 需外接閃光燈 |
| [187] **傑克．佛格** | [187] **下午 2 點** | 瑞耶斯大道 865 號 | 15 | 信用卡 | |
| [190] **布萊德．穆爾** | 下午 3 點 | [190] **佛爾路 262 號** | 10 | 支票 | |
| 艾倫．佐藤 | 下午 1 點 | 摩伊路 190 號 | 35 | 信用卡 | 熟客 |

- external (adj.) 外部的

http://www.jackfogelphotography.com/testimonials

**最新的客戶評價**

「身為不動產經紀人，我非常推薦這家公司。幾個星期前，[188] **我在事前很短的時間內預約拍照**，攝影師佐藤女士提早到達而且非常認真。[189] **才兩天，我就拿到了高品質的照片**，甚至還可以用公司支票付款。」

——麗莎．托拜亞斯，8 月 26 日星期二

「他們很專業但價格平實。我原本預約 10 張照片的方案，但在最後一刻，我決定拍 15 張照片。我很高興我這麼決定，[190] **攝影師穆爾先生很優秀**。[189/190] **拍完兩天後的今天，我剛收到照片**，它們看起來很棒。」

——[190] **賴瑞．霍吉斯，8 月 25 日星期一**

- with little notice 在短時間內
  affordable (adj.) 負擔得起的

**186. 確認事實與否**

何者未被列為佛格先生公司的獨有特色？

(A) 保證的交貨時間
(B) 接受的付款方式
**(C) 使用精密設備**
(D) 服務的價格結構

- sophisticated (adj.) 精密的

換句話說

next-day turnaround（隔天交件）
→ (A) guaranteed delivery times（保證交貨時間）
payment options（付款選擇）
→ (B) payment methods（付款方式）
Fixed pricing（價格固定）
→ (D) The price structure（價格結構）

**187. 推論或暗示**

在工作日程表中，關於上午 11 點的拍照工作，可看出什麼事？

(A) 它是那天量最大的工作。
(B) 它主要在室內拍攝。
(C) 它是老顧客的預約。
**(D) 它的時間不會超過三小時。**

- regular client (n.) 老顧客；熟客

---

**188. 同義詞考題**

在顧客評論中，第一段第二行的「notice」，意思最接近下列何者？

**(A) 提醒** (C) 辭職聲明
(B) 注意 (D) 公開貼文

---

**189. 整合題** 

張貼近期評價的客戶有什麼共同點？

(A) 他們的照片需要特殊編輯。
**(B) 他們的拍攝工作在星期六進行。**
(C) 他們在不動產經紀公司工作。
(D) 他們事先預付定金。

- deposit (n.) 定金；押金

---

**190. 整合題**

霍吉斯先生最可能為哪一間房子拍照？

(A) 鄧恩街 177 號 **(C) 佛爾路 262 號**
(B) 瑞耶斯大道 865 號 (D) 摩伊路 190 號

---

**191–195 使用說明與電子郵件**

特吉斯飯店

**朝陽四杯份咖啡機操作指南**

1. 將咖啡壺從電爐上取下。
2. 打開咖啡壺的蓋子，並以咖啡壺的指示線為準，倒入想要的水量。蓋上咖啡壺。
3. 把壺中的水倒入咖啡機頂部的水箱。
4. 把咖啡壺放回電爐上。
5. [192] **把濾紙放入咖啡機頂部的濾紙籃裡。**
6. 在濾紙中加入想要的咖啡粉量。我們建議每一杯咖啡需要 1 到 1.5 大匙的咖啡粉。
7. 蓋緊咖啡機的蓋子。
8. 按下「開關」按鍵，開始煮咖啡。等電源燈熄滅，再將咖啡壺從電爐取下。

[191] **在兩次使用之間必須清洗機器**，但我們請您不要嘗試自己清洗。[191] **清潔人員在每天進入房間打掃時，會清洗咖啡機。**

- instructions (n.) 操作指南；使用說明
  indicator (n.) 指示物；指標 reservoir (n.) 儲水槽
  securely (adv.) 牢固地 brew (v.) 煮（咖啡）

寄件人：維琪．史密特
收件人：崔維斯．彼得斯
主旨：咖啡機問題
日期：1 月 11 日

嗨，崔維斯：

[194] **我們收到一些關於我們透過布魯金斯有限公司購買的利文「朝陽」咖啡機的小小客訴。** 客人說，[192] **不先把濾紙籃拿出來，其實就沒辦法把濾紙放進去。** 但 [194] **我們提供的使用說明上並未明確說明這一點**，而且 [192] **濾紙有點難取出，所以客人不確定是否應該這麼做。**

[193] **我查看了商務套房的傑瑞斯家用咖啡機，以及早餐室的奎爾奇朵咖啡機的使用說明，** 得到的結果很混亂——奎爾奇朵提到要把濾紙籃取出，而傑瑞斯則沒說。但我們從來沒有收到關於傑瑞斯的抱怨。

你可以查看一下這個問題嗎？

謝謝。

維琪

- specify (v.) 明確說明

寄件人：崔維斯．彼得斯
收件人：維琪．史密特
主旨：關於：咖啡機問題
日期：1 月 12 日

嗨，維琪：

[194] **我打電話給製造商，他們證實使用說明應該明確說明那個額外步驟。** 他們覺得很抱歉，說打算修正產品的使用手冊。因此，我會把目前客房裡的使用說明換成正確的版本。

妳知道，[195] **這問題會發生，是因為我只是複製使用手冊裡的說明，而沒有真正試用。** 我們其他機器的說明都沒問題。但現在我了解那樣會有風險。我很抱歉，我不會再犯那樣的錯。

祝 好

崔維斯

- manufacturer (n.) 製造商
  apologetic (adj.) 抱歉的 current (adj.) 目前的

**191. 推論或暗示** 難

在使用說明中，暗示了朝陽咖啡機的什麼事？

(A) 它讓使用者可以調整煮咖啡的時間。
(B) 特吉斯飯店供應特殊的水給咖啡機用。
(C) 需要清洗時，它的指示燈會亮。
**(D) 特吉斯飯店預期一天只需使用咖啡機一次。**

換句話說
daily（每天的）→ (D) once per day（一天一次）

---

**192. 整合題**

史密特女士指出，使用者不確定的是哪一個步驟？

(A) 步驟二
(B) 步驟三
**(C) 步驟五**
(D) 步驟六

---

**193. 相關細節**

根據第一封電子郵件，特吉斯飯店有什麼東西？

(A) 洗衣服務
**(B) 專門用來吃早餐的地方**
(C) 分析客訴的電腦化系統
(D) 商務旅客的酬賓方案

- dedicated (adj.) 專用的

換句話說
the breakfast room（早餐室）
→ (B) A dedicated place for morning meals
（專門用來吃早餐的地方）

---

**194. 整合題**

彼得斯先生最可能聯絡哪一家公司？

**(A) 利文**
(B) 布魯金斯有限公司
(C) 傑瑞斯家用
(D) 奎爾奇朵

---

**195. 相關細節**

彼得斯先生為什麼道歉？

**(A) 自己未測試使用說明步驟**
(B) 未正確複製使用手冊的內容
(C) 沒有另外買不同的咖啡機
(D) 不理會同事的擔憂

- dismiss (v.) 對……不予理會

換句話說
without actually trying them out
（沒有真正試用）
→ (A) Not testing instructions himself
（自己未測試使用說明步驟）

---

**196–200 網頁、表格與電子郵件**

http://www.cityofrowder.gov/business/signs

**招牌規定**

羅德市的規畫開發服務局（DPDS）監管市政府關於商業招牌使用的執行規定。[196] **局內同仁致力於提供有利於商業的氣氛，同時也維持市民舒適的居住空間。**

市政府的詳細招牌法規列於此處，但為了方便閱覽，下面以簡易格式列出最常見的臨時招牌種類。

**盛大開幕招牌：**經 DPDS 批准後，新商家可以陳列宣傳開幕的招牌，最多 30 天。這是唯一准許獨立式戶外招牌的情況。

**假期宣傳招牌：**商家不需 DPDS 許可，即可陳列與耶誕節或新年有關的宣傳招牌，最多 15 天，而與其他六個特定假期有關的招牌則最多 5 天。

**其他大型宣傳橫幅：**所有其他 [197] **表面積超過 20 平方英尺的宣傳橫幅，都需要 DPDS 核准。這些橫幅一次最多可掛 14 天，一年三次。**

[200] **您不同意 DPDS 的決定嗎？點擊這裡以查明如何向市議會提出申訴。**

- regulation (n.) 規定　enforcement (n.) 執行
  favorable (adj.) 有利的　atmosphere (n.) 氣氛
  comprehensive (adj.) 詳盡的
  ordinance (n.) 法規；法令
  commercial (adj.) 商業的
  circumstance (n.) 條件　approval (n.) 批准
  promotional (adj.) 宣傳的
  file an appeal 提出申訴

羅德市
規畫開發服務局

**商業招牌許可申請**

**申請者：**蓋兒・布洛克
**地址：**48097 密西根州羅德市艾利斯路 922 號
**電話：**(810) 555-0124
**電子郵件：**gail.brock@ubi-mail.com
**店名：**閃亮寶石沙龍
**地址：**48097 密西根州羅德市緬因街 640 號
**統編：**0943-886
**計畫內容：**

[197] **我想要懸掛一個 24 平方英尺的橫幅，宣傳沙龍開業五週年及相關的促銷活動。**[198] **橫幅上會以大的字級文字顯示「閃亮寶石沙龍慶祝開業五週年」，以較小文字顯示「6 月 6 日至 8 日所有服務 85 折」**。橫幅將以粉紅色為底，字體是黑色。請見附件的實體模擬設計圖樣。我會把它掛在沙龍其中一扇窗的上半部直到 6 月 8 日止。

- mock-up (n.) 實體模型

**寄件人：**雷蒙・摩根
<ray.morgan@cityofrowder.gov>
**收件人：**蓋兒・布洛克
<gail.brock@ubi-mail.com>
**主旨：**回覆您的申請
**日期：**5 月 8 日

親愛的布洛克女士：

我很遺憾通知您，規畫開發服務局 [199] **（DPDS）無法核准您最近臨時商業招牌許可的申請。市中心商業區的市容標準不允許招牌使用明亮的顏色**（羅德市政法規 9.34.130）。[200] **請以處理過這個問題的設計，重新提出申請。**

[200] **若您對這個決定有任何問題的話，可以撥打 555-0186 給我。**

規畫開發服務局
副局長　雷蒙・摩根　謹啟

- municipal (adj.) 市的；市政的；市立的
  address (v.) 處理

**196. 確認事實與否**

關於 DPDS，網頁上陳述了什麼事？

(A) 它的員工都有很優秀的資格。
(B) 它是部門合併的結果。
**(C) 它努力滿足兩個團體的需求。**
(D) 它最近制定了新的招牌相關法令。

- merger (n.) 合併

**197. 整合題**

布洛克女士的招牌可能可以懸掛多久？

(A) 最多 5 天
**(B) 最多 14 天**
(C) 最多 15 天
(D) 最多 30 天

**198. 推論或暗示**

關於布洛克女士的店，她暗示什麼？

(A) 它出現在表格附件的照片中。
(B) 它位於十字路口。
(C) 它以前還有另一個老闆。
**(D) 它將提供顧客短期折扣優惠。**

**換句話說**
15% Off All Services June 6–8
（6 月 6 日至 8 日所有服務 85 折）
→ (D) a temporary discount（短期折扣優惠）

**199. 相關細節**

摩根先生為什麼駁回布洛克女士的申請？

(A) 設計裡缺少必要的文字。
**(B) 她招牌的顏色未遵照規定。**
(C) 城市的某一區不允許某種廣告方式。
(D) 她招牌的陳列位置未遵循安全標準。

- conform to 遵守

**換句話說**
cannot approve（無法核准）→ reject（駁回）
The city's appearance standards（市容標準）
→ (B) a regulation（規定）

**200. 整合題** 

文中未提及哪個布洛克女士可以採取的行動？

(A) 聯絡摩根先生
(B) 修改招牌的設計圖
(C) 要求市議會審查一個決定
**(D) 提出不同許可的申請**

- alter (v.) 修改；改變

換句話說

call me（打電話給我）
→ (A) Contacting Mr. Morgan（聯絡摩根先生）

a design that addresses this issue
（處理過這個問題的設計）
→ (B) Altering the plan for the sign
（修改招牌的設計圖）

file an appeal with the city council
（向市議會提出申訴）
→ (C) Asking the city council to review a decision（要求市議會審查一個決定）

# ACTUAL TEST 6

## PART 5 P. 148–150

**101. 人稱代名詞考題——主格**

潘妮洛普．史戴勒斯以她為安德魯斯廣場大樓的大廳所創作的藝術品為傲。

(A) 她的（東西） **(C) 她**
(B) 她的 (D) 她自己

- artwork (n.) 藝術品

**102. 名詞詞彙題——不定詞的受詞**

今天就打給克林特聯合事務所，安排和我們的資深律師進行初步諮詢。

(A) 顧問 (C) 諮詢
**(B) 諮詢** (D) 諮詢

- initial (adj.) 最初的
  experienced (adj.) 經驗豐富的
  attorney (n.) 律師 consult (v.) 諮詢

**103. 名詞詞彙題**

佩澤不動產的網站為每一筆列出的房地產，提供每月能源費用估算。

(A) 忠告 (C) 證據
**(B) 估算** (D) 優勢

- real estate (n.) 不動產 expense (n.) 費用；開支
  list (v.) 把……列入名單 property (n.) 房地產
  advantage (n.) 優勢；好處

**104. 介系詞詞彙題** 

多虧新的電視廣告，報名木工課的人數比上學期增加 22%。

(A) 比 (C) 遍及
(B) 在……之上 **(D) 從……**

- commercial (adj.) 商業的
  enrollment (n.) 報名人數 carpentry (n.) 木工
  semester (n.) 學期

**105. 動詞詞彙題**

麗娜．奧克斯將對迪爾福化妝品的總倉庫員工，進行本月生產力評估。

**(A) 評估** (C) 訓練
(B) 贈送 (D) 恢復

- productivity (n.) 生產力 warehouse (n.) 倉庫
  present (v.) 贈送 discipline (v.) 訓練
  resume (v.) 恢復

**106. 副詞詞彙題**

重新設計我們的網站也許有助我們吸引範圍更廣泛的客戶，因此而增加利潤。

(A) 接近地 (C) 典型地
(B) 很少 **(D) 因此**

- a broad range of . . . 範圍廣泛的……
  boost (v.) 增加；提高 profit (n.) 利潤

**107. 代名詞詞彙題**

位在緊急出口那一排的座位，是唯一配有收在扶手裡的折疊式桌面的椅子。

(A) 一些 (C) 那些人的
(B) 這些 **(D) 一些（東西）**

- emergency exit (n.) 緊急出口
  equipped with . . . 配備……
  armrest (n.) 扶手

**108. 相關連接詞詞彙題**

員工手冊提供可以接受的服裝和鞋子的指引，但沒有提到髮型。

**(A) 但是** (C) 或者
(B) 為了 (D) 甚至

- apparel (n.) 服裝

**109. 動詞詞彙題**

坐落於翡翠山山腳的賽威谷，以擁有全國最乾淨的天然泉水而自豪。

(A) 勝過 (C) 區別
(B) 強調 **(D) 以有……而自豪**

- situated (v.) 坐落在…… excel (v.) 勝過
  distinguish (v.) 區別

**110. 副詞詞彙題**

既然銀行已改用電子帳務系統，它的文具費用就明顯較低了。

(A) 非常 (C) 體貼地
(B) 沉重地 **(D) 明顯地**

- electronic billing (n.) 電子帳務系統
  heavily (adv.)（程度上）很大地；沉重地

**111. 動詞詞類變化題——語態——時態** 難

失物存放在健身房的櫃台最多兩個月，之後東西就會被丟掉。

**(A) 被丟棄**　(C) 將正被丟棄
(B) 已被丟棄　(D) 丟棄

- lost property (n.) 失物　discard (v.) 丟棄

---

**112. 動詞詞類變化題——現在分詞** 

因任何原因而辭職的所有員工，都必須交一封正式信函給人力資源部以留作紀錄之用。

(A) 辭職　**(C) 辭職**
(B) 辭職　(D) 辭職

- submit (v.) 呈遞；交出
  recordkeeping (n.) 整理儲存紀錄
  resign (v.) 辭職

---

**113. 副詞詞彙題**

飯店經理說，已經收到十則關於泳池畔整修工程噪音的投訴了。

(A) 所有的　(C) 除了
**(B) 已經**　(D) 和……一樣多

- complaint (n.) 投訴；抱怨　renovation (n.) 整修

---

**114. 形容詞詞彙題——修飾名詞** 

關於改變地區歷史的授課方式的爭議性教育，學校董事會將提案進行辯論。

(A) 爭議　**(C) 有爭議的**
(B) 有爭議地　(D) 爭議

- school board (n.) 學校董事會
  controversy (n.) 爭議

---

**115. 名詞詞彙題**

新病房以鈴木博士的名字來命名，以表彰他對醫院的重要貢獻。

(A) 關聯　**(C) 表彰**
(B) 義務　(D) 場合

- ward (n.) 病房
  name after . . . 以……的名字命名
  association (n.) 關聯　obligation (n.) 義務
  occasion (n.) 場合

---

**116. 名詞詞彙題——動名詞的受詞**

在七月離開哈丁家具執行長一職之前，葛萊迪先生會積極挑選他的繼任人選。

**(A) 繼任者**　(C) 繼任
(B) 繼任　(D) 成功

- step down 辭職；下台
  successor (n.) 繼任者　succeed (v.) 繼任

---

**117. 形容詞詞彙題**

夏天時，柯費克斯公立圖書館將放映小至三歲兒童都適合觀看的動畫電影。

**(A) 合適的**　(C) 謹慎的
(B) 相等的　(D) 暫時的

- equivalent (adj.) 相等的
  cautious (adj.) 謹慎的　tentative (adj.) 暫時的

---

**118. 介系詞詞彙題** 

為了確保有趣又輕鬆的旅程，和羅伊斯旅行社一起預約你的夏日假期吧。

(A) 到　(C) 圍繞
**(B) 和……一起**　(D) 用

- effortless (adj.) 輕鬆的；不費力的

---

**119. 動詞詞彙題**

卡羅巴製造公司實施嚴格的安全措施，防止工廠發生意外事故。

(A) 使必要　(C) 假定
(B) 生產　**(D) 實施**

- manufacturing (n.) 工業；製造業
  entail (v.) 使必要　presume (v.) 假定

---

**120. 動詞詞類變化題——語態——時態**

等工人趕來修理商店的屋頂時，大批商品已毀損。

(A) 已毀損　(C) 將被毀損
**(B) 已被毀損**　(D) 被毀損了

- merchandise (n.) 商品；貨物

---

**121. 副詞子句連接詞詞彙題**

博物館的南側廳暫時禁止遊客入內，因為正在布置新的史前化石展品。

(A) 遊覽　(C) 以便
**(B) 因為**　(D) 他們

- temporarily (adv.) 暫時地
  off-limits (adj.) 禁止進內的
  prehistoric (adj.) 史前的　fossil (n.) 化石
  exhibit (n.) 展覽品

### 122. 動詞詞類變化題——不定詞

在咖啡館的集點冊集滿 100 張貼紙的首位顧客，將得到一年份的免費咖啡。

(A) 填滿　　(C) **填滿**
(B) 正填滿　　(D) 填滿

- reward book (n.) 獎賞小冊；集點小冊

### 123. 副詞詞彙題——修飾動名詞

在新員工加入公司後，蘇萊曼先生比較喜歡親自訓練他們的顧客服務禮儀。

**(A) 親自**　　(C) 私人的
(B) 更私人的　　(D) 使具個人特色

- new hire (n.) 新員工　personalize (v.) 使個人化

### 124. 介系詞詞彙題 

被抓到在水域 50 公尺內亂丟垃圾的人，將處以 250 美元罰鍰。

(A) 在附近　　**(C) 在……範圍內**
(B) 在……期間　　(D) 在任何地方

- individual (n.) 個人　litter (v.) 亂丟垃圾
  body of water (n.) 水域；水體
  be subject to 遭受；承受　fine (n.) 罰金；罰鍰

### 125. 形容詞詞彙題——受詞補語 

曼索先生質疑，擴張是否真的能讓執行長的年度銷售目標在年底前達成。

(A) 達到　　(C) 達到
**(B) 可達到的**　　(D) 實現

- annual (adj.) 年度的；每年的

### 126. 副詞詞彙題

為了減少大眾的詢問，有些政府單位刻意不提供聯絡電話。

(A) 足夠地　　(C) 熟練地
(B) 正式地　　**(D) 刻意地**

- in an effort to . . . 為了　cut down 削減
  inquiry (n.) 詢問　proficiently (adv.) 熟練地

### 127. 名詞詞彙題 

許多速食餐廳已大幅更換菜單，以回應激增的素食者友善產品需求。

(A) 節奏　　**(C) 激增**
(B) 流動　　(D) 階段

- significantly (adv.) 顯著地　demand (n.) 需求
  vegan (n.) 嚴格素食者（不食用或不使用任何動物產品）　surge (n.) 遽增

### 128. 介系詞詞彙題

如果我們不在談判開始之前清楚定下我們的目標，我們將無法有效協商。

**(A) 在……之前**　　(C) 根據
(B) 代表……　　(D) 反對

- objective (n.) 目標　commencement (n.) 開始
  negotiation (n.) 談判；協商　bargain (v.) 協商

### 129. 名詞詞彙題——不定詞的受詞——複合名詞 難

歐文伯格新鮮空氣協會利用放置於城市各處的感應器，即時進行污染監測。

(A) 監測　　(C) 監測
(B) 監測　　**(D) 監測**

- sensor (n.) 感應器　place (v.) 放置
  carry out 進行；執行　monitor (v.) 監測

### 130. 動詞詞彙題

在音樂節的那個週末，市議會將不收取緬因街沿路的停車費。

(A) 競爭　　(C) 委派
**(B) 免除**　　(D) 彌補

- charge (n.) 費用　contend (v.) 競爭；爭奪
  delegate (v.) 委派　redeem (v.) 彌補；補救

## PART 6 P. 151–154

### 131–134 公告

**費爾法克斯公立圖書館會員請注意：**

使用圖書館的預約保留系統時，請記得書籍只在流通櫃台保留 24 小時。[131] **萬一**您沒有在那段時間之內取走預約保留的書籍，它就會被放回去，以供借閱。

[132] **有好幾種方法可以預約保留圖書館的書籍。**第一種，您可以告訴流通櫃台的人員。當您想借的書可供借閱時，會幫您將它放在一旁保管。您也可以使用館內到處都有 [133] **裝設**的資料庫終端機，或者透過我們的網站，提出預約保留的要求。

當您 [134] **預約保留**書籍時，請記住上面的時間限制。這是支持我們目標的準則之一，確保會員能享有許多不同書籍、雜誌和多媒體資料。

- bear in mind 記住
  circulation desk (n.)（圖書館的）流通櫃台
  set aside 把……放在一邊
  policy (n.) 準則；原則
  a wide selection of 各式各樣的；選擇眾多的

**131. 假設語氣——倒裝**

| | |
|---|---|
| **(A) 萬一** | (C) 然而 |
| (B) 雖然 | (D) 直到 |

**132. 句子插入題**

(A) 申請會員再簡單不過了。
(B) 我們的館藏可以親自到館內或上網瀏覽。
**(C) 有好幾種方法可以預約保留圖書館的書籍。**
(D) 請遵照這些步驟提出投訴。

- file a complaint 提出投訴

**133. 動詞詞類變化題——過去分詞** 難

| | |
|---|---|
| (A) 裝設 | (C) 裝設 |
| (B) 裝設 | **(D) 裝設** |

**134. 動詞詞彙題** 難

| | |
|---|---|
| (A) 購買 | (C) 歸還 |
| **(B) 保留** | (D) 閱讀 |

- reserve (v.) 保留；預約

**135–138 電子郵件**

**寄件者：**米娜．王
**收件者：**所有員工
**主旨：**客戶服務工作坊
**日期：**1 月 21 日

親愛的員工們：

我寫信是要提醒你們大家，關於我們 2 月 5 日第一場「與客戶積極互動（PCI）」工作坊的事。工作坊將由提姆．艾利森 [135] **主持**，他是有名的勵志演說家，也是《顧客滿意的關鍵因素》的作者。

我們已經要求艾利森先生討論能吸引、滿足及留住顧客的 [136] **最重要**態度與實施方式。由於是我們這系列的第一場，課程也會由我們的總裁霍華德．鮑亭 [137] **先**進行開場白，他會詳述工作坊的整體目標。每場工作坊的空間最多容納 100 人參加，報名將以先來先登記為原則。[138] **如果你有興趣參加，請到人事室。**

祝 好

人事部主任 米娜．王

- renowned (adj.) 有名的
  motivational (adj.) 激勵人心的
  practice (n.) 實行；實踐 retain (v.) 留住
  introductory (adj.) 介紹的
  registration (n.) 登記；報名
  first-come, first-served basis 先到先接待的準則

**135. 動詞詞類變化題——語態——時態**

| | |
|---|---|
| (A) 被主持 | (C) 正主持 |
| (B) 主持 | **(D) 將被主持** |

**136. 形容詞詞彙題——主詞補語** 難

| | |
|---|---|
| (A) 評論家 | (C) 危急地 |
| **(B) 至關重要的** | (D) 批評 |

- critically (adv.) 危急地；批評地

**137. 動詞詞彙題——過去分詞**

| | |
|---|---|
| **(A) 在……之前** | (C) 使結合 |
| (B) 主持 | (D) 記錄 |

- officiate (v.) 主持（儀式或其他公眾活動）

**138. 句子插入題** 

(A) 請放心，這些費用將用來增加你的經驗。
(B) 取消的研討會之後將補辦訓練課程。
(C) 可透過電話或電子郵件要求全額退費。
**(D) 如果你有興趣參加，請到人事室。**

- rest assured （用於安慰別人）請放心；別擔心
  enhance (v.) 增加；提高 makeup (n.) 補償；彌補

**139–142 信件**

5 月 22 日
蓋博艾拉．赫倫
93311 加州貝克斯菲爾德
戴頓大道 4827 號

親愛的赫倫女士：

謹此通知您，赫丘里斯健身中心為了擴建，預定進行整修工程。[139] **因此**，我們將從 6 月 3 日至 9 日暫停營業。我們已買下隔壁由倫提洛服飾近期空下的商用空間，將把它改成擴建的空間，主要包含許多不同規格的健身教室。[140] **這讓我們可以提供更多不同的運動課程。**本中心目前的可用空間將於 6 月 10 日上午七點如常重新開放營業，而新的空間將在下個月開始啟用。

我們為這次暫時 [142] **關閉**致歉，並感謝您的體諒。另外，我們也鼓勵您查看七月的課程表，看看新的活動課程。6 月 15 日起，可在我們的櫃檯或上網 www.herc-fitness.com/schedule 取得。

祝　萬事順心

赫丘里斯健身中心
蓋瑞．塞林格

- **please be advised that . . .** 謹此通知……；請知悉……
  **undergo (v.)** 經歷（不快的事或變化）
  **renovation (n.)** 整修　**acquire (v.)** 購得
  **adjacent (adj.)** 鄰近的　**vacate (v.)** 空出
  **specification (n.)** 規格；標準
  **offering (n.)** 課程

**139. 連接副詞**

(A) 偶爾　**(C) 因此**
(B) 在那之後　(D) 儘管如此

- **occasionally (adv.)** 偶爾

---

**140. 句子插入題**

**(A) 這讓我們可以提供更多不同的運動課程。**
(B) 有越來越多人改為較健康的生活方式。
(C) 現有停車場已不再有足夠的空間。
(D) 本地刊物盛讚我們機構。

- **sufficient (adj.)** 足夠的
  **publication (n.)** 刊物；出版物

---

**141. 名詞詞彙題——介系詞的受詞** 難

(A) 使用　(C) 使用
**(B) 使用**　(D) 使用者

---

**142. 名詞詞彙題**

(A) 搬遷　(C) 壅塞
(B) 疏忽　**(D) 關閉**

- **relocation (n.)** 搬遷　**negligence (n.)** 疏忽；粗心
  **congestion (n.)** 壅塞

---

**143–146 報導**

**密德蘭生物科學任命新研發總監**

密德蘭生物科學公司 143 **已選出**研發部的克里佛德．麥克斯威爾擔任公司的研發部新總監。這家生質燃料製造商昨天在它網站的一篇貼文中，宣布麥克斯威爾先生的 144 **任命**消息。文中引述密德蘭執行長艾倫．史坦的話：「我很榮幸歡迎麥克斯威爾先生加入我們的行政管理團隊。他的專長將使我們得以成功 145 **達成**我們的研發目標。」

根據網站的貼文，麥克斯威爾先生在獲得生物科技博士學位後不久即加入密德蘭公司。146 **雖然他一開始擔任初級研究員，但那個職位並沒有做太久**，由於他的勤奮與創新想法，他在公司的升遷管道內穩定往上爬升，在他即將於 12 月 10 日就任的新角色上，麥克斯威爾先生將決定並執行密德蘭的研發目標。

- **bioscience (n.)** 生物科學　**biofuel (n.)** 生質燃料
  **quote (v.)** 引述　**expertise (n.)** 專長
  **earn (v.)** 獲得　**doctoral degree (n.)** 博士學位
  **diligence (n.)** 勤奮　**assume (v.)** 就任
  **implement (v.)** 執行

**143. 動詞詞類變化題——語態——時態**

(A) 挑選　(C) 被選出
**(B) 已選出**　(D) 挑選

---

**144. 名詞詞彙題**

(A) 退休　(C) 倡議
(B) 候選資格　**(D) 任命**

- **retirement (n.)** 退休　**candidacy (n.)** 候選資格
  **initiative (v.)** 倡議

---

**145. 動詞詞類變化題——介系詞＋動名詞** 難

(A) 達成……的那個　**(C) 達成**
(B) 藉由……達成　(D) ……的達成

---

**146. 句子插入題** 難

(A) 這個行動反映出公司想變得更有效率的目標。
**(B) 雖然他一開始擔任初級研究員，但那個職位並沒有做太久。**
(C) 董事會正進行大規模的搜尋，以找到接替他的人選。
(D) 他的最新研究計畫得到許多業界人士的注意。

- **streamlined (adj.)** 優化效率後的
  **extensive (adj.)** 大規模的
  **replacement (n.)** 接替

## PART 7 P. 155–175

### 147–148 邀請函

邀請您觀賞一場只在薩利斯伯利烹飪學院才有的廚藝示範！

客座主廚：

**古斯塔夫．佩洛特**

紐約市五星級餐廳「鷓鴣小館」老闆

佩洛特主廚將於 6 月 14 日上午 9:15 至 11:45 在三號廚藝教室示範如何像專家一樣熟練地準備多道地中海料理。

[147] **這次示範是特別為目前註冊本學院高階烹飪課程的學生所安排。**[148] **場地僅限 250 人**，你必須在 6 月 8 日之前，和行政辦公室的伊布拉欣女士確認你的出席意願。

- exclusive (adj.) 獨有的 culinary (adj.) 烹飪的 expertly (adv.) 像專家地；熟練地 Mediterranean (adj.) 地中海的 enroll (v.) 註冊 advanced (adj.) 高階的

**147. 推論或暗示**

這份邀請最可能想發給誰？

(A) 烹飪教師 **(C) 有抱負的廚師**
(B) 美食評論家 (D) 餐廳的客人

- aspiring (adj.) 有抱負的

**換句話說**

those currently enrolled in the institute's advanced cooking courses
（目前註冊學院高階烹飪課程的學生）
→ (C) Aspiring cooks（有抱負的廚師）

**148. 確認事實與否**

關於這項活動，可由文中得知什麼？

(A) 每年都有。
(B) 出席者將參與活動。
(C) 將在下午結束。
**(D) 入場人數有限。**

- restricted (adj.) 受限制的

**換句話說**

limited（有限的）→ (D) restricted（受限制的）

### 149–150 優惠券

**里亞爾托寵物市場**

里亞爾托寵物市場想要答謝我們的忠實顧客，作為我們十週年慶祝活動的一部分。從 3 月 1 日到 3 月 14 日，[150] **您可以將這張優惠券交給任何一位收銀員，購物滿 50 元以上，就可以折抵 15 元。**[149] **這張優惠券不能兌現、無法在自動結帳機使用**，並將於 3 月 14 日晚上九點到期。完整的條款與條件，請上 www.rialtopetmart.ca/voucher。

- reward (v.) 獎勵 checkout operator (n.) 收銀員 terms and conditions (n.) 條款與條件

**149. 確認事實與否**

文中提到關於里亞爾托寵物市場的什麼事？

(A) 最近開了新分店。
(B) 目前正在徵收銀員。
(C) 它經營酬賓專案。
**(D) 它有自助結帳機。**

**換句話說**

automated checkout kiosks（自動結帳機）
→ (D) self-checkout machines（自助結帳機）

**150. 相關細節**

為了使用折價券，顧客必須做什麼？

**(A) 消費最低金額**
(B) 去店裡兩次
(C) 把它拿給店經理
(D) 在網頁上啟用它

**換句話說**

any purchase valued at $50 or more
（購物滿 50 元以上）
→ (A) Spend a minimum amount
（消費最低金額）

### 151–152 文字訊息串

蘇西．利維〔下午 2:04〕
秀夫，你還在下面三樓嗎？

藤田秀夫〔下午 2:05〕
是的，會議剛結束。妳需要什麼嗎？

蘇西．利維〔下午 2:06〕
[151] **我正試著要在我電腦上安裝那個新的平面設計軟體套件，但我遇到問題。**我本來希望你可以找到那個推薦這套軟體給我的人。

藤田秀夫〔下午 2:07〕
是我們公司這裡的人嗎？

蘇西．利維〔下午 2:08〕
是的，[152] **網站設計團隊的那位高個子**。

藤田秀夫〔下午 2:10〕
[152] **我們的網站設計團隊相當龐大。**

蘇西．利維〔下午 2:11〕
噢，抱歉。[152] **他留著金色短髮，可能是新來的。**

藤田秀夫〔下午 2:13〕
我想我知道妳說的是誰，他叫克里斯，對嗎？

蘇西．利維〔下午 2:14〕
對，聽起來是的！請他無論何時有空，就來我辦公室一下。謝了，秀夫。

- suite (n.)（電腦）軟體套件
  blond(e) (adj.) 金色頭髮的

**151. 相關細節**

利維女士的問題是什麼？

(A) 她開會要遲到了。
(B) 一個電子裝置無法開啟。
**(C) 她無法安裝某個軟體。**
(D) 有些圖像讓人看不懂。

**換句話說**
set up that new graphic design suite
（安裝那個新的平面設計軟體套件）
→ (C) install some software（安裝某個軟體）

**152. 掌握意圖**

下午 2:10，當藤田先生寫道：「我們的網站設計團隊相當大」，他意指什麼？

(A) 不需要僱用新員工。
**(B) 他需要更詳細的描述。**
(C) 他擔心某個空間的大小。
(D) 團隊裡的某個人很可能有某種技術。

**153–154 廣告**

**光亮洗車**
48213 蘭辛市金士曼街 3476 號

**試試我們的新型豪華洗車以及優質細緻洗車服務！**

**豪華洗車**
每車 25 元，約需 15 分鐘
- 預洗、清洗底盤、清洗外表
- 機器吹乾加上手工軟布擦乾

**優質細緻洗車**
每車 35 元，約需 45 分鐘
- 全車內裝清潔（以 X 壓力空氣技術去除所有縫隙和裂縫的灰塵和髒污）
- 保養座椅椅面並清洗鋪有地毯的區域
- 以手工打上 [154] **「X 聚合物」蠟，給車子烤漆最佳的保護及光澤**

[153] **若要求豪華洗車與優質細緻洗車套裝服務，只要 50 元！**

- approximately (adv.) 大約
  undercarriage (n.)（汽車的）底盤
  manual (adj.) 手工的　crevice (n.) 縫隙
  crack (n.) 裂縫
  condition (n.) 保養（髮質、皮膚等）
  upholstery (n.) 座椅椅面
  carpet (v.) 在……上鋪地毯
  supreme (adj.) 頂級的　on request 根據要求

**153. 確認事實與否**

關於光亮洗車，可由文中得知什麼？

(A) 它的豪華洗車需半小時。
**(B) 綜合服務有折扣。**
(C) 它專門服務某種汽車。
(D) 它販售某些清潔產品。

**換句話說**
Deluxe Wash + Premium Detailing Package Deal（豪華洗車與優質細緻洗車套裝服務）
→ (B) combined services（綜合服務）

**154. 相關細節**

產品「X 聚合物」用來做什麼？

(A) 保養汽車的內裝
(B) 除去汽車車窗上的水
**(C) 保護汽車的烤漆**
(D) 去除車子外表的髒污

**換句話說**
wax for supreme paint protection
（給車子烤漆最佳保護的蠟）
→ (C) Protecting a vehicle's paint job
（保護汽車的烤漆）

## 155–157 公告

**親愛的馬提諾健康食品顧客：**

過去五年來，我們老闆迪諾．馬提諾和馬提諾健康食品的其他團隊成員很高興在我們位於哈里遜街的店面為您服務，但現在該是改變的時候了。自從我們擴大進貨範圍，納入有機食品雜貨後，[156] **我們就一直努力要趕上需求。您可能已經注意到結帳的隊伍越來越長**，而且我們幾乎無法應付我們每天接到的市中心訂單數量。

因此，[155] **我們將在 7 月 1 日搬到市中心一棟較大的大樓**，如此一來，我們可以增加我們的庫存量，並能更有效率地服務顧客。更好的新馬提諾健康食品將坐落於舒拉許路 411 號。

別擔心，所有顧客的會員資格和獎勵仍然有效且不變。關於搬遷的更多細節將透過我們的每月通訊提供。[157] **如果您還沒有收過通訊，請到顧客服務中心訂閱**。

感謝您！

- stock (v.) 進貨　struggle to 努力
  keep up with 趕上；跟上　demand (n.) 需求
  barely (adv.) 幾乎沒有　cope with 處理
  rest assured that . . . 別擔心；請放心

### 155. 主旨或目的

這則公告的目的是什麼？

(A) 宣傳一種新商品
**(B) 宣布商店搬遷**
(C) 介紹新老闆
(D) 提供即將進行的整修工程細節

**換句話說**
move to a larger building（搬到一棟較大的大樓）→ (B) the store's relocation（商店搬遷）

### 156. 推論或暗示 難

關於馬提諾健康食品，下列何者最可能為真？

(A) 它徵求員工的意見回饋。
(B) 它是家族經營的企業。
(C) 它正經歷財務困難。
**(D) 它越來越受歡迎。**

- solicit (v.) 徵求
  financial (adj.) 財政的；金融的

### 157. 相關細節

這則公告鼓勵某些讀者做什麼？

**(A) 登記接收定期郵件**
(B) 推薦朋友加入會員
(C) 參加盛大開幕活動
(D) 快點使用紅利點數

**換句話說**
subscribe（訂閱）→ (A) sign up（登記）
the newsletter（通訊）→ (A) a regular mailing（定期郵件）

## 158–160 新聞稿

**聰明玩玩具公司官方新聞稿**

聰明玩得知最近有些報導和傳聞指出，本公司某一玩具系列的材質與做工低劣。可以理解的是，這些傳聞導致 [158] **許多顧客聯絡我們，詢問那些玩具是否真的品質較差，而且有些人還要求退款**。有爭議的系列是我們最近發行的 [159] **銀河海盜玩具系列，包含來自同名電視動畫節目的可動式玩偶和車輛**。在網路上流傳的謠言指出這些玩具在海外製造，由於結構粗糙和廉價塑膠之故，因此很容易斷掉，這已造成銷售額明顯下滑，而且 [159] **有好幾個網站甚至移除了我們這系列玩具的廣告**。

雖然，[159/160] **這些玩具的確是由一家國外的工廠所生產，**[160] **但聰明玩和工廠老闆密切合作，以確保使用高級原料，並遵守正確的生產步驟。**事實上，我們每週針對生產線執行品質保證檢查。我們可以明確聲明，這些玩具是由專業人員組裝，並且極為耐用。今早，我們在我們的網站上發布了一段影片，顯示銀河海盜玩具的完整製作過程。我們向所有顧客保證，聰明玩仍會盡全力生產市面上最好的玩具。

- workmanship (n.) 做工；手藝
  inferior (adj.) 較差的　circulate (v.) 流傳
  noticeable (adj.) 顯著的
  adhere to 遵守　unequivocally (adv.) 明確地
  assemble (v.) 組裝　committed to 致力於

### 158. 主旨或目的

這篇新聞稿的目的是什麼？

(A) 新系列玩具上市　(C) 描述如何獲得退款
(B) 發出產品召回令　**(D) 處理顧客的憂慮**

- obtain (v.) 獲得

### 159. 確認事實與否 難

文中並未提到關於銀河海盜玩具的什麼事？

(A) 它們是在不同國家生產的。
**(B) 它們已停產。**
(C) 它們曾在網路上廣告。
(D) 它們是根據某個娛樂媒體而製造的。

- discontinue (v.) 停止

**換句話說**

produced . . . overseas（在國外……生產）
→ (A) manufactured in a different country（在不同國家生產的）
Web sites（網站）→ (C) online（網路上）
the animated television show（電視動畫節目）
→ (D) some entertainment media（某個娛樂媒體）

### 160. 句子插入題 難

「事實上，我們每週針對生產線執行品質保證檢查。」最適合放在標示 [1]、[2]、[3]、[4] 的何處？

(A) [1]　　**(C) [3]**
(B) [2]　　(D) [4]

### 161–163 電子郵件

**寄件人：**琪娜妮．烏曼
**收件人：**全體員工
**主旨：**員工推薦獎金
**日期：**6 月 29 日

嗨，大家好：

由於 [161] **我們接受瑞博汀集團資金的條件之一是必須快速增加人力**，看起來似乎是提醒所有人我們員工推薦獎金計畫的好時機。員工順利為一個職缺推薦人選，就有權利得到 500 元獎金。如果你們有興趣參加，請定期查看我們網站上的「工作」頁面。

請注意，很重要的是，你們只能推薦符合該職缺所有條件的人。我們今年初制定了新的分級獎金系統，[162] **以削減無用的推薦**。你們可能還記得，發放推薦獎金必須分階段：

- [163] **當被推薦人獲選參加面對面的面試時，先發 20%**
- [163] **當應徵者被錄取時，再另發 30%**
- 經過 90 天後，當新進人員仍在職時，發放剩下的 50%

更多計畫詳情，請見員工手冊第 28 頁，包括如何提出推薦人選的說明。任何手冊中未包含的問題，可以打電話（分機 233）或寄電子郵件給我。

謝謝。

帕東多科技
人力資源總監　琪娜妮．烏曼

- referral (n.) 介紹；推薦
  entitle (v.) 給……權力或資格
  candidate (n.) 應徵者　qualification (n.) 資格
  institute (v.) 制定　tiered (adj.) 分層的
  entail (v.) 使必要

### 161. 確認事實與否 難

關於帕東多科技，可由文中得知什麼事？

**(A) 它最近吸引到外部資金。**
(B) 網站上已新增一個網頁。
(C) 它的員工手冊以電子版發放。
(D) 它今年第一次實施推薦獎金制。

- distribute (v.) 分發　implement (v.) 執行

**換句話說**

the funding we received from Ribdins Group（我們接受瑞博汀集團資金）
→ (A) outside investment（外部資金）

### 162. 推論或暗示 

烏曼女士暗示，過去的計畫有什麼問題？

(A) 透過錯誤的管道提出推薦人選
(B) 被推薦的人同質性太高
**(C) 為不適合的人選背書**
(D) 遲發獎金

- diversity (n.) 多樣性
  endorsement (n.) 背書；支持

### 163. 相關細節 

推薦人何時會剛好拿到一半獎金？

(A) 在完成應徵後
(B) 在已提出面對面的面試後
**(C) 在接受工作機會後**
(D) 在通過試用期後

- probationary (adj.) 試用的

**換句話說**

the candidate is hired（應徵者被錄取）
→ (C) a job offer has been accepted（接受工作機會）

## 164–167 線上聊天室

莉亞·楊〔下午 1:04〕
韋德和烏蘇拉，你們有空嗎？[164] **管理部剛剛告訴我，他們選了兩個新的目的地，要我們放進下一套歐洲探險家旅遊書中**——一個國家和一個城市。

韋德·柯賓〔下午 1:08〕
太好了！是哪裡？

莉亞·楊〔下午 1:10〕
[165] **他們想要關於盧森堡的完整指南，以及關於威尼斯的城市指南口袋書。**

烏蘇拉·艾瑞克森〔下午 1:11〕
噢，我在盧森堡住過很久，那是個令人讚嘆的地方。

莉亞·楊〔下午 1:14〕
的確是。那麼，[166] **我們要派兩名實地考察員從 5 月 1 日到 6 月 29 日待在盧森堡，一名從 6 月 1 日到 6 月 30 日在威尼斯**。我們會在七月的第一個星期收到他們所有的筆記，然後在預定出版和上市日之前，我們有大約一個月可以編輯資料。

烏蘇拉·艾瑞克森〔下午 1:16〕
那我們的時間相當充足。[167] **我這星期可以開始設計每一本的版面**，這樣一來，我們就能為書的編輯階段做好萬全準備。

韋德·柯賓〔下午 1:22〕
我不確定這是明智的作法，烏蘇拉。[167] **記得保加利亞那本嗎？**

烏蘇拉·艾瑞克森〔下午 1:23〕
[167] **有道理，韋德。我這次會等一等，看管理部到底想要書中包含什麼內容。**

莉亞·楊〔下午 1:25〕
聽起來不錯。好，等我明天和管理部開完會，我會給你們更多資訊。

- assignment (n.)（分派的）任務；工作

### 164. 主旨或目的

楊女士為何送出第一則訊息給她的同事？

(A) 詢問他們對競爭提案的意見
(B) 建議他們的出版品做些修改
(C) 感謝他們在一項專案的付出
**(D) 讓他們知道未來的工作**

- executive (n.) 行政主管

### 165. 推論或暗示

關於威尼斯的書，可由文中得知什麼？

(A) 會在 7 月出版。
**(B) 會是小巧型的書。**
(C) 是修訂過的版本。
(D) 是柯賓先生的工作。

- revised (adj.) 經過修訂的

**換句話說**
pocket-sized（口袋版的）→ (B) compact（小巧型的）

### 166. 相關細節

楊女士提供了什麼資訊？

(A) 某些考察人員的資格
(B) 某些作品的最大篇幅
**(C) 某些旅程的持續時間**
(D) 某些編輯的原因

### 167. 掌握意圖

下午 1:22，當柯賓先生寫道：「記得保加利亞那本嗎」，他的意思最可能為何？

(A) 艾瑞克森女士有另一項任務必須趕快完成。
(B) 艾瑞克森女士對一本新書成功的期待太高了。
(C) 艾瑞克森女士可以參考現有的版型。
**(D) 艾瑞克森女士不應該又太早開始某個工作流程。**

- template (n.) 範本，樣板

## 168–171 報導

**今年英國建築獎得主揭曉**

倫敦　訊（12 月 15 日）——今年，聲譽卓著的英國建築獎從大約 250 件決選作品中選出的 50 件非凡建築，贏得最富創新精神建築物獎，它們均出自英國建築師或事務所設於英國的外國建築師之手。邁入第 22 年的[168] **英國建築獎，今年與倫敦建築與設計博物館及英國城市規畫與藝術中心聯合頒發獎項**，他們表彰這些建築師設計出在許多方面形塑我們生活的卓越當代建築物，包括摩天大樓、企業總部、橋樑、公園涼亭、醫院、私人住宅和學術機構。

名列今年最大贏家的包括 [171] **賽門．索普的曼特蘭街汽車停車場**，這是一座位於曼徹斯特市中心迷人的停車場，擁有 9 層樓、768 個車位和許多環保功能；馬科斯．佛萊爾的水平橋，[169] **一座 195 公尺長、令人屏息的行人專用橋，裝設了獨一無二的 4,500 顆與音樂同步閃爍的 LED 星星**，還有 [170] **伊索貝兒．麥克杜夫的尖塔，一棟靠近愛丁堡繁忙購物區的優雅 28 層樓公寓大樓**，屋頂上有溫水游泳池。

一如之前幾年，由於得獎人數眾多，[170] **獎項頒發自 12 月 12 日星期五到 12 月 14 日星期日，經過三個晚上和三場典禮**。開幕夜頒發企業與商業類獎項，[170] **星期六的獎項頒給住宅與都市規畫類**，而最後一晚則表揚機構類。[171] **曼特蘭街停車場創下先例，成為第一個在同一年為建築師贏得兩個獎項的建築**：一個是城市規畫類，以及年度最創新設計獎的最高榮譽。

- **extraordinary** (adj.) 非凡的
  **shortlisted** (adj.) 列入決選名單的
  **prestigious** (adj.) 聲譽卓著的
  **innovative** (adj.) 創新的；富創新精神的
  **architecture** (n.) 建築學；建築風格
  **architect** (n.) 建築師 **recognize** (v.) 表彰；表揚
  **contemporary** (adj.) 當代的
  **skyscraper** (n.) 摩天大樓
  **corporate** (adj.) 公司的
  **pavilion** (n.)（公園、花園中的）涼亭
  **residence** (n.) 住宅
  **breathtaking** (adj.) 令人屏息的
  **pedestrian** (n.) 行人 **synchronize** (v.) 使同步
  **sheer** (adj.) 完全的（用以強調某物的數量或程度）

### 168. 確認事實與否

文中提到關於英國建築獎的什麼事？

**(A) 兩個組織合作頒獎。**
(B) 獎項有巨額獎金。
(C) 近期更新了獎項類別。
(D) 只有英國公民有資格獲獎。

- **collaborate** (v.) 合作 **eligible** (adj.) 有資格的

**換句話說**

**jointly presented by the London Museum of Architecture & Design and the British Centre for Urban Planning & Art**（與倫敦建築與設計博物館及英國城市規畫與藝術中心聯合頒發獎項）
→ **(A) Two organizations collaborate to issue**（兩個組織合作發）

### 169. 相關細節

根據報導，佛萊爾先生的設計有什麼特別？

(A) 與商業區整合 **(C) 結合光與聲音**
(B) 環保功能 (D) 令人印象深刻的高度

- **integration** (n.) 整合

**換句話說**

**4,500 blinking LED stars synchronized with music**（4,500 顆與音樂同步閃爍的 LED 星星）
→ **(C) combination of light and sound**（結合光與聲音）

### 170. 推論或暗示 

麥克杜夫女士最可能在何時領獎？

(A) 12 月 12 日 (C) 12 月 14 日
**(B) 12 月 13 日** (D) 12 月 15 日

### 171. 推論或暗示

關於索普先生，可由文中得知什麼？

(A) 他以前得過獎。
(B) 他在星期六頒獎。
(C) 他得到終身成就獎。
**(D) 他今年得到兩個獎。**

**換句話說**

**win its architect two awards in the same year**（在同一年為建築師贏得兩個獎項）
→ **(D) He received two awards this year.**（他今年得到兩個獎。）

### 172–175 電子郵件

**收件人：**連恩．高德曼 <lgoldman@whizzomail.net >
**寄件人：**崔美京 <mkchoi@summitsc.com>
**主旨：**火花輕型營火爐
**日期：**9 月 6 日

親愛的高德曼先生：

我很興奮收到 [172] **您最近申請到專利發明的**新聞資料袋。「火花輕型營火爐」看起來很棒，而且一定是我們會很有興趣在頂峰運動 & 露營商店銷售的產品。[172] **我們喜愛它輕便可攜帶，以及可選擇以太陽能充電**。然而，我有幾個關於設計的問題。首先，[175] **您可以再說明一下空氣噴嘴如何把氧氣抽入木頭燃起的火堆中嗎？**我們有些關於這個機械安全

的小小疑慮。還有，172 **資料袋中概述了火焰的強度可以透過智慧型手機的應用程式來控制**，這個應用程式相容於哪些作業系統？

雖然我很希望您儘快回答那些簡單的問題，但我也希望您能帶一個營火爐親自造訪我們總公司。我相信您知道，我們的行政主管比較喜歡在同意合約進行購買並銷售新產品前，先親眼看到新產品的使用狀況。173 **如果您可以參加 9 月 13 日下午兩點的會議，我們將不勝感激。您將有一個小時的時間展示這個裝置的用途與性能。**

根據產品規格和您寄給我的照片來看，更別提 174 **您的露營爐和多功能冷藏箱到現在仍名列我們的暢銷產品中**，我有信心，我們會決定進火花輕型營火爐。期待收到您的回音。

頂峰運動＆露營
採購部主管　崔美京　謹啟

- patented (adj.) 取得專利的
  portability (n.) 輕便；可攜帶
  air jet (n.) 空氣噴嘴
  pump (v.) 抽送（液體或氣體）
  intensity (n.)（電、熱、光等的）強度
  operation system (n.) 作業系統
  compatible with 與……相容
  at one's earliest convenience 儘快
  executive (n.) 行政主管
  firsthand (adv.) 直接地；第一手地
  allot (v.) 分配　multifunctional (adj.) 多功能的

**172. 確認事實與否** 難

關於火花輕型營火爐，下列何者非真？

(A) 可以使用再生能源。
(B) 方便運送。
(C) 連結行動裝置。
**(D) 正在等待專利批准。**

- renewable (adj.)（能源）可再生的

**換句話說**
solar charging（太陽能充電）
→ (A) renewable energy（再生能源）
portability（輕便可攜帶）
→ (B) easy to transport（方便運送）
be controlled via smartphone app
（透過智慧型手機的應用程式來控制）
→ (C) connects to mobile devices
（連結行動裝置）

**173. 相關細節** 難

崔女士要求高德曼先生做什麼？

**(A) 現場示範**
(B) 寄一個原型來
(C) 建議合約條款
(D) 造訪生產工廠

- prototype (n.) 原型

**換句話說**
showcase the device's functions and capabilities（展示這個裝置的用途與性能）
→ (A) Give a live demonstration（現場示範）

**174. 推論或暗示**

關於頂峰運動＆露營，可由文中得知什麼？

(A) 它計劃擴大運動服飾的品項。
(B) 是高德曼先生的前雇主。
**(C) 它供應高德曼先生設計的其他產品。**
(D) 它已下訂火花輕型營火爐的第一批訂單。

**換句話說**
are . . . among our top sellers（名列我們的暢銷產品中）→ (C) stocks（供應）
your camping stove and multifunctional cooler（您的露營爐和多功能冷藏箱）
→ (C) other products created by Mr. Goldman（高德曼先生設計的其他產品）

**175. 句子插入題**

「我們有些關於這個機械安全的小小疑慮。」
最適合放在標示 [1]、[2]、[3]、[4] 的何處？

(A) [1]　　(C) [3]
**(B) [2]**　　(D) [4]

**176–180 廣告與報名表**

**新創公司的成長策略**

你是否想要你的新公司成長、進步，但不確定要從哪裡著手？富爾布里其成長策略公司正是你該來的地方。我們提供一系列對新手老闆有幫助的研討會。176 **每一場的教授內容結合了經由數十年實務專業工作得來的智慧，以及對最新管理技巧與趨勢的了解。**以下是我們今年秋天將提供課程的實例：

---

**一起來**（研討會編號 #1809）
—費用：48 元
這個研討會提供 [177] **許多鼓勵員工一起有效工作的策略**。
➥9 月 3 日星期三上午 10 點至 12 點，主大樓 204 室

---

[179] **未來的市場（研討會編號 #3487）**
**—費用：95 元**
這個研討會提供如何為你的產品或服務吸引更多不同客戶的建議。
➥9 月 24 日星期三上午 10 點至下午 3 點，訓練中心 3 室

---

**開拓你的視野**（研討會編號 #2276）
—費用：149 元
這個研討會提供老闆 [177] **在打算開新分店時，要考慮什麼的必要祕訣**。
➥10 月 15 日星期三上午 10 點至下午 4 點，主大樓 206 室

---

**同步前進**（研討會編號 #3785）
—費用：109 元
這個研討會 [177] **介紹受歡迎的員工福利，例如** [177/178] **彈性上班時間，並解釋如何執行**。
➥11 月 5 日星期三上午 10 點至下午 4 點，訓練中心 4 室

更多詳情請上 www.fulbridge-gs.com。

- strategy (n.) 策略　novice (n.) 新手
  hands-on (adj.) 親身實踐的
  cutting-edge (adj.) 最新的；尖端的
  implement (v.) 執行

**富爾布里其成長策略——研討會報名表**

姓名：　羅賓．布基
地址：　98121 華盛頓州西雅圖市
　　　　巴勒克大道 84 號
電話：　555-0139
電子郵件：r.booky@globenet.net
研討會編號：[179] **#3487**
付款方式：銀行轉帳
意見：　我真的很期待九月時在你們訓練中心參加我的第一場富爾布里其研討會。[179] **我已按照要求將 59 元報名費匯到你們公司的帳號**，我唯一擔心的是我可能無法在早上十點前到中心，因為我住得很遠。[180] **如果有人能透過電子郵件告訴我，這是否會是個大問題，我會很感謝**。謝謝你。

- registration (n.) 註冊

**176. 推論或暗示**　難

關於富爾布里基成長策略，可由文中得知什麼？

(A) 它的網站上提供教材樣本。
**(B) 它的講師擁有商業實務經驗。**
(C) 若提出要求，它提供的課程可以客製化。
(D) 它每季舉辦同樣一套研討會。

**換句話說**
hands-on professional work（實務專業工作）
→ (B) practical business experience
（商業實務經驗）

---

**177. 確認事實與否** 

表列的研討會未涵蓋什麼主題？

**(A) 對顧客的採購決定提出建議**
(B) 培養員工間的團隊合作
(C) 增加公司的新工作場地
(D) 給員工某些福利

**換句話說**
encouraging your employees to work together
（鼓勵員工一起工作）
→ (B) Fostering teamwork between employees
（培養員工間的團隊合作）
to open a new branch（開新分店）
→ (C) Adding new work sites（增加新工作場地）
popular employee perks（受歡迎的員工福利）
→ (D) certain benefits to staff（給員工某些福利）

---

**178. 同義詞考題**

在廣告中，第五段第二行的「flexible」，意思最接近何者？

(A) 逐漸的　　(C) 可彎曲的
(B) 服從的　　**(D) 可變動的**

**179. 整合題**

布基先生最可能誤看了什麼資訊？

(A) 研討會的地點
**(B) 研討會的費用**
(C) 研討會的月分
(D) 研討會開始的時間

**180. 相關細節** 難

布基先生要求富爾布里基成長策略做什麼？

**(A) 確定一項風險的嚴重性**
(B) 一項規定的特例
(C) 彙整一些替代的選項
(D) 定期更新一個狀況

- seriousness (n.) 嚴重性　compile (v.) 彙整
  alternative (adj.) 替代的

換句話說
whether this would be a major problem
（這是否會是個大問題）
→ (A) the seriousness of a risk
（一項風險的嚴重性）

**181–185 手冊資訊與顧客評論**

卡斯特蘭特倉儲公司
家用儲藏空間

卡斯特蘭特家用儲藏空間有各種尺寸，租用期可以短到兩個星期，或你想要多長就多長。[181] **每一間儲藏室都在一樓，方便裝卸貨，而且有自己的警報器和攝影機。**[181] **你保管自己那間儲藏室的鑰匙，這樣就能在一星期的任何一天、任何時間拿取你的東西。**而且，[181] **我們內建的冷暖氣系統，能確保你的儲藏室絕對不會熱到或冷到有危險的程度。**

| 空間類型 | 尺寸 | 週／月費* | 適用於： |
|---|---|---|---|
| A | 13.6 平方公尺 | 52／208 英鎊 | 三房住家的物品 |
| B | 6.7 平方公尺 | 32／128 英鎊 | 單房公寓的物品 |
| [183] **C** | 3.4 平方公尺 | 18／72 英鎊 | [183] **幾件家具** |
| D | 1.6 平方公尺 | 10／40 英鎊 | 一些箱子 |

* 另需訂金 50 英鎊。如果在租用期滿時，[182] **卡斯特蘭特倉儲公司發現租用的空間骯髒或受損，可能會扣留全部或部分訂金。**

- residential (adj.) 住宅的
  a variety of 各種的
  ground floor (n.)〔英〕一樓
  access (v.) 有權擁有或使用
  belongings (n.) 財產；所有物
  built-in (adj.) 內建的　deposit (n.) 訂金；押金

http://www.birminghamsmartreviews.com/storage/0421

卡斯特蘭特倉儲公司評價

[184] **當我因為一項六個月的研究計畫而必須搬到德國時，我向卡斯特蘭特租了一個儲藏室存放我的財物。**我的經驗好得不得了。首先，我不確定需要多大的空間，因此 [185] **他們的業務代表親切地解釋各種選項**，沒有給我壓力。在我簽約之前，她也確認我了解租約條款。當 [183] **我把我的東西——一張床、一個梳妝台、一些小家電——搬過去時，**[185] **值班的工作人員幫我把它們卸下來，並很有效率地把所有東西排好。**六個月後，所有東西都在我原先放的地方，沒有破損、受潮。卡斯特蘭特是優良的自助倉儲公司。

綺拉．里茲於 12 月 2 日

- pressure (v.) 對……施加壓力
  terms (n.) 條款（恆用複數）
  appliance (n.) 家用電器　unload (v.) 卸貨

**181. 確認事實與否**

並未提及哪項各個儲藏空間的特色？

(A) 溫度控制
(B) 24 小時可使用
(C) 保全系統
**(D) 電源插座**

換句話說
heating and cooling systems（冷暖氣系統）
→ (A) Temperature control（溫度控制）
you can access your belongings at any time, on any day of the week（能在一星期的任何一天、任何時間拿取你的東西）
→ (B) 24-hour accessibility（24 小時可使用）
security alarm and camera（警報器和攝影機）
→ (C) A security system（保全系統）

**182. 相關細節**

根據資訊，為何會有額外收費？

(A) 選擇租期短於兩個星期
(B) 租用一樓的儲藏室
**(C) 使儲藏室的狀況不佳**
(D) 更換儲藏室的鑰匙

**換句話說**

if the rental unit is found to be dirty or damaged（如果發現租用的空間骯髒或受損）
→ (C) Leaving a unit in poor condition（使儲藏室的狀況不佳）

**183. 整合題**

里茲女士最可能租用哪一種儲藏室？

(A) A 類型　**(C) C 類型**
(B) B 類型　(D) D 類型

**184. 相關細節**

里茲女士為什麼需要儲藏一些物品？

**(A) 她暫時搬到國外住。**
(B) 她搬到較小的房子。
(C) 她的住家重新裝潢。
(D) 她因為新嗜好而買了一些用品。

- relocate (v.) 搬遷

**換句話說**

store my belongings（存放我的財物）
→ store some items（儲藏一些物品）
move to Germany for a six-month study program（因為一項六個月的研究計畫而搬到德國）→ (A) went to live abroad temporarily（暫時搬到國外住）

**185. 確認事實與否**

關於卡斯特蘭特倉儲公司，里茲女士暗示什麼？

(A) 它的設施空間很大。
**(B) 它的員工樂於幫忙。**
(C) 它的信譽良好。
(D) 它的合約很容易了解。

- reputation (n.) 信譽；聲望

**換句話說**

representative / worker（業務代表／工作人員）
→ (B) staff（員工）

**186–190 網頁與電子郵件**

http://www.rosensteinconcerthall.com/events

| 關於我們 | **活動** | 門票 | 地點 | 聯絡我們 |
|---|---|---|---|---|

**羅森斯坦音樂廳**
**即將舉行的活動**

點擊活動名稱以得知更多詳情及購票，或者探索我們的主題系列，例如羅森斯坦家族（適合所有年齡層樂迷的表演）和偉大的演奏家（展現來自全球各地的樂器演奏家），請點這裡。

| | |
|---|---|
| [186] **11 月 15 日星期六 下午 7:30–9:30 歡慶西莉雅．穆迪** [188] **波吉斯管弦樂團演奏此位知名作曲家的精選作品。** | [186] **11 月 22 日至 23 日 星期六至星期日 下午 7:30–10:00 演繹爵士 **** XO 爵士四重奏帶來當代流行金曲的爵士演奏版。 |
| [186] **11 月 29 日星期六 下午 7:00–8:30 記憶之夜** 男高音安東尼奧．畢昂奇演唱一些他的招牌作品。 | [186] **12 月 7 日星期日 下午 7:00–9:00 《綠谷》之歌 *** 波吉斯管弦樂團演奏此部經典電影的配樂。 |

*[190] **標記一個星號（*）的活動只開放訂閱會員參加。**點擊這裡查看成為羅森斯坦音樂廳會員的完整優惠清單。

** 標記兩個星號的活動不包含在訂閱會員優惠中，必須另外付費。

- alternatively (adv.) 或者
  instrumentalist (n.) 樂器演奏家
  composer (n.) 作曲家
  rendition (n.)（對音樂、詩歌等的）詮釋；表演
  spin (n.)（對資訊或狀況的）詮釋
  score (n.)（電影、歌舞等的）配樂
  asterisk (n.) 星號　subscriber (n.) 訂閱者

http://www.rosensteinconcerthall.com/events

| 關於我們 | 活動 | **門票** | 地點 | 聯絡我們 |
|---|---|---|---|---|

**羅森斯坦音樂廳**
**感謝您的購買！**

您的門票將郵寄到以下地址。不過，[187] **我們建議您將這一頁列印出來，或使用螢幕截圖，以防萬一您在活動之前需要更換別場活動或取消。**

預訂確認碼：59289289
姓名：韋恩．賈居
電子郵件：wjudge@solomail.com
地址：77014 德州波吉斯紅木公園 114 號
電話：555-0103

[188] **活動日期：** **11 月 15 日**

門票張數：2　　座位區：C

票價：100 元

付款方式：YowzaPay 線上支付

購票日期：10 月 20 日

請仔細核對您的訂票內容。若發現有誤，請寄電子郵件給我們：inquiries@rosenstein.com，以尋求協助。

**收件人：**<support@rosenstein.com>

**寄件人：**<wjudge@solomail.com>

**主旨：**音樂會

**日期：**12 月 18 日

哈囉：

在經歷過最近觀賞的一場美好演出後，[190] **我剛剛訂閱成為你們的會員**。現在，我正試著要買一場不在我訂閱內的節目門票。然而，[189] **當我在空格內輸入我的訂戶號碼，以獲得九折優惠時，我看到紅色字體寫著「無效的訂戶號碼」，而且沒有折扣。**我確定我輸入了正確的號碼。是否能請你們查一下，再回覆我？謝謝你們。

韋恩・賈居　謹啟

- invalid (adj.) 無效的　look into 調查

**186. 相關細節**

列在第一個網頁上的活動有什麼共同點？

**(A) 它們都在週末舉行。**
(B) 它們的演出時間一樣長。
(C) 它們的表演者都是團體。
(D) 它們每一場都只有一天。

**187. 相關細節**

第二個網頁指示賈居先生做什麼？

(A) 檢查他的電子郵件收件匣
**(B) 儲存他的訂票資料**
(C) 在家印出他的門票
(D) 注意取消的最後期限

**換句話說**
print or take a screenshot of this page（把這一頁列印出來或使用螢幕截圖）
→ (B) Save his booking information（儲存他的訂票資料）

**188. 整合題**　難

賈居先生在他參加的音樂會聽到什麼？

(A) 聲樂表演
(B) 為電影創作的音樂
(C) 轉換為另一種類型的歌曲
**(D) 由一個人所寫的音樂作品**

**換句話說**
selected works of the famous composer（這位知名作曲家的精選作品）
→ (D) Musical pieces written by one person（由一個人所寫的音樂作品）

**189. 主題或目的**

賈居先生為何撰寫這封電子郵件？

(A) 表達對一項服務的謝意
**(B) 報告技術性問題**
(C) 確認購買
(D) 詢問一項協議的條款

- terms of an agreement (n.) 一項協議的條款

**190. 整合題**　

關於賈居先生，下列何者最可能為真？

**(A) 他有資格出席專屬的表演。**
(B) 他會開始收到定期刊物。
(C) 他誤解了特殊身分的優惠。
(D) 他對適合兒童的娛樂節目有興趣。

- exclusive (adj.) 獨有的　publication (n.) 刊物

**換句話說**
only available（只開放）→ (A) exclusive（專屬的）

**191–195 公告、報導與電子郵件**

**查爾斯頓中央博物館**

我們將在 2 月 26 日主辦一場歡迎會，[192] **慶祝**三月的「隱形世界：微生物」**科學展開展**。[191] **我們希望，您身為過去多年來慷慨支持我們機構的贊助者，能與我們一起慶祝這個令人興奮的活動。**

**歡迎會詳情：**

2 月 26 日星期六下午 6:00 至 9:30
查爾斯頓中央博物館東廳
自助餐由銀星外燴公司提供

[194]**「隱形世界：微生物」從 3 月 3 日展出到 5 月 31 日**，主打超過 250 件描繪這些最小生命形式奇觀的展品。

- reception (n.) 歡迎會
  microorganism (n.) 微生物　depict (v.) 描繪

《中西報》

**查爾斯頓中央博物館贏得殊榮**
文／吉兒．布雷德福

梅里特　訊（4 月 20 日）——4 月 18 日，[193] **在首次舉辦的中西部藝術與科學獎頒獎典禮上，查爾斯頓中央博物館獲得科學文學獎**。由中西部知識基金會主辦的這場典禮，在華盛頓會議廳於約六千名藝術與科學界成員的面前進行。

查爾斯頓中央博物館以「隱形世界：微生物」展詳盡且具娛樂性的補充資料包贏得此獎。首席設計師高橋優衣上台領獎，感謝平面設計師雷蒙．施樂普，資料包中有許多插圖皆出自他之手。她也保證，這套資料會在博物館的新版網站上公開，網站目前正在建置中。

「隱形世界：微生物」的概念來自科學家湯瑪斯．艾爾森，[195] **他得到建築師費歐娜．華生的知識與專業所助，製作了這些展覽品**。這個展覽是博物館的一大成功，門票收入高於之前的所有展覽。[194] **在那裡的展期結束後，展覽將移往鄰近的喬治城**，在喬治城科學學院展出約兩個月。

- prestigious (adj.) 有名望的
  put on 舉辦（展覽）　supplement (n.) 補充
  under construction（網站）建置中
  conceptualize (v.) 概念化
  enlist (v.) 獲得（幫助、支持等）
  expertise (n.) 專門技能或知識
  tremendous (adj.) 巨大的　top (v.) 超過；高於
  neighboring (adj.) 鄰近的
  approximately (adv.) 大約

**收件人**：<jillbradford@midwestern.com>
**寄件人**：<kevinshaw@gomial.net>
**日期**：4 月 22 日
**主旨**：最近的文章

親愛的布雷德福女士：

一開始，我很高興看到妳最近關於查爾斯頓中央博物館獲得中西部藝術與科學獎成就的報導。然而，[195] **當我將報導從頭到尾讀過，興奮地期待看到我的名字出現在報導裡時，我發現我的工作被誤植到費歐娜．華生名下**，她在過程中只是我的顧問而已，這真是令人非常失望。我建議妳未來的報導能做更詳盡的調查。

凱文．蕭　謹啟

- coverage (n.) 新聞報導
  attribute (v.) 將……歸功於……
  merely (adv.) 只是　encourage (v.) 建議
  carry out 實行
  thorough (adj.) 詳盡的

**191. 相關細節**

這則公告預計發給誰？

(A) 博物館員工　**(C) 捐款人**
(B) 可能的參展者　(D) 大學生

**換句話說**
someone who has supported our institution with generous donations（身為過去多年來慷慨支持我們機構的贊助者）
→ (C) Financial donors（捐款人）

**192. 同義詞考題** 

在公告中，第一段第一行的「mark」，意思最接近下列何者？

(A) 為……的特徵　**(C) 認可**
(B) 評估　(D) 銘刻於

**193. 確認事實與否**

關於中西部藝術與科學獎頒獎典禮，可由文中得知什麼？

**(A) 之前沒有舉辦過。**
(B) 在查爾斯頓中央博物館舉行。
(C) 由高橋女士主持。
(D) 對現場觀眾轉播。

- dedicated (adj.) 專用的

**換句話說**
first-ever（首次的）→ (A) not been held previously（之前沒有舉辦過）

**194. 整合題** 難

6 月 1 日最可能發生什麼事？

(A) 某個獎項開始提名。
(B) 有些教材將於線上公開。
(C) 贊助機構將資助一場談話。
**(D) 有場展覽將移到不同城市去。**

- nomination (n.) 提名　release (v.) 發布

換句話說
it will be transported to neighboring Georgetown（展覽將移往鄰近的喬治城）
→ (D) An exhibition will move to a different town.（有場展覽將移到不同城市去。）

**195. 整合題** 難

蕭先生很可能做了什麼？

(A) 提供一套資料裡的插圖
(B) 代表一個機構接受一個獎項
(C) 發想某個展覽的概念
**(D) 建構一些博物館的展覽品**

- on behalf of 代表……　display (n.) 展覽品

換句話說
construct the exhibits（製作了這些展覽品）
→ (D) Constructed some museum displays（製作一些博物館的展覽品）

**196–200 申請表、電子郵件與附件**

索托里克市
臨時食品設施申請書

請繳交這份申請書以獲得在特殊活動期間，於索托里克市的限制內經營臨時食品以及／或飲料設施的許可。

| | | | |
|---|---|---|---|
| 申請人： | 琳恩．麥金利 | 活動名稱： | 環球工藝節 |
| 商家： | 琳恩的墨西哥玉米捲餅 | 主辦單位： | 索托里克觀光局 |
| 地址： | 47372 紐約州索托里克市西路 32 號 | 日期： | 5 月 8 日至 10 日 |
| 電話： | 555-0153 | 地點： | 索托里克大公園 |

附件資料（除另有説明外，必附）：

(a) 所有在現場準備與供應食品／飲料的設施與設備的照片
(b) 一份所有販售的食品／飲料品項以及所有非預先包裝品項食材的清單
(c)[196] **一張支付給索托里克市政府的 50 元支票，或者，如果在活動前十天內提出申請則為 100 元**
(d) [198] **索托里克衛生局的檢驗合格證書（只有欲於設施內使用瓦斯器具的攤販需要此項）**

申請人簽名：琳恩．麥金利

日期：4 月 19 日

- temporary (adj.) 臨時的　facility (n.) 設施
  ingredient (n.) 食材
  non-prepackaged (adj.) 非預先包裝的
  payable to（支票）支付給……
  certificate (n.) 證明；證書　inspection (n.) 檢查

**收件人：**安琪．穆諾茲及其他三人
**寄件人：**琳恩．麥金利
**日期：**5 月 3 日
**主旨：**環球工藝節攤位
**附件：**班表、工藝節地圖

嗨，各位：

謝謝大家答應在這個週末的環球工藝節裡代表琳恩墨西哥玉米捲餅。[197] **除了遵守附件班表中的指示外**，請注意 [199] **會有一張市政府發的食品安全檢查表，早班人員必須填寫好**，而星期五和星期六的晚班人員必須把食品仔細收好，並鎖好我們的攤位。真正賣餐的時間會比班表的時間晚半小時開始，早半小時結束，因此，我們應該有充足的時間做這些工作。

如果我們在晚餐的高峰時間前，庫存變得不夠，[198] **如果瓦斯烤爐罷工（以前發生過）**，或者如果出現別的問題，請聯絡我或葛萊迪，他整個週末都會監管餐廳。

謝謝。
琳恩

- shift (n.) 輪班工作時間
  run low 快要用完；不足

TEST 6 PART 7

琳恩墨西哥玉米捲餅

**環球工藝節班表**

| | 星期五 | 星期六 | 星期日 |
|---|---|---|---|
| [199] **早班** [200] **（早上 9:30 至下午 2:00）** | 琳恩 光善 | 琳恩 [199] **榮恩** | 達拉斯 光善 |
| **晚班**（下午 2:00 至 6:00） | 安琪 達拉斯 | 安琪 肯 | 達拉斯 琳恩 |

- 使用第四街的攤商停車區與入口。
- 帶一種身分證件（會核對你在攤商名單上的名字）。
- [200] **至少提早 15 分鐘到，這樣才有時間走到攤位。**

**196. 相關細節**

文中要求麥金利女士隨表格提供什麼東西？

(A) 員工名單
(B) 臨時設施的藍圖
(C) 公司執照的影本
**(D) 支付政府單位的款項**

換句話說

A check payable to Sotorik City Hall（一張支付給索托里克市政府的支票）
→ (D) A payment to a government office（支付政府單位的款項）

---

**197. 同義詞考題**

在電子郵件中，第一段第二行的「following」，意思最接近下列何者？

**(A) 遵守** (C) 伴隨
(B) 理解 (D) 隨後的

---

**198. 整合題** 難

文中提到關於麥金利女士的什麼事？
(A) 必須加速處理她的申請。
**(B) 她的設備通過檢查。**
(C) 她僱用專業的美食攝影師。
(D) 她選擇租用烹飪器具。

- expedite (v.) 迅速完成

**199. 整合題** 難

榮恩最可能和同事做什麼？

**(A) 完成一些文書工作**
(B) 共乘去節慶會場
(C) 保護一些公司財產
(D) 拿取一些庫存

換句話說

fill out（填寫）→ (A) complete（完成）
a city-issued food safety checklist（一張市政府發的食品安全檢查表）
→ (A) some paperwork（一些文書工作）

---

**200. 推論或暗示**

可在附件中得知關於環球工藝節攤商的什麼事？

(A) 他們依商品種類分組。
(B) 會發識別證給他們。
**(C) 他們每天可以在上午 9:30 前進場。**
(D) 他們可以在星期一拆除攤位。

- merchandise (n.) 商品；貨物
  disassemble (v.) 拆卸

# ACTUAL TEST 7

**PART 5** P. 176–178

**101. 所有格代名詞——介系詞的受詞** 難

因為羅伊女士的停車位離入口很遠，艾茲拉先生體貼地同意，在她的傷勢痊癒之前，讓她停他的車位。

(A) 他　(C) 他
**(B) 他的（東西）**　(D) 他自己

**102. 名詞詞彙題——動詞的主詞**

亞洛夫 -A 外套的布料所提供的強大保護力，確保你在全世界最冷的地方都能保持溫暖。

(A) 保護　(C) 保護地
(B) 保護　**(D) 保護**

- fabric (n.) 布料

**103. 名詞詞彙題** 難

羅倫會議中心是許多不同活動的理想場地，因為它的設計目的在於盡可能提供彈性運用。

**(A) 彈性**　(C) 提供資金
(B) 熱心　(D) 精確

- venue (n.) 舉辦活動的場地
  a wide variety of 各式各樣的
  financing (n.) 提供資金給……
  accuracy (n.) 精確

**104. 介系詞詞彙題**

多年來，派特森銀行一直提供基層工作機會給剛畢業的大學生。

(A) 在……內　**(C) 持續（一段時間）**
(B) 在……之後　(D) 在……期間

- opportunity (n.) 機會
  university graduate (n.) 大學畢業生

**105. 副詞詞彙題**

餐廳老闆不斷面臨新挑戰，尤其是在今日競爭激烈的商業環境下。

(A) 沉重地　(C) 不同地
**(B) 不斷地**　(D) 多變地

- competitive (adj.) 競爭的
  diversely (adv.) 各種不同地
  variably (adv.) 多變地

**106. 名詞詞彙題**

當防毒軟體進行更新時，可能暫時影響電腦的工作效能。

(A) 創新　**(C) 工作效能**
(B) 測量　(D) 代表

- innovation (n.) 創新　measurement (n.) 測量
  representation (n.) 代表

**107. 副詞詞彙題——修飾動詞——比較級**

市場報告指出，社群媒體行銷比電視廣告更能有效觸及年輕消費者。

(A) 有效的　**(C) 更有效地**
(B) 有效地　(D) 有效

- indicate (v.) 指出　consumer (n.) 消費者
  effectiveness (n.) 有效

**108. 動詞詞彙題**

克萊維瑞提克斯供應商旨在生產供專業廚師使用的最高品質廚房設備。

(A) 承諾　(C) 保持
(B) 賺得　**(D) 生產**

- aim (v.) 旨在　equipment (n.) 設備
  commit (v.) 承諾　earn (v.) 賺得
  remain (v.) 保持

**109. 連接詞、介系詞詞彙題**

你學彈吉他時，使用像法蘭摩 -5 這樣的耐用型號來練習。

(A) 是否　(C) 從……開始
(B) 從此　**(D) 當……時**

- durable (adj.) 耐用的

**110. 名詞詞彙題**

為了預防紀錄重複，如果相同的客戶編號輸入資料庫超過一次，就會顯示通知。

(A) 運輸　(C) 組織
**(B) 重複**　(D) 區別

- notification (n.) 通知　transportation (n.) 運輸
  differentiation (n.) 區別

**111. 副詞詞彙題——修飾不定詞** 難

隨著更多商家轉移到網路上，招牌和廣告布條的銷售量持續不斷下滑。

(A) 穩定的　　**(C) 不斷地**
(B) 穩固　　(D) 穩固

---

**112. 介系詞詞彙題**

安全顧問建議對室內地板進行表面防滑處理，以預防工作場所的意外事故。

**(A) 用（工具）**　　(C) 向
(B) 屬於　　(D) 直到……

- flooring (n.)（總稱）室內地板
  non-slip finish (n.) 表面防滑

---

**113. 形容詞詞彙題——過去分詞** 難

下次市民大會時，官員會就所規劃的社區中心工程進度提出報告。

**(A) 已計畫的**　　(C) 認識的
(B) 提名的　　(D) 放心的

- official (n.) 官員　acquainted (adj.) 認識的
  relieved (adj.) 放心的

---

**114. 動詞詞彙題——動詞的受詞**

智慧科技公司製造能幫助幼兒熟悉科學概念的教育性玩具。

(A) 親密地　　(C) 使熟悉的
**(B) 熟悉**　　(D) 更熟悉

- gain (v.) 得到　familiarize (v.) 使熟悉

---

**115. 副詞詞彙題** 難

雖然有些經理可能有不同的想法，但將舊的紙本文件存放在公司以外的地方是可負擔的解決方法。

(A) 尤其　　(C) 此外
**(B) 不同地**　　(D) 以前

- off-site (adj.) 工作場所以外的
  formerly (adv.) 以前

---

**116. 介系詞詞彙題**

很多企業家，無論經驗多寡，都可能犯了太快擴展業務的錯誤。

**(A) 無論**　　(C) 仍然
(B) 反而　　(D) 和……一樣多

- entrepreneur (n.) 企業家　expand (v.) 擴展
  nevertheless (adv.) 仍然

---

**117. 動詞詞類變化題——助動詞＋原形動詞——語態**

我們下次買辦公室家具時，我提議選擇能調整不同高度的桌椅。

(A) 正升起　　**(C) 被升起**
(B) 升起　　(D) 正被升起

- propose (v.) 提議
  a variety of 各式各樣的

---

**118. 動詞詞彙題**

蘇納拉食品市場的所有農產品，都來自當地的有機農場。

(A) 繼續做　　(C) 打算
(B) 成功　　**(D) 獲得**

- produce (n.) 農產品　proceed (v.) 繼續進行

---

**119. 受詞補語考題——過去分詞** 

要讓你的顧客總是百分之百滿意，大多仰賴以專業態度解決客訴的能力。

(A) 滿意　　(C) 正滿意
**(B) 感到滿意的**　　(D) 滿意

- depend on 視……而定　satisfy (v.) 使滿意

---

**120. 反身代名詞詞彙題** 

諾華瑞克科技公司的研究人員已開發出一種機器人，可以教它自己學會新的基本工作。

(A) 他們自己　　**(C) 它自己**
(B) 你自己　　(D) 我們自己

---

**121. 動詞詞類變化題——語態**

數位影片需要比大部分其他應用程式更大的資料量，尤其是以高畫質觀看時。

(A) 正需要　　(C) 已需要
(B) 需要　　**(D) 需要**

- high definition (n.) 高畫質

---

**122. 介系詞詞彙題**

路面改善工程已面臨數次延期，消息來源指出，這項工程可能會延續到六月之後。

(A) 沿著　　(C) 加上
(B) 在……之上　　**(D) 超過**

- source (n.) 消息來源

### 123. 形容詞詞彙題——受詞補語

近期美元貶值已使我們從美國進口的商品更有利潤。

**(A) 有利潤的**　(C) 獲利
(B) 獲利能力　(D) 利潤

- profitable (adj.) 有利潤的
  profitability (n.) 獲利能力

### 124. 連接詞詞彙題

新網站預計等開發人員一完成易用性測試就會推出。

**(A) 一……就……**　(C) 儘管
(B) 曾經　(D) 在……之上

- usability test (n.) 易用性測試
  whereas (adv.) 儘管

### 125. 副詞詞彙題

博物館人員和一組資訊科技專家，將合作設計一場虛擬實境展覽。

(A) 相對地　**(C) 合作地**
(B) 不尋常地　(D) 心不在焉地

- virtual reality (n.) 虛擬實境　exhibit (n.) 展覽
  relatively (adv.) 相當地；相對地
  absently (adv.) 心不在焉地

### 126. 形容詞詞彙題 難

雖然公司合併的討論進展緩慢，但公司的談判人員仍對達成協議很樂觀。

(A) 進行的　(C) 專心致志的
(B) 很有可能的　**(D) 樂觀的**

- merger (n.)（公司等的）合併
  negotiator (n.) 談判者　deal (n.) 協議
  ongoing (adj.) 進行的
  probable (adj.) 很有可能的
  dedicated (adj.) 專心致志的

### 127. 副詞子句連接詞

只要能趕上一般截止日，新政策允許選定的員工在家工作。

(A) 至於　(C) 關於
**(B) 只要**　(D) 如果

- meet a deadline 趕上截止期限
  provided that 只要　concerning (prep.) 關於
  in case of 如果

### 128. 動詞詞彙題

迷迭香是義大利料理最常用的香草植物之一，因為這種植物在當地溫暖乾燥的氣候下長得很茂盛。

**(A) 茂盛生長**　(C) 具有……的特徵
(B) 奉承　(D) 吸收

- flatter (v.) 奉承
  characterize (v.) 具有……的特徵

### 129. 簡化副詞子句——分詞構句 難

如果未正確安裝，軟體程式會在開始選單上顯示錯誤訊息。

(A) 安裝　**(C) 安裝**
(B) 安裝工具　(D) 安裝

### 130. 名詞子句連接詞 

卓女士以文字詳細記錄上次部門會議的討論事項。

(A) 那個　(C) 每件事
**(B) ……的事物**　(D) 它

- transcript (n.) 文字紀錄

## PART 6　P. 179–182

### 131–134 電子郵件

收件者：陳唐 <don-chen@mail.org>
寄件者：布蘭迪倉庫 <brundy-storage@mail.com>
日期：1 月 30 日
主旨：空間 1032 最新資訊

親愛的陳先生：

感謝您對我們布蘭迪倉庫的長期惠顧。

近來，由於這個地區對儲物空間的 [131] **需求**增加而調漲租金。基於這些市場狀況，1032 空間新的月租金 [132] **將**從 3 月 1 日星期日起調為 208 元。

這項 [133] **調整**相當於您的租金增加不到 2%。[134] **別擔心，即使是這個價格，您仍然享有划算的價格**，您的新租金仍低於第一次承租與您的空間相同大小儲藏單位顧客的現有租金。

我們再次感謝您長期對布蘭迪倉庫的惠顧。

敬祝　安康

布蘭迪倉庫管理部

- loyalty (n.) 忠實　rental rate (n.) 租金
  represent (v.) 相當於　grateful (adj.) 感謝的

**131. 名詞詞彙題**

(A) 範圍　　(**C**) **需求**
(B) 銷售　　(D) 整修

- sales (n.) 銷售（額）
  renovation (n.) 整修；翻新

---

**132. 動詞詞類變化題——時態**

(A) 將是　　(C) 已經是
(**B**) **將是**　　(D) 本來是

- file a complaint 提出投訴

---

**133. 名詞詞彙題——動詞對應的主詞**

(A) 調整　　(C) 可調整的
(B) 調停者　　(**D**) **調整**

---

**134. 句子插入題** 

(A) 我們要謝謝所有對這個問題提供意見的顧客。
(B) 我們想要強調，由於房客減少，我們現在正在裁員。
(C) 請注意，租約的條款可能有很大的更動。
(**D**) **別擔心，即使是這個價格，您仍然享有划算的價格。**

- emphasize (v.) 強調　tenant (n.) 房客
  downsize (v.) 裁減（員工）人數
  terms and conditions (n.)（合約）條款
  vary (v.) 改變　rest assured 別擔心；請放心
  receive a good value 很划算；物有所值

---

**135–138 網頁**

佩卓拉出版公司是教學指南書籍的領導品牌，135 **滿足**喜歡手作藝術與工藝嗜好讀者的**需求**。支持新人才與點子是我們公司所重視的部分。136 **因此**，我們積極尋找新書提案，希望能有助增加我們領域的書籍。137 **我們的編輯團隊可以把有希望做成一本書的想法化為現實**。對我們的許多作者來說，寫書只是個 138 **遙遠的**夢想，是他們希望有朝一日能做的事。有了我們的鼓勵和指導，他們開始創作出一本美麗的新作可供出版。請點擊這裡，看看我們的提案準則。

- publisher (n.) 出版公司
  instructional (adj.) 教學的；指導性的
  hands-on (adj.) 實際動手做的
  actively (adv.) 積極地
  addition (n.) 增加的人事物　guidance (n.) 指導
  submission (n.) 提出

**135. 動詞詞類變化題——現在分詞**

(A) 滿足需求　　(C) 將滿足需求
(**B**) **滿足需求**　　(D) 被滿足需求

- cater to 滿足或提供（個人或團體的）願望或需求

---

**136. 連接副詞**

(**A**) **因此**　　(C) 之後
(B) 相比之下　　(D) 或者

- by comparison 相比之下　afterward (adv.) 之後

---

**137. 句子插入題** 

(A) 在某些天裡，教育工作者可以要求幾本近期出版書籍供瀏覽。
(B) 我們會安排電話約訪，和你進一步談這件事。
(**C**) **我們的編輯團隊可以把有希望做成一本書的想法化為現實。**
(D) 研究顯示，童話仍對年輕讀者較有吸引力。

- title (n.) 書　appointment (n.) 約定會面
  editor (n.) 編輯　promising (adj.) 有希望的
  appeal (v.) 有吸引力

---

**138. 形容詞詞彙題** 

(**A**) **遙遠的**　　(C) 細微的
(B) 空白的　　(D) 深的

---

**139–142 報導**

多特朗德　訊（3 月 19 日）——上個星期六和星期日，第 25 屆多朗德民謠音樂節破紀錄吸引了六千餘人參加。根據主辦單位指出，這個令人印象深刻的 139 **到場人數**要歸功於今年活動的一些新特色，140 **例如，演出更多元的音樂風格。**有史以來首次，演出陣容不但包含受歡迎的民謠團體，還有古巴的曼波樂團、波蘭舞團，141 **甚至**還有爵士樂獨奏家。觀眾還有機會參加體驗工坊，教他們彈奏各種不同傳統樂器的技巧。主辦單位表示，明年的音樂節將會保留這兩項受大眾歡迎的改變。

- annual (adj.) 一年一度的　draw (v.) 吸引
  organizer (n.)（競賽、活動的）籌辦者
  credit (v.) 把……歸於　feature (n.) 特色
  lineup (n.) 陣容
  ensemble (n.) 劇團；舞團；樂團
  attendee (n.) 出席者　carry over 繼續存在

**139. 名詞詞彙題** 難

(A) 獎品　**(C) 到場人數**
(B) 資金　(D) 等級

---

**140. 句子插入題**

(A) 他們注意到，傳統文化未來可能會持續改變。
(B) 所有志工都有免費餐點和特製的音樂節 T 恤。
(C) 事實上，並不一定需要有音樂背景才更能欣賞音樂。
**(D) 例如，演出更多元的音樂風格。**

- background (n.) 背景；經歷
  appreciation (n.) 欣賞
  diverse (adj.) 各種各樣的

---

**141. 副詞詞彙題——強調名詞片語**

(A) 然而　**(C) 甚至**
(B) 非常　(D) 很多

---

**142. 動詞詞類變化題——過去分詞**

(A) 設計師　(C) 設計
**(B) 設計**　(D) 設計

---

**143–146 資訊**

HGA 在德州達拉斯的年度家用品貿易展——你為什麼應該參加

60 多年來，家用品協會（HGA）[143] **一直主辦**業界最大的貿易展，以來自全球頂尖製造商的家用品為特色。零售商店的採購經理每年參加，和批發商碰面，把握機會建立商業夥伴關係。你正在尋找原創商品，讓貴公司與競爭對手有所區別，並取得市場優勢嗎？[144] **只要**到貿易展會場走走，探索展示商品，你一定會 [145] **發現**創新的家用產品。[146] **此外，還有關於目前業界議題的演講和工作坊**。透過參加 HGA 貿易展，保證你得知家用品的最新趨勢。

- household goods (n.) 家庭用品
  trade show (n.) 貿易展
  manufacturer (n.) 製造商
  purchase (v.) 購買　retail store (n.) 零售商店
  wholesale supplier (n.) 批發商
  seize (v.) 抓住（時機等）
  original (adj.) 有獨創性的
  merchandise (n.) 商品　distinguish (v.) 區別
  competitor (n.) 競爭對手
  market advantage (n.) 市場優勢
  innovative (adj.) 創新的　attend (v.) 參加；出席
  stay up to date 了解最新情況

**143. 動詞詞類變化題——語態——時態**

**(A) 一直主辦**　(C) 正被主辦
(B) 被主辦　(D) 原本要主辦

---

**144. 副詞詞彙題**

**(A) 只要**　(C) 緊密地
(B) 近來　(D) 不久

---

**145. 動詞詞彙題** 難

(A) 利用　(C) 示範操作
(B) 航行　**(D) 發現**

- utilize (v.) 利用　navigate (v.) 航行

---

**146. 句子插入題** 難

(A) 料理一個家有其他幾種重要的方法。
**(B) 此外，還有關於目前業界議題的演講和工作坊。**
(C) 有些展示的復古商品歷史超過 50 年。
(D) 當你談完生意後，請享用我們的免費自助式午餐。

- complimentary (adj.) 免費贈送的

## PART 7 P. 183–203

**147–148 公告**

**會議室規定**

克里瑞市公共圖書館的會議室於下列情況下，免費供社區團體使用。所有在會議室舉行的社區會議必須免費且開放給大眾參加，會議室只在圖書館的一般開放期間使用，必需經由圖書館的線上預約系統提出預約申請。團體可以預約本月或下個月的會議室，任何團體都不得在 14 天內預約一間會議室召開一次以上的會議，[148] **預約採先來先受理的原則**。

請注意，[147] **所有會議室都備有椅子及會議桌。圖書館所有的視聽設備可在申請會議室時提出需求，且必須以借書證登記借用**。

- at no charge (= free of charge) 免費
  request (n.) 要求　via (v.) 經由
  reservation (n.) 預約
  under no circumstances 無論如何都不⋯⋯

on a first-come, first-served basis 以先到先得為原則
equipped with 配備有……
audiovisual equipment (n.) 視聽設備
application (n.) 申請 check out 登記借用

**147. 推論或暗示**

文中提到關於圖書館會議室的什麼事？

(A) 圖書館的讀者可以重排裡面的座位。
(B) 會議室的最大容納人數都不同。
**(C) 沒有視聽設備。**
(D) 可在圖書館的一般開放時間之外使用。

- patron (n.) 顧客；常客 capacity (n.) 容量

**148. 確認事實與否**

根據公告，關於會議室的預約，下列何者為真？

**(A) 會依照收件的順序預約。**
(B) 在某個時間點後取消會有罰款。
(C) 必須親自前往辦理。
(D) 必須在一個月前預約。

- penalty (n.) 罰款；處罰
  in advance 事先

**換句話說**

accepted on a first-come, first-served basis
（採先來先受理的原則）
→ (A) taken in the order they are received
（依照收到的順序預約）

**149–150 徵才廣告**

**誠徵：平面設計師（數位媒體）**
**公司／地點：**安大略省漢米爾頓市，史卓伯總公司

史卓伯公司正在尋找具有創意的人為我們的數位行銷計畫設計平面圖像。這些計畫內容包含公司網站、線上廣告、社群媒體和手機應用程式。錄取者也將代表公司參加業界的貿易展，並接受公司內的訓練，以持續獲知數位通訊的最新趨勢。[149] **應徵資格包括至少兩年的廣告公司平面設計師經歷**，並精通數位設計軟體。

史卓伯公司是家族經營的連鎖便利商店企業，為忙碌的顧客提供輕食與快餐。我們曾獲媒體認證為安大略省五大最佳公司之一，我們也以對所在社區的強大支持而聞名。[150] **公司每年贊助數間慈善機構的募款活動。**

- initiative (n.) 新計畫；新提議
  on one's behalf 代表…… acquire (v.) 獲得
  in-house (adj.) 在組織內部的
  qualification (n.) 資格
  proficiency (n.) 精通；熟練
  on the go 忙碌的 commitment (n.) 支持
  fundraising (n.) 募款
  charitable organization (n.) 慈善組織

**149. 確認事實與否**

文中提到這項工作所需的資格為何？

(A) 電腦程式設計的學歷
**(B) 之前在廣告公司任職**
(C) 證明可以設計公司內部訓練課程的能力
(D) 籌辦貿易展活動的經驗

- educational background (n.) 學歷
  organize (v.) 籌劃

**換句話說**

Qualifications（資格）
→ a requirement for the job（工作所需的資格）
a minimum of 2 years' experience
（至少兩年的經歷）
→ (B) Previous employment（之前任職）

**150. 確認事實與否**

關於史卓伯公司，可由文中得知什麼事？

(A) 它有許多員工認同計畫。
(B) 它的總公司最近搬遷。
(C) 它經營外送服務。
**(D) 它支持地方慈善團體。**

- recognition (n.) 認同 relocate (v.)（使）搬遷
  charity (n.) 慈善團體

**換句話說**

sponsors . . . several charitable organizations
（贊助數間慈善機構）
→ (D) supports local charities
（支持地方慈善團體）

## 151–152 票券

城市鐵路　票券 01 之 01　旅程中請保留票券

旅客姓名：史蒂芬．瑞格比　預定編號：834253　3 月 19 日
發票地：多佛　開票方式：人工
[152] **座位等級：商務車廂**　列車編號：192
出發地：多佛　目的地：維農高地
出發時間：下午 1:45　抵達時間：下午 3:44

[151] **在火車上需有附照片的身分證件**　總價：53 元 *
* 退票／換票會有罰款　* 更改時間或地點需付費

加入我們的常客方案，享受 [152] **從普通車廂升級尊貴車廂的折扣優惠**。更多詳情請上 www.city-railways.com。

- retain (v.) 保留　issue (n.) 發行　coach (n.)（火車）普通車廂　penalty (n.) 罰款

### 151. 推論或暗示

關於瑞格比先生，可由文中得知什麼？

(A) 他會在火車上用餐。
(B) 他是城市鐵路的常客。
(C) 他更改行程不需付費。
**(D) 他在旅程中必須出示身分證件。**

- itinerary (n.) 預定行程

換句話說
on board（在火車上）→ (D) during his trip（在旅程中）

### 152. 推論或暗示

關於城市鐵路，可由文中得知什麼？

(A) 它接受電話訂票。
(B) 它的網站最近剛升級。
**(C) 它的火車有許多不同等級的座位。**
(D) 在網路上預訂車票有折扣。

## 153–154 文字訊息串

陶德．米爾〔下午 1:23〕
嗨，梅莉莎，妳知道樓下的會議室今天下午是否可以用嗎？

梅莉莎．柯茲洛斯基〔下午 1:24〕
我知道，沒人用。你今天約了客戶碰面嗎？

陶德．米爾〔下午 1:24〕
沒有，[153] **我只是需要練習我在景觀設計研討會上要發表的簡報。我加了一張投影片，展示我最新的花園設計專案。**

梅莉莎．柯茲洛斯基〔下午 1:25〕
很好。噢，那間會議室的投影機用的是不同的遙控器，放在儲藏櫃裡，[154] **我可以拿下去給你。**

陶德．米爾〔下午 1:26〕
[154] **不用了，謝謝。我反正要去辦公室拿一些其他的資料。**

梅莉莎．柯茲洛斯基〔下午 1:27〕
好，祝你練習順利。

- landscape architecture (n.) 景觀設計

### 153. 推論或暗示

米爾先生最有可能是什麼身分？

(A) 一棟大樓的管理員
(B) 研討會籌辦人
**(C) 景觀設計師**
(D) 資訊科技專家

- superintendent (n.)（大樓的）管理員
  organizer (n.)（競賽、活動的）籌辦者

### 154. 掌握意圖

下午 1:26，當米爾先生寫道：「不用了，謝謝」時，他意指什麼？

(A) 他很會做簡報。
**(B) 他不需要更多協助。**
(C) 他有合用的儲藏空間。
(D) 他和客戶的合作關係很穩固。

## 155–157 網路文章

http://www.keys-to-success.com/articles/023421

### 一些專家常常分享的建議

[155] **要好好展示房子需要有所準備**，客戶必須信任 [155] **你對鄰近地區以及待售房屋的專業知識**。[156] **當你載著可能的買主去看一間房子時，確定你已事先記住行車路線，你甚至可能想要在帶看的前一天先練習開車去那間房子**，在去一間房子的路上迷路會讓人覺得不了解社區。當你帶可能的買主參觀房子時，[157] **帶幾份關於那間房子和鄰近地區的資料袋給買主是個好主意**，任何收到的人都會很感謝，而且在需要的時候，你能夠參考這些資料來回答問題，就算是一張當地的紙本地圖也有幫助。此外，確定你有進入房子的正確鑰匙，帶錯鑰匙，或沒帶鑰匙，都不會給人好印象。

- expertise (n.) 專業技術或知識
  property (n.) 房地產
  prospective (adj.) 可能的；潛在的
  memorize (v.) 記住
  en route to . . . 去……的途中
  surrounding (adj.) 周圍的　district (n.) 地區
  confirm (v.) 確定　access (v.) 進入

**155. 推論或暗示**

這篇文章最可能打算給誰看？

**(A) 不動產銷售員**
(B) 住宅修繕專家
(C) 導覽志工
(D) 房屋首購族

---

**156. 相關細節**

這篇文章的作者建議做什麼事？

(A) 多打幾組鑰匙
**(B) 事先熟悉行車路線**
(C) 在風景優美的地點稍做停留
(D) 調查社區服務的機會

- scenic (adj.) 風景優美的

**換句話說**

memorized the directions ahead of time
（事先記住行車路線）
→ (B) Mastering travel routes in advance
（事先熟悉行車路線）

**157. 句子插入題**

「任何收到的人都會很感謝，而且在需要的時候，你能夠參考這些資料來回答問題。」最適合放在 [1]、[2]、[3]、[4] 的何處？

(A) [1]　　**(C) [3]**
(B) [2]　　(D) [4]

---

## 158–160 信件

伊鳳・克拉克
60419 伊利諾州波溫市
貝茲街 803 號

親愛的克拉克女士：

身為波溫市青年足球聯盟的教練之一，妳應該知道即將召開的波溫市公園與遊憩委員會特別會議，它將在 2 月 4 日星期二下午 6:30 於市政府第五室舉行。

[158] **會議主題是公園處處長費歐列羅・索洛要撥出公園處的部分預算，更新洪曼公園休閒設施的提案**。尤其，[159] **在青年足球場器材室大樓拍到的照片呈現出裸露的釘子、壁板上的破洞，還有破裂的窗戶必須要處理**。

索洛處長也會討論球場計分板安裝現代電子照明設備的事，[60] **他已經拿到塞佛特電子公司關於這些計畫的總費用估價單**，在會議上，委員會將徵詢大眾對這個計畫的意見。

青年足球聯盟理事會敦促妳參加並分享妳寶貴的意見，因為妳會是受到這個專案影響的人之一。

波溫市青年足球聯盟理事會主席
克爾文・華特斯　謹啟

- allocate (v.) 分配　portion (n.) 部分
  amenity (n.)（常用複數）便利設施
  siding (n.) 壁板；牆板　cracked (adj.) 破裂的
  secure (v.) 獲得　estimate (n.) 估價單
  endeavor (n.) 努力　input (n.) 貢獻意見或建議
  urge (v.) 敦促；力勸

**158. 推論或暗示**

這場即將舉行的會議，目的最可能是什麼？

(A) 提供最新的公園活動日程表
**(B) 討論資助公園的改善計畫**
(C) 宣布一場公開競賽的結果
(D) 介紹一位新任命的公園處官員

- financing (n.) 提供資金　appoint (v.) 任命

**換句話說**

to allocate a portion of the Parks Department's budget（撥出公園處的部分預算）
→ (B) financing（資助）
to upgrade Hohman Park's recreational amenities（更新洪曼公園休閒設施）
→ (B) for park improvements（公園的改善計畫）

### 159. 推論或暗示

關於球場的器材室大樓，可由文中得知什麼？

(A) 它們有其他的功能。
(B) 它們將遷移到新地點。
(C) 它們可能可以花錢租用。
**(D) 它們需要修理。**

**換句話說**

must be taken care of（必須處理）
→ (D) in need of repair（需要修理）

### 160. 相關細節

根據這封信，索洛先生最近做了什麼？

**(A) 收到一份費用估價單**
(B) 拍了其他市立公園的照片
(C) 參加一場地方體育活動
(D) 修訂一本公園的小冊子

- revise (v.) 修訂

**換句話說**

has secured an estimate of the overall cost（已經拿到關於這些計畫的總費用估價單）
→ (A) Received a cost estimate（收到一份費用估價單）

### 161–163 網路評論

[161] **Book-bargains.com「最值得信賴的網路二手書賣家」**

**顧客評價書籍：《商標設計靈感》**| 平裝，148 頁

[161] 評價次數：**7 本在 Book-bargains.com 購買書籍中的 1 本**
點擊這裡看其他評價

**評論日期：**5 月 26 日

**顧客姓名：**傑夫．史塔克斯 ✓確認購買

**整體評價：**優良

**評論：**

這本小巧、便於攜帶的書，介紹了 55 個完全達到預期效果的著名商標設計。所有的商標都以全彩呈現，襯以白色背景，附上文字概述它們的創作過程，並分析它們的設計元素。除了主要內容，[162] **出版者貼心地提供了大約十頁的空白頁面，供記筆記之用**，這是很好的特色。這些商標選自許多不同公司，從軟體開發商到包裹運送服務公司都有，後者的報導是我認為書中最有趣的一章：「展示動作的圖案」。這個部分也特別解說我最喜歡的設計—— [163] **齊拉塔瑞克斯的動態商標，這是以創新聞名的運動器材製造商，**這本書對任何商業設計師來說都是寶貴的資源。

- secondhand (adj.) 二手的
  inspiration (n.) 靈感
  verify (v.) 證實　compact (adj.) 小巧的
  commercial (adj.) 商業的

### 161. 推論或暗示

關於史塔克斯先生，下列何者最可能為真？

**(A) 他在網路上買了好幾本二手書。**
(B) 他是某家書店的專業採購。
(C) 他最近加入一個書籍討論團體。
(D) 他為許多公司設計商標。

### 162. 確認事實與否

關於《商標設計靈感》，文中提及什麼事？

**(A) 它包含一部分的空白頁面。**
(B) 它也有電子書版本。
(C) 史塔克斯先生的一個朋友為這本書進行研究調查。
(D) 目前已絕版。

**換句話說**

ten empty pages（十頁的空白頁面）
→ (A) a section of blank pages（一部分的空白頁面）

### 163. 相關細節

齊拉塔瑞克斯是什麼樣的公司？

(A) 電腦軟體開發商
**(B) 健身器材製造商**
(C) 包裹運送服務公司
(D) 平面設計公司

**換句話說**

a maker of exercise machines
（運動器材製造商）
→ (B) A fitness equipment manufacturer
（健身器材製造商）

## 164–167 網頁公告

www.curiosom.com/news/0111

### 1 月 11 日─關於克里歐森公司更換支付服務商的正式公告——它對我們訂戶的意義

從將近 15 年前成立以來，克里歐森公司已成長為 [164] **攝影師與全球社群分享照片的首選之地**。當我們開始提供付費訂閱以獲得無限上傳照片的權利時，我們的管理部門選擇 [166] **布蘭納加支付服務處理我們訂戶的帳務**，我們的決定主要是基於布蘭納加能讓我們的一年和兩年訂閱方案自動續約。

然而，當 [165] **我們去年六月成為巴拿麥特公司的子公司**時，[166] **我們開始轉換到他們的支付服務公司迪吉特克斯特 -D**，以統一我們的帳務系統。遺憾地是，迪吉特克斯特 -D 已經通知我們，[166] **他們無法展延任何來自我們之前支付服務商的克里歐森公司訂閱服務**，這影響了 [166] **所有在去年 6 月 30 日或之前開始訂閱的克里歐森會員**。為了避開這個問題，[166/167] **我們鼓勵這些會員把握續約的早鳥八折優惠**，[167] **如果這麼做，您的訂閱將持續無間斷至它的中止日期為止，而且可以自動續約。若您不採取行動，在您目前的訂閱到期後，必須更新您的訂戶檔案和帳務資料。**然後將收取您選擇的訂閱方案的正常費用。因此，我們建議所有受影響的訂戶早早續約。

- **subscriber (n.)** 訂閱者
  **inception (n.)** 成立；創立
  **premier (adj.)** 首要的；最重要的
  **subscription (n.)** 訂閱　**privilege (n.)** 特權
  **renew (v.)** 續約；展期　**subsidiary (n.)** 子公司
  **unify (v.)** 統一；使相同　**originate (v.)** 來自
  **take advantage of** 利用
  **uninterrupted (adj.)** 不間斷的

### 164. 推論或暗示

克里歐森公司最可能是哪種公司？

(A) 視覺藝術家看的電子雜誌
(B) 廣告分析服務商
(C) 線上會計應用程式
**(D) 照片分享平台**

**換句話說**

venue for photographers to share their pictures
（攝影師分享他們的照片的地方）
→ (D) photo sharing platform（照片分享平台）

### 165. 相關細節 

根據公告，前一年發生了什麼事？

(A) 週年慶
**(B) 公司收購**
(C) 推出新產品
(D) 訂閱費調升

**換句話說**

we became a subsidiary of Panamat.com（我們成為巴拿麥特公司的子公司）
→ (B) A business acquisition（公司收購）

### 166. 相關細節 

目前誰有資格享受折扣優惠？

(A) 過去一週開始訂閱服務的訂戶
(B) 選擇續訂三年或更久的訂戶
**(C) 一開始由布蘭納普拉斯寄發帳單的訂戶**
(D) 也是巴拿麥特公司會員的訂戶

### 167. 句子插入題 難

「然後將收取您選擇的訂閱方案的正常費用。」最適合放在標示 [1]、[2]、[3]、[4] 的何處？

(A) [1]　(C) [3]
(B) [2]　**(D) [4]**

## 168–171 線上聊天室

奧瑞莉亞・瑞穆斯〔下午 2:04〕
嗨，各位，我只是來查看狀況。我們的顧客討論區網頁的腦力激盪進展得如何？有任何文章的構想嗎？

彼得・修〔下午 2:05〕
有，我想寫一篇如何讓倉庫變亮的正確指南。

奧瑞莉亞・瑞穆斯〔下午 2:06〕
很好。[168] **我們的確有很多跟我們買照明用品的商業客戶**，所以我們的討論區內容應該反映他們的需求。有其他點子嗎？

琳達・梅洛〔下午 2:07〕
[169] **就我們的消費客戶，我想要寫些如何為休閒娛樂室選擇最佳固定燈具的秘訣，有好多選擇。**

奧瑞莉亞・瑞穆斯〔下午 2:07〕
當然。

琳達・梅洛〔下午 2:08〕
[170] **我還可以寫一篇摩伊謝・魏茲的人物簡介**，他是那個用回收工業管材製作壁燈的手工藝人。

奧瑞莉亞・瑞穆斯〔下午 2:09〕
太好了。[170] **妳以前和他一起工作，對嗎？**

琳達・梅洛〔下午 2:10〕
是的，[170] **我是他的學徒。**

彼得・修〔下午 2:11〕
這讓我想到了，我還有另一個點子。[171] **我們應該寫一篇貼文，詳細說明一些常見的技術用語**，讓它們更容易理解。

奧瑞莉亞・瑞穆斯〔下午 2:12〕
那會有很幫助。[171] **你可以寫嗎？**

彼得・修〔下午 2:13〕
[171] **當然可以。**

奧瑞莉亞・瑞穆斯〔下午 2:14〕
很好，謝謝你們兩位貢獻意見，我這星期晚點再來查看你們的進度。

- brainstorming (n.) 集思廣益
  commercial client (n.) 商業客戶
  supplies (n.) 用品
  consumer client (n.) 消費客戶
  lighting fixture (n.) 固定燈具
  artisan (n.) 手工藝人　apprentice (n.) 學徒
  clarify (v.) 闡明　input (n.) 貢獻意見或建議

**168. 推論或暗示**

參與對話者最可能在哪種公司工作？

(A) 園藝工具製造商
**(B) 燈具用品販售商**
(C) 儲藏設備連鎖店
(D) 電氣技師看的商業刊物

- publication (n.) 刊物

**169. 掌握意圖**

下午 2:07，當梅洛女士寫道：「有好多選擇」，她的意思最可能是什麼？

(A) 某位同事可能需要更多時間做決定。
(B) 她不確定如何開始寫一篇文章。
**(C) 選擇太多可能令顧客不知所措。**
(D) 她對建議事項清單印象深刻。

- overwhelm (v.) 使無法承受

**170. 確認事實與否**

關於梅洛女士，可由文中得知什麼？

**(A) 她以前在魏茲先生指導下做事。**
(B) 她組織回收活動計畫。
(C) 她目前正在改造她的家。
(D) 她以前是雜誌記者。

- initiative (n.) 計畫

**換句話說**

I was his apprentice.（我是他的學徒。）
→ (A) She worked under Mr. Wietz's guidance.（她以前在魏茲先生指導下做事。）

**171. 相關細節**

修先生同意做什麼？

(A) 收集資料以衡量顧客的滿意度
**(B) 發想解釋一些用語的內容**
(C) 在共享日曆上貼出提醒備忘錄
(D) 監督一個實習生計畫

- customer satisfaction (n.) 顧客滿意度
  reminder (n.) 提醒物　supervise (v.) 監督

**換句話說**

create a post that clarifies some common technical terms（寫一篇貼文，詳細說明一些常見的技術用語）
→ (B) Develop content that explains some expressions（發想解釋一些用語的內容）

**172–175 文章**

《企業家新聞時報》　4 月 23 日

**咖啡館老闆應該知道……**
文／凱拉・利契

➢ 經營獨立咖啡館的人很快就會發現，他們決定所供應的餐點收費多寡對利潤將有重大影響，因為咖啡館競爭激烈，[172] **決定產品與服務的最佳定價很重要。**

➢ 當 [173] **我將近十年前開始經營「連結咖啡館」**時，我打算收取和主要連鎖咖啡店一樣的價格，但提供優質的服務。這個策略成功吸引了顧客，但並沒有帶來不錯的收入。在我開業一年後，我找人做了一次市場調查研究，發現大部分顧客已經認為獨立咖啡館會提供較高級的服務與產品品質。記住這一點後，我開始供應更高品質、更昂貴的優質咖啡飲品。

➢[174] 為了進一步證明我的較高定價合理，我努力開拓咖啡館的利基，成為鄰近地區的人約碰面的地方。[173] 我每個月為顧客舉行有趣的特別活動，例如調製咖啡工作坊或咖啡品嚐課程。這些聚會對咖啡館的形象有正面效果。

➢ 當然，收費也可以比競爭對手低，但這不一定保證能夠帶來足夠的額外業績讓獲利增加，[175] 畢竟，獨立咖啡館老闆已經投入大量金錢在設備與貨品上，因此必須讓利潤最大化。

---

**關於作者：[173] 利契女士是土生土長的迪市人，她在那裡經營一家很成功的咖啡館。**就在上星期，她提供給全球咖啡館與茶館老闆的線上資源網站 www.cafe-owners.com 開始上線營運了。

- offering (n.) 供銷售之物　optimal (adj.) 最佳的
  aim (v.) 打算　superior (adj.) 優越的
  decent (adj.) 像樣的；還不錯的
  earnings (n.) 收入　commission (v.) 委任
  perceive (v.) 認為；視為
  justify (v.) 證明……有理
  carve out a niche 努力開拓利基
  impact (n.) 衝擊　establishment (n.) 企業；機構
  profitability (n.) 獲利能力
  inventory (n.) （商店的）貨品／存貨
  returns (n.) 收益；利潤
  operational (adj.) （系統）運作中的

**172. 主旨或目的**

撰寫這篇文章的原因最可能為何？

(A) 解釋為何許多咖啡館無法獲利
(B) 提供管理咖啡館員工的祕訣
**(C) 提供咖啡館老闆定價建議**
(D) 概述咖啡館近來的業界趨勢

**換句話說**
prices for products and services（產品與服務的定價）→ (C) pricing（定價）

**173. 確認事實與否** 難

關於「連結咖啡館」，可由文中得知什麼？

(A) 已開業超過十年。
(B) 舉辦雙週特別活動。
(C) 有本行銷書籍寫了它的簡介。
**(D) 位於利契女士的家鄉。**

**174. 相關細節** 難

「連結咖啡館」做了改變的理由之一是什麼？

**(A) 讓它與競爭對手有所區隔**
(B) 縮短顧客的等候時間
(C) 減少它對環境的衝擊
(D) 讓它成為令人更愉快的工作場所

- differentiate (v.) 區別；使有差異

**175. 同義詞考題** 

第四段第三行的「good」，意思最接近何者？

(A) 令人滿意的　　**(C) 大量的**
(B) 可信任的　　(D) 有用的

**176–180 報導與網頁公告**

**考威市戲劇團將公演**
**《凱更街》**

考威市　訊（6 月 3 日）—— [178] **考威市劇團（CCTG）將以唐娜．曼森有趣的喜劇《凱更街》開啟它的夏季公演檔期，從 6 月 10 日**星期五演到 6 月 26 日星期日為止，星期五和星期六的演出在下午七點，而星期日則在下午兩點。

[176/180] **本劇以布萊德和瑪莉生命中的一天為中心，這一對年輕夫妻邀請他們的新鄰居**肯和珍妮絲過來吃烤肉晚餐。在燒烤時，這兩對夫妻得知，[176] **就在幾個星期前，他們分別參加了同一家旅行社的橫越非洲之旅，隨著劇中人物分享國際旅行的有趣、驚險和啟發人心的各種趣聞，[177] 戲劇帶領觀眾進入了一種奇幻感。**

演出陣容包括西城的艾瑞克．葛里菲、希爾塞德市的尹艾美、東谷的凱文．布萊達克和西城的貝茲．馬利基。[178] **在 6 月 10 日的演出結束後，觀眾可以和演員見面並拍照，**導演喬治．穆威也會在現場回答觀眾的問題。

更多關於 CCTG 的資訊，請上 www.colway-theater.org。可透過 CCTG 的網站或於售票口購票。

- kick off（活動等）開始
  center around . . . （話題或興趣）以……為中心
  overland (adj.) （旅行）橫跨陸地的
  anecdote (n.) 趣聞；軼事
  inspirational (adj.) 啟發人心的
  aspect (n.) 方面　audience (n.) 觀眾
  be on hand 在場　box office (n.) 售票處

http://www.colway-theater.org/home

**考威市劇團（CCTG）**

6 月 6 日更新：[179] **CCTG 管理部很高興宣布，我們將在每個星期六下午兩點加演我們夏季公演的第一齣戲《凱更街》**。星期五和星期六的晚場在下午七時，而星期日的日場是下午兩點。

[180] **這齣由考威市本地人喬治・穆威執導的戲，將由才華洋溢的凱文・布萊達克主演布萊德一角，和我們劇團首次合作登台，和他搭檔的有飾演瑪莉的尹艾美**、飾演凱文的艾瑞克・葛里菲和飾演珍妮絲的貝茲・馬利基。

- management (n.) 管理部門
  matinee (adj.)（電影或戲劇的）日場
  direct (v.) 執導　feature (v.) 由……主演
  talented (adj.) 才華洋溢的

**176. 相關細節**

《凱更街》的主題是什麼？

**(A) 有共同經驗的鄰居**
(B) 一個家庭的幽默烹飪錯誤
(C) 移民適應新文化
(D) 經常搬家的挑戰

- immigrant (n.) 移民　adapt to 適應

**177. 同義詞考題** 

在報導中，第二段第 11 行的「carries」，意思最接近下列何者？

**(A) 推動**　(C) 溝通
(B) 維持　(D) 捕獲

**178. 相關細節** 

《凱更街》的首演觀眾會得到什麼？

(A) CCTG 未來劇碼的預告
**(B) 和演員交流的機會**
(C) 參加劇院導覽的抽選
(D) 一份和戲劇主題有關的小禮物

- preview (n.) 預告　drawing (n.) 抽籤

**換句話說**
meet and take photos with the performers（和演員見面並拍照）
→ (B) interact with the cast（和演員交流）

**179. 主旨或目的**

公告的主要目的最可能為何？

(A) 鼓勵提早購票
(B) 向舞台劇導演致敬
(C) 宣布某位演員退休
**(D) 宣傳表演要加演的時程表**

- retirement (n.) 退休　publicize (v.) 宣傳
  expand (v.) 增加

**換句話說**
extra（額外的）→ (D) expanded（增加的）

**180. 整合題** 

關於布萊達克先生，可由文中得知什麼事？

(A) 他出現在 CCTG 網站的一支影片中。
(B) 他將演出 6 月 26 日下午七點的場次。
**(C) 他將扮演尹女士所飾角色的丈夫。**
(D) 他和穆威先生來自同一個城市。

**181–185 摘要與電子郵件**

高爾馬克研究公司

**四種奶昔飲料的市場調查**
**研究摘要**

**客戶名稱：**蒙特洛伊圓點
**說明：**高爾馬克研究公司受大型連鎖休閒餐廳「蒙特洛伊圓點」僱用，評估顧客對它的四種奶昔飲料的反應。[181] **調查於八月中到九月中在該公司位於俄亥俄州克里夫蘭和賓州匹茲堡的各餐廳進行**。參與者受指示前往他們所在區域的餐廳，[181] **隨機分派四種奶昔飲料的其中一種口味給他們試喝。然後，他們必須透過他們的手機點選一個連結，回答一份包含選擇題和開放式問題的調查。**

**所有調查結果：**

| | |
|---|---|
| 樣本 #1 | **香蕉與櫻桃口味**<br>回答者中表示「很好喝」的百分比—79%<br>[182] **最常見的意見：「香蕉味太重」、「喝不太到櫻桃味」** |
| 樣本 #2 | **鳳梨與芒果口味**<br>回答者中表示「很好喝」的百分比—82%<br>[182] **最常見的意見：「清爽的口味」、「鳳梨味不夠」** |

| | |
|---|---|
| 樣本 #3 | [184] 鹹味焦糖口味<br>[184] 回答者中表示「很好喝」的百分比—84%<br>最常見的意見：「味道很重」、「顏色很吸引人」 |
| 樣本 #4 | 椰子與香草口味<br>回答者中表示「很好喝」的百分比—87%<br>最常見的意見：「口感濃郁」、「甜味剛好」 |

- casual dining restaurant (n.) 休閒餐廳
  assess (v.) 評估　participant (n.) 參與者
  assign (v.) 分派；分配　sample (v.) 品嚐
  consist of 由……組成　finding (n.) 結果
  respondent (n.) 回答者
  refreshing (adj.) 清爽的
  texture (n.) 結構；質地

**收件人：**芭芭拉．密利根
<b.milligan@goalmarkkresearch.com>
**寄件人：**卡爾．佩拉
<c.pella@goalmarkkresearch.com>
**日期：**10 月 2 日
**主旨：**「蒙特洛伊圓點」的調查研究結果
**附件：**圖和表格

嗨，芭芭拉：

如妳所要求，我已附上「蒙特洛伊圓點」報告的圖和表格。[185] **妳設計的電子問卷讓受訪者說出意見回饋的效果非常好。我很高興調查過程順利，尤其是考量到我們公司以前從未用過這種線上格式的情況下。**

[183] **根據我們先前為這位客戶所做的調查，大部分的結果和我先前的預測相符。**然而，有個結果的確很突出，[184] **我原先以為最不受歡迎的口味，結果卻是第二受歡迎的，**我真的沒有預料到這個結果。

讓我知道妳是否需要更多資料，以支持我們給客戶的建議。

謝謝。

卡爾

- questionnaire (n.) 問卷
  effective (adj.) 有效的
  elicit (v.) 引出（尤指資訊或反應）
  consistent with 與……一致
  project (v.) 預測　stand out 突出；出眾
  anticipate (v.) 預期



**181. 確認事實與否** 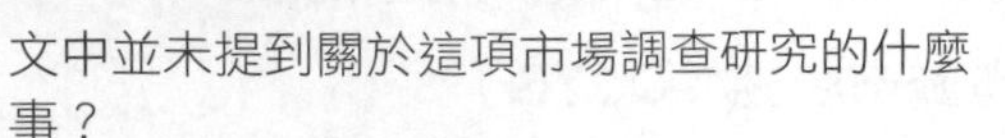

文中並未提到關於這項市場調查研究的什麼事？

(A) 它在兩個城市進行。
(B) 它需要使用行動裝置。
(C) 它的調查有選擇題。
**(D) 每位參與者都試喝了四種飲料。**

**182. 相關細節** 

有兩種試喝的飲料得到什麼共同的回饋意見？

(A) 太濃了。
(B) 口味很清爽。
**(C) 混合的口味不均勻。**
(D) 顏色很吸引人。

- uneven (adj.)（品質）不均勻的

**183. 推論或暗示**

關於「蒙特洛伊圓點」，下列何者最可能為真？

(A) 計劃擴展到其他地區。
(B) 從匹茲堡起家。
(C) 提供很多不同的瓶裝飲料。
**(D) 以前向高爾馬克研究公司諮詢過。**

**184. 整合題**

哪一個樣品得到的正面回饋意見比佩拉先生預期的多？

(A) 樣本 #1　　**(C) 樣本 #3**
(B) 樣本 #2　　(D) 樣本 #4

**185. 確認事實與否**

關於密利根女士，可由文中得知什麼事？

(A) 她以前在一家食品製造商工作。
**(B) 她設計了一家公司的第一份電子調查表。**
(C) 她會在 10 月和一位客戶碰面。
(D) 她修改了一份市場報告中的圖。

- manufacturer (n.) 製造業者；廠商

**換句話說**

The electronic questionnaire you designed
（妳設計的電子問卷）
→ (B) She created a . . . electronic survey.
（她設計了一份……電子調查表。）
our firm had never used the online format before（我們公司以前從未用過這種線上格式）
→ (B) a firm's first electronic survey
（一家公司的第一份電子調查表）

## 186–190 通訊文章、傳單與電子郵件

**《歐塔物業通訊》** **八月號**

芝加哥　訊——住戶的舒適與便利對歐塔物業來說很重要。正因如此，[186] **我們很高興地宣布，我們已經和「隆得利快洗」建立合夥關係**，這是一家隨選服務公司，會來取住戶的待洗衣物，並把洗乾淨的衣物放回便利的儲物櫃裡。

這項服務在我們的兩棟公寓大樓都有提供。曼沃斯大樓的儲物櫃將於 8 月 20 日安裝在住戶休息區，而考特威大樓則於 8 月 27 日安裝在健身中心對面。每位住戶會從大樓經理那拿到一把分配到的儲物櫃鑰匙。[187] **每棟大樓大廳的櫃檯服務人員將受托登記隆得利快洗人員的名字**。

透過隆得利的網站 www.laundry-flash.com 即可輕鬆安排取件服務的時間。處理時間是兩天，也有當天送回的快洗服務。[189] **洗衣費用每件襯衫 3 元、每件褲子 5 元，每件套裝或洋裝 15 元**。公司的廣告傳單上有折價券，可於大廳取得。

- property (n.) 房地產；物業
  on-demand service 隨選服務
  tenant (n.) 住戶；房客　garment (n.) 衣服
  installation (n.) 安裝　attendant (n.) 服務員
  entrust (v.) 委託　turnaround time (n.) 處理時間
  flyer (n.)（廣告）傳單

**隆得利快洗**

我們收取你的衣物，洗乾淨，並在兩天後送回——掛保證！

歐塔物業管理的大樓住戶請注意——
[188] **我們一切就緒，準備和你們做生意了！**

| 特惠券（提及代碼 166） |
|---|
| 曼沃斯大樓和考特威大樓的住戶服務費用總計 20 元或以上者，享九折優惠 |

- **如何申請服務**
  上我們的網站 www.laundry-flash.com，前往線上預定區。我們也可以透過電話 555-0129 預定。
- **取件時間**
  - [190] **北區（包括位在艾佛利街 5320 號的曼沃斯大樓）**星期一、星期三、星期五
  - 南區（包括位在迪克森路 1811 號的考特威大樓）星期二、星期四、星期六
- **價格**（標準兩日服務，包括取件與送件）
  [189] **襯衫 3 元，褲子 5 元，洋裝 8 元，套裝 15 元**。洗加摺，每磅 1.6 元。當天來回快洗服務，加收 10 元。
- **洗衣袋**
  每位顧客在第一次交件時，會收到一個免費洗衣袋——這是送給你的，留著之後需要服務時可用。可購買額外的洗衣袋，每個 14 元。

- surcharge (n.) 額外費用
  complimentary (adj.) 贈送的

收件人：雅各．葛里茲 <j-gritz@mail.com>
寄件人：<orders@laundry-flash.com>
主旨：隆得利快洗確認信
**日期：9 月 1 日**

感謝您申請服務——確認代碼 #22176158。

[190] **顧客姓名：雅各．葛里茲**　　**儲物櫃號碼：**12

[190] **地址：艾佛利街 5320 號**　　**取件日期：**9 月 2 日星期一

| 品項 | 價格 | 單項總金額 |
|---|---|---|
| 襯衫（清洗） | 3.00 元 × 4 | 12.00 元 |
| 褲子（清洗） | 5.00 元 × 4 | 20.00 元 |
| 洗衣袋 | 0.00 元 | |
| | −3.20 元 | 9 折券優惠碼 166 |
| | 總金額 | 28.80 元 |

付款方式：信用卡 末四碼 1362

- confirmation (n.)（常指書面的）確認

**186. 主旨或目的**

此篇通訊文章的主要目的為何？

(A) 徵求讀者的意見
(B) 謝謝住戶的忠實支持
(C) 報告整修工程的進度
**(D) 說明一項新服務的細節**

**187. 相關細節**

根據通訊文章，曼沃斯大樓和考特威大樓有什麼共同點？

(A) 有給住戶用的運動設施。
(B) 會在同一天安裝儲物櫃。
(C) 出租單位數相同。
**(D) 都附有櫃檯。**

換句話說
each building（每棟大樓）→ (B) the Menworth and the Courtway Buildings（曼沃斯大樓和考特威大樓）
The front desk attendant（櫃檯服務人員）→ (D) attended front desks（附有櫃檯）

**188. 同義詞考題**

在傳單中，第一段第二行的「set」，意思最接近下列何者？

(A) 估算的 **(C) 準備好的**
(B) 恢復的 (D) 固定的

**189. 整合題**

文章中的什麼資訊可能不正確？

(A) 快速處理的選項
**(B) 衣物清洗費用**
(C) 網址
(D) 優惠券的有無

- expedite (v.) 迅速完成

**190. 整合題**

關於葛里茲先生，下列何者最可能為真？

(A) 他要求多給一個洗衣袋。
**(B) 他住在曼沃斯大樓。**
(C) 他的衣服會在星期二送回。
(D) 他因為使用信用卡而有折扣。

**191–195 網頁、電子郵件與線上評論**

www.jerroldssupply.com/about

**傑洛德供應**

關於我們

我們是本地最大的餐飲業者會員制量販店。

任何符合資格 * 的業者都可免費入會。享有這些很棒的好處：

- **一站式購物**：我們備有所有主要品牌的食品與飲料，還有廚房設備，甚至是主廚服。只要走一趟就能買齊您所有的用品。
- **沒有最低消費要求**：我們和巴斯可俱樂部和其他 [193] **開放給大眾的**量販店最大的不同在於，[193] **在「傑洛德供應」，您永遠不需要大量購買**。
- **廣告專刊**：我們每月寄發電子郵件，持續告知會員最新的特賣活動。

* 備註：我們是批發市場，不開放給一般大眾。會員卡只發給擁有或管理餐廳者。在您第一次到店裡時，[192] **必須出示有效文件，顯示您有餐飲業者的執照**。然後會發給您 [191] **一張不可轉讓的卡**。不過，您每個月可以帶一位貴賓同行，只要他們在入店時出示有照片的身分證件即可。

- supply (n.) 供應；供應品；生活用品
  warehouse store (n.) 量販店
  operator (n.)（企業）經營者
  qualified (adj.) 合格的
  stock (v.)（商店或工廠）儲備有……可賣
  apparel (n.)（某種類型的）衣服 in bulk 大量
  wholesale (adj.) 批發的 valid (adj.) 有效的
  transferable (adj.) 可轉移的 present (v.) 出示

**收件人**：史黛拉．艾德森
**寄件人**：蒂娜．羅禮
**日期**：10 月 9 日
**主旨**：明天的差事——有興趣嗎？

嗨，史黛拉：

[194] **我明天早上必須去傑洛德供應，補充餐廳的餐巾和外帶餐盒**，妳有次曾表示有興趣看看量販店，因此我在想，不知道妳想不想要一起去，我可以在上午九點整到妳的公寓前面接妳。請回簡訊或寄電子郵件給我，告訴我妳是否能去。

要去的話，務必帶身分證件，並穿舒適的鞋子，量販店很大，所以要走很多路。還有，[195] **如果妳想參觀冷凍區，帶件外套**。裡面相當冷。

希望明天能見到妳。

蒂娜

- errand (n.) 差事；跑腿 stock up 儲備
  carry-out (adj.)（食物）外帶的
  container (n.) 容器
  outerwear (n.)（總稱）外套

**評論者：**史黛拉．艾德森
**評論日期：**10 月 11 日

我昨天第一次去「傑洛德供應」。就像巴斯可俱樂部一樣，它也是量販店，販售的商品價格超低。但是，[193] **不像那家店，它沒有賣平板電視或電腦設備**，而是供應一切經營餐廳所需的物品，我看到六千張的大包裝紙餐巾！更令人吃驚的是冷凍海鮮的選擇之多，我在那一區待的時間比我原先打算的久，[195] **讓我希望自己有帶毛衣來。**[195] **店裡擠滿人，排隊結帳的隊伍很長，但移動得很快**，我很幸運認識有會員身分的人，因此在她買東西時，我能以訪客的身分進來。

- flat-screen (n.)（電視或電腦）平面螢幕
  up and running 運行　vast (adj.) 大量的
  intend (v.) 打算

**191. 確認事實與否**

關於「傑洛德供應」，可由網頁中得知什麼事？

**(A) 會員資格不得轉移。**
(B) 每天開門營業。
(C) 舉辦給主廚的烹飪課。
(D) 有自動結帳站。

**換句話說**
not transferable（不可轉讓）→ (A) may not be transferred（不得轉移）

---

**192. 相關細節**

想要有「傑洛德供應」的會員卡，必須有什麼？

(A) 以電子郵件寄送的邀請函
(B) 每月最低購買量
**(C) 有效的營業執照**
(D) 兩種有照片的身分證件

**換句話說**
a valid document showing you are licensed as a food service business（有效文件顯示您有餐飲業者的執照）→ (C) A valid business license（有效的營業執照）

---

**193. 整合題** 難

文中未提到關於巴斯可俱樂部的什麼事？

(A) 它販賣消費性電子產品。
(B) 一般大眾可在那裡購物。
(C) 它的商品都是大分量販售。
**(D) 它和傑洛德供應屬同一家母公司。**

**194. 確認事實與否**

在電子郵件中，羅禮女士提到要買什麼？

(A) 廚房用具
(B) 用餐器具
**(C) 食品包裝材料**
(D) 原料

**換句話說**
carry-out containers for the restaurant（餐廳外帶餐盒）
→ (C) Food packaging（食品包裝材料）

---

**195. 整合題** 

關於艾德森女士，下列何者最可能為真？

**(A) 她沒有遵循羅禮女士的某些建議。**
(B) 她去「傑洛德供應」的行程延後了。
(C) 她最後沒有和羅禮女士一起去。
(D) 她去「傑洛德供應」那天，店裡異常忙碌。

---

**196–200 簡報講義、議程表與簡訊**

## 如何改善公司網站

**提案人：**葛瑞格．吳，網站顧問

**提案對象：**布雷科斯比自行車公司

**日期：**5 月 2 日

公司網站的強項：
- [196] **引人注目的配色**—瀏覽網站時，看起來很舒適
- [196] **各系列產品的照片都很吸引人**—大小和間隔都很恰當
- [196] **名為「為什麼開始騎單車？」那一區，很有說服力地概述騎單車對健康的好處**

公司網站的弱點：
- 每一頁的文字和資訊太多—可能讓人困惑
- 載入時間太長—有些顧客可能因此而離開網站
- 購物結帳過程太複雜—太多表格要填寫

行動方案——經公司同意，藉此改善網站：
- [198] **移除開啟網站時的一支數位影片，將大幅縮減載入所需的時間**
- 精簡結帳流程，同時以更明顯的圖形呈現付款選項（例如：信用卡、禮券、電子商務帳戶等）
- 在網站上另開一區，放置公司最新的電動自行車系列產品，其中將包含自行車如何充電的簡短說明

- color scheme (n.) 色彩搭配

appealing (adj.) 吸引人的　spacing (n.) 間隔
appropriate (adj.) 恰當的
persuasively (adv.) 有說服力地
complicated (adj.) 複雜的　approval (n.) 同意
streamline (v.) 精簡　prominent (adj.) 顯眼的
separate (adj.) 不同的

布雷科斯比自行車公司

**5 月 30 日策略會議 * 的建議議程**

| | |
|---|---|
| 下午 2:00 | 概述主題：持續努力升級公司網站 |
| 下午 2:15 | 第一項：仔細檢視目前的網站，[198] **一邊解釋顧問已實施（更快的載入時間、更顯眼的付款選項、增加最新產品區）與被拒絕（更短的結帳流程）的建議** |
| 下午 3:00 | 第二項：數位行銷總監特洛伊．維登簡報顧問來訪時，對網站所提其他較小的修改建議 |
| 下午 4:00 | 第三項：[197] **討論提供線上聊天支援的利弊**，由公司內部的網站開發人員佛瑞德．考洛威主持 |
| 下午 4:30 | [200] 第四項：**就網站可能的互動功能進行腦力激盪** |
| 下午 5:00 | 休會 |

* 由業務經理艾莉森．浩爾主持，[197] **與會者必須攜帶筆記型電腦**

- ongoing (adj.) 繼續進行的
  walk-through (n.) 仔細檢視
  implement (v.) 實施　modification (n.) 修改
  pros and cons (n.) 利弊
  in-house (adj.) 在組織內部的
  potential (adj.) 可能的；潛在的
  adjournment (n.) 休會

**發訊者**：佛瑞德．考洛威（5 月 30 日上午 10:17）

嗨，艾莉森。我剛剛研究了一個競爭對手的網站，發現了有趣的事情。有一區提供一個自行車的數位影像，可以 [199] **透過操作電腦滑鼠或觸控螢幕**將它「客製化」。我會在開會時把這個秀給大家看，因此 [200] **我想要在討論可能的互動功能時多加 15 分鐘**。謝謝。

- customize (v.) 客製
  manipulate (v.)（用手）操縱；控制
  allot (v.) 分配

**196. 確認事實與否**

關於布雷科斯比自行車公司網站的強項，文中未提及何者？

(A) 商品的圖像
(B) 顏色的選擇
**(C) 文字大小**
(D) 關於騎單車與健康的內容

**換句話說**

photos of all product lines（各系列產品的照片）
→ (A) image of merchandise（商品的圖像）
color schemes（配色）
→ (B) choice of color（顏色的選擇）
Section . . . outlines health benefits of cycling（……概述騎單車對健康的好處的那區）
→ (D) content on cycling and health（騎單車與健康的內容）

**197. 推論或暗示** 

5 月 30 日會議的與會者最可能做什麼？

**(A) 辯論提案的優點**
(B) 使用借來的筆記型電腦
(C) 注意聽顧問的簡報
(D) 決定某個專案的截止時間

**換句話說**

Discussion of pros and cons . . . of offering online chat support
（討論提供線上聊天支援的利弊……）
→ (A) Debate the merits of a proposal（辯論提案的優點）

**198. 整合題** 

布雷科斯比自行車公司的網站最近最可能做了什麼改變？

(A) 說明頁面縮短。
**(B) 刪除一支數位影片。**
(C) 簡化付款流程。
(D) 修改一個產品類別。

- eliminate (v.) 消除

**換句話說**

Removing a digital video（移除一支數位影片）
→ (B) A digital video was eliminated.
（刪除一支數位影片。）

**199. 同義詞考題**

在簡訊中，第四行的「manipulating」，意思最接近下列何者？

(A) 哄騙　　(C) 改變
**(B) 操作**　　(D) 安裝

---

**200. 整合題**

考洛威先生想為議程中的哪一個項目安排更多時間？

(A) 第一項　　(C) 第三項
(B) 第二項　　**(D) 第四項**

**換句話說**
**would like to allot 15 more minutes**
（想要多加 15 分鐘）
**→ want to schedule more time**
（想要安排更多時間）

# ACTUAL TEST 8

**PART 5** P. 204–206

**101. 所有格代名詞——主詞補語** 難

每一次團體旅行結束時，每位參加者會收到一張紀念照供留存。

(A) 他們　**(C) 他們的（東西）**
(B) 他們　(D) 他們自己

- participant (n.) 參加者；參與者
  souvenir photo (n.) 紀念照

---

**102. 名詞詞彙題——主詞補語**

經營民族風餐廳的成功關鍵在於道地性。

**(A) 道地性**　(C) 證實
(B) 道地的　(D) 道地地

- ethnic (adj.) 民族的
  authenticate (v.) 證明……是真實的
  authentically (adv.) 道地地；真實地

---

**103. 動詞詞彙題**

這座城市的景觀設計師，正想辦法要決定如何能將更多樹納入史賓塞運河計畫中。

(A) 反映　(C) 增強
(B) 鼓勵　**(D) 決定**

- landscape architect (n.) 景觀設計師
  canal (n.) 運河

---

**104. 介系詞詞彙題**

顧客若要求，可郵寄含有我們產品說明與照片的紙本目錄給他們。

(A) 在……之後　(C) 為了
**(B) 在……後立即**　(D) 沿著

---

**105. 副詞詞彙題**

桑德瑞克斯公司採礦機器的設計，是為了即使在最惡劣的狀況下也能確實運轉。

(A) 連續地　(C) 寬敞地
**(B) 確實地**　(D) 考慮周到地

- mining (n.) 採礦；礦業
  perform (v.)（機器）運轉

**106. 名詞詞彙題**

建議新手健行者以悠閒的速度行走，不要走太快，尤其在陡峭的山徑上。

(A) 程度　(C) 路徑
(B) 伸展　**(D) 步調**

- novice (n.) 新手　steep (adj.) 陡峭的

---

**107. 副詞詞彙題——修飾動詞**

府上的暖氣系統應該每六個月檢查一次，確保它的運轉效率盡可能好。

(A) 效率　**(C) 有效地**
(B) 有效的　(D) 更有效的

---

**108. 副詞詞彙題**

有要在東丘市蓋一個新的研發中心的計畫，但還沒有決定確切的位置。

(A) 足夠的　**(C) 尚未**
(B) 一次　(D) 較晚的

---

**109. 動詞詞彙題** 

柴提利亞的 X10 手機非常耐用，即使掉落在堅硬的表面上也不會受損。

(A) 終止　(C) 減少
**(B) 遭受**　(D) 犯錯

- terminate (v.) 終止　diminish (v.) 減少
  commit (v.) 犯錯；犯罪

---

**110. 形容詞詞彙題——修飾名詞**

拉克思邁科技公司以人人負擔得起的價格，開發令人印象深刻的個人及企業網站。

**(A) 令人印象深刻的**　(C) 令人印象深刻地
(B) 使人留下印象　(D) 印象

---

**111. 副詞子句連接詞詞彙題** 

費爾威市的新回收容器免費提供給居民，數量有限，送完為止。

(A) 朝向　**(C) 當……的時候**
(B) 在……期間　(D) 在……範圍內

- while supply last 售完為止；送完為止

**112. 介系詞詞彙題**

公司的使命宣言中，簡短概述了它的願景和目標。

(A) ……的　**(C) 在……中**
(B) 向　(D) 關於

- objective (n.) 目標　summarize (v.) 概述

**113. 形容詞詞彙題**

VT-5 健身腳踏車非常適合小公寓，因為它所占的空間很小。

**(A) 非常合適的**　(C) 有說服力的
(B) 謹慎的　(D) 能夠做……

- exercise bike (n.) 室內健身腳踏車
  occupy (v.) 占（時間、空間）
  deliberate (adj.) 謹慎的

**114. 副詞詞彙題** 

瑞納可公司的建築物模型套組的特色是每塊都標示得很清楚，可以毫不費力地組裝好。

(A) 非常　(C) 迅速地
(B) 遙遠地　**(D) 明確地**

- kit (n.) 成套的工具或物件　assemble (v.) 組裝
  minimum (adj.) 最少的

**115. 名詞詞彙題——動詞受詞**

攝影比賽的優勝者馬克．墨多說，他的靈感來自空無一人的沙漠景色。

(A) 得到靈感的　(C) 鼓舞人心的
(B) 啟發靈感　**(D) 靈感**

**116. 動詞詞類變化題——語態**

多虧新的教育應用程式，手機可以在課堂上當作學習工具使用。

**(A) 被使用**　(C) 已使用
(B) 正被使用　(D) 使用

**117. 介系詞詞彙題**

除了它自己使用生質燃料的遊覽車外，格林維德公園不允許任何車輛在它景色優美的道路上通行。

(A) 遍布　(C) 不管
**(B) 除了……以外**　(D) 沒有

- bio-fuel (n.) 生質燃料

**118. 形容詞詞彙題——分詞**

技藝超群的室內設計師艾爾豐索．克里柯為各種不同的客戶提供設計解決方案。

(A) 完成　(C) 完成
**(B) 有才藝的**　(D) 成就

**119. 代名詞詞彙題——介系詞的受詞——主詞動詞單複數一致性**

曼吉就業博覽會開放給任何在找新工作的人參加，不論目前的就業狀態。

(A) 每一個　(C) 那些
(B) 所有　**(D) 任何人**

- career fair (n.) 就業博覽會
  without regard to . . . 不論；不考慮
  employment status (n.) 就業狀態

**120. 名詞詞彙題**

最近的研究發現，社群媒體貼文對人們購物決定的影響有限。

(A) 價值　(C) 關聯
(B) 功能　**(D) 影響**

**121. 動詞詞彙題**

傑納貝克外燴公司讓客戶訂製他們的餐點選擇，以適合他們的確切口味。

(A) 繫緊　**(C) 訂製**
(B) 監測　(D) 贊助

- monitor (v.) 監測；監控　patronize (v.) 贊助

**122. 形容詞詞彙題——修飾名詞** 

會要求應徵者說出三位能為他們的專業度提供確實推薦的人。

(A) 優點　(C) 確實地
(B) 確實　**(D) 確實的**

- candidate (n.) 應徵者
  professional reference (n.) 專業上的推薦

**123. 名詞詞彙題——不定詞的受詞** 

行銷組人員正向網路新聞媒體管道投稿，以吸引大眾注意我們品牌。

**(A) 關注**　(C) 宣傳
(B) 公開地　(D) 大眾的

- contribute (v.) 投稿；撰稿
  news outlet (n.) 新聞媒體管道，新聞出處
  publicize (v.) 宣傳

**124. 副詞子句連接詞詞彙題**

布思女士打算等接替的人一完成適當的訓練，她就要調往海外公司。

(A) 從……開始　(C) 到……才……
**(B) 一……就……**　(D) 直到

- up to 直到

---

**125. 副詞詞彙題——修飾動詞**

當業務人員超越他們的季度銷售目標時，公司會用紅利給予他們財務獎勵。

(A) 財務的　(C) 財政
**(B) 財務地**　(D) 提供資金給……

- quarterly (adj.) 季度的　financial (adj.) 財政的
  finance (n.) 財政

---

**126. 與過去事實相反的假設語氣——語態** 難

若包裹在運送過程中遺失，貨運公司將給予補償。

(A) 本來可以被提供　(C) 已被提供
(B) 將已提供　**(D) 將已提供**

- compensate (v.) 補償

---

**127. 副詞子句連接詞詞彙題** 

不論你是出遊還是出差，重要的是選擇一間位置方便的飯店。

(A) 儘管　**(C) 不論……還是……**
(B)（兩者中）任一個　(D) 不論

- convenient (adj.) 便利的
  notwithstanding (adv.) 儘管

---

**128. 形容詞詞彙題** 

不幸地是，合約中含糊不清的措辭，導致對其中的意思有許多種解釋。

**(A) 含糊不清的**　(C) 普遍的
(B) 強而有力的　(D) 懷疑的

- interpretation (n.) 解釋　widespread (adj.) 普遍的
  skeptical (adj.) 懷疑論的

---

**129. 動詞詞類變化題——動名詞**

「FNR 金屬」已贏得許多認可，包括是本地第一家得到「環保工廠」證書的廠商。

(A) 是……的東西　**(C) 是**
(B) 是　(D) 將是

- ample (adj.) 大量的　manufacturer (n.) 廠商
  certification (n.) 證明

**130. 名詞子句連接詞詞彙題** 

「艾拉瑞克斯繪圖」可以印出所有種類的招牌，不論要求什麼形狀或尺寸都行。

**(A) 不論什麼**　(C) 對比
(B) 尤其　(D) 任何

- in particular 尤其　in contrast 相比之下

## PART 6 P. 207–210

### 131–134 電子郵件

收件者：現有客戶
寄件者：瑟夫樂貨運公司
主旨：最新消息
日期：11 月 30 日

**最新電子商務消息**——製作退貨標籤的解決方案

網路銷售交易不斷成長，代表電子商務公司可能也需要處理更多顧客想退回近期購買，卻 [131] **不想要的**商品這類要求。在每個寄出的包裹中附上一張退貨標籤，會使顧客的退貨過程 [132] **更容易**。退貨標籤是一張貼紙，上面寫有所購買商品的公司地址，[134] **也有條碼可追蹤退貨包裹**。瑟夫樂貨運的標籤解決方案軟體製作精緻且實用的退貨標籤，欲試用並在幾分鐘內就製作出標籤樣品，請點擊此處。然後，您可以決定要不要幫公司買這套軟體。

- e-commerce (n.) 電子商務
  ongoing (adj.) 持續的　transaction (n.) 交易
  outbound (adj.) 往外地的
  functional (adj.) 實用的

**131. 形容詞詞彙題——過去分詞**

(A) 取消的　(C) 無意的
**(B) 不想要的**　(D) 過期的

- unintended (adj.) 無意的　expired (adj.) 過期的

---

**132. 形容詞詞彙題——受詞補語** 

(A) 減輕　**(C) 較容易的**
(B) 容易地　(D) 減輕

---

**133. 關係副詞考題**

**(A) 在那裡**　(C) 那個
(B) 某人的……　(D) 那個

**134. 句子插入題** 難

**(A) 上面也有條碼可追蹤退貨包裹。**
(B) 對並不十分滿意的商品，你可以換貨。
(C) 為了達到更好的結果，我們建議顧客晚個幾天再把它寄出去。
(D) 作為網路商家，你可以在舒適的家中販售商品。

**135–138 網頁**

## 隆蒙不動產公司——線上看屋

多虧現今的數位科技，購屋者現在可以 [135] **不用**離開自己的居所，就能進行虛擬看屋導覽並查看房屋。透過為大部分的物件提供這樣的導覽，隆蒙不動產居於這項業界革命的最前線。

[136] **我們的所有線上虛擬房屋導覽，包括每個物件的照片與互動式影片。**這些虛擬看屋利用相機來 [137] **製作**，提供每間房屋裡所有空間的 3D 影像。這些影像讓觀看者就像親自參觀那樣，在屋內數位「移動」。

虛擬的房屋導覽一上傳到我們的網站，我們的客戶就能使用電腦或行動裝置，從 [138] **幾乎**任何地方查看虛擬導覽，這項科技保證為潛在的購屋者省下數小時的往返時間與數十元的油錢。

欲觀看我們目前可線上看屋的待售物件，請點擊這裡。

- **virtual (adj.)** 虛擬的 **property (n.)** 房地產
  **at the forefront** 在……的最前線
  **industry (n.)** 產業
  **revolution (n.)** 革命性劇變；革命
  **dimensional (adj.)** 維度的 **manner (n.)** 方法
  **in person** 親自 **guarantee (v.)** 保證
  **prospective (adj.)** 有希望的

**135. 介系詞詞彙題**

(A) 直到　**(C) 沒有**
(B) 裡面的　(D) 在……後面

**136. 句子插入題**

(A) 某些地區的房價持續上漲，但其他地區則維持穩定。
(B) 接受調查的顧客也表示，他們較喜歡親自去看屋。
**(C) 我們的所有線上虛擬房屋導覽，包括每個物件的照片與互動式影片。**
(D) 如果你對這間房子有疑問，我們其中一位專家可以幫你。

**137. 動詞詞類變化題——時態** 難

(A) 正被創造　(C) 本來可以被創造
**(B) 被創造**　(D) 將被創造

**138. 副詞詞彙題**

(A) 甚至　(C) 幾乎不
(B) 不　**(D) 幾乎**

**139–142 傳單**

## 探索佛羅罕市的自然步道——還有升級的設施！

佛羅罕公園與遊憩局很高興宣布，為期六個月的步道改善工程及時在夏天前完工了。[139] **我們的完整步道網現在又再次對遊客開放**，感謝您在工程期間的耐心等候。

升級工程包括一條新的木棧道，延伸橫越佛羅罕公園的池塘，讓人可以 [140] **安全**前往濕地區。[141] **還有**很多人走的藍色步道，這條受到本地居民與外地遊客喜愛的步道，現已拓寬以容納更多健行者，其餘步道也進行了許多其他的小型改善工程。

從具有挑戰性的攀爬上陡峭山坡，到沿著平緩草地的休閒散步，經過改善的自然步道讓各種 [142] **能力**的人都能來健行。互動式步道地圖可以瀏覽 www.florham-trails.org。

- **trail (n.)** 步道；鄉間或山林間的小徑
  **amenity (n.)** 便利設施 **wetland (n.)** 濕地
  **well-traveled (adj.)**（道路等）很多人使用的
  **accommodate (v.)** 容納 **leisurely (adj.)** 悠閒的
  **meadow (n.)** 草地

**139. 句子插入題** 難

(A) 公園處人員與志工密切合作。
(B) 組織良好的健行俱樂部越來越受歡迎。
**(C) 我們的完整步道網現在又再次對遊客開放。**
(D) 這座城市的公園系統歷史悠久又有趣。

- **organized (adj.)** 有組織的

**140. 副詞詞彙題——修飾現在分詞**

(A) 安全的　(C) 最安全的
(B) 安全　**(D) 安全地**

**141. 連接副詞**

(A) 仍然　　(C) 例如
(B) 反而　　**(D) 還有**

**142. 名詞詞彙題**

**(A) 能力**　　(C) 風景
(B) 假期　　(D) 利益

- landscape (n.) 風景　benefit (n.) 利益

**143–146 資訊**

**當地生產的食物——快速概要**

關於當地生產的食物，並沒有明確的定義。然而，一般的理解是指在離販售地點相當近的 [143] **地方**種植的糧食。購買當地生產的食物可以幫助地方經濟，[144] **因為**更多的錢會直接歸種植者所有。當地農民幾乎從來不需要外來經銷商的幫忙，好讓他們的農產品上市。[145] **因此，他們的收入更有可能留在當地。**一年大部分的時候，都 [146] **可**在農夫市集和戶外農場攤位**買到**當地生產的食物。農產品只有當令時節才會販售，所以它們都很新鮮且風味十足。這表示，購買當地生產的食物對消費者本身也有好處。

- generally (adv.) 一般地　relativety (adv.) 相當
  distributor (n.) 經銷商
  get . . . to market 讓……上市
  farmers' market (n.) 農夫市集
  produce (n.) 農產品　individual (adj.) 個別的

**143. 名詞詞彙題**

(A) 日期　　(C) 總量
**(B) 地方**　　(D) 方式

- volume (n.) 總量；總額　manner (n.) 方式

**144. 連接詞詞彙題** 難

**(A) 因為**　　(C) 由於
(B) 基於　　(D) 以防萬一

- base on 以……為基礎；基於　owning to 因為
  in case 以防萬一

**145. 句子插入題** 

(A) 此外，農夫可能會告訴遊客一些園藝祕訣。
(B) 事實上，吃很多加工食品可能不太健康。
(C) 因此，食品運輸業持續成長。
**(D) 因此，他們的收入更有可能留在當地。**

- processed food (n.) 加工食品
  transportation (n.) 運輸　earning (n.) 收入
  be more likely to . . . 更有可能……

**146. 動詞詞類變化題——時態**

(A) 可買到的　　(C) 以前可買到
**(B) 可買到的**　　(D) 將可買到

## PART 7 P. 211–231

**147–148 收據**

**艾亞利超級市場**
北威佛市分店
德文路 12 號
分店電話：555-0163

5 月 3 日下午 2:28

| | |
|---|---|
| 藍莓瑪芬（5 入） | 3.70 元 |
| 瓶裝水（12 入） | 4.90 元 |
| 蔬菜湯（小罐） | 2.20 元 |
| 水果乾（大包） | 5.80 元 |
| *** 總計 | 16.60 元 |
| 現金 | 20.00 元 |
| 找零 | 3.40 元 |

[147] **感謝光臨北威佛市分店！**

店經理：戴夫・索托
[147] **收銀員：自助結帳，機檯 #3**

[147] **至客戶服務處登記領取貴賓卡，**開始省錢！

*************************************************************

我們的服務如何？[148] **請上 www.ayali-survey.com，告訴我們您的意見，就有機會贏得 500 元 *。請以個人身分識別碼 334 05081 登入並完成調查。**

* 更多抽獎詳情，請至客戶服務處詢問

- inquire (v.) 詢問　prize drawing (n.) 抽獎

**147. 推論或暗示** 

文中未提到關於艾亞利超級市場的什麼事？

**(A) 烘焙食品是在店內烘烤的。**
(B) 發行會員卡給某些顧客。
(C) 有不止一家分店。
(D) 顧客可以自行處理購買流程。

- on the premises 在該場所
  loyalty card (n.) 會員卡

**換句話說**

a preferred shopper cards（貴賓卡）
→ (B) loyalty cards（會員卡）
our North Weaver City Branch/location（我們的北威佛市分店）
→ (C) It has more than one store location.（有不止一家分店。）
SELF-CHECKOUT（自助結帳）
→ (D) Its customers can process their own purchases.（顧客可以自行處理購買流程。）

---

**148. 相關細節**

文中指示顧客如何參加一項調查？

(A) 去客戶服務處拿一張表格
(B) 提供目前的電話號碼
**(C) 進入指定的網站**
(D) 直接和管理部門談

- access (v.) 進入　designated (adj.) 指定的　management (n.) 管理部門

**換句話說**

complete the survey（完成調查）
→ participate in a survey（參加一項調查）
Visit www.ayali-survey.com（上 www.ayali-survey.com）
→ (C) accessing a designated Web site（進入指定的網站）

---

**149–150 網頁**

**顧客評價對象：丹沃德公司**

**最新貼文：**6 月 9 日

**貼文者：**傑夫．安德森，標準紙業公司地區經理

丹沃德公司的服務非常出色。由於我們最近擴張業務，[149] **我必須在短時間內為生產與倉儲的新進員工另外訂購制服**，丹沃德公司給了我們所需的商品，而且他們的貨車司機史丹非常準時又有禮貌；他們的衣服品質優異，而且可以加上公司商標；他們總是快速回應客戶的需求。

➥ **公司回覆：**謝謝您，安德森先生！顧客的滿意永遠是丹沃德公司的第一要務。我們是我們這個地區第一家採用 [150] **ACPS（先進客戶處理系統）的公司，這是一套訂單管理程式，曾得過商用軟體開發者協會的獎項**。這套最新的解決方案使我們得以更快速、更正確地追蹤及分類訂單，讓我們的準時送達率達到 99.6%。

- owing to 由於　on short notice 在短時間內　punctual (adj.) 準時的　courteous (adj.) 有禮的　responsive (adj.) 反應積極的；反應敏捷的　utmost (adj.) 最大的　employ (v.) 使用；利用　cutting-edge (adj.) 最新的　sort (v.) 將……分類

**149. 推論或暗示**

丹沃德公司最可能是哪一種公司？

(A) 食物外送服務公司
(B) 紙製品廠商
(C) 建築物維修公司
**(D) 工作服供應商**

**換句話說**

uniforms for our newly hired production and warehouse staff（給我們生產與倉儲新進員工的制服）→ (D) work apparel（工作服）

---

**150. 確認事實與否**

可從文中得知關於 ACPS 的什麼事？

**(A) 它得到業界的表揚。**
(B) 它經過修改以符合安德森先生的需要。
(C) 它有好幾種上市的版本。
(D) 大家認為它很好用。

- recognition (n.) 表揚　tailor (v.) 修改　release (v.) 發行

**換句話說**

has won awards from the Business Software Developers Association（曾得過商用軟體開發者協會的獎項）→ (A) has achieved industry recognition（得到業界的表揚）

---

**151–152 文字訊息串**

**布萊德．伊克博**〔上午 10:40〕
瑪莉亞，[151] **我剛剛下來電腦室這裡安裝新軟體**，妳知道冷卻系統又怪怪的嗎？這裡相當熱。

**瑪莉亞．迪**〔上午 10:41〕
是，我們知道這個問題，我剛打給空調公司，派一個維修人員過來。

**布萊德．伊克博**〔上午 10:42〕
真的嗎？那 [152] **我會等到他們修好，再把這個工作做完**，這種溫度令人很不舒服。

**瑪莉亞．迪**〔上午 10:43〕
你確定嗎？[152] **他們明天才會來。**

布萊德．伊克博〔上午 10:44〕
噢，我知道了。[152] **我看只好在這種高溫下工作了。**

- HVAC (Heating, Ventilating, and Air Conditioning) (n.) 空氣調節系統（包括暖氣、通風及空調）
  assignment (n.) 工作；任務

**151. 推論或暗示**

伊克博先生最有可能是什麼身分？

(A) 空調維修人員
(B) 辦公室家具安裝人員
**(C) 電腦技師**
(D) 大樓管理員

- superintendent (n.) 大樓管理員

---

**152. 掌握意圖**

上午 10:43，當迪女士寫道：「他們明天才會來」，她的意思最可能是什麼？

(A) 她還沒有什麼消息。
(B) 她無法提供協助。
(C) 伊克博先生應該趕快完成工作。
**(D) 延誤的時間可能比伊克博先生預期的長。**

---

**153–154 電子郵件**

**收件人：**康士坦絲．貝勒 <constance-baylor@mail.com>
**寄件人：**<greenbrandtbooks@green-brandt.com>
**主旨：**您的訂單
**日期：**8 月 1 日

親愛的貝勒女士：

感謝您選購我們的商品。[153] **我們想通知您，由於我們的郵寄機器意外故障，您訂購的《新手木工手藝》一書在處理過程中受損。**然而，同樣這本書，我們確實有一本二手書，封底有點褪色，還有下緣有一小塊水漬，它的內頁很乾淨，沒有摺痕或任何記號。

如果您有興趣訂購這本替換的書，我們會在您的顧客帳號中存入七元，以反映它和新書間的價差。

[154] **請在星期一（8 月 4 日）之前回覆這封電子郵件**，讓我們知道您接下來想如何處理，**否則我們將自動取消您的訂單，並將訂單金額全數退還給您。**

感謝您的諒解。

格林布蘭特書店全體人員　敬啟

- carpentry (n.) 木工手藝　novice (n.) 初學者
  malfunction (n.) 故障　faded (adj.) 褪色的
  moisture (n.) 濕氣　stain (n.) 汙漬
  credit (v.) 將錢存入帳戶　proceed (v.) 繼續進行

**153. 主旨或目的**

撰寫這封電子郵件最有可能的原因為何？

(A) 提供一項新的折扣活動的資訊
**(B) 通知貝勒女士訂單的問題**
(C) 解釋漲價的原因
(D) 清楚說明購買珍本書的準則

- clarify (v.) 闡明　collectible (adj.) 值得收藏的

---

**154. 推論或暗示**

如果貝勒女士未在星期一之前回覆電子郵件，最可能發生什麼事？

(A) 她不會得到額外的紅利。
(B) 她會得到替換的商品。
**(C) 她會獲得全額退款。**
(D) 她會失去升級帳號的機會。

- substitute (n.) 取代；代替

**換句話說**
reply to（回覆）→ respond to（回答）
return the full amount of the purchase price（將訂單金額全數退還）
→ (C) a full refund（全額退款）

---

**155–157 新聞稿**

**史多利摩爾劇團首次推出線上節目**

立即發布（6 月 22 日）——史多利摩爾劇團（STC）的上一季以它備受好評的舞台喜劇《家族大團圓》成功連演多場畫下句點，[155] **這次帶來劇團史上最多觀眾的演出**，包括 [156] **演出後針對戲劇主題——家族聚會的歡樂面，進行的小組討論。這些熱烈的對話讓 STC 的公關主任葛洛莉亞．查特姆想出發展有聲播客的點子**，讓劇團的工作人員談論在劇團的創作過程。第一集名為〈設計為什麼重要〉於 6 月 19 日上線，它的主題是《家族大團圓》的服裝設計荷兒．布瑞迪和這齣戲的舞台設計蜜雪兒．林德利之間愉快而迷人的對談；第二集將於 6 月 26 日上線，會包含一段與本劇導演的對話。[157] **查特姆計畫持續每週上一集 30 分鐘的節目，或者一星期兩次，**然而，她指出，半小時的節目可能就要花好幾天製作。聽眾可以上 www.stc-theater.org/podcast 免費收聽這些播客。

- programming (n.)（電視、廣播等的）節目播送
  highly-praised (adj.) 備受好評
  lively (adj.) 熱烈的
  public relations (n.) 公共關係
  come up with 想出、提出（主意或計畫）
  engaging (adj.) 令人愉快的；迷人的

**155. 確認事實與否**

關於《家族大團圓》，可由文中得知什麼？

(A) 它的演員包括葛洛莉亞．查特姆。
(B) 它有兩個不同的導演。
**(C) 它創下觀賞人數紀錄。**
(D) 它的製作費高昂。

- attendance (n.) 出席人數

換句話說
brought in the biggest crowds in the company's history（帶來劇團史上最多觀眾）→ (C) set an attendance record（創下觀賞人數紀錄）

---

**156. 確認事實與否**

文中提到關於 STC 播客的什麼事？

**(A) 受到小組討論啟發。**
(B) 將由觀眾捐款贊助。
(C) 要求聽眾付費訂閱。
(D) 特別為記者開發。

- fund (v.) 提供資金　donation (n.) 捐款
  paid subscription (n.) 付費訂閱

換句話說
led . . . to come up with the idea（讓……想出點子）→ (A) inspired（受到啟發）

---

**157. 句子插入題**

「然而，她指出，半小時的節目可能就要花好幾天製作。」最適合放在標示 [1]、[2]、[3]、[4] 的何處？

(A) [1]　　(C) [3]
(B) [2]　　**(D) [4]**

**158–160 線上清單**

[158]**《源自奈及利亞》——西非最值得信任的商業期刊**　電子版

**一探奈及利亞最佳廣告公司**

**貼文：**一天前　[158] **文／瑪德琳娜．艾康達**
觀看次數 1242

近幾個月來，許多訂戶都建議我們刊登一份奈及利亞頂尖廣告公司的名單。以下列出的廣告公司是由 [158] **我過去為這份刊物採訪過的商業領袖所熱心推薦。**

「行銷觸及」——20 年前創立的行銷觸及公司，是奈及利亞最大的廣告公司之一，在拉哥斯和阿布札都有分公司。[159] **為了滿足一位主要客戶丹古敏食品製造公司的需求，**行銷觸及最近在塞內加爾開設了海外營業處，進行市場研究。

「融合科技」——開業四年來，這家在拉哥斯和阿布札都有營業處的本國公司，已因它的數位行銷活動而備受尊崇。去年，[159] **它的客戶群增加了泡麵廠商桑木魯牌。**為了這家公司，它創造了一系列得獎的網路廣告。

「歐魯瓦解決方案」——這家有十年歷史的專業廣告公司在奈及利亞、迦納和肯亞都有分公司，不像許多其他公司，它主要專注於幫助客戶的公司發展並引進新品牌。[159] **它最近才接下任務，要確保 BCC 企業的包裝零食系列成功上市。**這家公司也以和普羅斯派克特科技合夥開發「資訊麥特普拉斯」而聞名，[160] **這是一套讓公司可以設計線上顧客調查，以改善品牌形象的軟體。**

- subscriber (n.) 訂戶　publish (v.) 刊登
  advertising agency (n.) 廣告公司
  domestic (adj.) 國內的
  highly respected (adj.) 備受尊敬的；被看重的
  client base (n.) 客戶群
  award-winning (adj.) 得獎的　decade (n.) 十年
  specialty (n.) 專長　packaged (adj.) 包裝的

**158. 推論或暗示**

艾康達女士最有可能是什麼身分？

(A) 廣告公司老闆
(B) 書店經理
(C) 軟體開發商
**(D) 財經記者**

**159. 相關細節** 難

列出的廣告公司有什麼共同點？

(A) 在不止一個國家有分公司。
(B) 開業超過五年。
**(C) 與食品業的客戶合作。**
(D) 總公司在同一座城市。

- industry (n.) 產業
  be headquartered in . . . 將總公司設在……

---

**160. 推論或暗示** 難

「資訊麥特普拉斯」最可能用來做什麼？

(A) 追蹤大眾提及品牌的次數
**(B) 收集顧客的意見回饋**
(C) 分析市場研究資料
(D) 管理社群媒體帳號

> **換句話說**
> customer surveys（顧客調查）
> → (B) customer feedback（顧客回饋意見）

---

**161–163 資訊**

> **羅納特物業**
>
> **[161] 即將承租——丹摩爾大樓，位於史奈德街 2 號設施豐富的綜合出租大樓**
>
> 丹摩爾大樓面積延伸將近一整個街區，結合了舒適的公寓生活和豐富的便利設施，包括位於一樓附有室內游泳池的健身中心。寬敞的大廳可以作為房客的共享工作空間，而大樓距離鄰近的商店及餐廳只有幾步之遙。[162] **當初作為成衣廠之用而興建的丹摩爾大樓**，擁有復古的外觀和保存完好的建築細部，它的 38 戶包含各種格局的一房和兩房公寓。
>
> 7 月 1 日起可入住。[163] **於 6 月 5 日前申租，羅納特物業將免收新申租時慣例收取的 50 元處理費**。

- properties (n.) 房地產；財產
  an abundance of 大量　amenity (n.) 便利設施
  complex (n.) 綜合大樓　spacious (adj.) 寬敞的
  garment (n.)（一件）衣服；服裝
  facility (n.)（供特定用途的）場所
  architectural (adj.) 建築的
  consist of 由……組成　occupancy (n.) 居住
  waive (v.) 免除
  customary fee (n.) 慣常收取的費用
  application (n.) 申請

**161. 主旨或目的**

這則資訊主要是關於什麼？

(A) 開幕儀式
(B) 城市的街坊
**(C) 空屋**
(D) 商業機會

- vacancy (n.) 空房

---

**162. 確認事實與否**

關於丹摩爾大樓，可由文中得知什麼？

(A) 在兩條街上都有入口
(B) 有戶外的休閒設施
**(C) 以前是工廠**
(D) 位於歷史區域

> **換句話說**
> Built originally as a garment production facility（當初作為成衣廠之用而興建）
> → (C) previously a factory（以前是工廠）

---

**163. 推論或暗示** 

關於羅納特物業，可由文中得知什麼？

**(A) 通常對申租人收取費用。**
(B) 專做商業不動產。
(C) 提供短期租約給房客。
(D) 打算僱用更多員工。

---

**164–167 電子郵件**

> **寄件人：**營養學通訊 <healthnutrition-neswletter@maynard.edu>
> **收件人：**珍妮特．李 <j.lee@mail.com>
> **主旨：**MU 營養學通訊
> **日期：**3 月 1 日
>
> **梅納德大學營養學通訊**
>
> 親愛的李女士：
>
> 如今，我們都收到太多關於健康飲食的資訊。從電視節目到網路烹飪論壇，有大量的來源發送來自令人存疑的科學權威相互矛盾的營養建議。[164] **這讓我提出一個主要理由，讓您可以信任您在每個月的梅納德大學營養學通訊裡讀到的所有內容。**

167 **每一篇文章都經過編輯群和梅納德大學營養科學學院的頂尖營養學專家做過研究，並給出有科學根據且容易遵循的健康建議。**通訊內容總是以簡單的語言寫成，不會充滿複雜的醫學術語。更重要的是，165 **這份通訊不刊登任何廣告**，讓我們可以自由討論受歡迎食品的營養品質，而沒有義務要討好食品業的廣告企業客戶。

例如，我們這一期的通訊就包含一篇公正的指南，關於最健康的義大利麵種類。我們邀請您上 www.mu-health.com，輸入代碼「A12」試閱這一期的完整線上版，我們這麼做是希望您會想要 164 **訂閱我們卓越非凡的刊物**，有了我們的首購優惠，您可以用一年 32 元的價格訂閱紙本或電子版，會比我們的正常費率省下 35%。

我們會聯絡您，是因為 166 **我們的紀錄顯示，您目前接收從我們大學校友網站發出的免費「最新健康」電子郵件**，我們的每月通訊提供甚至更為詳盡的健康指引，因此我們敦促您把握這次特別優惠。

梅納德大學營養學通訊
編輯主任　大衛．阿邁德　謹啟

- **nutrition (n.)** 營養；營養學
  **overload (v.)** 超載；負荷過多
  **dispense (v.)** 分派　**questionable (adj.)** 可疑的
  **authority (n.)** 權威人士
  **bring up** 提起；談到　**editorial (adj.)** 編輯的
  **leading (adj.)** 最重要的　**obligation (n.)** 義務
  **corporate (n.)** 企業
  **advertiser (n.)** 刊登廣告的人
  **impartial (adj.)** 公正的　**entirety (n.)** 全部
  **extraordinary (adj.)** 非凡的
  **publication (n.)** 刊物；出版品
  **introductory (adj.)** 首次的
  **reach out to . . .** （透過電話或信件）和……聯絡
  **alumni (n.)** 校友
  **take advantage of** 利用……的機會

**164. 主旨或目的**

這封電子郵件的主要目的為何？

(A) 更新一份通訊的新編輯方針
(B) 比較許多專家的健康建議
**(C) 概述訂閱制刊物的好處**
(D) 提議在系列文章上的合作

- **policy (n.)** 方針　**outline (v.)** 概述
  **collaboration (n.)** 合作

**165. 確認事實與否**

關於這份通訊，下列何者最可能為真？

(A) 已不再販售紙本。
**(B) 沒有廣告。**
(C) 主要讀者群是科學家。
(D) 和某個電視節目有關聯。

- **aim at** 瞄準……　**associated (adj.)** 有關聯的

**換句話說**
the newsletter carries no advertising（這份通訊不登任何廣告）→ (B) It does not have advertisements.（沒有廣告。）

---

**166. 推論或暗示**

關於李女士，可由文中得知什麼？

**(A) 她畢業於梅納德大學。**
(B) 她教線上烹飪課程。
(C) 她以前和阿邁德先生一起工作。
(D) 她試圖取消一項免費服務。

**換句話說**
our university's alumni（我們大學的校友）
→ (A) graduated from Maynard University（畢業於梅納德大學）

---

**167. 句子插入題**　難

「通訊內容總是以簡單的語言寫成，不會充滿複雜的醫學術語。」最適合放在標示 [1]、[2]、[3]、[4] 的何處？

(A) [1]　　(C) [3]
**(B) [2]**　　(D) [4]

---

**168–171 線上聊天室**

**即時聊天**

阿米爾．納札里〔上午 9:22〕
嗨，各位，168 **我現在在會議室練習我們小組要發表的簡報，我剛剛檢查過原本的與新的商標並列比較的投影片**，上面有我們對所做變更的描述，看起來很好。

娜迪亞．戈森〔上午 9:23〕
169 **你有沒有把我那些展示我們選擇圖案理由的投影片加進去？**

阿米爾．納札里〔上午 9:24〕
有，169 **它們很有用**。

娜迪亞．戈森〔上午 9:25〕
影片在螢幕上看起來如何？

阿米爾．納札里〔上午 9:26〕
我們的問題就在這裡，影片無法播放。

琳達．韋德〔上午 9:27〕
[170] **試試更改格式。**

阿米爾．納札里〔上午 9:28〕
好，等我一下。

娜迪亞．戈森〔上午 9:37〕
可以了嗎？

阿米爾．納札里〔上午 9:38〕
有了，現在可以播了。

琳達．韋德〔上午 9:39〕
[170] **建議有派上用場嗎？**

阿米爾．納札里〔上午 9:40〕
[170] **一如以往。**

戴爾．康〔上午 9:41〕
也記得，[171] **你可以用遙控器暫停影片。你可能會想試個幾次**，按鈕可能不太靈光。

阿米爾．納札里〔上午 9:42〕
好主意，謝啦。

**168. 推論或暗示**

小組簡報的主題最可能是什麼？

**(A) 修改商標的設計**
(B) 現在和未來業績的預測
(C) 競爭品牌的概述
(D) 如何描述一個產品的特色

- **revision (n.)** 修訂　**forecast (n.)** 預測

---

**169. 推論或暗示** 難

可由文中得知關於納札里先生的什麼事？

(A) 他還沒看過某個宣傳影片。
(B) 他主持簡報策略的工作坊。
(C) 他僱用工作團隊裡所有的平面設計師。
**(D) 他把戈森女士的內容加入簡報中。**

- **incorporate (v.)** 包含；加上

**換句話說**
add my slides（加上我的投影片）
→ (D) incorporated Ms. Ghosn's content（把戈森女士的內容加入）

**170. 掌握意圖** 難

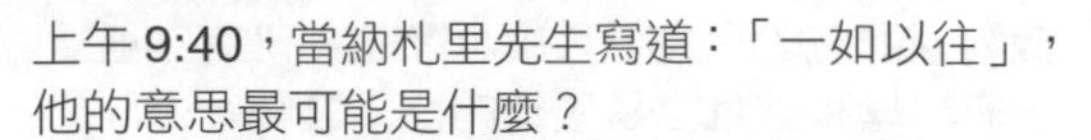

上午 9:40，當納札里先生寫道：「一如以往」，他的意思最可能是什麼？

(A) 這個小組經常必須在很短的時間內做出修改。
**(B) 一位同事給了可靠的疑難排解建議。**
(C) 有台電腦不斷重覆發生一個問題。
(D) 他常協助轉換影片格式。

- **dependable (adj.)** 可靠的
  **troubleshooting (n.)** 疑難排解

---

**171. 相關細節**

康先生建議納札里先生做什麼？

(A) 背下引言
(B) 腦力激盪觀眾可能提出的問題
(C) 在各段之間安排休息時間
**(D) 練習使用一個配件**

**換句話說**
try it out（試用）→ (D) Practice using an accessory（練習使用一個配件）
the remote control unit（遙控器）
→ (D) an accessory（配件）

---

**172–175 報導**

## 文化遺產博物館展示<br>日常生活紀念品

哈茲列特弗　訊——齊勒文化遺產博物館一直被探索過其龐大古董珍藏的遊客們稱為「一顆鮮為人知的寶石」。[172] **這間博物館擁有超過三萬件展品，陳列在一個由複合式農場改造而成的四棟大型建築物中，這些展品是** [174] **馬文．齊勒的個人收藏，他一輩子都住在哈茲列特弗，**從童年就開始收集當地的紀念品。現今，人們常看到他在博物館的花園涼亭放鬆休息，[172] **遊客可以在這裡首次嘗試操作展出的古董農場設備。**「成立博物館是齊勒先生的夢想，」博物館經理茱莉亞．哈斯泰德說，她現在帶領小型團體的導覽。

[173] **博物館的展品和歷史時間軸包含該地區日常生活的許多層面。**[172] **其中一部分展示出來自當地產業的紀念品，包括一組來自山卓利亞餐館的完整包廂座位和服務檯，這是齊勒先生一直經營到退休的餐館，**還有展出許多其他歷史物件，從古董印刷機到舊的學校制服。參觀博物館時，很多遊客會把這些展品和他們自己對過去時光的回憶連結在一起。

[174] **博物館位於山脊路 1100 號，就在哈茲列特弗小鎮外**，每週開放七天，從上午 8 點到下午 5 點。入場成人票 8 元，學生票 5 元，[175] **遊客應空出至少三小時，悠閒地參觀博物館的所有物品。**博物館也提供會員方案，得以參加一系列特殊活動。更多關於博物館的資訊，請上 www.keeler-mus.org。

- heritage (n.) 遺產（指具有歷史意義的傳統、語言、建築等）
  memorabilia (n.) 紀念品
  repurpose (v.) 重新利用；改變……的用途
  complex (n.) 綜合設施　gather (up) (v.) 收集
  pavilion (n.) 涼亭
  facility (n.)（供特定用途的）場所
  exhibit (n.) 展示品　industry (n.) 產業；行業
  intact (adj.) 完整無缺的
  printing press (n.) 印刷機　set aside 留出
  in a leisurely manner 悠閒地

### 172. 確認事實與否 難

關於博物館的收藏，文中未提及什麼？

(A) 以互動式展品為特色。
(B) 存放在好幾棟建築物裡。
(C) 展出齊勒先生以前商店的一部分。
**(D) 包含由之前遊客捐贈的物品。**

**換句話說**

try their hand at operating the antique farm equipment（首次嘗試操作古董農場設備）
→ (A) interactive exhibits（互動式展品）
displayed in four massive buildings（陳列在四棟大型建築物中）
→ (B) housed in multiple buildings（存放在好幾棟建築物裡）
an intact seating booth and service counter from Centralia Diner, which Mr. Keeler owned（一組來自山卓利亞餐館的完整包廂座位和服務檯，這是齊勒先生經營的餐館）
→ (C) sections of Mr. Keeler's former business（齊勒先生以前商店的一部分）

### 173. 同義詞考題 難

第二段第二行的「cover」，意義最接近下列何者？

(A) 暫代　(C) 圍住
**(B) 與……有關**　(D) 保證

### 174. 推論或暗示

關於齊勒先生，可由文中得知什麼？

(A) 他也在當地經營一家珠寶店。
(B) 他跟哈斯泰德女士買了一座農場。
**(C) 他成長的地方靠近他的博物館所在地。**
(D) 他以園藝為嗜好。

**換句話說**

just outside（就在……外）→ (C) near（靠近）

### 175. 相關細節

此篇報導的作者推薦做什麼？

**(A) 留出數小時參觀一個機構**
(B) 透過網站購買單程票
(C) 註冊一個新的會員方案
(D) 參加特別的團體導覽

**換句話說**

set aside three or more hours to view all of the museum's objects（空出至少三小時參觀博物館的所有物品）→ (A) Allowing several hours to look around a facility（留出數小時參觀一個機構）

### 176–180 線上評論與回覆

評論普拉斯　—本地最好的線上評論網站

阿雷羅小館的評論　文：麥特・布羅斯基

| 麥特・布羅斯基的檔案 | →評論普拉斯會員：5 年 7 個月<br>評論貼文總數：32　照片貼文：11 |
|---|---|

阿雷羅小館的食物品質很好，但考量到他們收取的價錢，品質還可以更好。我點了豆腐漢堡（13.00 元）、一碗蘑菇湯（7.00 元）、[179] **波浪薯條（8.00 元）**和一份「農場特製」沙拉（9.00 元），每一道都相當美味，有好幾種健康拉沙可選，但因為某些原因，菜單上刪掉了塔可沙拉。[177] **我以前來這裡吃過**，希望可以把它加回來。整體而言，[176] **這裡的食物會吸引注重健康的客人，他們對花俏的手作料理沒興趣**。我造訪過程裡最正面的部分是員工的快速反應，即使在我到的時候，小小的餐廳裡很忙碌，但我等不到一分鐘，就有服務人員來到我的座位。

- reasonably (adv.) 相當地
  appeal to 對……有吸引力
  health-conscious (adj.) 注重健康的
  be concerned with 對……有興趣
  artisanal (adj.) 傳統匠人手工製作的
  responsiveness (n.) 反應敏捷

TEST 8 PART 7

→ 回覆：阿雷羅小館總經理麗莎・崔帕尼

嗨，麥特：

謝謝您的回饋意見。我們以殷勤好客自豪，最重要的是，我們對於食材來源的高標準。尤其，[179] **我們所有的薯條都來自有機種植的馬鈴薯。**[178/179] **由於本季供貨量吃緊，我們最近不得不跟另一個農民進馬鈴薯，因此，帳單上並未收取那道菜的金額。**我們希望您注意到這一點，如果沒有，您可以查看您的收據確認。

我們相信能讓您有比最近一次造訪更好的體驗，因此我們想邀請您再度光臨我們的餐廳。[180] **您可以透過這個網站，傳一個訊息給我，並提供您的電子郵件信箱嗎？我們的客服主管想更了解您的用餐經驗。**

再次感謝您。

麗莎・崔帕尼，www.alerro-bistro.com

- hospitality (n.) 殷勤待客
  source (v.) 從（某地）獲取
  accordingly (adv.) 因此　supervisor (n.) 管理者

**176. 推論或暗示** 

關於阿雷羅小館的食物，布羅斯基先生暗示了什麼？

(A) 分量很大。
**(B) 準備功夫很簡單。**
(C) 價格驚人地低。
(D) 餐廳的裝潢不相配。

- portion (n.)（食物的）一份　décor (n.) 室內裝潢

**177. 確認事實與否**

關於布羅斯基先生，下列何者最可能為真？

**(A) 他以前曾在阿雷羅小館用餐**
(B) 他是本地一家健康食品商店的員工
(C) 他的每篇線上評論都附有照片
(D) 他在週間去阿雷羅小館

**換句話說**
had it here before（以前來這裡吃過）
→ (A) eaten at Alerro's Bistro previously（以前曾在阿雷羅小館用餐）

**178. 同義詞考題**

在回覆中，第一段第三行的「tight」，意思最接近下列何者？

(A) 嚴格的　(C) 塞得很緊
**(B) 缺乏**　(D) 固定得很牢

**179. 整合題**

哪個金額最可能從布羅斯基先生的帳單上刪除？

(A) 7.00 元　(C) 9.00 元
**(B) 8.00 元**　(D) 13.00 元

**180. 推論或暗示**

崔帕尼女士提議，如果布羅斯基先生回覆的話，她會做什麼？

(A) 全額退回他的餐費
(B) 告訴某位老闆他的抱怨
(C) 送他一張電子優惠券
**(D) 傳達他的詳細聯絡資料**

**181–185 網頁與電子郵件**

**歡迎光臨布萊特連出版！**
布萊特連出版是一家發行最新行銷策略指南書的出版公司。自將近 15 年前創立後，我們已出版了上百本受歡迎且實用的書籍。這裡是我們最新發行的書：

**《寫出更好的產品介紹》**在這本圖解書中，著名的廣告文案傑克・薛佛針對寫出能帶來銷量的產品介紹提出實用的建議。[181] **這是薛佛先生首次出版的作品**，我們確信會成為這個領域的經典作品。平裝本—— 27 元＋ 5 元運費，[181] **電子書** 13 元

**《開旅館》**這本啟發人心的書聚焦在創業能力上，[182] **使它和我們之前出過的任何書都不同**。活潑的文字出自餐旅業專家休・贊格拉斯之手，為順利設立旅館定下重要的原則，即使是開在觀光業不興盛的地區也一樣。平裝本—— 22 元＋ 4 元運費

**《提高你的電子商務業績》**本書作者洛伊絲・瑪札 [183] **認為**，在發展能獲利的網路商店時，行銷技巧甚至比專業技能還重要。她提供了增加網路業績的祕訣，並列出頂尖電子商務顧問的聯絡方式。平裝本—— 29 元＋ 6 元運費，[181] **電子書** 14 元

**《透過社群媒體銷售》**這本由《網路時代》編輯艾美・康所撰寫的詳盡書籍，[184] **提供透過社群媒體網站有效銷售的詳盡方向，並另外附上一本 24 頁的口袋書，列出已證實能增加業績的字詞**。精裝本—— 37 元＋ 7 元運費

- cutting-edge (adj.) 最新的；尖端的
  release (n.) 發行的書（或電影等）
  illustrated (adj.) 有插圖的　volume (n.) 書
  entrepreneurship (n.) 創業能力；創業精神

hospitality (n.) 餐旅業
lay down 制定（規則等）
get . . . off the ground (v.)（活動、事業等）開始；順利進行
expertise (n.) 專門技術；專門知識
comprehensive (adj.) 全面的；包羅萬象的

**寄件人：**艾瑞克．劉 <eric-liu@mail.com>
**收件人：**艾倫．崔蒙 <ellen-tremont@mail.com>
**日期：**10 月 18 日
**主旨：**實用的事物

嗨，艾倫：

184 **我跟布萊特連出版訂購要給我們員工訓練工作坊用的書剛剛送來，看起來很棒，隨書附贈的小冊子裡充滿了「賣出更多商品的有力字詞」**，等我看完，我就會把兩本都寄給妳。

還有，185 **請隨時告訴我，妳開發訓練模組的進展如何**。我想，還有很多事要做，不過妳的時間很充裕。

謝謝。

艾瑞克

- merchandise (n.) 商品　come along 進展
  module (n.) 模組

**181. 確認事實與否** 難

關於布萊特連出版，下列何者最不可能為真？

(A) 出版過一位作者的首部作品。
(B) 運費另外收取。
(C) 有些書有數位版。
**(D) 由一位雜誌編輯所創立。**

- impose (v.) 強制實行

**換句話說**
Mr. Schoeffel's debut book（薛佛先生首次出版的作品）
→ (A) a work by a first-time author（一位作者的首部作品）
shipping（運費）
→ (B) a separate charge for delivery（運費另外收取）
Electronic edition（電子版）
→ (C) digital editions（數位版）

**182. 推論或暗示**

關於《開旅館》，可由文中得知什麼？

(A) 它無法寄送到某些地區。
**(B) 這是這間出版公司出的第一本這種類型的書。**
(C) 受觀光業專家的推薦。
(D) 比其他新書的寫作時間都長。

**換句話說**
different from any of our previous releases（和我們之前出的書都不同）
→ (B) the first book of its type（第一本這種類型的書）

**183. 同義詞考題** 

在網頁中，第四段第一行的「holds」，意思最接近下列何者？

(A) 包含　**(C) 遵循**
(B) 獲得　(D) 懸掛

**184. 整合題**

劉先生最近最可能買了哪一本？

(A)《寫出更好的產品介紹》
(B)《開旅館》
(C)《提高你的電子商務業績》
**(D)《透過社群媒體銷售》**

**185. 相關細節**

劉先生要求崔蒙女士做什麼？

**(A) 給他一項計畫的進度報告**
(B) 為一個訓練課程找一位代班主持人
(C) 校對一位員工的簡報內容
(D) 核銷他的業務支出

- replacement (n.) 取代　proofread (v.) 校對
  reimburse (v.) 報銷

**換句話說**
keep me posted on how you are coming along with developing your training module（隨時告訴我，妳開發訓練模組的進展如何）
→ (A) Provide him with a progress report on a project（給他一項計畫的進度報告）

## 186–190 網頁、會議摘要與線上報名表

http://www.cityofstenley.gov/services/recycling-waste

**史丹利市**＞＞市民資源回收及廢棄物清除服務

➢ 史丹利市與葛倫比工業公司（GIC）簽約，清運本市各處的廢棄物，不可回收的廢棄物會先運到位於本市北邊的史丹利市轉運站（SCTF），再送到掩埋場。[186] **資源回收物則全部送到 GIC 經營的回收設施**，進行現場處理，資源回收物必須在每週指定的回收物清運日當天上午六點前放在人行道邊緣。[187] **市府提供每個家戶與公司每種回收桶各一個：**

➢ 藍——家庭回收物，包括罐頭與瓶子

➢ [187] **紅——可製堆肥的庭院廢棄物，例如雜草和樹葉 ***

➢ [187] **綠——其他庭院廢棄物，包括樹枝和大樹枝**

➢ [190] **黃——電子廢棄物，包括電腦及周邊設備、手機和電子配件**

* 清運時間從 3 月中到 12 月中

- **contract (v.)** 簽訂契約 **transfer (n.)** 轉移
  **transport (v.)** 運送 **landfill (n.)** 垃圾掩埋場
  **curb (n.)** 人行道的邊緣 **designated (adj.)** 指定的
  **compostable (adj.)** 可用作堆肥的
  **limb (n.)** 大樹枝
  **peripheral (n.)** （電腦的）周邊設備

**[188] 4 月 28 日星期二史丹利市定期週會摘要**

**出席：**市長雷．康利，廢棄物管理處處長德魯．蒙洛，預算委員會全體委員，GIC 代表尤妮絲．禹

**新的行動應用程式：**蒙洛先生宣布，由葛倫比工業公司（GIC）特別為本市居民開發的「回收提醒」手機應用程式，將於 5 月 1 日星期五啟用。[188] **這個應用程式的主要開發者禹女士示範導覽它的功能**，蒙洛先生證實，每週的資源回收物清運時間將分成下列幾區：[189] **第一區（地址為「北」的住家）為每星期二**；第二區（地址為「北」的商家）為每星期三；第三區（地址為「南」的住家）為每星期四；第四區（地址為「南」的商家）為每星期五。[189] **下個月第一、二、三和四區的第一個清運日分別為 5 月 5 日、6 日、7 日和 8 日。**

- **go live** （新系統）開始運作
  **demonstration (n.)** 實地示範
  **navigate (v.)** 操作導覽
  **respectively (adv.)** 分別地

**「回收提醒」**
註冊螢幕

**填寫下列欄位，然後按「提交」以登記提醒。**

今天的日期：[5 月 1 日]

居民姓名：[黛比．葛里尼] 電子郵件：[Debbie@mail.com]

[189] 地址：[**布萊德利街北 1736 號**]

[189] 不動產類型：[V] 住宅 [ ] 商用

（選填）詢問「回收幫手」問題。

[190] 我如何處理 [**電腦鍵盤和喇叭、電源線**] ？

[提交]

[189] **你會在每星期的清運日前一天收到提醒簡訊。**

「回收幫手」可用來告知你要用哪一個容器。

- **registration (n.)** 註冊 **field (n.)** 欄位
  **property (n.)** 不動產 **dispose (v.)** 處理

**186. 確認事實與否**

文中提到關於 GIC 的什麼事？

(A) 正擴充資訊科技部門。
**(B) 經營自己的回收設施。**
(C) 製造回收容器。
(D) 位在 SCTF 旁邊。

**換句話說**

**the GIC-managed recycling facility**（GIC 經營的回收設施）→ **(B) its own recycling facility**（它自己的回收設施）

**187. 推論或暗示** 難

關於史丹利市，下列何者最可能為真？

**(A) 很多住宅都有戶外土地。**
(B) 將不可回收廢棄物送往海外。
(C) 11 月時沒有清運某些回收物。
(D) 要求居民將玻璃和金屬分開處理。

**換句話說**
every home（每個家戶）→ (A) its residential properties（它的住宅）
yard（庭院）→ (A) outdoor land（戶外土地）

**188. 確認事實與否**

文中提到關於禹女士的什麼事？

(A) 她是財政委員會的一員。
(B) 她目前是史丹利市的居民。
**(C) 她在 4 月 28 日說明如何使用一個行動應用程式。**
(D) 她以前在康利先生的辦公室工作。

- illustrate (v.) 說明

**換句話說**
gave a demonstration（示範）
→ (C) illustrated how to use（說明如何使用）

**189. 整合題** 難

葛里尼女士最可能何時收到提醒訊息？

**(A) 5 月 4 日** (C) 5 月 6 日
(B) 5 月 5 日 (D) 5 月 7 日

**190. 整合題**

葛里尼女士詢問的廢棄物，需要使用什麼容器？

(A) 藍色桶子 (C) 綠色桶子
(B) 紅色桶子 **(D) 黃色桶子**

**191–195 公告、報名表與電子郵件**

**參加《巴貝多生活》雜誌攝影比賽！**

[191] **你的得獎照片會被我們雜誌七萬多名住在巴貝多及海外的讀者看見，**[193] **我們的攝影比賽開放給所有的業餘攝影師參加，也就是任何非以攝影賺取收入的人，**[193] **所有的參賽者都必須是巴貝多的居民。**[193] **每位參賽者可以在任何一個類別中，最多上傳十張照片。**

請確保你的報名表（可透過 www.magazine-contest.com 取得）以及 [193] **你的照片，最晚於 2 月 15 日之前以電子檔傳送。**

前三名的照片會刊登在我們六月的特刊《最好的巴貝多》上，而入選佳作者則會提及他們的名字。我們的編輯也會審閱佳作獎的照片，以便放入未來的月刊裡。[192] **如果我們想要在雜誌中刊登你的照片**，我們會聯絡你，安排一次使用權。

**每個類別的獎金：**

| | |
|---|---|
| **第一名：** 300 元現金 | **第三名：** 二年份《巴貝多生活》雜誌 |
| **第二名：** 150 元現金 | **佳作：** 一件《巴貝多生活》的 T 恤 |

有問題嗎？寄電子郵件給我們：
editor@barbados-mag.com

- entrant (n.) 參賽者
  honorable mention (n.) 佳作

**巴貝多生活攝影比賽**
**報名表**

**照片類別：** ____ 節慶（在活動中所拍）
__V__ 野生生物（動物、昆蟲或植物）
____ 風景（風景和遠景）

**姓名：** 艾達．西拉諾 **電子郵件：** serrano@mail.com

**每張照片請加標題與描述，詳細說明拍攝地點與時間。在下方的空間說明照片拍攝周圍情況的特色：**
[194] **這些照片是我當義工導遊帶團體旅遊時拍的。**

**簽名：** 艾達．西拉諾

- vista (n.) 遠景

**寄件人：** 詹姆斯．馬林 <marlin@barbados-mag.com>
**收件人：** 艾達．西拉諾 <serrano@mail.com>
**日期：** 4 月 17 日
**主旨：** 恭喜！

TEST 8 PART 7

親愛的西拉諾女士：

恭喜，[194]**《巴貝多生活》雜誌已認可您的其中一張照片，1 月 24 日在熱帶蝴蝶園所拍的（蝴蝶 #2）**，獲得佳作獎，[193]**我們已確認您符合所有的參賽資格**。欲領取您的獎項，請在五天內以電子郵件回覆我。在您的電子郵件中，[195]**請確認我們可以在我們的特刊中放進您的大名**。

若您有任何問題，也請寄電子郵件給我。

敬祝　安康

攝影編輯　詹姆斯．馬林

**191. 確認事實與否**

關於《巴貝多生活》雜誌，可由公告中得知什麼？

(A) 每兩個月出刊一次。
**(B) 有巴貝多以外地區的讀者。**
(C) 每一期都有攝影比賽。
(D) 贊助巴貝多的節慶。

**換句話說**

readers living in Barbados and internationally（住在巴貝多及海外的讀者）→ (B) readers outside of Barbados（巴貝多以外地區的讀者）

**192. 同義詞考題**

在公告中，第三段第三行的「run」，意思最接近下列何者？

| | |
|---|---|
| (A) 編輯 | (C) 評價 |
| (B) 監督 | **(D) 刊印** |

**193. 整合題** 

關於艾達．西拉諾，下列何者最不可能為真？

(A) 她提交十張照片或更少。
(B) 她的收入並不來自攝影。
**(C) 她的參賽作品在 2 月 15 日之後才寄達。**
(D) 她目前是巴貝多的居民。

**換句話說**

up to 10 images（最多十張照片）
→ (A) 10 or fewer images（十張照片或更少）
does not earn any income as a photographer（非以攝影賺取收入）→ (B) income does not come from photography（收入並不來自攝影）

**194. 整合題**

關於西拉諾女士的其中一張照片，可由文中得知什麼？

(A) 會是 T 恤圖樣的主要設計。
**(B) 在參觀一座花園時拍攝的。**
(C) 參加了兩個不同類別。
(D) 會得到獎金作為表揚。

**195. 相關細節**

馬林先生要求西拉諾女士做什麼？

**(A) 准許刊登她的名字**
(B) 列一張其他適合的替代獎項清單
(C) 將之後的詢問轉給另一個部門
(D) 確認她的住家地址，以供郵寄之用

- permission (n.) 許可　substitute (n.) 代替物

**換句話說**

confirm that it is OK（確認可以）
→ (A) Give permission（准許）
to include your name in our special issue（在我們的特刊中放進您的大名）
→ (A) for her name to be published（刊登她的名字）

## 196–200 報導、專欄文章與網頁

**柏里市新聞**　　**3 月 20 日**

**新任經理為柏里飯店帶來新行銷計畫**

文／財經記者莎拉．柯齊

坐落在分隔達爾曼郡和亨利郡的佛朗提吉路上，200 歲的柏里飯店被充滿綠蔭的花園環繞，提供客人一個令人放鬆的住處。

在我採訪時，[198]**飯店經理莫妮卡．胡**告訴我，她對飯店有目標遠大的行銷計畫，[196]**飯店老闆是當地企業家丹．克羅斯比**，克羅斯比先生去年底僱用她，好讓他能更專注在已經營三年、正在成長的咖啡館事業。

在我們談話時，我提到飯店的網站並未完全展現飯店的奢華便利設施，[197]**她微笑，拿起一個平板裝置，指出最近重新設計過的網站裡的一個頁面，展示著每一間裝潢精美的客房影像**。她接著詳述她努力將飯店推廣為探索亨利郡的起點，該郡擁有許多景點，但遊客卻比達爾曼郡少得多。她說，飯店的新廣告手冊鼓勵遊客「體驗亨利郡」。

胡女士表示，她也計畫修改柏里飯店的晚餐菜單，以包含「符合每個人的預算」的選項。目前，[196] **該飯店的禮品店販售克羅斯比先生手工製作的藥草及香料。**

- shaded (adj.) 遮蔭的
  ambitious (adj.) 志向遠大的
  entrepreneur (n.) 企業家
  amenity (n.) 便利設施
  launch point (n.) 起點
  artisanal (adj.) 傳統匠人手工製作的

柏里市新聞　　3月24日

**探索亨利郡**

文／旅遊專欄作家吉姆．史康達

柏里市　訊——我最近下榻柏里飯店並探索亨利郡的迷人景點，[198] **飯店經理安排我和亨利郡旅遊協會（HCTA）會長布萊恩．庫佐聯絡**，他帶領我在郡內一日遊，行程從萊特小館的美味早餐開始，這是飯店附近幾家高評價餐廳之一，然後，我們短暫造訪有名的藝術社區葛雷里鎮，並遊覽派克斯頓公園歷史村。[199] **行程中最精彩的部分是搭乘露天平底船沿派克斯頓運河而下的解說航程**，庫佐先生對這個地區抱有高度熱情，我非常推薦參觀此地的許多名勝。

- highly-rated (adj.) 高度評價的
  narrated cruise (n.) 解說航程　barge (n.) 平底船
  enthusiasm (n.) 熱情　sight (n.) 名勝；景色

www.birleyhotel.com/home

**下榻柏里飯店，體驗亨利郡**

| 放鬆<br>更多服務內容 | [197] 住宿<br>**觀看我們的房間** |
| --- | --- |
| 飲食<br>看菜單 | 發現<br>探索附近景點 |

* 柏里飯店歡迎團體活動。配備有投影機和音響系統的大型會議室可供租用。[200] **飯店也提供電動自行車與電動車用的充電站，房客免費，非房客 15 元。**

- charging station (n.) 充電站

**196. 推論或暗示** 難

關於柏里飯店，下列何者最可能為真？

(A) 最近調漲房價。
(B) 以復古家具裝潢。
(C) 提供房價折扣給一位專欄作家。
**(D) 販售老闆製作的食物相關產品。**

- occupancy (v.) 居住

換句話說

sells artisanal herbs and spices created by Mr. Crosby（販售克羅斯比先生手工製作的藥草及香料）→ (D) sells food-related products made by its owner（販售老闆製作的食品相關產品）

---

**197. 整合題**

胡女士展示哪部分的網站給柯齊女士看？

(A) 放鬆　(C) 飲食
**(B) 住宿**　(D) 發現

---

**198. 整合題** 難

關於庫佐先生，可由文中得知什麼？

**(A) 胡女士將他介紹給一位專欄作家。**
(B) 他在克羅斯比先生的一家咖啡館主持一場餐會。
(C) 他在觀光行程中和柯齊女士說話。
(D) 他為柏里飯店設計廣告手冊。

- refer A to B 將 A 轉介給 B

換句話說

put . . . in contact with（安排……聯絡）
→ (A) was referred . . . to（介紹給……）

---

**199. 確認事實與否**

關於亨利郡，可由文中得知什麼？

(A) 遊客比達爾曼郡多。
(B) 比達爾曼郡更早有人定居。
**(C) 遊客可以搭船遊覽。**
(D) 公園最近擴建。

- settle (v.) 使定居

換句話說

cruise down Paxton Canal in an open-air barge（搭乘露天平底船沿派克斯頓運河而下）
→ (C) boat tours（搭船遊覽）

TEST 8 PART 7

**200. 相關細節**

飯店免費提供什麼給房客？

(A) 使用影音設備
(B) 關於植物照護技巧的工作坊
**(C) 電動車輛用的充電設施**
(D) 某些衣物種類的洗衣服務

換句話說

free（免費）→ at no charge（免費）
charging stations for electric bikes and cars
（電動自行車和電動車用的充電站）
→ (C) Charging facilities for electric vehicles
（電動車輛用的充電設施）

# ACTUAL TEST 9

## PART 5 P. 232–234

**101. 形容詞詞彙題——主詞補語**

用沃謝特的線上聊天平台，能輕易為顧客提供良好的支援。

(A) 簡單地　(C) 簡化
**(B) 簡單的**　(D) 簡化

---

**102. 形容詞詞彙題**

因為價格平實且設計簡單，「遊艇 10」縫紉機是偶爾想縫紉的人的極佳選擇。

(A) 耐用的　**(C) 隨意的**
(B) 富裕的　(D) 新鮮的

- affordability (n.) 負擔能力
  straightforward (adj.) 簡單的
  sewing machine (n.) 縫紉機

---

**103. 動詞詞類變化題——語態——時態**

密斯公司期待下個月降價後，它的護髮產品業績可以提高。

(A) 將降低　(C) 已降低
**(B) 降低**　(D) 現在被降低

---

**104. 動詞詞彙題** 難

應徵者說，是因為可能常要出國出差，他才婉拒升為經理。

(A) 撤退　(C) 登記
(B) 隱瞞　**(D) 婉拒**

- prospect (n.) 可能性

---

**105. 副詞詞彙題**

雖然是個人的最佳紀錄，但波克女士的分數並沒有高到讓她夠格進入全國大賽。

(A) 無論如何　(C) 很多
**(B) 足夠**　(D) 向上

---

**106. 介系詞詞彙題**

除了「護理倫理」被移到星期二晚上，系上的所有秋季課程都會照原先排定的時間開課。

**(A) 除……之外**　(C) 為了
(B) 關於　(D) 在……期間

- initially (adv.) 最初　ethics (n.) 倫理學

---

**107. 反身代名詞考題** 難

威靈頓先生要求為他自己和兩位同事，訂一間在會議中心旁邊的飯店。

(A) 他　**(C) 他自己**
(B) 他自己的　(D) 他的

- adjacent to 鄰近……

---

**108. 形容詞詞彙題——修飾名詞**

因為辦公室是開放空間，員工必須利用無人使用的會議室講私人電話。

(A) 私下地　**(C) 私人的**
(B) 隱私　(D) 私有化的

- open floor plan (n.) 開放式隔局
  unoccupied (adj.) 未占用的
  privatize (v.) 使私有化

---

**109. 副詞詞彙題**

為了保養你的木製家具，海爾吉家居建議偶爾在家具表面擦椰子油。

(A) 草率地　(C) 意外地
**(B) 偶爾**　(D) 最近

---

**110. 關係代名詞考題——主格**

電影公司勉強同意導演選擇以其電視作品較為聞名的梅爾．佛萊瑟，擔任她的電影主角。

(A) 某個人　**(C) ……的人**
(B) 無論誰　(D) 那人

- studio (n.) 電影公司；電影製片廠
  reluctantly (adv.) 勉強地；不情願地

---

**111. 名詞詞彙題** 

公司規章載明值班主任有權分派工作給員工。

(A) 便利設施　(C) 意圖
(B) 調整　**(D) 權力**

- regulation (n.) 規章；規定　supervisor (n.) 主管

---

**112. 副詞詞彙題——修飾不定詞**

艾彭托的手機 APP 程式設計得很差，使用者每次打開程式，都要重複輸入登入資料。

**(A) 重複地**　(C) 重複的
(B) 重複　(D) 重複

- repetition (n.) 重複

**113. 介系詞詞彙題** 難

皮特曼集團的都會消費者調查中，很多受訪者喜歡知名品牌的產品，勝過自有品牌。

(A) 就像　　**(C) 超過**
(B) 下降　　(D) 向

- participant (n.) 參加者　urban (adj.) 城市的　generic (adj.) 一般的

---

**114. 動詞詞類變化題——介系詞的受詞**

經過幾年在有限預算下營運後，我們已習慣避免不必要的開支。

(A) 避免　　(C) 避免
(B) 避免　　**(D) 避免**

- restricted (adj.) 受限的　budget (n.) 預算　expense (n.) 開支

---

**115. 形容詞詞彙題**

由於謠傳有安全問題，乘客對使用地鐵系統的支付卡有疑慮。

(A) 重大的　　(C) 不合適的
(B) 敏感的　　**(D) 猶豫的**

- critical (adj.) 重大的　sensitive (adj.) 敏感的

---

**116. 名詞詞彙題——動詞的直接受詞**

貝利先生最新的書，提供對不動產投資有興趣的讀者，進入這個領域的實用指引。

(A) 指導　　(C) 可引導的
**(B) 指引**　　(D) 指導

- real estate (n.) 不動產

---

**117. 副詞詞彙題**

公司的政策必須讓員工容易了解，而且管理部門要貫徹執行。

**(A) 一貫地**　　(C) 不久
(B) 相對地　　(D) 據說

- management (n.) 管理部門　relatively (adv.) 相對地　shortly (adv.) 不久　supposedly (adv.) 據說

---

**118. 連接詞詞彙題**

雖然她的課吸引了將近 30 人，但佐藤女士仍盡力和每個人至少說到一次話。

(A) 儘管　　(C) 在……之前
**(B) 雖然**　　(D) 除……外

- endeavor (v.) 努力；盡力　nevertheless (adv.) 儘管　prior to 在……之前　apart from 除……外

---

**119. 名詞詞彙題** 難

建造大量自行車停車設施，只是史道維爾為推廣大眾騎自行車所採行的方法之一。

(A) 指示物　　**(C) 方法**
(B) 目標　　(D) 期限

- ample (adj.) 大量的　promote (v.) 推廣；宣傳　indicator (n.) 指示物　objective (n.) 目標

---

**120. 形容詞詞彙題——修飾名詞**

奧斯朋歌劇支持者俱樂部的會員，得到門票和商品的專屬折扣。

**(A) 專有的**　　(C) 把……排除在外
(B) 把……排除在外　　(D) 專有地

- access (n.) 使用；使用權　merchandise (n.) 商品　exclusively (adv.) 專有地

---

**121. 動詞詞類變化題——時態**

自從我們開始在《現在創業》上登廣告後，我們的飯店一直有大量商務旅客造訪。

(A) 造訪　　(C) 原本可能造訪
(B) 正造訪　　**(D) 一直造訪**

- business traveler (n.) 商務旅客

---

**122. 介系詞詞彙題** 難

儘管文化不同，菲利普斯女士仍和北京分公司的團隊建立了堅定的關係。

(A) 代表　　**(C) 儘管**
(B) 除……之外　　(D) 交換

- on behalf of 代表……　notwithstanding (prep.) 儘管　in exchange for 交換……

---

**123. 名詞詞彙題——動詞的主詞** 

工作坊延長為整天將讓每場工作坊都能涵蓋大量資訊。

**(A) 延長**　　(C) 延長
(B) 最漫長的　　(D) 長度

- significantly (adv.) 相當數量地　lengthen (v.) 延長

### 124. 動詞詞彙題 難

選擇專做婚禮規畫，證明是佛漢活動公司做過最好的決定之一。

(A) 使聯合　　(C) 展望
**(B) 證明**　　(D) 奮鬥

- envision (v.) 展望　strive (v.) 奮鬥；努力

### 125. 副詞子句連接詞詞彙題

即使津特服飾決定不找我們做它的行銷活動，本季仍有望成為我們有史以來最成功的一季。

(A) 在……之上　　(C) 為了……
(B) 一……就……　　**(D) 即使**

- quarter (n.) 季度
  on track 如預期；順利進行中

### 126. 副詞詞彙題——修飾過去分詞——比較級 難

事實上，走桑默斯路比大家常走的 24 號公路更容易到卡斯維瀑布。

(A) 更常的　　(C) 最常地
(B) 最常的　　**(D) 更常地**

### 127. 形容詞詞彙題 難

歡迎曼森咖啡的顧客，使用收據上的密碼連上我們的無線網路。

(A) 可能的　　(C) 建議的
**(B) 受歡迎的**　　(D) 有利的

- patron (n.) 顧客；老主顧　receipt (n.) 收據
  beneficial (adj.) 有利的

### 128. 動詞詞類變化題——(should) ＋原形動詞 

顧問建議這家店重新設計酬賓計畫，以提供更立即可得的獎勵。

**(A) 被重新設計**　　(C) 被重新設計
(B) 預定重新設計　　(D) 將正重新設計

- loyalty program (n.) 酬賓方案
  tangible (adj.) 明確的；真實的

### 129. 不定詞的慣用法

當工人即將達到每週工時上限時，電子時間追蹤系統會通知主管。

(A) 幾乎　　**(C) 即將**
(B) 接近　　(D) 在……之內

### 130. 名詞詞彙題 難

佛里吉哥的冷凍卡車確保食品在運送途中，不會經歷導致危險的溫度波動。

**(A) 波動**　　(C) 知覺
(B) 界限　　(D) 標準

- undergo (v.) 經歷；承受
  fluctuation (n.) 波動；起伏
  boundary (n.) 界限　sensation (n.) 知覺

## PART 6 P. 235–238

### 131–134 電子郵件

寄件者：<accounts@final-tally.com>
收件者：譚雅．貝爾
主旨：免費試用期結束
日期：2 月 7 日

親愛的貝爾女士：

您的費諾塔利免費試用期 [131] **預定**於 2 月 10 日結束，那表示您的全方位雲端會計解決方案只剩三天可用。我們希望，費諾塔利不僅幫助您將您的小企業的每日財務打理得井井有條，也了解 [132] **全面的**財務狀況。若您想要繼續使用費諾塔利，請登入您的帳號，成為付費訂戶。

若您未付費訂購，您將有 60 天的時間取回您儲存於費諾塔利的資料。[133] **之後**，所有與您的帳號連結的資料都會被刪除。此外，若您有特殊理由，最後決定不要訂購，請告訴我們，[134] **我們永遠尋求改進之道。**

感謝您。

費諾塔利團隊

- trial (n.) 試用　comprehensive (adj.) 包羅萬象的
  paid subscriber (n.) 付費訂戶
  subscription (n.) 訂閱　retrieve (v.) 收回

### 131. 動詞詞類變化題——時態

**(A) 被排定**　　(C) 已排定
(B) 被排定　　(D) 排定

### 132. 形容詞詞彙題

(A) 初步的　　**(C) 全面的**
(B) 各式各樣的　　(D) 頂尖的

- preliminary (adj.) 初步的
  assorted (adj.) 各式各樣的
  foremost (adj.) 頂尖的

**133. 連接副詞**

(A) 同時　(C) 因此
(B) 然而　**(D) 之後**

**134. 句子插入題** 

(A) 我們一直熱切地等候您的回覆。
**(B) 我們永遠尋求改進之道。**
(C) 我們有好幾個選項也許適合。
(D) 我們喜愛與我們團隊的其他成員分享讚美。

**135–138 說明**

**按壓指紋說明**

為了確認你有資格獲得長期簽證，必須有你手指和拇指的清晰印記；135 **為了取得**你自己的指紋，你需要一個黑色印台。將一根手指在印台上滾動，它才能均勻沾上墨水。在背景查核表上找到與那根手指 136 **相對應**的方框，將手指一側壓在框內，然後轉往另一側，維持同樣的力道，所有其他手指也重複同樣的步驟。只要正確的方框內 137 **剩下**的空間足夠的話，你可以試著重印不清楚的指印，138 **否則請用一張新的表格，重新開始這個流程。**

- fingerprint (v.) 採……的指紋
  impression (n.) 壓印；印記
  eligible for 有資格做……
  background check (n.) 背景查核
  sufficient (adj.) 足夠的

**135. 動詞詞類變化題——不定詞**

(A) 取得　(C) 已取得
**(B) 為了取得**　(D) 取得……

**136. 動詞詞彙題**

(A) 將……用於　**(C) 相對應**
(B) 指定　(D) 同意

- devote (v.) 將……用於　designate (v.) 指定

**137. 動詞詞類變化題——現在分詞**

(A) 剩下　(C) 剩餘的
**(B) 剩下**　(D) 剩下

**138. 句子插入題** 

(A) 這麼做會造成指紋的嚴重瑕疵。
(B) 在快到那個日期之前，你才需要再次按壓指紋。
(C) 最後，讓參加者把他或她的手完全擦乾淨。
**(D) 否則請用一張新的表格，重新開始這個流程。**

- imperfection (n.) 瑕疵　thoroughly (adv.) 完全地
  wipe off 擦掉

**139–142 備忘錄**

寄件者：傑瑞．摩爾
收件者：全體員工
關於：會計部

嗨，各位：

在近期的整修後，很多員工一直選擇穿過會計部，好從前門到休息室，或從休息室到前門。我了解這條路線 139 **最方便**，但這種習慣不准再繼續下去了，會計們已報告他們發現這樣非常令人分心，140 **更重要的是，他們必須能不受干擾地處理機密資料。**在我建議下，他們試著鎖門，還有直接要求這樣走的員工停止這麼做，但兩種方法都沒用。因此，大樓維修單位已同意以大型家具封住會計部和休息室間的門，這份備忘錄旨在通知你們大家，從明天開始，那扇門完全不能使用，請依此調整你們的 142 **路線**。

人力資源部主管
傑瑞．摩爾

- accounting (n.) 會計
  following (prep.) 在……以後
  distracting (adj.) 分心的
  maintenance (n.) 維修；保養　notify (v.) 通知
  accordingly (adv.) 相應地

**139. 形容詞詞彙題——主詞補語**

(A) 方便的　**(C) 最方便的**
(B) 方便　(D) 更方便地

**140. 句子插入題**

(A) 如果你也有類似的問題，我們可以一起去找管理階層談。
(B) 無論如何，休息室會是比較適合進行這類對話的地方。
(C) 請先敲門提醒他們，你要進來了。
**(D) 更重要的是，他們必須能不受干擾地處理機密資料。**

- confidential (adj.) 機密的

### 141. 限定詞詞彙題 難

(A) 這個　(B) 任何　(C) 他們的　**(D) 兩者都不**

### 142. 名詞詞彙題

**(A) 路線**　(B) 優先　(C) 預估　(D) 問候

### 143–146 報導

**《辦案》將播映路威茲這集**

路威茲　訊（10 月 2 日）——電視影集《辦案》中 [143] **主要**在路威茲拍攝的一集，今晚九點將於 NBO 頻道播出。

影集主角由琺麗達．艾保德和亨利．布萊恩特飾演警探，在全國各地解決犯罪案件。今晚這一集裡，他們到了 [144] **虛構的**芒恩戴爾鎮調查一起失蹤案。

路威茲的好幾個地點，包括法院、凱利公園和巴特勒雜貨店被選中，以具體呈現劇組人員想像出的地方，[145] **這幾場戲在八月花了一星期拍攝完成**。不過，依照慣例，這一集的開場和結束是在卓墨里市的拍攝場地拍的。

市鎮官員亞伯特．鄭表示，他希望這一集的播出吸引到其他製作團隊的 [146] **注意**：「我們歡迎更多電影和電視的拍攝企畫。」

- detective (n.) 警探；偵探　investigate (v.) 調查　embody (v.) 使具體化

### 143. 副詞詞彙題 難

**(A) 主要地**　(B) 非常　(C) 過度地　(D) 獨占地

### 144. 形容詞詞彙題

(A) 真實的　**(B) 虛構的**　(C) 鄰近的　(D) 各式各樣的

### 145. 句子插入題

(A) 其他的場地都需要路威茲政府的許可。
(B) 居民應預期這些區域的交通會受阻。
**(C) 這幾場戲在八月花了一星期拍攝完成。**
(D) 目前為止，這集得到評論家和觀眾的好評。

- traffic disruption (n.) 交通受阻　well-received (n.) 獲得好評　critic (n.) 評論家

### 146. 名詞詞彙題——動詞的受詞 難

(A) 侍者　(B) 最專心的　**(C) 注意**　(D) 參加

- attentive (adj.) 專心的　attend (v.) 參加　attending (v.) 參加；出席

## PART 7 P. 239–261

### 147–148 網頁

www.leampter.com/order
林特公司

**訂單摘要**

請在完成訂單前再檢查一次。

[148] 送貨地址：**38637 密西西比州波摩斯大學大道 1660 號 波摩斯大學維修部轉交德瑞克．麥奎爾**
[148] 付款方式：**信用卡　尾碼 0455**
帳單地址：同送貨地址
[148] 運送方式：標準陸運

| 產品 | 數量 | 單價 | 總價 |
|---|---|---|---|
| 中強度垃圾袋（一盒 200 入） | 5 | 25.00 元 | 125.00 元 |
| 13 瓦螢光燈泡（一盒 12 入） | 1 | 4.20 元 | 4.20 元 |
| [147] **12 伏特無線電鑽** | 1 | 129.00 元 | 129.00 元 |
| 耐化學性橡膠手套（一盒 10 入） | 2 | 10.40 元 | 20.80 元 |
| | | 運費 | 24.99 元 |
| | | **總計** | 303.99 元 |

促銷碼：＿＿＿＿＿＿

送出訂單

- c/o (= care of) 轉交
  fluorescent (adj.) 螢光的
  cordless (adj.) 無電線的
  chemical-resistant (adj.) 耐化學性的

### 147. 推論或暗示

林特公司最可能是何種公司？

(A) 家具店
**(B) 五金零售店**
(C) 辦公室用品經銷商
(D) 汽車零件廠商

**148. 確認事實與否**

麥奎爾先生沒有提供什麼資料？

(A) 訂的貨要送到哪裡
(B) 貨品應如何運送
(C) 他要用什麼付款
**(D) 他為什麼可以享有折扣**

換句話說
Ship to（送貨地址）→ (A) Where the order should be sent（訂的貨要送到哪裡）
Shipping preference（運送方式）
→ (B) How the goods should be shipped（貨品應如何運送）
Payment method（付款方式）→ (C)What he will use to make a payment（他要用什麼付款）

**149–150 線上聊天室**

茱蒂·克萊恩〔下午 2:14〕
艾瑞克，真高興在線上遇見你。[150] **我今天早上處理你的差旅費報銷時，遇到問題。**

艾瑞克·霍蘭德〔下午 2:15〕
嗨，茱蒂。是什麼問題？

茱蒂·克萊恩〔下午 2:16〕
抱歉，可以等我一下嗎？[149] **我以為表格就在這裡，但我從那時之後一直在處理一些其他檔案。**

艾瑞克·霍蘭德〔下午 2:16〕
當然可以。

茱蒂·克萊恩〔下午 2:19〕
好，[149] **我找到了**。在「雜項」欄，你在 5 月 25 日列了 24.38 元的費用，但我看不懂你寫在說明格裡的字，[150] **你還記得你在那裡寫了什麼嗎？**看起來像是「h」開頭的字。

艾瑞克·霍蘭德〔下午 2:20〕
嗯。[150] **我過去妳位子找妳。**

茱蒂·克萊恩〔下午 2:21〕
噢，那太好了。待會見。

- reimbursement (n.) 報銷
  miscellaneous (adj.) 混雜的
  description (n.) 敘述

**149. 推論或暗示**

文中提到關於克萊恩女士的什麼事？

(A) 她時常被同事的問題打斷。
(B) 她有時會打不開某個軟體程式。
(C) 她在談話前，從印表機取出幾張紙。
**(D) 她在談話中，一邊在找一些文件。**

- retrieve (v.) 收回

換句話說
the form（表格）
→ (D) some paperwork（一些文件）

**150. 掌握意圖**

下午 2:20，當霍蘭德先生寫道：「我過去妳的位子找妳」，他意指什麼？

(A) 他有個要求需要快點處理。
(B) 他偏好繳交實體的紙本表格。
**(C) 他不記得他如何花某些款項。**
(D) 他提議示範一個流程。

- physical (adj.) 實體的　recall (v.) 記得；回想起

**151–152 報導**

**接收新聞的新方法**

（10 月 15 日）—— 70 餘年來，《包德溫時報》一直是包德溫市民偏好的每日新聞來源。然而，現在人們想要在新聞事件發生時就得知消息，而不是一天一次。因此，[151] **我們今天早上推出了《包德溫時報》APP，作為我們網站之外，一個更方便的選擇。**

[152] **無論是地方報導，及全國新聞的深度分析，透過我們的 APP，讀者可以期待線上版與紙本都能獲得同等深度的閱讀內容。**然而，他們也可以利用它的客製化通知功能，接收他們有興趣的突發新聞提醒。APP 的內容首月免費，之後每月僅 4.99 元。今天就上各大應用程式商店下載。

- release (v.) 發行　alternative (adj.) 可供選擇的
  in-depth (adj.) 深入的　coverage (n.) 新聞報導
  insightful (adj.) 深刻理解的
  customizable (adj.) 可客製化的
  notification (n.) 通知　alert (n.) 通知
  breaking news (n.) 突發新聞

**151. 主旨或目的**

這篇文章的目的為何？

**(A) 宣傳一項數位產品**
(B) 告知一個地方上的趨勢
(C) 概述一家公司的歷史
(D) 宣布推出新專欄

換句話說
the Boldwin Times app（《包德溫時報》應用程式）→ (A) a digital product（一個數位產品）

**152. 確認事實與否** 難

可由文中得知關於《包德溫時報》的什麼事？

(A) 以前是該地區最受歡迎的刊物。
(B) 以財經新聞報導聞名。
**(C) 有好幾種方法可以看到它的內容。**
(D) 許多該報的讀者住在包德溫以外的地區。

---

**153–155 廣告**

**來赫斯麗電影院同時享受**
**晚餐和電影！**

赫斯麗電影院新的用餐影廳「放飛廳」開始營業了！[153/155] **買票在該影廳觀賞所有放映電影的觀眾可以吃到的不止有爆米花，還有不那麼傳統的電影院餐點**，像漢堡和披薩。而且這一切都只要按一個鈕就有，即使電影正在放映！我們的服務人員會幫你點餐，並將食物送到 [153] **你的座位，座椅超級寬敞**且有可收起來的餐桌。放飛廳獨特的用餐與觀影體驗是赫斯麗電影院一項令人興奮的新產物，[153] **已被《畢勒根先驅報》稱為「畢勒根電影愛好者的最佳選擇」**。

**赫斯麗電影院三月特別活動：**
《南國》的導演特映場：[153] **3 月 19 日來放飛廳，在全國上映前觀賞這部令人深思的新劇情片**。電影結束後，導演泰納夏．羅布森將討論電影並接受觀眾提問。

孩童的星期二：[154] **三月的每個星期二早上，家長可以帶六歲以下的兒童來觀賞適合孩童的電影，成人每人只要 5 元，兒童每人 2 元**。

- screening (n.) 上映電影
  retractable (adj.) 可收回的
  addition (n.) 增加的人或物
  enthusiast (n.) 愛好者　thoughtful (adj.) 深思的
  wide release 全國上映

**153. 確認事實與否** 

文中未提及關於放飛廳的什麼事？

(A) 是一個即將舉行試映會的場地。
(B) 客人可以點各式各樣的食物。
**(C) 在雜誌中受到評論。**
(D) 座位很寬敞。

換句話說

to see the . . . new drama before its wide release（在全國上映前觀賞這部……新劇情片）
→ (A) preview screening（試映會）
enjoy not just popcorn but also less traditional movie fare（不止吃到爆米花，還有不那麼傳統的電影院餐點）→ (B) order a variety of foods（點各式各樣的食物）
extra-wide（超級寬敞）→ (D) spacious（寬敞的）

---

**154. 確認事實與否**

關於三月的一項每週活動，可由文中得知什麼？

(A) 是給學童團體的活動。
**(B) 給有些觀眾的票價較低。**
(C) 活動時程包含互動式討論。
(D) 提供觀看較舊電影的機會。

換句話說

Every Tuesday（每個星期二）
→ weekly（每週的）
for just $5 per adult and $2 per child（成人每人只要 5 元，兒童每人 2 元）
→ (B) ticket prices are lower for some viewers（有些觀眾的票價較低）

---

**155. 句子插入題**

「而且這一切都只要按一個鈕就有，即使電影正在放映！」最適合放在標示 [1]、[2]、[3]、[4] 的何處？

**(A) [1]**　　(C) [3]
(B) [2]　　(D) [4]

---

**156–158 客戶評論**

www.tradespeoplereview.com

**首頁 > > 城市 > > 奧馬哈 > > 水管工人 > > 富爾頓水電**

**評論者：哈柏．昆泰羅　　發布日：3 月 22 日**

我朋友的浴室整修是找查德．富爾頓和他的團隊做的，她跟我推薦這一家。[156] **當我發現廚房的水龍頭就算整個關緊還是在滴水時，我聯絡富爾頓水電好解決這個問題**，和我談話的代表在電話上就能提供報價，而且是付得起的價格。[157] **但我想強調的是，工人有多快到達——就在我打過電話 20 分鐘之後**！這絕對是這次服務最棒的一點，[158] **即使在我這個案子裡不太需要，因為我的問題不可能造成淹水**，但我可以了解，那些處於緊急狀況的人真的會很感謝這一點。總之，富爾頓先生和跟他一起來的員工迅速又專業地完成工作，我當然推薦富爾頓水電。

- renovation (n.) 整修 faucet (n.) 水龍頭
  representative (n.) 代表
  estimate (n.) 估價，報價

**156. 相關細節**

昆泰羅女士為何僱用富爾頓水電？

(A) 改善家裡的水壓
**(B) 修理有問題的水龍頭**
(C) 整修浴室
(D) 連接一個廚房家電

- faulty (adj.) 有缺陷的 tap (n.) 水龍頭
  hook up 連接 appliance (n.) 用具

**換句話說**

water was dripping from my kitchen faucet
（我的廚房水龍頭正在滴水）
→ (B) a faulty tap（有問題的水龍頭）
resolve the issue（解決這個問題）
→ (B) have . . . repaired（修理……）

---

**157. 相關細節**

昆泰羅女士對富爾頓水電的哪一方面說得最詳細？

(A) 多種服務選項
(B) 員工的態度
(C) 工資
**(D) 回應時間**

---

**158. 推論或暗示**

關於富爾頓水電提供的服務，可由文中得知什麼？

(A) 是該公司的專長。
**(B) 昆泰羅女士不認為是緊急需求。**
(C) 昆泰羅女士之前從另一個供應商處獲得。
(D) 它包含到場諮詢。

- specialty (n.) 專長 consultation (n.) 諮詢

---

**159–160 廣告**

**唐娜**
**綠色植物大師**

你的辦公室會利用植物創造出促進工作的環境嗎？還是只有櫃檯的桌腳放了蕨類盆栽，而其他剩下的地方都用單調的畫作裝飾？

很遺憾，[159] **大部分的辦公室都錯失了植物充滿生氣的樂趣，因為他們擔心要讓植物存活並不容易**。但是，你知道有很多植物品種適應力非常強，不需要昂貴的土壤或常常澆水嗎？

[160] **讓唐娜推薦你要買哪些植物和如何布置**，好達到預期的最大效果。當她仔細挑選幾乎不需照顧的植物，重新設計你的辦公室時，你會很驚訝員工士氣和生產力的改善結果。今天就打給唐娜（990）555-0107，展開行動吧。

- greenery (n.) 綠色植物 fern (n.) 蕨類植物
  receptionist (n.) 接待人員
  be composed of 由……組成
  vibrant (adj.) 充滿生氣的
  assortment (n.) 各種各樣；混雜
  resilient (adj.) 適應性強的
  maximize (v.) 達到最大值
  upkeep (n.) 維修；保養 morale (n.) 士氣
  productivity (n.) 生產力

**159. 相關細節**

根據廣告，為何大部分的辦公室選擇不要有很多植物？

(A) 買起來很貴。
(B) 散發強烈氣味。
(C) 創造能量很低的氣氛。
**(D) 看起來很難好好照顧。**

- properly (adv.) 恰當地

**換句話說**

miss out on the joys of . . . flora
（錯失了植物……的樂趣）
→ not to have many plants
（不要有很多植物）
not be easy to keep the plants alive
（讓植物活著不容易）
→ (D) difficult to care for properly
（很難好好照顧）

---

**160. 相關細節**

文中廣告哪種服務？

(A) 定期到場照顧植物
**(B) 用植物裝飾的建議**
(C) 如何栽種植物的課程
(D) 清除不想要的植物

- tending (n.) 照料 disposal (n.) 清除

**換句話說**

recommend . . . how to arrange them
（推薦……如何布置）
→ (B) Advice on decorating with plants
（用植物裝飾的建議）

## 161–164 電子郵件

寄件人：道格拉斯．麥考伊
收件人：脇本愛美
主旨：試驗結果
日期：1 月 28 日
附件：報告

嗨，脇本女士：

我剛剛收到我們的新安全措施的試驗報告，結果很清楚：[161] **在建造工程開始前進行工作危害分析（JHA），在讓工程順利進行及降低成本上有正面效果**。完整報告如附件，但我在此概述重點。

[162] **過去兩年來，我們在三個工程案上執行這項措施——羅賓森塔、史巴克公寓及布萊恩市場，並請布洛斯利顧問公司將那些工程案與我們在同一時期進行的其他工程案加以分析和比較**。由於 JHA 預防了傷害及其他問題，[163] **羅賓森塔和布萊恩市場分別比其他類似工程快 8% 和 11% 完工，且成本各減少 6% 和 10%**。史巴克公寓在這兩項上只達到平均值，但考量到它面對異常的區域性天氣所致的主要問題，這已經很棒了。相較之下，遇到類似問題的胡柏大樓進度落後至少 15%，而成本比平均高出 13%。

別忘了，一開始花在執行 JHA 的時間與經費已經計入本次資料中，對我來說這相當清楚，我們應該儘快在所有工程上執行這項流程。等妳準備好，[164] **我們何不見面談談如何把這個想法提供給其他部門呢？**請告訴我。

道格　謹啟

- trial (n.) 試驗　measure (n.) 措施
  keep . . . on track 使……順利進行
  summarize (v.) 概述　implement (v.) 實施；執行
  unseasonable (adj.) （天氣）反常的
  regional (adj.) 地區的；區域的
  run into 遭遇（困難）
  factor A into B 把 A 作為因素計入 B
  present (v.) 提供；給

### 161. 推論或暗示

試驗中最可能測試的是什麼措施？

(A) 立刻調查傷害事故
**(B) 事前研究工人可能遇到的危險**
(C) 鼓勵工人建議改善安全的方法
(D) 某些職位需要額外的資格證明

- incident (n.) 事件　potential (adj.) 可能的
  qualification (n.) 資格證明

**換句話說**
conducting a job hazard analysis (JHA) before construction（在建造工程開始前進行工作危害分析〔JHA〕）
→ (B) Studying potential dangers . . . ahead of time（事前研究……的可能危險）

### 162. 確認事實與否

可由文中得知關於試驗的什麼事？

(A) 持續得比一開始規劃的久。
**(B) 涉及外部公司。**
(C) 結果出人意料。
(D) 資料將會公開。

- external (adj.) 外部的
  unexpected (adj.) 意外的　release (v.) 公開

**換句話說**
had Broseley Consulting analyze and compare（請布洛斯利顧問公司分析和比較）
→ (B) involved an external company（涉及外部公司）

### 163. 相關細節

哪個工程最順利完成？

(A) 羅賓森塔　**(C) 布萊恩市場**
(B) 史巴克公寓　(D) 胡柏大樓

### 164. 相關細節

麥考伊先生建議做什麼？

**(A) 設計宣傳策略**
(B) 調查服務供應商
(C) 複查某些計算結果
(D) 簡化執行的流程

- promotional (adj.) 宣傳的
  calculation (n.) 計算；計算結果
  streamline (v.) 使簡化

**換句話說**
why don't we . . .（我們何不……）→ suggest（建議）
how to present this idea to the other departments（如何把這個想法提供給其他部門）→ (A) a promotional strategy（宣傳策略）

## 165–167 備忘錄

### 備忘錄

收件者：傑姆時尚總監
寄件者：供應與控制經理 賴瑞．梅
日期：10 月 2 日
關於：最新營運狀況

如各位所知，今年對傑姆時尚的營業部來說，是忙碌的一年，[165] **我們監督了五間新製造中心開幕**，而我很高興宣布這五間現在全都全面運作中，商品快速生產，符合我們去年定下的目標。

然而，我們的業務中有個部分讓我格外擔心。與客戶服務團隊聯繫後，我清楚知道，[166] **我們的商品並未在我們答應顧客的時間內送達**，我私下調查這件事，發現我們目前僱用的貨運公司，貨車數量不夠，無法符合我們的需求，這造成訂單積壓和許多客訴。

因此，[167] **我提議與貨運公司老闆見面，討論我們和他們的合約條款，我們必須要他們為這個問題負責，且要求按照所需修改文件。**如果你們對採取這個步驟有任何疑慮或建議，請打分機 553 給我，或寄電子郵件到 larry.may@jem-fashion.com 給我。

賴瑞

- operational (adj.) 營運的　oversee (v.) 監督
  manufacturing hub (n.) 生產中心
  liaise (v.) 聯絡　investigation (n.) 調查
  insufficient (adj.) 不足的　backlog (n.) 積壓
  terms (n.) 條款
  hold A accountable for B 要 A 為 B 負責

### 165. 確認事實與否

文中提到關於傑姆時尚的什麼事？

(A) 去年的利潤創新高。
(B) 重組一個部門。
(C) 推出新系列的產品。
**(D) 最近進行擴張。**

- undergo (v.) 經歷　expansion (n.) 擴張

**換句話說**

the opening of five new manufacturing hubs（五間新製造中心開幕）→ (D) an expansion（擴張）

### 166. 確認事實與否

梅先生提到什麼問題？

**(A) 訂單未準時完成。**
(B) 有間生產設施尚未營運。
(C) 發現商品有瑕疵。
(D) 貨車經常故障。

- defective (adj.) 有缺陷的

**換句話說**

our goods are not being delivered within the timeframe promised（我們的商品並未在答應的時間內送達）
→ (A) Orders are not being completed on time.（訂單未準時完成。）

### 167. 相關細節

梅先生提議傑姆時尚做什麼？

(A) 客戶經理換人
(B) 修改客訴的流程
**(C) 重新談判一份協議**
(D) 公開道歉

**換句話說**

discuss the terms of our contract, demand changes to the document（討論我們合約的條款，要求修改文件）
→ Renegotiate an agreement（重新談判一份協議）

## 168–171 信件

### 古德溫地方公寓大樓管委員

N0G 1Y0 安大略省艾班托
布萊德利街 9070 號

8 月 18 日

503 號房
胡立歐．薩拉哲

親愛的薩拉哲先生：

你好，這裡是古德溫地方公寓大樓管委會。我們寫信來正式通知你，我們的公寓規章中新增了一條規定，從 9 月 1 日起，[168] **屋主不能再將他們房子裡的任何部分短期**（少於六個月）**出租出去。你可能很熟悉「使用 Owillo.com」就是這樣做**，但這項禁令適用於透過任何管道，甚至是私底下簽訂的短期租賃。

你可能知道，這項新規定是管委會成員經過數月討論後，正式投票的結果。因此它對所有住戶都具法律約束力，[171] **違反此項規定，就算只有一次也會帶來巨額罰款**，多次違規會引發管委會採取法律行動。[169] **詳情請見隨附的這條規定全文（第 9 條第 B 節第 12 款）**。

我們希望，[170] **你們之中投票反對禁令的人**記得不允許短期出租的許多好處。首先，它會消除因不斷有非住戶在我們的中庭進進出出而造成的安全問題。此外，它會維持古德溫地區是個鄰居友善社區的精神。

為了確認你了解這項改變，請在附件的表格上簽名並在 8 月 31 日前交回管委會辦公室。請注意，拒絕簽名並不會讓你免受這項規定的約束。

古德溫地方公寓大樓管委會主委
科特妮．葛拉漢　謹啟

附件

- condominium (n.)（各戶有獨立產權的）公寓
  bylaw (n.) 內部章程
  legally binding 具法律約束力的
  violate (v.) 違反　substantial (adj.) 大量的
  fine (n.) 罰款　enclose (v.) 隨信附上
  considerable (adj.) 相當多的　eliminate (v.) 消除
  constant (adj.) 持續的　stream (n.) 人流
  exempt (v.) 免除

### 168. 推論或暗示

人們最可能用 Owillo.com 做什麼？

**(A) 在他們的房產上安排付費住宿**
(B) 和鄰居通訊
(C) 回報公共空間的問題
(D) 瀏覽他們那一區房屋的估價

**換句話說**
let any part of their unit for . . . rental（將他們公寓的任何部分……出租）
→ (A) Arrange paid stays on their property（在他們的房產上安排付費住宿）

---

### 169. 相關細節

這封信附帶什麼？

(A) 投票的表格
(B) 某些維修工作的時間表
(C) 大量的統計資料
**(D) 一套規則的摘錄**

- statistics (n.) 統計資料　excerpt (n.) 摘錄

**換句話說**
is enclosed（隨信附上）→ come with（附帶）
the full text of the rule（規則的全文）
→ (D) An excerpt from a set of regulations（一套規則的摘錄）

---

### 170. 推論或暗示 難

關於某些古德溫地方的住戶，可由文中得知什麼？

(A) 他們要求安全檢查。
**(B) 他們對一項提案表達反對。**
(C) 他們受到一些財務上的處罰。
(D) 他們想要改裝他們的公寓。

- opposition (n.) 反對　incur (v.) 遭受
  alteration (n.) 改變

**換句話說**
those among you（你們之中那些人）
→ some residents（某些住戶）
voted against the ban（投票反對禁令）
→ (B) expressed opposition（表達反對）

---

### 171. 句子插入題 難

「多次違規會引發管委會採取法律行動。」最適合放在標示 [1]、[2]、[3]、[4] 的何處？

(A) [1]　(C) [3]
**(B) [2]**　(D) [4]

- provoke (v.) 激起；導致
  legal action (n.) 法律行動

---

### 172–175 線上聊天室

**布拉瑟公立圖書館 員工聊天室**

克利夫頓．山德斯〔上午 10:19〕
嗨，亞曼達和傑佛瑞。[172] **我正在仔細看上星期讀書俱樂部參加者寫的意見卡，有個問題，我想你們應該要知道**。

亞曼達．湯瑪斯〔上午 10:20〕
是什麼，克利夫頓？

克利夫頓．山德斯〔上午 10:22〕
超過一半的經典俱樂部參加者寫了：「主持人沒有控制好討論時段。」看起來那個團體的主持人莎賓娜讓一位參加者講太久。

亞曼達・湯瑪斯〔上午 10:23〕
啊，是的，[175] **那是道伊爾今年參加的團體，** 他是圖書館讀書俱樂部的固定參加者之一，[175] **如果主持人不堅定一點，他很容易就主導了對話。**

傑佛瑞・沈〔上午 10:24〕
噢，道伊爾！[173] **莎賓娜第一次帶讀書會就要應付他，真是太慘了。**

克利夫頓・山德斯〔上午 10:25〕
我應該照慣例只把回饋意見的摘要給她，還是這需要某種特別回應？

亞曼達・湯瑪斯〔上午 10:26〕
我們應該想想辦法，我會和她坐下來，給她一些讓參加者的發言更平衡的訣竅。[174] **但我現在得趕去開會。還有別的事嗎，克利夫頓？**

傑佛瑞・沈〔上午 10:27〕
我和莎賓娜的關係很好，而且 [175] **我以前曾帶過道伊爾參加的團體，也許應該讓我和她談談。**

亞曼達・湯瑪斯〔上午 10:28〕
當然，傑佛瑞。聽起來是個好主意。

克利夫頓・山德斯〔上午 10:29〕
謝啦，傑佛瑞。好，兩位，晚點聊。

- moderate (v.) 節制；使適中
  dominate (v.) 支配；控制
  assertive (adj.) 肯定的

**172. 主旨或目的**

參與聊天的人正在討論什麼？

(A) 一項即將舉行的活動的廣告
(B) 幫讀書俱樂部選書
**(C) 評估一項圖書館的計畫**
(D) 自動化流程的低效率

- evaluation (n.) 評估　inefficiency (n.) 無效率

**換句話說**
the comment cards（意見卡）
→ (C) Evaluations（評估）

**173. 確認事實與否** 難

可由文中得知關於莎賓娜的什麼事？

**(A) 她是某個角色的新手。**
(B) 她是個有抱負的作者。
(C) 她是無薪志工。
(D) 她有空接下一個任務。

- aspiring (adj.) 有抱負的
  take on an assignment 接受任務

**換句話說**
her first time leading a club（她第一次帶讀書會）→ (A) new to a role（某個角色的新手）

**174. 掌握意圖**

上午 10:26，當湯瑪斯女士寫道：「還有別的事嗎，克利夫頓」，她意指什麼？

(A) 她希望有別的方式可以解決一個問題。
(B) 她沒有足夠的資訊可以做決定。
(C) 她擔心她忘了一個任務。
**(D) 她想知道是否可以結束一段對話。**

**175. 相關細節**

沈先生說他經歷過什麼？

**(A) 處理一位難纏的讀者**
(B) 提供某項技術的訓練
(C) 導覽一棟大樓
(D) 編輯某種文字作品

**換句話說**
lead a group with Doyle（帶過道伊爾參加的團體）
→ (A) Handling a difficult patron（處理一位難纏的讀者）

**176–180 資訊與電子郵件**

**蒙塔拉營地**
露營設施資訊

蒙塔拉營地是蒙塔拉國家公園遊客的絕佳住宿選擇，[180] **園區管理員總是樂意推薦健行步道、釣魚地點和有趣的活動，甚至回答關於他們具代表性的帽子的問題！** [176] **營地的洗手間和淋浴設施為所有露營客共享**，下列的營地皆可租用（所有地點皆包含焚火台）：

- 拓荒者（每晚 15 元）：一頂帳篷和一輛車的空間
- 冒險者（每晚 20 元）：一頂帳篷和一輛車的空間（包含野餐桌）
- 探險者（每晚 18 元）：一輛露營車的空間
- [179] **開路者（每晚 26 元）：一輛露營車的空間（含水電）**

請注意，[177] **三月初當園區在當季首次開放以及國定假日時的需求都很高**，因此強烈建議提前預訂。

欲預訂蒙塔拉營地，請上 www.campingmontara.gov。

- lodging (n.) 借宿的地方
  ranger (n.) 公園管理員　iconic (adj.) 代表性的
  facility (n.) 設施　motor home (n.) 露營車
  advance booking (n.) 提前預訂

**收件人**：<info@campingmontara.gov>
**寄件人**：<s.kohl@kellipsco.com>
**日期**：6 月 29 日
**主旨**：蒙塔拉營地

敬啟者您好：

我最近在蒙塔拉營地住了一星期，雖然營地很美麗宜人，但我對供露營車使用的便利設施很失望，從我們住的第二天到那個星期結束，[179] **我們營地的電力都故障**。因此，[178] **我相信我們應該只付沒有水電的露營車營地的價錢，我想請你們將差價退還給我。** [180] **值班的園區管理員查德・雷恩哈特**人很好，給了我這個電郵地址，這樣我就可以找人協助。您可以回覆這封電子郵件聯繫我。

謝謝您。

香儂・科爾

- amenity (n.) 便利設施

**176. 同義詞考題**

在資訊中，第一段第四行的「shared」，意思最接近下列何者？

(A) 分割的　(C) 被公開
(B) 討論的　**(D) 共同使用**

**177. 推論或暗示** 難

可由文中得知關於蒙塔拉國家公園的什麼事？

(A) 位於一個氣候潮濕的地區。
(B) 遊客比其他國家公園都多。
**(C) 一年中有部分時間關閉。**
(D) 最近僱用了更多園區管理員。

**178. 主旨或目的**

科爾女士為何寫這封電子郵件？

(A) 建議修正一個說明
**(B) 要求退回部分款項**
(C) 解釋一則負評
(D) 查看一則客訴的狀態

- description (n.) 說明；描述
  partial (adj.) 部分的　status (n.) 狀態

**換句話說**

would like the difference to be sent back（想要退還差價）→ (B) request a partial refund（要求退回部分款項）

**179. 整合題**

科爾女士最可能預訂哪種營地？

(A) 拓荒者　(C) 探險者
(B) 冒險者　**(D) 開路者**

**180. 整合題** 

可由文中得知關於雷恩哈特先生什麼事？

**(A) 他工作時戴特別的帽子。**
(B) 他建議搬到另一個營地。
(C) 他暫時可以使用焚火台。
(D) 他在一座有名的山帶領健行。

**換句話說**

their iconic flat hats（他們具代表性的帽子）→ (A) a special type of headgear（特別的帽子）
on duty（值班）→ (A) at work（在工作）

**181–185 會議日程表與公告**

**零售藥房經理協會（ARPM）**
**第 11 屆年會**
[181] **日程表：第二天—— 12 月 4 日**

| 上午 8:00–9:00 | 指定飯店接駁服務 | |
|---|---|---|
| 上午 9:15–9:30 | ARPM 行政副總裁安妮塔・墨里森致詞 | 大禮堂 |
| 上午 9:30 – 10:45 | 上午課程一<br>「改善你的銷售與行銷策略」<br>卡魯索製藥解決方案顧問德魯・艾斯皮諾 | 大禮堂 |
| 上午 11:00–下午 12:15 | 上午課程二<br>「該升級你的銷貨點技術了嗎？」<br>「今日零售藥房」網站編輯凱莉・鮑威爾 | 大禮堂 |
| 下午 12:30–2:00 | 自助式午餐 | 南廳 |

| [183] 下午 2:00–3:15 | [183] 下午課程一「病人照護的有效員工訓練」歐斯沃斯藥房經理馬歇爾・霍洛威 | 大禮堂 |
|---|---|---|
| 下午 3:30–4:45 | 下午課程二「做好準備：零售藥房的未來趨勢」派克斯頓大學藥學院教授瑞卡・百里克 | 大禮堂 |
| 下午 5:00–8:00 | [181] **閉幕晚宴** | 大宴會廳 |

- 關於各講者與課程的資訊，請見 www.arpm-conf.com。
- [182] **每堂課程的最後半小時保留給觀眾問答。**
- 在上午與下午的休息時間，禮堂外有茶點供應。

- designated (adj.) 指定的　remark (n.) 言辭
  refine (v.) 改進　point of sale (n.) 銷貨點
  banquet (n.) 宴會　refreshment (n.) 茶點

## 公告

[183] **因私人因素，馬歇爾・霍洛威今天無法前來上預定課程**「病人照護的有效員工訓練」，[184] **我們的候補講者，同時也是 APRM 的營運長莎拉・休斯，將主持替代課程**。在名為「如何發現並消除無效率」的演講中，她會敘述她的五個步驟系統，用來找出與處理浪費藥房的時間與金錢問題，[183] **對這項變動感到非常不便、想要金錢補償而非參加休斯女士課程的與會者，必須在課程開始前至報到處提出這項要求。**

[185] **此外，會議中心的管理部已通知我們，南廳的外燴業者冰箱昨晚故障，許多今天午餐要供應的食物都壞了**，請改用所附的餐券到附近的餐廳購買午餐，今晚的晚宴會依預定進行。

我們為造成這些不便深致歉意，並請您們體諒。

—— ARPM 第 11 屆年會主辦單位

- standby (adj.) 備用的
  replacement (n.) 取代；更換
  eliminate (v.) 消除　inefficiency (n.) 無效率
  address (v.) 處理　attendee (n.) 參加者
  compensation (n.) 補償；賠償
  catering (n.) 餐飲業；外燴

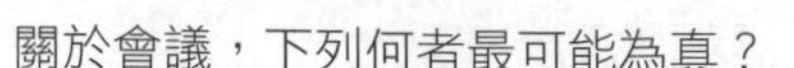

**181. 推論或暗示** 難

關於會議，下列何者最可能為真？

**(A) 舉行兩天。**
(B) 會場有提供住宿。
(C) 會錄影並在線上播放。
(D) 參加者主要是學者。

- venue (n.) 會場　accommodation (n.) 住處
  academic (n.) 學者

**182. 相關細節**

根據會議日程表，會議與會者可以做什麼？

(A) 帶某些飲料進大禮堂
(B) 試用新型零售設備
**(C) 在每節課程結束時提問**
(D) 以電子方式展現他們對會議內容的反應

- beverage (n.) 飲料

**換句話說**
audience（觀眾）
→ conference attendees（會議參加者）
be reserved for . . . Q&A（保留給……問答）
→ (C) Ask questions（提問）

**183. 整合題**

參加者最晚必須在什麼時間之前要求因不便而退費？

(A) 上午 9:30　(B) 上午 11:00　(C) 下午 12:30　**(D) 下午 2:00**

**換句話說**
would prefer financial compensation（較想要金錢補償）
→ ask to be reimbursed（要求退款）
feel strongly inconvenienced（感到非常不便）
→ for an inconvenience（因不便）

**184. 推論或暗示** 難

可由文中得知關於休斯女士的什麼事？
**(A) 她準備了演講以防緊急狀況。**
(B) 她會使用另一位講者的資料。
(C) 她的結束時間會比預定的晚。
(D) 她在 ARPM 之前的會議上演講過。

- in case of an emergency 以防緊急狀況

**185. 確認事實與否**

什麼造成通知中提到的第二個問題？

(A) 外燴訂單的錯誤
**(B) 家電故障**
(C) ARPM 成員的不良行為
(D) 附近街道意料之外的道路工程

- malfunction (n.) 故障

換句話說
the South Hall's catering fridge failed（南廳的外燴業者冰箱故障）→ (B) A malfunctioning appliance（家電故障）

**186–190 電子郵件與廣告**

寄件者：索爾．史崔克蘭
收件者：達琳．吉布森
主旨：迪克森教育科技
日期：7 月 6 日

嗨，達琳：

我寫信來是關於迪克森教育科技的事，那是我們前途看好的新創客戶之一。為防妳對他們還不熟，他們的主要產品是一個員工訓練平台，用類似遊戲的功能讓學習變得有趣，他們最近已成長到，除了我們的行銷服務外，還需要一家專屬的公關公司，**186/189 他們的通訊經理維克多．鮑斯威爾已問我們能否推薦合適人選，187 他們尤其想要一家和科技業有關係、負擔得起的公關服務公司**。由於妳是我們的資訊科技主管，**186 我想知道妳是否在這個領域有特別深入了解**。

非常感謝妳的任何想法。

謝謝。

佛尚行銷
行銷專員　索爾．史崔克蘭

- in regards to . . . 關於
  promising (adj.) 有前途的
  start-up (n.) 新創公司　dedicated (adj.) 專用的
  public relations (n.) 公共關係
  insight (n.) 深刻的理解

**倫戴夥伴**

公關服務

無論您的公司是剛起步或已是著名企業，倫戴夥伴都準備好提供您智慧又先進的服務。我們會花時間了解您的品牌、挑戰及目標，以便為您打造一套獨特、有效的公關策略。

以下是另外一些選擇倫戴夥伴的理由：

- 我們的各式服務包括從文案到活動支援的一切。
- 我們採用先進的數位工具，給您關於您的品牌如何被看待的寶貴資料。
- **187 我們與數個領域有特殊連結，包括不動產、科技和金融。**

**188 請上 www.luneday.com，看看來自許多滿意客戶的推薦。**

- established (adj.) 有名的
  cutting-edge (adj.) 最新的
  a wide range of 各式各樣的
  advanced (adj.) 先進的　perceive (v.) 看待
  testimonial (n.) 推薦；證言

寄件者：辛蒂．帕迪拉
　　　　<c.padilla@luneday.com>
收件者：維克多．鮑斯威爾
　　　　<v.boswell@dixon-edutech.com>
主旨：後續會議
**189 日期：8 月 2 日**

親愛的鮑斯威爾先生：

**189 很高興昨天在您辦公室與您談話**。如我當時所說，**190 我現在會根據所獲得關於您的處境及目標的資料，召集一群合適的專員負責您這位客戶**。接著，我們會在兩到三個星期內安排另一次會議，簡報我們建議的策略，讓您批准。若有需要，我們會照您的建議，和您在佛尚行銷的客戶經理互相配合。

如果您對這個流程有任何問題，請以電話或電子郵件與我聯絡。再次感謝您為您的公關需求選擇倫戴夥伴。

倫戴夥伴
客戶代表　辛蒂．帕迪拉　謹啟

- follow-up (n.) 後續（行動）　assemble (v.) 召集
  appropriate (adj.) 適當的　specialist (n.) 專員
  account (n.) 客戶　approval (n.) 認可；同意
  coordinate (v.) 互相配合　process (n.) 過程

**186. 主旨或目的**

第一封電子郵件的目的為何？

**(A) 要求協助客戶的詢問**
(B) 介紹員工訓練資源
(C) 報告和一位承包商之間的難題
(D) 表達對努力嘗試範圍的擔憂

- contractor (n.) 承包商　endeavor (n.) 努力

**187. 整合題** 難

為什麼吉布森女士最可能推薦倫戴夥伴給史崔克蘭先生？

(A) 價格範圍
(B) 科技工具
**(C) 和另一個產業的連結**
(D) 現場活動服務

**換句話說**

ties to the tech industry / special connections in several fields（和科技業有關係／與數個領域有特殊連結）→ (C) connections in another industry（和另一個產業的連結）

**188. 相關細節**

根據廣告，在倫戴夥伴的網站上可看到什麼？

(A) 預訂預約會面的表格
(B) 它的領域中目前趨勢的資料
**(C) 關於工作的正面回饋意見**
(D) 最高行政主管的簡介

- executive (n.) 行政主管

**換句話說**

at www.luneday.com（上 www.luneday.com）
→ on Luneday Partners' Web site（在倫戴夥伴的網站上）
testimonials from our many satisfied clients（我們許多滿意客戶的推薦）
→ (C) Positive feedback about its work（關於工作的正面回饋意見）

**189. 整合題**

帕迪拉女士 8 月 1 日和誰見面？

(A) 迪克森教育科技的一位業務代表
**(B) 迪克森教育科技的通訊經理**
(C) 佛尚行銷的資訊科技主管
(D) 佛尚行銷的一位行銷專員

**190. 確認事實與否**

帕迪拉女士表示她接下來會做什麼？

(A) 安排一場簡報會議
(B) 更新一項策略提案
(C) 確定一項計畫預算
**(D) 組織一個客戶團隊**

**換句話說**

assemble a crew of appropriate specialists（召集一群合適的專員）
→ (D) Form an account team（組織一個客戶團隊）

## 191–195 文章、手冊內頁與電子郵件

### 藝術在瑞斯戴爾

文／謝恩．威勒

瑞斯戴爾　訊（9 月 10 日）——兒童暑期課程結束後才幾個星期，瑞斯戴爾社區中心已開始規劃另一場令人興奮的活動。[194] **第 32 屆瑞斯戴爾社區年度藝術展，將於 10 月 22 日至 28 日當週在社區的禮堂舉行。**

這個活動從 32 年前開始，當時一位本地水彩畫家格蘭特．林賽邀請朋友和他一起在一場小型展覽上展出他們的畫作。在那之後，這變成一個所有瑞斯戴爾的專業與業餘視覺藝術家展現才藝的機會。

目前，[194] **藝術展的特色是有一場比賽，由**社區中心主任**蒂娜．喬丹所帶領的委員會擔任評審**，其中包括默克大學的藝術史學家艾德納．卡利夫。此外，展覽上的大部分藝術品都可供販售。[192] **每筆交易收入的 25% 歸入社區中心建築與土地的維護基金。**

[191] **社區中心休閒部副主任兼展覽籌備人**景惠蘭**鼓勵各種年齡、背景和藝術訓練的市民考慮參展**。有興趣者應瀏覽 www.rellsdaleart.com 查看說明。

- auditorium (n.) 禮堂　committee (n.) 委員會
  proceeds (n.) 收入
  upkeep (n.)（房屋、設備等的）維修；保養
  discipline (n.) 訓練

### 第 32 屆瑞斯戴爾社區年度藝術展

歡迎光臨瑞斯戴爾社區藝術展！
瑞斯戴爾社區中心很高興你加入我們
慶祝本社區的藝術才能。

**開幕夜歡迎會時間表**

下午五點——開門

下午六點——供應茶點，由瑞斯戴爾超市贊助

下午七點——[194] **評審委員會主席致歡迎辭並宣布比賽結果**

下午九點——關門

**其他有用資訊：**

✧ [193/195] **欲尋找某個藝術作品，請見第 3 及第 4 頁的完整參賽作品名單，以藝術家的姓名字母順序排列。**

✧ 欲詢問購買某件作品，請立刻找我們的工作人員談。記得，先搶先贏！

[195] **第一頁**

**寄件人：**山繆．麥修

**收件人：**尤拉利亞．普羅塞

**主旨：**詢問

**日期：**11 月 4 日

親愛的普羅塞女士：

哈囉，[195] **我朋友安．華森買了妳在瑞斯戴爾社區藝術展展出的木雕**。我覺得非常漂亮，想要買一件類似的作品放在我辦公室。因此，我從安購買的作品所附的名片上獲得妳的電子郵件信箱。可以請妳回信給我，告訴我妳是否有販售其他作品嗎？謝謝妳。

山繆．麥修　謹啟

- sculpture (n.) 雕刻品；雕塑品
  gorgeous (adj.) 極其漂亮的

**191. 主旨或目的**

這篇文章的目的之一為何？

(A) 敘述一場募款活動的成功
(B) 宣傳本地藝術家的成就
**(C) 邀請人們參加社區活動**
(D) 宣布社區中心的新課程

- publicize (v.) 宣傳　accomplishment (n.) 成就
  offering (n.) 課程

**換句話說**

urges citizens of all ages, backgrounds, and artistic disciplines to consider exhibiting（鼓勵各種年齡、背景和藝術訓練的市民考慮參展）
→ invite people to participate in a community event（邀請人們參加社區活動）

**192. 相關細節**

如何使用某些收到的資金？

**(A) 維護一個設施**
(B) 開設給年輕人的課程
(C) 出版歷史書籍
(D) 獎勵比賽的得主

**換句話說**

Twenty-five percent of the proceeds of each sale（每筆交易收入的 25%）
→ some collected funds（某些收到的資金）
funding the upkeep of the center's buildings and grounds（社區中心建築與土地的維護基金）
→ (A) To maintain a facility（維護一個設施）

**193. 相關細節**

根據手冊內頁，藝術品名單如何排列？

(A) 依藝術的種類
(B) 依藝術品的名稱
(C) 依藝術品的位置
**(D) 依創作者的名字**

**換句話說**

the full list of entries ordered（完整參賽作品名單排列）
→ a list of artwork organized（藝術作品名單排列）
alphabetically by artist（以藝術家的姓名字母順序排列）
→ (D) By the name of the creator（依創作者的名字）

**194. 整合題** 難

誰在 10 月 22 日公開講話？

(A) 林賽先生　(C) 卡利夫先生
**(B) 喬丹女士**　(D) 景女士

**195. 整合題** 難

關於普羅塞女士，下列何者最可能為真？

**(A) 她在資料手冊的另一頁裡被提及。**
(B) 她提供聚會的茶點。
(C) 她收到一封來自華森女士的電子郵件。
(D) 她是一位住在瑞斯戴爾的業餘視覺藝術家。

## 196–200 徵才廣告、會議紀錄與文章

### 夏季法律實習生

在吉爾維地區商事法領域越來越常出現的胡安聯合法律事務所，現在提供一個從 6 月 1 日到 7 月 31 日的法律實習工作。實習生將從事法律研究與分析、草擬許多不同的法律文件、參加客戶會議和完成特殊專案，好處是一切都有經驗豐富律師的指導與意見。

**必要條件**

- 現為法學院學生，至少在法學院讀完一年
- 能一星期在事務所位於華特福朗特區的辦公室工作 30 小時

**優先資格**

- 熟悉地方、州和聯邦商事法
- 精通 [197] **法律搜尋平台，例如羅倫托**

[196] **欲應徵者，請在 3 月 31 日前將下列文件以電子郵件**寄到 marlon.terry@huanelegal.com：[196] **一頁的自我推薦信、你的履歷表、你的法學院成績單和一份 3 到 5 頁的寫作範本。**

- presence (n.) 出現　commercial (adj.) 商業的
  draft (v.) 草擬　seasoned (adj.) 經驗豐富的
  attorney (n.) 律師　familiarity (n.) 熟悉
  proficiency (n.) 精通　transcript (n.) 成績單

| 實習證明文件——雙週會議紀錄 | |
|---|---|
| 日期：7 月 8 日星期三<br>實習生：蕾妮．華特斯<br>指導者：馬龍．泰瑞 | |
| 對之前專案／經驗的反思 | • 分析線上零售稅法：馬龍給了改進「摘要」部分的一般性意見和建議<br>• 和索馮鞋業開會：回應蕾妮的問題，馬龍討論處理客戶意外要求的選項 |
| 進行中專案的最新狀況 | • 關於保密協議歷史的部落格文章：[197] **蕾妮報告使用羅倫托有困難**；馬龍安排 7 月 10 日下午一點的訓練課程<br>• 草擬馬基塔咖啡館的工作合約：蕾妮一直無法安排和吉妮．威爾克森的必要會議；馬龍會就此事聯絡吉妮 |
| 新工作 | • [199] **草擬布雷爾—洛格有限責任公司的經營協議：暫訂 7 月 15 日完成**；蕾妮應該參考內部網路的「經營協議」檔案中的資源 |

- retailer (n.) 零售商　general (adj.) 一般的
  improve (v.) 改進　disclosure (n.) 公開
  employment contract (n.) 工作合約
  operating agreement (n.) 經營協議
  LLC (Limited Liability Company) (n.) 有限責任公司
  tentatively (adv.) 暫時地　resource (n.) 資源
  internal (adj.) 內部的

http://www.huanelegal.com/blog

### 向胡安聯合的第一位實習生道別

文／知念亮　　[199] **7 月 28 日星期二發布**

蕾妮．華特斯在我們事務所的實習將在本週結束。華特斯女士過去兩個月來，[198] **在馬龍．泰瑞律師指導下**，做了許多不同的工作。你們可能見過華特斯女士和泰瑞先生一起參加會議，或讀過她關於保密協議歷史的部落格文章。

當 [199] **她昨天完成一份經營協議的草約時**，華特斯女士告訴我，她在這裡得到的實際經驗非常有用。她也說她尤其感謝泰瑞先生的細心指導。

關於他的角色，泰瑞先生表示他非常喜歡指導華特斯女士，因為他「看到她即使在這麼短的時間內也成長了那麼多」。[200] **他說希望明年夏天能再次舉辦實習生計畫，讓甚至更多學生參加。**

邀請事務所的所有同仁參加星期五下午四點於 A 會議室為華特斯女士舉辦的歡送派對。

- supervision (n.) 監督　practical (adj.) 實際的

**196. 確認事實與否**

徵才廣告中沒有要求應徵者繳交什麼？

(A) 在學表現的紀錄
**(B) 專業推薦信**
(C) 工作經歷列表
(D) 寫作技巧的證明

換句話說

law school transcript（法學院成績單）
→ (A) A record of school performance（在學表現的紀錄）
résumé（履歷表）→ (C) A list of career experiences（工作經歷列表）
a writing sample（寫作範本）
→ (D) Evidence of writing skills（寫作技巧的證明）

**197. 整合題**

會議紀錄中指出華特斯女士有什麼困難？

(A) 安排和一位行政主管的會議
(B) 了解某些紙本的回饋意見
(C) 通勤到某個鄰近地區
**(D) 使用某個電子搜尋工具**

換句話說

reported difficulty（報告有困難）
→ had trouble（有困難）
research platform（搜尋平台）
→ (D) electronic research tool（電子搜尋工具）

**198. 同義詞考題**

在文章中，第一段第二行的「under」，意思最接近下列何者？

(A) 具有作為她的頭銜　**(C) 服從**
(B) 被……隱藏　(D) 少於

**199. 整合題** 

可由文中得知關於華特斯女士的什麼事？

(A) 她上傳一份文件到網路上的一個檔案夾。
(B) 她接受泰瑞先生關於和一位客戶往來的建議。
**(C) 她的一個專案的截止時間延後了。**
(D) 未進行提供給她的一個特別訓練課程。

- postpone (v.) 延後

**200. 相關細節** 

根據文章，泰瑞先生想如何改變實習生計畫？

**(A) 增加職位數量**
(B) 延長期間
(C) 有更多員工參與
(D) 給參加者更多責任

- extend (v.) 延長　duration (n.) 持續期間

換句話說

with even more student participants（讓甚至更多學生參加）→ (A) increasing the number of positions（增加職位數量）

# ACTUAL TEST 10

## PART 5 P. 262–264

**101. 名詞詞彙題** 難

外燴人員已接獲指示，只能在應要求的情況下，送上額外分量的甜點。

(A) 賓客　(C) 食譜
(B) 菜單　**(D) 分量**

- caterer (n.) 外燴人員　upon request 應要求

**102. 人稱代名詞考題——「所有格＋ own」**

海斯先生多年來一直是用報稅軟體，來準備他自己的所得稅報告。

(A) 他　**(C) 他自己的**
(B) 他　(D) 他自己

- income tax (n.) 所得稅

**103. 介系詞詞彙題**

所有欲參賽的作品，一定要在 2 月 11 日當天之前簽名提交出去。

(A) 在……以內　**(C) 在……之前**
(B) 直到……　(D) 從……起

- entry (n.) 參賽作品　submit (v.) 提交

**104. 副詞子句連接詞詞彙題**

為了能夠讓更多畢業生應徵柯勒普農業公司的專員職位，該公司同意為大學農業系的班級舉辦實地參訪。

(A) 如果　**(C) 為了能夠**
(B) 即使　(D) 儘快

- agricultural (adj.) 農業的

**105. 動詞詞類變化題——過去分詞**

連鎖大賣場處理宅配服務相關環境問題的方法之一，就是使用可重複利用的包裝。

**(A) 相關的**　(C) 把……聯繫在一起
(B) 生意夥伴　(D) 協會

- address (v.) 處理

**106. 副詞詞彙題**

隔壁大樓的施工噪音，大聲到我們幾乎無法聽見同事在說什麼。

(A) 仍然　(C) 最後
**(B) 幾乎無法**　(D) 從來

**107. 名詞詞彙題——動詞的主詞** 難

聽眾對該樂團新專輯所產生的熱烈迴響，令樂評大吃一驚。

(A) 收據　(C) 接收者
(B) 已接收　**(D) 迴響**

- recipient (n.) 接收者
  reception (n.) 迴響；反應

**108. 不定代名詞考題** 

來面試接待人員職位的幾位應徵者中，沒有任何人獲得聘雇委員會的青睞。

**(A) 沒有**　(C) 那些
(B) 沒有人　(D) 兩者

- candidate (n.) 應徵者
  receptionist (n.) 接待人員
  hiring committee (n.) 聘雇委員會

**109. 動詞詞彙題** 

計畫如有任何更新，專案領導人需負責通知組員。

(A) 協調　(C) 招聘
**(B) 通知**　(D) 相信

- coordinate (v.) 協調　recruit (v.) 招聘
  credit (v.) 相信

**110. 形容詞詞彙題**

亞洛銀行以吸引人的利率，向具有抱負的小型企業老闆提供貸款。

(A) 相較的　(C) 史無前例的
**(B) 有抱負的**　(D) 一如往常的

- interest rate (n.) 利率
  unprecedented (adj.) 史無前例的
  customary (adj.) 一如往常的

**111. 動詞詞類變化題——語態——時態**

冷氣機組一旦裝設好，每層樓均應指派一位員工來監督冷氣的使用狀況。

(A) 曾被裝設　(C) 裝設
(B) 已裝設　**(D) 被裝設**

- assign (v.) 指派　install (v.) 裝設

### 112. 副詞詞彙題 難

實驗室可能被有害的化學物質汙染，從那時起就開始消毒。

**(A) 從此**　(C) 尚未
(B) 因此　(D) 足夠

- laboratory (n.) 實驗室　contaminate (v.) 汙染
  hazardous (adj.) 有害的
  chemical substance (n.) 化學物質
  sterilize (v.) 消毒

---

### 113. 副詞詞彙題——修飾動名詞

此研究小組的主持人，因為能夠巧妙掌控艱深主題的探討走向而獲得好評。

(A) 技能　(C) 技巧優越的
(B) 熟練的　**(D) 巧妙地**

- moderator (n.) 主持人
  maneuver (v.) 掌控走向

---

### 114. 介系詞詞彙題 

畢戈爾通訊公司的業務代表，每賣出一組傳輸線就能獲得 100 元的固定佣金。

(A) 關於　(C) 超過
**(B) ……的**　(D) 朝……方向

- representative (n.) 代表　flat (adj.) 固定的
  commission (n.) 佣金

---

### 115. 名詞詞彙題——動詞的主詞

只有在出差回來後，公司才會處理差旅補助，而且核准與否需取決於主管。

(A) 補助中　**(C) 補助**
(B) 補助　(D) 已補助

- contingent on 取決於……
  managerial (adj.) 主管的　approval (n.) 核准
  reimburse (v.) 補助　reimbursement (n.) 補助

---

### 116. 介系詞詞彙題

有鑑於我們和佳斯通科技公司長久以來的關係，因此我們新應用程式軟體的開發過程中，該公司將扮演重要角色亦為意料之事。

**(A) 有鑑於**　(C) 超出……
(B) 儘管　(D) 代替

- longstanding (adj.) 長久以來的
  it is no surprise that . . . ……為意料之事
  notwithstanding (prep.) 儘管　in place of 代替

---

### 117. 副詞子句連接詞詞彙題

比諾飯店鼓勵老主顧，如需服務可以隨時聯繫櫃台。

(A) 那個　**(C) 隨時**
(B) 無論　(D) 好像

- patron (n.) 老主顧

---

### 118. 形容詞詞彙題——主詞補語 

臨床試驗顯示，此藥品可治療經證實對其他藥物產生抗藥性的症狀。

**(A) 有抵抗性的**　(C) 抵抗地
(B) 抵抗中　(D) 可抵抗的

- clinical trial (n.) 臨床試驗　symptom (n.) 症狀
  medication (n.) 藥物

---

### 119. 動詞詞彙題 

張女士獨特的設計風格雖然在她在世時沒有造成熱潮，卻對後世建築師造成極大的影響。

(A) 投資　(C) 主宰
(B) 商議　**(D) 造成**

- considerable (adj.) 極大的　confer (v.) 商議
  dominate (v.) 在……中占首要地位

---

### 120. 動詞詞類變化題——分詞構句——語態 

一般而言，主動提供過多選項時，顧客反而會有選擇障礙。

(A) 主動提供　(C) 主動提供
**(B) 被提供**　(D) 主動提供

- in general 一般而言

---

### 121. 副詞子句連接詞詞彙題

僅能在未上漆的表面，先塗上索根品牌的底漆之後，才能使用索根乳膠漆。

(A) 幾乎　(C) 超過
**(B) 之後**　(D) 以免

- primer (n.) 底漆　bare (adj.) 赤裸的

---

### 122. 名詞詞彙題

「專業藥妝超市」在小巧卻規劃良好的空間裡，陳列一系列令人滿意的健康產品。

**(A) 系列**　(C) 期望
(B) 替代　(D) 成果

- wellness (n.) 健康　substitute (n.) 替代
  outcome (n.) 成果

**123. 形容詞詞彙題**

富蘭克林書店購買此軟體的主要原因，在於軟體維護資料安全的效率。

**(A) 主要的** (C) 多產的
(B) 資訊豐富的 (D) 嚴格篩選的

- **informative (adj.)** 資訊豐富的
  **productive (adj.)** 多產的
  **selective (adj.)** 嚴格篩選的

---

**124. 副詞詞彙題**

據說中野小姐是柴田工程公司最努力工作的主管。

(A) 聲望 (C) 把……認為
(B) 有聲望的 **(D) 據說**

- **executive (n.)** 主管 **reputation (n.)** 聲望
  **reputable (adj.)** 聲譽良好的
  **reputedly (adv.)** 據說

---

**125. 形容詞詞彙題**

戶外夏季展「石雕藝術」受歡迎的程度，讓公園管理部門開始研究是否能改為常設展。

(A) 可行的 **(C) 永久的**
(B) 強制的 (D) 豐富的

- **feasible (adj.)** 可行的 **mandatory (adj.)** 強制的
  **abundant (adj.)** 豐富的

---

**126. 與過去事實相反的假設語氣——語態**

如果當初我們最新款的 V2 咖啡機原型有獲得產品測試人員的高分評鑑，科技商城早就會決定和我們簽訂長期合約。

(A) 已決定 **(C) 早就會決定**
(B) 可決定 (D) 早就會被決定

- **prototype (n.)** 原型 **long-term (adj.)** 長期的

---

**127. 介系詞詞彙題**

多虧有近期引進的自助報到機，讓天戟航空公司服務櫃台的等候時間縮減一半。

(A) 無論在哪裡 (C) 與此同時
(B) 與……一起 **(D) 多虧**

- **self-check-in kiosk (n.)** 自助報到機
  **introduce (v.)** 引進

**128. 副詞詞彙題** 

有些與會者對於主辦單位將唯二的統計學工作坊，安排在同一個時間感到不滿。

(A) 相同地 (C) 刻意地
**(B) 同時地** (D) 不利地

- **statistics (n.)** 統計學 **identically (adj.)** 相同地
  **intentionally (adv.)** 刻意地
  **adversely (adv.)** 不利地

---

**129. 連接詞考題——倒裝**

被用在部落格的攝影師作品，不僅沒有標出名字，攝影師也沒有因為貢獻照片而獲得報酬。

**(A) 也沒有** (C) 除此之外
(B) 相當 (D) 雖然

- **compensation (n.)** 報酬

---

**130. 動詞詞彙題** 

要指派給臨時會計員的下一個任務，就是徹底改進資助研究專案的制度。

(A) 核准 (C) 縮減
**(B) 徹底改進** (D) 實驗

- **assign (v.)** 指派 **interim (adj.)** 臨時的
  **accountant (n.)** 會計師 **fund (v.)** 資助
  **grant (v.)** 核准 **deduct (v.)** 縮減
  **experiment (v.)** 實驗

## PART 6 P. 265–268

**131–134 電子郵件**

寄件者：泰瑞莎・葉茲
收件人：厄瑪・希姆斯
主旨：格瑞爾玩具專案團隊
日期：9 月 2 日

嗨，厄瑪：

因應妳的要求，我有想過我退休時，該由哪位資深工程師來代替我擔任格瑞爾玩具團隊的主管。雖然凱倫能在必要時出任此位子，但我推薦的人選是崔佛，凱倫的工程領悟力也許 [131] **十分卓越**，但是她不一定具有清楚溝通的能力，而溝通是非常重要的管理能力。相反地，崔佛傑出的人際技巧則能讓他出色的專業工程知識更加分，以我之見，他 [133] **會是**很棒的專案團隊領導人。

如果妳需要更多資訊來做決定，或想親自討論我的建議，請跟我說。[134] **我這週都會在辦公室，把工作收尾。**

泰瑞莎

- grasp (n.) 領悟力　decent (adj.) 出色的
  outstanding (adj.) 傑出的
  interpersonal (adj.) 人際的　in person 親自

**131. 形容詞詞彙題**

| | |
|---|---|
| **(A) 卓越** | (C) 最大的 |
| (B) 緊急 | (D) 熱切的 |

**132. 動詞詞彙題** 難

| | |
|---|---|
| (A) 優先處理 | (C) 評估 |
| **(B) 增強** | (D) 指定 |

- prioritize (v.) 優先處理　amplify (v.) 增強
  designate (v.) 指定

**133. 動詞詞類變化題——時態**

| | |
|---|---|
| (A) 是 | (C) 已經被…… |
| **(B) 會是** | (D) 早就被…… |

**134. 句子插入題** 

(A) 再次謝謝妳給我這個令人雀躍的機會。
(B) 我沒有特別偏好誰，只要選妳喜歡的人就好。
**(C) 我這週都會在辦公室，把工作收尾。**
(D) 只需要再涵蓋幾個小重點。

- wrap up 收尾

**135–138 新聞稿**

**美樂品交響樂團**
**媒體公關部**

美樂品交響樂團自五月起，將每個月於《分享音樂》節目現場直播特別音樂會。

此節目得以成立的原因，在於獲得專為提升音樂普及度的「歐卡佛基金會」所提供的補助金，[135] **該協會的其他活動，包括為身障兒童舉辦的音樂營**，「分享音樂」節目雖然主要為行動不便的人所設計，將來亦會開放所有大眾會員參與。

音樂會開始 [136] **的時候**，大家可透過交響樂團的網站 www.melapinsymphony.com 的一個頁面免費觀賞。[137] **不過**，訪客可能需要建立並登入會員帳號，才能連至該頁面。

交響樂團成員與重要職員對於和歐卡佛基金會合作一事感到開心，總監佐野大樹表示：「實在是深感 [138] **榮幸**，能擁有這個機會與更多人分享我們的音樂，我們非常感恩。」

- livestream (v.) 直播　grant (n.) 補助金
  access (n.) 接觸　mobility (n.) 活動能力
  collaborate (v.) 合作　grateful (adj.) 感恩的

**135. 句子插入題** 

**(A) 該協會的其他活動，包括為身障兒童舉辦的音樂營。**
(B) 資助金甚至讓音樂會能夠在網路上串流播放。
(C) 美樂品交響樂音樂廳，之後也增設了輪椅空間。
(D) 在此之前，表演期間無法允許任何觀眾進入後台。

- disability (n.) 身障　patron (n.) 觀眾

**136. 副詞子句連接詞詞彙題**

| | |
|---|---|
| (A) 與此同時 | **(C) ……的時候** |
| (B) 除非 | (D) 然後 |

**137. 連接副詞** 

| | |
|---|---|
| (A) 也就是說 | (C) 同樣 |
| **(B) 不過** | (D) 取而代之的是…… |

- namely (adv.) 也就是說

**138. 名詞詞彙題** 

| | |
|---|---|
| (A) 已致敬 | **(C) 榮幸** |
| (B) 為了致敬 | (D) 致敬 |

**139–142 信件**

5 月 11 日

夏伊娜・辛
BN4 7DA 英國貝寧漢
包菲爾德街 83 號

親愛的辛小姐：

我最近收到您的來信，您提到住家所在街道的人行道狀態不佳，還有您 [139] **因為**鋪路板不平整而深受爆胎之苦的情況。您在信中指出，該社區的馬路和人行道急需維修已經好一陣子，[140] **請您安心，我會竭力改正此情況。**

從 5 月 18 日起，工程小組會拆除與重新鋪設包菲爾德街與該區其他幾條街的所有鋪路板，他們也會修繕許多機車騎士在三月社區會議所抱怨的路面坑洞。希望這對您與其他 [141] **居住**在該區的選民來說，會是一件好消息。

對於您車子的遭遇，我深感抱歉。我有信心，安排好的修路工程將可避免未來發生任何類似的 [142] **意外**。

市議員　麥可・杜克　謹啟

- pavement (n.)〔英〕人行道　flat tyre (n.) 爆胎
  paving slab (n.) 鋪路板　desperate (adj.) 迫切的
  pothole (n.) 坑洞　motorist (n.) 機車騎士
  constituent (n.) 選民

**139. 介系詞詞彙題** 難

(A) 藉由　(C) 在……期間
(B) 以下　**(D) 因為**

---

**140. 句子插入題** 

(A) 我引以為傲地宣布，工程終於完成。
(B) 不幸的是，街道維修不在我們今年的預算內。
**(C) 請您安心，我會竭力改正此情況。**
(D) 我們會考慮您的提議並試圖解決問題。

- rectify (v.) 改正

---

**141. 現在分詞**

(A) 居住　(C) 居民
**(B) 居住**　(D) 居住的

- reside (v.) 居住

---

**142. 名詞詞彙題**

(A) 不準確性　(C) 撤銷
(B) 誤會　**(D) 意外**

- cancelation (n.) 撤銷

---

**143–146 廣告**

鑽石改衣坊

555-0184 羅倫斯市第三街 308 號
www.diamondsewing.com

鑽石改衣坊十多年來，一直協助羅倫斯市的居民，在穿上其服飾後更顯 [143] **絕美亮眼**。無論是身形尺寸改變或新衣不太合身，我們的縫紉專家總是能夠隨時滿足您的改衣需求。[144] **我們提供改短長褲、幫襯衫打褶收窄等許多改衣服務。**

我們 [145] **特別**專攻婚紗、燕尾服與其他正式服飾，已有上百名新娘新郎穿著鑽石改衣坊修改過的禮服走上紅毯。

您的服飾有脫線、磨損或破裂的問題嗎？我們亦提供專業的 [146] **修補**服務！在您丟掉心愛的牛仔褲或復古夾克前，請先來找我們進行免費諮詢。我們的營業時間是週一至週五早上 9 點至下午 5 點，週六則是早上 9 點至中午 12 點。

- sewing (n.) 縫紉　purchase (n.) 購買物
  alteration (n.) 修改　specialize in 專攻……
  formalwear (n.) 正式服飾
  frayed (adj.) 脫線的　worn (adj.) 磨損的
  ripped (adj.) 破裂的　consultation (n.) 諮詢

**143. 形容詞詞彙題——主詞補語——現在分詞**

(A) 震驚　**(C) 絕美亮眼的**
(B) 被震驚的　(D) 驚人地

---

**144. 句子插入題**

(A) 完美合身的套裝是現今專業從商人員不可或缺的服飾。
(B) 甚至可完全透過我們的網站線上下單。
(C) 只要從我們的設計版型系列選擇即可。
**(D) 我們提供改短長褲、幫襯衫打褶收窄等許多改衣服務。**

- entirely (adv.) 完全地　template (n.) 版型
  dart (n.) 打褶收窄

---

**145. 副詞詞彙題**

(A) 理想上　(C) 極其
(B) 最近　**(D) 特別是**

- exceedingly (adv.) 極其，非常

---

**146. 名詞詞彙題** 

**(A) 修補**　(C) 洗衣服務
(B) 製造　(D) 做造型

- mend (v.) 修補　manufacture (v.) 製造
  launder (v.) 洗衣　style (v.) 做造型

**PART 7** P. 269–291

## 147–148 公告

**公告**

我們認為 [147] **健身腳踏車上方的監視器，是被**使用健身腳踏車又同時手拿啞鈴練舉的人**砸壞的**。我們無法確定的原因在於，監視器拍到的畫面，只看得出來此人是尾隨會員進來我們中心的非會員。[148] **請大家千萬別讓其他人跟著進入大樓**，如果有人宣稱自己的會員卡不見了或忘了帶而要求您這麼做，請告知對方在外等候，您會通知櫃台。謝謝大家。

杭斯勒健身中心管理團隊

- stationary bicycle (n.) 健身腳踏車
  shatter (v.) 砸壞　hand weight (n.) 啞鈴
  security camera (n.) 監視器

### 147. 推論或暗示

此公告最有可能出現在什麼地方？

**(A) 某種受損的機器上**
(B) 某大樓門口的外面
(C) 某些重訓器材旁邊
(D) 某接待區後方

**換句話說**
shattered（砸壞）→ (A) damaged（受損的）
stationary bicycle（健身腳踏車）
→ (A) machinery（機器）

### 148. 相關細節

此公告要求讀者做什麼事？

(A) 避免擋住監視器
(B) 一次使用一種器材
(C) 遺失會員卡時須立即通報
**(D) 避免讓他人進入設施**

- refrain from 避免

**換句話說**
do not allow other people to enter the building
（大家千萬別讓其他人進入大樓）
→ (D) Refrain from letting others into a facility
（避免讓他人進入設施）

## 149–150 文字訊息串

艾力克斯・懷特〔下午 3:09〕
布列提絲拉娃，[149] **很抱歉在妳休假的時候打擾妳**，但我想迅速問個問題，我們幾乎快用完手套了，妳上週不是有訂一些嗎？

布列提絲拉娃・柯維克〔下午 3:11〕
喔對，昨天到貨了，但我還沒來得及開箱，就在我桌上的箱子裡。

艾力克斯・懷特〔下午 3:13〕
好，我看到了，感謝妳！我們今天多了幾位未預約而直接過來看診的患者，所以手套消耗速度比預計的快。

布列提絲拉娃・柯維克〔下午 3:14〕
了解。不過我倒是需要記錄你取用了多少，還有是給誰使用。

艾力克斯・懷特〔下午 3:16〕
喔，[150] **我可以星期一再告訴妳嗎？**我已經回到接待櫃台這邊了。

布列提絲拉娃・柯維克〔下午 3:17〕
不好意思，[150] **那有點太晚了。**你可以寫在便利貼上，然後貼在我的門上嗎？ [150] **我覺得不要冒著我們兩個都忘記的風險比較好。**

艾力克斯・懷特〔下午 3:18〕
好，沒問題。布列提絲拉娃，再次感謝妳。

- unpack (v.) 開箱
  walk-in (n.) 未預約而直接過來的人
  patient (n.) 患者　sticky note (n.) 便利貼

### 149. 推論或暗示

關於柯維克女士的敘述，何者為真？

(A) 她用完了某些用品。
(B) 她沒有個人辦公室。
(C) 她出去辦事情。
**(D) 她目前沒在上班。**

- use up 用完　go on an errand 辦事情

**換句話說**
on your day off（在妳休假的時候）
→ (D) not currently on duty（目前沒在上班）

**150. 掌握意圖**

下午 3:17，柯維克女士回覆「那有點太晚了」是什麼意思？

(A) 她在爭論有人算錯數字。
(B) 她在批評某文件遭到修改的事。
(C) 她拒絕尋找某地點。
**(D) 她反對對方延後回覆的提議。**

- figure (n.) 數字　miscalculate (v.) 誤算
  modification (n.) 修改　oppose (v.) 反對

**151–153 同意書**

提卡德股份有限公司

**市場研究參與同意書**

感謝您同意參加本次 18 歲至 34 歲男性的研究。[151] **我們會讓您觀賞兩種版本的刮鬍刀電視廣告**，並請您針對各版本提出看法，整個過程大約需要 30 分鐘。

請閱讀以下事項，並於旁邊的框格內寫下您的姓名首字母縮寫，表示您同意各項內容。

- 我同意研究期間，研究方可錄音我的回答，並 [152] **可在移除我身分資料的狀態下，由提卡德公司內部使用此錄音內容**。 ☐
- 我了解當我有意隨時停止參與本研究，只要告知研究人員即可。 ☐
- 研究結束後，[153] **我不會向任何人談及此研究內容，或是建立任何與此研究內容有關的實體或數位資料**。 ☐
- 我已經向研究人員詢問過我對此研究產生的任何疑問。 ☐

**參與者姓名：**________　**簽名：**________
**日期：**________

- consent (n.) 同意　participate in 參加
  facial razor (n.) 刮鬍刀　entire (adj.) 整個的
  approximately (adv.) 大約
  adjacent (adj.) 旁邊的
  identifying information (n.) 身分資料
  internally (adv.) 內部地
  physical (adj.) 實體的

**151. 相關細節**

參加者將為此研究做什麼事？

(A) 試用產品　(C) 說明自己的習慣
(B) 比較兩種設計　**(D) 觀賞短片**

**換句話說**
be shown two versions of a television advertisement（觀賞兩種版本的刮鬍刀電視廣告）→ (D) Watch some video clips（觀賞短片）

**152. 相關細節**

根據表格的內容，研究結束後會發生什麼事？

**(A) 資料會匿名化處理。**
(B) 會銷毀某些錄音內容。
(C) 會寄出後續追蹤的問卷。
(D) 研究人員會回答參加者的問題。

- anonymize (v.) 匿名化

**換句話說**
with my identifying information removed（在移除我身分資料的狀態下）
→ (A) The data will be anonymized.（資料會匿名化處理。）

**153. 相關細節**

參加者務必同意什麼事？

(A) 誠實說出自己的看法
**(B) 保密與研究有關的資訊**
(C) 揭露自己是否以前有參加任何研究
(D) 保留此表的副本一段時間

- confidential (adj.) 機密的　disclose (v.) 揭露
  retain (v.) 保留

**換句話說**
not speak about or create any physical or digital materials about the contents of this study（不會向任何人談及此研究內容，或是建立任何與此研究內容有關的實體或數位資料）
→ (B) Keep information about the study confidential（保密與研究有關的資訊）

**154–155 電子郵件**

**寄件人：**柯迪．麥內爾
**收件人：**莎曼珊．尼爾森
**主旨：**關於：網速慢
**日期：**3 月 29 日

嗨，莎曼珊：

很遺憾聽到妳說，[154] **妳使用公司上週提供的筆記型電腦上網，速度卻很慢**，我們認為 [154] **這個問題跟妳家的網路服務無關**，因為妳不是第一個回報公司筆電網速慢的人。我們深入了解後，發現問題出在我們使用的虛擬私人網路（VPN），VPN 能讓我們安全的從其他地方連線至公司網路，因此是很重要的軟體而無法移除，我們目前在尋找比較不會影響網速的其他 VPN，如果決定更換服務供應商，一定會通知妳。

不幸的是，我們目前只能向妳提出這樣的說明，[155] **妳看看要不要將此電子郵件轉寄給妳的主管**，讓他了解妳所說的工作效率疑慮。如果妳還有其他疑問，請再跟我說。

祝　好

資訊科技部　柯迪．麥內爾

- virtual (adj.) 虛擬的　provider (n.) 供應商
  supervisor (n.) 主管
  in reference to 與……有關的
  productivity (n.) 工作效率

**154. 推論或暗示** 難

關於尼爾森女士的說明，何者為真？

(A) 她沒有存取部分網絡的權限。
(B) 她要求替換某些設備。
(C) 她沒有閱讀使用說明書。
**(D) 她目前在遠端上班。**

- authorize (v.) 授權　remotely (adv.) 遠端地

**155. 相關細節**

麥內爾先生允許尼爾森女士做什麼事？

(A) 從筆記型電腦解除安裝某程式
**(B) 將他的訊息分享給另一人**
(C) 如果再出問題，可在家聯絡他
(D) 替換另一家核准使用的供應商

- uninstall (v.) 解除安裝　reoccur (v.) 再發生
  alternative (adj.) 替代的

**換句話說**

forward this e-mail to your supervisor（將此電子郵件轉寄給妳的主管）
→ (B) Share his message with another person（將他的訊息分享給另一人）

**156–157 公告**

暴雪曲棍球

**記者會**

暴雪經紀公司以欣喜若狂的心情，讓各位有機會見到在新東家帶領球隊獲勝的負責人。[156] **暴雪經紀公司老闆桃樂絲．伊肯達，將主持介紹球隊新總經紀人的記者會**。記者會內容包括伊肯達女士的演說、新總經紀人的演說、問答時段以及合影機會。

**地點：** 沙瓦德劇院會議室（一樓，靠近北入口）
[157] **空間有限，請攜帶記者證以便進場。**

**時間：** 6 月 8 日星期三，上午 11:00。
請於 10:45 前入場就座。

**聯絡人：** 暴雪媒體公關部經理雷克斯．威爾契
rex.welch@blizzard-hockey.com

- task (v.) 分派任務
  press credential (n.) 記者證　entry (n.) 入場

**156. 相關細節**

記者會上會宣布什麼？

(A) 曲棍球隊主場搬遷
**(B) 任命某運動主管**
(C) 與某專業運動員簽約
(D) 建造新打球空間的計畫

- relocation (n.) 搬遷　appointment (n.) 任命

**換句話說**

to introduce the team's new general manager（介紹球隊新總經紀人）
→ (B) The appointment of a sports executive（任命某運動主管）

**157. 推論或暗示** 難

文中提及記者會的哪些資訊？

**(A) 會優先讓記者進場。**
(B) 有機會參觀某設施。
(C) 威爾契先生會在伊肯達女士演說後發言。
(D) 會發送宣傳禮物。

- priority (n.) 優先順序

**換句話說**

to ensure entry（以便進場）
→ (A) Priority admission（優先進場）

### 158–160 信件

12 月 7 日

V54 1R9 卑詩省溫哥華
日落街 1520 號
迪森內特飯店

親愛的先生／女士：

[159] **我於 12 月 2 日至 4 日到訪溫哥華而下榻貴飯店**，我想和您分享住宿期間的難忘體驗。

[159] **我住宿的最後一天，正要開我租的車前往機場，卻發現電瓶沒電**，我雖然有聯絡租車公司，但 [160] **業務表示無法派人來協助處理兩小時**，這情況可能會讓我錯過班機。幸好，因為我是在飯店大廳講手機，[159] **貴飯店的櫃檯人員德瑞．史考特，聽到了我的談話內容，他主動用他自己的車和電瓶夾線，用借電的方式發動我租的車，我心懷感激的接受他的幫忙，而他親切又效率高的處理態度，讓我及時抵達機場。**

雖然我對貴飯店的許多面向均感到滿意，但這樣的體貼舉止，最讓我最印象深刻，[158] **史考特先生願意用自己有用的額外能力來協助有難的房客，真的值得獎勵**。我希望你們有制定這類的政策。

崔維斯．昆恩　謹啟

- memorable (adj.) 難忘的
  overhear (v.) 碰巧聽到　jump-start (v.) 借電發動
  cheerful (adj.) 和樂的　efficient (adj.) 有效率的
  establishment (n.) 企業
  deserve (v.) 應得　reward (v.) 獎勵
  supplementary (adj.) 額外的
  in place 制定

**158. 主旨或目的**

此信函的主要目的為何？

(A) 建議附加服務
(B) 客訴某項設施
**(C) 傳達對某員工的讚賞**
(D) 詢問政策的細節

- convey (v.) 傳達

**159. 推論或暗示** 難

史考特先生最有可能在 12 月 4 日做了什麼事？

**(A) 暫時離開他被指定的工作站點**
(B) 在私人區域充電行動裝置
(C) 請某位房客移開停好的汽車
(D) 在某機場網站搜尋某些資訊

**160. 句子插入題**

「這情況可能會讓我錯過班機。」最適合放在標示 [1]、[2]、[3]、[4] 哪個位置？

(A) [1]　　(C) [3]
**(B) [2]**　　(D) [4]

### 161–163 徵才貼文

**職稱：**送貨銷售員（兼職）　**公司名稱：**羅特諾股份有限公司

**工作地點：**加州斯托克頓區　**徵才張貼時間：**10 天前

**詳細說明：**羅特諾係屬家族自營的食品製造商，專為注重健康的消費者製作零食，[161] **我們的所有產品至少採用 80% 天然成分製成，我們致力為超過 1,100 名員工打造健康又能樂在其中的工作環境，羅特諾股份有限公司去年獲得「斯托克頓商業協會」（SBA）頒發的「身心友善職場獎」。**

送貨銷售員需負責將羅特諾產品配送到特定區域的大賣場，其他必要職務也包括盤點存貨，以及監督公司產品在店頭架上的存貨狀態，銷售員必須擁有深厚的溝通技能，因為必須定期與店長互動，提出最合適的羅特諾產品混搭方案。

錄取的應徵者需要駕駛 22 英尺貨車往返指定路線，[162] **值班時，員工亦需使用平板電腦輸入存貨資料**，指定工時為週四至週日下午 4 點到晚上 10 點（每週工作 24 小時）。

如需應徵此職位，請至 www.rotunnos.com/jobs 並遵循說明上傳履歷。[163] **應徵者必須先進行大約 20 分鐘的基本電腦能力測驗，並且達到特定分數方能符合面試資格。**

- route salesperson (n.) 送貨銷售員
  health-conscious (adj.) 注重健康的
  ingredient (n.) 成分　committed to 致力於
  essential (adj.) 必要的　conduct (v.) 進行
  inventory (n.) 庫存盤點　stock (v.) 存貨
  successful candidate (n.) 錄取的應徵者
  assigned (adj.) 指定的　instruction (n.) 說明
  quality for 符合……資格　proficiency (n.) 能力

**161. 確認事實與否** 難

文中並未提及羅特諾股份有限公司的什麼事？

(A) 產品多以天然成分製成。
(B) 獲得某商業團體的肯定。
**(C) 會定期張貼許多徵才資訊。**
(D) 員工超過 1,100 人。

- recognize (v.) 肯定

換句話說
at least 80%（至少 80%）
→ (A) mostly（大多）
was presented with a "Workplace Well-being" award from the Stockton Business Association（獲得「斯托克頓商業協會」〔SBA〕頒發的「身心友善職場獎」）
→ (B) has been recognized by a business group（獲得某商業團體的肯定）
more than 1,100 employees（超過 1,100 名員工）→ (D) over 1,100 people（超過 1,100 人）

---

**162. 確認事實與否**

徵才廣告中提及此職位需要負責什麼職務？

(A) 爭取新商業客戶
(B) 在商展設置展示物品
**(C) 將資料輸入攜帶型裝置**
(D) 向該職位人員的主管提供更新資訊

換句話說
to input inventory data（輸入存貨資料）
→ (C) Entering data（輸入資料）
a tablet computer（平板電腦）
→ (C) a portable device（攜帶型裝置）

---

**163. 相關細節**

應徵者必須做什麼事？

(A) 承諾會保護機密資料
(B) 提交專業執照的副本
(C) 在電話面試中表現良好
**(D) 展現技術能力**

換句話說
achieve a certain score in a basic computer proficiency test（進行基本電腦能力測驗並且達到特定分數）→ (D) Demonstrate technical skills（展現技術能力）

**164–167 廣告**

**哈里斯與權氏集團**

哈里斯與權氏集團以合理的價格提供高品質的英語及韓語服務。我們位於首爾市中心，已協助各種規模的國內、海外與國際公司，橋接語言溝通方面的斷層。

164 **我們的服務包括紙本及數位資料翻譯、謄錄影片檔和錄音檔的逐字稿**，以及實體會議和大型活動現場的口譯。164 **我們亦可出租能確保向至多 300 名與會者順暢傳輸口譯內容的音訊系統**。

自動化的筆譯和口譯軟體仍常出錯而造成嚴重的混淆情況，而職業筆譯師與口譯師的專業程度不一定可靠，即使是擁有翻譯產業相關學位的人也是一樣，這就是 165 **哈里斯與權氏集團為何僅僱用同時在英語和韓語環境下長大、流利度如母語的語言專業人士**。我們保證翻譯成品不僅零錯誤，還能敏銳掌握與傳達文化上的細微差異。

請至我們的網站 www.hkgroup.co.kr 了解更多翻譯委託流程，以及滿意的客戶所回饋的見證。若您想針對僱用哈里斯與權氏集團負責專案的部分進行討論，請使用「聯絡我們」此區的便利聯絡表格，167 **我們很樂意先提供可靠的服務報價**。此外，166 **如果您代表公益服務團體來詢價，即可洽詢我們為非營利組織所提供的特別費率**。

- domestic (adj.) 國內的　translation (n.) 筆譯
  transcription (n.) 逐字謄錄
  interpretation (n.) 口譯　transmission (n.) 傳輸
  expertise (n.) 專業　degree (n.) 學位
  guarantee (v.) 保證　capture (v.) 掌握
  sensitively (adv.) 敏銳地　testimonial (n.) 見證
  quote (n.) 報價　up front 提前
  nonprofit (n.) 非營利機構

**164. 確認事實與否**

以下何者未列入哈里斯與權氏集團的服務項目？

(A) 出借專業設備
(B) 轉換文字檔的語言
(C) 為錄音資料製作書面文檔
**(D) 對商業環境的文化差異提供建議**

- conversion (n.) 轉換

換句話說

rent out audio systems that can ensure the smooth transmission of interpretations（出租能確保順暢傳輸口譯內容的音訊系統）
→ (A) Lending of specialized equipment（出借專業設備）
translation of printed and digital materials（筆譯紙本及數位資料）→ (B) Conversion of the language of a text（轉換文字檔的語言）
transcription of . . . audio clips（謄錄……錄音檔的腳本逐字稿）→ (C) Making a written copy of audio materials（為錄音資料製作書面文檔）

**165. 確認事實與否**

文中提及哈里斯與權氏集團員工的特性為何？

(A) 豐富的工作經驗
**(B) 在完全雙語的環境下長大**
(C) 審慎進行某學科的學術研究
(D) 接受過某技術的廣泛訓練

- substantial (adj.) 充足的　upbringing (n.) 養育
  extensive (adj.) 廣泛的

換句話說

grew up using both English and Korean with native fluency（同時在英語和韓語環境下長大、流利度如母語）→ (B) A completely bilingual upbringing（在完全雙語的環境下長大）

**166. 推論或暗示**

文中可看出哈里斯與權氏集團的哪些資訊？

(A) 在不只一個國家設有分公司。
(B) 專門服務特定領域的公司。
**(C) 會對業務項目有益社會的客戶提供折扣。**
(D) 近期增加員工人數。

換句話說

our special rates for nonprofits（我們為非營利組織所提供的特別費率）
→ (C) a discount（折扣）

**167. 相關細節**

根據廣告內容，哈里斯與權氏集團能為新顧客提供什麼服務？

**(A) 事先預估價格**
(B) 研究對方產業的術語
(C) 提供主管層級的個人參考經驗
(D) 建立客製化的工作流程

- terminology (n.) 術語　executive (n.) 主管
  customized (adj.) 客製化的

換句話說

provide a reliable quote for the cost . . . up front（先提供可靠的……報價）
→ (A) Supply a price estimate in advance（事先預估價格）

**168–171 線上聊天室**

蓋伊．瓦勒斯〔上午 11:24〕
嗨，大家好。很抱歉打擾大家，我想說要到哪裡取得可以張貼在我們網站上的圖片，我需要在我們部落格上的最新貼文放些圖片。

傑瑞．葛倫特〔上午 11:25〕
抱歉，我不清楚。

桑妮亞．奈賈爾〔上午 11:26〕
我想馬克都用「照片農場」來下載免費圖庫的照片。[168] **他沒有給你那個網站的登入資料嗎？**

蓋伊．瓦勒斯〔上午 11:26〕
我看一下。

蓋伊．瓦勒斯〔上午 11:28〕
啊有，[168] **我看到了！**謝謝妳，桑妮亞。

彼得．陳〔上午 11:29〕
[169] **蓋伊，你對於暫時代理馬克的職務有什麼感覺？**

蓋伊．瓦勒斯〔上午 11:30〕
滿有難度的。常發生這種情況，例如他職務所需的資料不齊全或沒有清楚標示。

彼得．陳〔上午 11:31〕
我去年接管羅賓的職位時也遇到相同的問題，[170] **我們真的要更清楚記錄工作過程，畢竟這有列在公司手冊裡。**

蓋伊．瓦勒斯〔上午 11:32〕
喔，真的嗎？我都不知道。

彼得．陳〔上午 11:33〕
多數員工都不清楚這件事，我要去跟艾咪談一下，關於鼓勵大家撥點時間養成建立文檔的習慣。

傑瑞．葛倫特〔上午 11:34〕
這個點子很棒，也 [171] **請別猶豫問我們問題，蓋伊，這樣會比自己猜測該怎麼做和犯錯還好**。

蓋伊．瓦勒斯〔上午 11:35〕
謝謝你，[171] **我很感激**。

- fill in for 暫時替補某人
  available (adj.) 可用的　label (n.) 標示
  after all 畢竟　be aware of 清楚知道
  appreciate (v.) 感激

**168. 相關細節**

上午 11:28，瓦勒斯先生發現了什麼？

(A) 數位圖片的檔案
(B) 網路文章的草稿
**(C) 使用者名稱和密碼**
(D) 某部落格文章的留言

- draft (n.) 草稿

**換句話說**
the log-in information（登入資料）
→ (C) A user name and password（使用者名稱和密碼）

---

**169. 推論或暗示**

可從文中得知瓦勒斯先生的哪些資訊？

**(A) 他暫時處理同事的職務。**
(B) 他是新進員工。
(C) 他最近剛請假回來上班。
(D) 他之前不知道有公司內部網站。

- temporarily (adv.) 暫時　leave of absence 請假

**換句話說**
filling in for Mark（暫時代理馬克的職務）
→ (A) temporarily handling a colleague's duties（暫時處理同事的職務）

---

**170. 掌握意圖** 

上午 11:31，陳先生的訊息「畢竟這有列在公司手冊裡」是什麼意思？

(A) 他指示瓦勒斯先生再多查詢資料。
(B) 他在說明自己被禁止協助瓦勒斯先生處理工作的原因。
**(C) 他在強調工作責任感的重要性。**
(D) 他指出公司政策過時。

- instruct (v.) 指示　outdated (adj.) 過時的

---

**171. 相關細節** 

瓦勒斯先生感謝葛倫特先生什麼事？

(A) 確認某些指引的準確性
(B) 分享某些紀錄文件的位址
(C) 原諒他誤解某工作項目
**(D) 讓他安心，他不會造成大家不便**

- assignment (n.) 工作項目　reassure (v.) 使人安心

**換句話說**
to ask us questions（問我們問題）
→ (D) potentially causing inconvenience（不會造成大家不便）

---

**172–175 通訊文章**

《地區新聞論壇報》　　10 月 22 日

藤山區的三家公司——巴斯戴爾烘焙坊、三歐羅烤肉店以及雷利洗衣店——近期紛紛關店。[174] **在巴伯亞購物中心亦設有分店的地區連鎖事業巴斯戴爾烘焙坊，於 10 月 9 日關閉藤山分店**。公司發言人布蘭達．邱表示，[172] **「公司於該區面臨激烈的競爭」，因為許多社區咖啡廳已經開始拓展烘焙食品的品項**。

[173] **三歐羅烤肉店屬於墨西哥結合日式料理的創意餐廳，已關閉兩週，且大門目前掛上「出租」告示**。這家熱門餐館一直開在露水街 56 號，[173] **而老闆安東尼奧．克魯茲表示，他會在艾爾文公園附近較大的店面重新開張**。

雷利洗衣店則是上週關閉，該店為顧客提供投幣式的自助洗衣機，還有洗衣精販賣機。老闆桃樂絲．雷利表示：[172] **「最近許多開發，讓整個社區鄰里都在改變。例如像德爾頓這樣的新公寓大樓**，公寓內都有附設洗衣機和烘衣機，因此我們店裡洗衣需求量就減少了。」她補充說明，[175] **為了因應趨勢，幾家當地洗衣店已經開始轉型為餐廳**。<u>的確，一間義大利餐酒館很快會遷移至她這個空店面</u>。

雷利女士已將洗衣店遷往巴特勒大道 17 號，她亦開始提供商業洗衣服務。[172] **藤山區目前僅剩一家名為「微風洗衣」的自助洗衣店**。

此區亦只剩下一家供應墨西哥料理的餐館「潭皮可墨西哥捲餅」，以及 [172] **提供日式料理的「艾薇快餐」餐車**。

- district (n.) 區　laundromat (n.) 洗衣店
  regional (adj.) 地區的　eatery (n.) 餐館
  establishment (n.) 公司
  coin-operated (adj.) 投幣式的
  vending machine (n.) 販賣機　convert (v.) 轉型

TEST 10 PART 7

**172. 推論或暗示** 難

文中未提及藤山區的什麼事？

(A) 屬於烘焙坊競爭激烈的市場。
**(B) 現在已有數家投幣式洗衣服務。**
(C) 有新蓋好的住家。
(D) 有行動美食設施。

- competitive (adj.) 具有競爭力的

**換句話說**
difficult to compete（面臨激烈的競爭）
→ (A) competitive（競爭激烈的）
The new apartment buildings（新公寓大樓）
→ (C) newly-built housing（新蓋好的住家）
a food truck . . . offers . . . food（提供……食物的餐車）
→ (D) is served by mobile food facilities（有行動美食設施）

**173. 確認事實與否**

文中提及三歐羅烤肉店的什麼資訊？

(A) 最近易主。
(B) 以咖啡飲品聞名。
**(C) 並非完全歇業。**
(D) 是該區第一家創意混搭餐廳。

**174. 相關細節**

哪一個店家位於藤山區以外的地區？

**(A) 巴伯亞購物中心**
(B) 德爾頓
(C) 微風洗衣
(D) 潭皮可墨西哥捲餅

**175. 句子插入題** 難

「的確，一間義大利餐酒館很快會遷移至她這個空店面。」最適合放在 [1]、[2]、[3]、[4] 哪個位置？

(A) [1]
(B) [2]
**(C) [3]**
(D) [4]

**176–180 資訊與電子郵件**

**阿堤夏機構的秋季課程**

9 月 25 日這週開課。[178] **每種課程的每週上課日子相同**，總共八堂課。學費包含所有必要材料費。[176] **在秋季梯次期間，學生如參加第二種／第三種／第四種課程，學費可享八折。**

| 課程／價格 | 說明 | 上課日子／時間 |
|---|---|---|
| 人物素描課（285 元） | [177] **建議中等程度的學生參加**，此課程每週會請不同的模特兒來到現場。 | 每週二 晚上 6:30 至 7:30<br>每週三 晚上 7:00 至 8:00<br>每週四 晚上 6:30 至 7:30 |
| [178] **陶藝課**（300 元） | 學生將學會手拉坏技巧，來製作碗、花瓶等物品。[177] **歡迎所有程度的學生參加。** | [178] **每週一 晚上 6:30 至 8:30**<br>**每週四 晚上 6:30 至 8:30** |
| 水彩畫課（260 元） | 專為初級生所設計，此課程教導基本的水彩技巧，並以風景畫為主。 | 每週一 晚上 6:00 至 7:00<br>每週三 晚上 6:00 至 7:00<br>每週四 晚上 7:00 至 8:00 |
| 網版印刷課（280 元） | 學習網版印刷步驟來製作自己的 T 恤。專為初級生所設計，以往從未開過此課程。 | 每週二 晚上 6:30 至 8:00 |

如需註冊課程或了解更多資訊，請至 www.artesiainst.com/autumn。註冊截止日為 9 月 12 日。強烈建議大家及早註冊。

- institute (n.) 機構 intermediate (adj.) 中級的
  wheel-throwing (n.) 手拉坏
  intend for 專為……

**收件人：** 辛西亞．羅培茲 <c.lopez@artesiainst.com>
**寄件人：** 朴泰宇 <t.park@artesiainst.com>
**日期：** 11 月 22 日
**主旨：** 意見反饋問卷

親愛的辛西亞：

我已經將最後一天上課發給學生的意見反饋問卷回應都彙整好了。妳的課程獲得壓倒性的正面評價，所有學生都表示會向其他人推薦。[178] **由於妳的教學方式很受歡迎，我覺得每梯次開兩班不夠**。如有可能，[179] **我希望妳冬季梯次可再多開一班**，我們可以在這週五晚上的員工聚餐進一步討論。聚餐地點離我們機構只要走路就可以到，時間暫定晚上七點。[180] **帕布羅會負責安排，看妳要自己參加或帶另一半參加，跟他說就可以了。**

感謝妳辛勤教課！

泰宇

- compile (v.) 彙整　distribute (v.) 分發
  overwhelmingly (adj.) 壓倒性地
  within walking distance 走路就會到的距離
  tentatively (adj.) 暫時地　arrangement (n.) 安排
  spouse (n.) 配偶

**176. 相關細節**

學生能如何獲得折扣？

(A) 向朋友推薦此機構
(B) 提前付清學費全額
(C) 在註冊截止日前及早報名
**(D) 報名超過一種課程**

換句話說
are charged 80% of the class fee（學費可享八折）→ get a discount（獲得折扣）
for second/third/fourth classes（參加第二種／第三種／第四種課程）
→ (D) By enrolling in more than one class（報名超過一種課程）

---

**177. 確認事實與否** 

關於秋季課程的說明，何者為真？

**(A) 有兩種課程適合中等程度的學生參加。**
(B) 有兩種課程首次開課。
(C) 有一種課程每週由不同講師教授。
(D) 有一種課程單日的上課時間，比其他課程的時間都短。

---

**178. 整合題**

羅培茲女士最有可能教哪種課？

(A) 人物素描課　(C) 水彩畫課
**(B) 陶藝課**　(D) 網版印刷課

---

**179. 相關細節**

朴先生希望羅培茲女士怎麼做？

(A) 訓練新進講師
(B) 審核一些問卷結果
**(C) 增加工時**
(D) 要求下一梯次的用品

換句話說
teach an additional class（再多開一班）
→ (C) Increase her working hours（增加工時）

---

**180. 相關細節**

關於晚上聚餐的事，帕布羅需要何種資訊？

(A) 參加者是否有食物過敏的問題
(B) 大家哪一個時段最方便
(C) 大家偏好哪一家餐廳
**(D) 大家是否會攜伴**

換句話說
if you will attend alone or with your spouse（看妳要自己參加或帶另一半參加）
→ (D) Whether a guest will be brought（大家是否會攜伴）

---

**181–185 行動裝置螢幕截圖與網路文章**

**愛聊聊**
**手機版本 3.0**

使用者好評

**凱莉．盧卡斯 ★★★★☆（4.5 顆星）**
「愛聊聊」非常適合用來與世界各地的親友保持聯絡。我已經試過「奧立方塔」上面的許多視訊聊天應用程式，「愛聊聊」最好用。[184] **我只希望可以自訂或隱藏選單——選**單的顏色滿傷眼的。

**多明尼克．法瑞斯爾 ★★★★☆（4 顆星）**
[183] **我很高興「愛聊聊」再度推出「隱藏」狀態功能**，不過 [182/184] **貼圖的數量還真有限，應該要讓其他公司為這個平台製作貼圖，就像「史班格勒」一樣。**

**阮錢 ★☆☆☆☆（1 顆星）**
[181/184] **儘管「木斯」比交出信用卡資料還安全，卻無法使用「木斯」來儲值帳戶**，我會解除安裝此應用程式。

**尤蘭達．卡斯提洛 ★★★★☆（4 顆星）**
[184] **請讓使用者別再自動啟用這個應用程式！**我的提特斯手機電池壽命不是很好，而「愛聊聊」會讓手機更快沒電，不然我沒有其他可抱怨的了，視訊和音訊品質都很可靠。

- keep in touch with . . . 和……保持聯絡
  customize (v.) 自訂　hand over 交出
  automatically (adv.) 自動地

## 「平台方程式」推出「愛聊聊」手機應用程式 3.1 版

安德里安娜·羅素 4 月 8 日 上午 10:35 發文

「平台方程式」本週稍早推出手機裝置可用的「愛聊聊」視訊聊天軟體最新版本。[184] **3.1 版具有可隱藏的簡化選單**，可騰出更多視訊畫面空間，亦支援更棒的整合功能，[184] **讓使用者可透過「木斯」來儲值帳戶**，並且匯入「星信箱」的聯絡人。「平台方程式」的更新公告更誇口 [184] **「愛聊聊」能讓使用者從第三方開發商購買貼圖**，不過目前還不存在這類功能。此外，電腦版本的「愛聊聊」所大受歡迎的「分享畫面」功能，現在終於出現在手機版了。

[185] **「平台方程式」三年前從「愛聊聊」創辦人葛斯·丹尼爾森手上買下此應用程式的開發商**。該公司率先推出的更新版 2.0，受到使用者的強烈批評。[183] **幾種既有功能都從該版本移除，例如能讓使用者狀態設為「隱藏」的功能，不過 3.0 版本又恢復了此功能**。

目前為止，3.1 版本的網路評價均十分正面。「平台方程式」預計接下來會更新「愛聊聊商用版」的手機版本。

- launch (v.) 推出　feature (v.) 具有……功能
  integration (n.) 整合　import (v.) 匯入
  spearhead (v.) 做……的先鋒
  criticism (n.) 批評　preexisting (adj.) 既有的
  restore (v.) 恢復

**181. 確認事實與否**

阮先生表達了什麼樣的疑慮？

**(A) 他金融資料的安全性**
(B) 網路活動的不健全狀態
(C) 聊天服務與日俱增的費用
(D) 刪除手機應用程式的難度

**換句話說**

credit card information（信用卡資料）
→ (A) financial information（金融資料）

---

**182. 確認事實與否**

文中提及「愛聊聊」的競爭對手是何者？

(A) 奧立方塔　(C) 木斯
**(B) 史班格勒**　(D) 提特斯

**183. 整合題** 難

文中提及法瑞斯爾先生的什麼資訊？

(A) 他的部分評價有提到「愛聊聊」的電腦版。
**(B) 他有用過 2.0 版的「愛聊聊」。**
(C) 他的工作是讓他使用「愛聊聊」的主要原因。
(D) 他付費下載「愛聊聊」。

---

**184. 整合題** 難

「愛聊聊」的更新版未採納何者的建議？

(A) 盧卡斯女士　(C) 阮先生
(B) 羅素女士　**(D) 卡斯提洛女士**

---

**185. 確認事實與否** 

文中提及「平台方程式」的哪些資訊？

(A) 於三年前成立。
(B) 曾由丹尼爾森先生帶領。
**(C) 並非「愛聊聊」的原創者。**
(D) 外包部分開發工作。

- outsource (v.) 外包

---

**186–190 電子郵件與不動產清單**

**寄件人：**艾德華多·韋斯特
**收件人：**蘇珊·巴克
**主旨：**物件資訊
**日期：**1 月 16 日

嗨，蘇珊：

前幾天我們開會後，妳有提到願意看一下我替我的莫威瑞大樓物件所寫的說明。說明如下：

莫威瑞大樓現有專業辦公空間可出租。位於邊間，具有 [187] **開放式的中央區域和三個隔間**（其中一間有水槽）、兩個單間廁所和 [187] **儲藏室**。附設專用暖氣和冷氣系統，以及防汙地毯。方便進出電梯，[187] **全日都有良好自然採光**！

然後我會加入我們平常介紹莫威瑞大樓的說明，妳覺得怎麼樣？[186] **身為資深房仲的妳，如果能給我任何建議，我真的感激不盡**。

謝謝妳。

艾德華多

- look over 看一下　single-stall (n.) 單間
  storage closet (n.) 儲藏室
  dedicated (adj.) 專用的
  stain-resistant (adj.) 防汙的

www.property-finder.com/commercial/9320

**佛洛伊德大道 416 號**
**（莫威瑞大樓）二樓**

照片

平面圖

**地圖**

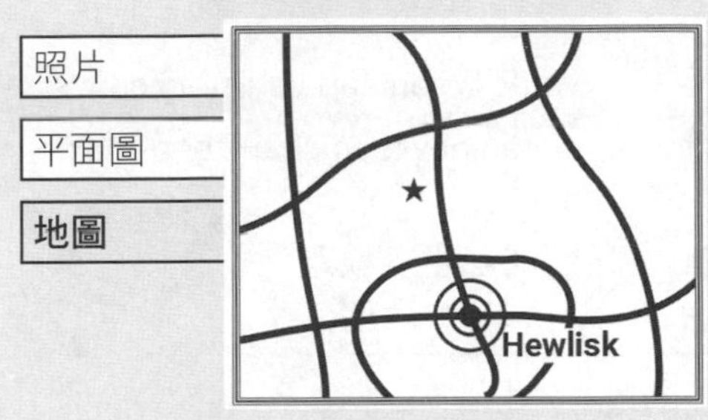


**大小：1,512 平方英尺　　樓層：二樓**
**租期：三年**
[190] **租金：每年 27,972 元（每年每平方英尺為 18.50 元）**

**說明：**優質莫威瑞大樓現有專業辦公空間可出租。[187] **絕佳的邊間位置，全天都能擁有自然採光。**[187] **寬敞的開放式中央區域，加上兩間辦公室／會議室和一間廚房／休息室**、兩個單間廁所，以及 [187] **安全的儲藏室**。附設專用的節能暖氣及冷氣系統，位置方便進出電梯。

**地點：**莫威瑞大樓位於高速公路 320 旁繁忙的帕瑞德斯商業大樓區，距離休里斯克市區北邊三英里。五年前新建成，且具有寬敞的平面停車場。[188] **租金包含大樓維護費與大廳保全人員薪資，但不含水電費。**

**聯絡人：**拉比內房屋仲介公司
艾德華多．韋斯特

- generous (adj.) 寬敞的　secure (adj.) 安全的
  energy-efficient (n.) 節能的　surface (n.) 平面
  lease (n.) 租金　personnel (n.) 人員
  utility (n.) 水電設施

**寄件人：**達琳．布拉德
**收件人：**艾米爾．雷米道尼
**主旨：**可行的辦公空間
**日期：**1 月 19 日

嗨，艾米爾：

我知道你喜歡 [189] **我週一給你看的那間吉巴多街辦公室，不過我剛剛發現一個可能更適合貴公司的新空間，位於莫威瑞大樓二樓的邊間，採光良好。**[189/190] **雖然比吉巴多街辦公室大，但每平方英尺的價格一樣。**吉巴多街辦公室離市區比較近，但由於莫威瑞大樓就在高速公路旁，在交通便利度方面不會差太多。還有莫威瑞大樓的租期比較短，如果你不喜歡，就不用租太久。

我真的覺得你應該看一下這個新空間，如果你感興趣，再跟我說，我可以安排看屋的時間。

敬祝　安康

達琳

**186. 推論或暗示**

可從文中得知巴克女士的什麼資訊？

(A) 她是韋斯特先生的現任主管。
**(B) 她的工作經驗比韋斯特先生多。**
(C) 她寫了某辦公大樓的說明。
(D) 她在某會議上給了一份工作任務。

**換句話說**
as a senior agent（身為資深房仲）
→ (B) has more work experience（有較多的工作經驗）

**187. 整合題** 難

第一封電子郵件中所出現的資訊，有哪一項沒有出現在在空間的公開說明？

(A) 第三個密閉空間　(C) 保全系統
**(B) 地板類型**　(D) 有日照

- enclosed (adj.) 密閉的
  exposure to 暴露在……

**188. 推論或暗示**

莫威瑞大樓的租客最有可能需要額外支付什麼費用？

**(A) 使用水利基礎設施的費用**
(B) 溫度控制系統的維修費
(C) 進出室外停車場的費用
(D) 大樓入口的保全服務

- infrastructure (n.) 基礎設施

**換句話說**
utilities（水電設施）→ (A) Usage of water infrastructure（使用水利基礎設施）

**189. 推論或暗示**

布拉德女士最有可能是什麼身分？

(A) 雷米道尼先生的事業夥伴
(B) 雷米道尼先生的法律顧問
**(C) 雷米道尼先生的房仲**
(D) 雷米道尼先生的行政助理

---

**190. 整合題** 難

可從文中得出吉巴多街辦公室相關資訊的什麼結論？

(A) 空間超過 1,500 平方英尺。
(B) 距離休里斯克市區超過三英里。
(C) 租期需要超過五年。
**(D) 每年租金低於 28,000 元。**

---

**191–195 手冊、電子郵件與公告**

### 柯林戴爾歷史博物館

**主要展覽**

| 木材、鋼鐵與水泥<br>了解柯林戴爾從小型住宅、店面到工廠與摩天大樓等建物背後的迷人故事。 | 柯林斯女士的圖書館<br>[191] **深入探索在柯林戴爾土生土長、創作出《奇拉·史密斯》系列的作家迪安娜·柯林斯的一生，絕對是粉絲最開心的事——即使是已經長大成人的粉絲也是一樣。** |
|---|---|
| 50 年的動物歷史<br>專為最近歡慶柯林戴爾動物園 50 週年慶所辦，此展覽能追溯動物園的歷史與其令人驚豔的生物。 | 山岳之上<br>你或許還沒聽過尼可拉斯·維卡瑞歐的名號，但當你看過他以附近真心山脈為主題的美麗畫作後，一定會永遠忘不了他的名字。 |

**注意事項**

- 雖然我們歡迎團體前來參觀，但 [192] **如果參觀人數超過八人，請提前 24 小時預約**。請至 www.corlingdalehistory.com 的網路預訂系統。
- 導覽服務僅有英語，不過自助語音導覽服務則有其他幾種語言。

- fascinating (adj.) 迷人的 storefront (n.) 店面
  skyscraper (n.) 摩天大樓
  anniversary (n.) 週年紀念 trace (v.) 追溯
  facility (n.) 設施 in advance 提前

寄件人：<verag@corlingdalehistory.com>
收件人：<chiranjeevi.somchai@ben-mail.net>
主旨：關於：今天要參觀嗎？
日期：7 月 15 日

親愛的頌柴先生：

感謝您告訴我們今天下午會來參觀本館。雖然 [192] **像您這樣的團體人數，我們通常需要至少來訪前一天先告知**，不過幸運的是此時館內空間有辦法接待您們。

[194] **由於您提到通常位於三樓的「山岳之上」展覽，我想先跟您說一下，該展覽目前外借至英國的米漢博物館**。雖然一樓禮品店有相關的商品，但 [193] **如果此展覽是主要吸引貴團體前來的原因，請您考慮將來訪時間改至八月**，屆時我們將在此再次展出。

若您仍決定前來，我們期待今天下午見到您。

敬祝　安康

柯林戴爾歷史博物館
營運部經理　薇拉·戈登

- accommodate (v.) 協助 currently (adv.) 目前
  related merchandise (n.) 相關商品
  reschedule (v.) 重新安排時間

### 不好意思！

[194] **平常在此空間展出的展覽，目前外借至倫敦的米漢博物館**，預計於 8 月 1 日再度展出。您的團體如需再次來訪，請詢問服務台 [195] **了解屆時免費入場的資訊**。我們對此不便深感抱歉。

柯林戴爾歷史博物館職員

- house (v.) 提供空間 admission (n.) 入場

---

**191. 相關細節**

根據手冊的說明，某主要展覽的主題為何？

(A) 紡織製造業　　(C) 某都市的畫作
**(B) 童書作者**　　(D) 當地野生生物

**192. 整合題**

關於頌柴先生的團體，以下何者為真？

**(A) 超過八人。**
(B) 團體裡的某些人是某藝術家的親戚。
(C) 團體裡的某些人不說英語。
(D) 會接受個人導覽的服務。

換句話說

bring more than eight people（參觀人數超過八人）→ (A) consists of more than eight individuals（超過八人）

---

**193. 相關細節**

戈登女士建議頌柴先生什麼事？

(A) 預約觀賞某表演
(B) 購買一些限量商品
(C) 聯絡海外組織
**(D) 延後參觀博物館的日期**

換句話說

rescheduling your visit for August（將來訪時間改至八月）→ (D) Touring the museum on a later date（延後參觀博物館的日期）

---

**194. 整合題**

此公告最有可能張貼在柯林戴爾歷史博物館的哪一樓？

(A) 一樓　　**(C) 三樓**
(B) 二樓　　(D) 四樓

---

**195. 同義詞考題**

在公告中，第一段第四行的「party」，意思最接近何者？

(A) 慶祝　　(C) 參與
**(B) 一群人**　　(D) 休假

---

**196–200 網頁、電子郵件與報導**

http://www.shalkon.gov/council/foster

**奧琳．福斯特**
第四區的代表（區地圖）

雖然這是奧琳首度擔任市議員，但她的事業生涯一直投入在公眾服務中。[196] **她在桑特瑞長大與就讀大學**，以政治學系學位畢業後，她先在維金斯的非營利組織工作，該組織負責推廣平價的大樓住家。她後來搬遷至蕭克恩市，成為前任市議員米契爾．布雷爾的幕僚。在擔任幕僚時期，她協助進行 SETIP 稅務誘因配套措施等專案，讓住宅和商業房地產能在環境友善方面有所進步。

自從加入市議會，奧琳著重於改善往返蕭克恩市的交通堵塞問題，包括預計拓寬楊恩大道。[197] **她致力和選民維持開放的溝通管道，且專為民眾保留每週二上午和每週四下午的會面時間。**

委員會：交通預算審核　　聯絡資料

- representative (v.) 代表
  public service (n.) 公共服務
  nonprofit (adj.) 非營利的
  affordable (adj.) 平價的
  tax incentive (n.) 稅務誘因
  residential (adj.) 住宅的
  commercial (adj.) 商業的
  property (n.) 房地產
  traffic congestion (n.) 交通堵塞
  constituent (n.) 選民　exclusively (adj.) 特有的

**寄件人：**奧利佛．柯提斯
**收件人：**奧琳．福斯特
**主旨：**關於：轉寄：瑋柏斯特路標誌
**日期：**9 月 2 日

親愛的市議員您好：

[197/198] **布坎南總幹事將您詢問的事項轉交給我，因為我的團隊負責本市的路標。**

先回答您的主要問題——是的，路標的設計有限制條件，必須符合一般 [199] **交通號誌的形式（綠底白字），或是蕭克恩市指引類標誌的形式（淡金色底加上白色字體與市標）。此外，請注意後者僅適用於矗立在路旁的標誌。**

我這週很樂意與您會面，深入討論標誌選擇的細節，[197] **我週四下午和週五早上都有空，**請問您偏好哪一天討論呢？

蕭克恩市交通部
奧利佛．柯提斯　謹啟

- inquiry (n.) 詢問　general (adj.) 一般的
  informational (adj.) 含有資訊的

## 市政府將把瑋柏斯特路的延伸路段命名為「康明思」

（[200] **9 月 29 日**）——瑋柏斯特路介於柯爾曼街與楊恩大道的某路段與市長同名，原因在於向蕭克恩市第一位女性市長法蘭西絲．康明思致敬。

提議此致敬之舉的蕭克恩市議員 [200] **奧琳．福斯特，與已故康明思市長的家人及其他人，昨日在瑋柏斯特路和柯爾曼街的交叉路口附近聚集，進行小型的揭幕儀式。**

防水油布從 [199] **橫跨瑋柏斯特路的新橋式路標**拉下時，可看見後續半英里路命名為「法蘭西絲．康明思大道」，群眾皆開心歡呼。會選擇以市長的名字命名此路段，是因為這裡靠近塔爾梅奇公園，當年康明思市長任期時的知名之舉，就是復甦這座公園。

[200] **市議員福斯特與康明思市長之子艾德蒙．康明斯均發表演說，強調市長為蕭克恩市帶來的正面影響。**

- stretch (n.) 延伸
  name A after B 以 B 命名 A
  in honor of 向……致敬　tribute (n.) 致敬
  intersection (n.) 十字路口　unveiling (n.) 揭幕
  tarp (n.) 防水油布　proclaim (v.) 顯示
  subsequent (adj.) 接續的　proximity (n.) 附近
  revitalize (v.) 復甦　tenure (n.) 任期
  highlight (v.) 強調　impact (n.) 影響

**196. 確認事實與否**

網頁內容透露了福斯特女士的什麼資訊？

**(A) 她不是蕭克恩市土生土長的居民。**
(B) 她已經被選上很多次。
(C) 她在楊恩大道上有房產。
(D) 她的工作領域跟自己的學位無關。

---

**197. 整合題** 難

柯提斯先生最有可能和福斯特女士在何時開會？

(A) 週四上午　**(C) 週五上午**
(B) 週四下午　(D) 週五下午

---

**198. 同義詞考題**

在電子郵件中，第一段第一行的「passed」，意思最接近何者？

**(A) 傳達**　(C) 婉拒
(B) 實施　(D) 超越

---

**199. 整合題** 

關於完工的路標，以下何者為真？

(A) 具有市標。
(B) 可從某公園入口看見此路標。
(C) 位於市界以外的地方。
**(D) 背景是綠色的。**

---

**200. 相關細節**

福斯特女士在 9 月 28 日發表什麼演說？

(A) 科學嘗試的未來
**(B) 某當地政治人物的成就**
(C) 環境保護的重要性
(D) 某社區鄰里的獨特性

- endeavor (n.) 嘗試；努力
  accomplishment (n.) 成就
  conservation (n.) 保護
  characteristics (n.) 特性

**換句話說**

gave speeches（發表演說）→ speak（演說）
the mayor's positive impact on Shalkon
（市長為蕭克恩市帶來的正面影響）
→ (B) The accomplishments of a local politician（某當地政治人物的成就）

## ACTUAL TEST 01

| READING SECTION | | | | | | | | | | | | | | | | | | | |
|---|---|---|---|---|---|---|---|---|---|---|---|---|---|---|---|---|---|---|---|
| 101 | Ⓐ Ⓑ Ⓒ Ⓓ | 111 | Ⓐ Ⓑ Ⓒ Ⓓ | 121 | Ⓐ Ⓑ Ⓒ Ⓓ | 131 | Ⓐ Ⓑ Ⓒ Ⓓ | 141 | Ⓐ Ⓑ Ⓒ Ⓓ | 151 | Ⓐ Ⓑ Ⓒ Ⓓ | 161 | Ⓐ Ⓑ Ⓒ Ⓓ | 171 | Ⓐ Ⓑ Ⓒ Ⓓ | 181 | Ⓐ Ⓑ Ⓒ Ⓓ | 191 | Ⓐ Ⓑ Ⓒ Ⓓ |
| 102 | Ⓐ Ⓑ Ⓒ Ⓓ | 112 | Ⓐ Ⓑ Ⓒ Ⓓ | 122 | Ⓐ Ⓑ Ⓒ Ⓓ | 132 | Ⓐ Ⓑ Ⓒ Ⓓ | 142 | Ⓐ Ⓑ Ⓒ Ⓓ | 152 | Ⓐ Ⓑ Ⓒ Ⓓ | 162 | Ⓐ Ⓑ Ⓒ Ⓓ | 172 | Ⓐ Ⓑ Ⓒ Ⓓ | 182 | Ⓐ Ⓑ Ⓒ Ⓓ | 192 | Ⓐ Ⓑ Ⓒ Ⓓ |
| 103 | Ⓐ Ⓑ Ⓒ Ⓓ | 113 | Ⓐ Ⓑ Ⓒ Ⓓ | 123 | Ⓐ Ⓑ Ⓒ Ⓓ | 133 | Ⓐ Ⓑ Ⓒ Ⓓ | 143 | Ⓐ Ⓑ Ⓒ Ⓓ | 153 | Ⓐ Ⓑ Ⓒ Ⓓ | 163 | Ⓐ Ⓑ Ⓒ Ⓓ | 173 | Ⓐ Ⓑ Ⓒ Ⓓ | 183 | Ⓐ Ⓑ Ⓒ Ⓓ | 193 | Ⓐ Ⓑ Ⓒ Ⓓ |
| 104 | Ⓐ Ⓑ Ⓒ Ⓓ | 114 | Ⓐ Ⓑ Ⓒ Ⓓ | 124 | Ⓐ Ⓑ Ⓒ Ⓓ | 134 | Ⓐ Ⓑ Ⓒ Ⓓ | 144 | Ⓐ Ⓑ Ⓒ Ⓓ | 154 | Ⓐ Ⓑ Ⓒ Ⓓ | 164 | Ⓐ Ⓑ Ⓒ Ⓓ | 174 | Ⓐ Ⓑ Ⓒ Ⓓ | 184 | Ⓐ Ⓑ Ⓒ Ⓓ | 194 | Ⓐ Ⓑ Ⓒ Ⓓ |
| 105 | Ⓐ Ⓑ Ⓒ Ⓓ | 115 | Ⓐ Ⓑ Ⓒ Ⓓ | 125 | Ⓐ Ⓑ Ⓒ Ⓓ | 135 | Ⓐ Ⓑ Ⓒ Ⓓ | 145 | Ⓐ Ⓑ Ⓒ Ⓓ | 155 | Ⓐ Ⓑ Ⓒ Ⓓ | 165 | Ⓐ Ⓑ Ⓒ Ⓓ | 175 | Ⓐ Ⓑ Ⓒ Ⓓ | 185 | Ⓐ Ⓑ Ⓒ Ⓓ | 195 | Ⓐ Ⓑ Ⓒ Ⓓ |
| 106 | Ⓐ Ⓑ Ⓒ Ⓓ | 116 | Ⓐ Ⓑ Ⓒ Ⓓ | 126 | Ⓐ Ⓑ Ⓒ Ⓓ | 136 | Ⓐ Ⓑ Ⓒ Ⓓ | 146 | Ⓐ Ⓑ Ⓒ Ⓓ | 156 | Ⓐ Ⓑ Ⓒ Ⓓ | 166 | Ⓐ Ⓑ Ⓒ Ⓓ | 176 | Ⓐ Ⓑ Ⓒ Ⓓ | 186 | Ⓐ Ⓑ Ⓒ Ⓓ | 196 | Ⓐ Ⓑ Ⓒ Ⓓ |
| 107 | Ⓐ Ⓑ Ⓒ Ⓓ | 117 | Ⓐ Ⓑ Ⓒ Ⓓ | 127 | Ⓐ Ⓑ Ⓒ Ⓓ | 137 | Ⓐ Ⓑ Ⓒ Ⓓ | 147 | Ⓐ Ⓑ Ⓒ Ⓓ | 157 | Ⓐ Ⓑ Ⓒ Ⓓ | 167 | Ⓐ Ⓑ Ⓒ Ⓓ | 177 | Ⓐ Ⓑ Ⓒ Ⓓ | 187 | Ⓐ Ⓑ Ⓒ Ⓓ | 197 | Ⓐ Ⓑ Ⓒ Ⓓ |
| 108 | Ⓐ Ⓑ Ⓒ Ⓓ | 118 | Ⓐ Ⓑ Ⓒ Ⓓ | 128 | Ⓐ Ⓑ Ⓒ Ⓓ | 138 | Ⓐ Ⓑ Ⓒ Ⓓ | 148 | Ⓐ Ⓑ Ⓒ Ⓓ | 158 | Ⓐ Ⓑ Ⓒ Ⓓ | 168 | Ⓐ Ⓑ Ⓒ Ⓓ | 178 | Ⓐ Ⓑ Ⓒ Ⓓ | 188 | Ⓐ Ⓑ Ⓒ Ⓓ | 198 | Ⓐ Ⓑ Ⓒ Ⓓ |
| 109 | Ⓐ Ⓑ Ⓒ Ⓓ | 119 | Ⓐ Ⓑ Ⓒ Ⓓ | 129 | Ⓐ Ⓑ Ⓒ Ⓓ | 139 | Ⓐ Ⓑ Ⓒ Ⓓ | 149 | Ⓐ Ⓑ Ⓒ Ⓓ | 159 | Ⓐ Ⓑ Ⓒ Ⓓ | 169 | Ⓐ Ⓑ Ⓒ Ⓓ | 179 | Ⓐ Ⓑ Ⓒ Ⓓ | 189 | Ⓐ Ⓑ Ⓒ Ⓓ | 199 | Ⓐ Ⓑ Ⓒ Ⓓ |
| 110 | Ⓐ Ⓑ Ⓒ Ⓓ | 120 | Ⓐ Ⓑ Ⓒ Ⓓ | 130 | Ⓐ Ⓑ Ⓒ Ⓓ | 140 | Ⓐ Ⓑ Ⓒ Ⓓ | 150 | Ⓐ Ⓑ Ⓒ Ⓓ | 160 | Ⓐ Ⓑ Ⓒ Ⓓ | 170 | Ⓐ Ⓑ Ⓒ Ⓓ | 180 | Ⓐ Ⓑ Ⓒ Ⓓ | 190 | Ⓐ Ⓑ Ⓒ Ⓓ | 200 | Ⓐ Ⓑ Ⓒ Ⓓ |

## ACTUAL TEST 02

| READING SECTION | | | | | | | | | | | | | | | | | | | |
|---|---|---|---|---|---|---|---|---|---|---|---|---|---|---|---|---|---|---|---|
| 101 | Ⓐ Ⓑ Ⓒ Ⓓ | 111 | Ⓐ Ⓑ Ⓒ Ⓓ | 121 | Ⓐ Ⓑ Ⓒ Ⓓ | 131 | Ⓐ Ⓑ Ⓒ Ⓓ | 141 | Ⓐ Ⓑ Ⓒ Ⓓ | 151 | Ⓐ Ⓑ Ⓒ Ⓓ | 161 | Ⓐ Ⓑ Ⓒ Ⓓ | 171 | Ⓐ Ⓑ Ⓒ Ⓓ | 181 | Ⓐ Ⓑ Ⓒ Ⓓ | 191 | Ⓐ Ⓑ Ⓒ Ⓓ |
| 102 | Ⓐ Ⓑ Ⓒ Ⓓ | 112 | Ⓐ Ⓑ Ⓒ Ⓓ | 122 | Ⓐ Ⓑ Ⓒ Ⓓ | 132 | Ⓐ Ⓑ Ⓒ Ⓓ | 142 | Ⓐ Ⓑ Ⓒ Ⓓ | 152 | Ⓐ Ⓑ Ⓒ Ⓓ | 162 | Ⓐ Ⓑ Ⓒ Ⓓ | 172 | Ⓐ Ⓑ Ⓒ Ⓓ | 182 | Ⓐ Ⓑ Ⓒ Ⓓ | 192 | Ⓐ Ⓑ Ⓒ Ⓓ |
| 103 | Ⓐ Ⓑ Ⓒ Ⓓ | 113 | Ⓐ Ⓑ Ⓒ Ⓓ | 123 | Ⓐ Ⓑ Ⓒ Ⓓ | 133 | Ⓐ Ⓑ Ⓒ Ⓓ | 143 | Ⓐ Ⓑ Ⓒ Ⓓ | 153 | Ⓐ Ⓑ Ⓒ Ⓓ | 163 | Ⓐ Ⓑ Ⓒ Ⓓ | 173 | Ⓐ Ⓑ Ⓒ Ⓓ | 183 | Ⓐ Ⓑ Ⓒ Ⓓ | 193 | Ⓐ Ⓑ Ⓒ Ⓓ |
| 104 | Ⓐ Ⓑ Ⓒ Ⓓ | 114 | Ⓐ Ⓑ Ⓒ Ⓓ | 124 | Ⓐ Ⓑ Ⓒ Ⓓ | 134 | Ⓐ Ⓑ Ⓒ Ⓓ | 144 | Ⓐ Ⓑ Ⓒ Ⓓ | 154 | Ⓐ Ⓑ Ⓒ Ⓓ | 164 | Ⓐ Ⓑ Ⓒ Ⓓ | 174 | Ⓐ Ⓑ Ⓒ Ⓓ | 184 | Ⓐ Ⓑ Ⓒ Ⓓ | 194 | Ⓐ Ⓑ Ⓒ Ⓓ |
| 105 | Ⓐ Ⓑ Ⓒ Ⓓ | 115 | Ⓐ Ⓑ Ⓒ Ⓓ | 125 | Ⓐ Ⓑ Ⓒ Ⓓ | 135 | Ⓐ Ⓑ Ⓒ Ⓓ | 145 | Ⓐ Ⓑ Ⓒ Ⓓ | 155 | Ⓐ Ⓑ Ⓒ Ⓓ | 165 | Ⓐ Ⓑ Ⓒ Ⓓ | 175 | Ⓐ Ⓑ Ⓒ Ⓓ | 185 | Ⓐ Ⓑ Ⓒ Ⓓ | 195 | Ⓐ Ⓑ Ⓒ Ⓓ |
| 106 | Ⓐ Ⓑ Ⓒ Ⓓ | 116 | Ⓐ Ⓑ Ⓒ Ⓓ | 126 | Ⓐ Ⓑ Ⓒ Ⓓ | 136 | Ⓐ Ⓑ Ⓒ Ⓓ | 146 | Ⓐ Ⓑ Ⓒ Ⓓ | 156 | Ⓐ Ⓑ Ⓒ Ⓓ | 166 | Ⓐ Ⓑ Ⓒ Ⓓ | 176 | Ⓐ Ⓑ Ⓒ Ⓓ | 186 | Ⓐ Ⓑ Ⓒ Ⓓ | 196 | Ⓐ Ⓑ Ⓒ Ⓓ |
| 107 | Ⓐ Ⓑ Ⓒ Ⓓ | 117 | Ⓐ Ⓑ Ⓒ Ⓓ | 127 | Ⓐ Ⓑ Ⓒ Ⓓ | 137 | Ⓐ Ⓑ Ⓒ Ⓓ | 147 | Ⓐ Ⓑ Ⓒ Ⓓ | 157 | Ⓐ Ⓑ Ⓒ Ⓓ | 167 | Ⓐ Ⓑ Ⓒ Ⓓ | 177 | Ⓐ Ⓑ Ⓒ Ⓓ | 187 | Ⓐ Ⓑ Ⓒ Ⓓ | 197 | Ⓐ Ⓑ Ⓒ Ⓓ |
| 108 | Ⓐ Ⓑ Ⓒ Ⓓ | 118 | Ⓐ Ⓑ Ⓒ Ⓓ | 128 | Ⓐ Ⓑ Ⓒ Ⓓ | 138 | Ⓐ Ⓑ Ⓒ Ⓓ | 148 | Ⓐ Ⓑ Ⓒ Ⓓ | 158 | Ⓐ Ⓑ Ⓒ Ⓓ | 168 | Ⓐ Ⓑ Ⓒ Ⓓ | 178 | Ⓐ Ⓑ Ⓒ Ⓓ | 188 | Ⓐ Ⓑ Ⓒ Ⓓ | 198 | Ⓐ Ⓑ Ⓒ Ⓓ |
| 109 | Ⓐ Ⓑ Ⓒ Ⓓ | 119 | Ⓐ Ⓑ Ⓒ Ⓓ | 129 | Ⓐ Ⓑ Ⓒ Ⓓ | 139 | Ⓐ Ⓑ Ⓒ Ⓓ | 149 | Ⓐ Ⓑ Ⓒ Ⓓ | 159 | Ⓐ Ⓑ Ⓒ Ⓓ | 169 | Ⓐ Ⓑ Ⓒ Ⓓ | 179 | Ⓐ Ⓑ Ⓒ Ⓓ | 189 | Ⓐ Ⓑ Ⓒ Ⓓ | 199 | Ⓐ Ⓑ Ⓒ Ⓓ |
| 110 | Ⓐ Ⓑ Ⓒ Ⓓ | 120 | Ⓐ Ⓑ Ⓒ Ⓓ | 130 | Ⓐ Ⓑ Ⓒ Ⓓ | 140 | Ⓐ Ⓑ Ⓒ Ⓓ | 150 | Ⓐ Ⓑ Ⓒ Ⓓ | 160 | Ⓐ Ⓑ Ⓒ Ⓓ | 170 | Ⓐ Ⓑ Ⓒ Ⓓ | 180 | Ⓐ Ⓑ Ⓒ Ⓓ | 190 | Ⓐ Ⓑ Ⓒ Ⓓ | 200 | Ⓐ Ⓑ Ⓒ Ⓓ |

## ACTUAL TEST 03

**READING SECTION**

| No. | Answer | No. | Answer | No. | Answer | No. | Answer | No. | Answer | No. | Answer | No. | Answer | No. | Answer | No. | Answer | No. | Answer |
|---|---|---|---|---|---|---|---|---|---|---|---|---|---|---|---|---|---|---|---|
| 101 | Ⓐ Ⓑ Ⓒ Ⓓ | 111 | Ⓐ Ⓑ Ⓒ Ⓓ | 121 | Ⓐ Ⓑ Ⓒ Ⓓ | 131 | Ⓐ Ⓑ Ⓒ Ⓓ | 141 | Ⓐ Ⓑ Ⓒ Ⓓ | 151 | Ⓐ Ⓑ Ⓒ Ⓓ | 161 | Ⓐ Ⓑ Ⓒ Ⓓ | 171 | Ⓐ Ⓑ Ⓒ Ⓓ | 181 | Ⓐ Ⓑ Ⓒ Ⓓ | 191 | Ⓐ Ⓑ Ⓒ Ⓓ |
| 102 | Ⓐ Ⓑ Ⓒ Ⓓ | 112 | Ⓐ Ⓑ Ⓒ Ⓓ | 122 | Ⓐ Ⓑ Ⓒ Ⓓ | 132 | Ⓐ Ⓑ Ⓒ Ⓓ | 142 | Ⓐ Ⓑ Ⓒ Ⓓ | 152 | Ⓐ Ⓑ Ⓒ Ⓓ | 162 | Ⓐ Ⓑ Ⓒ Ⓓ | 172 | Ⓐ Ⓑ Ⓒ Ⓓ | 182 | Ⓐ Ⓑ Ⓒ Ⓓ | 192 | Ⓐ Ⓑ Ⓒ Ⓓ |
| 103 | Ⓐ Ⓑ Ⓒ Ⓓ | 113 | Ⓐ Ⓑ Ⓒ Ⓓ | 123 | Ⓐ Ⓑ Ⓒ Ⓓ | 133 | Ⓐ Ⓑ Ⓒ Ⓓ | 143 | Ⓐ Ⓑ Ⓒ Ⓓ | 153 | Ⓐ Ⓑ Ⓒ Ⓓ | 163 | Ⓐ Ⓑ Ⓒ Ⓓ | 173 | Ⓐ Ⓑ Ⓒ Ⓓ | 183 | Ⓐ Ⓑ Ⓒ Ⓓ | 193 | Ⓐ Ⓑ Ⓒ Ⓓ |
| 104 | Ⓐ Ⓑ Ⓒ Ⓓ | 114 | Ⓐ Ⓑ Ⓒ Ⓓ | 124 | Ⓐ Ⓑ Ⓒ Ⓓ | 134 | Ⓐ Ⓑ Ⓒ Ⓓ | 144 | Ⓐ Ⓑ Ⓒ Ⓓ | 154 | Ⓐ Ⓑ Ⓒ Ⓓ | 164 | Ⓐ Ⓑ Ⓒ Ⓓ | 174 | Ⓐ Ⓑ Ⓒ Ⓓ | 184 | Ⓐ Ⓑ Ⓒ Ⓓ | 194 | Ⓐ Ⓑ Ⓒ Ⓓ |
| 105 | Ⓐ Ⓑ Ⓒ Ⓓ | 115 | Ⓐ Ⓑ Ⓒ Ⓓ | 125 | Ⓐ Ⓑ Ⓒ Ⓓ | 135 | Ⓐ Ⓑ Ⓒ Ⓓ | 145 | Ⓐ Ⓑ Ⓒ Ⓓ | 155 | Ⓐ Ⓑ Ⓒ Ⓓ | 165 | Ⓐ Ⓑ Ⓒ Ⓓ | 175 | Ⓐ Ⓑ Ⓒ Ⓓ | 185 | Ⓐ Ⓑ Ⓒ Ⓓ | 195 | Ⓐ Ⓑ Ⓒ Ⓓ |
| 106 | Ⓐ Ⓑ Ⓒ Ⓓ | 116 | Ⓐ Ⓑ Ⓒ Ⓓ | 126 | Ⓐ Ⓑ Ⓒ Ⓓ | 136 | Ⓐ Ⓑ Ⓒ Ⓓ | 146 | Ⓐ Ⓑ Ⓒ Ⓓ | 156 | Ⓐ Ⓑ Ⓒ Ⓓ | 166 | Ⓐ Ⓑ Ⓒ Ⓓ | 176 | Ⓐ Ⓑ Ⓒ Ⓓ | 186 | Ⓐ Ⓑ Ⓒ Ⓓ | 196 | Ⓐ Ⓑ Ⓒ Ⓓ |
| 107 | Ⓐ Ⓑ Ⓒ Ⓓ | 117 | Ⓐ Ⓑ Ⓒ Ⓓ | 127 | Ⓐ Ⓑ Ⓒ Ⓓ | 137 | Ⓐ Ⓑ Ⓒ Ⓓ | 147 | Ⓐ Ⓑ Ⓒ Ⓓ | 157 | Ⓐ Ⓑ Ⓒ Ⓓ | 167 | Ⓐ Ⓑ Ⓒ Ⓓ | 177 | Ⓐ Ⓑ Ⓒ Ⓓ | 187 | Ⓐ Ⓑ Ⓒ Ⓓ | 197 | Ⓐ Ⓑ Ⓒ Ⓓ |
| 108 | Ⓐ Ⓑ Ⓒ Ⓓ | 118 | Ⓐ Ⓑ Ⓒ Ⓓ | 128 | Ⓐ Ⓑ Ⓒ Ⓓ | 138 | Ⓐ Ⓑ Ⓒ Ⓓ | 148 | Ⓐ Ⓑ Ⓒ Ⓓ | 158 | Ⓐ Ⓑ Ⓒ Ⓓ | 168 | Ⓐ Ⓑ Ⓒ Ⓓ | 178 | Ⓐ Ⓑ Ⓒ Ⓓ | 188 | Ⓐ Ⓑ Ⓒ Ⓓ | 198 | Ⓐ Ⓑ Ⓒ Ⓓ |
| 109 | Ⓐ Ⓑ Ⓒ Ⓓ | 119 | Ⓐ Ⓑ Ⓒ Ⓓ | 129 | Ⓐ Ⓑ Ⓒ Ⓓ | 139 | Ⓐ Ⓑ Ⓒ Ⓓ | 149 | Ⓐ Ⓑ Ⓒ Ⓓ | 159 | Ⓐ Ⓑ Ⓒ Ⓓ | 169 | Ⓐ Ⓑ Ⓒ Ⓓ | 179 | Ⓐ Ⓑ Ⓒ Ⓓ | 189 | Ⓐ Ⓑ Ⓒ Ⓓ | 199 | Ⓐ Ⓑ Ⓒ Ⓓ |
| 110 | Ⓐ Ⓑ Ⓒ Ⓓ | 120 | Ⓐ Ⓑ Ⓒ Ⓓ | 130 | Ⓐ Ⓑ Ⓒ Ⓓ | 140 | Ⓐ Ⓑ Ⓒ Ⓓ | 150 | Ⓐ Ⓑ Ⓒ Ⓓ | 160 | Ⓐ Ⓑ Ⓒ Ⓓ | 170 | Ⓐ Ⓑ Ⓒ Ⓓ | 180 | Ⓐ Ⓑ Ⓒ Ⓓ | 190 | Ⓐ Ⓑ Ⓒ Ⓓ | 200 | Ⓐ Ⓑ Ⓒ Ⓓ |

## ACTUAL TEST 04

**READING SECTION**

| No. | Answer | No. | Answer | No. | Answer | No. | Answer | No. | Answer | No. | Answer | No. | Answer | No. | Answer | No. | Answer | No. | Answer |
|---|---|---|---|---|---|---|---|---|---|---|---|---|---|---|---|---|---|---|---|
| 101 | Ⓐ Ⓑ Ⓒ Ⓓ | 111 | Ⓐ Ⓑ Ⓒ Ⓓ | 121 | Ⓐ Ⓑ Ⓒ Ⓓ | 131 | Ⓐ Ⓑ Ⓒ Ⓓ | 141 | Ⓐ Ⓑ Ⓒ Ⓓ | 151 | Ⓐ Ⓑ Ⓒ Ⓓ | 161 | Ⓐ Ⓑ Ⓒ Ⓓ | 171 | Ⓐ Ⓑ Ⓒ Ⓓ | 181 | Ⓐ Ⓑ Ⓒ Ⓓ | 191 | Ⓐ Ⓑ Ⓒ Ⓓ |
| 102 | Ⓐ Ⓑ Ⓒ Ⓓ | 112 | Ⓐ Ⓑ Ⓒ Ⓓ | 122 | Ⓐ Ⓑ Ⓒ Ⓓ | 132 | Ⓐ Ⓑ Ⓒ Ⓓ | 142 | Ⓐ Ⓑ Ⓒ Ⓓ | 152 | Ⓐ Ⓑ Ⓒ Ⓓ | 162 | Ⓐ Ⓑ Ⓒ Ⓓ | 172 | Ⓐ Ⓑ Ⓒ Ⓓ | 182 | Ⓐ Ⓑ Ⓒ Ⓓ | 192 | Ⓐ Ⓑ Ⓒ Ⓓ |
| 103 | Ⓐ Ⓑ Ⓒ Ⓓ | 113 | Ⓐ Ⓑ Ⓒ Ⓓ | 123 | Ⓐ Ⓑ Ⓒ Ⓓ | 133 | Ⓐ Ⓑ Ⓒ Ⓓ | 143 | Ⓐ Ⓑ Ⓒ Ⓓ | 153 | Ⓐ Ⓑ Ⓒ Ⓓ | 163 | Ⓐ Ⓑ Ⓒ Ⓓ | 173 | Ⓐ Ⓑ Ⓒ Ⓓ | 183 | Ⓐ Ⓑ Ⓒ Ⓓ | 193 | Ⓐ Ⓑ Ⓒ Ⓓ |
| 104 | Ⓐ Ⓑ Ⓒ Ⓓ | 114 | Ⓐ Ⓑ Ⓒ Ⓓ | 124 | Ⓐ Ⓑ Ⓒ Ⓓ | 134 | Ⓐ Ⓑ Ⓒ Ⓓ | 144 | Ⓐ Ⓑ Ⓒ Ⓓ | 154 | Ⓐ Ⓑ Ⓒ Ⓓ | 164 | Ⓐ Ⓑ Ⓒ Ⓓ | 174 | Ⓐ Ⓑ Ⓒ Ⓓ | 184 | Ⓐ Ⓑ Ⓒ Ⓓ | 194 | Ⓐ Ⓑ Ⓒ Ⓓ |
| 105 | Ⓐ Ⓑ Ⓒ Ⓓ | 115 | Ⓐ Ⓑ Ⓒ Ⓓ | 125 | Ⓐ Ⓑ Ⓒ Ⓓ | 135 | Ⓐ Ⓑ Ⓒ Ⓓ | 145 | Ⓐ Ⓑ Ⓒ Ⓓ | 155 | Ⓐ Ⓑ Ⓒ Ⓓ | 165 | Ⓐ Ⓑ Ⓒ Ⓓ | 175 | Ⓐ Ⓑ Ⓒ Ⓓ | 185 | Ⓐ Ⓑ Ⓒ Ⓓ | 195 | Ⓐ Ⓑ Ⓒ Ⓓ |
| 106 | Ⓐ Ⓑ Ⓒ Ⓓ | 116 | Ⓐ Ⓑ Ⓒ Ⓓ | 126 | Ⓐ Ⓑ Ⓒ Ⓓ | 136 | Ⓐ Ⓑ Ⓒ Ⓓ | 146 | Ⓐ Ⓑ Ⓒ Ⓓ | 156 | Ⓐ Ⓑ Ⓒ Ⓓ | 166 | Ⓐ Ⓑ Ⓒ Ⓓ | 176 | Ⓐ Ⓑ Ⓒ Ⓓ | 186 | Ⓐ Ⓑ Ⓒ Ⓓ | 196 | Ⓐ Ⓑ Ⓒ Ⓓ |
| 107 | Ⓐ Ⓑ Ⓒ Ⓓ | 117 | Ⓐ Ⓑ Ⓒ Ⓓ | 127 | Ⓐ Ⓑ Ⓒ Ⓓ | 137 | Ⓐ Ⓑ Ⓒ Ⓓ | 147 | Ⓐ Ⓑ Ⓒ Ⓓ | 157 | Ⓐ Ⓑ Ⓒ Ⓓ | 167 | Ⓐ Ⓑ Ⓒ Ⓓ | 177 | Ⓐ Ⓑ Ⓒ Ⓓ | 187 | Ⓐ Ⓑ Ⓒ Ⓓ | 197 | Ⓐ Ⓑ Ⓒ Ⓓ |
| 108 | Ⓐ Ⓑ Ⓒ Ⓓ | 118 | Ⓐ Ⓑ Ⓒ Ⓓ | 128 | Ⓐ Ⓑ Ⓒ Ⓓ | 138 | Ⓐ Ⓑ Ⓒ Ⓓ | 148 | Ⓐ Ⓑ Ⓒ Ⓓ | 158 | Ⓐ Ⓑ Ⓒ Ⓓ | 168 | Ⓐ Ⓑ Ⓒ Ⓓ | 178 | Ⓐ Ⓑ Ⓒ Ⓓ | 188 | Ⓐ Ⓑ Ⓒ Ⓓ | 198 | Ⓐ Ⓑ Ⓒ Ⓓ |
| 109 | Ⓐ Ⓑ Ⓒ Ⓓ | 119 | Ⓐ Ⓑ Ⓒ Ⓓ | 129 | Ⓐ Ⓑ Ⓒ Ⓓ | 139 | Ⓐ Ⓑ Ⓒ Ⓓ | 149 | Ⓐ Ⓑ Ⓒ Ⓓ | 159 | Ⓐ Ⓑ Ⓒ Ⓓ | 169 | Ⓐ Ⓑ Ⓒ Ⓓ | 179 | Ⓐ Ⓑ Ⓒ Ⓓ | 189 | Ⓐ Ⓑ Ⓒ Ⓓ | 199 | Ⓐ Ⓑ Ⓒ Ⓓ |
| 110 | Ⓐ Ⓑ Ⓒ Ⓓ | 120 | Ⓐ Ⓑ Ⓒ Ⓓ | 130 | Ⓐ Ⓑ Ⓒ Ⓓ | 140 | Ⓐ Ⓑ Ⓒ Ⓓ | 150 | Ⓐ Ⓑ Ⓒ Ⓓ | 160 | Ⓐ Ⓑ Ⓒ Ⓓ | 170 | Ⓐ Ⓑ Ⓒ Ⓓ | 180 | Ⓐ Ⓑ Ⓒ Ⓓ | 190 | Ⓐ Ⓑ Ⓒ Ⓓ | 200 | Ⓐ Ⓑ Ⓒ Ⓓ |

## ACTUAL TEST 05

| READING SECTION | | | | | | | | | | | | | | | | | | | |
|---|---|---|---|---|---|---|---|---|---|---|---|---|---|---|---|---|---|---|---|
| 101 | Ⓐ Ⓑ Ⓒ Ⓓ | 111 | Ⓐ Ⓑ Ⓒ Ⓓ | 121 | Ⓐ Ⓑ Ⓒ Ⓓ | 131 | Ⓐ Ⓑ Ⓒ Ⓓ | 141 | Ⓐ Ⓑ Ⓒ Ⓓ | 151 | Ⓐ Ⓑ Ⓒ Ⓓ | 161 | Ⓐ Ⓑ Ⓒ Ⓓ | 171 | Ⓐ Ⓑ Ⓒ Ⓓ | 181 | Ⓐ Ⓑ Ⓒ Ⓓ | 191 | Ⓐ Ⓑ Ⓒ Ⓓ |
| 102 | Ⓐ Ⓑ Ⓒ Ⓓ | 112 | Ⓐ Ⓑ Ⓒ Ⓓ | 122 | Ⓐ Ⓑ Ⓒ Ⓓ | 132 | Ⓐ Ⓑ Ⓒ Ⓓ | 142 | Ⓐ Ⓑ Ⓒ Ⓓ | 152 | Ⓐ Ⓑ Ⓒ Ⓓ | 162 | Ⓐ Ⓑ Ⓒ Ⓓ | 172 | Ⓐ Ⓑ Ⓒ Ⓓ | 182 | Ⓐ Ⓑ Ⓒ Ⓓ | 192 | Ⓐ Ⓑ Ⓒ Ⓓ |
| 103 | Ⓐ Ⓑ Ⓒ Ⓓ | 113 | Ⓐ Ⓑ Ⓒ Ⓓ | 123 | Ⓐ Ⓑ Ⓒ Ⓓ | 133 | Ⓐ Ⓑ Ⓒ Ⓓ | 143 | Ⓐ Ⓑ Ⓒ Ⓓ | 153 | Ⓐ Ⓑ Ⓒ Ⓓ | 163 | Ⓐ Ⓑ Ⓒ Ⓓ | 173 | Ⓐ Ⓑ Ⓒ Ⓓ | 183 | Ⓐ Ⓑ Ⓒ Ⓓ | 193 | Ⓐ Ⓑ Ⓒ Ⓓ |
| 104 | Ⓐ Ⓑ Ⓒ Ⓓ | 114 | Ⓐ Ⓑ Ⓒ Ⓓ | 124 | Ⓐ Ⓑ Ⓒ Ⓓ | 134 | Ⓐ Ⓑ Ⓒ Ⓓ | 144 | Ⓐ Ⓑ Ⓒ Ⓓ | 154 | Ⓐ Ⓑ Ⓒ Ⓓ | 164 | Ⓐ Ⓑ Ⓒ Ⓓ | 174 | Ⓐ Ⓑ Ⓒ Ⓓ | 184 | Ⓐ Ⓑ Ⓒ Ⓓ | 194 | Ⓐ Ⓑ Ⓒ Ⓓ |
| 105 | Ⓐ Ⓑ Ⓒ Ⓓ | 115 | Ⓐ Ⓑ Ⓒ Ⓓ | 125 | Ⓐ Ⓑ Ⓒ Ⓓ | 135 | Ⓐ Ⓑ Ⓒ Ⓓ | 145 | Ⓐ Ⓑ Ⓒ Ⓓ | 155 | Ⓐ Ⓑ Ⓒ Ⓓ | 165 | Ⓐ Ⓑ Ⓒ Ⓓ | 175 | Ⓐ Ⓑ Ⓒ Ⓓ | 185 | Ⓐ Ⓑ Ⓒ Ⓓ | 195 | Ⓐ Ⓑ Ⓒ Ⓓ |
| 106 | Ⓐ Ⓑ Ⓒ Ⓓ | 116 | Ⓐ Ⓑ Ⓒ Ⓓ | 126 | Ⓐ Ⓑ Ⓒ Ⓓ | 136 | Ⓐ Ⓑ Ⓒ Ⓓ | 146 | Ⓐ Ⓑ Ⓒ Ⓓ | 156 | Ⓐ Ⓑ Ⓒ Ⓓ | 166 | Ⓐ Ⓑ Ⓒ Ⓓ | 176 | Ⓐ Ⓑ Ⓒ Ⓓ | 186 | Ⓐ Ⓑ Ⓒ Ⓓ | 196 | Ⓐ Ⓑ Ⓒ Ⓓ |
| 107 | Ⓐ Ⓑ Ⓒ Ⓓ | 117 | Ⓐ Ⓑ Ⓒ Ⓓ | 127 | Ⓐ Ⓑ Ⓒ Ⓓ | 137 | Ⓐ Ⓑ Ⓒ Ⓓ | 147 | Ⓐ Ⓑ Ⓒ Ⓓ | 157 | Ⓐ Ⓑ Ⓒ Ⓓ | 167 | Ⓐ Ⓑ Ⓒ Ⓓ | 177 | Ⓐ Ⓑ Ⓒ Ⓓ | 187 | Ⓐ Ⓑ Ⓒ Ⓓ | 197 | Ⓐ Ⓑ Ⓒ Ⓓ |
| 108 | Ⓐ Ⓑ Ⓒ Ⓓ | 118 | Ⓐ Ⓑ Ⓒ Ⓓ | 128 | Ⓐ Ⓑ Ⓒ Ⓓ | 138 | Ⓐ Ⓑ Ⓒ Ⓓ | 148 | Ⓐ Ⓑ Ⓒ Ⓓ | 158 | Ⓐ Ⓑ Ⓒ Ⓓ | 168 | Ⓐ Ⓑ Ⓒ Ⓓ | 178 | Ⓐ Ⓑ Ⓒ Ⓓ | 188 | Ⓐ Ⓑ Ⓒ Ⓓ | 198 | Ⓐ Ⓑ Ⓒ Ⓓ |
| 109 | Ⓐ Ⓑ Ⓒ Ⓓ | 119 | Ⓐ Ⓑ Ⓒ Ⓓ | 129 | Ⓐ Ⓑ Ⓒ Ⓓ | 139 | Ⓐ Ⓑ Ⓒ Ⓓ | 149 | Ⓐ Ⓑ Ⓒ Ⓓ | 159 | Ⓐ Ⓑ Ⓒ Ⓓ | 169 | Ⓐ Ⓑ Ⓒ Ⓓ | 179 | Ⓐ Ⓑ Ⓒ Ⓓ | 189 | Ⓐ Ⓑ Ⓒ Ⓓ | 199 | Ⓐ Ⓑ Ⓒ Ⓓ |
| 110 | Ⓐ Ⓑ Ⓒ Ⓓ | 120 | Ⓐ Ⓑ Ⓒ Ⓓ | 130 | Ⓐ Ⓑ Ⓒ Ⓓ | 140 | Ⓐ Ⓑ Ⓒ Ⓓ | 150 | Ⓐ Ⓑ Ⓒ Ⓓ | 160 | Ⓐ Ⓑ Ⓒ Ⓓ | 170 | Ⓐ Ⓑ Ⓒ Ⓓ | 180 | Ⓐ Ⓑ Ⓒ Ⓓ | 190 | Ⓐ Ⓑ Ⓒ Ⓓ | 200 | Ⓐ Ⓑ Ⓒ Ⓓ |

## ACTUAL TEST 06

| READING SECTION | | | | | | | | | | | | | | | | | | | |
|---|---|---|---|---|---|---|---|---|---|---|---|---|---|---|---|---|---|---|---|
| 101 | Ⓐ Ⓑ Ⓒ Ⓓ | 111 | Ⓐ Ⓑ Ⓒ Ⓓ | 121 | Ⓐ Ⓑ Ⓒ Ⓓ | 131 | Ⓐ Ⓑ Ⓒ Ⓓ | 141 | Ⓐ Ⓑ Ⓒ Ⓓ | 151 | Ⓐ Ⓑ Ⓒ Ⓓ | 161 | Ⓐ Ⓑ Ⓒ Ⓓ | 171 | Ⓐ Ⓑ Ⓒ Ⓓ | 181 | Ⓐ Ⓑ Ⓒ Ⓓ | 191 | Ⓐ Ⓑ Ⓒ Ⓓ |
| 102 | Ⓐ Ⓑ Ⓒ Ⓓ | 112 | Ⓐ Ⓑ Ⓒ Ⓓ | 122 | Ⓐ Ⓑ Ⓒ Ⓓ | 132 | Ⓐ Ⓑ Ⓒ Ⓓ | 142 | Ⓐ Ⓑ Ⓒ Ⓓ | 152 | Ⓐ Ⓑ Ⓒ Ⓓ | 162 | Ⓐ Ⓑ Ⓒ Ⓓ | 172 | Ⓐ Ⓑ Ⓒ Ⓓ | 182 | Ⓐ Ⓑ Ⓒ Ⓓ | 192 | Ⓐ Ⓑ Ⓒ Ⓓ |
| 103 | Ⓐ Ⓑ Ⓒ Ⓓ | 113 | Ⓐ Ⓑ Ⓒ Ⓓ | 123 | Ⓐ Ⓑ Ⓒ Ⓓ | 133 | Ⓐ Ⓑ Ⓒ Ⓓ | 143 | Ⓐ Ⓑ Ⓒ Ⓓ | 153 | Ⓐ Ⓑ Ⓒ Ⓓ | 163 | Ⓐ Ⓑ Ⓒ Ⓓ | 173 | Ⓐ Ⓑ Ⓒ Ⓓ | 183 | Ⓐ Ⓑ Ⓒ Ⓓ | 193 | Ⓐ Ⓑ Ⓒ Ⓓ |
| 104 | Ⓐ Ⓑ Ⓒ Ⓓ | 114 | Ⓐ Ⓑ Ⓒ Ⓓ | 124 | Ⓐ Ⓑ Ⓒ Ⓓ | 134 | Ⓐ Ⓑ Ⓒ Ⓓ | 144 | Ⓐ Ⓑ Ⓒ Ⓓ | 154 | Ⓐ Ⓑ Ⓒ Ⓓ | 164 | Ⓐ Ⓑ Ⓒ Ⓓ | 174 | Ⓐ Ⓑ Ⓒ Ⓓ | 184 | Ⓐ Ⓑ Ⓒ Ⓓ | 194 | Ⓐ Ⓑ Ⓒ Ⓓ |
| 105 | Ⓐ Ⓑ Ⓒ Ⓓ | 115 | Ⓐ Ⓑ Ⓒ Ⓓ | 125 | Ⓐ Ⓑ Ⓒ Ⓓ | 135 | Ⓐ Ⓑ Ⓒ Ⓓ | 145 | Ⓐ Ⓑ Ⓒ Ⓓ | 155 | Ⓐ Ⓑ Ⓒ Ⓓ | 165 | Ⓐ Ⓑ Ⓒ Ⓓ | 175 | Ⓐ Ⓑ Ⓒ Ⓓ | 185 | Ⓐ Ⓑ Ⓒ Ⓓ | 195 | Ⓐ Ⓑ Ⓒ Ⓓ |
| 106 | Ⓐ Ⓑ Ⓒ Ⓓ | 116 | Ⓐ Ⓑ Ⓒ Ⓓ | 126 | Ⓐ Ⓑ Ⓒ Ⓓ | 136 | Ⓐ Ⓑ Ⓒ Ⓓ | 146 | Ⓐ Ⓑ Ⓒ Ⓓ | 156 | Ⓐ Ⓑ Ⓒ Ⓓ | 166 | Ⓐ Ⓑ Ⓒ Ⓓ | 176 | Ⓐ Ⓑ Ⓒ Ⓓ | 186 | Ⓐ Ⓑ Ⓒ Ⓓ | 196 | Ⓐ Ⓑ Ⓒ Ⓓ |
| 107 | Ⓐ Ⓑ Ⓒ Ⓓ | 117 | Ⓐ Ⓑ Ⓒ Ⓓ | 127 | Ⓐ Ⓑ Ⓒ Ⓓ | 137 | Ⓐ Ⓑ Ⓒ Ⓓ | 147 | Ⓐ Ⓑ Ⓒ Ⓓ | 157 | Ⓐ Ⓑ Ⓒ Ⓓ | 167 | Ⓐ Ⓑ Ⓒ Ⓓ | 177 | Ⓐ Ⓑ Ⓒ Ⓓ | 187 | Ⓐ Ⓑ Ⓒ Ⓓ | 197 | Ⓐ Ⓑ Ⓒ Ⓓ |
| 108 | Ⓐ Ⓑ Ⓒ Ⓓ | 118 | Ⓐ Ⓑ Ⓒ Ⓓ | 128 | Ⓐ Ⓑ Ⓒ Ⓓ | 138 | Ⓐ Ⓑ Ⓒ Ⓓ | 148 | Ⓐ Ⓑ Ⓒ Ⓓ | 158 | Ⓐ Ⓑ Ⓒ Ⓓ | 168 | Ⓐ Ⓑ Ⓒ Ⓓ | 178 | Ⓐ Ⓑ Ⓒ Ⓓ | 188 | Ⓐ Ⓑ Ⓒ Ⓓ | 198 | Ⓐ Ⓑ Ⓒ Ⓓ |
| 109 | Ⓐ Ⓑ Ⓒ Ⓓ | 119 | Ⓐ Ⓑ Ⓒ Ⓓ | 129 | Ⓐ Ⓑ Ⓒ Ⓓ | 139 | Ⓐ Ⓑ Ⓒ Ⓓ | 149 | Ⓐ Ⓑ Ⓒ Ⓓ | 159 | Ⓐ Ⓑ Ⓒ Ⓓ | 169 | Ⓐ Ⓑ Ⓒ Ⓓ | 179 | Ⓐ Ⓑ Ⓒ Ⓓ | 189 | Ⓐ Ⓑ Ⓒ Ⓓ | 199 | Ⓐ Ⓑ Ⓒ Ⓓ |
| 110 | Ⓐ Ⓑ Ⓒ Ⓓ | 120 | Ⓐ Ⓑ Ⓒ Ⓓ | 130 | Ⓐ Ⓑ Ⓒ Ⓓ | 140 | Ⓐ Ⓑ Ⓒ Ⓓ | 150 | Ⓐ Ⓑ Ⓒ Ⓓ | 160 | Ⓐ Ⓑ Ⓒ Ⓓ | 170 | Ⓐ Ⓑ Ⓒ Ⓓ | 180 | Ⓐ Ⓑ Ⓒ Ⓓ | 190 | Ⓐ Ⓑ Ⓒ Ⓓ | 200 | Ⓐ Ⓑ Ⓒ Ⓓ |

## ACTUAL TEST 07

| READING SECTION | | | | | | | | | | | | | | | | | | | |
|---|---|---|---|---|---|---|---|---|---|---|---|---|---|---|---|---|---|---|---|
| 101 | Ⓐ Ⓑ Ⓒ Ⓓ | 111 | Ⓐ Ⓑ Ⓒ Ⓓ | 121 | Ⓐ Ⓑ Ⓒ Ⓓ | 131 | Ⓐ Ⓑ Ⓒ Ⓓ | 141 | Ⓐ Ⓑ Ⓒ Ⓓ | 151 | Ⓐ Ⓑ Ⓒ Ⓓ | 161 | Ⓐ Ⓑ Ⓒ Ⓓ | 171 | Ⓐ Ⓑ Ⓒ Ⓓ | 181 | Ⓐ Ⓑ Ⓒ Ⓓ | 191 | Ⓐ Ⓑ Ⓒ Ⓓ |
| 102 | Ⓐ Ⓑ Ⓒ Ⓓ | 112 | Ⓐ Ⓑ Ⓒ Ⓓ | 122 | Ⓐ Ⓑ Ⓒ Ⓓ | 132 | Ⓐ Ⓑ Ⓒ Ⓓ | 142 | Ⓐ Ⓑ Ⓒ Ⓓ | 152 | Ⓐ Ⓑ Ⓒ Ⓓ | 162 | Ⓐ Ⓑ Ⓒ Ⓓ | 172 | Ⓐ Ⓑ Ⓒ Ⓓ | 182 | Ⓐ Ⓑ Ⓒ Ⓓ | 192 | Ⓐ Ⓑ Ⓒ Ⓓ |
| 103 | Ⓐ Ⓑ Ⓒ Ⓓ | 113 | Ⓐ Ⓑ Ⓒ Ⓓ | 123 | Ⓐ Ⓑ Ⓒ Ⓓ | 133 | Ⓐ Ⓑ Ⓒ Ⓓ | 143 | Ⓐ Ⓑ Ⓒ Ⓓ | 153 | Ⓐ Ⓑ Ⓒ Ⓓ | 163 | Ⓐ Ⓑ Ⓒ Ⓓ | 173 | Ⓐ Ⓑ Ⓒ Ⓓ | 183 | Ⓐ Ⓑ Ⓒ Ⓓ | 193 | Ⓐ Ⓑ Ⓒ Ⓓ |
| 104 | Ⓐ Ⓑ Ⓒ Ⓓ | 114 | Ⓐ Ⓑ Ⓒ Ⓓ | 124 | Ⓐ Ⓑ Ⓒ Ⓓ | 134 | Ⓐ Ⓑ Ⓒ Ⓓ | 144 | Ⓐ Ⓑ Ⓒ Ⓓ | 154 | Ⓐ Ⓑ Ⓒ Ⓓ | 164 | Ⓐ Ⓑ Ⓒ Ⓓ | 174 | Ⓐ Ⓑ Ⓒ Ⓓ | 184 | Ⓐ Ⓑ Ⓒ Ⓓ | 194 | Ⓐ Ⓑ Ⓒ Ⓓ |
| 105 | Ⓐ Ⓑ Ⓒ Ⓓ | 115 | Ⓐ Ⓑ Ⓒ Ⓓ | 125 | Ⓐ Ⓑ Ⓒ Ⓓ | 135 | Ⓐ Ⓑ Ⓒ Ⓓ | 145 | Ⓐ Ⓑ Ⓒ Ⓓ | 155 | Ⓐ Ⓑ Ⓒ Ⓓ | 165 | Ⓐ Ⓑ Ⓒ Ⓓ | 175 | Ⓐ Ⓑ Ⓒ Ⓓ | 185 | Ⓐ Ⓑ Ⓒ Ⓓ | 195 | Ⓐ Ⓑ Ⓒ Ⓓ |
| 106 | Ⓐ Ⓑ Ⓒ Ⓓ | 116 | Ⓐ Ⓑ Ⓒ Ⓓ | 126 | Ⓐ Ⓑ Ⓒ Ⓓ | 136 | Ⓐ Ⓑ Ⓒ Ⓓ | 146 | Ⓐ Ⓑ Ⓒ Ⓓ | 156 | Ⓐ Ⓑ Ⓒ Ⓓ | 166 | Ⓐ Ⓑ Ⓒ Ⓓ | 176 | Ⓐ Ⓑ Ⓒ Ⓓ | 186 | Ⓐ Ⓑ Ⓒ Ⓓ | 196 | Ⓐ Ⓑ Ⓒ Ⓓ |
| 107 | Ⓐ Ⓑ Ⓒ Ⓓ | 117 | Ⓐ Ⓑ Ⓒ Ⓓ | 127 | Ⓐ Ⓑ Ⓒ Ⓓ | 137 | Ⓐ Ⓑ Ⓒ Ⓓ | 147 | Ⓐ Ⓑ Ⓒ Ⓓ | 157 | Ⓐ Ⓑ Ⓒ Ⓓ | 167 | Ⓐ Ⓑ Ⓒ Ⓓ | 177 | Ⓐ Ⓑ Ⓒ Ⓓ | 187 | Ⓐ Ⓑ Ⓒ Ⓓ | 197 | Ⓐ Ⓑ Ⓒ Ⓓ |
| 108 | Ⓐ Ⓑ Ⓒ Ⓓ | 118 | Ⓐ Ⓑ Ⓒ Ⓓ | 128 | Ⓐ Ⓑ Ⓒ Ⓓ | 138 | Ⓐ Ⓑ Ⓒ Ⓓ | 148 | Ⓐ Ⓑ Ⓒ Ⓓ | 158 | Ⓐ Ⓑ Ⓒ Ⓓ | 168 | Ⓐ Ⓑ Ⓒ Ⓓ | 178 | Ⓐ Ⓑ Ⓒ Ⓓ | 188 | Ⓐ Ⓑ Ⓒ Ⓓ | 198 | Ⓐ Ⓑ Ⓒ Ⓓ |
| 109 | Ⓐ Ⓑ Ⓒ Ⓓ | 119 | Ⓐ Ⓑ Ⓒ Ⓓ | 129 | Ⓐ Ⓑ Ⓒ Ⓓ | 139 | Ⓐ Ⓑ Ⓒ Ⓓ | 149 | Ⓐ Ⓑ Ⓒ Ⓓ | 159 | Ⓐ Ⓑ Ⓒ Ⓓ | 169 | Ⓐ Ⓑ Ⓒ Ⓓ | 179 | Ⓐ Ⓑ Ⓒ Ⓓ | 189 | Ⓐ Ⓑ Ⓒ Ⓓ | 199 | Ⓐ Ⓑ Ⓒ Ⓓ |
| 110 | Ⓐ Ⓑ Ⓒ Ⓓ | 120 | Ⓐ Ⓑ Ⓒ Ⓓ | 130 | Ⓐ Ⓑ Ⓒ Ⓓ | 140 | Ⓐ Ⓑ Ⓒ Ⓓ | 150 | Ⓐ Ⓑ Ⓒ Ⓓ | 160 | Ⓐ Ⓑ Ⓒ Ⓓ | 170 | Ⓐ Ⓑ Ⓒ Ⓓ | 180 | Ⓐ Ⓑ Ⓒ Ⓓ | 190 | Ⓐ Ⓑ Ⓒ Ⓓ | 200 | Ⓐ Ⓑ Ⓒ Ⓓ |

## ACTUAL TEST 08

| READING SECTION | | | | | | | | | | | | | | | | | | | |
|---|---|---|---|---|---|---|---|---|---|---|---|---|---|---|---|---|---|---|---|
| 101 | Ⓐ Ⓑ Ⓒ Ⓓ | 111 | Ⓐ Ⓑ Ⓒ Ⓓ | 121 | Ⓐ Ⓑ Ⓒ Ⓓ | 131 | Ⓐ Ⓑ Ⓒ Ⓓ | 141 | Ⓐ Ⓑ Ⓒ Ⓓ | 151 | Ⓐ Ⓑ Ⓒ Ⓓ | 161 | Ⓐ Ⓑ Ⓒ Ⓓ | 171 | Ⓐ Ⓑ Ⓒ Ⓓ | 181 | Ⓐ Ⓑ Ⓒ Ⓓ | 191 | Ⓐ Ⓑ Ⓒ Ⓓ |
| 102 | Ⓐ Ⓑ Ⓒ Ⓓ | 112 | Ⓐ Ⓑ Ⓒ Ⓓ | 122 | Ⓐ Ⓑ Ⓒ Ⓓ | 132 | Ⓐ Ⓑ Ⓒ Ⓓ | 142 | Ⓐ Ⓑ Ⓒ Ⓓ | 152 | Ⓐ Ⓑ Ⓒ Ⓓ | 162 | Ⓐ Ⓑ Ⓒ Ⓓ | 172 | Ⓐ Ⓑ Ⓒ Ⓓ | 182 | Ⓐ Ⓑ Ⓒ Ⓓ | 192 | Ⓐ Ⓑ Ⓒ Ⓓ |
| 103 | Ⓐ Ⓑ Ⓒ Ⓓ | 113 | Ⓐ Ⓑ Ⓒ Ⓓ | 123 | Ⓐ Ⓑ Ⓒ Ⓓ | 133 | Ⓐ Ⓑ Ⓒ Ⓓ | 143 | Ⓐ Ⓑ Ⓒ Ⓓ | 153 | Ⓐ Ⓑ Ⓒ Ⓓ | 163 | Ⓐ Ⓑ Ⓒ Ⓓ | 173 | Ⓐ Ⓑ Ⓒ Ⓓ | 183 | Ⓐ Ⓑ Ⓒ Ⓓ | 193 | Ⓐ Ⓑ Ⓒ Ⓓ |
| 104 | Ⓐ Ⓑ Ⓒ Ⓓ | 114 | Ⓐ Ⓑ Ⓒ Ⓓ | 124 | Ⓐ Ⓑ Ⓒ Ⓓ | 134 | Ⓐ Ⓑ Ⓒ Ⓓ | 144 | Ⓐ Ⓑ Ⓒ Ⓓ | 154 | Ⓐ Ⓑ Ⓒ Ⓓ | 164 | Ⓐ Ⓑ Ⓒ Ⓓ | 174 | Ⓐ Ⓑ Ⓒ Ⓓ | 184 | Ⓐ Ⓑ Ⓒ Ⓓ | 194 | Ⓐ Ⓑ Ⓒ Ⓓ |
| 105 | Ⓐ Ⓑ Ⓒ Ⓓ | 115 | Ⓐ Ⓑ Ⓒ Ⓓ | 125 | Ⓐ Ⓑ Ⓒ Ⓓ | 135 | Ⓐ Ⓑ Ⓒ Ⓓ | 145 | Ⓐ Ⓑ Ⓒ Ⓓ | 155 | Ⓐ Ⓑ Ⓒ Ⓓ | 165 | Ⓐ Ⓑ Ⓒ Ⓓ | 175 | Ⓐ Ⓑ Ⓒ Ⓓ | 185 | Ⓐ Ⓑ Ⓒ Ⓓ | 195 | Ⓐ Ⓑ Ⓒ Ⓓ |
| 106 | Ⓐ Ⓑ Ⓒ Ⓓ | 116 | Ⓐ Ⓑ Ⓒ Ⓓ | 126 | Ⓐ Ⓑ Ⓒ Ⓓ | 136 | Ⓐ Ⓑ Ⓒ Ⓓ | 146 | Ⓐ Ⓑ Ⓒ Ⓓ | 156 | Ⓐ Ⓑ Ⓒ Ⓓ | 166 | Ⓐ Ⓑ Ⓒ Ⓓ | 176 | Ⓐ Ⓑ Ⓒ Ⓓ | 186 | Ⓐ Ⓑ Ⓒ Ⓓ | 196 | Ⓐ Ⓑ Ⓒ Ⓓ |
| 107 | Ⓐ Ⓑ Ⓒ Ⓓ | 117 | Ⓐ Ⓑ Ⓒ Ⓓ | 127 | Ⓐ Ⓑ Ⓒ Ⓓ | 137 | Ⓐ Ⓑ Ⓒ Ⓓ | 147 | Ⓐ Ⓑ Ⓒ Ⓓ | 157 | Ⓐ Ⓑ Ⓒ Ⓓ | 167 | Ⓐ Ⓑ Ⓒ Ⓓ | 177 | Ⓐ Ⓑ Ⓒ Ⓓ | 187 | Ⓐ Ⓑ Ⓒ Ⓓ | 197 | Ⓐ Ⓑ Ⓒ Ⓓ |
| 108 | Ⓐ Ⓑ Ⓒ Ⓓ | 118 | Ⓐ Ⓑ Ⓒ Ⓓ | 128 | Ⓐ Ⓑ Ⓒ Ⓓ | 138 | Ⓐ Ⓑ Ⓒ Ⓓ | 148 | Ⓐ Ⓑ Ⓒ Ⓓ | 158 | Ⓐ Ⓑ Ⓒ Ⓓ | 168 | Ⓐ Ⓑ Ⓒ Ⓓ | 178 | Ⓐ Ⓑ Ⓒ Ⓓ | 188 | Ⓐ Ⓑ Ⓒ Ⓓ | 198 | Ⓐ Ⓑ Ⓒ Ⓓ |
| 109 | Ⓐ Ⓑ Ⓒ Ⓓ | 119 | Ⓐ Ⓑ Ⓒ Ⓓ | 129 | Ⓐ Ⓑ Ⓒ Ⓓ | 139 | Ⓐ Ⓑ Ⓒ Ⓓ | 149 | Ⓐ Ⓑ Ⓒ Ⓓ | 159 | Ⓐ Ⓑ Ⓒ Ⓓ | 169 | Ⓐ Ⓑ Ⓒ Ⓓ | 179 | Ⓐ Ⓑ Ⓒ Ⓓ | 189 | Ⓐ Ⓑ Ⓒ Ⓓ | 199 | Ⓐ Ⓑ Ⓒ Ⓓ |
| 110 | Ⓐ Ⓑ Ⓒ Ⓓ | 120 | Ⓐ Ⓑ Ⓒ Ⓓ | 130 | Ⓐ Ⓑ Ⓒ Ⓓ | 140 | Ⓐ Ⓑ Ⓒ Ⓓ | 150 | Ⓐ Ⓑ Ⓒ Ⓓ | 160 | Ⓐ Ⓑ Ⓒ Ⓓ | 170 | Ⓐ Ⓑ Ⓒ Ⓓ | 180 | Ⓐ Ⓑ Ⓒ Ⓓ | 190 | Ⓐ Ⓑ Ⓒ Ⓓ | 200 | Ⓐ Ⓑ Ⓒ Ⓓ |

## ACTUAL TEST 09

| READING SECTION | | | | | | | | | | | | | | | | | | | |
|---|---|---|---|---|---|---|---|---|---|---|---|---|---|---|---|---|---|---|---|
| 101 | Ⓐ Ⓑ Ⓒ Ⓓ | 111 | Ⓐ Ⓑ Ⓒ Ⓓ | 121 | Ⓐ Ⓑ Ⓒ Ⓓ | 131 | Ⓐ Ⓑ Ⓒ Ⓓ | 141 | Ⓐ Ⓑ Ⓒ Ⓓ | 151 | Ⓐ Ⓑ Ⓒ Ⓓ | 161 | Ⓐ Ⓑ Ⓒ Ⓓ | 171 | Ⓐ Ⓑ Ⓒ Ⓓ | 181 | Ⓐ Ⓑ Ⓒ Ⓓ | 191 | Ⓐ Ⓑ Ⓒ Ⓓ |
| 102 | Ⓐ Ⓑ Ⓒ Ⓓ | 112 | Ⓐ Ⓑ Ⓒ Ⓓ | 122 | Ⓐ Ⓑ Ⓒ Ⓓ | 132 | Ⓐ Ⓑ Ⓒ Ⓓ | 142 | Ⓐ Ⓑ Ⓒ Ⓓ | 152 | Ⓐ Ⓑ Ⓒ Ⓓ | 162 | Ⓐ Ⓑ Ⓒ Ⓓ | 172 | Ⓐ Ⓑ Ⓒ Ⓓ | 182 | Ⓐ Ⓑ Ⓒ Ⓓ | 192 | Ⓐ Ⓑ Ⓒ Ⓓ |
| 103 | Ⓐ Ⓑ Ⓒ Ⓓ | 113 | Ⓐ Ⓑ Ⓒ Ⓓ | 123 | Ⓐ Ⓑ Ⓒ Ⓓ | 133 | Ⓐ Ⓑ Ⓒ Ⓓ | 143 | Ⓐ Ⓑ Ⓒ Ⓓ | 153 | Ⓐ Ⓑ Ⓒ Ⓓ | 163 | Ⓐ Ⓑ Ⓒ Ⓓ | 173 | Ⓐ Ⓑ Ⓒ Ⓓ | 183 | Ⓐ Ⓑ Ⓒ Ⓓ | 193 | Ⓐ Ⓑ Ⓒ Ⓓ |
| 104 | Ⓐ Ⓑ Ⓒ Ⓓ | 114 | Ⓐ Ⓑ Ⓒ Ⓓ | 124 | Ⓐ Ⓑ Ⓒ Ⓓ | 134 | Ⓐ Ⓑ Ⓒ Ⓓ | 144 | Ⓐ Ⓑ Ⓒ Ⓓ | 154 | Ⓐ Ⓑ Ⓒ Ⓓ | 164 | Ⓐ Ⓑ Ⓒ Ⓓ | 174 | Ⓐ Ⓑ Ⓒ Ⓓ | 184 | Ⓐ Ⓑ Ⓒ Ⓓ | 194 | Ⓐ Ⓑ Ⓒ Ⓓ |
| 105 | Ⓐ Ⓑ Ⓒ Ⓓ | 115 | Ⓐ Ⓑ Ⓒ Ⓓ | 125 | Ⓐ Ⓑ Ⓒ Ⓓ | 135 | Ⓐ Ⓑ Ⓒ Ⓓ | 145 | Ⓐ Ⓑ Ⓒ Ⓓ | 155 | Ⓐ Ⓑ Ⓒ Ⓓ | 165 | Ⓐ Ⓑ Ⓒ Ⓓ | 175 | Ⓐ Ⓑ Ⓒ Ⓓ | 185 | Ⓐ Ⓑ Ⓒ Ⓓ | 195 | Ⓐ Ⓑ Ⓒ Ⓓ |
| 106 | Ⓐ Ⓑ Ⓒ Ⓓ | 116 | Ⓐ Ⓑ Ⓒ Ⓓ | 126 | Ⓐ Ⓑ Ⓒ Ⓓ | 136 | Ⓐ Ⓑ Ⓒ Ⓓ | 146 | Ⓐ Ⓑ Ⓒ Ⓓ | 156 | Ⓐ Ⓑ Ⓒ Ⓓ | 166 | Ⓐ Ⓑ Ⓒ Ⓓ | 176 | Ⓐ Ⓑ Ⓒ Ⓓ | 186 | Ⓐ Ⓑ Ⓒ Ⓓ | 196 | Ⓐ Ⓑ Ⓒ Ⓓ |
| 107 | Ⓐ Ⓑ Ⓒ Ⓓ | 117 | Ⓐ Ⓑ Ⓒ Ⓓ | 127 | Ⓐ Ⓑ Ⓒ Ⓓ | 137 | Ⓐ Ⓑ Ⓒ Ⓓ | 147 | Ⓐ Ⓑ Ⓒ Ⓓ | 157 | Ⓐ Ⓑ Ⓒ Ⓓ | 167 | Ⓐ Ⓑ Ⓒ Ⓓ | 177 | Ⓐ Ⓑ Ⓒ Ⓓ | 187 | Ⓐ Ⓑ Ⓒ Ⓓ | 197 | Ⓐ Ⓑ Ⓒ Ⓓ |
| 108 | Ⓐ Ⓑ Ⓒ Ⓓ | 118 | Ⓐ Ⓑ Ⓒ Ⓓ | 128 | Ⓐ Ⓑ Ⓒ Ⓓ | 138 | Ⓐ Ⓑ Ⓒ Ⓓ | 148 | Ⓐ Ⓑ Ⓒ Ⓓ | 158 | Ⓐ Ⓑ Ⓒ Ⓓ | 168 | Ⓐ Ⓑ Ⓒ Ⓓ | 178 | Ⓐ Ⓑ Ⓒ Ⓓ | 188 | Ⓐ Ⓑ Ⓒ Ⓓ | 198 | Ⓐ Ⓑ Ⓒ Ⓓ |
| 109 | Ⓐ Ⓑ Ⓒ Ⓓ | 119 | Ⓐ Ⓑ Ⓒ Ⓓ | 129 | Ⓐ Ⓑ Ⓒ Ⓓ | 139 | Ⓐ Ⓑ Ⓒ Ⓓ | 149 | Ⓐ Ⓑ Ⓒ Ⓓ | 159 | Ⓐ Ⓑ Ⓒ Ⓓ | 169 | Ⓐ Ⓑ Ⓒ Ⓓ | 179 | Ⓐ Ⓑ Ⓒ Ⓓ | 189 | Ⓐ Ⓑ Ⓒ Ⓓ | 199 | Ⓐ Ⓑ Ⓒ Ⓓ |
| 110 | Ⓐ Ⓑ Ⓒ Ⓓ | 120 | Ⓐ Ⓑ Ⓒ Ⓓ | 130 | Ⓐ Ⓑ Ⓒ Ⓓ | 140 | Ⓐ Ⓑ Ⓒ Ⓓ | 150 | Ⓐ Ⓑ Ⓒ Ⓓ | 160 | Ⓐ Ⓑ Ⓒ Ⓓ | 170 | Ⓐ Ⓑ Ⓒ Ⓓ | 180 | Ⓐ Ⓑ Ⓒ Ⓓ | 190 | Ⓐ Ⓑ Ⓒ Ⓓ | 200 | Ⓐ Ⓑ Ⓒ Ⓓ |

## ACTUAL TEST 10

| READING SECTION | | | | | | | | | | | | | | | | | | | |
|---|---|---|---|---|---|---|---|---|---|---|---|---|---|---|---|---|---|---|---|
| 101 | Ⓐ Ⓑ Ⓒ Ⓓ | 111 | Ⓐ Ⓑ Ⓒ Ⓓ | 121 | Ⓐ Ⓑ Ⓒ Ⓓ | 131 | Ⓐ Ⓑ Ⓒ Ⓓ | 141 | Ⓐ Ⓑ Ⓒ Ⓓ | 151 | Ⓐ Ⓑ Ⓒ Ⓓ | 161 | Ⓐ Ⓑ Ⓒ Ⓓ | 171 | Ⓐ Ⓑ Ⓒ Ⓓ | 181 | Ⓐ Ⓑ Ⓒ Ⓓ | 191 | Ⓐ Ⓑ Ⓒ Ⓓ |
| 102 | Ⓐ Ⓑ Ⓒ Ⓓ | 112 | Ⓐ Ⓑ Ⓒ Ⓓ | 122 | Ⓐ Ⓑ Ⓒ Ⓓ | 132 | Ⓐ Ⓑ Ⓒ Ⓓ | 142 | Ⓐ Ⓑ Ⓒ Ⓓ | 152 | Ⓐ Ⓑ Ⓒ Ⓓ | 162 | Ⓐ Ⓑ Ⓒ Ⓓ | 172 | Ⓐ Ⓑ Ⓒ Ⓓ | 182 | Ⓐ Ⓑ Ⓒ Ⓓ | 192 | Ⓐ Ⓑ Ⓒ Ⓓ |
| 103 | Ⓐ Ⓑ Ⓒ Ⓓ | 113 | Ⓐ Ⓑ Ⓒ Ⓓ | 123 | Ⓐ Ⓑ Ⓒ Ⓓ | 133 | Ⓐ Ⓑ Ⓒ Ⓓ | 143 | Ⓐ Ⓑ Ⓒ Ⓓ | 153 | Ⓐ Ⓑ Ⓒ Ⓓ | 163 | Ⓐ Ⓑ Ⓒ Ⓓ | 173 | Ⓐ Ⓑ Ⓒ Ⓓ | 183 | Ⓐ Ⓑ Ⓒ Ⓓ | 193 | Ⓐ Ⓑ Ⓒ Ⓓ |
| 104 | Ⓐ Ⓑ Ⓒ Ⓓ | 114 | Ⓐ Ⓑ Ⓒ Ⓓ | 124 | Ⓐ Ⓑ Ⓒ Ⓓ | 134 | Ⓐ Ⓑ Ⓒ Ⓓ | 144 | Ⓐ Ⓑ Ⓒ Ⓓ | 154 | Ⓐ Ⓑ Ⓒ Ⓓ | 164 | Ⓐ Ⓑ Ⓒ Ⓓ | 174 | Ⓐ Ⓑ Ⓒ Ⓓ | 184 | Ⓐ Ⓑ Ⓒ Ⓓ | 194 | Ⓐ Ⓑ Ⓒ Ⓓ |
| 105 | Ⓐ Ⓑ Ⓒ Ⓓ | 115 | Ⓐ Ⓑ Ⓒ Ⓓ | 125 | Ⓐ Ⓑ Ⓒ Ⓓ | 135 | Ⓐ Ⓑ Ⓒ Ⓓ | 145 | Ⓐ Ⓑ Ⓒ Ⓓ | 155 | Ⓐ Ⓑ Ⓒ Ⓓ | 165 | Ⓐ Ⓑ Ⓒ Ⓓ | 175 | Ⓐ Ⓑ Ⓒ Ⓓ | 185 | Ⓐ Ⓑ Ⓒ Ⓓ | 195 | Ⓐ Ⓑ Ⓒ Ⓓ |
| 106 | Ⓐ Ⓑ Ⓒ Ⓓ | 116 | Ⓐ Ⓑ Ⓒ Ⓓ | 126 | Ⓐ Ⓑ Ⓒ Ⓓ | 136 | Ⓐ Ⓑ Ⓒ Ⓓ | 146 | Ⓐ Ⓑ Ⓒ Ⓓ | 156 | Ⓐ Ⓑ Ⓒ Ⓓ | 166 | Ⓐ Ⓑ Ⓒ Ⓓ | 176 | Ⓐ Ⓑ Ⓒ Ⓓ | 186 | Ⓐ Ⓑ Ⓒ Ⓓ | 196 | Ⓐ Ⓑ Ⓒ Ⓓ |
| 107 | Ⓐ Ⓑ Ⓒ Ⓓ | 117 | Ⓐ Ⓑ Ⓒ Ⓓ | 127 | Ⓐ Ⓑ Ⓒ Ⓓ | 137 | Ⓐ Ⓑ Ⓒ Ⓓ | 147 | Ⓐ Ⓑ Ⓒ Ⓓ | 157 | Ⓐ Ⓑ Ⓒ Ⓓ | 167 | Ⓐ Ⓑ Ⓒ Ⓓ | 177 | Ⓐ Ⓑ Ⓒ Ⓓ | 187 | Ⓐ Ⓑ Ⓒ Ⓓ | 197 | Ⓐ Ⓑ Ⓒ Ⓓ |
| 108 | Ⓐ Ⓑ Ⓒ Ⓓ | 118 | Ⓐ Ⓑ Ⓒ Ⓓ | 128 | Ⓐ Ⓑ Ⓒ Ⓓ | 138 | Ⓐ Ⓑ Ⓒ Ⓓ | 148 | Ⓐ Ⓑ Ⓒ Ⓓ | 158 | Ⓐ Ⓑ Ⓒ Ⓓ | 168 | Ⓐ Ⓑ Ⓒ Ⓓ | 178 | Ⓐ Ⓑ Ⓒ Ⓓ | 188 | Ⓐ Ⓑ Ⓒ Ⓓ | 198 | Ⓐ Ⓑ Ⓒ Ⓓ |
| 109 | Ⓐ Ⓑ Ⓒ Ⓓ | 119 | Ⓐ Ⓑ Ⓒ Ⓓ | 129 | Ⓐ Ⓑ Ⓒ Ⓓ | 139 | Ⓐ Ⓑ Ⓒ Ⓓ | 149 | Ⓐ Ⓑ Ⓒ Ⓓ | 159 | Ⓐ Ⓑ Ⓒ Ⓓ | 169 | Ⓐ Ⓑ Ⓒ Ⓓ | 179 | Ⓐ Ⓑ Ⓒ Ⓓ | 189 | Ⓐ Ⓑ Ⓒ Ⓓ | 199 | Ⓐ Ⓑ Ⓒ Ⓓ |
| 110 | Ⓐ Ⓑ Ⓒ Ⓓ | 120 | Ⓐ Ⓑ Ⓒ Ⓓ | 130 | Ⓐ Ⓑ Ⓒ Ⓓ | 140 | Ⓐ Ⓑ Ⓒ Ⓓ | 150 | Ⓐ Ⓑ Ⓒ Ⓓ | 160 | Ⓐ Ⓑ Ⓒ Ⓓ | 170 | Ⓐ Ⓑ Ⓒ Ⓓ | 180 | Ⓐ Ⓑ Ⓒ Ⓓ | 190 | Ⓐ Ⓑ Ⓒ Ⓓ | 200 | Ⓐ Ⓑ Ⓒ Ⓓ |

# Answer Key

## Actual Test 01

| 101 (C) | 121 (D) | 141 (B) | 161 (D) | 181 (A) |
|---|---|---|---|---|
| 102 (D) | 122 (C) | 142 (D) | 162 (A) | 182 (D) |
| 103 (B) | 123 (A) | 143 (D) | 163 (B) | 183 (A) |
| 104 (A) | 124 (D) | 144 (A) | 164 (C) | 184 (C) |
| 105 (C) | 125 (D) | 145 (D) | 165 (A) | 185 (D) |
| 106 (D) | 126 (C) | 146 (B) | 166 (B) | 186 (C) |
| 107 (A) | 127 (C) | 147 (C) | 167 (D) | 187 (B) |
| 108 (A) | 128 (B) | 148 (A) | 168 (C) | 188 (A) |
| 109 (B) | 129 (B) | 149 (B) | 169 (C) | 189 (D) |
| 110 (C) | 130 (B) | 150 (C) | 170 (B) | 190 (A) |
| 111 (A) | 131 (B) | 151 (D) | 171 (D) | 191 (C) |
| 112 (B) | 132 (D) | 152 (A) | 172 (C) | 192 (B) |
| 113 (D) | 133 (A) | 153 (D) | 173 (B) | 193 (C) |
| 114 (B) | 134 (B) | 154 (A) | 174 (A) | 194 (A) |
| 115 (A) | 135 (C) | 155 (B) | 175 (D) | 195 (B) |
| 116 (B) | 136 (C) | 156 (B) | 176 (A) | 196 (D) |
| 117 (C) | 137 (A) | 157 (D) | 177 (D) | 197 (B) |
| 118 (D) | 138 (B) | 158 (B) | 178 (C) | 198 (A) |
| 119 (C) | 139 (A) | 159 (C) | 179 (B) | 199 (C) |
| 120 (D) | 140 (C) | 160 (D) | 180 (A) | 200 (C) |

## Actual Test 02

| 101 (D) | 121 (B) | 141 (A) | 161 (C) | 181 (C) |
|---|---|---|---|---|
| 102 (C) | 122 (C) | 142 (C) | 162 (A) | 182 (A) |
| 103 (A) | 123 (D) | 143 (C) | 163 (C) | 183 (D) |
| 104 (C) | 124 (A) | 144 (A) | 164 (A) | 184 (D) |
| 105 (B) | 125 (C) | 145 (B) | 165 (A) | 185 (C) |
| 106 (A) | 126 (A) | 146 (B) | 166 (B) | 186 (D) |
| 107 (D) | 127 (A) | 147 (C) | 167 (A) | 187 (C) |
| 108 (B) | 128 (D) | 148 (D) | 168 (A) | 188 (A) |
| 109 (A) | 129 (B) | 149 (D) | 169 (D) | 189 (B) |
| 110 (C) | 130 (C) | 150 (A) | 170 (A) | 190 (B) |
| 111 (D) | 131 (B) | 151 (D) | 171 (B) | 191 (D) |
| 112 (B) | 132 (D) | 152 (A) | 172 (B) | 192 (A) |
| 113 (A) | 133 (A) | 153 (B) | 173 (A) | 193 (C) |
| 114 (B) | 134 (D) | 154 (C) | 174 (C) | 194 (D) |
| 115 (D) | 135 (B) | 155 (B) | 175 (D) | 195 (C) |
| 116 (A) | 136 (D) | 156 (C) | 176 (B) | 196 (A) |
| 117 (D) | 137 (C) | 157 (D) | 177 (A) | 197 (B) |
| 118 (D) | 138 (A) | 158 (B) | 178 (B) | 198 (C) |
| 119 (B) | 139 (D) | 159 (B) | 179 (C) | 199 (D) |
| 120 (C) | 140 (D) | 160 (C) | 180 (D) | 200 (B) |

## Actual Test 03

| 101 (A) | 121 (D) | 141 (C) | 161 (B) | 181 (D) |
|---|---|---|---|---|
| 102 (B) | 122 (C) | 142 (D) | 162 (C) | 182 (D) |
| 103 (B) | 123 (A) | 143 (B) | 163 (A) | 183 (B) |
| 104 (C) | 124 (B) | 144 (A) | 164 (C) | 184 (B) |
| 105 (A) | 125 (D) | 145 (B) | 165 (D) | 185 (C) |
| 106 (B) | 126 (C) | 146 (D) | 166 (A) | 186 (D) |
| 107 (C) | 127 (B) | 147 (D) | 167 (A) | 187 (A) |
| 108 (D) | 128 (A) | 148 (A) | 168 (A) | 188 (B) |
| 109 (C) | 129 (C) | 149 (A) | 169 (B) | 189 (B) |
| 110 (D) | 130 (B) | 150 (B) | 170 (C) | 190 (C) |
| 111 (A) | 131 (C) | 151 (B) | 171 (B) | 191 (C) |
| 112 (D) | 132 (B) | 152 (D) | 172 (B) | 192 (D) |
| 113 (A) | 133 (A) | 153 (D) | 173 (D) | 193 (B) |
| 114 (B) | 134 (C) | 154 (B) | 174 (B) | 194 (D) |
| 115 (D) | 135 (A) | 155 (C) | 175 (C) | 195 (A) |
| 116 (A) | 136 (D) | 156 (A) | 176 (C) | 196 (B) |
| 117 (D) | 137 (C) | 157 (B) | 177 (A) | 197 (C) |
| 118 (B) | 138 (A) | 158 (A) | 178 (D) | 198 (C) |
| 119 (D) | 139 (A) | 159 (D) | 179 (C) | 199 (A) |
| 120 (C) | 140 (B) | 160 (D) | 180 (C) | 200 (D) |

## Actual Test 04

| 101 (D) | 121 (B) | 141 (C) | 161 (B) | 181 (B) |
|---|---|---|---|---|
| 102 (A) | 122 (A) | 142 (C) | 162 (D) | 182 (D) |
| 103 (B) | 123 (A) | 143 (B) | 163 (B) | 183 (A) |
| 104 (C) | 124 (D) | 144 (A) | 164 (A) | 184 (C) |
| 105 (C) | 125 (C) | 145 (A) | 165 (B) | 185 (C) |
| 106 (B) | 126 (C) | 146 (D) | 166 (A) | 186 (D) |
| 107 (C) | 127 (B) | 147 (B) | 167 (C) | 187 (C) |
| 108 (D) | 128 (C) | 148 (C) | 168 (B) | 188 (B) |
| 109 (B) | 129 (A) | 149 (A) | 169 (C) | 189 (B) |
| 110 (A) | 130 (D) | 150 (D) | 170 (A) | 190 (A) |
| 111 (D) | 131 (D) | 151 (C) | 171 (D) | 191 (D) |
| 112 (B) | 132 (C) | 152 (D) | 172 (C) | 192 (A) |
| 113 (D) | 133 (B) | 153 (B) | 173 (D) | 193 (A) |
| 114 (A) | 134 (B) | 154 (A) | 174 (B) | 194 (D) |
| 115 (C) | 135 (C) | 155 (B) | 175 (C) | 195 (B) |
| 116 (A) | 136 (D) | 156 (D) | 176 (A) | 196 (A) |
| 117 (B) | 137 (A) | 157 (B) | 177 (C) | 197 (D) |
| 118 (B) | 138 (D) | 158 (D) | 178 (D) | 198 (C) |
| 119 (D) | 139 (A) | 159 (A) | 179 (D) | 199 (A) |
| 120 (C) | 140 (B) | 160 (C) | 180 (A) | 200 (C) |

## Actual Test 05

| 101 (B) | 121 (C) | 141 (C) | 161 (B) | 181 (B) |
|---|---|---|---|---|
| 102 (D) | 122 (A) | 142 (C) | 162 (B) | 182 (C) |
| 103 (A) | 123 (C) | 143 (C) | 163 (C) | 183 (D) |
| 104 (C) | 124 (A) | 144 (A) | 164 (A) | 184 (A) |
| 105 (B) | 125 (C) | 145 (B) | 165 (D) | 185 (C) |
| 106 (D) | 126 (B) | 146 (C) | 166 (A) | 186 (C) |
| 107 (C) | 127 (D) | 147 (C) | 167 (C) | 187 (D) |
| 108 (D) | 128 (B) | 148 (D) | 168 (D) | 188 (A) |
| 109 (A) | 129 (A) | 149 (D) | 169 (B) | 189 (B) |
| 110 (D) | 130 (B) | 150 (A) | 170 (B) | 190 (C) |
| 111 (B) | 131 (B) | 151 (B) | 171 (A) | 191 (D) |
| 112 (D) | 132 (A) | 152 (A) | 172 (C) | 192 (C) |
| 113 (A) | 133 (C) | 153 (A) | 173 (D) | 193 (B) |
| 114 (C) | 134 (B) | 154 (B) | 174 (A) | 194 (A) |
| 115 (C) | 135 (D) | 155 (A) | 175 (C) | 195 (A) |
| 116 (B) | 136 (B) | 156 (D) | 176 (A) | 196 (C) |
| 117 (D) | 137 (A) | 157 (C) | 177 (D) | 197 (B) |
| 118 (A) | 138 (B) | 158 (A) | 178 (D) | 198 (D) |
| 119 (A) | 139 (A) | 159 (C) | 179 (B) | 199 (B) |
| 120 (B) | 140 (D) | 160 (B) | 180 (B) | 200 (D) |

## Actual Test 06

| 101 (C) | 121 (B) | 141 (B) | 161 (A) | 181 (D) |
|---|---|---|---|---|
| 102 (B) | 122 (C) | 142 (D) | 162 (C) | 182 (C) |
| 103 (B) | 123 (A) | 143 (B) | 163 (C) | 183 (C) |
| 104 (D) | 124 (C) | 144 (D) | 164 (D) | 184 (A) |
| 105 (A) | 125 (B) | 145 (C) | 165 (B) | 185 (B) |
| 106 (D) | 126 (D) | 146 (B) | 166 (C) | 186 (A) |
| 107 (D) | 127 (C) | 147 (C) | 167 (D) | 187 (B) |
| 108 (A) | 128 (A) | 148 (D) | 168 (A) | 188 (D) |
| 109 (D) | 129 (D) | 149 (D) | 169 (C) | 189 (B) |
| 110 (D) | 130 (B) | 150 (A) | 170 (B) | 190 (A) |
| 111 (A) | 131 (A) | 151 (C) | 171 (D) | 191 (C) |
| 112 (C) | 132 (C) | 152 (B) | 172 (D) | 192 (C) |
| 113 (B) | 133 (D) | 153 (B) | 173 (A) | 193 (A) |
| 114 (C) | 134 (B) | 154 (C) | 174 (C) | 194 (D) |
| 115 (C) | 135 (D) | 155 (B) | 175 (B) | 195 (D) |
| 116 (A) | 136 (B) | 156 (D) | 176 (B) | 196 (D) |
| 117 (A) | 137 (A) | 157 (A) | 177 (A) | 197 (A) |
| 118 (B) | 138 (D) | 158 (D) | 178 (D) | 198 (B) |
| 119 (D) | 139 (C) | 159 (B) | 179 (B) | 199 (A) |
| 120 (B) | 140 (A) | 160 (C) | 180 (A) | 200 (C) |

## Actual Test 07

| 101 (B) | 121 (D) | 141 (C) | 161 (A) | 181 (D) |
|---|---|---|---|---|
| 102 (D) | 122 (D) | 142 (B) | 162 (A) | 182 (C) |
| 103 (A) | 123 (A) | 143 (A) | 163 (B) | 183 (D) |
| 104 (C) | 124 (A) | 144 (A) | 164 (D) | 184 (C) |
| 105 (B) | 125 (C) | 145 (D) | 165 (B) | 185 (B) |
| 106 (C) | 126 (D) | 146 (B) | 166 (C) | 186 (D) |
| 107 (C) | 127 (B) | 147 (C) | 167 (D) | 187 (D) |
| 108 (D) | 128 (A) | 148 (A) | 168 (B) | 188 (C) |
| 109 (D) | 129 (C) | 149 (B) | 169 (C) | 189 (B) |
| 110 (B) | 130 (B) | 150 (D) | 170 (A) | 190 (B) |
| 111 (C) | 131 (C) | 151 (D) | 171 (B) | 191 (A) |
| 112 (A) | 132 (B) | 152 (C) | 172 (C) | 192 (C) |
| 113 (A) | 133 (D) | 153 (C) | 173 (D) | 193 (D) |
| 114 (B) | 134 (D) | 154 (B) | 174 (A) | 194 (C) |
| 115 (B) | 135 (B) | 155 (A) | 175 (C) | 195 (A) |
| 116 (A) | 136 (A) | 156 (B) | 176 (A) | 196 (C) |
| 117 (C) | 137 (C) | 157 (C) | 177 (A) | 197 (A) |
| 118 (D) | 138 (A) | 158 (B) | 178 (B) | 198 (B) |
| 119 (B) | 139 (C) | 159 (D) | 179 (D) | 199 (B) |
| 120 (C) | 140 (D) | 160 (A) | 180 (C) | 200 (D) |

## Actual Test 08

| 101 (C) | 121 (C) | 141 (D) | 161 (C) | 181 (D) |
|---|---|---|---|---|
| 102 (A) | 122 (D) | 142 (A) | 162 (C) | 182 (B) |
| 103 (D) | 123 (A) | 143 (B) | 163 (A) | 183 (C) |
| 104 (B) | 124 (B) | 144 (A) | 164 (C) | 184 (D) |
| 105 (B) | 125 (B) | 145 (D) | 165 (B) | 185 (A) |
| 106 (D) | 126 (D) | 146 (B) | 166 (A) | 186 (B) |
| 107 (C) | 127 (C) | 147 (A) | 167 (B) | 187 (A) |
| 108 (C) | 128 (A) | 148 (C) | 168 (A) | 188 (C) |
| 109 (B) | 129 (C) | 149 (D) | 169 (D) | 189 (A) |
| 110 (A) | 130 (A) | 150 (A) | 170 (B) | 190 (D) |
| 111 (C) | 131 (B) | 151 (C) | 171 (D) | 191 (B) |
| 112 (C) | 132 (C) | 152 (D) | 172 (D) | 192 (D) |
| 113 (A) | 133 (A) | 153 (B) | 173 (B) | 193 (C) |
| 114 (D) | 134 (A) | 154 (C) | 174 (C) | 194 (B) |
| 115 (D) | 135 (C) | 155 (C) | 175 (A) | 195 (A) |
| 116 (A) | 136 (C) | 156 (A) | 176 (B) | 196 (D) |
| 117 (B) | 137 (B) | 157 (D) | 177 (A) | 197 (B) |
| 118 (B) | 138 (D) | 158 (D) | 178 (B) | 198 (A) |
| 119 (D) | 139 (C) | 159 (C) | 179 (B) | 199 (C) |
| 120 (D) | 140 (D) | 160 (B) | 180 (D) | 200 (C) |

## Actual Test 09

| | | | | |
|---|---|---|---|---|
| **101** (B) | **121** (D) | **141** (D) | **161** (B) | **181** (A) |
| **102** (C) | **122** (C) | **142** (A) | **162** (B) | **182** (C) |
| **103** (B) | **123** (A) | **143** (A) | **163** (C) | **183** (D) |
| **104** (D) | **124** (B) | **144** (B) | **164** (A) | **184** (A) |
| **105** (B) | **125** (D) | **145** (C) | **165** (D) | **185** (B) |
| **106** (A) | **126** (D) | **146** (C) | **166** (A) | **186** (A) |
| **107** (C) | **127** (B) | **147** (B) | **167** (C) | **187** (C) |
| **108** (C) | **128** (A) | **148** (D) | **168** (A) | **188** (C) |
| **109** (B) | **129** (C) | **149** (D) | **169** (D) | **189** (B) |
| **110** (C) | **130** (A) | **150** (C) | **170** (B) | **190** (D) |
| **111** (D) | **131** (A) | **151** (A) | **171** (B) | **191** (C) |
| **112** (A) | **132** (C) | **152** (C) | **172** (C) | **192** (A) |
| **113** (C) | **133** (D) | **153** (C) | **173** (A) | **193** (D) |
| **114** (D) | **134** (B) | **154** (B) | **174** (D) | **194** (B) |
| **115** (D) | **135** (B) | **155** (A) | **175** (A) | **195** (A) |
| **116** (B) | **136** (C) | **156** (B) | **176** (D) | **196** (B) |
| **117** (A) | **137** (B) | **157** (D) | **177** (C) | **197** (D) |
| **118** (B) | **138** (D) | **158** (B) | **178** (B) | **198** (C) |
| **119** (C) | **139** (C) | **159** (D) | **179** (D) | **199** (C) |
| **120** (A) | **140** (D) | **160** (B) | **180** (A) | **200** (A) |

## Actual Test 10

| | | | | |
|---|---|---|---|---|
| **101** (D) | **121** (B) | **141** (B) | **161** (C) | **181** (A) |
| **102** (C) | **122** (A) | **142** (D) | **162** (C) | **182** (B) |
| **103** (C) | **123** (A) | **143** (C) | **163** (D) | **183** (B) |
| **104** (C) | **124** (D) | **144** (D) | **164** (D) | **184** (D) |
| **105** (A) | **125** (C) | **145** (D) | **165** (B) | **185** (C) |
| **106** (B) | **126** (C) | **146** (A) | **166** (C) | **186** (B) |
| **107** (D) | **127** (D) | **147** (A) | **167** (A) | **187** (B) |
| **108** (A) | **128** (B) | **148** (D) | **168** (C) | **188** (A) |
| **109** (B) | **129** (A) | **149** (D) | **169** (A) | **189** (C) |
| **110** (B) | **130** (B) | **150** (D) | **170** (C) | **190** (D) |
| **111** (D) | **131** (A) | **151** (D) | **171** (D) | **191** (B) |
| **112** (A) | **132** (B) | **152** (A) | **172** (B) | **192** (A) |
| **113** (D) | **133** (B) | **153** (B) | **173** (C) | **193** (D) |
| **114** (B) | **134** (C) | **154** (D) | **174** (A) | **194** (C) |
| **115** (C) | **135** (A) | **155** (B) | **175** (C) | **195** (B) |
| **116** (A) | **136** (C) | **156** (B) | **176** (D) | **196** (A) |
| **117** (C) | **137** (B) | **157** (A) | **177** (A) | **197** (C) |
| **118** (A) | **138** (C) | **158** (C) | **178** (B) | **198** (A) |
| **119** (D) | **139** (D) | **159** (A) | **179** (C) | **199** (D) |
| **120** (B) | **140** (C) | **160** (B) | **180** (D) | **200** (B) |

# 多益分數換算表

## 聽力測驗

| 答對題數 | 分數 |
| --- | --- |
| 96-100 | 480-495 |
| 91-95 | 435-490 |
| 86-90 | 395-450 |
| 81-85 | 355-415 |
| 76-80 | 325-375 |
| 71-75 | 295-340 |
| 66-70 | 265-315 |
| 61-65 | 240-285 |
| 56-60 | 215-260 |
| 51-55 | 190-235 |
| 46-50 | 160-210 |
| 41-45 | 135-180 |
| 36-40 | 110-155 |
| 31-35 | 85-130 |
| 26-30 | 70-105 |
| 21-25 | 50-90 |
| 16-20 | 35-70 |
| 11-15 | 20-55 |
| 6-10 | 15-40 |
| 1-5 | 5-20 |
| 0 | 5 |

## 閱讀測驗

| 答對題數 | 分數 |
| --- | --- |
| 96-100 | 460-495 |
| 91-95 | 410-475 |
| 86-90 | 380-430 |
| 81-85 | 355-400 |
| 76-80 | 325-375 |
| 71-75 | 295-345 |
| 66-70 | 265-315 |
| 61-65 | 235-285 |
| 56-60 | 205-255 |
| 51-55 | 175-225 |
| 46-50 | 150-195 |
| 41-45 | 120-170 |
| 36-40 | 100-140 |
| 31-35 | 75-120 |
| 26-30 | 55-100 |
| 21-25 | 40-80 |
| 16-20 | 30-65 |
| 11-15 | 20-50 |
| 6-10 | 15-35 |
| 1-5 | 5-20 |
| 0 | 5 |

◆ 以上換算表是依據本書收錄的試題訂定，建議使用該表格，推算自己取得的分數。舉例來說，若聽力部分答對 61 至 65 題，對應分數會落在 240 至 285 區間。計分方式並非答對題數為 61 題，對應分數就是 240 分、或是答對題數為 65 題，對應分數就是 285 分。**請注意，本換算表僅用於幫助考生判斷自己的英語實力大致落在哪個區間，並不適用於實際多益測驗成績換算。**

# 新制多益
# 閱讀高分金榜演練
## 關鍵10回滿分模擬1000題


| | |
|---|---|
| **作　　者** | YBM TOEIC R&D |
| **譯　　者** | 蔡裴驊／賴祖兒／劉嘉珮<br>關亭薇（前言及各題考點） |
| **編　　輯** | 陳彥臻 |
| **校　　對** | 陳慧莉／申文怡／許嘉華 |
| **主　　編** | 丁宥暄 |
| **內文排版** | 蔡怡柔／林書玉 |
| **封面設計** | 林書玉 |
| **製程管理** | 洪巧玲 |
| **出 版 者** | 寂天文化事業股份有限公司 |
| **發 行 人** | 黃朝萍 |
| **電　　話** | +886-(0)2-2365-9739 |
| **傳　　真** | +886-(0)2-2365-9835 |
| **網　　址** | www.icosmos.com.tw |
| **讀者服務** | onlineservice@icosmos.com.tw |
| **出版日期** | 2022 年 10 月 初版一刷 |





郵撥帳號 1998620-0 寂天文化事業股份有限公司
訂書金額未滿 1000 元，請外加運費 100 元。
〔若有破損，請寄回更換，謝謝。〕





**國家圖書館出版品預行編目 (CIP) 資料**

新制多益閱讀高分金榜演練：關鍵 10 回滿分模擬 1000 題 /YBM TOEIC R&D 著；蔡裴驊，賴祖兒，劉嘉珮，關亭薇譯. -- 初版. -- [臺北市]：寂天文化事業股份有限公司，2022.10

面；　公分

ISBN 978-626-300-154-1( 平裝 )

1.CST: 多益測驗

805.1895　　111013608